Choices

By Lyn Gardner

Dedication

To Duke–

For some, it may seem odd to see that I'm dedicating this book to a cat, but then again, you didn't know Duke. He was special in so many ways, from his demanding need for attention while I tried to write, to the fact he couldn't sleep at night unless he was touching me; he was as strong as he was soft, as beautiful as he was devilish, and as unforgettable as the day is long. There wasn't one person who met my four-year-old tuxedo who didn't fall in love with his gentlemanly nature, and there wasn't one who didn't cry when cancer took his life.

I miss you, boy.

Prologue

Twenty paces from her home, she stopped and looked back at the door. Inside on a peg was her cloak, and on the shelf above it were gloves made for their winters, but other than her scarf, she had left all else behind. She didn't need to be warm any longer. She only needed to be invisible.

She turned and continued along the path, thankful for the full moon that illuminated everything around her, its brilliance dimmed only slightly by translucent clouds as they drifted by. Much snow had fallen in the past few weeks, and packed down by those who had come before her, its surface now glistened a warning, and it was one she heeded. She could not afford to slip. Bruises and bumps could be easily overcome, but an ankle twisted or snapped would end her journey, and the questions that would have followed she was unprepared to answer.

As she walked past a stand of conifers, the wind gusted and a branch, no longer able to withstand the weight of the snow precariously perched on its tip, bent with strain. The mass of flakes fell to the ground, and landing with a muted thump, it cratered itself into a drift. She stopped and stared at the depression, saddened that the pristine surface of the snowy mound had been marred, but then again, so had she. Scarred by secrets too heinous to reveal, each time they had harrowed up, she had tried to push them away, but she knew she would never win the battle. She had fought it for far too long.

She resumed her journey, and as she filled her lungs with the frigid air, the scent of pine found its way to her. A thin smile appeared on her face. The fragrance of the boughs reminded her of her beloved mother, and the remembrances found their way to her heart. In only a few weeks, her mother's favorite season would be upon them. A season when the house would smell of goose and potato, and sprigs of evergreen would drape the mantle and wreath the door. It always seemed to her to be the warmest time of the year, although it was hardly that.

Consumption had taken her mother away. It had started so innocently, just a fever with some chills, and her mother assured her the broth and blankets would cure it, but then the coughing began, and before too long, her mother was gone. She had wailed at the loss, mourning the woman she loved so dearly, but deep inside, there was also relief. Not for the passing of her mother, but for the freedom it brought with it.

As those around her tittered and chattered, growing up to be what was expected of them, she hid in the shadows of her new duties. Complaisant, she perfected each and every one of her obligations in hopes she would become indispensable. Her mornings began early and her nights ended late, and never once did she bemoan her lot in life for it protected her from the inevitability of her gender.

So, the years slipped by. As she had hoped, lost in his grief and active in his teachings, he hadn't noticed as winters came and went, but as his hair grayed, his mind cleared. She was his to protect, and to safeguard her from a future, bleak and empty, he made a decision. He would ensure her a life that included a roof, food, and companionship.

She stopped again as she reached the turn toward town and looked at the little homes lining the road. Their windows were dark for those inside slumbered under quilts of down or blankets of wool. Snuggled in the warmth, they were oblivious to her presence just outside their doors, but even if one had awoken, peered out into the moonlit snow to stare at the sky smattered with stars, she would have gone unnoticed. Her neighbors had guaranteed that.

No one had raised eyebrows when the news had spread through their town, and those knowledgeable in the needle had volunteered to assemble the frock she would wear. In the color of dandelion fluff with sleeves long and neck high, the broadcloth was not embellished with anything to taint the purity of the rite, and even the tiny buttons that held it fastened to her form were in the hue of frost. Standing in the sheen of the moon, with her brown hair hidden under a scarf the shade of cream, her persona and her truth had melded. She was as unseen as her secret.

A burst of wind caused her to hunch her shoulders and pulling the knot of her scarf even tighter, she moved through town like a ghost in the breeze.

There had been many a night she had lain awake, silently damning herself for the bent that had dogged her, but his edict had given her no choice. She would no longer be able to melt into the background as her duties would soon change, and it was those duties that had led her to this. Unable to stomach what was to come, like him, she had also made a choice.

Mindless of the cold that was burrowing into her bones and of the frost forming on her lips and nose as the moisture of her breath froze instantly, she crept along in boots laced in the front and scuffed on the sides. Her fingers had grown stiff, and her skin had become tinged with a hue matching a spring sky, but unyielding, when she reached the end of town, she turned right and kept going.

She would soon be forever free, forever unfettered from the decorum expected, and as her legs grew heavy, she shortened her gait to a shuffle for she was unwavering in the pursuit of her independence.

The solution to her distress had come to her easily for it was but a mirror, a reflection of things pained, things past, and things never to be forgotten. It hadn't been her choice. It wouldn't have *been* her choice, but the location was indeed poetic. Within its label was a memorial, and within its memory, a sonnet of sorts, the stanza holding hushed words spoken in the shadows, gazes secret and revealing, and a finality that would be anything but. She knew the connection would be invisible. The tides were her safeguard, disguising in death as she had disguised in life.

A rush of air whistled through the trees and no longer feeling in need of protection from the briskness of the wind, with frozen fingers she tugged at the knot on her scarf until it loosened. She pulled the cloth from her head, and it fell to the ground, and as if it was controlled by the strings of a puppeteer, it swirled here and there as it danced its way into the darkness.

She turned her attention to the west and looked out over the inky, undulating waves of the Straits. She paused for only a moment before she precariously stepped out onto the round rocks and pebbles lining the water's edge. She held out her arms for balance as she traversed stones smoothed by centuries of tides, and when her feet suddenly felt warm, she lowered her eyes. The water was nipping at the hem of her dress, and the soles of her boots were not stitched tightly enough to prevent it from entering. It was so much warmer than she had expected. Warmer than the air or a fire in a hearth, it gave her comfort, and she moved deeper into the water. As she knew it would, her dress grew weighty and relishing the anchor it was becoming, she turned to face the world she was leaving. Relaxing back into the water, she floated upon its surface and waited for her final sleep.

On this side of town, only two homes existed. As she stared at their silhouettes against the gray-blue sky, her eyes were drawn to the one familiar. She noticed a flickering light in a window, and she wondered if it was an early riser or perhaps one in need of relief. Her answer came soon as the yellow glow moved from one window to the next. Yes, indeed it was an early riser. Someone to warm the house and ready the meal before privileged feet would find their slippers, the person moved as silently as she floated.

She followed the light until her eyes fluttered closed. It would be soon now, and she took a stuttered breath and awaited her demise, but the quietude of the night was broken by the bark of a dog. She was acquainted with that bark, and she opened her eyes and peered at the house again. The door was now open, and the light from inside created a rectangle of brilliance against the blackness that would soon be dawn, and she became transfixed as memories flooded her mind. It looked so warm in the house, so friendly and welcoming as it had been once before. It called to her like a beacon in the night...and then she was gone.

Chapter One

"So, it's true. You're running away."

Robin Novak looked up from the box she was kneeling in front of, and her eyes flew open wide. "Gabby!"

Scrambling to get to her feet, Robin rushed over to the woman and pulled her into a bear hug. While her arms were not quite long enough to match her friend's circumference, the hug was as heartfelt as they came. "What in the world are you doing here?"

After returning the embrace, Gabriella Passarelli stepped back and glanced around the condo. "I came down to talk some sense into you, but it seems I'm too late."

Robin scrunched up her face and then remembered what Gabby had said seconds earlier. "What are you talking about? I'm not running away."

"No?" Gabby said.

"No," Robin blurted, and spinning around, she returned to her packing. "And how did you find out I was moving anyway?"

"I was speaking to Declan earlier this week, arranging some book signings, and he mentioned what you were planning to do."

"And he said I was running away?"

Robin had been in and out of the condo all morning. Seeing no need to waste the air-conditioning, she had shut it off two hours earlier, and the effect showed on Gabby's face. With her cheeks now red and sweat sprouting on her forehead, Gabby took off her suit jacket and hung it on the doorknob. "No," she said as she rolled up her sleeves. "He said your aunt had died, and you decided you were going to move a thousand miles away...just like that."

"It wasn't just like that," Robin said, shaking her head. "I thought about it."

"For what? Like a minute?"

"No, for a few days, and the more I thought about it, the more it made sense."

"Because you're running away."

Robin jammed a wad of newspaper in the box, ensuring her precious coffee maker would make the trip safely. "I am *not* running away! Gabby, I need a change. Okay? I need fresh air and—"

"You live in fucking Florida, for God's sake," Gabby said, waving her arms about. "You can't get much fresher than that."

They had had many conversations over the years. Discussions, debates, and at times even arguments, so Gabby was surprised when instead of replying, Robin sat back on her haunches, hung her head, and stared at the television remote she was holding. With a frown, Gabby gazed at the woman who had been her friend for over twenty years.

It had been a chance meeting that had brought Gabby, Robin, and Declan together. Two had enrolled at Central Michigan University to follow their dreams of becoming writers while one had enrolled only because her parents told her she had to.

Gabby took the required courses, but unsure of what she wanted to do, she bounced from one seminar to another hoping something would click. Nothing did, so while her afternoons were spent in school, her evenings were spent in bars, crying into her beer and moaning she would forever be a loser. Stumbling back to the dorm one night toward the end of her freshman year, she passed a bulletin board filled with scraps of paper fellow students had stapled and thumbtacked to the cork. It was the usual stuff, just kids looking for study partners, tutors, and roommates, but amidst the Post-Its of poorly written pleas from freshmen was a neatly typed and grammatically correct notice. Two students in the English Lit program were looking for avid readers to critique their work. The only requirement was they couldn't be enrolled in the same program, and their criticism had to be constructive.

Gabby knew all about criticism. Long before attitudes had begun to soften, she had remained true to herself. Butch, round, and pierced, with her hair high and tight and a wardrobe purchased in the men's departments of stores and shops, she had worn her sexuality on her sleeve for as long as she could remember, and she *had* been criticized for it. She had been called names on playgrounds and shoved to the ground. In high school she had fingers pointed at her and slurs painted on her locker, and although college students weren't as obvious, they, too, at times had treated her like a leper. To associate with her meant they condoned or worse yet, they were the same.

With her lack of friends and ambiguity about her future, Gabby had spent much of her life lost in books, so ripping the notice from the cork, she trudged back to her room. The next morning, she called the number on the paper, and that afternoon she strolled into Starbucks holding her head high and her breath in. She exhaled seconds later when a smile creased Declan's face, and after shaking her hand, offering her a seat, and introducing her to Robin, he scurried to get Gabby her espresso. Through it all, he was a gentleman. Through it all, she noticed no eyebrows raised or eyes rolled, and through it all, the dazzling smiles on the faces of her soon-to-be-best-friends were the most encouraging and truest she had ever seen.

Before too long, the three were inseparable. Declan and Robin would write, and Gabby would read, and before the end of her sophomore year, Gabby had found her career. Enthralled with the words her friends could pen, she had become their biggest fan and adding classes on contractual law and editing to her curriculum, she became a self-proclaimed literary agent. Upon graduation, with two up-and-coming authors now under verbal contracts, Gabby headed to New York with her sights set high while her friends, craving beaches and sunshine, traveled to Florida for a summer vacation.

"It's not just about air," Robin said, placing the television remote in the box.

Broken from her thoughts, Gabby said, "What?"

"It's not *just* about air," Robin said. "It's about starting over. Starting fresh. Getting out of the rat race."

"You live thirty minutes from some of the best beaches in Florida, and if you want to get out of the rat race, move somewhere else."

"I am."

"I mean in this state."

"You hate this state."

"I do not!"

"You complain about the heat every time you come down."

"I don't complain. I just state the obvious. It's fucking hot down here, but that doesn't mean I want you to run away."

"For the last flipping time, I am *not* running away!" Robin said. Snagging a package of coffee filters off the floor, she crammed it into the box. "I'm making a change. I've had an opportunity dropped in my lap, and I'm going to take it and see where it leads me." By the dirty look Gabby was giving her, Robin could tell the woman wasn't convinced. "What?"

"What what?"

"My mom used to give me that same exact look every time she doubted what I was saying was true, which means you don't believe me."

"I'm trying to, but after all you've been through, honestly how can I *not* think you're doing this because of her?"

Robin let out a sigh, and getting to her feet, she approached her friend. "Look, I'm not going to lie and say that what happened over the past several months didn't play a part in my decision, but I'm not running away because I'm afraid of her. I'm moving because I *need* a change. We both know I have two very poorly written manuscripts withering away on my laptop, and I haven't been able to get any work done on either of them because I've lost my focus. I've been doing everything in my power just so I don't have to sit down and write, and that's not me. I need to find myself again...and I can't do that here."

"But what if you can't do it there either?"

"Then I'll move somewhere else," Robin said, taking Gabby by the shoulders. "But the point is, I'm not running away from any*one* or any*thing*. I'm running toward finding that author I used to be. I would think *you* would appreciate that given the fact that if I don't write books, you don't get paid."

Gabby snorted. "This has never been about the money, and you know it."

"I know," Robin said, kissing Gabby on the cheek. "It was just my clever way of changing the subject."

"It wasn't that clever."

"Yes, but it worked," Robin said, waggling her eyebrows for a second before she returned to her packing.

"Sorry about your aunt, by the way."

Robin looked up. "Thanks. I wanted to go to her service, but I had the damn flu."

"That sucks."

"Yeah, especially since I know my mom would have wanted me there."

"So, she was your mother's sister?"

"Yes, and they were pretty close, and now I'm kicking myself for never taking the time to get to know her better."

"Why didn't you?"

"Stupidity mostly," Robin said as she closed the box and got to her feet. "When I was a kid, I went with Mom to see Adele a couple of times, but I always had my nose stuck in a book. Mom decided she wasn't going to have me miss out on my childhood just because I loved to read, so she started sending me to summer camp instead. And when I grew up, I got busy with my own life. My mom adored her though, and from what I can remember about her, she was a nice woman. Quiet and little reserved, but nice."

Gabby nodded an acknowledgment and then scanned the starkness of the empty condo. "What did you do with all your stuff?"

Robin glanced over her shoulder at the barren space. "I put what I wanted to keep into one of those cube thingies and the rest I sold or donated. I figure once I get up there, I'll arrange to have what's in storage delivered and buy whatever else I need." Robin looked at the cartons at her feet. "And once I get this into the car and gather the cats, I'll be on my way."

Gabby's eyes flew open and darting to the door, she peeked outside. "Oh my God!" she said, spinning around. "Please don't tell me you sold your Z4!"

"I don't really need a sports car where I'm going," Robin said, smiling. "The 4Runner is more practical."

"But it's an SU*Veeee*."

Robin narrowed her eyes. "What's your point?"

"Soccer moms drive SUVs."

"No, they don't."

Gabby flopped one arm over the other and pursed her lips.

"Okay," Robin said, snickering. "Okay, maybe some of them do, but they have to haul kids around, and I have to haul stuff. It made sense to get one."

"You could have got a truck."

"I don't need a truck."

"*Everyone* needs a truck, Robin. A big, badass truck with lots of power and tons of bling. You'll be the envy of every dyke in Florida. You can haul their Harleys. Come on. What do you say? Swap the soccer-mom-mobile for something with a little more oomph. There're some dealers down the street. What say we drive over—"

"I don't want a truck, Gabby," Robin said. "I hate bling. I have no desire to haul motorcycles *or* be the envy of anyone, so drop it. Okay?"

Gabby let out a long sigh. "You're really going to do this, aren't you?"

"Yep. I'm *really* going to do this, but it's not going to be easy if I don't have you on my side."

"You'll always have me on your side," Gabby said, walking toward the boxes surrounding Robin. "But don't expect me to visit until the spring thaw."

"Absolutely not," Robin said, holding up her hands. "And by that time I should have a manuscript for you to read."

"You better have two."

"I'll do my best."

"So," Gabby said, pointing to the boxes. "You want some help loading these?"

Robin's face split into a grin. "I thought you'd never ask."

Gabby picked up one of the boxes and immediately groaned at the weight. "Holy crap," she groused as she lugged it to the door. "Where the hell is Declan when you need him? He's got muscles coming out of his ears."

"We said our goodbyes last night," Robin said, lifting a carton. "He's got the final edits for *Emerald Axes* to work on and there was no need for us to get all emotional again."

"He cried?"

"We *both* cried. Declan's my best friend, and I'm his, and I'm no longer going to be just around the corner and that...well, that hurts, but he and I both know this is for the best." Seeing that Gabby's eyes were rapidly becoming glassy, Robin said, "I'm not moving to another planet, Gabby, and Declan knows that. I'll always be there for him, and he'll always be there for me. Now chill, will you?"

"*I'm* not the one who's going to be chilled," Gabby said, summoning a smile as she sniffled back her tears. "I hope your SU*Veeee* has heated seats."

"As a matter of fact, it does," Robin said, sashaying out the door.

***

Concentration had never been a problem for Declan Kennedy. He could write with music blaring in his ears or the television screaming in the background and never miss an adjective or a noun, but noise was easier to block out than loss.

Unlike most eighteen-year-old boys, when Declan first set eyes on Robin Novak, he wasn't enamored by her blue eyes or her blonde hair. While he couldn't argue that her face was more radiant than any he had ever seen and her form, tall and slim, was probably the envy of many of the girls on campus, what attracted Declan to Robin were her words.

The class had been entitled Introduction to Creative Writing, and toward the end of the course, those attending had been required to stand and read aloud a short story of their own creation. His had been welcomed and appreciated, with a smattering of applause, but hers had a cadence that had mesmerized everyone in the hall, including Declan. After the class had ended, he practically body blocked those in the way as he hurried to catch up to Robin before she exited the building and became lost forever in the sea of students roaming about.

Although the woman seemed reluctant to even acknowledge the bear of a man as he towered over her five-foot-seven-inch frame babbling his praises, by the time Declan had ended his accolades, he had convinced Robin he was harmless. She accepted his invitation for coffee, and when Declan finally escorted Robin back to her dorm near midnight, they were in complete agreement. They were both writing geeks.

Declan ran his fingers through his wealth of black hair as he leaned back on the sofa. He sighed and rubbed the back of his neck, trying to relieve the tension overthinking can cause. He knew they'd always be friends. He knew it would only take a couple of flights to get him to where she would be, and he knew this was the right thing for her, but convincing his heart was another matter. He hated she wouldn't be there when he needed to vent about dialogue he couldn't get *just* right. He hated she wouldn't be calling him at all hours of the night, excited about a new idea or one silly little line that one of her characters would be speaking. But most of all, he hated that for the first time since his freshman year in college, he wouldn't be able to see Robin's smiling face anytime he wanted.

"Jesus Christ, dude, you need to get a grip," he mumbled, pushing himself off the couch. Grabbing the empty bottle sitting on the coffee table, Declan headed to the kitchen to get another beer, but he came up short when there was a knock at the door. He glanced at his watch and frowned. There were only two people who were crazy enough to show up at his house at eleven o'clock at night without calling first, and if Robin had stayed true to her plans, she was already heading north.

Declan strode over, yanked open the door and immediately let out an exaggerated sigh. "Seriously?" he said, glaring at the woman. "What the fuck is wrong with you?"

"Where is she?"

With one hand on the doorjamb and another holding onto the door, Declan let out yet another sigh as he filled the space remaining. "That's none of your business."

"She won't text me back or answer any of my e-mails, and I went by her house, and it's empty."

Declan jerked back his head. "What the hell did you do, peer in the windows? Do we need to add Peeping Thomasina to your list of charges?"

"Just tell me—"

"Listen, you poor excuse for a human being. She's not replying to your texts *or* to your e-mails because she *doesn't* want to have *anything* to *do* with you!"

"I just need to talk to—"

"She *doesn't* want to talk to you!" Declan bellowed. "Are you that stupid that I need to explain to you what a restraining order is because if Robin *did* want to talk to you, I doubt she'd have gone to those lengths."

"Don't you dare call me stupid!"

Declan eyeballed the scrawny brunette and noticed that her hands were now fists. "What? You going to hit me again?"

"It's not like you're going to stop me," Pamela Burton said, intruding into Declan's space. "You're not man enough for that."

"I was taught never to hit a girl," he said, glaring at the woman. "But if you do it again, I'm going to call the police—*again*—and you're going to go to jail—*again*. So, if that's what you want to do, then take your best shot because I'm not afraid of you, Pam. All you are is a coke head who's gotten caught in so many lies it's not even funny, and I, for one, am not going to waste another minute on you, your bullshit, *or* your threats."

Taking one step backward, Declan was about to shut the door when Pamela Burton stuck her foot into the opening. "Not so fast."

Declan hung his head, allowing his annoyance the time it needed to dissipate. "Are we *really* going to do this all over again?" he said, raising his eyes.

"I want to know where she is."

"And I want to win a Pulitzer," Declan said with a laugh. "But I'll tell you what I'm going to do. When I win that Pulitzer, I'll tell you where she is. How's that?"

"Look, you son-of-a-bitch, either you tell me where she is, or I'll make your life a living hell, and when I get done with you, no one on earth will *ever* buy one of your books again!"

Declan's hearty guffaw echoed down the street. "Jesus Christ, do you hear yourself? Better yet, do you actually *believe* the crap you're shoveling? I hate to break it to you, Pam, but you aren't the queen of the planet, and whatever friends you do have left are probably only there because you're a pyscho and they're afraid to piss you off, but I'm *not* your friend, and I'm *not* cowering at your threats. My publisher has more lawyers than you have lies, Pam, so do us both a favor. Get the fuck off my porch."

Before Pamela Burton could say another word, Declan Kennedy slammed the door in her face.

***

As they had done on the two previous nights in hotels along I-75, as soon as Robin set the carrier on the floor, the occupants announced their existence loudly. "Geez, hold on," she said, chuckling as the meows and wails spewed forth. "Give me a second."

Unzipping her suitcase, she pulled out the remaining cardboard tray and the last baggie of kitty litter, and after setting up the temporary litter box, she unlatched the carrier door. "Okay, guys. You do your thing, and I'm going to do mine," she said, grabbing her toiletry bag. "And don't make a mess."

A short time later, Robin emerged from the bathroom with one towel wrapped around her body, and another wrapped around her hair. Before she took two steps, she was met by another chorus of meows. "Okay,

okay," Robin said, and rummaging around in the luggage, she was soon emptying two tiny cans of food into stainless steel bowls and putting them on the floor. "Here you go, sweeties."

The two cats wasted no time in devouring their dinner, and Robin wasted no time in making a beeline for the bed. She flopped down on the mattress and stared at the ceiling. She was doing okay, but there was one question continuing to nibble at her brain. Did insanity run in her family?

Her mother had never talked about a barmy cousin four times removed who had barked at trees or a great-great-grandparent known for · wearing their clothes inside out, yet Robin had packed up her life in less than fourteen days on a *whim*. A whim offering new. A whim offering different. A whim offering her freedom from the same old, same old. She really didn't even think twice about it. She merely reduced the size of her world to a storage cube, a cargo hauler jam-packed with totes, and a 4Runner filled with her luggage and laptops…just like that.

Of course, some things were thought out. Robin had traded phone calls with her aunt's lawyer to get as much of the paperwork as possible sorted before her appointment with him on Friday. She had called the local utility and cable companies to get those balls rolling, and she had made reservations at three pet-friendly hotels along the turnpike, so she had places to stay for the night as she headed north. And in between filling the cube, organizing a quick garage sale, and calling a local pet shelter to donate what was left, she had managed to spend a few hours on the Internet researching her new home, but only a few.

Robin wasn't a total stranger to the area her mother used to refer to as a godsend. She had made the trip twice with her mom, the last time being when she was nine-years-old. Thirty-five years had passed since then, and Robin's memories were a bit foggy, but there was one that was as crystal clear as it had ever been. Tomorrow, Robin was going to travel back in time.

Chapter Two

"Hi. It's me."

"Good morning," Declan said, his voice gravelly and low.

"I just wanted to let you know I made it in all right. I was going to call you last night, but it was late."

Declan glimpsed at the clock on his nightstand. "So you decided to call me at seven-freaking-o'clock in the morning? Oh wait, have you slipped into another time zone?"

"No, I'm still in the same time zone. I just didn't look at the clock. I'm sorry."

"It's okay," Declan said, scrubbing his hand over his face. "Speaking of okay, are you?"

"I'm fine."

"You don't sound fine."

"I'm still not getting a lot of sleep."

"You know, they make drugs for that."

"I don't like drugs."

"You know, they make alcohol for that."

Robin snorted. "Thanks. You're just what I needed."

Declan didn't have to ask what Robin was talking about. She didn't laugh easily anymore, and smiles were rare as well. Not the quick, flash of a smile when she was just being polite, but the one that brightened a room and warmed his heart. Those had disappeared months ago. Declan's brow furrowed. He wanted his friend back. "What's wrong, Robbie?"

Robin closed her eyes, and bowing her head, she pinched the bridge of her nose. "I guess I'm still trying to wrap my head around what I'm doing."

"Well, if you're expecting me to tell you to come back, that's not going to happen."

"Some best friend you are."

"Is that what you want me to do? Tell you to run back to Florida?"

"Honestly?"

Declan scowled. "Do you even have to ask that?"

"No, I don't. I think I just needed to hear a friendly voice."

"Oh yeah? Who'd you call?"

Robin grinned. "My best friend who's over fourteen hundred miles away, but he's giving me a hard time."

"That's because he loves you and wants you to be happy," Declan said softly. "And that wasn't happening here, and we both know it."

"I miss you."

"It's been four freaking days, Robbie. Grow the fuck up," Declan said, his merriment traveling over the phone line to Robin's ear.

"Okay," she said, smiling into the phone. "So, what about you? How are you doing? Did you get the edits finished?"

Declan paused for a second, debating on whether to tell Robin about the night crawler who had visited him the day she left. Clearing his throat, he said, "No, not yet, but I should have them done by the middle of next week."

"You slacker! You usually whip through those things."

"Yeah, well, Natalia came over the other night, and one thing led to another—"

"TMI, Declan. *TMI!*"

"Well, you asked."

"When are you going to marry her anyway?"

Declan pulled his iPhone away from his ear and stared at it for a moment before placing back it against his ear. "Where the hell did that come from?"

"It came from the fact you've been dating her for over three years, and you love her. Why don't you just marry her and get it over with?"

"She's Catholic, Robbie."

"*What?*" Robin said, jumping to her feet.

Instantly, Declan realized his mistake. "No!" he yelled into the phone. "No. No. No. *No*, that's not what I meant. Jesus Christ, you know I don't have a problem with any religion. It's just that all her brothers and sisters have bambinos coming out the wazoo and we'd be expected to keep up."

"So? You love kids, and you wouldn't be expected to do anything other than to love her. You forget I've met her parents, and they love you as much as I do. All they want is for their daughter to be happy, so put a damn ring on her finger already. You know you want to." Robin knew the connection was still good because she could hear Declan breathing. "*Hello*?" she said, her smile growing wider. "Cat got your tongue?"

"No, you took the little bastards with you," Declan grumbled. "I can forgive *you* for leaving, but you didn't have to take the cats."

"They're *my* cats, Declan," Robin said with a laugh. "And you can visit them whenever you'd like."

"Suppose that means I'd have to see you, too—huh?"

"Yep, afraid so."

Declan let out an exaggerated sigh. "I guess I could put up with you for a few days for the sake of the cats since they've always liked me better than you."

"They do not!"

He was trying to keep the conversation light because the sadness that had crept into Robin's tone months before still seemed to be lingering like a bad cold. Even when she was feigning shock, melancholy lurked just under the surface.

"All right, Robbie, all joking aside. Are you really okay? If you want, I can catch a flight—"

"Don't you dare, Declan. I'm fine. I just needed to hear your voice."

"If you say so," Declan said as he stood up, and going to the window, he pulled back the drapes. "Jesus-flipping-*Christ*!"

"Oh, my God, what's wrong?"

"It's fucking blinding outside," he said, recoiling from the sunlight. "What the hell does a person do at this hour of the morning anyway?"

"Well, if I'm not mistaken, *we* used to get up and go to class."

"That's true, but if you remember I didn't like it back then either," he said, closing the drapes. "So, what do you have planned for the day?"

"I'm meeting the lawyer at noon and..." Robin looked at her watch. "Crap, Declan I need to get a move on. I have a boatload of stuff to get done before then. I'll call you when I get there. Okay?"

"Or you could just text."

"Yeah, that'll be the day."

"I tried."

"There are some things you just need to let go of, Declan," Robin said, grinning as she began stuffing things into her suitcase."

"Robbie?"

"Yeah?"

"Right back at you."

***

"Well, I think that's about it," Howard Underhill said as he placed the last piece of paper in a folder and handed it to Robin. "Like I told you on the phone, your aunt had set up the living trust a few years ago so you should be set."

"I still can't believe she did that. I never even knew about it," Robin said, slipping the folder into her laptop case.

"Some people don't until it's all said and done," Howard said as he gathered up a few loose paperclips and dropped them into a tiny crystal bowl. "Adele always struck me as a very no-nonsense kind of woman. She knew what she wanted. She knew who she wanted to give it to, and she was smart enough to research everything before she called me. Adele knew by setting up this trust and adding your name to her accounts and the deed to the Inn, when she passed away, it would automatically transfer to you without the courts having to get involved. Less paperwork, less money, and a lot fewer headaches."

"Wow," Robin said, shifting in her chair. "So, that's it then?"

"Yes, except for these," Howard said, handing Robin a set of keys. "Those will get you into the Inn. The rest you'll find inside."

The jumble of brass and nickel was weighty in her hand, and as Robin read the words Safe Harbor Inn engraved onto the silver surface of the anchor-shaped key fob, she got to her feet. "I'm confused about one thing though."

"What's that?"

Robin put on her coat and dropped the keys into her pocket. "I'm embarrassed to say this, but the last time I visited my aunt was over thirty years ago. She owned a small house up on a hill, but you keep referring to it as an inn. I was wondering why?"

Howard's mouth dropped open, and as it closed, a smirk formed. "Oh, to be a fly on the wall today."

"What's that supposed to mean?" Robin said, eyeing the man. "What aren't you telling me?"

"Do you like surprises?"

"I suppose," Robin said, cocking her head to the side. "Why?"

"Well, you're about to get one, and I'm not going to ruin it," Howard said, and getting to his feet, he walked toward the door. "And I apologize again for not being able to take you over, but I handle divorces, too, and right now my client is involved in a messy one."

"That doesn't sound like fun," Robin said, slinging her laptop bag over her shoulder.

"No, but it beats flipping burgers," Howard said, reaching for the doorknob. "Leo is going to meet you and get you where you need to be, but if you need anything, anything at all, you have my card."

"But an explanation as to why you keep calling my aunt's place an inn isn't one of them?"

Howard's grin reached his eyes and then some. "Trust me, you'll understand soon enough."

Before Robin had walked into Howard Underhill's office, she already knew she was going to like the man. Over the past two weeks, they had had many conversations, and not one had been texted via the smartphones they both owned.

Robin was as techno-savvy as the next person, but having been burned by more than one woman hiding behind coy texts and well-thought-out e-mails, Robin was now wary of tiny typed messages. Voices, Robin believed, were more easily read than rapidly typed words, shortened to acronyms or misspelled entirely. With the right inflection, the spoken word can become a question or an answer. It can be happy or sad or somewhere in-between, and at times, it can prove intelligence or the lack thereof, but with Howard Underhill, it proved even more.

They had traded over a dozen calls, and while the multi-syllable words he had often used proved his education and profession, his tone had never held a hint of arrogance when she had asked a question. He was courteous. He was accessible, and on more than one occasion, he was downright funny, so her smile wasn't the first she'd worn when dealing with Howard. It was just the first he had seen.

"Well, you haven't given me a reason not to trust you, so I guess we'll just leave it at that," Robin said.

"Good idea."

"And again, I can't thank you enough for all the help," Robin said as she walked into Howard's outer office. "You've been great."

"Any time," Howard said, but as he watched Robin walk toward the exit, he blew out his cheeks. "Robin, hold up for a minute, will you?"

Robin stepped away from the door and waited for Howard to come over. "What's up?"

"Look," he said, lowering his voice so his secretary couldn't hear. "Um...you know how they say you can choose your friends, but you can't choose your family?"

"Sure."

"Well, Leo, he's my brother-in-law, and God help my sister, she loves him, but..." Howard stopped and hung his head for a moment. "But he can somewhat...somewhat pushy."

"Pushy?"

"He sees himself as the be-all and end-all when it comes to realtors, and when he finds out you've inherited Adele's place, well..."

"Ohhhh," Robin said with a wink. "Gotcha."

"He doesn't mean any harm, but I thought I should at least warn you."

"Well, since I don't even know what I've inherited, he's not going to get very far."

***

Robin sat near the window and stared out the glass. Her breath was steaming, and flipping up the collar of her navy blue pea coat, as she filled her lungs with the fresh autumn air, she thought back to her childhood. To piles of leaves in need of raking and to rainy fall mornings with skies the color of ash. To pumpkins on doorsteps and bags filled with candy, and to sleds and hills monstrous in the eyes of a child of three or four or five. Dressed in a snowsuit of yellow and her mittens tied on a string so they wouldn't get lost, she would giggle as her nose became red and her cheeks grew rosy, oblivious that her plastic boots were filling with snow. Her mother would call her inside, and wearing a frown, she would tut at Robin and then laugh, finding it impossible to discipline the gaiety that comes from innocence. After the layers of protection were removed and feet and hands were warmed, Robin would sit at the kitchen table and drink hot chocolate while her mother prepared a lunch of tomato soup and grilled cheese sandwiches for two.

A chill ran down Robin's spine, and she rubbed her hands over her arms to ward it off. Glancing at the carrier at her feet, she knelt to look inside, smiling instantly when she saw her cats doing an excellent impression of the symbol representative of Yin and Yang.

"We'll be there soon. I promise," Robin whispered, and covering the crate, she stood back up and looked once again through the water-spotted glass. How many times had her mother sat like this, staring out across water glistening from the sun? How many times had her mother visited this place only to return home somewhat sad, yet somewhat happy? How many times did her father visit or had he ever?

Robin's recollections of her father had been thinned by the passage of time, and it was only on the rarest of occasions when he came into her thoughts. She'd see a stubbly-faced man in a commercial or on a billboard, and she'd get a flicker of an image of her father's face, his chin shadowed by whiskers unstoppable, and his eyes, dark brown and penetrating. In a crowd, she would sometimes catch a whiff of an aftershave, classically blue and crisp in scent, and she didn't have to look to know the man wearing it would be old just like her father would have been…if he hadn't died.

He had been born and raised on a farm in southwest Indiana. The son of a corn farmer, his days had been long and hard, helping to grow a crop that would eventually be used as feed. His father loved the feel of earth in his hands and sun on his face, but he did not. He didn't want to rise before dawn or slumber with muscles aching and brow burned, so instead, much to the disapproval of his father, he became the first in his family to attend college. He hadn't told his father he had no intention of returning to till the soil again or repair tractors in rain or shine, but he never got the chance to break the old man's heart. An aneurysm had done that on a balmy, sunny day in April, just like a heart attack had taken his mother four years earlier. Less than a year after burying his father and graduating from college, he sold the family farm and stocked the money away for his retirement. His parents had worked themselves to death, and he had no intention of following in their footsteps. No intention at all.

Having earned a degree in accounting, he took a job at Newberg Wire and Cable in Fort Wayne, Indiana spending his days punching numbers, tallying columns, and making sure debits and credits balanced behind the short walls of the newest in business furnishings—the cubicle. The faux office, while tiny, was better than the open floor plan the company had used before, and hidden behind the panels, he could do his work without being disturbed by gum-smacking typists and other pencil-sharpening accountants. There was only one problem. Directly across from his cubicle was another and its occupant was blonde, blue-eyed, and beautiful. Like him, she also had a degree in accounting, so casual conversation came naturally, and so did what followed. In less than a year, they were married, and ten months to the day after Constance Novak and Billy Cook said their vows, Robin Catherine Cook was born.

A mini-me of her mother, Robin's hair was the color of corn silk and her eyes, the shade of the sky. She was a happy little baby as most babies are, cooing and gurgling and wanting nothing more than her mother's breasts and a heartbeat to listen to as she fell asleep. At such a tender age, she had no idea there was an undercurrent of tension between her parents, arguments over money becoming forefront in Constance's and Billy's daily conversations.

Determined never to end up like his father, working into his sixties with nothing to show for it except a bent spine and calloused hands, Billy squirreled away every penny he could. His wife and daughter never went without. There was always food on the table and heat in their apartment, but more often or not it was casseroles stretched by the addition of rice or potatoes, and temperatures requiring more than one layer of clothing to ward off the chill.

Constance wasn't accustomed to this level of frugality. She had lived on her own before marrying Billy, and she was used to watching her pennies, but Billy was taking it to the extreme. She would turn up the heat, and he would turn it down. She would say they needed something at the grocery store, and he would dart out the door, worried she would spend too much of his hard-earned money, and when Robin began to grow, Billy started bringing home clothes purchased at the local thrift stores, circumventing the shopping trip to Sears Constance had planned.

Yet, even though their relationship was becoming more strained as each month passed, neither had ever let their true feelings show around their daughter. They both adored Robin more than life itself, and while Billy was genuinely cheap, the love he bestowed on his daughter was not. All anyone had to do to get Billy to smile was mention his daughter's name.

Robin grew from one to two and from two to three without a worry in the world. Her parents loved her, and she loved them, but a few months after her third birthday, her mother grew sad. Robin didn't understand the tears or the visitors who seemed to walk over their doorstep for days on end, and her little brow wrinkled during a gathering at their church on a blustery Sunday. Why was everyone dressed in black, and what was in that box?

Late on a Thursday night as Billy traveled familiar roads returning from a quick trip to the grocery store, another man who had spent his evening swallowing gin and tonics ran a stop sign. Billy barely had time to utter an expletive before the Cadillac T-boned his faded green 1974 Pontiac Ventura, and in a blink of an eye, Billy was gone, leaving Constance to raise their daughter on her own.

The next few months were rough on Constance. No sooner had her daughter begun to accept that her daddy wouldn't be coming home when Constance had to explain that she no longer could spend her days with Robin. She had managed to get her job back at Newberg Cable and Wire, which meant Robin had to go into daycare, and it wasn't a smooth transition. More than a few mornings had been filled with tantrums and more than a few nights overflowed with tears, but slowly Robin adapted to daycare just as she had adapted to no longer having a father, and eventually, they settled into their new routines.

The following year, Constance bought a small two-bedroom house in Monroeville, a little town just outside of Fort Wayne. It was all the mother and daughter needed, and while its size usually deemed it a starter home for couples just beginning their lives together, it would remain Constance's home until the day she died.

Chosen by Constance for its hometown values and its small population, Monroeville was a place where everyone knew everyone, and everyone liked it. Neighbors helped neighbors. Churches were filled with familiar faces, and on warm Saturday nights, crowds would gather outside the soft ice cream shop at the end of the street, and under buzzing street lights, people would lick swirls of vanilla, chocolate, and strawberry while they caught up on each other's lives.

The years went by, and as they did, Constance watched as her daughter grew into a profession that was inevitable. As soon as Robin had learned how to read, books held her interest like a swinging pendant transfixes those hypnotized, so it was no surprise when Robin announced over dinner one night she wanted to be a writer when she grew up.

It's a parent's job to listen to their children's dreams. To smile and appease their offspring's aspirations to become astronauts, doctors, superheroes, or ballerinas, but Constance had never placated Robin, and she wasn't about to start. Instead, she asked Robin to explain why she wanted to be a writer.

Robin's exuberance bubbled over in an instant as if she needed to get all the words out or explode. She said she wanted to spin tales and keep readers on the edge of their seat. She wanted to weave her words much like the yarn her grandmother had used for the afghans draping the backs of their chairs and sofa, and she wanted her stories to be as complex as geometry, yet as addicting as chocolate-chip cookies fresh out of the oven.

Her breath taken away by her twelve-year-old's words, Constance gazed in awe at her daughter. It was the first and last time she ever questioned Robin about her career choice.

The sound of the ferry's horn jolted Robin from her thoughts, and looking around, she saw the other passengers beginning to gather their things. She peered back through the glass to the place she was about to call home and waited while the ferry came to a stop.

Unlike a few of the travelers who didn't seem to care about the instructions to remain seated, Robin did just that as the workers rolled all the carts off the boat. Stationed toward the back, each held the luggage and belongings of those traveling, but once the last was moved onto the dock, Robin got to her feet and took a deep breath. She slung the strap of her laptop case over her shoulder, and picking up the cat carrier, made her way off the boat. She stopped on the dock and squinted up at the brilliant blue fall sky. The sun was shining. The breeze was brisk, and suddenly Robin's face spread into a smile. She felt alive for the first time in months.

Chapter Three

At the eastern end of the Straits of Mackinac, between the upper and lower peninsulas of Michigan is an island not quite four square miles in size.

It had been home to the Ojibwa and the Huron tribes before being discovered by the French in 1634 when Jean Nicolet passed through the Straits in search of the Northwest Passage. Because of the hump-backed appearance of the island, its bluffs rising one hundred and fifty feet in the air, the Indians had named it Michilimackinac, meaning large turtle. The French, however, feeling the name was far too long, shortened it to Mackinac and while the name of the island ends in *nac*, keeping with the French pronunciation, it would be forever known as Macki*naw*.

From the time the French traders and Jesuit missionaries arrived in 1670, the island had been claimed by many. The French discovered it, but the British took control after the French and Indian War. The United States acquired it through the Treaty of Paris in 1783, and then promptly lost it back to the British during the War of 1812. However, in 1815 the Treaty of Ghent forced the British to return the tiny island measuring a mere eight miles in circumference back to the United States of America.

Men and women looking to escape the horrors of the years spent in a Civil War began to make their way to Mackinac to lose themselves in its history, its rocky beaches, and its scenic beauty. Ten years after the end of the Civil War and three years after Yellowstone National Park was named the *first* national park in the United States, seventy-four percent of Mackinac Island was named the second.

Boat and railroad companies began building hotels, and souvenir shops sprung up, and those who could afford it began construction of the summer cottages that would eventually line the bluffs of the island. Business was booming, and more and more people were visiting, but fearing the newest of inventions, in 1896 the people of Mackinac made a decision. The Village Council and the Mackinac Island State Park Commission voted that except for a few emergency vehicles, the use of automobiles on the island would be banned. A ban that still stands today.

***

Whether it's from an apartment, a condo, or a house, when someone moves, it usually involves either friends filling the trunks of their cars or beds of their trucks with everything you own, or moving vans driven by burly men who will eventually place your furniture wherever you'd like it. However, when a person moves to Mackinac Island, things are a *little* bit different.

Before leaving Florida, Robin had already arranged for long-term parking and a packet of ferry tickets, so her first stop that morning was to the dock station on the mainland in St. Ignace. She emptied the cargo hauler and the contents of her 4Runner onto a wheeled, aluminum cart and arranged for its delivery to Mackinac later that day. After that, she was off to the local U-Haul dealer to get rid of the annoyance she had towed for four days, and Robin ended her morning by walking up and down the aisles at Family Fare, filling not one, but two carts with everything she thought she'd need for the next few weeks.

Like most stores in the area, Family Fare was accustomed to making deliveries to the ferries for their customers, so after making those arrangements, and being assured her purchases would arrive on time, Robin was off to meet Howard Underhill. Shortly after noon, Robin climbed back into her SUV and returned to the hotel where she gathered her things and her cats before finally ending up back at the docks for the second time that day. So, as Robin made her way through the throng of tourists and dock porters, all she wanted was a nap…and a beer.

Robin stopped at the cart containing her belongings. Deciding what was essential and what could wait for another hour or two, with her laptop case draped over one shoulder, she slung a backpack over the other and then tugged a sizeable black suitcase from the pile. Listing slightly off her axis, she carried her luggage and the cat carrier over to a man holding a clipboard. "Excuse me. Can you help me?"

"What can I do for you, miss?" the man said.

"I was wondering how I can arrange to have my groceries delivered."

It was an odd question for a tourist to ask, and Glen Ramon eyed Robin for a few seconds. "Groceries?" he said, slipping his pencil behind his ear. "Where are you staying?"

Robin took a moment to set everything at her feet before reaching into her pocket "Here," she said, handing the man the Post-It Howard had given her.

As Glen Ramon read the address, the lines across his weathered forehead deepened. "This is the address for the Safe Harbor Inn."

An image of the key fob popped into Robin's head. "Yeah, that's right."

Glen let out a sigh and handed the note back to Robin. "I'm sorry, miss, but the Safe Harbor closed a few years—" The words died in Glen's throat as he stared at the woman in front of him. There was something about her face that was eerily familiar. It wasn't just the square jaw or the blue eyes or her sun-washed blonde hair, but when he noticed the sprinkle of freckles on the bridge of the woman's nose, another woman came to mind, and his eyes flew open wide.

"Well, I'll be damned," Glen said as he tossed his clipboard on a nearby box. "As I live and breathe!"

Before Robin could say a word, she found herself being hugged by the leathery-faced man. Her first instinct was to pull away, but when the smell of a familiar aftershave made its way to her, she relaxed and waited to be released.

After a moment or two, Glen took a step backward and held Robin at arm's length. "You're the spitting image of your mother."

It was Robin's turn to widen her eyes. "You knew my mother?"

"I've worked this dock for over thirty years and like clockwork, every summer and every winter, she'd come off that ferry like she didn't have a care in the world. I hope you don't mind me saying this, but when I see a pretty lady like your mom, I don't forget them too easily," Glen said with a smile, but it slowly faded from his face. "I'm sorry. I heard she passed away."

"Yes, she did," Robin said, offering the man a weak grin. "A couple of years ago."

"Well, her beauty won't soon be forgotten with you around."

"Thank you," Robin said, the rosiness on her cheeks no longer being caused by the chilly air. "So, I guess that means you knew my aunt, too?"

"Of course. Everyone knows *everyone* on Mackinac," Glen said. "Adele was quite a character. A little quiet, but she had a wit sharper than a razor blade. There weren't many around here who didn't cry when they found out she had passed, so you've been quite the talk of the town ever since we heard you were coming."

"What?" Robin said, flinching back her head. "How did you know I was coming?"

"Let me give you a piece of advice," Glen said, taking a step closer. "If you don't want anyone to know what you're doing or who you are, do not live on Mackinac."

Robin's face clouded with confusion and Glen chuckled. "You had the utilities turned on, and that lawyer...um...Mr. Underhill. He came here once or twice with some workers to make sure there were no problems with the plumbing or electricity at the Inn."

"Oh, I see," Robin said, smiling. "And word apparently travels fast."

"Faster than a yacht in the Straits on a windy day."

Just then a gust of wind came along, and Robin laughed as she combed her fingers through her hair to get it out of her face. "I'll have to remember that."

"So, you mentioned you had groceries on board?"

"Yes, and I actually have quite a bit more luggage, but I couldn't carry it all."

"Oh, you don't have to do that," Glen said as he scanned the dock. "Zayne, can you come here for a minute."

A boy Robin guessed to be in his late teens hurried over. "Yeah, Glen. What do you need?"

"Can you make a delivery to Safe Harbor?"

"Sure. I've just got to take that stuff to Bayview," he said, pointing across the way to his overloaded bike. "After that, I'm free until the next ferry. What am I getting?"

"Groceries and some luggage that matches that," Robin said, pointing to the suitcase at her feet. "They should all be tagged with the name Novak. Robin Novak."

"All right. Cool," Zayne said with a thumbs-up. "I'll see you there in about an hour."

"That'll work," Robin chirped. "Thanks!"

"My pleasure," Zayne said, and flashing a quick smile, he hustled back to his bike.

"Well, now that that's taken care of," Glen said, turning back to Robin. "Is there anything else I can help—"

"*Are you Robin Novak?*"

Robin cringed. Glen scowled, and in unison, they turned to consider the man who had just interrupted their conversation with his nasally shrieked question.

"I'm sorry?" Robin said, looking down at the short, beak-nosed man.

"Geez," Leo Valentine said, his eyes flicking toward the sky. "I said, are *you* Robin *Novak?*"

Robin suddenly remembered what Howard Underhill had said about his brother-in-law, and two and two equaled four. "You must be Leo."

"The one and only," Leo said, and grabbing Robin's hand, he shook it as if trying to dislocate her shoulder. "Howie told me you'd be coming in on the one-thirty. I've got a taxi waiting." Leo glanced at the luggage at Robin's feet and quickly snatched up the backpack. "I'll meet you at the taxi."

Robin watched as the man waddled away, his open black trench coat flapping like wings on a bird unable to get itself off the ground.

"Well, that was interesting," Robin said, turning back to Glen. She reached down and picked up the carrier, but when she went for the suitcase, Glen beat her to it.

"I'll get this stuff," he said, easily slinging the laptop case over his shoulder before picking up the suitcase. "Some of us were raised better."

***

With her things safely strapped down in the back of Mackinac's version of a taxi, Robin climbed into the red and yellow carriage and placed the cat carrier on the floor at her feet. The carriage dipped as Leo clambered in from the other side and plopped down on the bench seat, and a second later, it dipped again when the driver climbed into the front seat.

"So, where we going folks?" the man said, looking over his shoulder.

"To here," Robin said, handing the man the Post-It.

"This is the Safe Harbor Inn."

A wave of déjà vu washed over Robin, and she smiled. "That's right. It belonged to my aunt."

"Holy moly, you're Adele's niece," the man shouted, and tugging off his gloves, he held out his hand. "Sheldon Graham."

"Robin Novak," Robin said, shaking the man's hand. "You knew my aunt?"

"Sure as hell did," Sheldon said as he let go of Robin's hand. "Then again, everyone around here knew her. The island's not that big."

"So I've heard."

"And rumor has it you inherited the Safe Harbor?"

Leo hated favors. He had no problem asking for them, but when it came to paying them back, that was another story. It didn't matter he had met a client earlier on Mackinac, a wannabe islander frothing at the mouth to buy a house they couldn't afford. What mattered was that Leo wanted to be home in his slippers and comfy clothes, waiting for the dinner his wife would be fixing. It was Friday. That meant chicken and dumplings, and Leo loved chicken and dumplings, but there was one thing Leo loved even more. Money.

When Leo heard what Sheldon said, his ears matched those of a Doberman. Leo was all too familiar with the Safe Harbor Inn. A few years earlier when he heard Adele had fallen ill, he had made a special trip to Mackinac only to have Adele throw him out on his ear. Adele was a plucky old broad who refused to even listen to his sales pitch, but as he slyly glanced in Robin's direction and took note of her blonde hair, Leo made a judgment based on a myth. *This* was going to be a piece of cake.

"Hey, buddy, how about you do your job and let the little lady and I talk?" Leo snapped as he pointed down the street. "I believe it's that way."

Sheldon raised an eyebrow and giving Robin a nod, he turned back to the horses. With a click of his tongue and a flick of the reins, the two magnificent Percherons began to clip-clop their way through town.

Robin rested back in the seat as the carriage began to move, but before she could appreciate the hustle and bustle of a Mackinac day, Leo chimed in.

"So, before you can put the place on the market, you'll need to have an estate sale, and I'm an expert at those."

"Excuse me?" Robin said, swiveling on the seat.

Leo sucked in his cheeks and rolled his eyes. Reaching into the inside pocket of his coat, he pulled out a business card. "I'm a realtor, and I've been through this a dozen times. The first thing we need to do is have an estate sale. It's easy, trust me. You just place a couple of ads in the newspapers and put some notices up in the supermarkets. People love old stuff, so we can probably have the place emptied in a weekend."

Robin stared at the card Leo had forced into her hand. "What makes you think I want to sell?"

"Are you kidding me?" Leo said, following it with a loud guffaw. "Look around you. You really want to smell horse poopy all the live long day?"

It was hard not to notice the smell. As soon as Robin got off the ferry, the aroma wafted into her senses, but other than the initial shock of it, it hadn't really bothered her.

"It's not that bad."

"You say that now, but wait until the season starts," Leo said with a snicker. "And don't forget about the tourists. Come May, this place will be crawling with them. It's going to be noisy and busy, and there are going to be so many bikes and carriages, you won't be able to spit without hitting one of them."

"Well, I guess I'll have to try not to spit then," Robin said, handing him back his card.

Leo pushed the card back into Robin's hand. "Trust me, you're going to change your mind, especially if you plan to stay the winter," he said with a cold, humorless laugh. "You have no idea what you're in for."

"Maybe not, but I guess I'm going to find out," Robin said, turning in her seat. "Now if you don't mind, I'd like to take in the view."

"Why bother?" Leo said, and slouching on the bench, he crossed his arms. "It's not like it ever changes."

Robin refused to let Leo's brashness get in the way of her first day on the island, but when she returned her attention to the town, she realized it was already behind her. The horses guided the carriage around a turn, and with Leo sitting on her right, blocking her view of the homes lining the street, Robin looked to the left. She smiled as they passed the small building deemed the Public Library, wondering if any of her books sat on its shelves, but no sooner had the thought entered her mind when it was swept away as the Straits came into view. The water shimmered in the brilliance of the September day, and gulls plunged and swooped above the water, hunting for their lunch. Small waves lapped against the shore, but unlike the beaches she was used to, the one surrounding Mackinac was covered with rocks and stones. Entranced by the view, Robin sat mesmerized until the carriage was no longer moving.

"Why'd we stop?" she said, turning to Leo.

"Because we're here," he said, motioning with his head.

Robin looked past Leo, and at first, all she could see was a low wall of brick running parallel to the sidewalk. With the fringed fabric top of the carriage blocking her view, Robin slowly leaned forward, and as she did, she saw atop the brick was a short, white picket fence. She followed it with her eyes until she noticed a gated opening down on the left, and inside was a brick path leading to a set of stairs covered in blue indoor-outdoor carpeting. White, wooden handrails flanked the stairs, and at the top of the eight steps was a porch, and except for the several rounded columns supporting the roof, its balustrade system matched that on the stairs.

"What the heck?" Robin said under her breath, but unable to bend any further as her chest was now pressed against her lap, she hopped out of the carriage. Walking around the back of it, she looked up and up...and up.

Chapter Four

When the first homes were built on Mackinac, they were simple cabins used to house the missionaries and fisherman who called the island their home, but as the well-to-do began traveling to Mackinac, cottages were soon being erected.

At first, they were unadorned, modest homes where those slightly more fortunate could retreat for the summer. Little rectangles and squares, they dotted the town and hills sparingly; however, in the early 1880s, things began to change. The affluent, influenced by the resurgence of the Gothic Revival, started building houses far more substantial. Porches wrapped around the spacious two and three-story homes, roofs became steeply-pitched, and the dormers and eaves were decorated with scrollwork and gingerbread.

In 1886, recognizing the little island's appeal, a steamship company joined forces with two railroad companies to form the Mackinac Island Hotel Company. They purchased a piece of land on the West Bluff, and had constructed what, to this day, is the most notable and recognizable piece of architecture on the island. It took almost six hundred workers to build the wood-framed, two-hundred room structure...and they did it in only ninety-three days.

In July of 1887, the Grand Hotel opened its doors. It offered not only comfort but a six hundred sixty foot front porch which would eventually be deemed the longest in the world. In no time at all, tycoons of railways and barons of lumber were not the only ones flocking to the island. Notables such as Thomas Edison and Mark Twain were frequent guests at the hotel, and in future years, the likes of Truman, Kennedy, Ford, Bush, and Clinton would also make the trip. Not quite one hundred years after it was completed, the illustrious hotel would become the backdrop for the movie *Somewhere in Time*, and in 1989, it would be deemed a National Historic Landmark.

Around the same time as the Grand Hotel was welcoming its first guests, the new homes erected on Mackinac changed again. With the popularity of Victorian Queen Anne architecture in its heyday, two stories became three, and the simplistic gave way to picturesque castles of wood with turrets and sweeping verandas. Windows throughout the new homes now varied in size, and the colors used on the exteriors were rich and vibrant.

Lyman Majors was one of several who had made his fortune off the forests of Michigan during the nineteenth century. Its expanse of timber so large, the millionaires created during California's Gold Rush paled in comparison to those born from the Michigan woodlands. Trees of white pine, three hundred years old and two hundred feet high were felled, and by the end of the Civil War, the state of Michigan had produced more lumber *and* more millionaires than any other state in the Union.

Having made more money than he or his family could spend in their lifetimes, after visiting Mackinac with his associates to partake of whiskey and cigars at the Grand Hotel, Lyman bought a parcel of land near Julia Point. He thought it the perfect place for a summer home, and he spared no expense in having one built. In 1894, he and his wife and their six children arrived on Mackinac to spend their first summer in their new home, but in 1898 Majors sold the house and he and his family never returned to the island. For the next ninety-five years, the house would have numerous owners until in 1982 it was purchased by Adele Anderson and soon afterward, she named it the Safe Harbor Inn.

***

Robin held her hand up, blocking the sun out of her eyes as she looked up at the biggest dollhouse she had ever seen. In the timeless elegance of Victorian fashion, the blue-gray exterior was a mixture of clapboard siding and fish scale cedar shake, and the rooflines were as imposing as they were multi-faceted. Windows of various sizes and shapes dotted the façade, and while the woodwork surrounding them was as white as the rails on the porch, burgundy had been used as the accent, the color repeating on the bargeboards, frieze boards, as well as around the stained glass insert on the front door. Showcasing the wealth of the original owner, elaborate gingerbread details decorated the stately front-facing gable and intricate, turned spindles ran the length of the roof overhanging the porch.

"Jesus," Robin said under her breath, captivated by the house that was now her home.

"*You got keys?*"

Robin winced at the volume of what appeared to be Leo's normal talking voice. "What?"

"Do you have keys?" he said, pointing over at the house.

"Oh, yeah, Howard gave them to me." Robin fumbled in her pocket, intending to have the keys at the ready when she reached the front door, but as soon as they were free from her jacket, Leo snatched them out of her hand.

"I'll just go open it up for you."

Before Robin could react, Leo was scurrying up the sidewalk as fast as his portliness would allow.

"Seriously?" Robin said, shaking her head.

"He's a little pushy."

Robin turned to Sheldon and grinned. "You think?"

Sheldon's expression matched Robin's as he reached for the straps holding Robin's luggage in place. "Why don't you go catch up with him, and I'll get this."

"You sure?"

"Yeah, go ahead," Sheldon said with a wave of his hand.

"Thanks," Robin said, and spinning around she trotted after Leo, not at all surprised that he had already disappeared into the house.

As Robin made her way down the sidewalk and onto her property, she began to see the telltale signs of a house that had been empty for far too long. The front gardens were overgrown with weeds, their density choking out any perennial that had ever been planted. Withered leaves from the oaks and birch on the property were everywhere. Blown by the wind, they had drifted into the corners of the fence and mounded against the latticed foundation of the screened-in porch on the right side of the Inn, forming berms of brown, red, and orange.

The dried foliage crunched under her feet as she made her way up the stairs, and as Robin reached the door, she paused to read the words on a sign in the shape of an anchor mounted on the wall. *Safe Harbor Inn Built 1894.*

"Wow," she whispered just before walking through the open door. No sooner had she stepped inside when she saw Leo marching toward her from the back of the house.

"Nothing back there except the kitchen, dining room, and the innkeeper's suite," he said, whizzing past. "The good stuff must be upstairs."

For a moment, Robin stood there watching as the little man began to dart up the steps, but the stress of the last few days finally bubbled over. "Leo, stop!"

Robin waited for a second, but when Leo reached the landing of the L-shaped staircase and continued upward, Robin shouted. "Leo, I said *stop!*"

Leo jerked to a standstill, and looking like he had just sucked on a lemon, he glared down at Robin. "What?" he said, holding up his hands. "I'm just gonna go up and look around. Take a chill pill. I'll be down in a minute."

"No!" Robin yelled, seeing him take another step. "Look, I appreciate you taking time out of your day to meet me at the ferry, but I've had a very long week, and I still have a lot to do today." Robin pulled Leo's business card out of her pocket. "I have your card, and if I decide to sell, I'll call you."

"But it'll *only* take a minute," Leo said, glancing back and forth from the second floor to Robin.

"I'm sorry, but not today," Robin said, waving him down. "Not today."

Leo pressed his lips into a flat, white line and stomped down the stairs. "Fine," he said, placing his hands on his hips when he reached the foyer. "But you *will* call me when you're ready to sell—right?"

"*If* I decide to sell, you'll be the first to know," Robin said, holding up one hand. "I promise."

Leo pursed his lips, his eyes becoming slits as he stared at Robin. With a huff, he jammed his hand into his pocket and pulling out a wad of business cards, he fanned them out across the high-top reception podium by the stairs. "I'll just leave these here, so you don't lose them."

Robin sighed and motioned to the door. "That's fine, Leo. Have a nice day. Okay?"

"Yeah, you, too," Leo said, and with no intention of paying for a taxi ride, he trudged out the door to make his way back to the ferry.

"Everything else is on the porch, but I thought you'd want this inside."

Having forgotten all about Sheldon, when Robin spun around and saw what he was carrying, her shoulders fell. "Oh my, God," she said, taking the cat carrier from him. "I can't believe I left them outside."

"By the sounds of their meows, they're fine," Sheldon said, grinning.

"Thank you," Robin said, and putting down the carrier, she reached into her back pocket and pulled out her wallet.

"No need for that," he said, holding up his hands. "Today is on the house."

"What? Are you sure?"

"Yeah. Adele was a friend. It's the least I can do," Sheldon said, handing her his business card. "But I will give you one of my cards just in case you need anything, but *only* one. High-pressure sales, I'm not."

Robin's face brightened. "I can't tell you how much I appreciate *that*, and I'll definitely call you the next time I need a taxi," Robin said, placing the card alongside Leo's handful. "And thanks for bringing up the luggage and all. I really appreciate it."

"Not a problem," he said, turning to leave. "You have a nice one, and I'll see you around."

"You, too," Robin said as she watched him walk to the taxi. "And thanks again!"

Sheldon waved over his shoulder before climbing into the carriage, and with a snap of the reins, he headed off down the street.

Robin took a minute to gather her things from the porch, and after everything was stacked in the foyer, she closed the door and turned around. For the first time, she could take in her surroundings, and when she did, her eyes opened to the extreme.

White pine was the driving force behind Michigan's lumber boom. Structurally, it was the perfect wood. Easy to cut and shape, its timbers formed the framework of most of the homes on Mackinac, but for interior decoration, pine was much too soft to take the wear and tear of foot traffic or the occasional bump of furniture. For that, hardwoods were used, and a lumber tycoon in the late 1800s had no problem finding hardwoods.

The opulence of vintage red oak was not only visible on the hefty newel posts and balusters running up the stairs, but also in the floor and on the lower half of the walls of the entryway. Thick, raised panels of the hardwood acted as the wainscoting, and after being capped by a rail of walnut, the plaster walls above it were painted in a soft, creamy tan. The oak crown molding blended with the beams running to and fro to create the coffered ceiling, but while the crosspieces were oak, they had all been trimmed with the darker walnut. The plaster of each inset had been covered in wallpaper in a subtle design barely noticeable from where Robin stood. The background matched the color of the walls, but the minuscule dots of what appeared to be flowers were in the palest of greens.

Robin glanced at the brass lantern dangling from a sculpted medallion in the center of the ceiling, but its incandescence wasn't necessary at the moment. Natural light was streaming in through a stained glass window at the bottom of the stairs as well as its twin, lighting the landing halfway up, the oval shapes having backgrounds of rippled, clear glass and centers displaying purple irises with leaves of brilliant emerald. The last dash of color in the room came from the tapestry runner on the stairs. On a background of deep forest green, stems of sage and leaves of gold wound their way toward the second floor, and Robin found herself leaning to one side as she followed their ascent.

She debated for a second on whether to follow the path of the runner, but deciding to leave the upper floors for later, Robin went over to the double doors on the far right of the foyer. It took her a few seconds to figure out how to work the inset handles, but when she finally freed the latch from its keeper and slid the doors apart, her jaw almost hit the ground. Victorian parlors tend to do that.

At the time the house was built, parlors were used by many to depict their place in society. Extravagant and spacious, they proved the owner's worth in not only the furnishings they contained but the decorations as well. Adele spent years making the Safe Harbor Inn a showplace, and her hard work had paid off. The parlor was the first room her guests would view, and the impression had always been a lasting one.

The front wall kicked out like a bay window, and housing three chairs draped in sheets and two tiny tables holding lamps, it was the perfect place to read a book or sip coffee in the morning. The double-hung windows were tall and wide, and with the help of the transoms above each, they almost reached the ceiling. The sunlight was tempered by ivory sheers, and framing the windows were thick drapes in garnet.

The wallpaper Adele had chosen, while it would have been overpowering in a small room, held its own in the sizable lounge. Vertical stripes of tawny acanthus against a backdrop the color of currant ran from floor to ceiling and even with the addition of the accompanying border wrapping the room, Robin could find no fault with it. Opposite the doors was a fireplace, not quite the width of the room, and to the left and right of the brick hearth were slender bookcases, the shelves on one holding novels while the other housed board games and boxes filled with jigsaw puzzles.

Robin went over and lifted the corner of the sheet covering one of the two sofas in the room. Careful not to disturb the thin layer of dust on the cotton, she looked underneath and smiled. She had expected to see an old-fashioned chaise, its fabric buttoned and proper and its edges finished in wood, but instead, she discovered an overstuffed sofa, modern in design, yet having upholstery flowery enough to stay true to the room.

With the need for a bathroom becoming forefront in her mind, Robin left the parlor and headed in the direction Leo had come from a few minutes earlier, but she only made it a few steps before she stopped again. Diagonally set between the wall of the parlor and the dining room was another door and to the right of it was a small brass plaque in the shape of an anchor with White Birch engraved on its surface. Having stayed at a few bed-and-breakfasts over the years, Robin knew many used names instead of numbers for their rooms, and confident she had just discovered the first of many bedrooms in the Inn, she couldn't help but open the door.

Robin's eyes creased at the corners at the sight of the white four-poster bed sitting against one wall. Its turned posts reached almost to the ceiling, and even without bed linens covering the mattress or sheers draped over the canopy, it was still something to behold. Flanking the bed was a pair of nightstands, each holding tall brass lamps standing proudly atop lace doilies, and in one corner of the room was a chest of drawers, but it was the other corner that grabbed Robin's attention. Tucked into an alcove was a bathtub and right next to it was a door. Robin rushed over and looked inside. It was indeed a cute little bathroom holding all the necessities a guest would need, except for one thing. Defeated by an empty cardboard roll hanging in the holder, Robin let out a sigh, closed the door, and returned her attention to the bedroom.

She knew enough about Victorian architecture to know the bay window filling the far wall would most likely not be the last she discovered in the house, and going over, Robin pushed aside the yellowed lace curtains and peered out the glass. The side yard was not overly wide, and toward the front, she could see the back side of the screened-in porch, but instead of latticework hiding the foundation, there was a set of doors. Deciding she'd make her way outside later to investigate, Robin turned back to the room.

Except for the wall holding the bay window, the lower two-thirds of the rest of the walls were covered in vertical strips of wood planking painted the color of cooked cabbage. Quickly deciding she needed to add the washed-out green to her list of least favorite colors, Robin went over to some of the artwork dotting the walls. Most were watercolors of white-barked saplings in various stages of growth, some leafless as winter had already set in and others filled with greenery reaching toward the clouds, but one was different. A faded photograph in a no-frills, dark frame hung above the dresser. Its image void of life, it showed only an empty beach along a birch-lined lake. Thinking back to the plaque outside the room, Robin nodded as she made the connection. White Birch.

Her inquisitiveness satisfied for the moment, Robin left White Birch and rounding the corner, she went into the dining room. Like the foyer, the lower parts of the walls were again covered in oak panels, but the plaster above had been painted a stony blue. If Adele's decorating had stayed true to the extravagance of the Victorian era, the dining room set should have been ornate. With tufted chairs and intricate carvings in the walnut or rosewood, it would again have spoken the affluence of its owners, but Adele had known bed-and-breakfasts required functionality. The table filling the center of the room was more like something found in a country kitchen. Although not rustic, its trestle base and bow-backed chairs afforded comfort and support to those sitting around its perimeter and the two sideboards on opposing walls added to the hominess of the room. It was clearly a place designed to enjoy meals with friends, old and new.

At the opposite end of the room were two windows framed by long burgundy drapes, and between them was another set of double doors; however, this set was diminutive in width compared to those in the parlor. Her curiosity piqued, Robin went over, opened them and found herself looking at another pair identical to the first at the end of a short hallway. It only took three steps to reach them, and when Robin pushed the second set open, a wave of cold air washed over her as she stepped onto a glassed-in porch.

Robin was surrounded by hazy panes of glass running from floor to ceiling, their thickness doing nothing to stop the outside temperature from reaching the room. Above her head were two sizeable wicker-bladed ceiling fans affixed to the beaded paneling covering the ceiling, and on the floor were oversized squares of ceramic tile in the darkest of greens. Across the far wall were three tiny sets of bistro tables and chairs, their white cast iron design acting as a perfect accent against the floor, while the remaining two larger tables in the center of the room were constructed of rattan with glass tops, both of which were surrounded by bulky wicker chairs with thick flowery cushions. In the summer, it would be the perfect place to enjoy that first cup of coffee in the morning, except summer had already ended, and the chill in the air was all Robin's bladder needed to announce itself again. Backtracking, she continued to the kitchen with a little more pep in her step.

In sharp contrast to the medium and dark tones used in the front of the house, all the cabinets in the kitchen were white, and as soon as Robin entered the room, she momentarily had to squint. Sunlight was streaming in through a long bank of squatty windows to her left, and the black pearl granite countertops were acting like a mirror, sending laser beams of light in every direction.

Several of the wall cabinets had seeded glass inserts in lieu of wooden panels, and behind the decorative panes Robin could make out the shapes of dishes and cups. Tiny mosaic tiles of blue, white, and silver covered the walls between the cabinetry and countertops, and the blue repeated in the spatterware canisters nestled in one corner of the counter as well as on the base of the island in the center of the room. Opposite of where Robin stood was the stove, wider than any she had ever owned, and like the rest of the appliances in the room, its surface was stainless steel.

Still in search of a bathroom, Robin spent only a few moments admiring the kitchen before walking the length of the room to an alcove which housed three more doors. She opened the first, and a moment later she closed it, the smell of musty earth a clear indication that it led to the basement. The next took a bit more investigation, but once she found the light switch the mystery was solved. With file cabinets along one wall and a small desk off to the side, the room apparently was used by her aunt as an office. Seeing a narrow door off to her right, Robin was momentarily elated when she opened it to find a tiny powder room, except, again, all that remained was an empty cardboard roll. "I see a trend that I really don't want to see," she muttered.

Stepping back into the intersecting hallway, Robin glared at the remaining door. "Third time's the charm?" she said, and opening it, the corners of her mouth drooped when she saw the pale tangerine walls of the hall in front of her. Of all the colors in the world, her aunt had picked Robin's least favorite for the innkeeper's suite.

"Thank God I like to paint," she said, and strolling down the short hallway, she opened the first door she came upon. Crinkling her nose at the smell of camphor, other than a few hangers dangling from a wooden rod and an old mop and straw broom, there was nothing else to hold her attention, so shutting the door, Robin opened the next. Stepping into a room void of furnishings, but abundant in space, Robin's face lit up. It was large enough to hold all the bedroom furniture she currently had in storage and then some, and there was also a bay window completely filling one wall.

Instead of draperies, wooden slatted shutters covered each pane of the bay, and at that particular moment, Robin appreciated the lack of sunlight making its way into the room. Not only was the area rug a rusty orange, but the abstract design of the fabric covering the cushions on the window seat held more shades of orange than Robin knew existed.

"I need to start making a list," Robin mumbled as she went over to the only other door in the room. Pushing it open, she instantly did a fist pump. This bathroom had *everything* she needed.

Chapter Five

Robin dried her hands on her jeans as she stood in the bathroom and stared at the framework of a shower that had never been completed. To the right of the toilet, studs ran from floor to ceiling, the wood covered by the newest in tile boards awaiting their finish. The mortared shower pan had also been installed, and a dirty rag was stuffed in the drain hole, preventing the loss of tools or perhaps odor from escaping. Poking through some holes on one side were the stems of a faucet yet to receive their trim and on the floor at her feet was the fixture along with a couple of boxes containing grab bars.

Suddenly, sadness swept over Robin. Behind her was a large stained glass window and below it was an equally substantial claw-foot tub, but a woman in her seventies no doubt would have found it difficult to climb in and out of something like that. Adele had been planning for a future that had never happened.

"Shit," Robin said, and taking a deep breath, she shook her head and headed back to the suite to see what it contained.

In dire need of the facilities, Robin hadn't paid any attention to the innkeeper's apartment, so when she stepped outside the bedroom and saw a tiny kitchen a few steps away, she wrinkled her brow. The need for two kitchens in such close proximity escaped her, and the lines on her forehead grew even deeper as she looked around. The flooring was the same oak

Robin had seen throughout the house, and although dusty, it seemed in good condition. The rest of the suite though...not so much.

The kitchen cabinets were old, the finish around the handles having been worn away by continual use, and the countertop was the most basic of laminates, its white and gold speckled surface nicked in some spots and scratched in others. The stove was tiny, barely having enough room for two pots or pans, and the refrigerator reminded Robin of those she had seen in antique stores, although thankfully, it wasn't turquoise.

The only other door in sight was opposite the kitchen, and going over, Robin stepped inside a room that wasn't overly large or overly small. With an empty built-in bookcase in one corner and a small window in the other, she guessed it had been used as a spare bedroom, but with nothing more to see, Robin moved further into the suite.

Just past the little bedroom was the dining room, evident by a small chandelier hanging low in the middle of the space. Across the back wall was a set of French doors, and careful not to hit her head on the dangling light, Robin went over and looked through panes of glass much in need of cleaning.

Amidst the tall blades of grass was a vintage metal table and chairs, lying on their sides as if blown over by a storm. The red and white paint once covering their surfaces was now flaked and chipped, and rust was eating away at all the metal exposed. At the back of the property, Robin could see a shed, its gambrel roof adding several feet to its height, and propped against the building were a few forgotten lawn tools, their handles shooting up like sprouts amongst the weeds and grass.

Again, Robin decided to leave investigating the outdoors until another time, and backtracking, she stepped through the wide arched opening leading to the living room. It was easily the largest space in the apartment, but other than two mismatched dining room chairs off to one side, it was empty. However, even though it lacked in furniture, it more than made up for it with what it *did* contain.

The wall to her right held a fireplace. The brick above the hearth was stained from years of heat and smoke and the mantle, while thick and lengthy, held nothing on its surface except for dust. The far wall had yet another bay window centered in its length. The glass was hidden behind shutters, and the seat was covered with cushions, but instead of varying shades of orange, her aunt had chosen purple and chartreuse. Robin grimaced at the combination, but then she noticed something at the far end of the room, and her frown turned upside down.

So intent on finding a bathroom a few minutes earlier, when Robin was in the glassed-in porch, she hadn't paid attention to what was outside the windows. If she had, she would have seen the private entrance leading into her apartment. Built to copy the angles of the bay windows, the entryway protruded out into the side yard. The door and flanking sidelights were filled with opalescent glass, the swirls and streaks in the panes providing complete privacy while still allowing sunlight to enter.

Ordinarily, Robin loved the sun. It provided warmth, and it provided light, but at the moment, while one aspect was appreciated, the other was not. As if the cushions on the bay weren't enough to assault her taste in decorating, most of the oak flooring in the room was hidden underneath a thick baby blue shag carpet. The pale azure fibers were now thinned and dingy from years of traffic, and Robin curled her lip. "I *seriously* need to start making a list."

As Robin turned to leave, the fireplace caught her eye again, and going over, she studied the mesh fireguard propped in front of the hearth. She moved it just enough to eliminate the gap at the edges so her cats couldn't investigate the sooty alcove and then headed back to the front of the house where she was met with deafening meows.

***

It took Robin three trips to get everything from the front of the house to the back, but after the final one was made, her first priority was the two felines still trapped in the carrier. Pulling a plastic tray and a box of kitty litter from the largest of her suitcases, she temporarily set up their bathroom near the French doors across from the kitchen and finally let them out of their cage. "Welcome to your new home, guys."

The two cats slinked out of the plastic crate, and rubbing against Robin's legs, they meowed their appreciation for the freedom she had given them. She sat down on the floor and crossed her legs, and scratching their heads, Robin delighted in the purrs of love rumbling in their throats. After a few minutes, they sidled off to investigate their new surroundings, and climbing to her feet, Robin headed for the kitchen to do the same.

Robin's first stop was the refrigerator, and praying it was clean and turned on, she held her breath as she opened the door. Seeing a box of baking soda on one shelf and a bowl filled with quartered lemons on another, Robin exhaled. "Thanks, Howard."

"He didn't do it. I did."

Robin jumped a foot in the air, and spinning around, she took a step backward, all the while eyeballing the old woman now standing in her kitchen. She was barely five feet tall and wearing an over-sized powder blue sweat suit and a puffy down vest to match. Her silver-gray hair was short and curly, and her eyes were twinkling, and even though Robin guessed the woman was in her mid-seventies, she didn't shy away from bright colors. Peeking out from under her baggy sweats was a pair of neon yellow running shoes and on her lips was the rubiest of ruby red lipsticks.

"My God, you scared the living daylights out of me," Robin said, placing her hand on her chest.

"I'm sorry, but the front door was open and old habits die hard."

"Old habits?"

"Yes, Adele was my best friend. I was in this house almost more than my own," the woman said, extending her hand. "Maxine O'Connor, but most people just call me Maxi...like in the pad."

Tiny lines appeared at the corners of Robin's eyes as she burned the woman's given name into her memory. "It's very nice to meet you...Maxine."

"It's nice to finally meet you, too."

"Finally?"

A smile played at Maxine's mouth as she looked toward the living room. "That one's Fred isn't it?" she said, pointing at the tuxedo cat in the doorway. "And the white one is Ginger—right?"

Robin's mouth fell open. "How did you know that?"

Maxine waved her dainty, age-spotted hand in the air. "I told you. I was your aunt's best friend. We talked about everything, and your name came up all the time."

"Really? But...but—"

"I know," Maxine said, narrowing her eyes for a second. "You never visited other than when you were a child, but that doesn't mean your aunt didn't know anything about you. You forget your mother and Adele were as thick as thieves, so Adele was always up on what was happening in your life. I spent many an afternoon listening to her going on and on about you. How you lived in Florida. How you were a writer. How successful you were, and oh...of course, when you came out, *that* was the topic of many conversations. She was so proud of you. Said she thought you were very strong to do it."

"What?"

Robin's naiveté added rosiness to Maxine's cheeks. "There were no secrets between your mother and Adele, Robin, and there were none between Adele and me either." Noticing Robin's deer-in-the-headlights look, Maxine laughed. "Sweetie, I'm way too old to worry myself over who you sleep with. What's that they say nowadays? Love is love is love?"

Robin's face split into a grin. "Yeah, that's exactly what they say."

"Well, they're right whoever the hell *they* are. Life's just too damn short to worry about what or *who* your neighbors are doing," Maxine said. "But I should warn you there are some old fogies on the island who probably don't agree with me, but they already have one foot in the grave, so don't give them a second thought."

"I'll remember that," Robin said, now wearing an unwavering smile. "So, since you already know about me and the fact I haven't been here in forever, can you tell me when exactly Adele bought this place? I thought I inherited a small house up on a hill with a few rooms I could rent out to the seasonal workers. I definitely wasn't expecting this."

"She bought it in 1982 during the recession," Maxine said. "Adele had always wanted to own a B&B, and she'd had her eye on this place for years. The people who owned it had bought it for an investment, so they never considered any of the offers she made, but when the real estate market crashed, suddenly the property was worth less than what they had paid for it. Adele made them another offer, and they snatched it up quicker than a dog can lick a dish, so they could get out from under the mortgage."

"But how could someone who worked in a bank afford this?" Robin said as she grabbed her backpack off the floor and put it on the counter. "Recession or not, it couldn't have been that cheap."

"Oh, well…well, she did get some money when Stanley died."

"Stanley?"

"Her husband."

"Shit," Robin said, hanging her head. "I totally forgot about him. He was killed in Vietnam."

"That's right," Maxine said. "And between the money she received from the government and what she had saved, it was enough for the down payment."

"Now things are starting to make sense," Robin said as she unzipped a compartment on her backpack and pulled out two bottles of water. "Would you like one? I'd offer you some coffee or tea, but the rest of my stuff isn't here yet."

"I actually need to get going," Maxine said, glancing at her watch. "Poor Violet over at the fudge shop twisted her ankle this morning, so I need to go fill in."

"Well, the least I can do is walk you out."

Maxine strode through the house with Robin in quick pursuit, all the while enjoying what appeared to be the woman's endless energy.

When they reached the foyer, Maxine stopped by the reception podium and glanced at the business cards. "Valentine was here?"

"Yes, he met me at the ferry. The lawyer arranged it."

Maxine's shoulders fell. "I'm sorry to hear that you're going to sell Safe Harbor. Your aunt put her heart and soul into this house and—"

"I'm not going to sell it. At least, I don't think I am. Honestly, I haven't had enough time to wrap my head around all of this, so I don't really know what I'm planning to do right now," Robin said, tugging her coat closed. "Except to find out how to turn on the blasted heat."

The frown that had formed on Maxine's face faded away, and the tiniest of dimples appeared on her cheeks. "That's easy," she said, pointing into the parlor. "There are controls on all the baseboard units. You just need to turn the dial, and the heat will come on."

"Thanks," Robin said, rubbing her arms. "Heat wasn't something I normally had to worry about in Florida."

Maxine's eyes held a glimmer of humor as she opened the door and stepped out onto the porch. "Can I give you some advice?" she said, turning around.

"I'll take all I can get," Robin said, leaning on the doorframe.

"Dress in layers. You're going to need it." After giving Robin an adorable yet devilish smirk, Maxine made her way down the stairs, and climbing onto an old three-wheeled Schwinn, she pedaled away.

"What a character," Robin said with a grin, and closing the door, she walked back through the house.

As soon as she got to the suite, Robin took the time to adjust the dials on the baseboard heater in the kitchen, but before she could think of what to do next, the thundering clang of the doorbell drove its way through her bones. "Jesus," she said, and running out to the small hall, she glared at the chime box on the wall above the door. "You are *so* coming down as soon as I find some tools," she said before heading back to the foyer.

Robin opened the front door just in time to see Zayne Johnson stack the last of her things on the porch. "Wow, you managed all of that in one trip?"

Zayne glanced at the eight banana boxes filled with groceries and the stack of luggage by the door. "That's nothing. Piece of cake," he said, gesturing toward the oversized cart attached to the back of his bike. "The more you haul, the more you...um...make."

Charmed by the blush appearing on the young man's face, Robin reached into her back pocket and pulled out her wallet. "Is this okay?" she said, handing him some cash.

"Yeah, it's great," he said. After stuffing the money into his jeans, he pulled out a business card. "Can I give you this? It's got my cell number on it, so if you need any help, just text me. I'm an islander so even in the winter, I'm around."

"Good to know," Robin said, taking the card. As she slipped her wallet back into her pocket, she noticed beads of sweat on Zayne's forehead. "Hey, do you want a bottle of water?" she said, pointing to a case sitting on the porch. "You look a little warm."

"No, I'm fine. Thanks," Zayne said, looking at his watch. "The next ferry is coming in soon, and I need to get back. The best thing about the season coming to an end is there aren't as many dock porters around to compete with, but I can hustle your stuff inside if you want. It'll only take a second."

"Oh, that's not necessary," Robin said, realizing the boy probably made most of his money on tips. "I can handle it."

"Okay, well, see you around," Zayne said, and skipping down the steps, he swung his leg over his bike and rode down the street.

***

An hour after Zayne had dropped off her groceries and luggage, the rest of Robin's belongings showed up on a dray pulled by two imposing chestnut-colored Belgian Draft horses.

The driver, who introduced himself as Woody Murdock, was almost as massive as the animals. His chest barreled and his shoulders broad, the man appeared to be a six-foot-five tower of strength, but nevertheless, he had brought along his two young sons to assist. Miniature versions of their father, neither seemed to be older than twelve, but like colts on legs still spindly from youth, their height far outreached their age.

Woody explained that most of his deliveries were curbside, but like all the other locals, he had heard about Robin and her connection to Adele Anderson, so curbside was *not* going to happen. Instead, he and his sons carried all the totes into the foyer, and although he refused a tip, Robin did manage to slip some money to his sons, their gratitude quickly showing itself through broad, gap-toothed smiles.

When Robin had packed up her condo, she had done it methodically, purchasing as many plastic totes as were needed to store her things safely, but by seven o'clock that evening, Robin wished she had sold more and packed less.

After searching through the totes for the essentials, she lugged five back to the innkeeper's suite, leaving the others piled in the entryway to be dealt with later. The next few trips involved carrying her suitcases to the bedroom until finally, the only thing left was the banana boxes filled with her groceries and essentials. Given the size of the larger kitchen, Robin used it as her staging area, spreading the cardboard crates out atop the counters, so she could easily view their contents, and after she placed the perishables into the old fridge in the suite, with shoulders sagging, she slunk back to the front of the house one more time.

Her first stop was White Birch, but a quick search told her there were no sheets or blankets for the bed, and having no desire to climb stairs after trekking through the house a zillion times, Robin headed to the parlor. Standing in the doorway, she looked at the room and nodded. For a while, it was going to have to act as her bedroom.

She carefully removed the sheets covering the sofas and tables, and after turning on the baseboard heaters, Robin traipsed back to the suite again. She was hungry. She was thirsty, and by the sounds of it, so were her cats.

***

A short time later, Robin returned to the parlor, instantly wrinkling her nose at the smell of the dust being burned off the elements of the heaters. She cracked open a window to let in some fresh air before sitting on the sofa and ending her evening by sipping her beer in between bites of her ham and cheese sandwich, all the while wondering if she should just pack up and move back to Florida.

The house was huge and so much more than she had bargained for. Her plans had only been to hunker down in a small cottage on a hill, content in allowing life to pass her by while she wrote her books, but how could she do that here? One person living in something so big seemed a waste. Then again, could she really sell it? Her mother had loved

Mackinac, and her aunt had spent over thirty years renovating Safe Harbor, but Robin couldn't help but think that if she called Leo right now, he'd have the house listed by the morning.

Robin put down her beer, and reaching over, she turned off the end table light behind her. For a second, she debated on turning off the other lamp across the room, but its bulb was dim, and she was tired, so stretching out across the sofa, she covered herself with one of the blankets she had packed and stared into the shadows. As she listened to the occasional clink of metal baseboards expanding from the heat, she let down her guard, and her mind did the rest.

She had once had so much energy, and the words she wrote flowed from her like water from a spigot, and then her mother died. The loss was unimaginable, and for months Robin walked around in a daze, but the reality of what she was becoming hadn't settled in until her forty-third birthday. Surrounded by friends at a local bar, they toasted her, their impromptu roast bringing tears of laughter to her eyes, but when Robin walked into her empty condo later that night, she realized that she was becoming just like her mother.

Constance had lived a solitary life, never going on dates or tripping the light fantastic with someone tall, dark, and handsome. She'd only venture out with friends for drinks or dinner, seemingly content with her lot in life, and now Robin was doing almost the same thing. True, she had dated lots of women, but only a few had remained in her life longer than a couple of weeks and then, one way or another, the relationship would come to an end. More often than not, the decision had been Robin's. Some were too clingy and some, too aloof. Some liked to drink far too much while others tutted when she ordered a beer, and then there were those who either wanted all the control in the bedroom or none of it. Robin had had lots of reasons to walk away from relationships, but as she sat alone on her bed in the condo that night, she made a decision. Next time, she would try harder.

Robin flinched, wincing at the headache now boring into her temples. She flexed her fingers, working out the stiffness caused by having her hands fisted for so long, and sitting up, she let out a sigh as she reached for her beer. Emptying it in one swallow, she fell back onto the sofa, took a deep breath, and tried to push away the thoughts that, once again, had burrowed their way into her brain like a cancer.

They had been the same ones that had dogged her for months, turning her dreams into nightmares and her mornings into pots of coffee overflowing with caffeine. They had sucked the words from her mind, her skill as a writer evaporating with every sleepless night until there was nothing left except endless days and endless nights filled with contempt.

Robin pressed her palms against her temples, groaning out loud her frustration at the throbbing in her head. She closed her eyes and again focused on the crackling of the heating system, counting the tiny pings and snaps of the metal as it expanded, but when something else made a noise, Robin stopped counting. She stopped breathing, too.

Slowly, Robin opened her eyes and looked at the ceiling, peering at the plaster as if slitting her eyes would somehow heighten her hearing. As silently as possible, she drew in a breath, but before the air exited her lungs, Robin heard the noise again and bolted upright on the sofa.

Robin had taken physics in high school and while not her favorite subject, she was familiar with the concept of heat rising. Molecules, less dense when warmed, rise above their cooler counterparts, but since turning on the heat in the parlor, the temperature in the room had yet to raise ten degrees, so physics had nothing to do with the floorboards creaking above her head. Her eyes darted to the chair across the way, and Robin was more than a little disappointed to see Fred and Ginger still snuggled on the cushion. If they were there...who was upstairs?

She paused, silently praying that the house was just settling or perhaps the winds had grown strong. It didn't matter that she knew the house was over a hundred years old, and its settling days were most likely over, and it didn't matter that the sheers covering the window she'd cracked open were stock-still. All that mattered was as long as Robin could come up with excuses for the groans of the floorboards above her head, there would be no need to investigate. Unfortunately, Robin couldn't come up with anything to explain why the sounds suddenly seemed to be traveling, and when the distant squeak of a hinge resonated against her eardrums, rationalization was lost, and Robin leapt to her feet.

Robin had seen dozens of horror movies. She had sat in theaters, munching on popcorn as madmen slashed, strangled, and dismembered their victims in every way, shape, and form possible. She had, on occasion, jumped in her seat or turned away when the blood gushed, but more often than not, she'd just roll her eyes at the stupidity of the prey. They'd climb into unlocked cars without checking the back seats. They'd find a hiding place that any toddler could discover without even trying. They'd always fall when they ran and instantly lose the ability to right themselves. Their cell phones were *never* charged, and seriously, who walks into a room without turning on a light?

Robin rushed around the room, turning on every lamp along the way, but when she returned to the sofa and went for her cell phone, she stopped mid-reach. Hanging her head, a strained titter slipped from her lips. She had just become the lead in a Hollywood thriller. Her phone was charged, of that, Robin was sure because it was currently plugged into an outlet...in the master bedroom of the innkeeper's suite.

Weapon instantly became the next word taking up space in Robin's head, and with adrenaline now coursing through her veins, her brain began firing on all cylinders. She scanned the room, mentally crossing off items as she went. There was a pretty little chair sitting in the corner, its seat cushion covered in tapestry upholstery. It appeared light enough for her to carry, but unless her only intent was to make kindling, she doubted its ability to protect. The tambour mantle clock was undoubtedly hefty enough to make a dent in anyone's skull, but its bulk made it impossible to use as a club, and the cherub candleholders situated to the right and left of it were far too fragile to even consider. She looked from one hurricane lamp to another, dismissing them all because of their glass bases and shades, and for a fraction of a second, her eyes locked on Fred and Ginger. They were light. They had claws. They didn't like strangers. "What the hell is wrong with you?" Robin said in a whisper. "Get a grip, woman. Think, damn it. Think."

Robin returned to focusing on the room, her breath catching in her throat when she spotted a lamp atop a table near one of the bookcases. Its base was bronze and its design slim, so rushing over, she carefully removed the tulip-shaped glass shade and yanked the plug from the wall. The accent lamp was heavier than she had imagined, but its weight gave her courage. Turning it upside down, Robin gripped the neck of the lamp, raising and lowering it until it was comfortable in her hand before tiptoeing to the doorway. She stepped into the foyer, running her hand down the wall until she found the switch, and flipping it up, she quietly snorted. Of the three bulbs in the brass lantern, only one was working, and the light it cast was laughable.

"Shit," Robin said in a whisper and creeping toward the dining room, she felt for the light switch. She flicked the toggle up and then down and then up again. "Oh, you gotta be kidding me. Seriously?"

Frowning at the thought of traveling through the pitch-black dining room, Robin returned to the entry and glanced back and forth between the stairs, the parlor, and the front door. "Oh, this is ridiculous," she mumbled. "What am I going to do? Run screaming down the street?"

It only took a moment for Robin to convince herself she had watched too many movies, and squaring her shoulders, she climbed the stairs; however, the closer she got to the second floor, the slower and quieter she became. Flicking on the switch at the top of the steps, she let out the breath she'd been holding when the four ceiling lights came on without incident.

"Now what?" Robin said as she looked up and down the long hallway. There were five doors, all of which were open, a set of stairs leading to the third floor, and two archways. One was at the far end of the corridor and the other, only a few steps away, was to her right. Holding the lamp in a death grip, Robin went over and peeked through the opening, the sound of her heart pounding in her ears fading almost instantly as soon as the small sitting area came into view. In front of the three windows looking out over the street was two overstuffed chairs flanking a petite table, and from where Robin stood, she could see the lights of St. Ignace across the water. Confident there was nothing in the nook that could have made the noise she heard, Robin turned around and headed for the nearest open door, the tiny plaque next to it engraved with the words Sunset Shores.

Robin took a deep breath, her knuckles whitening as she raised the base of the lamp above her head. Snaking her other hand into the darkness, she found the switch, flipped it on, and jumped into the room like a warrior ready for battle. A second later the room was flooded with light and Robin lowered her impromptu weapon. When she came upstairs, Robin's intent hadn't been to tour the house, but drawn to the two windows opposite the bed, Robin went over and smiled as she saw the lights of St. Ignace again. It wasn't hard to imagine how beautiful the view would be in the morning with sunlight dancing on the water.

Turning her attention to the wallpaper, Robin ran her hand over the pattern of small pale pink roses on stems the color of faded mint. There was also a hint of Aegean blue in the design, and as Robin looked around the room, she saw that Adele had chosen that color as the accent in Sunset Shores. The shade was repeated in the quilt and the area rug covering the floor, as well as on most of the frames of the paintings on the walls. Given the size of the room, it was minimally decorated, holding only a full-size bed housed in an iron frame, two tiny nightstands, and an armoire tucked into one corner, all of which were as white as the trim in the room. With the addition of a vase of flowers or perhaps a crystal bowl of potpourri, contrary to her orange apartment, as Robin left the room, she couldn't think of anything else Sunset Shores could possibly need other than a fresh coat of white paint on the trim.

The plaque alongside the next door in line announced Central Lake, and returning to her defensive posture, Robin repeated her surprise attack. Leaping into the room as soon as she turned on the light, she was ready for battle, and while a small yelp of fright *did* slip from her lips, it had nothing to do with an intruder.

Unlike Sunset Shores, the paper covering the walls in Central Lake was anything but muted. Carnations of varying shades of fuchsia could be seen everywhere above the white chair rail and below it was stripes of white and a pink reminiscent of the hue found on plastic flamingos. Tatted doilies covered the tops of the bureau and nightstands, and lace curtains draped the windows, adding yet even more froufrou to the space. The darkly-stained walnut bureau and nightstands glaringly opposed the pink frilliness of the room, yet even with the less-than-desirable color combinations, it was clear to Robin the room had some finer points.

The southeast wall jutted out much like the bays on the ground floor, allowing for a small seating area complete with two cushioned chairs and a coffee table, and Robin had no doubt that the three tall windows behind the set would fill the room with natural light. The queen-size bed was surrounded by an elegant brass and bronze frame, its antique finish repeating throughout the room, and with the two other doors in Central Lake open, Robin could see it contained not only a bathroom but a small closet as well. Failing to find anything that could have caused the sounds she heard, Robin closed the door to Central Lake and walked across the hallway to a room labeled Bayview.

***

Robin descended the stairs an hour later, flicking off lights as she went. Battle ready, she had walked in and out of every room on the upper two floors. She had discovered several she adored and several she didn't, but other than jumping out of her skin twice when full-length mirrors in bathrooms surprised her with her own reflection, Robin hadn't found anything that could have caused the noises she had heard.

As soon as Robin opened the doors leading to the parlor, her cats greeted her by weaving in and out of her legs, and ushering them back into the room with some kind, whispered words, she adjusted the doors until they were only opened a crack. She made her way around the room, turning off all the lights she had switched on in a panic, and after returning her faux club to the table by the bookcase, she headed back to the sofa.

Robin sank into the cushions, combing her fingers through her hair as she let out a sigh. She reached over and yanked on the brass chain dangling from the lamp on the end table. When the room went black, Robin realized she'd forgotten to turn on the little light with the dim bulb, but before she could swing her legs off the sofa, Fred and Ginger jumped up and began looking for a place to sleep. A smile graced her face as she felt them settle in against her, their throaty purrs quickly fading away as sleep took hold again, and letting out a long breath, Robin pulled the blanket over her and closed her eyes.

The heater still popped and cracked occasionally, but Robin's heart no longer raced. Old houses make noise. It was just that simple, and as slumber weighed down upon her, pulling her into a chasm noiseless and safe, Robin's mind fired a few more times. Why hadn't her mother told her about Safe Harbor...and why had the creaks of the floorboards stopped as soon as she had gone upstairs?

Chapter Six

Robin opened her eyes and seeing nothing but black, her first thought and her first words were identical. "Shit, not again." She scrubbed her hand over her face, but when something brushed against her skin, her eyes widened, and very slowly Robin pushed away the blanket covering her face.

The sun was blazing its way across the parlor, the sheers no match for the early morning light or for the arctic air making its way through the window Robin had opened the night before. "Oh, that was stupid," she said, seeing the lightweight panels flapping in the breeze. Totally forgetting she was wearing only a T-shirt and a thin pair of pajama bottoms, she tossed aside the blanket and regretted the decision instantly.

"Fuck!" Robin yelled as the frigid air found its way to her skin. Darting across the room, she closed the window with a bang and then ran back to the sofa to grab the blanket. Mindless of the two cats who had taken up residence in the warmth, she snatched up the thermal fleece and sent Fred flying in one direction while Ginger soared in the other.

"Crap, sorry guys," she said as she cocooned herself in the blanket. "Momma will make it up to you. I promise."

Fred and Ginger stared back at Robin through eyes black as coal. After reprimanding her with several swishes of their tails, they forced themselves through the crack in the pocket doors and scampered up the stairs leading to the second floor.

"Shit!" Robin said, running after them. "Fred. Ginger. Get your asses down here!" The few seconds Robin waited seemed like a lifetime to her full bladder. "Come on, guys. Momma has to pee," she said, squeezing her legs together. "Please?" Another minute passed before nature's call became too great, and remembering she had closed all the doors the night before, Robin stomped toward the innkeeper's apartment as she mumbled under her breath, "They listen like stepchildren."

Robin took the time she needed to use the bathroom, brush her teeth, pull on a hoodie, and set up her coffee maker before she made her way back to the front of the house. With no cats in sight, she climbed the stairs, but just before she reached the top, she found herself scrambling for the railing when Fred and Ginger dashed between her legs and sprinted down the stairs. "What the hell?" she muttered as she plopped down on the step. "You guys see a ghost or what?"

***

"Hi, it's me."

"Hello me."

"Thanks for the flowers. How did you know where to send them?"

"A couple of days after you left, I called that lawyer you've been dealing with," Declan said before pausing to take a sip of coffee. "He hooked me up with your address and the name of a local florist."

"Well, they're beautiful," Robin said, glancing over at the arrangement of yellow, bronze, and russet chrysanthemums sitting on her kitchen counter.

"I'm glad you like them. I hope they brightened your morning."

"They did."

"So, how's the house? Just like you remembered?"

"Not exactly," Robin said as she poured herself a cup of coffee. "Declan, this place is huge."

"What the hell are you talking about? You said it was a little three-bedroom cottage."

"It *was* a little three-bedroom cottage until Adele sold that one and bought this thing. Declan, it's a three-story Victorian bed-and-breakfast."

"Oh, my God, you're shitting me."

"No, I'm not!" Robin said, waving her hand in the air. "It's freaking huge, Declan. I mean big. Massive. Colossal. *Gargantuan*!"

As Declan's eyebrows went up, the corners of his mouth went down. "Robbie, I'm fairly schooled in all the synonyms used to describe large, so it sounds to me like there's something wrong."

"Nothing's wrong. Why would you think that?"

"Besides the fact that you just answered my question with a question, you mean?"

Robin sighed. "Declan, I came up here to write, and this place is more than I can handle. A shitload more than I can handle."

"You don't give yourself enough credit, kiddo," Declan said. "You were a wreck after your mom died, but you pulled yourself together and did what had to be done. How many times did you fly back and forth between Indiana and Florida to handle her estate? And what about all the crap Pam put you through? You handled that."

"Barely."

"Maybe so, but you did it."

"Yeah, but that was just about getting through the day or the week or the month. This is about changing my career, and I don't want to do that."

"Who the hell said you had to?"

"Declan, this place is—"

"Huge! I know. You've said it in all kinds of ways, but other than that, what's wrong with it?"

"What?"

"Is it falling down?"

"No."

"Does it need a lot of work?"

"Not really. Some of the rooms probably could use a facelift, and the innkeeper's suite needs some serious changes, but other than that, it's gorgeous."

"Are the neighbors homophobic?"

Robin set her jaw. "Since when do I give a damn about homophobes?"

"That's my girl," Declan said, hearing a hint of pluckiness in Robin's tone. "So knock off trying to find lame excuses not to stay."

"What lame excuses?"

"It's too hard," Declan said in a nasally voice. "It's too big. I wanna write. Boo hoo hoo."

"Well, I do!"

"Then write, goddamn it," Declan shouted. "No one said you had to run the freaking place. Hire someone, for Christ's sake."

Robin bowed her head. "I didn't think of that."

"That's what you have me for," Declan said, smiling. "Now, putting aside all your big, huge, colossal, *gargantuan* house worries and your redecorating tasks, I've noticed there's one thing you haven't said."

"What's that?"

"Do you like it up there? I know it's only been a day, but what do you think? Is it somewhere you could call home?"

Robin took the time she needed to think about the question. "Yeah, I like it and..."

Declan glanced at his phone to make sure the connection hadn't been lost. "And?" he said, putting the phone against his ear.

"And I slept through the night, Declan," Robin said quietly. "For the first time in months, I didn't have a nightmare. I didn't wake up screaming. I fell asleep in just a few minutes, and I slept until the sun came up."

Declan took a deep breath, letting it out slowly as his grin grew large. "Robbie."

"Yeah?"

"Find someone to run that place...because you're staying."

***

Robin sat on one of the mismatched dining room chairs halfway between her living room and her kitchen, looking back and forth between the two areas, deciding what she liked and what she didn't. The private entry had possibilities, but the shutters covering the bay had seen better days. One set listed to the right while another slanted to the left, and if Robin was going to stay, crooked wasn't an option. The fireplace was rustic and cozy, and she could imagine sipping cocoa in front of the flames, but the surround would have to be replaced, and the brick scrubbed to remove the years of soot. The two ceiling fans centered over each end of the living room, their blades drooping from either age or grime hidden from view, would also have to go, and there wasn't a chance in hell the shag carpet would remain.

She knew the kitchen cabinets could be salvaged with sandpaper and paint, but the counters had lived well past their prime as had the harvest gold appliances. She glanced over at the dining area, her eyes first finding the minuscule chandelier before she slowly considered the French doors and then the kitchen.

"I must be crazy," Robin said, sniggering as she got to her feet. After taking another gulp of her rapidly-cooling coffee, she placed the cup on the counter and made her way to the basement. She had a lot of work ahead of her, and she was going to need a lot of tools to do it.

The hinges squeaked as she opened the door, and flicking on the light, Robin looked down at the old steps as the smell of musty dampness wrapped itself around her. She crept downward, listening to the treads creak as she moved from one to the next, dancing her fingers over the handrail for fear the old wood would splinter and pierce.

When she reached the bottom, Robin took in what was around her. With only four naked bulbs hanging from the joists, much of the basement was still in shadows, yet it was hard to miss the two chest freezers off to the side, their lids open like large-mouth bass. Robin went over and let out a sigh of relief. Both were empty except for a thin coating of dust on their otherwise pristine white interiors. After making a mental note to clean them before turning them on, Robin headed toward the washer, dryer, and three water heaters lined up against a wall. She tilted her head for a moment and then she saw numbers written on the top of each heater, designating the floor they controlled. "Well, that explains that, now doesn't it."

Having reached the end of the illumination the closest bulb afforded, Robin had no choice but to leave whatever existed in the shadows for another day. Going back the way she came, she noticed a large workbench on the other side of the stairs. Above it were several shelves filled with cans and bottles of various sizes, each labeled with what it contained, and Robin soon knew that if she was in the market for a nail, screw, picture hanger, hook, bolt, or nut, this was where she was going to shop first.

At the far end of the bench was a tall tool chest, its red surface dented and rusted, and for the next few minutes, Robin opened and closed all the drawers until she found what she needed. Clipping a measuring tape on her belt loop and stuffing a screwdriver and utility knife into the back pocket of her jeans, she turned to scan the shadowy basement again. Although tempted to spend the next hour rummaging around to discover what secrets it held, when Robin saw a stack of ladders propped up against a support column, she got back on track. Going over, she grabbed the one closest to her height and carefully made her way back up the stairs. The basement wasn't going anywhere, and Robin had things to do.

***

For the rest of the morning, Robin was a cleaning machine. Between the supplies left under the sinks and the ones she had purchased the day before, by lunchtime, the parlor had been *almost* returned to its former glory. The drapes and area rug would have to be professionally cleaned, and while there was a laundry room on the second floor with three washers and dryers standing at the ready, it seemed pointless to wash the sheers at the moment, so she focused her attention on the rest of the room. By the time Robin's stomach began to growl, the bookcases and tables were shining, the windows were streak free, and all the knickknacks had been carefully washed and returned lovingly to the spots her aunt had last placed them. Satisfied she had done all she could do, Robin returned to the kitchen to devour another ham and cheese sandwich before proceeding to attack the apartment with the same velocity...albeit not with the same results.

Her intent had been first to remove the shutters on the bay in the living area, but screws with stripped heads had caused her to mutter more than one expletive until, defeated, she turned her attention to the shag rug. At almost the length of the room, Robin spent the better part of an hour wrestling with it before it finally ended up like a beached blue whale across the living room floor. The soot and stains on the fireplace stood strong against every cleaner in her arsenal, and when she stripped away the cushions of the two bay windows and discovered hinged seats underneath, she was bested by locks for which she didn't have keys.

By the time the sun went down, Robin was a wet dishrag. Her fingers were pruned. Her deodorant had long since failed, and she knew if she bent down one more time, she wouldn't be standing straight anytime soon. She opened the refrigerator, considering the beer on the top shelf for only a second before she closed the door and trudged back to the totes stacked in the foyer. A minute later, she returned to the kitchen with a bottle of wine in one hand and a corkscrew in the other.

After filling a red plastic cup with a Cabernet that deserved crystal, Robin grabbed a notepad and began jotting down things she needed to do and needed to buy. The list snowballed, her mind still firing even though her body had long since fizzled, but when she felt Fred and Ginger rubbing themselves against her legs, Robin set the list aside.

"You hungry, guys?" she said, looking down. "Give me one second."

Robin opened a can of food, divvying it up between two bowls before placing them on the floor in the dining room. Watching as her felines lapped up their turkey and liver pâté, she said, "Okay, kids. Now that you're satisfied, Momma is going to go take a much-needed bath."

Pouring a tad more than a splash of wine into her half-empty cup, Robin dragged herself into the bedroom. She grabbed her pajamas and a hoodie, and going into the bathroom, she turned on the taps clamped to the edge of the tub. A short time later, Robin was up to her shoulders in the hottest water she could handle.

***

With the window closed and Fred and Ginger cuddled alongside her, when Robin opened her eyes the next morning, she wasn't in any rush to move. For two nights in a row, no nightmares had roused her in her sleep and no thoughts, dark and heavy, had prevented her eyes from closing. Slumber, it seemed, had once again become her friend.

She took a deep breath, enjoying the scent of lemony polish as it made its way to her nose. Both cats climbed on her chest demanding attention, and accustomed to their morning routine, Robin petted both as she closed her eyes and listened to their purrs of appreciation.

Fred and Ginger were a gift from her mother. Their names given to them because of their colors and Constance's appreciation of old movies, their fur had held so many of Robin's tears over the past couple of years she had lost count. She had hugged them tightly as she wailed for the loss of her mother and had pulled them close when frustration, fear, and anger had pressed down on her like an unbearable weight, and through their rubs, purrs, and playful nips, they had always managed to stop her tears.

Feeling a sandpaper tongue doing its best to lick off her skin, Robin opened her eyes and looked down at Fred. "Are you telling me I'm going to be breakfast if I don't get my ass in gear?"

Fred lifted his eyes and licked his lips. "Yeah, I thought so," Robin said with a smile. "Okay, kids. Move your butts, and I'll get you some food."

At the sound of one of their favorite words, the two cats jumped off the couch and dashed down the hall, leaving their owner behind to snicker at their eagerness as she sat up and swung her legs off the sofa. Robin took the time to stretch, working out the kinks that had settled in during the night, and getting to her feet, she headed out of the room, but before she made it across the foyer, the doorbell rang. Unlike the one in the apartment, its volume equaling that of an ocean liner's horn, the chime at the front of the house was quiet and melodic, and Robin's appreciation of the difference showed on her face as she opened the door. "Hey there, Maxine. Good morning!"

"Drat," Maxine said, seeing Robin's rumpled pajamas and disheveled hoodie. "I always forget that you young people sleep in. I'll come back later."

"Don't be silly," Robin said, waving the woman inside. "I wasn't really sleeping. I was just going to feed the cats and put on some coffee. Would you like a cup?"

"Is it decaf?" Maxine said, unzipping her jacket.

Robin's shoulders fell. "Oh no. Sorry, all I have is regular."

"Good," Maxine said, hanging her jacket on the coat tree near the door. "That other shit will kill you."

***

Once Maxine was comfortable in the parlor with a freshly brewed cup of coffee, Robin excused herself long enough to brush her teeth, comb her hair, and exchange her pajamas for a pair of jeans and a long-sleeved Henley. By the time she returned to the front of the house, Robin was awake, aware, and filled with questions.

"It's nice to see this all uncovered again," Maxine said as Robin walked into the room.

"I bet," Robin said, taking a seat on the sofa. "Hey, do you mind if I ask you a few things? The longer I'm here, the more questions I'm starting to have."

"Of course not. I don't mind at all," Maxine said, resting back against the cushions. "Shoot."

"Okay," Robin said, scanning the parlor. "Why did Adele only cover the stuff in this room? I did a quick tour of the house yesterday and other than quilts covering the mattresses, everything else was just left out in the open. I would have thought she would have wanted to protect everything."

"Oh, that's an easy one. Like a lot of the B&Bs on the island, Adele used a service for her sheets, and when she decided to close the Inn, she canceled the service. The only sheets left were the ones from her apartment. They barely covered the things in here, but it was better than nothing."

"All right, that makes sense, but it leads me to my next question."

"Which is?" Maxine said, tickled by Robin's sudden exuberance.

"Every room seems to be completely furnished down to the paintings on the walls *except* for her apartment. Why? Where did all her stuff go?"

Maxine stared at the cup in her hands for a moment. "She gave it all away."

"But why?"

"Because everything back there was as out-of-date as I am," Maxine said, giving Robin a weak grin. "Adele poured her heart, soul, and money into the Inn, but as far as that apartment, it was just a place to hang her hat. When she first moved here, she spruced it up, but that was in the eighties. Those styles went the way of the dinosaur, thank the Lord, and since she never updated anything back there, when she decided to close the Inn, she called a couple of charities on the mainland and had everything hauled away. Adele figured it would be easier for you to sell the place without having to deal with all the old crap nobody would ever want."

"Wait. You knew about the trust?"

"Of course. I told you, Adele and I never had any secrets."

Robin relaxed back on the couch. "And she thought I'd sell it just like that?"

"She didn't have a reason not to, but I think, deep down in her heart, she hoped you wouldn't."

"What makes you say that?"

Maxine paused, and her eyes began to sparkle. "Just a guess."

Impressions, whether they are first, second, or third, are often opinions formed without any conscious thought. Perceptions based on nothing more than appearance or perhaps a look, they can create friendships as effortlessly as they can create enemies. When they first met, Robin thought Maxine to be a marvelous old woman with a lot of spunk and an attitude to match, but now she had a funny feeling there was more to meet the eye when it came to Maxine. Robin wasn't exactly sure what was lurking behind the glint in the senior citizen's eyes, but she would have had to be blind not to see it.

Entrenched in her own thoughts, it wasn't until she heard her name when she realized Maxine had been talking to her. "I'm sorry," Robin said, a hint of red coloring her cheeks. "My mind was somewhere else. What did you say?"

"I was saying that I know that you've only been here a couple of days, but I was wondering if you've decided whether you're going to stay or...or if you were going to leave."

Robin took a deep breath, and letting it out slowly, she said, "I'm going to stay."

Maxine threw herself at Robin, giving her the strongest hug she owned. "Oh, you just did this old woman's heart good. Do you know that?" she said. Pulling away, Maxine held Robin at arm's length. "And your aunt...oh, Adele would have been over the moon."

"I keep telling myself I must be crazy, but crazy or not, I'm not going to be able to do this without your help."

"My help?" Maxine said as her smile faded away. "Oh, Robin, I work in the fudge shops a couple of hours a week just to keep busy. I'm way too old—"

"No, not to work here, silly," Robin said with a laugh. "I need your help when I start setting up interviews."

"Interviews?"

"Maxine, I'm a writer, and I want to write, and I can't very well do that and try to run this place all by myself. When I said I was going to stay, that's contingent on me finding someone to manage the Inn," Robin said, crossing her legs. "What I'm thinking is that I'm going to place some ads online. That way, I can reach out across a few states, and if and *when* I get responses, I would have you look over them. You were Adele's best friend, and you're going to know the type of person she'd approve of *and* the type who'd fit in on Mackinac. I don't have a clue about any of that, at least not yet."

Robin waited for a response, and when saw the corners of the woman's mouth drooping as she stared off into space, Robin's shoulders fell. "Maxine, I'm sorry if you thought I was going to step into Adele's shoes, but my passion is writing and—"

"I think I already know of someone."

"What?"

"A few years ago, Adele took a spill. She got banged up pretty badly, but that didn't stop her guests from showing up for their reservations. One of the ladies in town, her name's Judy, took over until Adele could get back on her feet. She was here for a while, and I know Adele really liked her. I also know that Judy's filled in at other B&Bs on the island when the owners went on vacation or an emergency came along. She'd be perfect for Safe Harbor. She's hardworking. She knows the island, and this would give her the break she needs."

"The break?"

Maxine paused long enough to take a sip of her coffee. "I'm not one to tell tales, but Judy's husband up and left her about five years ago. He owned one of the bike shops in town, but after the divorce, he sold it and...well, he kind of left Judy high and dry."

"That's shitty. Oh, sorry. Pardon my French."

"That's okay. I've been known to speak that language fluently myself," Maxine said with a wink. "Don't get me wrong, Scott wasn't a total ass. I heard he split the profits, but Judy moved here when she married him. This is her home now, so since then, she's worked at a few of the shops, but I don't think she's married to any one of them. I see her in town all the time. If you'd like, I could mention it to her. She'd be perfect."

"That would be great," Robin said. "At the very least, it's a start, and if she's not interested, I'll put out some ads and go from there."

"Good," Maxine said, patting her lap. "Then that's what I'll do."

Chapter Seven

Monday morning, Robin walked up the ramp to the shed in her back yard, and swinging open the doors, she looked inside. The smell of grass, earth, and gasoline was the first thing she noticed, and the next was the three bicycles just inside the door, exactly where Maxine told her they'd be. One by one, Robin wheeled them out, propping them up on their kickstands as she took a look at them in the sunlight.

The first was a three-speed ladies' Schwinn with a neon pink frame and fenders to match, and hanging over both sides of the back tire were wicker baskets with purple and yellow plastic carnations intertwined in the weave. Robin shook her head at the girly bling and quickly decided of the three, that one would be the last to receive a tune-up. She was more femme than she was butch, but she was not *that* femme.

The next was a tad more understated in color. The frame and fenders the classic green and white found on vintage bicycles, and while it too had baskets, they were of the standard aluminum variety hardly deserving a second glance.

The last was the one Robin was most interested in seeing. It was Adele's beater bike, as Maxine had called it, and it was primarily used for hauling groceries and the like from the ferry to the Inn. The oldest in design, its candy-apple red frame was bulkier than the other two, but then it had to be. Attached to the rear wheel was a cargo hauler, extending the overall length of the Raleigh mountain bike by at least four feet, and atop the cart was a neon green cover with signs affixed to both sides announcing Safe Harbor Inn. Baskets hung over the rear tire as well as between the handlebars, and with the addition of lights on both the front and back fenders, trips could be made safely no matter what time of the day or night. With her list on the kitchen counter rapidly growing, Robin put the other two bikes back into the shed, and after buttoning her coat, she walked the beater bike into town.

***

It was less than a mile from the Inn to the bike shop, but by the time Robin reached her destination her shopping list, at least mentally, had grown to include a warmer coat, a knit cap, and a pair of gloves. The sun had been up for a couple of hours, so the frost of the evening had melted away, but the chill in the air had remained. After spending so many years in Florida, while many of the people she had passed seemed comfortable in their lightweight jackets or down vests, Robin needed more…a lot more.

Robin left the bike at the curb and entered a shop smelling of parts cleaner, grease, and rubber tires. She approached the counter and smiled at the clerk. "Good morning. Maxine O'Connor—"

"You must be Adele Anderson's niece," the man said, extending his hand. "Maxine stopped by earlier and said you'd be bringing in Adele's bikes to get them looked at. Name's Eddie Cowell."

"Robin Novak," Robin said, chuckling as she shook the man's hand. "She's fast. I'll give her that."

"Hell, you should have seen her when she was younger," Eddie said with a loud guffaw. "She was something to be reckoned with. Come to think of it, she still is."

"Yeah, I'm beginning to see that," Robin said. "And she was right. I brought over the first of the three I found in the shed. I was hoping you could look at it. I can tell you it needs new tires, but I'm not sure about the brakes or the gears."

Eddie looked through the shop window, instantly recognizing the red Raleigh parked just outside. "That won't be a problem," he said, turning back to Robin. "You want me to check the Burley, too?"

"The Burley?"

"The cargo hauler," Eddie said, pointing to the cart behind Robin's bike. "Adele used to keep everything in pretty good working order, but with the horse pee, the tires might need to be looked at."

"Oh…um…yes, please."

Eddie glanced up at the clock and then back down to the appointment book on the counter. "I should have it ready to go by tomorrow morning at the latest. Will that work?"

"Yeah, that'll be great," Robin said, pulling out her wallet. "Do you need a deposit or—"

"Hell, no," he said as he came out from behind the counter. "If I asked for a deposit, Maxine would have my hide. We'll settle up when you pick it up."

"That works for me," Robin said, putting her wallet away. "Well, I guess I'll see you tomorrow."

"I'll be here," Eddie said, and with that, his attention returned to the paperwork on his counter.

Robin had two more errands to run, but when she walked outside and felt the sun on her face, she decided she could handle the cold for a little while longer. Instead of backtracking to Hoban Street as Maxine suggested she do, Robin pulled up the collar of her coat and stuffing her hands in her pockets, she continued down Main Street.

Main Street housed most of the tourist shops on Mackinac, and both sides of the road were lined with multi-colored one, two, and three-story buildings. Their façades differed much like their contents, but most of the businesses had stayed true to the ambiance of the island. Clapboard siding of yesteryear could be seen on nearly all, and although some had been painted in beachy pastels, others were in the hues of colonial times, the smoky blues and grays similar to those worn on uniforms during the Civil War. Fabric awnings in various colors hung above several of the entrances, touting the name of the business or their wares, while others had signs jutting out from the buildings or dangling from overhangs. Behind the sizable plate glass windows filling the storefronts were mountains of T-shirts, coffee mugs, and practically any other memento a tourist could ever want to obtain and intermingled amongst the souvenir shops were restaurants and pubs with tables waiting for the weary.

From May to October, the tourists making their way to Mackinac could number up to fifteen thousand on any given *day*, but with just over three weeks left of the season, the crowds had thinned. The fragrance in the air still signified horses lived on the island, but as Robin made her way down the sidewalk, the aroma blended with that of fudge, the island's claim to confectionery fame. She had already passed one shop selling the tasty treat, but when she reached the next, she caved to the call of sugar.

Robin wandered inside, blending with the people milling about, and breathing in the decadence of all things fudge, she perused the glass cases. Marveling at all the flavors offered, she settled on a small pre-packaged assortment, and after paying the clerk, she slipped the pink box into the inside pocket of her coat. Robin headed back to the street to resume her walking tour of Main Street, but when she saw a familiar storefront up ahead, her mouth dropped open. She had just found the only store on the island that belonged to a chain, and inwardly, Robin did a fist pump. Mackinac had a Starbucks. A few minutes later, Robin meandered up the road with a white and green paper cup in her hand, the heat of the featured dark roast warming her palm nicely.

Ever since leaving the house that morning, Robin had felt as if she was walking in a bubble, a surreal slow-motion world where life crept along without a worry or a fear. That feeling had yet to leave her, and Robin didn't understand why. It wasn't because people passing her on the street hadn't smiled their hellos or mouthed the word, because they had, and the clerks couldn't have been more friendly and accommodating, so that didn't play into the conundrum causing her eyebrows to knit. There was *something* else. Robin just couldn't put her finger on it.

When she reached the white benches near the Tourist Bureau, Robin took a seat and sipping her coffee through the plastic lid, she watched the people stroll by, easily chatting with their friends or partners as they made their way down the sidewalk. Tethered to their music by earbuds, bicyclists pedaled down the street, the click of their shifting gears making it to Robin's ears, and a few joggers loped down the road, their footsteps padding lightly across the pavement.

Robin leaned back on the bench, crossed her legs, and was about to take another sip of her coffee, but as she brought the cup to her lips, she stopped. As if frozen in place, she remained still except for her eyes, which darted back and forth between the riders and the walkers until finally she tipped back her head and laughed out loud. A few passersby turned to look, but Robin paid them no mind for she had just solved the puzzle she'd been working on all morning. She was simply a product of her environment.

Like those living in northern climates adapting to the cold and those in the south familiar with the heat, Robin had become accustomed to the cacophony of the modern age. To the sound of car engines and diesel trucks, to buses and taxis rushing to their next stop, and to car horns, screeching brakes, and mufflers manufactured to rumble and roar. She had learned to block them all out, to pay no attention to car doors slamming or sirens announcing emergencies or even to the expletives born out of road rage that was shouted from windows because it was the clatter she had grown up with…but now it was gone.

Enthralled, Robin sat on the bench for almost an hour listening to the sounds of Mackinac. From the low hum of a ferry's engine off in the distance and the calls of the gulls flying over the town to the steady clip-clop of horses' hooves and the occasional ring of a biker's bell as they signaled their existence. Like a serene melody, the sounds filled her ears, but just barely, and Robin's smile grew. She liked the concord of Mackinac. She liked it a lot.

***

The bell over the door rang as Maxine entered Brushstrokes, a small art gallery on Market Street, and before the door could close behind her, Maxine saw Judy Dunnigan grinning back at her from the counter. "Good morning, Judy."

"Good morning, Maxi," Judy said, closing the book she'd been reading. "What are you doing up this way?"

"Just visiting," Maxine said, unbuttoning her jacket as she scanned the shop. "Are Walt or Sally around?"

"No, with things slowing down, they're using the time to get a jump on packing up for the winter. Why, do you need them? I can call them," Judy said, reaching for the phone.

"That's not necessary," Maxine said. "I was actually hoping they wouldn't be here."

Judy raised an eyebrow. "Why?"

"Because I'm about to steal their favorite employee away from them," Maxine said, rubbing her hands together.

"I'm their *only* employee, and you know it," Judy said, setting aside the book. "And what do you mean steal me away?"

"How'd you like to manage the Safe Harbor Inn?"

"What?"

"I don't know if you heard, but Adele's—"

"Maxi, you and I both know if Mackinac's grapevine were any thicker, we'd be producing wine instead of fudge," Judy said with a laugh. "Of course, I've heard. She's a writer. Her name's Robin, and she moved into the Inn last week, but what in the world does a writer know about running a B&B?"

"Nothing, which is why she's looking for someone to manage it, so I told her about you."

"Me? I've never run a B&B."

"No, but you helped out Adele when she needed it, and you've filled in at most of the others, too. And I thought..." Maxine stopped and looked around the empty shop. "I thought maybe you'd want something a little more challenging than this."

"What makes you think I'm looking for something more challenging?"

"Because you've worked in just about every shop on the island since your divorce."

"Maybe I just like change," Judy said with a shrug.

"Or maybe you're bored out of your mind," Maxine said, leaning on the counter. "You and I both know you were the driving force behind The Wheelhouse. Sure, Scott could wrench bikes with the best of them, but when it came to everything else, it was all you."

"Yes, and it was crazy and hectic, and non-stop from May to October."

"And you loved every minute of it," Maxine said, tapping her finger on the counter. "The people who live on this island are a special breed, and you may not have been born here, Judy, but you live and breathe the chaos of the tourist season just like the rest of us. It's in our blood."

Judy couldn't argue Maxine's point because, for the past twenty-five years, she had experienced it firsthand...and she *did* miss it.

Like a crocus emerging from the winter frost, Mackinac came alive in the spring. Shop owners, not brave enough to spend the winter, would begin arriving in April as would the teams of horses returning from their stay on the mainland. Shortly after that, ferries loaded with freight would pull into the docks and carts jam-packed with boxes of souvenirs, books, and supplies would be delivered by dray. The boards and plywood over the storefront windows would be taken down, and anything and everything that needed a fresh coat of paint would receive it. Neighbors would reacquaint themselves with neighbors. Windows on the B&Bs would be opened, allowing fresh air to replace stale, and gardens would be weeded and prepped for the spring. Like racehorses readying themselves for a dash, the people of Mackinac were champing at the bit for the season to start and on the first of May, it would do just that.

Every hour, a ferry horn would be heard, announcing the arrival of the next group of visitors, and after hundreds disembarked, bikes were rented, shops were visited, and bed-and-breakfasts and hotels across the island would begin to fill. Sightseers would clamber onto carriages, anxious to visit Fort Mackinac, Arch Rock, and the Grand Hotel, while others would set out on foot or bicycles, wanting to experience the beauty of the island at their own leisurely pace.

Rain or shine, seven days a week, and from dawn to dusk Mackinac was a bustling melting pot of young and old, but the island also had another vibe, and that came out at night. With fourteen bars on the island, the pub crawls of Mackinac had become a tradition for many. Those hardy enough, or perhaps *fool*hardy enough, could be found walking, weaving, or stumbling from one pub to the next, collecting the bartender's signatures and earning them boasting rights once their hangovers wore off. Late into the night, music, dancing, and the boisterous camaraderie born from friendship could be heard throughout the town until eventually, all would go quiet until the morning…and then it would start again.

Judy sighed as she looked around the gallery. The same pegboard-covered walls had stared back at her for the past six months, their surfaces thickened by the fresh coat of white paint that Walt and Sally always applied in the spring. Watercolors hung in every available inch of the little gallery, each framed to accent the swirls of transparent colors depicting local scenery, wildlife, and lighthouses within its confines. Some had caught and held Judy's attention for weeks, the artist so adept with washes, glazes, and edges that the watercolor clouds appeared as soft as cotton balls and the autumn colors were the truest she had ever seen. She was always sad to see them leave the shop, yet there were others Judy would have gladly given away if it had been up to her for their hues were too splotchy or their perspective too skewed.

Crates along the floor held small pieces of artwork, each matted and wrapped in cellophane for an easy sale, and in the center of the room was a rack filled with larger paintings, protected in the same way so customers could fan through them to their heart's content. Most of Judy's time had been spent kneeling at those crates or standing at the rack, sorting and rearranging what others had disordered, and she had never been more bored in her life. She was used to the hubbub of candy stores and souvenir shops, and to the waves of people jockeying for position as they scrambled to rent bikes. She was used to chatting with customers eager to listen to stories about the island, but those who visited galleries spoke in whispers or not at all. Judy wasn't sure she wanted to manage a bed-and-breakfast, but she did know that next year, come hell or high water, she wouldn't be working at the gallery.

***

Robin wiped the sweat from her forehead with the sleeve of her shirt, and sitting back on her haunches, she admired her handiwork.

Maxine had been a wealth of information that morning, answering as many questions as Robin could think to ask, and by the time the woman left, Robin's day was planned. After visiting the bike shop and ambling down Main Street, Robin headed up to Market Street to complete her errands for the day. Her first stop was the police department where she renewed the licenses required for each of the three bikes that were now hers, and her next stop was the Department of Public Works.

Robin had always thought of herself as an environmentally conscious person, recycling her newspapers, bottles, and cans like most everyone else, and any old paint, batteries, and chemicals were always taken to the designated disposal areas. However, after listening to Maxine, Robin realized she needed to step up her game because Mackinac Island had no landfill.

Whatever trash was generated had to be sorted in one of four ways. Plastic bins were still made available for recyclable materials, but the rest had to be put into clear, tan, or blue bags, all of which had to be purchased at the Department of Public Works. The clear sixty-gallon bags were used for yard waste while the tan thirty-three-gallon ones were for any compostable materials, both of which would be taken to the island's composting center where they'd be emptied and sorted. The blue bags held everything else, and since they had to be hauled off the island by ferry to a landfill on the mainland, the cost of those bags was double that of the tan, helping to offset the transportation charges while also acting as an incentive for the residents to sort their trash appropriately.

Robin had spent her afternoon slicing up the shag carpet into squares small enough to fit neatly into one of the blue bags, and then she attacked the shutters covering the bay window in the living room with the same fervor. More than one expletive slipped from Robin's lips, and a few were even shouted, but by the time the sun went down, she could see moonlight through the glass.

Blowing a strand of hair from her face, Robin got to her feet and headed to the kitchen, rewarding herself with an ice-cold beer before grabbing the notepad to add a few more things to her shopping list.

"Where the hell is my pen?" she mumbled, and as shuffled through the papers on the counter, she noticed Fred lazily making his way through the kitchen. Robin's eyes turned to slits. "You know better than to get on the counters, now give me back my pen."

Without so much as a side-eyed glance in her direction, Fred swished his tail and moseyed on his way.

"I have more pens than you have lives, you little bastard," Robin said with a laugh, and fishing around in her laptop bag, she pulled out another rollerball and began jotting down notes. A minute later, the cataclysmic doorbell in the hallway of her apartment rang out, its shrieking volume echoing off the empty walls and sending Robin a foot in the air in one direction while her pen flew like a missile in the other.

"Oh, you are so going to die," she mumbled, and snagging the hammer off the counter, Robin marched up the hallway with demolition on her mind. Like a point guard going for a slam dunk, she leapt through the air, and a moment later pieces of plastic and chime were raining down on her. Delighted she had killed her siren nemesis, Robin was about to go in search of the broom when she heard the front chime sounding again. "Crap," she said, and with hammer in hand, Robin jogged to the foyer.

After ringing the doorbell twice, Judy Dunnigan debated on ringing it again. Maxine had forgotten to get Robin Novak's number, and the landline to Safe Harbor had yet to be reconnected, so when Judy left the gallery that night, she thought she'd just stop by and introduce herself. It seemed the right thing to do at the time, but standing in the shadows of the porch light, Judy suddenly felt like an intruder. Technically, she hadn't received an invitation to visit, but then again, did she need one? What if this woman went to bed early or worse yet, she was enjoying a late dinner and didn't want to be disturbed? Judy nibbled on her bottom lip for a moment, but just as she was about to leave, she saw through the stained glass a silhouette approaching the front door. Taking a deep breath of the crisp, night air, Judy displayed her best smile as the door opened…and then a moment later it was all she could do to force it to remain.

Seeing a short figure through the rippled glass, Robin assumed her visitor was Maxine, but when she swung open the door, Robin drew in the longest breath of her life. For a split-second, the world stood still as she gazed upon the woman who had haunted her dreams for over two decades. Robin's heart began to race, and her palms grew damp, and it felt as if someone had placed an anvil on her chest. Her mind swirled with muddled thoughts, the past and present fusing into something both joyous and terrifying, and as Robin exhaled, she carried on her breath only two words. *"Miss Lawton?"*

Chapter Eight

It can happen at any age, that intense, most often short-lived admiration for someone known as a crush. Whether it is over the exchange of cardboard hearts in kindergarten or an innocent glance in high school or perhaps even just the scent of perfume or cologne wafting over cubicle walls, the minds of those affected fill with daydreams. Scenarios based solely on romantic obsession, time is lost to imaginations wild and free, and hearts beat faster at the possibilities the mind has created.

By the time Robin was eighteen, she had experienced only two crushes in her life. Freddy McDonald was her first. A little buck-toothed boy she met in first grade, she found his lisp as adorable as his smile. In second grade, her interest was piqued by his sister, Louisa. Freckle-faced and chubby, her giggles were music to young Robin's ears, but her interest in Louisa dwindled when books became Robin's obsession.

In the beginning, the written word sated her young imagination, filling it with images of little girls on prairies and a friendship between a spider and a pig, but as she grew older, books began offering Robin comfort in a different way. With her nose pressed deep into the pages, she could avoid what she was not yet willing to face.

For the most part, her years in primary and secondary school went by without fanfare. The slew of studies, field trips, finals, and whatever bestseller she could get her hands on filled her days and her nights, leaving no room for anything or anyone else, much to her mother's dismay. More than once the subject had come up over dinner, the questions raised by a parent who didn't understand their offspring's detachment from youthful companionship, but once again, Robin's brilliance quieted Constance's worries. She told her mother that books didn't argue or compete, they held no grudges and possessed no ulterior motives, and when Robin opened her latest fixation in the morning, it hadn't changed overnight, morphing into something she could no longer recognize. Just like Robin's career choice, Constance never questioned her again. Robin wasn't exactly telling the truth, but she wouldn't face *that* until college.

On her first day as a senior at Heritage High, Robin had ambled into her homeroom and slipping into a chair, she began reading the schedule she'd been given. She looked up occasionally, acknowledging those she recognized as they straggled in, their clothes newly purchased, but their expressions lacking the same crispness. She glanced down at her schedule again, confirming the location of her first class, and as the bell rang, Robin lifted her eyes…and then *she* walked in.

Petite, with a pixie haircut, vivid blue eyes, and a smile that created dimples in her cheeks, Judith Lawton was positively the prettiest woman Robin had ever seen. As she made her way to her desk, grinning at the roomful of students, Robin tried not to stare. For a moment, she acted nonchalantly and looked around the room, but unable to stop herself, her eyes found their way back to the teacher. And once everyone was settled, and Judith Lawton spoke for the first time, Robin couldn't help but shift in her seat.

Miss Lawton went on to introduce herself, informing all she was a newly-hired member of the Phys Ed department. Her classes would revolve around health and fitness, but her extra-curricular activities would include coaching the girls' soccer and softball teams, and Robin silently damned herself for never taking an interest in sports.

A minute later, Miss Lawton moved from behind her desk, and as she started calling off names from the attendance sheet, Robin found herself entranced. Dressed in a pleated dark blue short skirt and red polo top, the woman's vocation was clearly seen in her muscled calves and defined biceps, and Robin noticed every toned line. Lost in her admiration, it wasn't until Robin heard the class tittering when she realized Miss Lawton was calling her name, and as scarlet stung at her cheeks, Robin raised her hand…and so it began.

From that day forward, Robin began arriving at school earlier. She told her mother it was to get a jump on the day, but she didn't spend those extra minutes in the library cramming for a test or huddled in a corner, reading the newest novel. She spent them sitting in her homeroom, craving every second she could spend in Miss Lawton's presence. The words they exchanged in the mornings were purely obligatory greetings at first, but as the weeks went by, their conversations grew. Sometimes it was only about the goings-on at school, the score of the latest football game, or attendance at a pep rally, but on more than one occasion, one or the other would bring up the latest headlines in the newspaper, and they would comfortably chat until other students began to show up.

Those were the mornings Robin liked the best for they made her feel more like a friend and less like a student, but what made her blossom, what made her cheeks cherry and her eyes gleam were the few times when Miss Lawton complimented Robin on how she looked. When that happened, Robin would float through the rest of her day at school, her feet barely touching the floor as her head rose high above the clouds. But in clouds there are storms, and one was brewing that Robin knew nothing about until she returned from Christmas break to find Judith Lawton had resigned from Heritage High to get married.

Robin was devastated, and feigning illness, she didn't return to school for a week. Under her covers in her room she hid, waiting until her mother left for work before allowing her tears to fall, but eventually, those tears dried up. They left a residue of sadness that took months to overcome, but when Robin entered college that fall, she held her head high and looked toward the future. Judith Lawton still plagued her dreams, but Robin believed sooner or later, they would disappear, too. She was wrong.

***

Judy took a step back, and then she took another, her brain working overtime trying to keep up with her thoughts. The woman standing in the doorway was disheveled; her blonde hair more out of the clip than in, and errant strands were going in every direction. Her jeans were torn, and her T-shirt was ragged and stained, and in her hand, she clutched a hammer. The combination resembled that of someone deranged, yet the scale of surprise hadn't been tipped by the woman's appearance, but rather by something else.

Judy kept her eyes fixed on Robin while she got her thoughts in order. "I'm sorry, but...but do we *know* each other?"

Up until that moment, Robin had been lost in a vortex of memories that spun through her mind like a tornado. Flashes of a to-die-for smile, eyes of brilliant blue, short pleated skirts, and the melody of a voice Robin would never forget sucked her into a whirlpool it took all her strength to escape from. Robin cleared her throat, and taking a deep breath, she let it out ever so slowly. Unfortunately, she needed a hell of a lot more time than that to return her to adulthood.

"Um...yes. Um...I...I went to Heritage High when...when you were there."

"Oh," Judy said, continuing to stare at Robin. "I'm sorry. Your name...your name doesn't ring a bell."

Robin didn't allow the pain of that particular revelation to show on her face. "Well, it was Robin Cook back then, and I wasn't really a student. I mean...I mean I *was* a student, but not one of yours. Well, actually, I guess technically I was one of yours. You were...uh...you were my homeroom teacher."

Before another word could be said, a gust of wind came out of nowhere, its force strong enough to make Judy widen her stance to steady herself while Robin raced to stop the door from slamming into the wall.

"Geez, get in here before we're both blown down the street," Robin said, quickly waving Judy inside.

Judy darted into the house, her shoulders hunched against winds suddenly too strong for her fleece-lined jacket. "Thanks," she said, and waiting until Robin closed the door, she held out her hand. "And speaking of names, it's Dunnigan now. Judy Dunnigan."

When Robin had looked into the bathroom mirror while brushing her teeth that morning, she had seen the person she had become. In her teens, she was often mistaken for someone older, her intelligence and maturity overshadowing that of her peers. Blessed with good skin and a healthy body, she had been carded in bars until her mid-thirties, and when her forties arrived, while a few aches and pains had begun to show up when she pushed herself too hard, they hadn't slowed her down for long. Yes, Robin was lucky not to look or feel her age, but when she stared at Judy Dunnigan's extended hand, Robin's luck ran out. Suddenly, she was eighteen again with all the awkwardness, uncertainty, and lack of social skills that came with it.

Robin knew a handshake was merely a gesture used in greetings, a ritual in which two people grasp hands and say hello, and she had done it literally hundreds of times before, but this wasn't just *any* handshake. This would be the first time she had ever touched Judith Lawton, and as she reached out to take the woman's hand, a murder of crows flapped their wings in Robin's stomach.

Robin dared not make eye contact, knowing if she did her cheeks would flush scarlet and words would fail her like they'd never failed before. She slipped her hand in Judy's, and although the time it took was immeasurable, the effect was not. The texture, warmth, and strength would be something Robin never would forget. Judy's skin was soft and cool, and her grip was firm yet feminine, and unable to stop herself any longer, Robin raised her eyes. She had to make sure this wasn't a dream, and when she saw her twelfth-grade homeroom teacher smiling back at her, for more than a few seconds, Robin forgot how to breathe.

Like all good things, their handshake came to an end. Judy waited for what she thought was an appropriate time, but when Robin seemed content in just staring at her, her arms dangling at her sides, Judy pointed to the hammer in the woman's hand. "Doing a little renovation?"

Robin looked down and paled. Not only was she still gripping the hammer, but the jeans she was wearing were also the most ripped up pair she owned, and her white T-shirt had lost every bit of its whiteness hours before. "Oh, God. I'm so sorry," she said, raising her eyes. "I must look like a wreck."

"Don't be silly. It's me who's sorry," Judy said, taking a step toward the door. "Maxine O'Connor mentioned you may be looking for a manager for Safe Harbor, but she didn't have your number. I was on my way home, so I thought I'd just stop by, but it's obvious you're busy. I'll just come back at another—"

"No," Robin blurted a mere decibel lower than the chime she had just destroyed. "I mean, please don't. I just need a couple of minutes to get cleaned up."

"Are you sure?"

"Absolutely," Robin said before pointing in the direction of the innkeeper's suite. "Would you like to come back? I only have a couple of chairs at the moment, but you're welcome to one of them, or if you'd rather just make yourself comfortable in the parlor, that's fine, too. It's totally up to you. Oh, and would you like something to drink? I have water, of course, and coffee or tea, and...and beer if that sounds better. And I also have wine. Would you like some wine?"

It wasn't until she saw the humor in Judy's eyes when Robin realized she had just rambled off a few dozen words in less than a breath. Pressing her lips together, she prayed her cheeks weren't as dark as they felt.

Amused that the nervousness she had felt a few minutes earlier while standing on the front porch seemed to be catching, Judy took off her jacket. "What kind of wine?"

"What?" Robin said, snapping back her head. "Oh...um...Cabernet."

"That'll work," Judy said as she walked over and hung her jacket on the coat tree.

"Yeah?"

"Yes, Robin, that'll work just fine."

It was only two syllables. A name given to her at birth, but when Robin heard it spoken by Judith Lawton, it lit a fuse that sizzled all the way through her body, igniting Robin's core while extinguishing her ability to speak...again.

A few moments passed before Judy pointed toward the back of the house. "Um...shall we?"

"Oh, yeah, of course," Robin said, confident she would never need to buy anything to highlight her cheekbones again. "Follow me."

The walk through the house was uneventful. One woman was content in just admiring her surroundings while the other was absorbed in mentally scolding herself for acting like such an idiot. It wasn't until they stepped into the apartment when Robin was torn from her thoughts by the sound of Judy's voice.

"I was wondering what the hammer was for."

Halfway down the hall, Robin turned around to see Judy looking back and forth between the shattered pieces of plastic on the floor and what was left of the chime above the door. "Oh, yeah, it...it was—"

"Obnoxious?"

"How'd you know?" Robin said, flinching back her head.

"When Adele was recovering from her fall, I stayed here. On the island, the front doors of the B&Bs are rarely locked. Most of the guests know just to walk in, but the newbies would always ring the bell. I swear that thing scared me so many times if I had been a cat, I would have used up all my lives in about a week."

"Well, you don't have to worry about that anymore."

"Um...you do know those things have electricity running through them, don't you?" Judy said, pointing to the chime. "Beating them to death with a hammer could be hazardous to your health."

Robin grinned. "That's why I aimed for the chime and not the transformer."

"You know electricity," Judy said, catching up. "I'm impressed."

"Don't be," Robin said with a laugh. "I know just enough not to permanently curl my hair."

Robin rounded the corner and waited for Judy to catch up. "So...the wine is right there, and the glasses on that towel are clean," she said, pointing to the far corner of the countertop. "Feel free to help yourself, and I'll be back in a couple of minutes. Okay?"

"Take your time, Robin," Judy said with a smile. "I'll be here."

Robin's heart did a flip, and after giving Judy a quick smile of her own, Robin made a beeline for her bedroom.

After snagging a clean sweatshirt and jeans out of one of the open suitcases on the floor, Robin rushed into the bathroom, closed the door and ran to the sink. While she waited for the water to get warm, she stripped out of her T-shirt and then stared into the mirror. "Oh my God," she whispered as reality hit home. "Oh—my—*God*!"

Time had dulled Robin's memory just a tad, so she had forgotten some of the subtler points of having a crush, but not any longer. Her heart was pounding, and her palms were sweaty, and it was, as it always had been, because of the woman who was now standing in her kitchen. A woman Robin thought she'd never see again, a woman who had appeared in Robin's dreams more times than she could remember...and a woman who had hardly changed at all.

True, Judy's chestnut brown hair had strands of gray now running through it and the lines once only appearing when the woman laughed, now seemed permanent, but as far as Robin was concerned, they enhanced Miss Lawton's beauty. Her eyes were still as blue as the sky and her form, still as slender, and Robin swallowed hard. Acting nonchalant was going to take some practice.

Who was she kidding? It was going to take lots and *lots* of practice.

***

Fifteen minutes later, preferring the comfort of a soft sofa over the two old wooden chairs in Robin's apartment, the women returned to the parlor.

Taking up opposite corners on the couch, they each took a sip of their wine before the silence was broken by Judy.

"I've always loved this room."

By the time Robin had returned to the kitchen, she had convinced herself that her teenage infatuation was under control. She was an adult. Judy *Dunnigan* was an adult, and there was no reason to be nervous, but Robin was still having a hard time keeping her mind on the present. She looked over at Judy, and in a barely audible tone, Robin spoke the only word taking up space in her head. "Beautiful."

"What?" Judy said, tilting her head just a bit.

"The room...the room is beautiful," Robin said, quickly following it up with a gulp of wine.

"Most of them are," Judy said, taking a sip of her wine.

"Most?"

"It's been a few years, and I adored your aunt so don't take this the wrong way, but there were a couple of rooms upstairs that made me wince when I walked into them. I'm not a big fan of yellow."

"I'm the same way about orange."

Judy's face split into a grin. "Guess you'll be painting the apartment then—huh?"

"*That* is the second thing on my list. Trust me."

"What's the first?"

"Finding someone to manage this place, which I hope I already have," Robin said, eyeing Judy. "Interested?"

"I don't know," Judy said. "What did you have in mind?"

One of the greatest gifts a writer can have is an overactive imagination. With it, they can conjure up stories filled with twists and turns, create dialogue that flows effortlessly, and develop characters with more than one dimension. Robin had always considered herself blessed to have such an imagination. At times, she could close her eyes and write scenes by viewing the movie playing in her mind, but right now, Robin wished the reel would stop spinning. Inwardly groaning at the adult-rated images filling her head, she took a healthy swallow of wine in hopes she could drown them, and then snuggled back into her corner of the sofa.

"Okay, here goes," Robin said, turning to Judy. "I haven't been on Mackinac since I was a kid, and I came up here expecting a small house where I could spend my days writing. Instead, I inherited a bed-and-breakfast that is way too big for just one person, but I can't bring myself to sell it either. Over the years, I've stayed in a couple of places like this, so I know kind of what they're about, but I'm fairly clueless when it comes to running one. That's where you'd come in."

Judy arched her eyebrows. "Robin, I don't know what Maxine told you, but I've never actually managed a B&B. I've just worked in a few to help out."

"I know that."

"So, as far as experience goes, I have very little."

"You have a hell of a lot more than me."

"Maybe so, but regardless of the experience either of us has, running a bed-and-breakfast isn't a one-person operation, and you just said you came up here to write."

"I did, but I can't write twenty-four-seven," Robin said, tucking her leg under her. "What I was thinking is that we'd have to hire a few people to help with the cleaning and getting rooms ready for the next guests, and as far as breakfasts are concerned, I'm a good cook. Granted, I've never made breakfast for two dozen people, but it's not like I can't learn how or at least lend a hand while you're doing it. And as for reservations and bookkeeping, I'm usually a whiz at software programs, so I'm sure we can find something that could work for us."

Judy studied Robin as she took the last sip of her wine. "So much for being clueless."

Robin could feel her cheeks beginning to heat. "Actually, up until last night, I was."

"An epiphany?"

"No, lots of Google searches," Robin said with a snort. "If I had had that back in school, I would have aced everything."

"You didn't?"

Robin's cheeks went from warm to scalding. "As a matter of fact, I did, but Google would have made it a *lot* easier."

"Well, if there's one thing I've learned about life is that it's not always easy."

Robin raised her glass in the air. "I'll second you on that one."

Judy clinked her glass against Robin's before taking another sip. "So...speaking of Google, I should tell you that I tried to look you up today?"

"Yeah? Can I ask why?"

"I was curious as to what kind of books you wrote, but when I searched—"

"You didn't find an author named Robin Novak," Robin said, leaning back on the sofa. "And now you probably think I'm some struggling writer hoping and praying that one day I'll finally get published."

"I didn't say that. I just couldn't find you."

"That's because I write under R. C. Novak."

Judy's eyebrows drew together. "Anyone ever tell you that you have a lot of names?"

"I just have two," Robin said, smiling. "Since there was already a well-known writer by the name of Robin Cook, once I signed with a publisher, they suggested I change it, so I took my mother's maiden name. It's all legal. Trust me."

"I see...and the initials?"

Robin's eyes twinkled. "So people couldn't search for me on the Internet."

Judy threw back her head and laughed, and a few seconds passed before she spoke again. "So, back to Safe Harbor," she said, placing her glass on the table. "What were *you* looking for on Google?"

"Anything and everything I could find about B&Bs," Robin said, shrugging. "I wanted to make sure I wasn't getting in over my head."

"I see," Judy said, relaxing back on the sofa. "And you don't think you are?"

"Do you?"

"I think you can do anything you set your mind to."

"Thanks for the vote of confidence, but you don't really know me all that well."

"I know enough."

"Is that so?"

"Okay, maybe not enough, but Adele wouldn't have left this place to you if she didn't think you could handle it. You just said you aced school, which means you have a brain in your head, and since I'm assuming you *are* a published author, that takes talent."

"Writing a book is not the same as running a B&B."

"I wouldn't know."

"Neither would I, which is why I need your help."

Judy pulled in a long breath and letting it out slowly, she got to her feet. "Robin, I appreciate the offer. I really do, but I'm not getting any younger—"

"You are *not* old," Robin said, jumping off the sofa.

"Tell me that when you get to be my age," Judy said before heading to the foyer. When she reached the coat tree, she turned around. "And I'm not saying I'm ancient. I'm just saying that I'm not sure I want to start a new career at this point in my life. I appreciate you were willing to give me a shot, but I think you'd be better off finding someone with more experience."

Robin's shoulders fell. "What can I say to change your mind?"

Judy shook her head as she slipped into her jacket. "Robin—"

"Look, just take some time to think about it. Okay?" Robin said, and reaching out, she touched Judy on the arm. "It's not like I'm going to open this place tomorrow. I've got rooms to paint and wallpaper to buy, and I've never wallpapered in my life, so that alone should give you a month or two. Please? Come on. What do you say? Just think about it?"

"You don't give up easily, do you?" Judy said, looking up at the woman smiling down at her.

"No," Robin said, shaking her head. "There have been a few times when I've regretted *not* giving up, but I don't think this is going to be one of them."

Chapter Nine

Judy walked down the concrete stairway and unlocking the door at the bottom, she flicked on the light and stepped inside her two-room apartment. Located in the basement of a house owned by Larry and Kay Wilson, it was small and contained only the necessities, but Judy had done her best to make it her home.

The caramel brown concrete floor was now concealed behind oversized beige area rugs in both the living and bedroom areas and keeping with earth tones, Judy had chosen a pale olive green for three of the walls, while the last was two shades darker. She hung up various pieces of artwork she had gathered over the years and added more depth to the small space with a few second-hand accents, but when it came to decorating the corner of the apartment deemed the bedroom, Judy had purchased everything new.

No longer having to worry about greasy fingers or the clumsiness of her ex, the platform bed, dresser, and chest of drawers were white and still pristine after five years. Atop the bed was a quilt, the Morning Star pattern a blend of rose and pink against a background of pearl was as unblemished as the day it was bought, and delicate lamps were perched on.the nightstands, their bases crystal and their shades bell-shaped and diminutive.

The living room held an over-stuffed faux suede sofa against one wall and a meager entertainment unit along another, both of which she got in the divorce, but neither of which she used very often. Preferring books over television, besides the end tables flanking the couch, the only other piece of furniture in the room was a sturdy bookcase she purchased at last year's bazaar. Tall and wide, and stained a dark walnut, it was a struggle for her and her friends to get it down the stairs, but it had been well worth the trouble. Like sardines in a can, novels now filled the shelves, and sitting at the ready on one of them was Judy's iPad. While she still preferred printed books over electronic ones, when one lives on an island that's basically closed for five months of the year, adaptation is required...and Judy had adapted.

She had adapted to a divorce she hadn't seen coming. She had adapted to losing a business she had called her own for over twenty years, and she had adapted to being single again. That actually had been the easiest part. She no longer had to wait, to ask, to check, or to alter her plans to fit another's, and Judy quickly discovered that there was something to be said for independence, even at her age.

There were still times when she missed her best friend, the one who she had shared such easy banter with over meals and chores. Since meeting at Central Michigan University their lives had become intertwined, and even though their marriage ended badly, Judy found a way to forgive him. Scott had simply come full circle...as some people do.

Scott Dunnigan was a typical jock in college. More concerned with basketball than his classes, he spent every spare minute he had on the court, running sprints, dunking baskets, and practicing his three-point shot. Although majoring in business, his only intention was to eventually run the one his father had started so he paid very little attention to his grades, but his coaches did. Threatened with dismissal from the team, Scott did what most jocks do. He went in search of a tutor and found Judy Lawton.

Judy, a physical education major, was well aware of Scott Dunnigan before he ever walked into the library that day. Tall, handsome, and rippling with muscles, there hadn't been a basketball game she had attended where the bleachers weren't filled with sports groupies, clucking and cooing at the young man's physique like pigeons begging for seed, so her reception of him was less than warm. Judy didn't like jocks. She didn't like their cockiness, their self-importance, or their supercilious egos, so without as much as a longing glance in his direction, she opened a book and got down to business.

Before Scott met Judy, his interests had only numbered three—bicycles, basketball, and babes. Born and raised on Mackinac, like other kids on the island, Scott had attended the Mackinac Island Public School from preschool through twelfth grade. With an enrollment of fewer than one hundred students and the average graduating class being anywhere between two and six, Scott's boyhood conquests were nonexistent. There had been only three girls close to his age, two of which were his cousins, so Scott did what boys do throughout their teenage years, but when he reached Central Michigan University, he no longer needed magazines.

Physically fit due to the miles he had pedaled as a dock porter, and tanned by the Michigan sun, when he sauntered his tall, lanky, muscled self onto that campus, pretty little heads began to turn, and Scott noticed each and every one.

All through his first year at CMU and halfway through his second, Scott spent his mornings in classes, his afternoons in the gymnasium, and his evenings hopping from bed to bed sampling all that the university had to offer. His appetite was sated with a smorgasbord of curvy young women, but his tastes changed when he met Judith Lawton.

Unlike the girls flouncing across campus lawns with their bouffant flowing manes blowing in the wind, Judith wore her hair in a style that was not mussed by the weather. Short on the back and sides and a smidge longer on the top, the cut directly opposed those modeled after the latest television sensations or pop stars. Instead of skin-tight stirrup pants or equally snug miniskirts, Judy preferred khaki slacks or crisp blue jeans, and while other girls covered their torsos in oversized sweatshirts with extraordinarily long costume necklaces, Judy could usually be seen wearing polos sedately embellished with an alligator logo, and a sweater draped around her shoulders. She didn't wear the brightly-colored hoop earrings that were all the rage or the Espadrilles in stripes of orange, red, and brown, but rather her pierced ears only held tiny studs of gold, and the shoes on her feet were usually solid white cross-trainers.

Judith Lawton was everything the other girls were not, and Scott was totally smitten, except there was one teeny-tiny issue. Other than tutoring him in English, Judy didn't give Scott the time of day. If they passed in the halls, she didn't acknowledge him. If they attended the same sporting event, she never looked in his direction, and on the two occasions when they had shown up at the same party, before Scott could make it across the room to say hello, Judy had made her exit.

His pearly-toothed smile had no effect on the woman nor did his towering frame or faddish cologne, and he was at a loss on how to get Judy's attention, but when he passed his next English exam, and Judy smiled after hearing the results, Scott had found his answer. From that day forward, Scott studied harder than he ever had before.

Smiles eventually turned into celebratory drinks at trendy local bars catering to the college crowd, and by the middle of their junior year, Scott and Judy had become a couple. Theirs was a casual yet exclusive relationship, and Scott never looked at another woman again...until he was forty-seven.

Upon graduation, Scott went back to Mackinac, but with no teaching positions available on the island, Judy returned to her home state of Indiana to look for work. They settled into a long-distance relationship, seeing each other whenever they could, and for Judy, that was enough. For Scott, it was not.

Every time they saw each other, Scott began to propose. He did it on one knee and on two. He did it in bed, in restaurants, and on ferry rides across the Straits. He pleaded, promised, and pushed, even dangling children in front of what he assumed were maternal hormones ready to let loose, but it wasn't until a cold December night when Judy finally said yes. Twenty-four hours later, fearing she would change her mind, Scott purchased two airplane tickets to Nevada and two days after that, they were married in a small chapel on Las Vegas Boulevard.

Judy bent down, adjusting the dial on the baseboard heater before she shrugged out of her coat and hung it on a hook on the wall. She headed over to the kitchenette in the right corner of the apartment, and opening the refrigerator, she scanned the shelves for anything even remotely appetizing. She loved to cook, but making meals for one seemed tedious at best. Spying the leftover sausage from the day before, fifteen minutes later Judy was standing at her kitchen sink, eating fried eggs and re-heated sausage out of a skillet.

***

Cocooned in the bubbles floating atop the hottest water she could handle, Robin rested against the back of the double slipper claw-foot tub and stared at the wall in front of her. She wasn't examining the plaster for defects or condemning the shade of pale carrot Adele had chosen for the bathroom. Robin was just stupefied. Totally and utterly stupefied.

Was this dumb luck? Was this fate? Was this divine intervention? After all these years, what in the universe had shifted so perfectly to allow her teenage crush to once again become a part of her life...and a much bigger part at that.

Their time together would no longer have to be based on Robin showing up early for school. It wouldn't hinge on a chance meeting in a crowded hallway where Robin would crane her neck just to steal a glance. She wouldn't have to sit on metal bleachers, blinded by the sun or drenched by the rain, in order to watch the woman run up and down the sidelines of a soccer field, clapping her hands, shouting instructions, or huddling with her players. If Judy Dunnigan took the job, Robin could see her every day without question or camouflage. She could stand next to her in the kitchen, learning the meals they would serve for their breakfasts, and she could hover over her as Judy worked at mastering software they had yet to buy. She could comment on the entries, make suggestions, or perhaps even laugh at a typo, and it all hinged on only one thing. *If* Judy said yes.

Robin jerked in the tub, sending a splash of water over the sides. *If* wasn't an option. It couldn't be. Something or someone had brought them back together, and Robin refused to believe anything else. This *wasn't* happenstance. This *couldn't* be an accident. She had pined for this woman for decades, never able to truly shake the memories of only a few short months from her mind. In dreams, blurred and fractured, the sound of Judy's voice floating over athletic fields had always found its way to her, and on crowded beaches, it only took one glance at the cloudless Florida sky for Judy's eyes to come back to her, their blue so pure and clear. Alligator logos always brought smiles, pleated skirts forever received second glances, and when pixie haircuts came into view, Robin's heart rate had uncontrollably and consistently quickened.

Robin relaxed back in the tub again. She closed her eyes, welcoming the warmth of the water covering her shoulders as much as she welcomed her own convictions. This wasn't a coincidence. This was meant to be, and it only hinged on one thing, and it was that one thing that caused Robin's eyes to pop open. What if Judy said *no*?

"That is *not* going to happen!" Robin said, and scrambling out of the tub, she grabbed a towel and dried off in record time.

Neglecting her nightly routine of moisturizer and body lotion, she tugged on a pair of sweatpants, pulled a hoodie over her head, yanked on a pair of socks and darted from the room. She ran into the kitchen and snagged her phone from the counter, intending to run a search on the average salary of a bed-and-breakfast manager, but before she could type in one letter, Robin stopped. Could she actually stoop that low? Could she actually try to buy off Judy Dunnigan by waving a hefty salary in front of her face? Is that what her once innocent infatuation had become? An obsession whereby she would do anything, say anything, *pay* anything just to have the woman in her life?

Robin hung her head, and feeling like she needed another bath, she tossed her phone on the counter. She knew what it was like to be manipulated, and the memory of it caused bile to rise in her throat. For over a year, Robin had been on the receiving end of a master, and through deception, verbal abuse, and unscrupulous tactics, she had been unknowingly molded like wet clay. Turned and smoothed, shaped and grooved, helped along by a smattering of cursory charm, the occasional guilt trip, and several violent outbursts, toward the end of that relationship, Robin didn't even know who she was. Her interests fell by the wayside. Her needs were inconsequential, and she had become an expert on how to walk on eggshells.

A chill ran down Robin's spine, and rubbing her arms, she tried to calm the goosebumps prickling at her skin. This was not who she was, and with a sneer, she shoved the phone farther away. Robin could not deny what she felt for Judy Dunnigan. She could not rebuff the dreams or the fantasies she had had over the years, but none had ever been based on control because love *isn't* about control. It's not about deceit or holier-than-thou attitudes or pushing buttons just because you know you can. Love is about caring. It's about sharing and trust and honesty, and it's about putting others' needs before your own.

Robin didn't know if it had been a stroke of luck, a twist of fate, or God just playing God that had brought Judy back into her life, but Robin did know one thing. She had never been in control of the circumstances surrounding it, and she wasn't about to start now. Snatching up the bottle of wine, Robin poured what was left into a glass and went back to the parlor, leaving her phone on the counter, where it would remain all night.

***

The Wilsons had already gone to Florida, preferring to spend the winter in their RV near sun and surf rather than being snowed in on Mackinac for months, so when Judy stepped out of the bathroom, a plume of steam followed her. The Wilson's four children had moved off the island years before, but during the spring and summer, they and their horde of kids would visit Larry and Kay, and the water heater never kept up with the demand. Unless Judy got up at four in the morning or waited until midnight for a shower, the best she could hope for when she stepped into the tiny corner stall was water just warm enough so her teeth wouldn't chatter. Winter provided few luxuries, but ample hot water was more than enough to make up for the solitude of an island abandoned by most from November to April.

Dressed in flannel pajamas and bulky gray socks, Judy scrubbed a towel over her head, ridding her hair of most of the water before hanging the terrycloth back on the rod. Making her way to the bed, she slid beneath the covers and sheets, flicked off the light and stared into the darkness.

Robin Novak's proposal had popped in and out of her head since leaving Safe Harbor Inn a few hours before, but it had never stayed there for long. She had told Robin she would reconsider her decision, and Judy had done just that while pedaling back to her apartment, but what was there to rethink?

Bed-and-breakfasts were almost a twenty-four-seven job. Guests came and went daily, leaving behind messes that would have shamed their parents, yet complaining if one speck of dust was present when they checked in. Breakfasts had to offer a selection for varying palates, and if requested when reservations were made, special dietary needs would have to be met. There would be guests who would plunder the breakfast buffet, filling their coolers and backpacks with what they believed they were due, while others didn't know the meaning of the word guest. Intruding into areas they weren't allowed, they'd try to investigate every closet, nook, and cranny and Judy would be the one who would have to paint on a false smile and politely explain why a cabinet or perhaps a door was locked. She would face the ire of some unable to fathom why they couldn't borrow the bikes or Burley belonging to the Inn and others who'd turn indignant when they were told they couldn't use the kitchen to cook a meal. Guests would call at all hours of the day and night, and late check-ins would show up much later than they had promised, and when the weather turned foul, so would the guests. Grumpy that their plans had changed, they would grumble and growl and ask for snacks as if the Inn had suddenly turned into a hotel.

Judy let out a long sigh. She knew she was concentrating on the bad instead of the good. She knew when it came to running a bed-and-breakfast, especially one on Mackinac Island, the pros still outweighed the cons, but she couldn't risk thinking about the benefits. If she did, she'd change her mind, so as Judy drifted off to sleep, she just kept telling herself she was too old to start again.

Chapter Ten

Judy stood up as her best friend, Rita Hutchinson approached the booth, and wrapping her arms around the big-boned woman, she said, "Happy birthday!"

"Thanks, sweetie," Rita said, returning the hug. "Another year older and still no wiser."

"I know what you mean," Judy said with a laugh, and pulling out of the hug, she gestured for Rita to sit down.

"So, any exciting plans for you today?" Judy said, sliding a menu toward Rita. "Is Hank doing anything special?"

"No, just the usual," Rita said, picking up a menu. "He'll take me over to the Village Inn for dinner, and I'll come home to a lopsided cake he spent all morning trying to make."

"You love his lopsided cakes."

"I know, damn it. If the son-of-a-bitch weren't so good in bed, I'd find myself a new cake maker," Rita said, and as she looked up from her menu, she saw a young waitress approaching. "And speaking of cake makers," she said, turning back to Judy. "Anybody tasting your frosting lately?"

Judy didn't have to turn her head to know the waitress was standing next to the table, and no doubt had heard what Rita had said. With a sigh, Judy raised her eyes and saw the buxom brunette smiling down at her, the young woman's cheeks nearly as red as Judy's. Without looking in Rita's direction, Judy placed her order, and Rita followed suit. Once the waitress walked away, Judy glared at Rita. "Why do you *always* do that to me?"

Rita's boisterous guffaw echoed through the restaurant. "Because it's fun, and these youngsters need to know that they aren't the only ones getting any. Just because we have some gray in our hair, doesn't mean we have it in our beds."

The smile Judy wore had appeared in her heart long before it reached her face. She first met Rita a few years before moving to Mackinac when Scott brought her to the island on spring break. It was a friendship born in an instant, and when Judy moved to the island, Rita was there to greet her with open arms. Over the years, some friends had come and gone, leaving when retirements were reached, or new opportunities presented themselves, but Rita wasn't going anywhere, and neither was Judy.

A third-generation islander, Rita's family had opened one of the first candy stores on Mackinac. In a little inconspicuous store on Main Street in the late eighteen hundreds, they began producing peanut brittle and fudge based on old family recipes, their only marketing technique being the fans they placed by the front door to push the aroma of confectionery heaven onto the street. It wasn't long before those stepping off ferries came in search of fudge, and by the time Rita became the CEO of the company, Schockling's Sweets had opened additional stores in St. Ignace, Mackinack City, and Cheboygan.

At five-foot-ten and solidly built, Rita was quite an imposing figure. She could have easily used her appearance *and* her lineage to her advantage, like some on Mackinac who allowed their genealogy to fuel their level of self-importance, but Rita owned not one ounce of pretension. She loved her job. She loved her family. She loved her church, and she loved Mackinac Island, and it showed in everything she did. From the bounce in her step to the enduring laugh lines at the corners of her eyes and mouth, Rita went through her life enjoying every minute of it. She had an earthiness about her and one of the most charming smiles a person could ever hope to see, and while her voice was strapping and throaty, she was just a playful pussycat at heart, and as always, Judy was on the receiving end of Rita's innuendo-filled humor.

Judy leaned across the table and whispered, "You are incorrigible!"

"Yes, I am," Rita said, reaching for a glass of water. "And you wouldn't have it any other way. Without me, your life would be boring."

"All right, you've got me there," Judy said, slumping back into her seat.

"And speaking of boring, how's the gallery doing? Still as active as ever?"

"It's a thrill a minute," Judy said, narrowing her eyes. "And don't you dare tell me 'I told you so.'"

"Would I do that?" Rita said, pointing to herself.

"In a heartbeat."

Rita glanced at her watch. "Time's up. I told you so."

"See!"

Rita laughed, and more than a few patrons turned their heads toward the sound of her hearty chortle. "Hey, don't get mad at me because you took a job I told you that you'd hate. After all those years working at The Wheelhouse, plus at the candy stores, there's no way in hell you could handle the slower pace of the galleries. Granted, they can get busy, but not like the rest of us do."

"I know," Judy said, letting out a sigh.

"You could come back to Schockling's. There'll always be a place for you there."

"Thanks, hon, but I think I'm burned out when it comes to selling fudge. At least for a little while."

"So, what next then? Scrimshaw? T-shirts? Carriage tours?"

"Actually, I was offered a job earlier this week," Judy said as she played with the corner of her folded napkin.

Rita sat up in the booth, her backbone stretched to its limits as her eyes opened wide. "What are you talking about? You're not leaving the island, are you?"

"No," Judy said, flinching back her head. "Of course not."

"Then who in the hell is offering you a job at the end of the season?"

"Did you hear that Adele's niece inherited Safe Harbor?"

"Please," Rita said, rolling her eyes. "I swear, one of these days I'm going to look up into the sky and see a plane dragging a banner with Mackinac's gossip printed on it. Of course, I've heard about it. Her name's Robin Novak. She's tall, blonde, and a writer, but I already knew the last part because Adele used to talk about her every once in a while. Why?"

"She's the one who offered me the job."

"What job?"

"To manage Safe Harbor."

"What?" Rita said, her voice rising above the chatter in the restaurant. "That's great!"

"You think?"

"You don't?"

"I'm not sure."

"Why the hell not? Adele never had an empty room through the season. If you want to keep busy, that's the place to be. And it's not like you don't have the experience."

"I've just filled in—"

"Oh, bullshit," Rita said, waving her hand. "Whenever you worked at any of the B&Bs, you practically took over, and the owners loved it. They didn't have to worry about one goddamned thing when you were there."

"I suppose," Judy said as she returned her attention to the corner of her napkin.

Rita frowned. "What's wrong?"

"Nothing," Judy muttered.

"At the risk of repeating myself—bullshit."

Judy took a moment and got her thoughts together before she looked at Rita. "I just think I'm a little too old to start a new career."

"Where in the hell did that come from?" Rita said, sitting straight in her seat. "Since when is fifty-five old, and when exactly did your age start bothering you? In all the years we've known each other, I can't remember one time when you ever let it get in the way of anything. It's just a fucking number, and using it as an excuse so you can throw away this opportunity is crap."

"It's *just* a job."

"It is *not* just a job," Rita said, and leaning forward, she tapped her finger on the table. "It's a fantastic opportunity, and you and I both know it."

"We do, do we?"

"Yes, we do," Rita said, and resting back in the booth, she crossed her arms. "So, stop trying to kid a kidder and tell me the real reason why you don't want to take this job?"

Judy returned to picking at her napkin. "Robin went to Heritage High when I was there, and I think it would be kind of weird to work for a student. That's all."

The lines on Rita's forehead deepened as seconds ticked by. "She was...she was one of your students?"

"No. I was her homeroom teacher in her senior year. At least, that's what she says."

"So, you're saying you don't remember her?"

"No," Judy said, looking up. "No, I don't."

Before Rita could speak, the waitress appeared with their meals. Thankful for not only the food but the time it gave her to get her thoughts together, Rita didn't say another word until the brunette sashayed away from the table. "Then what's the problem?" she said, reaching for the ketchup. "She was just a kid in your homeroom."

"That's exactly my point. She was a kid."

"Well, she's not one anymore. I mean, unless her name's Dorian Gray, she has to be in her forties by now—right?"

"Yeah, I guess so," Judy said, picking up the salt shaker. "I just keep thinking it would be weird."

"You want to know what I think?"

Judy stopped salting her fries long enough to look up. "Do I have a choice?"

"Nope."

"How'd I know that?" Judy said, putting the condiment aside. "Okay, go ahead."

"I think you should take the job," Rita said as she wrapped her hands around her burger. "You know I'm not one to play the age card, Judy, but you're right. You and I aren't getting any younger, and something like this doesn't come along very often. Do you really want to pass up it up only to look back in a few years and regret never taking the chance to...to be happy?"

"You don't think I'm happy?"

"I think you're content. I think you settled into the monotony of your life years ago, and I think you've brainwashed yourself into believing you're okay with it, but as far as being happy? No, I don't think you've been happy for a long time. So go for it, Jude. Life's too fucking short not to."

***

As Judy stood on the front porch of the Inn late on Friday night, she chuckled to herself. Five days before she had been at the same door, ringing the same bell, and doing the same thing...debating on whether to stay or to leave.

Until she had talked to Rita earlier that afternoon, Judy's mind had been made up, but as she stood with her shoulders hunched against the cold wind, she let out a sigh. She knew she *could* do this, but the question was...should she?

Her thoughts broken by the sound of rain beginning to fall, Judy rushed out to her bike. Quickly covering the seat with the plastic bag she always kept tucked under it, she grabbed her backpack from the basket between the handlebars and ran back to the porch.

At times, the weather on Mackinac could be unpredictable, and since there were no cars parked in driveways or stationed at curbs, the islanders knew to be prepared. Most never left their homes without backpacks slung over their shoulders, and neatly folded inside the zippered compartments would be rain suits to protect them against storms and extra sweaters just in case the temperature dropped unexpectedly.

The next blast of wind answered the question on Judy's mind, and cringing as a spray of rain found its way to her face, she yanked the canary yellow rain suit out of her backpack. After stepping into the vinyl pants, she slipped on the jacket, flipped up the hood, and tugged the drawstring until it was tight around her face.

Less than five minutes had passed since Judy had run back to the porch, but in that short amount of time the clouds had let loose, and the sound of the storm was becoming deafening. The rain was slamming against the roof, and as puddles formed on the street and sidewalk, their surfaces began to jump and ripple, taking on lives of their own courtesy of Mother Nature.

Resigned to remaining under cover until at least the worst of the storm had passed, Judy leaned against the wall and watched the rain come down. Even at its worst, Judy always enjoyed a good rainstorm. She loved listening to the sound of it, the cadence created by water drumming against roofs and porches and windows, and how the scent of pine, earth, and grass would suddenly become enhanced, momentarily drowning out the aroma of manure, a constant on the island.

A distant sound caught her attention, and for a second, Judy thought it was a wind chime dangling on the porch of a neighbor's house until she heard it again. She stepped closer to the edge of the porch and looking down the street, she saw a bicyclist towing a Burley with a neon green cover. Judy couldn't help but giggle. "Oh, my God. She's going to be soaked."

There hadn't been a day that had gone by since arriving on the island when Robin hadn't learned something and today was no different. Today's lesson was proper planning...or the lack thereof.

When Robin left the house that morning, she rode her beater bike to the dock, all the while enjoying the balmier-than-normal October temperature on the island. She locked up her bike and boarded the ferry, and a short time later she was on her way to Petoskey to do some shopping. She spent the morning buying paint and assorted sundries and then toured every furniture store in the area. With only her bedroom set and some odds and ends in storage, Robin browsed what was available, taking photos with her phone, jotting down measurements, and grabbing various brochures as she went. Robin loved to decorate, so when she boarded the ferry to come home, her spirits were up. When she reached the island...not so much.

She had just finished zipping the cover on the Burley when the deluge started, and before Robin was a block from the dock, she was soaked to the skin. By the time she rounded the corner at the end of Main Street, her jeans had shrunk a size, her hoodie had grown at least three, and her favorite pair of lace panties had turned themselves into a thong.

Robin squinted through the blackness as water cascaded down her face, and with no more street lights illuminating her way, she concentrated on the meager ray of light coming from the headlight on her bike. When she spotted the small gate leading to the Inn, she slowed to a crawl and maneuvered the Raleigh onto the path that ran between her house and the next. Stopping under a tree, Robin climbed off and flipped down the kickstand.

"You need help?"

There are many levels of fear. There's the anxiety that can occur when viewing a thriller in a theater and the music begins to build. There's the uneasiness that happens when the written word ignites imaginations to the point that locks on windows and doors need to be double-checked. There are phobias that can cause shivers to snake down spines for everything from spiders to clowns, and then there is the fear created from the unexpected. That one's called terror.

Standing in practically total darkness with rain pouring down on her, Robin let out a scream so shrill and so loud, there was a good chance that it made it across the island. Her fight response told her to turn toward the danger, but as she spun to face the intruder, Robin's flight response kicked in. She needed to run, and she needed to run now, but caught halfway between a pirouette and a sprint, Robin's feet went out from under her, and she landed with a splat in the mud. "*Fuck!*"

Robin's fear gave way to the muck oozing into her jeans, and she shot a look at the canary-coated stranger meant to cause instant death. When she realized it was Judy Dunnigan, in the blink of an eye, Robin was transported back in time, and she cowered like a teenager about to be reprimanded for her language…and then Robin blinked again. She wasn't a child. *She* was an adult, and she was an adult who was now sitting in a puddle of mud because of the woman standing over her.

"*You scared the shit out of me!*" Robin bellowed. "What the fuck were you *thinking*?"

Judy opened her mouth to speak, but as she gazed down at the woman sitting up to her hips in a puddle, all that came out was laughter, lots and lots of laughter. Bending at the waist, Judy covered her mouth as she tried to rein in mirth that seemed to have no end.

For some, it is the coo of babies. For others, it is the sounds of Christmas carols sung by choirs high up in the lofts of drafty old churches, but up until that moment, Robin had never had a favorite sound. She did now, and she was prepared to sit in the puddle until spring just so she could listen to Judy's laughter.

Judy gasped for air as she fought to get herself under control, but every time she opened her eyes and saw Robin on the ground, the hilarity hit her again. The sound of Robin's shriek kept repeating in her head, and the sight of the bedraggled woman only made it worse. With the hood of her sweatshirt halfway down her face, Robin looked like something out of a horror movie.

After almost a minute, Judy stood straight and cleared her throat. "Are you okay?" she shouted over the rain.

"You know," Robin said, taking a moment to look down at her soggy self before looking up again. "I've been better."

Judy snorted as she held out her hand. "Let me help you up."

"Thanks," Robin said, and slipping her hand in Judy's, she was on her feet a second later.

"I'm really sorry," Judy said, raising her voice to be heard over the storm. "I didn't mean to startle you."

"You didn't startle me. You scared the ever-living *shit* out of me," Robin shouted back. "And now, not only am I wet, but I also have mud where there should *never* be mud."

Judy looked down at the brown stain covering Robin's posterior. "Oh, that *cannot* be comfortable."

"It's not. Trust me," Robin said, and turning, she began to fumble with the zipper on the cover of the Burley with fingers now stiff from the cold and spattered with muck.

"Here, let me do that," Judy said, stepping in front of Robin.

"I can do it."

"I'm sure you can," Judy said staring up at the chin peeking out from under the hood. "But I'm beginning to prune here, and you have mud in your...um...*jeans*. You really want to dawdle?"

Robin was about to argue, but when she shifted her stance, and a significant amount of mud shifted too, she changed her mind almost as quickly as her face distorted at the sensation. "Good point."

It took three trips to empty the cargo hauler and the baskets on the bike, but ten minutes later, eight gallons of paint and six bags of brushes, rollers, and assorted household items were stacked just inside the front door of the Inn.

After placing the last bag atop the pile, Judy turned around, her eyes immediately drawn to the mud and water puddling at Robin's feet. "You really need to get out of those clothes," she said, pointing toward the back of the house. "Go get cleaned up and I'll take care of this."

Robin was about to argue, but when she pushed the hood off her head, a splash of water hit the floor. "Shit," she said, looking at her feet. "Maybe you're right."

"I expect to be hearing that more often than not, just to let you know," Judy said as she unzipped her jacket.

Robin scrunched up her face. "Huh?"

"That is...if your offer to run this place is still good."

"Really?" Robin squeaked as a smile spread across her face.

"Yes, Robin," Judy said, grinning as she hung up her coat. "Really."

Chapter Eleven

Having worked at the Inn before, Judy knew that while Adele used a service for her linens, she had her own supply of towels. Once Robin went to change her clothes, Judy kicked off her shoes, rid herself of her vinyl rain suit and then ran upstairs to the laundry room on the second floor.

A few minutes later, Judy carried a stack of terrycloth back to the entrance hall and proceeded to wipe up the trail of water and mud that led all the way from the front door to Robin's apartment. After making short work of the mess Robin had created, Judy tossed another towel near the coat tree to catch the water dripping from her rain jacket before going back upstairs.

Robin had the body to wear skinny jeans, but as she yanked, tugged, and stumbled around the bathroom trying to pull the denim down over her damp legs, she swore she'd never buy another pair again. If her shower had been in working order, she would have been in and out of the bathroom in record time, but baths take longer, especially when the first lasted only a few minutes before Robin needed to drain the brown water and replace it with clear.

Forty-five minutes after dashing into the bathroom, Robin dashed back out with her hair clean, her clothes, dry, and her socked feet still not touching the floor. She rushed into her kitchen and snagging two glasses, a bottle of wine, and a folder off the counter, Robin exited the apartment only to stop as soon as she reached the other kitchen. The oak flooring was shiny and dry with not a drop of water or speck of mud anywhere in sight. With a heavy sigh, Robin headed toward the entry, reaching it just as Judy came down the stairs.

"You didn't have to clean it all up," Robin said, gesturing toward the kitchen. "I could have done it."

"Don't worry about it," Judy said with a wave of her hand. "I put everything in one of the washers upstairs, but you'll need to remember to get it into the dryer later."

"I can do that," Robin said, nodding. "Speaking of washers and dryers, do you have any idea why there's another set in the basement? It seems to me to be a little overkill. Don't you think?"

"Not really," Judy said, shaking her head. "True, this is your home, but it's also a B&B, and you lugging your dirty laundry through the house doesn't exactly fit the mood we're trying to set for our guests."

Stuck on the word *our*, it took Robin a moment to respond. "Oh, yeah. Good point."

"And just to let you know, we will have the occasional guest thinking they can use the washers and dryers, so, during the season, the door is kept locked for that reason."

"Why would they think that? You can't do it in hotels."

Judy smiled at her employer's naiveté. "Are you planning to offer me a glass of that?" Judy said, pointing to the bottle in Robin's hand.

"Yes. Would you like some?"

"After the day I've had? Most definitely," Judy said, gesturing toward the pocket doors. "Parlor work for you?"

Robin grinned. "I'm right behind you."

A minute later, curled up in opposite corners of the sofa, both women sipped their Cabernet, taking time to savor the earthiness and tannins of the dark ruby wine. As Judy breathed in the aroma, she noticed Robin seemed to be staring at her socks. "Um, I hope you don't mind," Judy said, unconsciously wiggling her toes. "My boots were soaked, and I didn't want to track mud through the house."

Robin didn't mind. Robin didn't mind one little bit. While she had no fetishes, kinks, or quirks, the sight of Judy's toes moving inside gray and orange socks affected Robin in a way she hadn't expected. Her body tingled, her stomach fluttered, and adulthood went *right* out the window.

"No," Robin said, snapping up her head. "No, not at all. Totally understandable. I mean, I'm wearing socks, why can't you? Right? Personally, I really like moccasins, but I need to get a new pair. I have to add that to my list. Come to think of it, I'll probably just get a couple of pairs, so I always have them."

Robin watched as Judy's eyebrow arched, confirming what Robin already knew. She had prattled on like an idiot...again.

"So," Robin said, pausing to take a quick gulp of her drink. "You mentioned having a bad day?"

Judy's mind had drifted while Robin had been babbling, but rubbing the back of her neck, Judy got herself back on track. "Oh...um...no, not really a *bad* day, it was just a slow one. Right now, I'm working at Brushstrokes. It's an art gallery up on Market Street. The owners, Walt and Sally Ford, leave the island during the winter, so it's time to sort, clean, and inventory everything before it gets packed up and stored. I love Walt and Sally to death. They're super people, but they're both approaching eighty, so they move a little slow, and they're kind of set in their ways. They came in this morning to help me with the process, but every time I cleaned something, Sally needed to clean it again, and every time I inventoried something, Walt had to check it, and then Sally had to check him because she didn't think he was doing it right," Judy said, snickering. "It made for a *very* long day."

"Well, from what I've read, that probably won't happen around here."

Judy's eyes crinkled at the corners. "It sounds like someone's been Googling again."

Robin smiled and reached for the folder she had set on the coffee table. "I figured whether you accepted my offer or not, I should at least be a little better prepared than I was the last time you were here," she said, and pulling out some papers, she shifted closer to Judy.

"What's all this?" Judy said, staring at the colorful spreadsheets in Robin's hands.

"I've been doing research on the other B&Bs on the island."

"Didn't Adele keep records?"

"Yeah, but I couldn't figure out her filing system, and everything I saw was a few years old, so instead I checked out the room rates of our competition and what they offer guests versus what we could offer," Robin said, handing Judy the papers.

"Wow," Judy said, looking at all the data. "You've *obviously* done your homework."

"I guesstimated using their rates as a baseline, and these are the numbers I came up with for us, adjusting them up and down depending on the size, location, and amenities in each room. Using higher rates for the months that are busier and lower ones for the slower part of the season, the number I highlighted at the bottom is what I think we could pull in, in a year."

Judy took her time as she glanced from one chart to the next, and as she studied the numbers, she found herself becoming excited. It wasn't due to the amount of money the Inn could make, but rather the depth of Robin's analysis. Her notes were clear. Her assumptions were sound, and Judy was duly impressed. "You've got a good business sense."

"I'm basically winging it," Robin said, grinning.

"Well, keep it up," Judy said, placing the papers on the table. "I mean, we still have a lot to look into, but this gives us a great starting point."

"And speaking of starting points, I wasn't exactly sure what you wanted as a salary, but what I'm thinking is that the profits from the first year would be split three ways. One part will be for you. One part will be for the house to cover all the expenses, and one part will be for me. I know you're going to be basically running this place once the season starts and you deserve more, but the Inn needs some work, and this will help me recoup what I'm going to be spending this winter to get things in order. After that, I'd increase your share and reduce mine. Hopefully, that'll be okay with you. If not, we can—"

"Robin, stop rambling," Judy said with a laugh. "I honestly hadn't even thought about a salary until now, but trust me, this is a hell of a lot more than I was making at the gallery."

"Yeah?"

"Yes," Judy said, and after taking a sip of wine, she thought about what they had just talked about. "Of course, this is all conjecture until we can take a look at Adele's records. Even when she was out sick, she handled all the finances, so I can't tell you if you're close or not until we can take a look at that stuff."

"Well, wanna go take a look?"

Judy glanced at her watch. It was almost ten, and she needed to work the next day, but suddenly that didn't seem significant. "Sure, let's go."

***

Having aired out her apartment and most of the ground floor, when they walked into Adele's office, Robin noticed the difference immediately. Without a window to allow in fresh air, the mustiness of the room had been trapped behind the closed door, and while a ceiling fan dangled above their heads, the amount of dust on the blades stopped Robin from turning it on.

"Where do you want to start?" Robin said.

"I think for now we should just see what's in these and go from there," Judy said, and walking over, she opened the top drawer of the first of three filing cabinets.

For the next hour, Judy browsed through the cabinets, and it didn't take long for her to agree with what Robin had said. When it came to a filing system, it didn't appear Adele ever had one, but what she lacked in order, she more than made up for in paperwork. The first cabinet overflowed with receipts for everything Adele had purchased, leased, or had repaired since purchasing the Inn, along with the stub of all the utility bills paid over the years. The next was filled with accounting journals, guest books, and employee records, and the last held a hodgepodge of out-of-date business licenses, insurance information, and bank statements.

While Judy perused the files, Robin was having a hard time doing the same. The Inn belonged to her now and this room, like every other, was hers to do with what she wanted, but the innkeeper's suite had been empty. Void of whatever life had lived there, it had been easy for Robin to open and close cabinets, and clean away the dust and dirt, but standing in the middle of her aunt's office, she felt like an intruder. Was Adele the last person who had ever opened one of those filing cabinets? Was she the last person who had ever sat at the desk or a hung a key on the board affixed to the wall? Going over, Robin looked at the keys dangling from the L-shaped hooks jutting out from the plywood. In her haste to find the ones fitting the locks on the window seats, she didn't really pay much attention to the room names neatly printed above each hook or the anchor-shaped fob attached to each key, and now it pained her to do so. It was all so neat and orderly, exactly like Robin would have done it if the Inn had been hers. Everything had a place, and everything was in its place...yet everything wasn't here.

With a sigh, Robin slipped into the chair behind the desk, the leather groaning as she sunk into its softness. The blotter centered in front of her had seen better days, its mocha felt center showing a half-dozen stains left behind by wet glasses, and the leather corners were cracked and worn. Tucked into one of them were a few business cards and pulling them out, Robin read the names of dock porters, grocery stores, and maintenance people, most likely all having serviced the Safe Harbor Inn at one time or another. An empty coffee mug sat off to the side, and picking it up, Robin looked inside, hoping it wouldn't contain remnants of a long-forgotten drink. Thankfully, the white ceramic was stained with only ink and pencil, and Robin smiled to herself. She used mugs the same way, too.

Robin slowly opened the pencil drawer to look inside. There was an assortment of paper clips and rubber bands in one compartment along the edge, and a jumble of loose change in another. A mishmash of blank Post-It notes and steno pads filled the rest of the space, yet there wasn't one touch of personal. True, at one time it had all belonged to Adele, but Robin was hoping for more. She wanted to find a handwritten reminder or a keepsake, something to connect her with her aunt, though as Robin glanced around the room, the office seemed just like her apartment. There were no signs her aunt had ever been here. Why? Why had everything in the innkeeper's suite and the office been stripped so bare of personal belongings?

Robin swiveled around, her eyes finding the prosaic oil painting hanging on the wall above the filing cabinets. Long and narrow, the landscape it presented was elementary, containing only the most basic blends of blues, greens, and browns, and Robin tilted her head. It seemed familiar, but it was far too primitive to be a copy of some masterpiece she had seen hanging in a museum. Unable to place it in her memory, Robin looked past the painting to three simply-framed certificates hanging next to it. Even though they looked official, most likely something to do with the business, they didn't hold Robin's interest. She knew whatever they were, they were most likely expired, so she rotated the chair toward the back wall. There was a bulletin board, the cork dark in some places yet light in others, but there were no notes attached, no reminders or calendars, just a row of thumbtacks neatly arranged along the bottom edge. Having run out of walls, Robin turned her attention back to the filing cabinets...and to the person standing in front of one.

Confident she could quickly avert her eyes if Judy turned around, Robin relaxed back in the chair and took in the view. The sweater Judy was wearing reminded Robin of ones often seen on ski slopes. A pale blue Nordic print against a background of ivory, it hugged her torso just enough to hold Robin's interest for almost a minute before her eyes moved lower. Judy's blue jeans weren't snug, much to Robin's disappointment, but they still managed to define Judy's slender waist and rounded hips before tapering to short, straight legs. Vertically disadvantaged, to browse through the highest drawer, Judy was standing on her tiptoes and Robin was transported back in time, imagining the muscles in Judy's calves pulled just as taut as they had been so many years before. Content in her daydream, Robin had no idea Judy had turned around until she heard the woman clear her throat.

Robin raised her eyes, and when they met Judy's, only one thing popped into Robin's mind. How in the hell was she going to explain the salacious grin she knew was plastered all over her face? Robin scanned the room, her eyes darting from one object to the next until her answer was found. "Oh, hey," she said, pointing at the wall. "Cool painting."

Judy looked over her shoulder at the lackluster artwork of non-descript trees and an all-too-perfect lake. "You actually like that?" she said, turning back around.

"Well, I don't know," Robin said, getting to her feet. "It's kind of scenic. Don't you think?"

"Most paint-by-numbers are."

As soon as Judy's words settled in Robin's brain, the puzzle pieces came together. "*That's* where I've seen it!"

"What?"

"I was just thinking that stupid thing looked familiar, and now I know why. My mother had something just like it hanging in her bedroom. She painted it when I was a kid. Adele must have done one, too."

"Probably, there's not a lot to do on the island when the snow starts to fall," Judy said, again glancing at the painting.

Satisfied that her ruse had worked, Robin gestured toward the filing cabinets. "Did you find anything helpful in there?"

"Yeah, it looks like she kept practically everything, but you're right about her filing system," Judy said, swallowing a yawn as she closed a drawer. "That's going to take me some time to figure out, but at least we're not starting in the dark. Do you know if she had a computer? Like I said, she handled all the finances, so I just assumed she had it with her."

"There wasn't one here when I moved in. Why?"

"I was hoping she didn't do everything longhand, but if she did, we're going to have to look into getting one, I think."

"That's doable. I'll just add it..." Robin stopped when she noticed Judy yawning again. Glancing at her watch, Robin's shoulders fell. "Geez. Look at the time. I'm sorry. It's late, and you worked today."

"I wouldn't exactly call it work, but I was up at five."

"Five!"

"I'm an early riser. By the time the sun comes up, I'm usually on my second cup of coffee. I normally don't even have to set an alarm," Judy said, following Robin to the door. "And speaking of work, I have to be at the gallery bright and early tomorrow, but I'm free on Sunday. How about I stop by in the morning, and we can talk some more?"

"Sounds good to me," Robin said, and as she walked past the keys hanging on the wall, she stopped long enough to pluck a set dangling under the label Spare Front. Dropping them in Judy's hands, she said, "I've always considered myself a morning person, but I do hereby relinquish my claim."

***

By six thirty on Sunday morning, Judy was pacing her apartment. The sun wasn't going to be up for another hour and a half, but with two cups of coffee in her stomach and more energy than she knew what to do with, she made it only halfway across the apartment again before she gave up and put on her rain suit. Grabbing her backpack off the kitchen counter, she flicked off the lights, shut the door, and climbed the steps.

Known as "the village" by the locals, Harrisonville was where most of the nearly five hundred full-time residents of Mackinac lived. Located just up the hill from the Grand Hotel, it contained an assortment of single-family homes, most of which were modest compared to the cottages lining the bluffs. In various shapes and sizes with white picket fences around some and chain-link surrounding others, the houses were like many found in small towns across America. The only difference was those in Mackinac had no need for driveways.

As Judy reached the top of the stairs, she paused and took a deep breath of the cold, damp air. By the time she left Safe Harbor on Friday night, the rain had eased up, and Saturday had remained dry for most of the day, but the skies had opened up again sometime during the night. With a steady drizzle pattering against the autumn foliage of trees as background noise, Judy removed the plastic bag covering the seat of her blue and white Giordano road bike. She stored it away for yet another rainy day, and climbing onto her bike, she pedaled out from under the small overhang along the house and headed for the street.

The season having all but ended, the village had yet to awaken. Most locals were now enjoying the luxury of sleeping in, so other than the hum of the streetlights, all Judy could hear was the melodic rhythm of her bike tires as they rolled over the pavement and the sound of rain as it pelted dried leaves. With the elevation of the town two hundred feet above Main

Street, for the most part, she allowed the steepness of the hill to assist in her descent as she made her way down Cadotte Avenue. She kept her head bowed, looking out from under her hood occasionally so she could avoid as many puddles as possible, but even the spritz of rain upon her face could not dampen Judy's mood. Since leaving the Safe Harbor Inn on Friday night, it had remained high, even though Walt and Sally had seriously tried to test it the day before.

Saturday had been tedious and at times frustrating. Brushstrokes had officially closed at noon that day. Saying goodbye to the tourist season with little fanfare, Walt and Sally flipped the Open sign to Closed, pulled down the blinds, and then at a snail's pace, they spent the afternoon methodically finishing up what needed to be done. For Judy, the day moved along like molasses rolling up a hill. Paintings she had carefully wrapped in brown paper had been unwrapped to check what they contained, and boxes she had meticulously filled with artwork had been emptied and filled again, Sally and Walt triple-checking what they had double-checked on Friday. The septuagenarians prattled on, filling Judy's ears with endless recollections of the past as one hour moved like a snail toward the next, and while she tried to nod at all the right times and laugh when the response was called for, her thoughts were somewhere else. A somewhere void of watercolors and walls covered in white pegboard.

As Judy's speed picked up when she neared the bottom of the hill, she gripped the hand brakes, slowing herself just enough to easily make the right turn, and as she did, she acknowledged the truth. The rapid beat of her heart had nothing to do with a brand-new day. Judy was excited for the possibility of a future she never thought she'd have.

Chapter Twelve

Judy winced as she went inside. The hinges screeched like fingernails down a blackboard, and holding her breath, she closed the door as slowly and silently as she could. While discussing the Inn with Robin two days earlier, she had noticed a pillow and blanket on a chair in the parlor, so after hanging up her rain suit, Judy grabbed her backpack and tiptoed over to the partially opened pocket doors. Peering through the crack, she did a double take when she saw the heads of the two cats pop up instantly from their place on the sofa, but there was no movement from the occupant under the blanket.

Pleased she hadn't awoken Robin, Judy went on her way, slowing up just a bit as she moved through the dining room. It now smelled of polish and pine, and the haze she had noticed on the windows had disappeared. There were several stacks of tablecloths and runners piled on the buffets, and even the upholstery on the cushions of the chairs seemed more colorful than it had on Friday night.

The kitchen also had its share of aromas, a blend of cleaners and cleansers finding their way to her nose as soon as Judy crossed the threshold. By the stacks of dishes and glassware laid out on towels across the counters, it appeared Robin had cleaned this room as well. One quick glance at the windows and glass on the cabinet doors showed they were all streak-free and shining, and the coffee maker she had seen in Robin's apartment was now sitting on the counter. Spying the coffee and filters nearby, Judy pulled a bag from her backpack and turned on the oven.

***

Robin's eyes fluttered open, and she drew in a slow, contented breath when she saw sunlight streaming through the curtains. Out of habit, she reached down to rub the head of whichever cat was the closest, and when she came up empty, Robin checked under the blanket. Finding neither snuggled underneath, she cocked her head to the side, straining to hear even the slightest noise, but again, she came up empty. Why weren't they meowing for their breakfast or chasing each other from room to room as was their morning ritual? Robin bolted upright. "I swear to God, if you two went upstairs and are getting into trouble, I'm going—" Robin's words died off when the smell of coffee found its way to her. "What the hell?"

Robin tossed aside the blankets, immediately regretting her action when the coolness of the room swept over her. She rubbed her hands over her arms, and in socked feet, Robin padded through the house in search of a smell. When she reached the dining room, yet another aroma filled her senses, and noticing the kitchen door was slightly ajar, Robin went over and pushed it open with her finger. A second later, her breath caught in her throat.

The blink of an eye is as quick as a camera shutter, and snapshots of life are burned into memories without even trying. A diamond ring held by someone on bended knee or the first smile appearing on a swaddled baby's face is eternally embedded into gray matter. The gaiety around tables at holidays and even the sadness etched into the expressions of mourners grieving at grave sites are things never forgotten, and as Robin stood there, she took a snapshot that would forever remain in her mind.

The sun poured in from the bank of windows behind Judy and cascading over her shoulders, it made her appear like an angel, haloed in brightness. Her hair sparkled in the light, and the V-neck of her dark green sweater exposed a shadow plunging deliciously between her breasts as she leaned on the counter reading a cookbook. Robin had never seen anything so beautiful.

Feeling as if she was being watched, Judy lifted her eyes and grinned. Robin was standing in the doorway, her face puffy from sleep and her long blonde hair, loose and tousled. Her sweatpants had settled halfway down her hips, and her long-sleeved T-shirt wasn't quite long enough to hide a bit of the toned stomach underneath it. Judy's grin widened as her eyes met Robin's. "Good morning."

Judy's tone was honey sweet and soft, and while Robin was sure she hadn't meant the words to sound so sensual, Robin's first attempt at speech failed in an unintelligible squeak. Clearing her throat, she tried again. "Good morning."

"I hope you don't mind that I let myself in. I thought I'd get a jump on the paperwork."

"You've already started?"

"No," Judy said with a laugh. "I found you had moved your coffee maker in here, so I made a pot, grabbed one of Adele's cookbooks, and I've been reading ever since."

"Find anything good?" Robin said as she walked across the room.

"Yes, your coffee. What's the brand? It's delicious."

"I blend it myself," Robin said as she filled a mug. "It's just a mix of beans, but I like it."

"That makes two of us."

"And speaking of like," Robin said, taking a deep breath. "What in the world is that smell?"

"Oh," Judy said, glancing at the timer on the oven. "I had a couple of bananas on their last legs, so I whipped up a small loaf of banana bread this morning. I figured you might like breakfast."

"You made banana bread?"

"Yeah."

"*Fresh* banana bread?"

"Is there any other kind?"

"Yeah, the kind I buy at the store which, I might add, never lives up to my expectations."

"Well, here's hoping I do."

Robin swallowed hard, not allowing herself to exhale for fear it would come out as a lust-filled sigh. Taking a sip of her coffee, she gathered her composure and changed the subject. "So," she said, looking around. "You didn't happen to see a couple of cats roaming about, did you? They usually sleep with me, but when I woke up, they weren't there."

"Yes, I saw them," Judy said, smiling. "They scurried back to your apartment when I got here. They're adorable."

"Thanks."

"What are their names?"

"Fred and Ginger." When Robin saw Judy's eyebrows rise, she said, "They were a Christmas present from my mother, and she loved old movies. Since Fred looks like he's wearing a tuxedo and Ginger is all white, she had her mind made up on their names before she even gave them to me. I offered to dedicate all my books to her if she'd let me change them to something else, but she wouldn't hear of it."

"I think it's cute," Judy said, flicking off the timer on the oven seconds before it was ready to sound.

Robin had never believed herself to be a perv. Sure, she had scoped out women in bars wearing provocative outfits or at the beach as they strutted past in their string bikinis, but her attention had always been fleeting. A casual glance to admire, a brief gander to acknowledge, or a cursory glimpse of interest that faded almost as quickly as it began, she did without even thinking. It was part of being a woman who appreciated women, and for Robin, it was as natural as breathing. Nevertheless, when Judy bent over to pull the bread out of the oven, and Robin caught herself eyeing the woman's backside, she inwardly scolded her body for its reaction. "I think I should go get dressed," she announced, placing her mug on the counter. "I'll be back in a few."

"Take your time," Judy said, looking over her shoulder. "This has to cool down for a while anyway."

Robin forced a grin before heading back to her suite knowing full well the bread wasn't the *only* thing needing a cooling-off period.

***

By the time Robin returned to the kitchen, her mind *and* her body were under control. After enjoying a breakfast of coffee and warm banana bread slathered in butter, the two women made their way to Adele's office. Their intention had only been to find all the licensing, insurance, and other legal documents they would need to ensure they could reopen the Inn without any issues, but once they began, one by one the file cabinets were emptied. Utility bills were separated by the service they provided. Receipts from vendors were sorted alphabetically. Old employee records were set off to the side, and all the receipts Adele had kept for miscellaneous items were stacked as best they could be in the middle of the desk. By the time Judy and Robin were done, there wasn't a horizontal space in the office that wasn't covered in paperwork of some kind or another, and they both agreed, getting a computer had to move to the top of Robin's list.

Their breakfast long since digested, shortly after twelve, they returned to the parlor carrying bottles of water and paper plates loaded down with sandwiches and potato chips.

"I have a question," Judy said, in between bites. "The other night when I was here, it looked like you had all your stuff in the kitchen in the suite, but now everything's been moved into the larger one. Not that it's any of my business, but I was just wondering why?"

"Because everything in the apartment needs to be painted, plus I want to refinish the kitchen cabinets and get a new countertop. Things will go a lot faster if I don't have to work around stuff, so I moved it all the other night."

"Oh, that makes sense."

"Thanks. I thought so," Robin said before taking a massive bite of her sandwich.

Tickled that Robin looked very much like a squirrel storing nuts in the winter, Judy returned to hers as well until, with her belly full and her plate empty, she sat back and took a swig of her water. "You know, it seems only fair that since you offered me this job, I offer you something in return."

Other than the one ogling incident in the kitchen, for the rest of the morning, Robin had acted like the mature, non-pervy woman she had grown up to be. She hadn't gawked or gaped. She hadn't imagined or daydreamed, and she had kept her mind on the task at hand, but as soon as Judy's innocent words found her ears, Robin felt a flutter between her legs. "Such as?" she managed to say before gulping down some water.

"I'd like to help you."

Inwardly, Robin groaned, and tucking her legs underneath her, she tried to suffocate her libido. "How so?"

"You said last week some rooms need painting or new wallpaper."

"That's right."

"Well, how about when I get back from vacation, I give you a hand with that?"

Robin's shoulders fell just a tad. "You're going on vacation?"

"Yeah. I'm leaving for Indiana on Wednesday."

"Wednesday?" Robin said, sinking heavier into the sofa. "This Wednesday?"

"Yep."

Robin tried her best to seem interested. "What's in Indiana that's so exciting?" she said, with absolutely no inflection in her tone.

"I wouldn't say they're all that exciting, but my family lives there," Judy said, smiling. "Every fall it's a tradition that we all get together and spend a few weeks helping out at the orchard. Actually, it's probably more like a duty, but since a lot of my nieces and nephews travel in, it's nice to see them and catch up."

"Your family owns an orchard?"

"Yes," Judy said with a bob of her head. "Originally, we just grew Gala apples, but as my father bought up more land, he added other varieties of apples, plus raspberries and plums. Then, about ten years ago, my brothers bought the adjoining farm and not only extended the orchard, but also the market."

"The market? You mean like a farmer's market?"

"Exactly. It started out as just a roadside produce stand that my grandparents ran. They sold apples and vegetables from their garden, stuff like that, but over the years, it's grown just like the orchard. It went from a just a simple stand to a few sheds my father built when they kept getting busier, and then my brothers replaced those with a huge metal building, so they'd have the room to sell local produce, too."

"It sounds popular *and* hectic."

"Oh, it is," Judy said. "And between the apple picking, the pumpkin patch, the hay rides, and a corn maze my brothers put in a few years back, this time of year the place is overrun with kids and families, which is why they need all the help they can get."

"Do you ever take a real vacation? I mean one where you aren't working?"

"Yes, it's called winter," Judy said with a laugh. "And it's not really like work. I grew up doing it, so it's second nature, but by November, I'll be ready to come back."

Robin tallied the days until November, and if she could have sunk into the sofa any further, she would have found herself underneath it. Lowering her eyes, she quietly said, "Wow, that's a long vacation."

"True, but like I said, it's a tradition and getting out of it isn't an option."

"I suppose."

"Are you okay?" Judy said, noticing how Robin's expression seemed to have saddened.

"What?" Robin said, returning her focus to Judy. "Oh, yeah. I'm fine. I guess I was kinda looking forward to going through all the rooms with you and seeing if we agreed on what needs to be done, but if you're leaving in a few days, that'll have to wait until you get back."

"No, it doesn't. I don't have to pack until Tuesday, so we have until then," Judy said, and getting to her feet, she held out her hand. "That is unless you can't keep up."

The broadest smile Robin owned spread across her face, and taking Judy's hand, Robin sprang to her feet...at the same time Judy tugged her arm.

Action and reaction are the subjects of Newton's third law of motion. The force of a push or a pull upon any given object can result in an interaction with another object, so when Robin pushed, and Judy pulled, interaction was inevitable.

Robin plowed right into Judy, and like two football players celebrating a touchdown, the two women chest-bumped, the force of which sent Robin scrambling to stay upright.

"Shit," Judy said, and reaching out, she grabbed Robin by the hips to steady her. "I'm sorry. Are you okay?"

It was yet another snapshot Robin would forever have embedded in her mind. They were standing so close she could see the threads of sapphire in Judy's pale cobalt eyes, the edge of the blue beautifully defined by the thinnest rim of black. Her eyelashes needed no enhancement for they were long and thick, and when Robin finally managed to remember how to inhale, she breathed in the bouquet of the woman's perfume. It was crisp like a spring morning, yet had just enough of a hint of cinnamon to add a touch of sultry, and it was that touch of sultry that caused Robin's body to ignite. As if she'd been burned, Robin took a quick step backward. Her body was on fire. Her face was on fire, and Robin had two choices. Either stand there and smolder or get the hell out. Robin chose the latter.

"No, it was totally my fault," she said, straightening her sweatshirt. "But since you have time, I'll meet you upstairs." Like a speeding bullet, Robin raced toward the stairs, taking them two at a time and reaching the top at breakneck speed. She knew she had forgotten her list. She knew she had forgotten her measuring tape, and she knew she had forgotten her pen, but the one thing Robin would never forget was still burning...into her hips.

Chapter Thirteen

The Safe Harbor Inn wasn't the largest bed-and-breakfast on Mackinac Island nor was it the smallest; however, its Victorian architecture and location drew tourists to its door like moths to a flame. Overlooking Julia Point, the tourists aboard the ferries from St. Ignace could see the Inn from the boat once their attention moved from the spectacular Grand Hotel. While appearing minuscule compared to the magnificent landmark to its north, Safe Harbor still garnered its fair share of attention and even those having no reservations would often find their way to its porch, if only for a photo opportunity.

Some would wander inside, hoping for a tour or possibly a vacancy they could fill, but all they ever managed to see were the few guest areas on the ground floor. They would ooh and ahh at what little they saw, vowing to return sometime in the future, and for those who did, they were not disappointed when they climbed the stairs.

In 1982, when Adele bought the home that would become Safe Harbor, it contained only five bedrooms and four baths, but within three years, she had more than doubled her rentable space. The study across from the dining room soon became White Birch, and walls were constructed on the second floor, dividing the most massive bedrooms, until two became four. The third floor, originally designed as a playroom for Lyman Major's six children, and used by other owners for storage, was Adele's most significant undertaking. Massive, and with windows throughout, by the time the workmen had finished in the winter of 1985, Adele had not only added three more suites, but she also ensured the guests in those rooms would be afforded awe-inspiring views of the island, something not always found in other B&Bs.

Adele knew her competition. She had visited all the bed-and-breakfasts on the island, as well as others on the mainland. She had studied what they offered their patrons, so when Adele began her renovations of Safe Harbor, she included in her plan private bathrooms in each. The four existing bathrooms were spacious, and each held all the conveniences, including claw-foot tubs, but with the only remaining space Adele had to work revolving around closets of varying sizes, the bathrooms she added required a little ingenuity. Tubs unable to fit into converted closets were placed into alcoves in the suites themselves, while angled showers were installed in others. Although modern in design, with the help of china pedestal sinks, high-tank toilets, and tile work reminiscent of vintage bathrooms, Adele accomplished what she had set out to do, and the historic flavor of the old Victorian cottage was never lost. It could be seen in the paint and the wallpaper, in the antique sconces on the walls, in the window treatments and the woodwork, and even in the pattern of the carpet running down the hallways upstairs. A carpet, which, as Judy climbed the steps, appeared to have Robin's full attention.

"You forgot something," Judy said as she reached the second-floor landing. "I saw this stuff on the reception desk and figured we were going to need it."

Robin had only been upstairs for a minute, but it was enough time to get back on track. Even though she jumped when Judy appeared and interrupted her thoughts, at least they had returned to being *chaste* thoughts. A definite plus.

"Thanks," Robin said, and slipping the notepad under her arm, she clipped the measuring tape to her belt, but as she began to slip the pen in her pocket, her eyebrows drew together. "Where did you find this?" she asked, holding up the ballpoint.

"Oh, I didn't see one on the desk, so I grabbed it out of my backpack. Why?"

"Because I've lost at least a dozen since I moved in, and I thought you may have found my cats' stash. I have no idea why they've developed a fixation on pens and pencils, but if I don't find some soon, I'm going to be writing in eyeliner."

Judy pressed her lips together to smother her smile, but there was no stopping the twinkle in her eyes from appearing. "Well, if I had to guess, I'd say it wasn't the cats."

"Oh yeah? Why's that?"

"Because it was probably Isobel."

Robin leaned her head to the side. "Who's Isobel?"

"The ghost," Judy said nonchalantly, and completely ignoring the fact Robin's mouth had just dropped open, Judy walked toward Sunset Shores. "How about we start in here?"

Robin wanted to laugh. She *really* wanted to laugh, but her mirth was being strangled by a noose in the form of a memory.

On her first night in the house, gripping a lamp for protection, Robin had crept upstairs in search of a noise. It was a noise that had traveled down this hallway, the oaken planks creaking as if they were being walked on, and it was a noise Robin had never identified. She had methodically checked every room, and she had also closed every door along the way.

Robin's heart began to race as she looked down the hallway, her eyes shifting from one open door to the next. The hairs on the back of her neck sprang to attention, and she slowly calmed them with a swipe of her hand.

The drizzle of the morning had long since gone, and sunlight was flooding the hall from the windows at each end. Everything that would have been lost in shadows was illuminated, and Robin had never been so happy to see dust bunnies in her life. Gathered like tumbleweeds in the corners and under accent tables, they lay motionless, and Robin breathed a little easier. Nothing was lurking in the hallway except for her.

Judy was standing near the window, and she grinned when the scent of Robin's cologne alerted her that she had finally made it into Sunset Shores. "I don't know about you," she said without turning around. "But I think the only thing this room needs is some fresh paint on the trim and maybe a little updating in the bathroom."

"Tell me you're kidding."

Judy's heart sank. She adored the color scheme in Sunset Shores, and with a heavy sigh, she turned around. "You don't like this room?"

"I'm not talking about the room," Robin said, taking another step inside. "I'm talking about what you said in the hallway?"

"Huh?"

"The ghost?"

"Oh, you mean Isobel," Judy said with a wave of her hand. "Don't worry about her. She's harmless."

Robin opened her mouth to speak, and then closed it, and then opened it again. "I'm...I'm not sure what's more ridiculous here. You saying there's a ghost in this house or the fact it doesn't seem to bother you."

"It doesn't really bother anybody. You kind of get used to it."

"Wait," Robin said, holding up her hands. "Are you saying that everyone on the island knows there's a ghost living in my house?"

"No, of course not."

"Thank goodness."

"I'm saying that everyone on the island knows there are ghosts all *over* Mackinac."

"What!"

It was clear by the disappearance of Robin's eyebrows into her hairline, she wasn't too keen on the idea of ghosts, and Judy tried not to laugh. "Why is this news to you?" Judy said, sitting down on the bed. "I know you haven't been here since you were a kid, but didn't you at least research Mackinac before moving here?"

"I did, but there weren't any mention of ghosts on the island's website."

Judy's smile rose to the surface. "That's the *only* site you went to?"

"I was in the middle of packing and rearranging my flipping life," Robin said, waving her hands in the air. "I didn't delve into the deep, dark secrets of the island. I just found out what I needed to know to move here."

"Well, it's hardly a deep, dark secret, Robin. Mackinac is known all over the world as having one of the largest ghost populations around. Some even say there are more ghosts here than there are residents."

"Okay, now you're shitting me."

"I am not!" Judy said, amused that Robin's complexion was getting whiter by the second. "There are dozens of books written about the hauntings on Mackinac. Paranormal groups come up here all the time to do research, and even one of those ghost hunting shows on television was here to film an episode not too long ago. I'm serious, Robin. When it comes to ghosts, Mackinac has most everybody beat."

"I think I need to sit down," Robin said, and going over to the bed, she sat next to Judy.

"Are you okay?" Judy said, her smile fading as she placed her hand on Robin's leg. "You look a little pale."

"I just need a minute," Robin said softly.

"Are you afraid of ghosts?"

Robin had heard the question, and she did indeed need a minute to get her head around the concept of living on a ghost-infested island, but once she felt the warmth of Judy's hand on her leg, Robin decided to take as much time as she needed.

Between the black of belief and the white of doubt is an area called gray. A zone that exists in all, it holds the teeter-totter of possibilities that fluctuate as information is provided. For some, the black of belief is unwavering. Whether it is in God or in country they go forth in faith, yet for those doubtful or ambiguous, until the belief is etched in stone in front of their eyes, until they are given proof, they live comfortably in a fog of gray...and Robin was no longer comfortable.

There was no reason to doubt what Judy was saying. It if had been a stranger, some practical joker just trying to get a rise out of her, Robin would have easily laughed it off, but this wasn't a stranger. This was a woman who had lived on Mackinac for twenty-five years. A woman who had no reason to lie. A woman who had rattled off facts easily checked if Robin so desired, and a woman whose hand now felt like a brand on Robin's thigh.

"Robin, I'm sorry. I didn't mean to scare you. I didn't know you were afraid of ghosts."

"I-I'm not. Not really," Robin said, raising her eyes to meet Judy's. "It's just...um...well, a minute ago, I didn't believe in ghosts, and now I find out I'm living with one. It kind of takes the wind out of your sails, you know?"

"Yeah. Been there, done that," Judy said, sniggering under her breath. "When I first moved here, I think it was three months before I took a bath with the lights on."

The modicum of color that had returned to Robin's face faded in an instant, and closing her eyes, she fell back onto the bed. "Oh crap. I didn't even *think* about that. I'm never going to be able to take a bath again."

Judy got to her feet, waving her hand through the air to disperse the billion particles of dust Robin had dislodged from the blanket. "Sure you will. You'll just do it in the dark for a while until you get used to the idea of being spied on by the spirits of the dead."

Robin opened one eye. "You're not helping. I hope you know that."

"I'm sorry. I'll behave," Judy said, giggling as she held out her hand. "No more talk about ghosts."

"No," Robin said, and taking Judy's hand, she allowed herself to be pulled back into a sitting position. "I can't believe I'm saying this, but I want to talk about ghosts. I want to know what's going on."

"What do you mean?"

"Well..." Robin stopped for a moment. "For starters, what makes Mackinac a magnet for poltergeists? Why not St. Ignace or Lansing or Chicago, for Christ's sake? Why here?"

Merriment danced in Judy's eyes. "You mean besides the fact that almost the entire island was once an Indian burial ground?"

Robin's jaw went slack. "I swear to God, if the next thing out of your mouth is that coffins have popped out of the ground on this flipping island, I'm seriously out of here."

Judy threw back her head and laughed. "I can honestly say *that's* never happened on Mackinac, but the residents still get a kick out of that movie."

"Hits a little close to home, does it?"

"Maybe just a little," Judy said with a shrug. "And to tell you the truth, it's really not the whole island that was a burial ground, but between the areas that were and all the people who died here during the wars and plagues and stuff, there are a lot of bodies buried on Mackinac. Actually, it's rumored when the Grand Hotel was being built, they discovered so many bones they just decided to build the hotel on top of them instead of moving them all."

Robin wrinkled her nose. "Oh, that's gross."

"Yeah, but it's just a rumor. It's never been proven as far as I know."

"Except for all the disembodied spirits, you mean."

"Yeah, well there is that," Judy said, grinning as she gave the room one last glance. "So, what do you think? Are we done in here?"

"Yep," Robin said as she stood up. "Let's head to the next."

"Well, if it's as easy as this one, it's going to be a piece of cake."

"That's what you think," Robin said, and with a snicker belonging to the devil, she left the room and headed down the hall. Once Judy caught up, Robin pushed open the door leading to Central Lake. "Then again, maybe you're a girly-girl."

It had been a few years since Judy had worked at Safe Harbor, but as soon as she saw the nameplate next to the door, she groaned. She had a few secrets in her closet, but being a girly-girl had never been one of them.

Even though Judy's go-to had always been slacks and polos, back in the day she had worn her fair share of sundresses. Flowered and flowing in the breeze, they were designed to catch a suitor's eye and had done that more than once. However, when she moved to Mackinac, Scott no longer seemed to care what she wore, so the dresses hung in her closet until they became outdated. Although none had been purchased simply because they contained the hue deemed feminine, Judy had always liked the pale pinks and roses printed on the chiffons and linens. They were subdued and gentle to the eye, but there wasn't anything subdued about Central Lake.

It was all Judy could do not to recoil from the electrifying combination of fuchsia and magenta splattered all over the room, but as she turned to . Robin to express her horror, Judy remembered what Robin had said. "What?" she said, placing her hands on her hips. "You don't think I'm a girly-girl?"

Instincts are natural. Innate behaviors brought on by sight, sound, taste, and smell, they cause newly-hatched turtles to race toward the water, babies to search out their mother's teat...and eyes to travel when a question is asked.

There was nothing Robin could do to stop herself from drinking in Judy's body. As if searching for a gem, her eyes moved slowly up her form, absorbing as they went, and it wasn't until Robin found herself gazing into Judy's eyes when she realized what she had just done. She had blatantly and unequivocally ogled Judy like a lust-filled lesbian and the only thing Robin *hadn't* done while doing it was to lick her lips. Thank *God*!

The thought of hurling herself out of one of the windows crossed Robin's mind for a split-second, but that seemed a bit melodramatic for her breach of etiquette, so she did the next best thing. She pushed aside her guilt, stood tall...and answered Judy's question.

"Honestly, you don't really strike me as a girly-girl, but I'm not saying that's a bad thing. I like you just the way you are. I always have. I only hope you're not a fan of hot pink."

Judy was fully expecting Robin to bumble. Since the night they first met, it was clear that the woman who said she once sat in Judy's homeroom was struggling with their new relationship, and Judy found Robin's reactions adorable. She had purposely said things over the past two weeks she knew were laced with innuendo just to see the woman stammer, and Judy had done the same with her playful question, but Robin's response took her by surprise. Her tone was clear and her words, unfaltering. Gone was the student and in her place was the woman, and that woman's words kept echoing in Judy's head. '*I always have.*'

It was Judy's turn to feel like a teenager. Robin's honesty, while appreciated, had taken all the fun out of the game and put Judy in a place she hadn't been in a very long time. She had no idea what to do. She had no idea what to say, and how in the hell was she supposed to respond to something like '*I always have*?' It took a few moments for Judy to find her answer, and it was the simplest of them all. Just move on...and do it quickly.

"I'm not a fan of hot pink *or* this wallpaper," Judy said, matter-of-factly. "I say that we change everything except the furniture. You?"

Robin beamed. "*Complete* agreement."

"Good. What's next then?" Judy said, and without waiting for an answer, she walked from the room and went down the hall.

Once Robin caught up to her at the next door in line, Judy pushed it open and instantly smiled. "Please don't tell me you want to change this one."

Similar to what she had done in the dining room, Adele had strayed from traditional Victorian design when decorating Whitefish Falls. With only one window on the back wall bringing in natural light, Adele had chosen to use the colors of sand and surf instead of the darker tones reminiscent of a queen named Victoria.

Atop a background of soft aqua, the silvery-gray metallic design on the textured damask wallpaper amplified the limited sunlight, and all the furniture was painted seafoam green. Accents of white had been used throughout, giving the room a light and airy feel, and the pewter tone of the iron bed mellowed the weightiness of the classically-curved head and footboard. The area rug seemed an afterthought, its gray pile bland compared to the duck egg hues used in the room, but other than that, Robin hadn't found anything wrong with Whitefish Falls.

"I'd love to find another carpet, but everything else is perfect," Robin said, and reaching in front of Judy, Robin closed the door and motioned toward the room across the hallway. "However, I think *that* one needs lots of help."

Judy stared at the door leading to Bayview, trying to remember what existed behind it. Coming up blank, she went over and looked inside. "Oh," she said, her shoulders sagging. "I remember this one. Yuck."

Robin followed Judy into one of the more spacious suites in Safe Harbor. Large enough to hold two beds, like Central Lake, the far wall in

Bayview was pushed out in the shape of a bay window, but instead of a seating area, the queen bed backed up into the space. Just inside the door, a twin bed ran along one wall and adjacent to another was a large bureau. The remaining wall housed two doors, one leading to a tiny closet and the other to the bathroom, and while the burled walnut frames of both beds were marvelous, the colors in the room were not. The scalloped valances and drapes surrounding the windows were garnet in color, held open by thick golden ropes with tassels tangling at the ends, and the walls were in the shade of Picholine olives.

"I wonder why she chose to paint in here rather than wallpaper," Judy said, still wearing the grimace she walked in with.

"I don't know, but it's gotta change. I don't even like martinis."

Judy snorted as she made the connection. "Truth be known, neither do I."

Robin returned Judy's smile with one of her own. "Seems like we're agreeing more than we're disagreeing."

"Did you think we wouldn't?"

"Um...no, actually. I didn't. I guess I still have a little self-doubt hanging on. My track record when it comes to dealing with women hasn't been too good recently."

"In what way?"

Robin had long ago become content with who she was and what she was, and it was rare that it gave her pause speaking the words, but they caught in her throat for a second. "Oh...um...well, it's no secret. I mean, I don't hide it, but...but I guess you should know that I'm gay." The few seconds it took for Judy to respond, were the longest in Robin's life.

That little tidbit came as no surprise to Judy for the leaves of Mackinac's grapevine were plentiful. Years before, a proud aunt had told all who would listen how pleased she was her niece was so strong. It had made the rounds and then was forgotten, replaced by other rumors far juicier, but fertilized by the news of Robin's arrival, the stories had spread again. Judy had heard them, but it wasn't until she learned of Robin's pen name, when hearsay became fact.

Intrigued as to the type of books Robin wrote, Judy had run her Internet search, discovering that Robin was, in fact, quite an accomplished author, but along the way, one click on a link led to another and then to another, and before Judy knew it, she was reading R. C. Novak's biography. It was the standard, condensed version which appeared on any site selling books, and even though some differed slightly from the others, in all of them, Robin made no secret about her sexuality.

Judy shifted in her stance as she thought about how to respond. "You're right," she said, quietly. "It's not a secret."

"You knew?"

"Yep."

"And it's okay?"

Judy cocked her head to the side. "Can you change it?"

"What? No, of course, I can't change it."

"Well then, I guess it's okay."

With that, Judy moseyed down the hall, and Robin admired the sway of the woman's hips every step of the way.

Chapter Fourteen

Horn's Gaslight Bar and Restaurant is a Mackinac staple, and it has been for almost a hundred years. During prohibition, it was just a snack shop for weary tourists, but once liquor was legal again, it became well known as one of the island's night spots. Tourists and locals alike gravitated toward the eclectic eatery, enjoying the southwestern and American fare, all the while listening to music provided by bands small enough to fit on Horn's tiny stage.

For those who wanted to dance, to trip the light fantastic with their spouses, dates, or partners, Horn's offered what many on the island did not. However, with the majority of the floor space taken up by tables, chairs, and booths, and a bar that ran down an entire wall, the only spot left for a dance floor was directly in front of the small stage just to the left of the front door. Patrons were often surprised to find gyrating bodies in front of them as they entered, but like Robin had done, they would weave through the swaying couples, sometimes dancing their way into the restaurant. When Robin came inside, she could have easily tripped the light fantastic on her way to the table. Her spirits were high and her mood bright, but as the waitress placed a glass of wine next to Robin's iced tea, Robin's attitude had changed. Glancing at her watch, she picked up the Chardonnay.

For Robin, the day had been surreal. From waking up and finding Judy in her kitchen to touring the house discussing decor and design, she had gone through the day so easily, so comfortably...so naturally.

By late morning, Robin's stutters and stammers had all but stopped. Quieted by the confidence in a friendship that seemed to be blossoming, the butterflies of her teenage infatuation stilled their wings, giving way to casual conversation, the occasional grimace at colors less than pleasing, and laughter that rang through the house. They had prattled on about colors, fabrics, and patterns until they had run out of words, and they had chuckled when they returned to rooms already visited to write down measurements they had forgotten to take. At times, they said nothing, each scrutinizing a room from every angle, but when one finally spoke, uttering their approval or just the opposite, for the next hour, they'd sit on dusty bedcovers excited about the changes they were planning to make.

As the sun began to set, the two women walked down the stairs hip-to-hip, and although Robin was sorry to see the day come to an end, she knew there would be others. Some would be filled with conversations about the ins and outs of running a bed-and-breakfast, and some would be spent papering and painting and cleaning. And once the renovations were complete, once the rooms were pristine and tidy and ready for guests, there would still be *more* days. Robin's future now included Judy Dunnigan and that fact, that *reality*, was all she needed. So, watching as Judy had gathered her things, Robin didn't suggest a dinner of sausage and eggs or even a drink of coffee or wine, but as Judy walked to her bike with her backpack slung over her shoulder, she turned and did the unexpected. *She* invited Robin on a date.

Okay, so it wasn't an *actual* date, but that didn't stop Robin from sprinting to her bathroom as soon as Judy pedaled out of view. Robin washed and dried and primped and preened and did all the things she would have done if it *had* been a real date. She even showed up early at the designated restaurant to secure a table, but as Robin looked at her watch, she let out a long sigh. Had she got the place wrong or even the time or the day? Had she somehow misunderstood Judy's invitation? Was it definitive or had her teenage jitters returned without her knowing, jumbling the words Judy had spoken and turning them into something Robin *wanted* to hear?

Robin took a healthy gulp of her wine and setting the glass hard against the table, she mentally scolded herself. It was now twenty after six and twenty minutes of feeling like a fool was *all* Robin could take.

Launching herself out of the booth, she turned the corner to leave and ran straight into Judy. Robin's hands found their way to the woman's waist and as her eyes locked with Judy's, time stood still.

Robin knew she should let go. She knew this accidental touch was just that, but Judy didn't seem to want to break away from the connection. She was merely smiling up at Robin just as Robin was smiling down at her.

"I'm sorry I'm late," Judy said in a whisper. "I tried to call, but you didn't answer."

It took a few seconds for Judy's words to sink in, and forcing herself to release her hold on Judy, Robin patted the pockets of her jeans. "Oh...um...I must have left my phone at home. I'm sorry."

"That's all right," Judy said, motioning to the booth. "Shall we?"

Robin quickly slipped back into the booth, and a moment later they were sitting opposite one another, both still wearing their smiles.

"Were you going to leave?" Judy said, noticing the empty wine glass.

"I...um..." Robin hung her head, taking a deep breath before she raised her eyes again. "Yeah, I thought maybe I got the wrong place or...or time."

"I am *really* sorry. Eric called just as I was about to leave."

Robin straightened her backbone. "Eric?"

"Yeah, he's my youngest brother," Judy said, glancing down at the menu. "He wanted to make sure I didn't forget to get him some fudge."

"Oh," Robin said, her posture relaxing as she opened her menu. "You said youngest. You have more than one?"

"Yeah, I have three," Judy said, looking back at Robin. "Patrick is the oldest, then Douglas, and then Eric, who we affectionately call an accident."

"An accident?" Robin said with a laugh. "Why's that."

"Because Patrick is fifty-nine. Doug is fifty-seven. I'm fifty-five, and Eric is *forty*-five."

"Wow, that is a difference."

"Yeah, I know," Judy said. "Mom and Dad used to hate when we called him an accident, but he really was, not that he wasn't loved or anything. He was just a big surprise, and we still rub it in whenever we can."

"I see," Robin said, closing the menu. "And your parents? I take it they're not alive?"

"No. Mom died from a heart attack ten years ago, and my dad passed away the year I graduated high school. He was a heavy smoker, and it finally caught up to him."

"That's too bad. I'm sorry."

"It's life, but I still have my memories of them," Judy said with a shrug. "And how about you? Any brothers or sisters?"

"No. My dad died when I was really young and my mother never remarried. Luckily, I grew up in a small town so if I wanted to go out and play, there were always kids around."

"One of the plusses of coming from a small town," Judy said, scanning the menu again. "So, what looks good to you?"

Robin gazed at Judy, but before she could speak the waitress returned.

"Judy, I didn't see you dance your way in. You're looking good," the strawberry-blonde woman said, placing a coaster in front of Judy.

"Thanks, Nancy," Judy said as she glanced around the crowded room. "And I almost *had* to dance my way in. What's with all the people? Don't they know the last ferry already left?"

"Yeah, they know," Nancy said, rolling her eyes. "It's a big birthday bash for a mainlander. They all checked in at Mission Point this afternoon and showed up here a few hours ago, so it's going to be a long, noisy night."

"Sounds like you can't wait for this month to end."

"You got that right," Nancy said, motioning toward the menus on the table. "You two decided on what you'd like?"

"Honestly, I think we need a few minutes," Judy said. "We've been talking more than reading."

"That's fine," Nancy said as she pointed at Robin's empty glass. "You want another Chardonnay, sweetie?"

"Yes, please," Robin said, sliding the glass in Nancy's direction.

"How 'bout you, Judy?" Nancy said, placing Robin's glass on her tray.

"Make it two, Nancy. Thanks."

Nancy turned around, zigzagging her way around tables and patrons as she made her way back to the bar.

"What happens at the end of this month?" Robin said, raising her voice to get over the ever-intensifying volume of the party-goers.

"This place closes for the year. Actually, other than the Village Inn and the Mustang, all the other bars and restaurants close, too."

"Really? All of them?"

"Yep, come winter this place becomes a ghost town," Judy said, and when she saw Robin immediately squint back at her, Judy's dimples appeared. "No pun intended."

"Like I believe that," Robin muttered as she began rereading the menu.

Both sat quietly for a few minutes, their heads bowed as they scanned the entrees on the list until Judy broke the silence. "Hey," she said, lifting her head. "Do you have any plans tomorrow?"

Robin looked up, more than willing to cancel a quadruple-bypass if she had had one scheduled. "No. Why?"

"I was...um...I was wondering if you'd like to go on a tour of the island?" Judy said, quickly looking back down at the menu.

"You mean like one of those carriage tours?"

Judy nibbled on her lower lip as she focused on the menu she knew by heart. Over the years, she had suggested to hundreds of visitors that to truly discover Mackinac, the best place to start was in a carriage drawn by horses. She had done it herself the first time she had come to the island...much to the chagrin of her suitor.

Scott had wanted to take her on a private tour, and he had made his intentions more than known. With a leer and his best smile, he offered to guide her around the island on a bicycle built for two. He wanted to be alone with her to coo and cuddle when they stopped to admire the scenery, but Judy wouldn't budge. Insisting they would have plenty of time to be alone to do what she knew Scott had on his mind, she pouted, and Scott caved in like a sinkhole. So, they climbed aboard a horse-driven carriage with a dozen other tourists on a sunny Saturday morning. Scott draped his arm around her shoulders and pulled her close, claiming ownership to all those aboard while Judy, oblivious to his show of machismo, lost herself in the stories and history of Mackinac told by the coachman.

It had been a good day, and it was a good memory, but as Judy thought back upon it, upon the camaraderie of strangers in a crowded carriage with a fringed top, her expression grew pensive. Did she really want to spend tomorrow surrounded by tourists clambering to cram everything they could into one day? Did she really want to jockey for position while others scrambled in and out of the carriage, anxious for photo opportunities? Did Judy really want the serenity of their day to be interrupted again and again as tourists peppered the coachman with endless questions? Was that *really* the way Judy wanted to spend the day?

Judy looked up, apologizing by way of a sheepish grin for her delay in answering. "Actually, if it's all the same to you, I thought maybe we'd just go it alone."

**

They had spent the day alone, touring the house, and that was fine. They had spent dinner basically alone at a table for two, and that was fine, but as Robin stroked Ginger's fur, she stared up at the ceiling. Why would the thought of being alone with Judy tomorrow make her suddenly feel so on edge?

Her body answered the question with a throb so intense it forced Robin to squeeze her legs together. "Oh, Jesus Christ," she muttered. "Really?"

Since Judy had come back into her life, Robin had felt a few twinges of awareness. A little pulse, a minor flutter, the tiniest shiver of awakening in her feminine core, but this was the first time Robin wanted to do something about it.

Her relationship with Pam more off than on for months before Robin finally ended it, nearly a year had passed since sex had played any part in Robin's life. A year of celibacy and a year of feeling nothing except emptiness, her peace, her confidence, her everything all but swept away by vile words and so many lies, Robin had lost count. She had forgotten what it was like to want. She had forgotten what it was like to need, to hunger, and to feel, but in one throb, it had all come back...and it felt good.

It felt good to feel her inner self pulse. It felt good to feel the nectar seep from her body, and it felt good knowing the hollowness was ending. Closing her eyes, Robin swallowed hard and opened her mind.

The most improbable or impossible are what fantasies are all about. Erotic scenarios involving strangers or celebrities, friends or enemies, current lovers or those in the past, they fill thoughts and drive imaginations to the extreme. Some are puritanical and tempered by guilt or shame, they barely reach the rating of PG, while others are risqué. Featuring sexual smorgasbords of positions or people, they can heat blood until it boils.

Robin was trying her best *not* to do the latter, *not* to imagine Judy naked under her, her body heated and soaked with sweat, the scent of her sex heady in the air, but Robin was quickly losing the battle. Her once hormone-infused teenage fantasies had sprung to life, and they had matured just as she had. Far from PG, they were no longer based on a young girl's innocence, but rather on a woman's knowledge. A woman who knew what a female body felt like. A woman who knew the heat it contained, the wetness it could exude, the feel of breasts, round and full, and the taste of something salty...yet oh so sweet.

A groan slipped from Robin's lips as she felt a rush of desire course through her body. There was no turning back from what she had just created, and slipping her hands under the blanket, she loosened the tie on her sweatpants. Pushing them from her hips, the smell of her arousal rose in the air, but as she opened her legs, craving her own touch, the floorboards on the second floor creaked.

Up until a few years earlier, Robin had had her fair share of girlfriends and her fair share of sex. She had danced on the line of impropriety a few times, consummating a one-night stand in the back of a car and another in the bathroom of a club. She had experienced drunken sex, standing sex, bathing sex, and wham-bam-thank-you-ma'am sex, but there was one line she had never wanted to cross. For Robin, masturbation was a private affair, so she had never pleasured herself in front of anyone...nor did she ever intend to.

Robin slowly opened her eyes, and staring at the ceiling, she tried to reconcile her dilemma. Her core pulsed with something she hadn't felt in so long, and if memory served, when it was released, it would feel positively glorious, but Robin had a ghost in her house. A ghost named Isobel who liked to steal pens and pencils and roam about making floors squeak and hinges squawk wherever she went. Supposedly, Isobel was innocent, just a spirit who had yet to move on, but what if Judy was wrong? What if Isobel wasn't Isobel, but rather *Ichabod*?

Robin bolted upright and buried her face in her hands. How many baths had she taken since arriving? How many times had she stood nude in the bathroom, primping and preening in all her naked glory? How many times had nature called?

"Oh my God," Robin muttered, and refusing to open her eyes, her mind took her down a different path.

Would there be an apparition floating above the floor when she dared to look? A weathered, bearded face with leering eyes and drool on his lips, or would his eyes be smiling for he was now aware of her form, her curves, and her habits? Would he make a sound? A throaty, ghoulish guffaw that would cause shivers to run down her spine or would he remain silent, sneering and repugnant?

Over a minute passed before Robin found the courage to split her fingers and look around the room. Fred was snuggled in what was becoming his favorite chair and Ginger was now nestled at her hip, but there wasn't anything menacing. Robin hung her head, huffing out a laugh under her breath as her posture relaxed. She felt like a fool, and her creative imagination had just eliminated the need to take care of something that had already disappeared, washed away by an Ice Bucket Challenge in the form of a ghost.

"Great," she said as she fell back onto the sofa. "Not only *don't* I want to do it, I'll probably *never* want to do it again."

Robin scrubbed her hand over her face, and glancing at the lamps on the tables, she debated whether to get up and turn them off. It had been years since she had felt the need to sleep with lights on, but then again, she had never lived with a ghost. Robin sighed again. *This* was going to take some getting used to

***

"Good morning."

Robin's expression instantly outshined the sun, and looking over her shoulder, she saw Judy standing in the doorway. "Good morning."

Judy came into the kitchen, her smile wavering when she noticed the dark circles under Robin's eyes. "Pardon me for saying this, but you look tired."

"A little," Robin said with a shrug. "Just give me a few minutes for another cup, and we can be on our way."

"Take all the time you need because our plans have changed."

"What? Why?"

"Have you looked outside?"

Robin had been wincing since she had come into the kitchen, so she didn't need to look out the windows to know the sun was shining. "It's not raining."

"No, it's not, but twenty to thirty mile an hour wind isn't exactly good biking weather."

"What!" Robin whirled around and went to the window, her shoulders falling when she saw all the trees in view slanting heavily to the west. "Well, shit."

Judy chuckled as she opened a cabinet to grab a mug. "I said the same thing when I was almost blown off the road while I was coming down here."

"Oh, geez, I'm sorry. You should have called to cancel."

"I could have," Judy said as she poured herself a cup of coffee. "But then I thought that maybe...maybe you'd like to go to the mainland. Look for paint and wallpaper? I know there're some stores in Petoskey, but it's an hour away, so if you — "

"No, I think that's a great idea!" Robin said a little louder than she intended. "Let me just go put on some shoes and grab my jacket, and we can be on our way. Oh, and I guess I should grab the list, too? Do you think we'll need the measuring tape? No, probably not, but then again, I'll grab it just in case. Better safe than sorry. Don't ya think?"

Judy pressed her lips together as she watched Robin trot toward the innkeeper's suite. "Um...Robin?"

Robin turned around. "Yeah?"

"Exactly how much coffee have you had this morning?"

Robin's cheeks flamed instantly. She opened her mouth to speak, to utter some made-up explanation for her juvenile prattling, but when her lips parted, the only sound slipping through them was a high-pitched giggle. With crimson now flooding her face, Robin managed a weak grin before disappearing into her suite.

"You are *such* an ass," Robin said under her breath as she strode into her bedroom and flopped down on the window seat. "You spent all day yesterday acting like an adult, and suddenly you're a child again. Really?"

Scanning the shoes she unpacked, her choice was a no-brainer and grabbing the pair of suede ankle boots in the color of camel from the pile, she tugged them on her feet. "I mean seriously," she mumbled. "Last night, you were all about..."

Robin didn't think her face could get any redder, but as she remembered what she had *almost* done the night before, hot blood stung at her cheeks. "Oh crap," she muttered, hanging her head. "And you thought being alone with her on a bike ride was going to be bad."

Chapter Fifteen

"This is nice," Judy said, breathing in the new car smell as she ran her hand over the dash. "Have you had it long?"

"Nope," Robin said as she checked the side view mirrors. "Got it just before I left Florida. Probably a little overkill since I can't drive it on the island, but I needed a change."

"Oh, yeah? What did you drive before?"

"A Z4."

"Wow, that's quite a change."

"It was no longer who I was, so it was an easy decision," Robin said, glancing at the GPS.

"What do you mean?"

"Huh?"

"You said it was no longer who you were. I was just wondering what that meant?"

Like the tide, Robin's persona ebbed and flowed when she was around Judy. An hour earlier, she had walked from her bedroom barely able to look at the woman for fear of blushing again, but since then, Robin had slipped back into adulthood. She didn't quite know when or why or how, but by the time they had climbed into her metallic black 4Runner, Judy was just a friend she was going shopping with, so answering the question came easily. "Girls like convertible sports cars," Robin said, flashing her passenger a quick smile.

Judy cocked her head to the side, her eyebrows squishing together as she pondered Robin's answer. A few seconds later, Judy flinched. "Oh," she said, quickly staring out the windshield. "You mean...you mean—"

"It wasn't like I trolled for them or anything, but a sleek, shiny, cherry red Z4 had a tendency to make a few heads turn," Robin said with a laugh. "Sorry, did I shock you?"

"What?" Judy said, glancing in Robin's direction. "No. No...I just forgot...I forgot..." Judy sighed and tried again. "What I meant to say is that I wouldn't think...I wouldn't think you'd need a sports car to do that."

Maturity brings with it many things. Knowledge from lessons learned over the years, confidence brought on by experiences, good and bad, and caution when traveling down paths unknown, but some paths are far too intriguing not to follow blindly. Robin arched an eyebrow as she stole a glance of Judy. "And why would you think that?"

Judy's expression went blank for a second, and then forcing a smile, she ran her hands down the denim covering her legs as she looked through the windshield again. "It's just that you're...well, come on. You're an attractive woman. I wouldn't think you'd ever have a problem getting dates. That's all."

A sizzle of awareness slinked its way through Robin's body, and shifting in her seat, she gripped the wheel tightly as she focused on the road. After a few moments, she cleared her throat. "Glad you think so," Robin said without daring to look in Judy's direction. "But finding dates and finding the *right* ones are two different things."

"And the right ones like sports cars?"

Robin's face split into a grin. "No, but it increased my chances."

Judy returned Robin's grin with one of her own. "So, why get rid of it then?" Judy waited for Robin to answer, and as she did, Judy's expression drooped. "Oh," she said, quietly. "Or *is* there a right one? I mean someone...a special someone back in Florida, who just hasn't moved here yet?"

"No," Robin said, the tone of her voice lowering much like Judy's. "There's no one special, and there won't be."

"Why?"

Robin glimpsed at the GPS and pointed toward the upcoming road signs. "I turn up here—right?"

Judy looked through the window. "Yeah. Make a left on Pleasantview Road."

"Okay, thanks," Robin said, flicking on the turn signal as she lifted her foot off the gas pedal.

Judy had never been a meddlesome person. Preferring to turn a deaf ear to the random bits of hearsay on Mackinac, she had always refused to delve deeper into the tidbits bantered about regarding skeletons in the closet or who was doing who and who wasn't. The personal goings-on of others was none of her business, and even with her closest friends, Judy rarely pried past what people were willing to share freely. It was just not in her nature to attempt to extract information, but as she looked over at Robin, Judy found herself facing a conundrum.

Robin's body language screamed anger. Her jaw was now clenched, and the tendons in her neck were corded and taut, and by the white appearing on her knuckles, Robin was gripping the steering wheel as if she was driving on ice.

Judy's brow furrowed, finding it impossible to do something she'd always done. With Robin, she couldn't look the other way.

"I'm sorry if I hit a sore spot," Judy said quietly, watching intently for Robin's reaction. "I didn't mean to upset you."

Broken from her thoughts, Robin gave Judy a fleeting look. "What?"

"I said I was sorry if I upset you about why you weren't looking for a special someone."

"You didn't upset me."

Judy tipped her head to the side. "No? Well, you changed the subject pretty quickly."

"Did I?" Robin said with a shrug. "Sorry, I was just paying attention to the road. Didn't want to miss the turn."

"I see." Judy tapped her finger against her knee as she studied Robin. "Well, just to let you know, I don't believe you," Judy said, and changing position, she stared out the window. "But it's none of my business, so I'm just going to apologize for intruding and leave it at that."

Declan could do it with a sarcastic retort and a few well-placed expletives. Her mother had done it with comforting hugs and smiling eyes, but never in Robin's life had her mood been altered so quickly just by the tone of someone's voice. Judy's had turned soft, her hushed timbre holding within its resonance the chords of penitent and somber, and Robin sagged in her seat. She took a long, deep breath, and then she took another before finally finding her voice. "Have you ever been disappointed in someone? Believing they were one thing and then finding out they were something totally different?"

An image of her ex-husband instantly came to mind as Judy turned toward Robin. "Yes. Why?"

"Because most of my disappointments have revolved around women, so even if Mackinac has a hidden lesbian population, I don't want any part of it. It's just not worth the trouble."

"That's awfully gloomy coming from someone so young."

"Are you looking?"

"Huh?"

"For a man. Someone to hold your hand or...or share your bed."

"No, but then again, I'm not your age."

"What's that got to do with it?" Robin said, looking in Judy's direction for a second. "You're not exactly a dried-up prune, and I know Mackinac is small, but there has to be a hell of a lot more single men living on it than there are lesbians. Why aren't you out there looking for a partner or a husband?"

"Been there, done that. Have absolutely no interest in doing it again."

"Why not?"

"Because I'm not interested in sharing my life with anyone," Judy snapped. "You're right. There are lots of single men living on the island, and I've known most of them almost as long as I knew Scott, so getting together with any of them would be just way too weird. And I've reached a point in my life where a partner or a...a husband is the furthest thing from my mind. I like living alone. I like the silence. I like the freedom, and I like not having to answer to anyone, to explain my reasons, my thoughts, my ideas, or my moods!"

"Are you having a mood right now?"

"What?"

"You seem a little snippy."

"Look who's talking."

"I'm not snippy."

"You were a minute ago."

"No, I wasn't," Robin said, and pressing her lips together, she paused for a moment. "I was moody."

For a fraction of a second, Judy stared blankly back at Robin with her mouth open before she grinned. "Nice one."

"I thought so," Robin said just before she stifled a yawn.

"Are you tired? Would you like me to drive?"

"No, I'm fine. I just didn't get much sleep last night, and I haven't rebounded yet. Once we get to Petoskey, I'll find a coffee shop, and I'll be fine."

"Caffeine isn't a replacement for sleep, just to let you know."

"Well, up until I found out a ghost was living in my house, I was actually sleeping through the night for the first time in months."

"Really? What's up with that?"

"I guess I just haven't become as nonchalant about disembodied souls as the rest of you."

"No, I meant about you not sleeping in months."

"Oh," Robin said, frowning. "Can you just forget I said that?"

If it had been a demand, Robin's tone would have been loud, and a suggestion would have come across easily, without inflection or change in volume, but Robin had made the request in a whisper, signaling it wasn't an appeal, but rather a plea.

"Sure, consider it forgotten," Judy said with a nod.

"Thanks."

For a couple of minutes neither said a word, but having no interest in the scenery she had seen hundreds of times, Judy turned to Robin again. "So, what was Isobel doing last night that stopped you from sleeping?"

"Okay, so here's the thing," Robin blurted, quickly looking at Judy before returning her attention to the road. "How come you're sure this ghost is a woman named Isobel? What makes you think it's not some guy named Michael or Jason or...or Hannibal?"

If Robin had spoken matter-of-factly, Judy could have kept it together. If Robin had kept both hands on the wheel instead of waving one about as if trying to swat a fly, Judy could have kept it together. And if Robin had picked any names other than those, Judy could have kept it together, but between Robin's bug-eyed expression and her bug-swatting antics, Judy knew she was about to lose it. Her amusement was bubbling up like a geyser ready to blow, and clamping her hand over her mouth, Judy tried to muffle it, but one giggle escaped and then another, and then all hope was lost.

Robin's mouth fell open as she watched Judy double over in the passenger seat, the woman's side-splitting howls erupting unrestrained and echoing in the quiet of the 4Runner. "It's not that funny," Robin said, hitting the palm of her hands against the steering wheel. "I'm serious!"

Judy held up her hand, silently asking for a moment to get herself together, but the more she thought about Robin's name choices, the funnier it became.

"Fine! Laugh all you want, but *you're* not the one living with a serial killer."

"Oh my, God," Judy said, wiping the tears from her eyes. "Will you get a grip on yourself? It's a ghost, not a maniac wearing a hockey mask."

"How do you know?"

Judy sniffled back her mirth. "Because if it were, Adele wouldn't have survived for twenty-five plus years, now would she? She would have been slashed into a hundred pieces or...or served for dinner."

Robin gaped at Judy for a millisecond before focusing on the road again, and a few moments later, titters began slipping through Robin's lips. It wasn't long before those morphed into hilarity, and for nearly two miles, neither dared to speak for fear their funny bones would be tickled again.

"So, I see you like horror movies, too," Robin said, finally breaking the silence.

"No, but Scott couldn't get enough of them. The more gore and blood, the happier he was."

"Oh, he sounds like a great guy."

"He was at times," Judy said with a shrug. "That is when he wasn't acting like a child."

"Ouch."

"I don't mean that the way it sounds. He was my best friend, and I enjoyed his playfulness in the beginning, but I grew up, and he never did. He was just one big kid, looking for the next thrill or the next joke or the next challenge, and I guess it got old."

"Is that why you two split?" As soon as the words left Robin's mouth, she wanted to kick herself. "I'm sorry. You don't have to answer that. It's none of my business."

"It's okay," Judy said, looking out the window. "It's water under the bridge now." Judy took a deep breath and turned to face Robin. "Remember what you just asked about being disappointed in someone?"

"Yeah."

"Scott and I split up because I found out he was sleeping around and had been for quite a while."

"Oh shit."

"Not exactly what I said, but honestly, I wasn't angry. I was just...I was just empty."

"I'm sorry."

"It is what it is. Our marriage hadn't been on an even keel for years. Like I said, we were best friends, so we were comfortable, and for the most part, we were happy, but whatever spark we did have fizzled a long time ago. We were just going through the motions and eventually, I guess, he found someone else to give him what we didn't have."

"That's still sad."

"Yeah, but, like I said, it is what it is," Judy said. "And I'm no longer living above a bike shop, so that's a plus."

"Above the bike shop? Oh, I guess I just assumed you had a house."

"No. I always wanted one, but since we never had any children, there wasn't really any point in pushing the subject. The apartment above the shop was more than enough for both of us. He had his space, and I had mine, and it was really convenient during the busy months. I could just roll out of bed, pour some coffee, and head downstairs."

"Can I ask why you never had children? Didn't you want them?"

"I did for a while in the beginning," Judy said, softly. "And it wasn't like we were trying *not* to have them, but it just never happened."

"Sorry."

"Don't be," Judy said with a hint of a grin. "I'm a firm believer in what's meant to be is meant to be, and apparently having children wasn't in my future. It's not for me to question why."

"Sounds like you believe in God."

"Don't you?"

"Yes, actually I do," Robin said, glancing at the GPS. "I don't go to church and all that, but yeah, I believe in God. Not saying I haven't questioned Him at times though, because I have."

"Has He ever answered?"

Robin smiled instantly. "Yeah," she said softly. "I think He's answered me more than I even realize.

***

"By the way, you never answered me."

Judy lifted her eyes just in time to see Robin snag the last crab rangoon from the plate. "Answered you about what?"

"About why you think my ghost couldn't be named Hannibal."

"Is this becoming an obsession?" Judy said with a laugh as she picked up her iced tea.

"No. I'm just trying to find out how someone figured out my ghost was a woman and not a man."

"Does it really matter?"

"Yes," Robin said, leaning closer to Judy so she could keep her voice down. "Look, I've dropped my drawers in front of plenty of women, but dropping my drawers in front of some pervy old geezer, ghost or not, isn't on my bucket list, if you know what I mean."

Judy stared at Robin for a second before picking up her drink. "Gotcha," she muttered into the glass before taking a sip, and then placing her iced tea on the table, she rested back in the booth and crossed her arms. "Well, I can't tell you if anyone has ever *seen* Isobel, but as far back as I remember, she's always been called Isobel. If you want to know anything more than that, I guess you'll just have to hit the library on the island and read up. They have a whole section on the ghosts of Mackinac that will keep you busy for weeks."

Robin's eyebrows knitted. They had spent the entire morning together, hitting every home center and paint store in or around Petoskey and through it all, there had never been a misstep. Their tastes in wallpaper and colors had been the same, and their exuberance over finding the perfect style and shade of both caused smiles to appear on their faces in unison. They laughed. They joked, and as far as Robin could tell, Judy had enjoyed herself, but that had suddenly changed. Judy's expression had turned pinched and the blue of her eyes sparked with anger.

Robin was at a loss. She took a moment and then another, and resigned to accept her own confusion instead of pressing the issue, Robin lowered her eyes. "Yeah, I guess I'll have to do that."

The aroma of spices and stir-fry wafting from the kitchen had made Judy's stomach growl with anticipation since they had walked into the eatery a short time earlier. A cuisine not served on Mackinac, Thai was Judy's favorite, but suddenly, the last thing she wanted was food. Bowing her head, she pinched the bridge of her nose, took a deep breath, and then raised her eyes. "I'm sorry. I didn't mean to snap. I'm hungry. I need more than an appetizer."

"No, I'm the one who's sorry," Robin said, looking up. "You're right. I should just read the books and not keep pestering you about ghosts. You probably get it from the tourists all the time. You don't need it from me, too."

"They do have a tendency to go on and on about it," Judy said, snickering. "But they don't have a ghost living in their house, and you do. I forgot about that, and you have a right to be curious, so the least I can do is tell you what I know."

"Don't worry about it," Robin said, looking over her shoulder. "I'm sure our food will be here any minute, and we can't eat and talk at the same time."

Judy pressed her lips together, her eyes narrowing as she stared back at Robin. "Harvey, Lucy, Charlie, and Aunt Ida."

Robin turned back around, and as she tilted her head, her eyebrows squished together. "Excuse me?"

"You wanted to know about ghosts, so add those names to your list."

"Seriously?" Robin said, perking up in her seat. "Those are all ghosts?"

"Yep," Judy said as her eyes began to sparkle. "I can't tell you if they're actually their real names or not, but that's what everybody calls them."

"But who are they and more importantly, *where* are they? Please don't tell me they're hiding in my closets because if you do—"

"Relax," Judy said, thoroughly entertained by Robin's rambling. "As far as I know, Isobel is your only deceased tenant. Harvey and Lucy are over at Mission Point. Charlie is at the Island House, and Aunt Ida hangs out at Bayview. And before you ask, I'm talking about the B&B on the island. Not one of our guest rooms."

"I figured." Robin paused for a second before clasping her hands together like an excited child. "Tell me about them. Who's Harvey?"

"Oh, rumor has it that back in the late sixties or early seventies, he shot himself behind Mission Point when his girlfriend dumped him. His body wasn't found for almost six months, but since then he's usually seen on the bluffs just wandering about, although there have been some reports that he's poked or tickled young women staying at the hotel. Apparently, he fancies himself a practical joker."

"Wow, and Lucy was his girlfriend?"

"No," Judy said, shaking her head. "It's believed she was a little girl who lived during the eighteen hundreds, but while her parents were away, she somehow died. She's been seen on the balcony at the Point or sometimes in the theater, and more than one person has said they've heard her calling for her mummy or daddy during their stay at the resort."

"Yikes," Robin said, running her hands over her arms to quiet her goosebumps.

Laugh lines sprung to life on Judy's face. "Shall I go on?"

"Yes, please. This is fascinating."

"Okay, so Charlie is called the Gentleman Ghost," Judy said, smiling. "He lives at the Island House where he's been known to turn on faucets, open and close doors, and move things around occasionally. Aunt Ida basically does the same thing, only over at Bayview, except I do remember hearing that when some renovations were going on over there, Ida would make it a point of hovering over the workers or slamming doors to announce her displeasure at the changes, but other than that, for the most part, they're all harmless."

"For the most part? Are you saying there are some that aren't?"

"Robin, it's not like they're walking around with axes in their hands or sucking poor unsuspecting children into televisions or through sewer grates," Judy said, whimsy dancing in her eyes. "But yes, some are a little bit more...um...active, shall we say."

"Active in what way *exactly*?"

"Well, some of the beds in the hotels have been bolted down because there are stories of them being shaken so violently that the occupants were thrown out of them. I've also heard that more than one family has left the island because they couldn't handle the disembodied voices or their stuff being knocked off of mantles or bookcases, but as far as I know, that's as demonic as it gets. Trust me, once you see a few of them, it'll become old hat."

The waitress suddenly appeared out of nowhere, putting a stop to Robin's line of questioning for as long as it took to place the two steaming plates of food on the table. After thanking the slim Asian woman, Robin waited until the waitress was out of hearing range before continuing. "Are you saying that you've literally *seen* a ghost?" Robin said, the hushed words tumbling out of her mouth as she tapped her finger on the table.

"Yeah, I've actually seen more than one," Judy said as she picked up her fork and prepared to dive into her Pork Pad Thai. "Mostly up near the Fort or around the cemeteries at night when I go for a ride, but I haven't done that in a while."

Robin's eyes bulged. "I'm surprised you'd do *that* at all."

"I'm not afraid of the dark or of ghosts, and besides it's a really nice ride. You'd probably like it."

"You honestly want me to bike around a ghost-infested cemetery...in the dark?" Robin said, picking up her fork. "You *really* don't want me to *ever* get a good night's sleep again. Do you?"

"I wasn't suggesting that we go at night, but maybe one morning after I get back from Indiana, we can go take a look. What do you think?"

Out of nowhere, a wave of jealousy washed over Robin, and staring down at the plate of Thai Orchid Duck in front of her, she prayed that the chef had been heavy-handed. She wasn't a fan of hot and spicy food, preferring to appreciate the flavors without the burn, so she always asked for medium spices. It was just enough to make a difference, but not enough to require dousing the flames Thai seasonings could create. Yet, Robin now craved the heat for it would incinerate the feelings she had no right to feel. She knew it was stupid. She knew it was infantile, and picking up her fork, Robin stabbed it into a piece of duck. "I think we should eat before it gets cold."

Chapter Sixteen

"Are you okay?"

"What do you mean?"

"You've been awfully quiet since lunch."

"Have I?" Robin said, glancing at Judy. "Sorry, I've just been thinking about all the stuff I have to do over the next few weeks."

"How about I cross one thing off your list? I'll stop by the wallpaper place on my way back from Indiana. It's just a small detour, and since some of the paper is going to take a few weeks to get in, it'll save you the trip."

"You don't mind?"

"No, of course not, and if you think of anything else, just text me, and I'll pick it up."

"I don't text."

Judy's eyebrows drew together. "You don't text?"

"Not unless it's absolutely necessary. It's always seemed very one-dimensional to me, and it's easy to miss someone's mood in a text. It's got me into trouble more times than I can remember, so if you don't mind, if I need anything, I'll just call. Okay?"

"That's fine. It'll be nice to hear your voice."

Robin's heart did a flip, and she snapped her head to the right. "Yeah?"

Judy quickly returned to looking out the windshield. "What I meant to say is that we've been spending a lot of time together, and other than Rita, I don't really have a lot of people I talk to regularly, so it would be nice to hear a friendly voice. That's all."

"Oh, gotcha," Robin said, returning her eyes to the road. "Who's Rita?"

"She's my best friend," Judy said, smiling. "She's a super nice person. I'll have to introduce you. I think you'd like her."

"I'm sure I would," Robin said, giving Judy a quick glance.

"So, feel free to call any time you'd like. Okay?"

Puzzled, Robin looked over at Judy again. "How come that sounds more like a plea than a suggestion? I thought you wanted to see your family."

"I do, but catching up with them doesn't take that long because nothing ever really changes. They'll ask me how I'm doing and what I've been doing, and then they'll talk about the orchard and sales and what changes they want to do next year. Oh yeah, and they'll try to persuade me to move back. That happens every time."

"It does?"

"Yep. Like clockwork," Judy said. "Even when I was married to Scott, they never understood why I'd want to live on Mackinac, and after the divorce, it just got worse because I have two brothers who can't take no for an answer."

"Wait. I thought you had three brothers?"

"I do, but Eric is on my side. After he graduated college, he took a job in North Carolina, but whenever he comes home, he gets bombarded with the same questions. Why do you need to live there? What does fill-in-the-blank have that Indiana doesn't? Blah, blah, blah, blah, blah. Trust me, when November comes around, Eric and I will be ready to bolt."

"So, you're saying that you wouldn't mind if I call…just to chat?"

Judy's eyes met Robin's. "Honestly?"

"Yeah."

"I'm already looking forward to it."

***

Judy shut the door behind her, and leaning against it, she looked around her apartment. It was just as she had left it earlier that day. The television remote was precisely where she liked it on the end table, near one of the only two coasters she owned, their stone surfaces featuring the same faded lighthouse. The dish rack by the sink was empty save for the coffee cup she had used that morning, and the two suitcases on her bed were gaping, waiting for more clothes to be put inside. There was a faint hint of patchouli in the air courtesy of the candle Judy lit the night before and shrugging out of her jacket, she went over to the bookcase and lit the candle again.

Robin wasn't the only one who had had trouble sleeping the night before. After Judy had scoured the Internet at two in the morning in search of R. C. Novak, she ended up scrubbing her bathroom and kitchen with bleach and pine-scented products, their aroma eventually masked by what the candle had produced.

Judy had never been anxious about going to Indiana before. The drive was long and lonely, but she always looked forward to it. It gave her time to sort out her thoughts, to listen to music as loud as she'd like, to binge on fast food, and to even try to make peace with some inner demons that occasionally rose to the surface, but last night those demons had risen early. Appearing in her head and burrowing into her brain, the cacophony they produced had made slumber impossible, and as Judy approached the bed, she let out a sigh. She doubted she'd get much sleep tonight either.

She had made light of her brothers' incessant nagging with Robin, but that badgering had played a part in her sleeplessness. The solitude of an eight-hour drive would be enjoyable, as would the music and greasy fries and hamburgers, but at the end of the road, Judy would once again face those endless questions. Questions that were getting harder to answer honestly as the years went by. She could no longer use the excuse of having a business to run or even a husband who tethered her to the rock surrounded by water, and when she mentioned this new venture, this opportunity to run Safe Harbor with Robin, Judy knew her two older brothers would scoff. They would smirk and then spew a list of reasons why they believed her stupid or foolish or both, before pouring on the guilt…again. Words like family, birthright, and responsibility would be bandied about, and fading photos of her parents would be pointed at, her brothers using every trick in the book to change her mind, and Judy would remain silent and take it. She would hold back her feelings just like she'd done her entire life because she had to. They were her family, and she loved them.

Judy rubbed the back of her neck, releasing the tension that had begun to creep into her muscles, and taking a deep breath she went over and opened the closet door. She stared at the hangers filled with sweaters and the shelves holding neatly folded jeans and knit turtlenecks, and slamming the door on it all, she headed for the kitchen. It wasn't often that Judy needed a drink, but tonight she *needed* a drink.

After saying goodbye to Robin, Judy found herself welcoming the distance she put between them as she pedaled away from Safe Harbor. Other than with Rita, Judy never freely shared with anyone her own thoughts, feelings, or personal information. Bits and pieces about her life, her failures, her regrets, and her marriage had always been off limits. Yet, with a woman she barely knew, she had spoken openly about Scott's adultery. It was so easy. So uncomfortably…comfortable.

Judy learned early on that it was better to remain quiet than to open herself up to scrutiny or ridicule. Her father had been an assertive man, strong in his convictions and physique, and those traits had been passed down to his first and second born. By the time Judy became a teenager, her older brothers' domineering personalities had taken hold. Both were obstinate and dogmatic, and using their towering heights, broad shoulders, and bellowing voices to their advantage, they would browbeat anyone who got in their path.

Her mother tried to protect her, to shield her from the testosterone running rampant in the house, but Harriet had been born in a different time. In an era where women were second-class citizens to the breadwinners of the family, her job had been to stay in the background, cooking, cleaning, and raising the children. For the most part, she had done just that, but they didn't know about the words she'd whisper to her daughter when she tucked her in at night or the hushed conversation while dishes were being washed and dried. Harriet knew Judy would always be a little reserved, the lessons ingrained for too many years, but Harriet also knew there was more to her daughter than met the eye…much more.

Judy grabbed the step stool from the corner of the kitchen, and carefully climbing the two steps, she opened the cabinet over the refrigerator. Inside was what remained of Scott's liquor collection, left behind in the divorce. She considered the dusty bottles of vodka, gin, and rum for only a moment before pushing them aside and reaching toward the back. A minute later, Judy was pouring a healthy splash of Jack Daniels into a glass filled with ice.

As she lifted the tumbler to her lips, the earthy aroma of the coppery liquor invaded her senses. It reminded her of Scott, the oaken scent always clinging to his breath longer than she would have liked, and forgetting the potency of Tennessee whiskey, Judy took a quick gulp to erase that memory...and immediately regretted it. The liquor engulfed her mouth and throat in a heat that took her breath away, and placing the glass on the counter, Judy coughed and sputtered until she could finally fill her lungs with air. She eyed her drink, giving it the evilest look she owned, but as she glanced up at the cabinet above the fridge, Judy shrugged, picked up her tumbler of Jack and headed back the way she came.

***

Robin limped into the parlor the most wounded of wounded warriors, except hers wasn't a battle fought on a soccer field or in a ring surrounded by ropes. Hers had involved a skirmish with the clawed foot of a bathtub and a razor sharper than she remembered, in a bathroom as dark as pitch.

She slowly lowered herself onto the sofa, groaning as a few of the Band-Aids stretched against her skin, and staring daggers at the ceiling, Robin dared one floorboard to creak. As if on cue, an old oak plank on the second floor groaned under an invisible weight.

"Oh, you are *so* going to have a piece of my mind!" she shrieked, and launching herself off the couch, Robin flew out of the parlor and right up the stairs. Flicking on the light switch, she stared down the hallway. "Okay, where the hell are you?"

Robin stood motionless, her eyes darting back and forth between all the closed doors in front of her. "I said, where the *fuck* are you!"

Hell-bent on standing there the entire night if she had to, Robin didn't hear Fred scamper up the stairs behind her, but when he casually walked across her foot, Robin lost every ounce of sense God had ever given her.

Her scream reverberated through the house, the pitch so shrill that Fred instantly hunched his back before he dashed past, and taking the shortest route, he traveled over Robin's foot again.

Robin spun to her left, her hand flying to her chest in an attempt to keep her heart from exploding through her rib cage. Out of the corner of her eye, she saw her cat, but it was too late. Her momentum was too strong, and the wall was too close.

Like a pinball hit by a flipper, Robin careened off the plaster and was sent spinning in the direction of the stairs. She scrambled to grab hold of anything to stop her from cascading head first down the steps, and when her hand wrapped around something sturdy, Robin held on for dear life.

A few seconds later, she found herself dangling at arm's length from the railing like a puppeteer's marionette.

"Fred, I'm going to freaking kill you," she mumbled, looking around for her sneaky black cat. Spying him at the bottom of the stairs, Robin shot him an evil look. "Yeah, that's right. You sure as hell better keep your distance, you little shit."

Robin straightened her pajamas and climbed back up the two steps she had just fallen down. As she reached the top, the hairs on the back of her neck stood at attention. The hallway was colder than it had been a few seconds earlier...much colder.

Robin swallowed hard and looked down the corridor again, and the color drained from her face. Two of the doors leading to the bedrooms were now wide open. "Shit," she said under her breath. "Shit. Shit. Shit."

Courage comes in several forms. Spiritual courage is provided by a person's beliefs, and emotional courage can be brought on by the euphoria of the moment. The resolve and ethics of some give birth to moral courage, making them resolute in the face of temptation, and familiarity with surroundings or people grants a person what is known as social courage. The last is physical courage. Encompassing not only strength but resiliency and awareness, it is an integral part of every hero or heroine. Facing danger without flinching, some run into burning buildings to save the lives of strangers. Some walk down darkened alleys searching for a suspect not knowing if they are armed or not, and some throw themselves on grenades to save their fellow man all because their courage is unshakable...unlike Robin's knees, which were currently making her pajama bottoms appear as if they were flapping in the wind.

"Hello?" Robin said in a whisper as every muscle in her body tightened. "Isobel, is...is that you?"

One minute passed and then another before Robin took an uneven breath and spoke. "Um...my name's Robin. I'm...um...I'm Adele Anderson's niece. I don't know...I don't know if you're aware of it, but Adele passed away, and I inherited Safe Harbor."

The door to Whitefish Falls suddenly slammed shut, the thunderous bang causing Robin to jump a foot into the air, but when her feet found the floor again, she stood her ground for only one reason. She was too afraid to move. The color had drained from her face. Her heart was pounding in her ears, and even though she wanted to bolt down the stairs more than she wanted the air she was breathing, Robin couldn't move. She just *couldn't* move.

Chapter Seventeen

Judy reached for her drink and drained what was left in the glass in one swallow. She grimaced at the sting, the intensity of the eighty proof still not to her liking, but clambering out of bed, Judy headed to the kitchen to pour another glass.

An hour earlier, after her suitcase was packed and sitting by the door, Judy stood under a steaming spray in her shower until her fingers pruned. She thought it would dissolve the rest of her anxieties, yet when she exited her bathroom, her mind was still ablaze with thoughts she could not extinguish. She paced. She tried to read. She even attempted to play some games on her phone until her frustration reached the next level, and anger is *not* a good bedfellow.

Judy stood at the kitchen sink, sipping her drink and looking around her apartment. Why in the hell did she have to be so neat? With a huff, she stormed back to her bedroom, having just enough time to set her drink on the nightstand before her cell phone rang. Glancing at the screen, Judy pinched her lips together before she accepted the call and put the phone to her ear. "For the last flipping time, I know you want fudge, and before you ask, yes, I know what your favorites are. Yes, I already bought it, and yes, I already packed it, so unless I forget my luggage tomorrow which, by the way, is stacked next to the flipping door, you're good. Okay?"

"Whoa. You sure as hell are in a mood. What the fuck, Judy?"

Judy let out a sigh and sinking onto the bed, she rubbed her forehead. "I'm sorry, Eric. You didn't deserve that. I've been having some problems sleeping over the last couple of days, and I guess it's getting to me."

"You guess?"

Judy snorted. "Okay, so it *is* getting to me, but I'm having a drink, so hopefully that'll help."

"I hope it's a big one."

"Big enough," Judy said, grinning into the phone. "I have a question for you. Do you ever think about not doing this? I mean, not going home for the autumn festivities?"

"Are you *kidding* me? All the time," Eric said. "And then I remember the crap Thing One and Thing Two put me through every time I didn't make it when my kids were small, moaning about how busy they were and bitching that I ruined the family get-together. It's easier to just bite my lip and do it than to have another guilt trip laid on me for years to come."

"See," Judy said, slapping her hand on the bed. "That's exactly what I mean. Why do we keep doing this to ourselves?"

"Because they're our brothers, and we love them."

"It's a lame excuse."

"You'll get no argument from me."

"They are definitely two of a kind, aren't they?"

"Yep, and unlike wine, age isn't doing one goddamned thing to mellow them."

A smile stretched across Judy's face. "True."

"So, why the question? You thinking about not going?"

"No, I told you, I'm already packed, but..." Judy hesitated for a moment. "Okay, so I have something to tell you, but you can't mention it to Pat or Doug. All right?"

"Sure. Are you okay?"

"Yeah, I'm fine. I've just taken a new job and...and, well, it's..." Judy stopped and sighed. "You know what? Never mind, I'm just being stupid."

"Wait. You can't just say you've got a new job and then drop it. What is it? Is it off the island?"

"No, it's here."

"Then what the hell are you doing? Running a plow?"

"No, managing a bed-and-breakfast."

"Hey, that's great!" Eric said. "But what's that got to do with going home? I thought all those places were closed by now."

"They are or will be by the end of the month."

"Then what's the issue?"

"There isn't any. I told you. I'm just being stupid."

"Jude, you are the least stupid person I know, so come on, tell your baby brother what's on your mind."

Judy took a sip of her drink and letting out a long breath, she relaxed back across the bed. "Okay, so...so this place, it's called Safe Harbor Inn."

"Hey, I remember that one. On the turn at the end of the street? A big Victorian?"

"That's right," Judy said, staring at the ceiling. "Anyway, the lady who owned it died and left it to her niece. She's the one who gave me the job, and she and I both agree there are a lot of renovations that need to be done, so we plan to spend the winter doing them."

"So, what's the problem? It's not like the winter up there doesn't last until April. Isn't that enough time?"

"It is, which is why I said I was being stupid. There are plenty of things to keep me busy all winter. There's no need to rush."

Eric pulled the phone away from his ear for a second. "Do you have any idea how long I've waited for this?"

"For what?

"For you to be actually excited about something."

"What in the world are you talking about?"

"Sis, the Judy I grew up with could never sit still. If you weren't helping Mom in the kitchen, you were working in the orchard or riding your bike to God knows where, and you were the only kid I knew who got excited when school started. You joined every sport you could, and nothing ever slowed you down, but once you married that prick, it was like...it was like you got into a rut you couldn't climb out of."

"I was happy."

"Yeah, right," Eric said, rolling his eyes. "Tell that to someone who believes you."

"Eric—"

"Don't worry, no one else picked up on it. Doug and Pat are way too focused on the orchard to ever see past it long enough to notice that you had changed."

"People change, Eric. It's called growing up."

"Or maybe it's because you were miserable."

"Please stop."

Eric closed his eyes, the underlying plea in his sister's tone telling him he had gone too far. "I'm sorry. So...what kind of renovations are you planning at the B&B? I'm pretty good with a hammer if you need help."

"Nothing like that, and thanks, you're a sweetie," Judy said, her eyes crinkling at the corners. "The Inn's actually in fairly good shape for being closed for a couple of years. Mostly, it's just going to be a lot of new paint and wallpaper. It shouldn't really take us that long, but I know she'll be more comfortable once I get back from Indiana."

"Why's that? Is she old?"

"No, she's a hell of a lot younger than me," Judy said with a laugh. "But the Inn has a permanent house guest in the form of a ghost named Isobel and Robin hasn't quite wrapped her head around that yet."

"Oh, you gotta be kidding me. That's awesome! Book me a room and do it now!"

Judy smiled. Most of her family had visited her one time or another on Mackinac, but other than Eric, they had only stayed for a few days. Eric would stay for a week, and while she was the main reason for his visit, his second was to overindulge in his favorite confection, and his third was ghosts. "Well, for you it's awesome, but for Robin, not so much."

"Let me guess. She's afraid of ghosts?"

"She says she isn't, but she's clearly weirded out by it," Judy said, giggling. "And I've told her a dozen times Isobel is completely harmless, but between you and me, I think Robin has just seen too many movies."

***

Robin bolted into the parlor, stopping long enough to pull the pocket doors closed with a bang before continuing toward the center of the room. She whipped around, and gasping for air, her hands turned into fists as she fixated on the doors.

A minute earlier, she had tried once again to talk to Isobel, but she had only managed a few words before a wave of icy air washed over her, stopping her mid-sentence. She had felt a few strands of her hair flutter in the breeze of ghostly travel, and as the chill burrowed its way into her bones, it froze Robin's thoughts, her movements, and her breath. Ten seconds seemed like a lifetime, but that's all the time that had passed before the door to Sunset Shores, the room only a few feet behind where she stood, slammed closed so violently that a vase on a nearby table crashed to the floor. Like a shot from a gun signaling the race to begin, it was all Robin needed to find her feet, and find them, she did. Dashing to the steps, she bounded down them three at a time as she fled to what she hoped would be her sanctuary.

Sanctuary, in the truest meaning of the word, is the most sacred place in a church or temple. Consecrated, it is the holiest of holy places, and it is where many find answers, where some find God, and others finally find the refuge they've been searching for. The parlor was neither consecrated nor holy, and within its walls, an altar did not exist, but it had doors, which were now locked. It had windows that could quickly be climbed out of, and there were enough lamps and knickknacks to be used as ammunition if the need arose.

Lines formed on Robin's forehead as she realized her plan was flawed. Isobel had no form, no shadow or glimmering aura allowing Robin to see her target. A target not at all as Judy had described. "Wait until I see her," Robin said under her breath. "Harmless my ass."

Only a few minutes had passed since Robin entered the parlor, but during that time, Robin's ability to think clearly had returned. Her hands relaxed, and her breathing returned to normal, but a few seconds later, she went rigid again. The doors hadn't opened, and the windows were closed, but suddenly Robin could see her breath.

Robin had two choices. She could either make a mad dash for the doors or try for the windows, but just as she made her decision, she heard a noise. It was a familiar noise, and it was a noise she could not leave behind.

The intuitive phenomenon to protect those held dear is possibly the most formidable force to be reckoned with. Educated or not, rich or poor, human or animal, while a biological link for this behavior does not necessarily have to exist, some believe the most dangerous place to be is between a mother and her child.

It took Robin only a moment to spy Fred and Ginger huddled under a chair, the hair on their backs and tails puffed out like she had never seen it before. Their ears were plastered against their heads and with every swish of their tails, they were hissing in unison. As the room grew even colder and Robin's hair began to dance in the breeze, an instinct she never knew she possessed took over her very soul.

"*Enough!*" she screamed at the top of her lungs. The wind began to gust, and Robin fisted her hands. "Goddamn it, I said enough!"

The wind died in an instant, and Robin waited for a moment before speaking again. "I get that you don't like me," she said, glancing around the room. "I get that you're angry Adele died, and I'm here now, but you know what? Too *fucking* bad! I'm not leaving no matter how many doors you slam or how many times you traipse up and down hallways, because this is *my* house now, and *you're* going to just have to get *used* to it!"

Robin could feel a few wisps of her hair beginning to move, and standing tall, she folded her arms. "That's not going to work anymore. I'm not afraid of you."

A gust of wind appeared out of nowhere, and Robin had to steady herself against the burst. "Okay, so I *am* afraid of you," she yelled. "You're a ghost, for God's sake, and the fact that you don't need doors to get into rooms is way more than a little freaky, let me tell you, but no matter how many you slam or how much wind you create, I'm not going anywhere. I don't know why Adele left me this place, but she did, and I'm going to stay. So, either you and I come to some sort of agreement, or you can continue to huff and puff until the cows come home, but you are *not* going to drive me from this house!"

Robin barely had time to take a breath before a gale like no other swept through the room. Lamps fell from the tables and papers swirled in the current of air so powerful and icy, Robin felt as if it sliced right through her. Her fingers and lips numbed instantly, and wincing at the squall as it stabbed at her eyes, she held her hands to her head, trying to keep her hair from flying into her eyes.

She had no idea how long it took before the room quieted again, but when it did, Robin straightened her backbone and shook her head. "Nice try, but like I said, I'm *not* going anywhere. You're just a disembodied soul that, for whatever reason, can't get on with whatever dead people do when they die. Well, do us both a favor. Go toward the *fucking* light!"

Robin stomped to the doors, and sliding them open with a bang, she went to the kitchen and opened the bottle of wine sitting on the counter. The neck of the bottle rattled against the rim of the glass as she filled the tumbler almost to the top, and letting out the breath she'd been holding, she chugged down half of what she had poured before the temperature in the kitchen plummeted.

Robin hung her head and let out a long, dramatized sigh. "I gotta tell ya," she said as she turned around. "This is getting—"

The drink in Robin's hand slipped from her fingers. The glass shattered upon impact, sending the robust Cabernet all over the floor and cabinetry, but Robin didn't hear the crash or see the mess. She was too intent on praying her bladder wasn't going to release.

Isobel peered at the stranger. She bore no resemblance to her old friend. A friend with dark eyes and hair that had been the color of strong tea until the years had turned it to the shade of smoke, its unruly natural waves defiant even then. She missed her old friend dearly. She had been the only one who had never feared her, never scolded or shouted out harsh language to try to drive her from the house. Then again, neither did the other.

Isobel cocked her head to one side and studied the woman standing near the sink. Her face held a familiarity, a reflection of someone else, someone with the same stature, though perhaps a bit shorter, a bit rounder, a bit older. Isobel's eyebrow raised, the one word Robin had said earlier now finally having significance, its definition simple, but its meaning considerable. *This* was the woman Adele had been so proud of. *This* was the woman who her old friends loved so much. *This* was the woman they had spoken of so many times. *This* was the *niece*.

With the connection now made, Isobel's apprehension waned. She had never given Adele a reason to be wary of her for her old friend had unknowingly bestowed upon Isobel something she had been searching for all these many years. Something this stranger, this niece...could provide as well.

Robin could not tear her eyes away from the image floating in the doorway. The details were blurred as if it was behind a film, hazy and rippled, and even though she tried to discern the features of the face framed by long, dark hair, all Robin could make out was the color of the woman's clothes. Her dress was white, and a shawl, a few shades darker than the dress, draped her shoulders, but all else was obscured by the aura surrounding Isobel. It was shimmering around the edges of her body as if behind her was a thousand-watt spotlight, and then Robin's breath caught in her throat. The two dark specks on the woman's face were aimed directly toward her, and there was no doubt in Robin's mind, Isobel was staring at her.

"I-I gotta tell ya, it's...um...it's good to s-see you're a woman," Robin said with the weakest of grins. "I-I was kind of worried about that. I kept thinking you were some pervy old guy." Robin frowned. "Oh, do you know what...do you know what pervy means? I-I'm not sure how long you've...um...been around, but pervy means...it means vulgar or...or like a voyeur."

Robin waited, and when Isobel's image began to flutter, Robin braced herself, preparing for another ghostly show of anger, but then she heard a meow and looked down to see Fred standing at her feet. Again, instinct reigned supreme, and squaring her shoulders, she glared back at Isobel.

"Look," Robin said, holding up her hands. "I'm sorry I yelled, and I'm sorry you're not happy, but you and I, we...we have to find a way to meet in the middle here. I mean you no harm and...and I'll give you whatever space I can, but I need space, too. I-I need to be able to sleep at night knowing you're a friend, not a foe. I need to be able to trust that you won't do harm to my cats or...or to me. I swear to God, I'm not your enemy. I'm just a woman who's trying to start over. Okay?"

A few seconds later, the spectral particles embodying all that was Isobel...fizzled into nothingness.

Chapter Eighteen

Robin's face fell as she approached the door. The silhouette she could see through the stained glass was much too tall to belong to Judy. Shaking off her disappointment, Robin opened the front door and grinned at the big-boned woman standing on her front porch. "Can I help you?"

"That depends," the woman said, displaying an infectious smile. "Are you Robin Novak?"

"That's me," Robin said, her eyes darting back and forth between the towering stranger and the bags she was carrying.

The woman juggled the packages in her arms and held out her hand. "Rita Hutchinson. Judy's best friend and the unofficial Welcome Wagon for Mackinac Island."

Robin's eyes flew open wide. "Oh, hi!" she said, shaking Rita's hand. "Judy's mentioned you more than once. I'm so glad to finally meet you."

"The feeling's mutual," Rita said, rearranging the bags again. "And these are for you."

Robin stared at the two handled shopping bags Rita was now holding in front of her. "What?"

"This one is from the ladies at the church," Rita said, handing Robin the first. "Tillie made you a batch of oatmeal cookies. Delores contributed two loaves of freshly baked bread. Vivian tossed in a few bottles of her homemade relish, and Madge, God bless her heart, baked you a cherry pie."

"Oh, my God," Robin said as she peeking inside the bag. "That was so nice of them."

"And this one is from me," Rita said, holding up the other bag. "I hope you like lasagna."

Robin's eyes opened to their extreme. "I love lasagna!" she said, taking the bag. "Are you kidding me? It's like my favorite meal."

"Well, you should have enough in there to last you at least the week," Rita said with a laugh.

"I don't know what to say," Robin said, looking back and forth between the bags and Rita. "This is totally unexpected."

A glint of humor came into Rita's eyes as she gazed at Robin. "Most good things are."

For a second, they stood smiling at each other until Robin came to her senses. "Please...please come in," she said, stepping aside.

"I'd love to," Rita said, and striding into the house, she waited for Robin to catch up.

After closing the door, Robin gestured toward the dining room. "I'm just going to put this stuff in the kitchen. Would you like a cup of coffee or...or I can make tea?"

"Coffee is my middle name."

"Coffee it is then," Robin chirped. "Follow me."

A few minutes later, Rita watched as Robin put away the last of her gifts, the tray of lasagna taking up more than its fair share of space in the refrigerator. When Robin turned around, Rita grinned. "It's uncanny how much you look like your mother."

Robin beamed. "It constantly surprises me that so many people here remember her."

"Why?"

"Because she only visited a few times a year."

"True, but haven't you heard it's the quality, not the quantity that matters?"

"What do you mean?"

"Robin, as you'll soon learn, we get thousands of tourists every year. They pile off the ferries and schlepp around the island, and don't get me wrong, most of them are really nice, but your mother...your mother was different. She was Grace Kelly different." Rita paused to set her coffee on the counter before continuing. "Constance was elegant and sophisticated, a true lady in a world of wannabe ladies. I can't ever remember her not having a clutch bag tucked under her arm, and her hair was always done up in a perfect chignon without a strand out of place."

Robin chuckled. "I can't tell you how many times I tried to get her to change that hairstyle, but she never would. Never."

"That's because it was part of who she was, *what* she was, and it's one of the reasons why we all remember her," Rita said with a soft smile. "Your mother was a lady, through and through. She had an air about her that others couldn't buy with all the money in the world, and she didn't even have to work at it. She stood tall, always wearing those flowing dresses, yet she didn't possess one goddamn ounce of snobbery. She was literally a breath of fresh air each and every time she stepped off the ferry."

In an instant, Robin shifted her focus to the floor, her face falling as her brow creased.

"I'm sorry," Rita said, noticing Robin's hardened expression. "Did I say something wrong?"

"No. I was just trying to remember the last time I told my mother she was beautiful," Robin said, her features softening as she raised her eyes. "She was, wasn't she?"

"You'll get no argument from me," Rita said as she picked up her water. "That's why we were all shocked when she and Ted didn't work out. They were quite a stunning couple."

Robin's forehead wrinkled again. "Um...don't take this the wrong way, Rita, but you must be talking about someone else. My mother didn't date."

Rita tilted back her head, and then a sly smile spread across her face. For a town known for its grapevine, she suddenly realized that there was more than one secret yet to be discovered by the inhabitants of Mackinac Island. Never being one to pull punches, Rita took a sip of coffee before speaking.

"Yes, she did, and she and Ted were an item for years," Rita said, resting against the counter. "Every time she visited, I'd see them out and about, having dinner at one of the restaurants or walking arm-in-arm around the island, whispering like two little lovebirds."

"No," Robin said, shaking her head. "I'm telling you, she didn't date."

"Maybe she didn't *tell* you she was dating, but visiting her sister wasn't the only reason she came up here, Robin. Ask anyone, and they'll say the same thing. Ted Owens and your mother were hot and heavy. We all figured they would eventually get married, but about fifteen years ago,

Ted up and sold his jewelry store and left the island. Everyone assumed he had finally popped the question and...and she popped his bubble."

"That can't be," Robin said under her breath.

"It is, honey, and I'm sorry if it upsets you?"

Robin struggled to find the right words. Her feelings were balanced on a razor blade. Lean one way and there was happiness. Her mother *hadn't* spent the last forty-plus years alone. She had enjoyed the company of men. She had dated, maybe kissed, maybe more, and isn't that what Robin had always wanted for her? Yet, lean the other, and there was annoyance. Agitation caused by a secret that shouldn't have been, it gnawed at Robin, causing her body to stiffen and her expression to darken.

"I'm just confused as to why she didn't tell me," Robin said, trying to ease the anxiety showing on her face as her eyes met Rita's. "I mean, she never dated when I was growing up. Not once. Call it the romantic in me, but I always thought it was because she loved my father so much, that he was her one and only."

"Well, now you're describing your aunt, not your mother."

"I am?"

Rita nodded. "Adele was the sister who only had one love in her life. She adored Stanley, and when he died, she was a basket case for years. I still remember walking into my parent's candy store and finding this young woman in the back room, bawling her eyes out. I was only thirteen or fourteen at the time, and I had no idea what was going on, so I asked my mom. She told me that the lady had lost her husband a few months earlier and was still having a hard time."

"Oh, God, it must have been awful for her."

"Yes, it was," Rita said softly. "But you know I never really understood just how much she loved him until years later."

"What happened?"

"Well, like I said, I was only a teenager when I first met her, so she and I didn't exactly travel in the same circles, but when I got back from college, our paths began to cross. By that time, she had bought Safe Harbor and was well on her way to being a successful businesswoman. One of her tricks was to always buy some fresh fudge for her guests. Just a small assortment, nothing extravagant, but every afternoon like clockwork, she'd show up at the shop to buy whichever flavor we had just finished making. I had four years of college business skills under my belt, and I was eager to put them to use, so I suggested instead of buying our fudge, Schockling's would give her the assortments and in exchange, she'd put some of our business cards in her dining room next to the plate of fudge. She agreed, and that was the start of our friendship."

Rita paused long enough to take another taste of her coffee. "At first it was just casual conversation when she stopped in to get the fudge, but eventually we started meeting up for a quick lunch or an occasional dinner. It's funny though, Adele never talked about herself. It was always about business or the island, or things she wanted to change at Safe Harbor. She was one focused woman."

"It sounds like it."

"Yeah," Rita said, setting aside her cup. "Anyway, I guess it was probably a few years after we became friends when she first invited me to have dinner with her at her place. I showed up with a bottle of wine, and we had a great meal, and as always, the conversation was easy and all about business. After we were done eating, she banished me to the living room while she straightened up the kitchen, and that's when I saw the mantle over the fireplace. It was practically a shrine to Stanley."

"You're kidding? When I moved in, it was empty. The whole place was empty."

"I don't know what to tell you about that, but back then it was far from empty. In the center was the American flag in one of those triangular cases along with some photographs of him, and a bunch of letters tied in a ribbon off to one side. There was even a pipe propped up in a stand like it was waiting for its owner to come home."

"Wow," Robin whispered. "I wonder what happened to all of it."

"I don't know," Rita said softly. "But when she came in with some coffee, I guess she noticed what I was doing, and she just started talking about Stanley. It was so unlike her. So different than the women I had come to know, but I wasn't about to stop her."

"What did she say?"

"She said they had met in college. Stanley was a couple of years ahead of her, but apparently love at first sight does exist because that's the way she described it. One look and that was it for both of them."

All too familiar with love at first sight, Robin bobbed her head in acknowledgment.

"She said they spent every minute they could together and when he graduated, he proposed, and she accepted. Adele told me she was going to quit college because being his wife was the only thing she wanted to be, but he wouldn't hear of it. Instead of returning to his home in Detroit like he had planned, Stanley stayed in Lansing so they could continue to be together until she finished school. Unfortunately, a few months before Adele was set to graduate, Stanley got drafted, and the big wedding they had planned in the spring got pushed up. They went to a Justice of the Peace, said their vows, and a few weeks later he was in boot camp. They saw each other only one more time before he was shipped off to Vietnam, and he never came back."

"God, that's sad."

"I know. Adele said she couldn't bear to think of ever being with another man. She always felt as if Stanley was going to walk through the door one night, and they'd be together again."

"Jesus."

"So, you see, your aunt was the one who had found her soul mate. Your mom, on the other hand, had more than one beau on this island."

"There were others?" Robin said, the tone of her voice climbing the scale with each syllable.

"Oh yeah," Rita said, grinning. "There was a maître d at the Grand named Ronnie she dated for a couple of years, and there was...oh, what was his name?" Rita paused and tapped her finger against her chin. "John, no wait...Joseph, Joseph Eastburn. He worked as a bartender over at the Mustang for a few seasons."

"Do you know if they're still on the island?"

"Why? It's a little late to make sure their intentions were pure."

Robin forced a smile. "No. I'm just a little curious to see the kind of men my mother dated, especially since she didn't see the need to tell me about them."

"Well, it wasn't because they were ugly. I can tell you that," Rita said with a laugh. "But as for meeting them, I'm afraid they were both just seasonal workers. They stayed for a few years and then headed back to civilization."

"Oh. Okay."

Rita looked at her watch. "Damn it all to hell. Look at the time," she said, quickly moving her cup from the counter to the sink. "I told Judy I'd get her to the ferry by one, which gives me fifteen minutes to get my sorry ass to her house."

"The ferry?" Robin said, trotting to catch up to Rita as she made her way to the front door. "But she's not leaving until tomorrow."

"She's getting on the road tomorrow," Rita said, grabbing her coat. "But she likes to leave at the crack of dawn's ass, and the ferries don't run that early. She's staying at a motel in St. Ignace tonight so she can leave first thing in the morning."

"Oh, I didn't know that," Robin said, her voice dropping to a whisper. "I thought...I thought I'd see her today."

Rita frowned. She hadn't missed Robin's inflection, or rather the lack thereof, and it gave her pause. As she buttoned her jacket, she kept her eyes on Robin, secure in the fact the woman would never know she was staring since Robin seemed intent on looking at the floor. By the time Rita reached the last button, her frown had disappeared. "You know, if there's something you need while she's gone, I'm always around or...or did you want to tell her something? I can give her a message, or you can come along. Up to you."

The last time Robin had experienced the sensation washing over her, she was a child. A mere toddler, she had been confused and saddened by the loss of her father, and swirling amidst her grief and anger was the feeling of being abandoned. Deserted by someone she had loved so much, even though she still had her mother by her side, it had taken a long time before Robin got over the hurt of being left behind.

Robin had heard Rita speak, but it took several seconds before she managed to raise her eyes. "No. That's okay."

"You sure? It's a short ride, and I'm sure she'd like to see you."

"Actually, I have a lot of things to do," Robin said, placing her hand on the door. "Just tell her I'll...I'll call her in a few days. Okay?"

"All right," Rita said, opening the door. "I'll catch you later, and I'll be sure to let Judy know to expect your call."

"Yeah, you do that."

Robin watched as Rita made her way down the steps of the porch, but as she was about to close the front door, another feeling washed over Robin. It was one she'd had for over twenty-five years, and rushing onto the porch, Robin called out, "And please tell her to drive carefully!"

***

"I'm so sorry I'm late."

Judy looked at her watch. "You're not."

"I'm not? Well, I'll be damned. I guess this old broad's legs still got some life left in them."

"And I'm sure Hank is thrilled to know that."

It wasn't often Judy could turn the tables on Rita, but when the woman's cheeks flamed, Judy clapped her hands together like a gleeful child. "What's wrong, honey? Don't like it when the shoe's on the other foot?"

Rita tried to conceal her smile by pressing her lips together, but she could do nothing to hide the merriment in her eyes. Pointing to the suitcases Judy had stacked near the house, Rita said, "Shut up and help me with your luggage."

Judy continued to giggle as they loaded the cargo hauler attached to Rita's tandem bike. "So, at the risk of opening myself up to yet another one of your sexual innuendos, I hope the reason you were almost late didn't have anything to do with Hank."

"No, I was talking to Robin, and I lost track of time."

"Robin? Where'd you see her?"

"At Safe Harbor," Rita said, standing straight after pulling the last bungee cord tight. "The ladies at church put together a bag of munchies, and I took it over this morning, along with a tray of my lasagna."

"Well, shit," Judy said, stomping her foot. "Now I really don't want to take this trip. I love your lasagna."

"Don't worry. I'll make you some when you get back. How's that?"

Judy sighed. "That'll work, I guess."

Rita rocked back in her stance. "Is it me, or aren't you feeling this whole return to Indiana thing...again?"

Judy ran her fingers through her hair, exhaling what seemed to be an endless breath as she picked up the bottle of water she had set aside. "To tell you the truth," she said as she unscrewed the cap. "It's getting old."

"That's because you've never had the balls to tell your brothers to shut the hell up."

"Have you ever tried talking to a wall? Because that's what it's like when I try to say anything to them," Judy said, bringing the bottle to her lips. "It's just easier to do what's expected and then get the hell out as soon as I can. Creating waves has never been my thing."

Everyone has a breaking point. An invisible line, crossed when stress or situations become extreme, it can cause suspects to admit guilt, the introverted to pull back into their shells, or the extroverted to explode like volcanoes, finally letting loose their lava in the form of opinions they had kept to themselves, and Rita had kept this opinion to herself for far too long. Believing her best friend now had a future filled with everything she deserved, Rita's name became Vesuvius.

"Well, it may not have been your thing when you were twelve, but you're not a child anymore, woman!" Rita said, widening her stance as jammed her hands on her hips. "Grow some big brass ones and tell them to stick it where the sun don't shine. Start living your goddamned life and the hell with anyone who thinks differently! I know they're your family, and I know you love them, and I know, God help me, you think this is some sort of family responsibility, but there's a difference between responsibility and constant guilt trips. If you ask me, it's time you start living your life and if those two morons can't handle it, then fuck 'em!"

Judy's eyebrows disappeared into her hairline. She had just taken a swig of water, and even though she knew she looked like a squirrel storing nuts for the winter, she couldn't make herself swallow. She was accustomed to Rita speaking her mind, but she wasn't used to an expletive-laced outburst like the one she had just heard. When she could swallow, Judy's gulp was audible. "What crawled up your butt and died?"

"What the hell are you talking about?" Rita snapped.

"Even for you, that was a little over the top. Don't you think?"

"No. I don't think it was at all. Every year you bitch and moan about this trip and every year, you end up going," Rita said, and walking over, she placed her hands on Judy's shoulders. "Judy, I love you. You're my best friend, and you deserve to be happy, and the kind of happy *I'm* talking about, you're not going to find in Indiana."

Judy jerked back her head. "What exactly is that supposed to mean?"

Rita took a step backward, her expression growing pensive as she looked at her friend. "It just means that you love Mackinac and...and if you ever left, you'd be miserable. That's all."

"I have no intention of leaving the island, at least not for good. You know that."

"I know that's what you've always said, but I also know that you were on the fence about taking the job at Safe Harbor, and I figured if you and Robin weren't hitting it off or...or if you were uncomfortable for any reason that you might...you might—"

"Run away?"

Rita's shoulders sagged. "The thought did cross my mind."

"But why? Wait," Judy said, and a second later, her face fell. "Don't you like her?"

"Who?"

"Robin?"

"No, I like her a lot," Rita said, her expression softened by a grin. "Of course, I only just met her, but she seems really nice."

"Oh. Okay. Good..." Judy said, her voice sinking to a whisper as she glanced at her watch.

"And what if I didn't like her? Are you saying you'd quit the job?"

"What? No, of course not. Well, maybe...I don't know."

"Judy, honey, we're best friends, and we're best friends because we have the same taste when it comes to people. If they're good, we like them, and if they're bad, we don't, and you wouldn't have taken the job if you thought Robin was a bad person, or am I wrong?"

"No, you're not wrong."

"Imagine that."

Waving off Rita's comment with a flick of her wrist, Judy walked to the bike. "We really should be going," she said, taking her place on the rear seat. "You coming?"

"Well, you're too short to reach my pedals, so I guess I'll have to," Rita said, taking her place at the front. "Oh, and by the way, Robin wanted me to tell you to drive carefully, and she'll call you in a few days."

Rita climbed on, and the two women started pedaling into town, one enjoying the scenery while the other was enjoying the moment.

***

Having taped off everything the day before, every piece of trim in the apartment was now outlined in strips of blue tape, and while the painter's masking guaranteed nothing would leak through, Robin saw no need to test its promise. A perfectionist by nature, she sat on her living room floor, inching her way along as she painstakingly cut in the paint above the baseboard. Her spirits had been dampened knowing she wouldn't see Judy for a few weeks, but as soon as Robin opened the first can of paint, they lifted. To turn old into new, to change dingy into vivid, and to freshen what had once been forgotten had always put a smile on her face, and it did again.

Robin put the handle of the brush in her mouth long enough for her to scooch another few feet, but as she went to reload the brush, she stopped. She had kept the heating system in the apartment on low, warm enough to remove any chill, but cool enough to warrant the sweatshirt she was wearing, yet all of a sudden, the fleece-lined pullover wasn't enough. Robin glanced at the fireplace. She wasn't close enough for the draft from the chimney to find its way to her, and there were no windows or doors open to allow in the crisp autumn air, which left her with only one other possibility.

Robin swallowed hard and looked over her shoulder to the emptiness behind her. "Good afternoon, Isobel." She wasn't expecting a response, but that didn't stop Robin from continuing. "I hope you like blue," she said, dipping her brush in the paint can. "It's my favorite color."

She turned her attention to the wall, but as Robin moved the brush closer to the plaster, she noticed her hand was shaking. "Damn it," she said under her breath. Balancing the brush on the edge of the can, Robin crossed her legs under her and pivoted to face the room. "So, here's the thing. I-I don't...I don't mind you watching or being around. Okay? I really don't. It's just going to take some time to get used to, but I *can* get used to it. I *will* get used to it. I *have* actually gotten used to it because I'm here talking to you right now even though I feel a little foolish. All right?"

Robin paused, slowly scanning the room for any sign of Isobel's aura. Coming up empty, she let out the breath she'd been holding. "So, this is what I'm going to do," Robin said, picking up her paintbrush. "I'm going to talk to you when you're around. I don't expect you to answer. I don't even know if *you* can answer, but I figure this is the best way for you to get to know me a little better."

With her brush fully loaded, Robin got back to work, admiring the shade of paint she had chosen as it concealed the orange. "So...like I was saying, blue's my favorite color, so I've picked a few different shades for the apartment. This one's called Dolphin, which makes perfect sense given the color, though I guess it's as much gray as it is blue, but I like it. What about you?"

Robin scooched until she was directly under the bay window, and dipping her brush in the paint, she was about to continue when she noticed the small, brass keyway mortised into the trim just under the window seat. "Hey?" she said over her shoulder. "You wouldn't happen to know where the keys for these locks are, would you? The one in the bedroom won't open either."

Her hand had remained steady all the while Robin was rambling, but suddenly it was trembling again. Robin scowled and then she stiffened. She wasn't nervous. She was cold. Very, *very* cold.

"Shit," she whispered, her breath steaming in the air. "Here we go again."

Robin hunched her shoulders, and gripping the brush in hopes it wouldn't fly out of her hand, she waited for the hurricane named Isobel. One minute passed and then another, but it wasn't until Robin's legs began to cramp when she finally uncrossed them and dared to look behind her.

The room was empty...and growing warmer by the second.

Chapter Nineteen

Two days after Judy had left the island, there wasn't a muscle in Robin's body that didn't ache, and there wasn't one ache she didn't welcome.

With only the bathroom and spare bedroom left in the innkeeper's suite to paint, Robin was far ahead of her own schedule, so that morning she decided to do what she hadn't done in almost a year. She went for a run.

In her younger years, Robin had always used running to burn off excess energy, and as she grew older, it had become her form of meditation. Others would jog through parks or over trails with earbuds pumping in their favorite tunes, but the cadence of her steps was the only melody Robin had ever needed. Focused on the rhythm she created, she had written many a chapter in her head during those times, but this run wasn't about conjuring up characters or dialogue. Robin already had those. This run was about pummeling her self-doubt into submission and allowing her confidence as a writer to rise again. Somewhere in the wasteland of what another had created, R. C. Novak *did* exist, and Robin was going to find her, come hell or high water.

On the front porch, Robin stretched and flexed like she always did, and wearing her favorite pair of running shoes, she left the house and headed north up M-185. She started out slow, breathing in the cold, clean air as she admired the scenery as it crept by, and when she came upon a small plaque at the road's edge, Robin stopped. Reading the sign, she quickly made a mental note to Google Devil's Kitchen when she got home. Between the name and the fact it had been formed three hundred fifty million years ago, there had to be at least one story behind it, or maybe even two.

She continued on, and as she relaxed into a comfortable jog, Robin turned her thoughts to the reason she was running. On her laptop were two unpublished novels awaiting her return and no amount of painting, wallpapering, cleaning, renovating, or running would make them disappear. She had opened each manuscript more than once over the past year, praying they didn't contain what she knew they would, but Robin had never made it past a few pages, before she slammed her laptop closed and walked away. The author's voice was unrecognizable as her own. The words had been written by a woman who had been teetering on the edge, a woman careless of tense and grammar, she had just puked out the words taking up space in her head, all the while lying to herself that they actually made sense.

Her annoyance became her fuel, and Robin picked up the pace. Oblivious to the glorious autumn colors painting the forest in yellows, reds, and oranges, she sprinted up the road. The leaves littering the path crunched beneath her feet, disintegrating into dust as she pounded over them, but she didn't hear their demise. She had become single-minded, and the more Robin thought, the faster she ran.

***

"Hey, you," Robin said, placing the phone against her ear.

"I do have a name, you know?"

"Yes, I know. It's Declan Fitzgerald Kennedy," Robin said in the poshest accent she could muster. "But to me, you'll always be you."

Declan's old friend had returned, and his grin reached the state of Texas. "You sound good, Robbie. Really good."

"That's because I *feel* good," Robin said, stretching out her legs. "A little sore, but it's a good kind of sore."

"Holy crap, you got laid. *Wahoo!*"

Robin looked toward the ceiling as she shook her head. "Not that kind of sore, you pervert. I went for a run today."

"You should have gotten laid. It's way more fun."

"Yeah, well, there's no laying material around here at the moment, so a run had to do, and guess what I realized?"

"What?"

"You were right."

Declan held his chin high. "Seriously, Robbie, when am I not?"

"Well, I can remember a certain redhead—"

"All right. All right. Let's not go there," Declan said, his ears reddening at the mention of the dominatrix he once dated. "I still have a few scars left from that one."

"I know. I've seen them. I still can't believe you allowed her to—"

"Subject change!"

Robin rolled to her side on the sofa, laughing until she couldn't breathe.

The more Robin roared, the more Declan smiled, and it wasn't until she got herself under control when he spoke again. "So, what was I right about this time?"

Wiping the tears from her eyes, Robin sat up and cleared her throat. "When I first told you about coming up here, you said you thought I was running away, and you were right, but I wasn't running from Pam. I was running from writing."

"That makes no sense."

"That's because you didn't see the two books I wrote last year. Declan, they're crap, and the more I looked at them, the more I thought I had lost my mojo. They don't even sound like me, and there are a ton of mistakes. Stupid, *stupid* mistakes that an amateur wouldn't even make."

"Well, you did have a few things on your mind."

"Yes, I know, but I kept telling myself it didn't matter. I've never struggled to write. It's always come naturally to me, so I thought I—"

"Could just hammer out a few best-sellers without any problem?"

"Something like that."

"Do you know how stupid that sounds?"

"Trust me, *I know*! I was an idiot. I was so engrossed in all that other shit, I blocked everything else out. I totally forgot the basics. Whether it comes naturally or it doesn't, what we do takes work. It takes concentration and dedication, and a shitload of time."

"Robbie, that's Writing 101."

Robin jumped from the sofa. "I know," she said, waving her arm in the air. "And it's everything I wasn't doing because I wasn't focused. I wasn't committed. I was just angry...and I'm not anymore."

"No?"

"No," Robin said, sitting back down. "I ran eight miles today. I practically killed myself, and I'll be paying for it tomorrow, but I think I burned off the hurt and the regrets and the doubts. I *am* a good person, and I *am* a good writer."

"You're a fucking excellent writer," Declan growled. "Don't you ever forget that, Robin. Your books don't sell the way they sell because you write crap, and they sure as hell don't show up on all those bestseller lists just because people like your looks. They sell because you're good, and you think things through, and you have more dedication in your goddamned pinkie than I have in my whole body."

"That's a lie, and we both know it."

Declan's eyes began to twinkle. "Okay, so maybe I'm exaggerating."

"Typical author."

"Takes one to know one."

For a few moments, neither said a word. Their expressions were identical, and they both knew it.

"I love you," Robin said softly. "You know that—right?"

"Yeah, I have that effect on women. What can I say? I'm a chick magnet."

Robin's grin grew larger. "Don't you mean you *used* to be a chick magnet?"

"What? Are you saying I've lost my touch?"

"No, I'm saying if another woman comes near you, Natalia is going to have their hide."

"Oh yeah, well, there is that."

"How are things going with you two anyway? Still smooth sailing," Robin said, resting back against the sofa.

"Not a ripple on the water."

"Good to know."

"Um…speaking of ripples, I had one just the other day. My place was broken into."

"What?" Robin said, sitting up straight. "Why didn't you call me? Are you okay? Oh, my God, Declan, if you—"

"Relax, woman. I'm fine," Declan grumbled. "I wasn't even home when it happened. I went out to run an errand, and when I got back, the kitchen door was open, and my office was torn apart."

"Oh, shit."

"Not exactly what I said, but close," Declan said, pausing to take a sip of his drink. "Anyway, I called the police and filled out all the necessary paperwork, but that was basically useless."

"Why?"

"Because whoever broke in, didn't take anything."

"You're kidding."

"Nope. They didn't touch my computer or my printer, and my freaking Rolex was still sitting right smack-dab in the middle of the desk where I had left it. The only thing they did was empty out all the drawers from my desk and filing cabinet onto the floor."

"Why the hell would they do that?"

Robin didn't need to look at her phone to make sure the call hadn't dropped. She could hear Declan breathing, and the longer she waited, the more Robin sensed something was wrong.

"What aren't you telling me?" she said softly. "And don't even think you're going to blow me off because that's not going to happen."

Declan slumped back into the pile of pillows in the corner of his sofa, rubbing his stubble-covered chin as he stared at the ceiling. "Robbie...I think it might have been Pam."

It was almost a full minute before Robin found her voice. "Why do you say that?"

"Because ever since you left, any time I walk into one of our old haunts for a drink, the bartenders tell me the same thing. Pam's been in. She's asking everyone where you are, and when she doesn't get answers, she starts threatening, and when that doesn't work, Pam gets shit-faced or somehow gets higher than she was when she walked into the place. Some of the bars even flagged her."

"That doesn't mean she'd break into your home, Declan."

"She broke into yours, didn't she?"

Robin hung her head, remembering the damage the drunken woman had done to her garage when Robin had changed the locks. "Okay, so if it was Pam, what could she have possibly been looking for?"

"Your address, honey, but before you panic, the only place it's written down is in my phone, which never leaves my side, so don't worry."

"Honestly, Declan, I'm not panicked or worried. I'm upset that she may have trashed your place, and I'm pissed that she's hassling the people we used to hang out with, but if Pam shows up here, it will go way beyond those idiotic texts and emails she sent me. She'd seriously be breaking the restraining order then, and even she's not *that* stupid."

"You give her a hell of a lot more credit than I do," Declan said with a snort. "All I see is a bitch with a bone that refuses to let go of it."

"Did you just call me a bone?"

"Well, you are a bit on the skinny side."

"Fuck you, Declan."

An instant later, Robin was yanking the phone away from her ear as Declan's loud, rumbling guffaw erupted from her mobile. Enjoying the sound, Robin waited until he settled down before placing the phone against her ear. "It's good to know I can still make you laugh."

"Oh, Robbie, there's no denying that," Declan said, wiping the tears from his eyes. "And speaking of knowing, *I'd* like to know when you're planning to open those manuscripts and get back to work?"

"Probably next week."

"Why wait that long?"

"Because I still have two rooms left to paint in my apartment and the stuff I had in storage is being delivered next Wednesday. That's only going to take care of the bedroom, so tomorrow I need to go back to the mainland to see about buying some living room furniture. And, if that's not enough, I also need to look into getting a new countertop for my kitchen and maybe even replace a couple of the appliances. They're really old."

"Don't look now, Robbie, but it sounds to me like someone is putting down some roots."

Robin's shoulders sagged. "Is that okay?"

"Of course, it's okay, kiddo. I'm happy for you. Hell, I'm ecstatic. You're starting to sound like your old self again, and I'm not going to lie, for a while there, I'd thought I lost you."

"For a while there, I thought I'd lost me, too."

Again, they grew quiet, one paling as memories flooded his mind while the other did everything in her power not to reflect.

"So..." Declan said, rubbing the back of his neck to release the tension brought on by the past. "Now that you've decided you're a writer, have you given any more thought to finding someone to help run that place for you?"

Robin opened her mouth and then shut it just as quickly. When it came to secrets, at least between each other, they didn't have any. It wasn't a conscious decision on either's part, but over the years as their trust grew, their lips loosened. She knew about his loves and his failures, and he knew about hers...including a crush on a particular teacher.

Declan pulled his phone away long enough to ensure their connection hadn't dropped. "Robbie, you still there?"

Robin scraped her fingers through her hair, thankful Declan couldn't see her rapidly reddening cheeks. "Oh...uh...yeah, I'm still here. As a matter of fact, I think...um...I think I've already found someone."

"Hey, that's great!"

"Yeah, I think...I think she and I will make a good fit. Every time we get together, it seems like the ideas just keep coming," Robin said, immediately scrunching up her face at the sexual innuendo only she could hear.

"Hey, anyone who can get the old juices flowing is a winner in my book."

Robin inwardly groaned. "Exactly," she forced out as she glanced at her watch. "Listen, I'm going to let you go. I still have some things to do before I call it a night. Okay?"

"Sure thing. Take care and good luck with that new lady. I hope it's a match made in heaven."

"Thanks," Robin managed to squeak before ending the call, and dropping her phone on the sofa, she buried her heated face in her hands. "No worries on the old juices, Declan," she mumbled into her palms. "No worries at all."

***

Robin stared at the two overwhelmed laundry baskets in her bedroom and knew she had avoided the inevitable long enough. If she didn't start laundry tonight, she'd be going commando tomorrow. She'd done it before in sleek outfits and running clothes, but in jeans, the damn center seam always rubbed her the wrong way—literally.

A minute later, Robin set the baskets down long enough to flip on the basement light, but before she could pick her laundry back up, she heard a series of pops. The lighting in the basement dimmed dramatically, as did Robin's patience. "*Seriously?*"

Robin stood there, trying to mentally persuade the bulbs to come back on as she glared at the ominous shadows awaiting her at the bottom of the stairs. She tapped her fingers against the door jamb as her eyes traveled from her laundry to the basement and then back again.

She had sensed Isobel's presence once or twice over the past few days, the temperature in a room suddenly dropping or a chilly breeze appearing out of nowhere, reminding Robin she wasn't alone, but there hadn't been another windy exhibition of anger since the painting incident. Then again, did Robin really want to tempt fate by going upstairs to use those machines? She was tired. It was late, and she needed to get some sleep. Sleep that wouldn't be interrupted by a ghost's temper tantrum in the form of gale-force winds if Robin intruded on what Isobel apparently believed to be her own personal space.

"Yeah. I'm thinking no."

Stepping around the baskets, Robin went into the big kitchen, rummaging through all her purchases until she returned with light bulbs in one hand and a flashlight in the other. Putting both on top of her laundry, she took a deep breath, picked up the baskets and made her way down the stairs.

Robin winced with every step, her muscles groaning in time with the old wooden treads under her feet. She had put her body through the mill today, pushing it further than she should have, but it was good to know she could still run. It was good to know running could still clear her mind, and it was good to know...she had more light bulbs upstairs.

Where once there were four lit bulbs, now the only one remaining was hanging over the washer and dryer, and it had to be the lowest wattage available on the market. Robin set down the baskets, and gathering what she needed, she turned on the flashlight and carefully made her way toward the workbench. She knew there was a light fixture somewhere in that area, and waving the beacon back and forth across the ceiling, she inched along until the burned-out bulb came into view. With one good stretch, she reached it, and a minute later Robin was blinking away the spots caused by a hundred watts of power.

It didn't take long before Robin managed to replace the remaining bulbs, and once her first load of laundry was in the washer, she was about to go back upstairs when something caught her eye. On the back of the post holding up the ladders was a light switch, one that had been hidden in the shadows until now.

With nothing but darkness filling whatever was left of the basement, Robin paused for a second before she went over and flipped on the switch. She expected to see a bit of clutter and maybe some old furniture she'd need to step around, but when the rest of the lighting around the basement sprang to life, Robin said the first word that came into her head. "Wow." Not only was the basement as large as the rooms above it, other than a few cobwebs dangling from some of the joists, but it was almost as well-kept as the house had been on the day she'd moved in.

There was no chaos created by boxes stacked haphazardly here and there, with contents overflowing their confines. There was no hodgepodge of mismatched tables or chairs piled high along the walls, waiting to be discarded or refinished, and where Robin expected to see little, grimy windows around the perimeter, their sills no doubt littered with dead insects, she found herself admiring ones perfectly framed by flowery kitchen curtains with nary a bug in sight.

In the center of the cellar was a large work table, its plywood surface speckled with drips of paint long since dried, and going over to it, Robin knelt by its side. Underneath were cubicles holding a collection of old paint cans in varying sizes, and when she saw another cubby filled with a stack of roller trays and at least a dozen brushes, she sighed. "That would have saved me some money."

As she stood back up, Robin groaned as the muscles in her thighs announced themselves again, and grimacing at the ache, she made her way slowly around the table toward a section of the stone foundation that had been cut away. As soon as steps came into view, her curiosity was satisfied, and feeling no need to investigate the abyss that was the outside entrance to the basement, Robin turned around...and gasped.

The far wall, easily the length of the dining room and entry combined, was entirely filled with shelves, each containing boxes and totes labeled with the names of holidays. A few called out the Federal ones, Memorial Day and Labor Day deserved of only one, while the Fourth of July warranted three. Halloween and Thanksgiving fared better, and Christmas was over the top. In an instant, Robin knew she had more in common with her aunt than she realized.

Unable to stop herself, Robin went over and opened one of the plastic totes. She smiled at the assortment of Christmas decorations piled inside for a moment before closing the lid, and stepping back, she scanned the rows again. She was hoping for something labeled Mementos or Photographs that would help to satisfy her curiosity about an aunt she hardly knew, but the longer she looked, the more her posture drooped. If it didn't have to do with a holiday, it was not going to be found here.

Abandoning all hope Adele had left anything behind even remotely personal, Robin turned to leave until she saw something in the far corner of the basement. She hesitated before moving toward it, and the closer she got, the more Robin's brow began to furrow. Concealing an area roughly the size of a small bedroom was heavy black curtains running from floor to ceiling.

Over the centuries, the genres in literature have adapted to the times. In Ancient Greece, the stories penned by authors and playwrights initially fell under the headings of poetry, drama, and prose, and as years passed, subgenres were born. Poetry was divided into epic, lyric, and dramatic, and dramas began to include both comedy and tragedy, its division based on the Greek plays of old. However, when it came to prose, the style in which the author wrote in sentences, paragraphs, and chapters, its subcategories expanded and expanded, and expanded again until eventually it became known as fiction.

Fiction, a story based on imagination rather than fact, is the most popular form of written entertainment in the modern world. Like its predecessors, poetry and drama, which it eventually consumed, it too has its subgenres. There are short stories and fairy tales, realistic fiction and fantasy, romance and horror, science fiction and westerns, thrillers and suspense...and then there are mysteries.

A mystery, by definition, is fiction involving a crime and its eventual solution, and Robin's passion for the genre had been ignited in her youth by Nancy Drew and the Hardy Boys. Poring over the pages, she would become the detective intent on cracking the case, but it wasn't long before her interest in solving the mysteries gave way to her interest in creating her own.

Robin's technique when it came to writing a mystery novel was sound and eventually proved to be award-winning. Her goal was always to take the reader on a ride they wouldn't forget. Much like the roller coasters she loathed, Robin incorporated in her plots unforeseen twists, abrupt turns, and sudden drops. However, unlike some mystery writers, who wouldn't unveil much-needed clues until the final few chapters, Robin always gave her readers all the information they would need to solve the crime. However, by weaving her words carefully, most were left scratching their heads until the last chapter was read.

The protagonists in Robin's stories were always strong, intelligent women. They'd approach the crime and the clues with clear heads, using logic and science as their methodology. They wouldn't shriek in terror when a dead body was discovered, or lose their lunch over a decomposing corpse. Their heart rate rarely increased at the first sign of trouble, and their palms remained dry when they entered darkened alleyways or abandoned warehouses. They were calm, cool, and collected, but fixated on the black curtain in front of her, Robin wasn't calm. She wasn't cool, and collected was still up for grabs.

Suddenly, Robin no longer appreciated the imagery her mind could create. Visions of rotting cadavers, skeletons dangling from nooses, and assorted body parts stuffed into little glass jars swirled in her head, and taking a step backward, she shook off the shiver that had just run down her spine.

Robin rubbed the back of her neck as she stared at the drapes. Her mind began to wander again, and this time it took her to a place that caused a different reaction. Decaying bodies were one thing, but what if Adele hadn't been hiding the dearly departed? What if she'd been hiding her proclivity for bondage?

As soon as the thought crossed Robin's mind, she laughed out loud, the few seconds of mirth erasing her worries in an instant. Her aunt wasn't a serial killer, and if she had possessed a penchant for leather, gags, and bindings, it would be a secret Robin would take to her grave. She filled her lungs as she stepped up to the wall of black fabric, deciding it was time to rip off the Band-Aid. She flung open the drapes...and a nanosecond later, Robin's scream shook loose the dust clinging to the joists above her head.

Chapter Twenty

Pam Burton sat on her sofa with her laptop balanced on her legs as she took another sip of coffee the shade of buttermilk. She glanced at her watch and smirked. It was still too early to make the phone call, and after waiting for four days, Pam wasn't about to jump the gun now. Her eyes returned to the screen, and as she clicked from one page to the next and then back again, her lips twisted into a snarl as she viewed the photos of floral finery. Throughout her life, Pam had professed to like flowers, to appreciate their beauty, their fragrance, and all the sentiments connected with them. She was a woman, and it was expected, but flowers were merely another ploy in Pam's repertoire. Another trick she'd use to deceive, she'd bestow her latest victim with long-stemmed beauties, for what better way to prove her love. After all, it worked in the movies.

The oldest of four daughters born to a construction laborer and a waitress, for the first few years of Pam's life, she shared her parents with no one. She was the center of their tiny world in their tiny trailer, and while her surroundings would change as they moved from one state to another for her father to find work, Pam didn't care. Her playmates were just that, trailer park children who came and went with the rise and fall of the sun, so leaving them behind caused not one flicker of emotion to appear on her chubby face. There would be more at the next place, more clueless little children anxious to find a new friend to play with, and Pam would easily slip into that role...at least for a little while.

All was right in Pam's little world until one summer morning her mother informed the four-year-old she was going to be a sister, and in an instant, Pam's attitude toward her parents changed to one of repugnance. She didn't want to share her life with a stranger, with some annoying, smelly baby demanding attention with every cry, coo, or gurgle that erupted from its splotchy, cherub face. She wanted things just as they were, and Pam made that blatantly clear. In the first of what would become dozens of tantrums she would throw over the coming years, she flailed and wailed, tossing out all the bluffs and demands her infantile mind could come up with. She threatened. She pleaded. She promised, and she lost.

As her mother's belly grew, Pam was fawned over by her parents as they tried to convince her all would be okay. They treated her to ice cream, and stuffed animals bought at the dollar store, and it was at that time a ritual was born. A ritual that eventually provided Pam the knowledge about all the emotions she did not possess.

A fan of romance, when Pam's mother wasn't tending to her firstborn's demands, she'd spend her afternoons reading gothic love stories and her nights, watching old Hollywood classics on a television, atop which were rabbit ears wrapped in foil.

One night, after an unusually lengthy tantrum, to calm her four-year-old daughter down, Pam's mother placed her on the sofa, turned on the TV, and introduced her child to movies. Immediately, Pam quieted. These weren't cartoons, stupid little animations of odd-shaped characters with whiny voices. These were real. These were snippets of someone's life she was watching, and she was enthralled. Her picture books taught her colors and shapes, but movies...movies could teach her so much more.

Over the next several years, her parents would continue to produce offspring until eventually, Pam had three younger sisters, but she refused to allow their existence to interrupt her life. She still threw tantrums, outbursts of anger supposedly based on her siblings' annoyingly screechy voices as they cackled and tittered their way through their days, but at night, her obsession with films and eventually books silenced her hatred for her family.

Movies and paperbacks became her dictionaries, explaining with words and images concepts as foreign as breathing water instead of air. Sympathy, the feeling of pity or sorrow for someone else's problems, seemed preposterous. In her young and rapidly warping mind, Pam had enough problems of her own without caring about another's misfortunes.

Did they have three annoying siblings living with them in a tiny trailer in an RV park overrun with weeds, beer-bellied men, and women prancing around in skimpy outfits two sizes too small? Were their clothes purchased at second-hand stores? Did they eat oatmeal every morning for breakfast, or gobble down pasta and potatoes every night of the week because it was cheap, and it went far? Those were the only things important to her, so movies taught Pam what she had to do in order to *pretend* to be sympathetic. Acknowledge the pain, appear concerned, offer condolences, and perhaps when she got older she could even deliver a home-cooked meal...and sympathy would be shown.

The idea of empathy was farcical to Pam. To be empathic required putting aside her own views for those of another, and to not only listen but to also *accept* that another person's perspective was as viable as her own. That would have required Pam to admit she was wrong about something, and Pam was never wrong about anything. Luckily, her mother's collection of romance novels contained stories that gave Pam a clue as to what she had to do. A headstrong heroine, beautiful and svelte, meets a debonair swashbuckler, athletic and brash, but their views are as distant as the North and South Poles, so a battle begins. Neither wants to listen. Neither wants to understand. They only want to judge, but once they put aside their egos and open their ears, their hearts would follow, and they would live happily ever after. That gave Pam the answer she was looking for. Behind false validation and quiet nods of understanding, she could appear empathic even though she didn't give a damn about anyone else's opinion except her own.

By far, the hardest emotion for Pam to comprehend was love. Without a doubt, it was the most common four-letter word appearing in all the books and movies. It was even bandied about by her parents and siblings, so she had learned to respond in kind, but her response was mere mimicry.

Love is often explained as an intense feeling for someone or something. It can be as inconsequential as adoring that first cup of coffee in the morning or as monumental as devotion so undying and unyielding, countries fall in the name of it, lives are lost because of it, and families divide as a result of it. And while Pam understood the enjoyment she got from eating her favorite ice cream, to have a feeling so intense for another that nothing else mattered left a foul taste in her mouth. It was self-deprecating and beneath her to ever put someone before herself, to downplay her superiority and intelligence simply because of *love*? What could love ever possibly bring her?

It would take several years before Pam began to grasp the potency of the emotion called love, but by the time she reached her early twenties, her playbook was glutted with tidbits gathered from novels and films. Like scraps of meat, she devoured every morsel, chewing on the perception each would give until they were forever etched in her twisted mind.

Diamonds were the most influential, but far too expensive for Pam to ever give to another, so she settled on the usual suspects, most of which could be purchased in dollar stores or markets if she were lucky. Greeting cards gushing sonnets were perfect if she wanted to produce tears of understanding and forgiveness. Chocolates, dark and easy on the palate, would ensure her a night of rapture when their sweetness was blended with wine, and then, of course, there were flowers.

Each variety held in its petals underlying meanings, and Pam had memorized them all. Calla Lilies symbolized beauty as did the vibrant amaryllis, while asters embodied patience and chrysanthemums, fidelity and joy. The iris signified wisdom, and the snapdragon, graciousness and strength, but the flower that had always worked to Pam's advantage, exemplifying the unmistakable expression she was pretending to convey, was the red rose. Its bouquet was sweet and delicate and its color, dark and sensual, and with a dozen of those in her hand, Pam knew between the roses and the sugary little promises she would have to whisper, she'd get her way. It was a skill she had honed to a razor's edge in her youth.

Lessons are learned by trial and error, and throughout Pam's childhood, she learned some invaluable ones. Scream loud, and you will get heard. Threaten to tell on your siblings, and they become your servants, and by weaving the most ingenious of lies, you can almost guarantee in getting anything you want. But Pam had learned other lessons too, the ones taught in school which she absorbed like a sponge, so by the time she headed off to community college, Pam knew how to read, write, multiply, divide...*and* manipulate.

Pam slurped down what was left of her coffee and looked at her watch again. It was five minutes to four, so it was time to do what Pam did best. She had spent every night that week studying the flower shop's website. She knew what they offered. She knew their hours. She knew they weren't open on weekends, and if their employees were anything like most of the blue-collar peasants in the world, they were looking forward to their upcoming weekend. A last-minute call would delay their escape, and they'd do and say anything to end it as quickly as possible. Picking up her phone, Pam tapped in the number and waited for the call to go through.

"Thank you for calling The Flower Patch. How can I help you?"

"Oh, thank *God*," Pam blurted. "Look, I know you're about to close, but if I don't get these flowers ordered my boss is going to kill me!"

Fiona Phillips pulled the phone away from her ear for a second, her eyes widening at the dread in the caller's tone. "Calm down, dear," she said softly. "I'm sure it's not that bad."

"You don't know my boss. He's a tyrant, and if he finds out I didn't order these flowers, he's going to fire me."

"He will do no such thing," Fiona said as she pressed the power button on her computer. "And we're open until I say we aren't. Just give me a second while my computer warms up, and we'll get your order placed. How's that?"

"Oh, I can't thank you enough. You're a life saver!"

"I'm just trying to brighten the world, one petal at a time."

Pam curled her lip. She had seen their motto on the website, and it was all she could do to keep the bile from rising in her throat. "That's so sweet."

"Thank you," Fiona said, tapping away on the keyboard. "And now that this goofy thing has finally decided to work, we can get your flowers ordered. Have you ever ordered from us before?"

"Yes...um...a few weeks ago. While I was out sick, my boss managed to place an order all by himself, but now that I'm back, it's beneath him to do it again. Typical man. If the pay weren't so good, I'd tell him where he could put this job."

"I see," Fiona said quietly. "And his name would be?"

"Oh, gosh, I'm sorry. It's Declan. Declan Kennedy," Pam said, glancing at the credit card statement in her hand. "He placed the order in late October."

"I found it. The Sun and Roses bouquet delivered to a Miss Robin Novak."

A sneer snaked its way across Pam's face. "That's it."

"All right, so what arrangement would you like to order now?"

"The Harvest Sunset centerpiece."

"Oh, that's lovely," Fiona said as she entered the information for the most expensive flower arrangement she had. "And that centerpiece comes in three sizes. Do you know—"

"He wants the biggest. Like I said, he's a typical man. The bigger, the better."

Fiona arched one sliver-thin eyebrow. "Yes, well, I have the order entered. Should I assume this is being delivered to the same person? Miss Novak?"

"That's right."

"Good. Well, we have her information, so all I need is a credit card number, and we'll be good to go."

Pam had planned to call back on Monday to cancel the order so it wouldn't appear on Declan's credit card, but this was even better. This was perfect. Letting out an exaggerated sigh, Pam said, "Oh, darn."

"Is that a problem?"

"He's already left for the day. I guess he thought you'd have it on record."

"I'm sorry, but once the orders are processed through the bank, we destroy all credit card information. In this day and age, you can't be too careful."

Superiority oozed from every pore Pam owned, and puffing out her chest, she said, "Yeah, I guess that's true, but you know what? I have an idea. Can you keep the order until next week? That way, you already have all the information."

"I can do that. I'll just put it in my pending file."

"Great, and while I have you on the phone would you mind confirming Miss Novak's address? That woman seems to move every other week. I just want to make sure it matches what I have."

"Of course," Fiona said, looking back at her computer. "It's 7760 Main Street on Mackinac."

***

Judy felt as if she was in a vacuum being sucked back through time, through birthdays and holidays, and marriages and wakes, for this was the room where her family had always gathered. Around a lengthy table of oak, its edges now worn and its surface faded and scratched, presents were opened, candles on cakes were extinguished, toasts were made, and the fond memories of the dearly departed were shared.

The old Windsor bow back was still as uncomfortable as it had been in her youth, and shifting in the chair, Judy looked around the room. The walls were as beige as they'd ever been and family photographs filled every void available like they had done throughout her life. The doilies her grandmother had tatted still lined the shelves of the hutch and showcased on top of them was her mother's prized China, the vintage porcelain having never been used, and Judy doubted it ever would be.

The sound of silverware clinking got her attention, and it was all Judy could do not to laugh. In her mind was the voice of her father, bellowing that children were to be seen and not heard at the dinner table. He had always believed silence was golden and Patrick had not fallen far from his father's tree, and this was his house now.

Patrick had just turned twenty-two when he, along with his siblings and mother, stood beside a hospital bed, listening as their father took his last, ragged breath. It was a time of tears and mourning, and countless casseroles being delivered by neighbors, but life does go on...and it did.

No one questioned when Patrick assumed the role of patriarch. He, like his brother, Doug, had been groomed to one day take over the family business, so Patrick lost no time in making the business *and* the family home his own. His mother didn't balk. She welcomed her eldest and his new bride, Louise, with open arms, and when Doug graduated college two years later, he, too, moved back home, taking his place at his brother's side.

Neither ever wanted to do anything else. Since they had first walked the orchard with their father, his plans became ingrained in them and the future he imagined soon became theirs. Their family would forever be together. Grandparents, parents, and children would work side-by-side just as they always had, creating a legacy to be handed down again and again, but castles in the air don't always come to fruition. Astronauts become accountants. Firefighters become financial planners. Ballerinas become brain surgeons, and daughters of orchardists sometimes become teachers.

If it had been up to her older brothers, Judy would never have gone to college. Patrick and Doug adored their little sister, but like their father, they believed women to be the weaker sex. So, in the kitchen one night a few months after their father had died, they rattled off reasons to their mother as to why their little sister couldn't possibly go to college. How could she get along without them to protect her? Who would help her with decisions much too complicated for her to understand, and when young men came calling, whispering promises of love and forever after, how could little Judy possibly comprehend their true, crotch-driven intentions?

Harriet Lawton was no fool, and she saw through her sons' smokescreens in an instant. There was no doubt in her mind they truly loved their sister, but this had nothing to do with love. This had to do with her husband's pipe dream, an absurd notion she had had to listen to for nearly thirty years, and it was one she had never agreed with. Children aren't supposed to blindly follow the paths carved out for them by their parents. They're supposed to discover their own passions, chase after their own desires, and create their *own* dreams, and Harriet knew her daughter's.

How many times had they whispered in the kitchen, Harriet drying the dishes Judy had washed while she hung on every word her daughter spoke? Words about furthering her education and going out into the world made Judy's dimples grow large, and she'd prattle on about wanting to be a high school coach. The values instilled by sports equally as important as those found in classrooms, Judy wanted to mold not only young bodies but young minds as well. To teach them commitment and responsibility, teamwork and friendship, and pride in not only themselves, but in others as well, Judy wanted to be a part of making future generations of women stronger than she knew she'd ever be.

Well-versed on all her children, Harriet knew that Patrick and Doug could be bullies at times and more often than not, they did get their way for her husband's opinion was the only one that had ever mattered. She thanked God her youngest was nothing like them, and she knew there was no way in hell Judy was going to end up like she did. She wanted her daughter to have a better life, a life outside the orchard and the market and the kitchen. A life of new and different. A life of freedom and equality, and a life overflowing with all the opportunities an education could provide. It was the one and only time Harriet stood up to Patrick and Doug. By the time she was done, they slunk from the room with their tails tucked between their legs as she strolled out, her head higher than she had ever held it before.

Later that year, as the leaves began to turn, Harriet waved as Judy and Doug drove off to college. She paid no attention to the scowl painted on the face of her oldest son. At her hip, was her youngest, and draping her arm over Eric's shoulders, Harriet pulled him closer. Her eyes grew glassy as she thought about how quickly the years had passed. In what seemed like no time at all, Patrick and Doug had become men, and Judy had grown into a woman, and Harriet's face softened with a secret smile. She had just given her daughter the one thing her sons had always taken for granted. Judy had finally been given a choice, and Harriet knew her daughter had chosen wisely.

For as long as their mother was alive, Patrick and Doug said not one word to Judy about moving home. They offered lackluster congratulations when she graduated college and feigned excitement when she took a teaching position in Indianapolis. When she took another a few years later, moving over a hundred miles away to Monroeville, they hid their annoyance behind thin-lipped grins, and when she married, they begrudgingly sent her gifts. The only time her brothers were honest about their excitement was when Judy came home for a visit. They'd welcome her with open arms and hugs that never seemed to end, for she was finally where *they* thought she should be, and all was well...until she would leave to go back to her own life.

It wasn't until after their mother passed when Judy's brothers' animosity bubbled to the surface. Whenever Judy visited, they began putting demands on her, dictating she needed to be home more often. Her place was in the market behind the register for that had always been *her* place, and the orchard was as much her birthright as theirs. *That* is what their father wanted. *That* was what they wanted, and for her not to do so would dishonor her father's memory.

In the beginning, Judy was amused by her brothers' preposterous ideas, and she shrugged them off with a laugh before climbing into her car and making her way back to Mackinac. She had no idea that her brothers' sermons would be repeated each and *every* time she visited.

For the past five minutes, Judy had been staring at her plate, absorbed in her own thoughts and memories, but she suddenly noticed the room seemed even quieter. She looked up and found that all eyes were now on her, and Patrick, sitting at the head of the table, appeared as if his face had turned into a tomato.

Years in the sun had done its damage to Patrick. His once handsome profile was now etched with lines, deep and craggy, deserved of someone twenty years his senior. His love of fried chicken could be seen around his waist, and his enthusiasm for hard cider had colored his cheeks and nose permanently red, accentuating the blemishes left behind from his adolescent acne. His hair had receded and grayed, and the wire-rimmed glasses he once only used occasionally, now never left his face, and at that moment, he was peering over them at his sister.

"I'm...I'm sorry," Judy said, glancing around the table. "Did I miss something?"

"I was just saying how nice it was to have you home. You didn't seem to miss a step in the market these past few days."

"Well, it's not like the steps change, Pat," Judy said, putting down her fork. "Other than a few prices, everything's the same as it always is."

Patrick pushed his glasses up his nose. Crossing his arms, he rested back in his chair. "So...is your room comfortable?"

As if on cue, Louise and Doug's wife, Beverly, rose from their chairs, gathered up as many dishes as they could hold and disappeared into the kitchen like Siamese twins.

Tickled by the sight of the two women making their escape, Judy shook her head and then tossed her napkin on the table. "Well, Pat, since it's the same room I use every year, *and* it's the same room I grew up in, why wouldn't it be comfortable?"

"There's no reason to get snippy," Patrick said, reaching for his cider. "I just asked a—"

The blast of a ferryboat horn suddenly filled the room, cutting Patrick off in mid-sentence and causing both Doug and Judy to jump. With a snicker, Judy got to her feet and scrambled to get her cell phone out of her back pocket. Glancing at the display, she accepted the call. "Hello."

"Hi, it's Robin."

"Hi," Judy said as she slid her chair under the table. "Um...could you give me a second?"

"Sure. No problem."

Robin could hear voices in the background, and while the words were garbled, someone appeared to be shouting. Several seconds later, she heard some rustling and then what sounded like a door opening and closing.

"You still there?" Judy said, cradling the phone between her shoulder and ear while she zipped up her jacket.

"Yeah, but if I'm interrupting, I can always call back at another time. I just needed to hear a friendly voice."

"Are you kidding? You just saved me from a fate *almost* worse than death, and what do you mean about a friendly voice? Is something wrong?"

Robin inwardly sighed. Even though she was inches away from sitting down in the parlor, Judy's question was all it took for Robin to do an about-face and return the way she came. She strode back to the well-lit dining room, peeked inside, and then spun around. "Um…no," Robin said, heading toward the parlor again. "Not really."

"Not really?"

Robin could feel her cheeks beginning to heat as she nibbled on her lip. "Forget I said anything."

"Not until you tell me what's wrong."

"There's nothing wrong." Robin threw herself onto the sofa, and in an instant, the muscles in her thighs reminded her of the damage she had done to them. They also gave her the subject change she was looking for. "I...um...I got it into my head to start running again, and I'm just a little sore. No worries. It'll pass."

Judy wasn't at all surprised to hear Robin liked to run. She guessed the woman was a size six, if that, and since meeting her a few weeks earlier, Judy had seen Robin wear at least three different pairs of well-worn, high-end running shoes. Still, Robin's tone seemed off. "Are you sure?"

"Positive, and besides, by the sound of it, there's something wrong with you. What's this about a fate worse than death?"

"*Almost* worse than death," Judy said as she took a seat in one of the rockers on the front porch. "And it was just my brothers, being my brothers."

Robin's eyebrows squished together, and feeling like she was reading one of her own novels, she replayed Judy's words in her head, striving to solve the mystery. After a few seconds, she gave up. "Um...I feel like I need to buy a vowel here."

Judy threw back her head and laughed, rocking so hard in the chair it slammed against the wall. "Oh God, I can't tell you how much I needed that," she said, sliding the rocker away from the clapboard siding.

"Glad I could help," Robin said, her face turning rosy at the sound of Judy's laughter. "But I still need that vowel, if you don't mind."

"Remember how I told you Pat and Doug are always trying to get me to move home?"

"Yeah."

"Well, Pat was about to start something at the dinner table when you called, so you saved me from yet another lecture."

Robin's smile wavered. "Okay, so maybe this isn't my place, but can't you just tell them to knock it off?"

"I've tried, but they only hear what they want to hear. It's easier to let them ramble on than to get into a full-blown argument. One, I know, I'd never win."

Robin unconsciously dipped her head in agreement. She had looked the other way with Pam more times than she could remember only because arguing would have been pointless. It's hard to disagree with someone who's always right. "I get that."

"You do?"

"Yeah. Been there."

Robin's voice had sunk to a whisper, and even though Judy had wanted to ask, she didn't. For almost a minute, neither woman said a word.

"So...how's the weather?" Judy said, instantly rolling her eyes at the question.

Asking about the weather was one of Robin's go-to questions whenever conversations stalled. It was lame, right up there with 'what's your sign,' but it was a surefire way of keeping a chat moving, especially one you didn't want to end. Unable to stop herself, Robin read more into Judy's innocent query, and her heart doubled in size. "It's good, but the nights are getting really chilly. I have a funny feeling my tank tops and shorts are never going to see the light of day again."

"Oh, don't be ridiculous," Judy said, grinning. "There're a few weeks in the summer you'll be able to wear them."

"A few weeks!"

Judy laughed. "Okay, maybe more than a few."

"Then I guess it's a good thing I stocked up on more winter clothes yesterday during my shopping spree in Petoskey."

"You went on a shopping spree for clothes?"

"No, for furniture," Robin said, relaxing back into the cushions. "But one thing led to another, and I ended up spending the entire day going from one store to another. By the time I got back, I had to run, so I didn't miss the last ferry."

"Been *there*, done that," Judy said, chuckling. "And correct me if I'm wrong, but it sounds like you still had a fun day."

The sound of Judy's throaty chuckle affected Robin much like a glass of fine wine, warming her body and lowering her inhibitions and her guard. "I did," she breathed into the phone. "Except it would have been much funner if you'd been there. I missed you."

As soon as the words slipped from her lips, Robin wished her name was Hoover. Squeezing her eyes shut, she waited for Judy to respond. As the soundless seconds ticked by, the only thing taking up space in Robin's mind was one word, and it kept repeating. Stupid. Stupid. *Stupid*!

"Is funner even a word?"

Robin's eyes flew open, and her body sagged as she let out the breath she'd been holding. "No, but just go with it. Okay?"

"All right, and...and I wish I could have been there. I think I would have enjoyed myself. Rain check?"

"Definitely," Robin said, popping to attention on the sofa. "I've got plenty more to buy."

"Something tells me you like shopping a little too much."

"There's no such thing as 'too much.'"

"Uh oh."

"What? Something wrong?"

"Other than the fact my employer is a compulsive shopper, absolutely nothing."

"I'm not a compulsive shopper, and I'm not your employer."

"Huh?"

"What I mean is, this thing with Safe Harbor is going to be a team effort between you and me, and I don't want you ever to think you work for me."

"But I do."

"No, you don't. As far as I'm concerned, you're my business partner. Okay?"

"Robin, I haven't contributed any money toward—"

"You're going to contribute your time and your energy, so stop arguing. You won't win."

"Is that so?"

Robin couldn't contain her grin. "Yes, that's so. I want you to be my partner, Judy." A second later, Robin's eyes flew open wide. "I-I mean, business...business partner," she quickly said as she pounded her fist on the sofa. "I want you to be my *business* partner."

"Are you going to keep repeating that until I say yes?"

"If I have to."

"Then I guess I'll let you put this win in your column since my fingers are starting to freeze."

"Oh crap, I'm sorry. I didn't know you were outside."

"Don't worry about it. I just forgot my gloves."

"Then go inside and get warm."

"I will," Judy said, and getting up, she looked through one of the glass sidelights by the door. "I just want to make sure the coast is clear first. That way, I can make a mad dash upstairs before anyone sees me."

"Is it?"

Before Judy could answer, her phone beeped in her ear. Looking at the screen, she sighed. "Robin, my battery is about to die, too."

"That's okay," Robin said, glancing at her watch. "I have a few things I need to finish around here before I hit the hay anyway."

"Call me in a few days? I promise to keep my phone charged."

An unstoppable smile made its way across Robin's face. "Absolutely."

"Great," Judy chirped. "So...good night, Robin."

"Good night, Judy. Sweet dreams, when you get there."

***

When Robin awoke the next morning, she did it with a groan. She'd been sleeping on the sofa for over a month, and the once comfortable cushions were no longer. After her trip to Petoskey on Friday, she had spent most of Saturday meeting with contractors about the kitchen and the unfinished shower, so as Robin got to her feet, she already was planning her day. First was to set up the coffee maker, second was to visit the bathroom, third was to feed Fred and Ginger, and fourth was to finish what she had started on Thursday.

An hour later, dressed in her painting clothes, Robin opened the door to the spare bedroom and repeated the process she had used in the living room and bedroom. She took down the curtains and rods and placed them in the appropriately-colored garbage bags, and then pulling a screwdriver from her back pocket, the drapery hardware was next. Moving around the room, all the covers for switches and outlets were removed until the only thing left was the bookcase in the corner. Unembellished and boxy, it seemed out of place, its plainness in direct contrast to the rest of the house. She scratched her head, wondering what color she'd paint it when she noticed a gap around the edges. Taking hold of a shelf, she gave it a tug, and her eyes widened when the bookcase easily slid toward her. "What the hell?"

Robin carefully inched the unit out of the alcove, and when she peeked behind it, her mouth dropped open. The niche wasn't a niche at all. It was three times deeper than the bookcase and on the left was another door. "Not again."

For almost a minute, Robin stared at the door. A few days earlier, she had whipped aside black drapes to reveal what they had hidden, and as she remembered that night, she rubbed the back of her neck. The last thing

Robin wanted was to uncover another secret, especially if it was anything like the one she had found in the basement.

Robin looked over her shoulder at the door leading out of the room and then back at the one she had yet to open. With an escape plan now in place, she cleared her throat, held her breath, and placed her hand on the knob. Freeing it from its latch, she jumped backward as the door swung open.

Cool, musty air enveloped Robin in an instant, and dust particles, released from their confines, floated around her like weightless stars. She took a hesitant step and then another, her jaw dropping open as her eyes followed the ascent of a narrow, winding set of stairs.

Robin's curiosity went into overdrive. She didn't know where to look first. So many things were grabbing her attention, but something on the fourth step held it. In the middle of the tread was a twist tie and within its loops were two tiny brass keys.

Chapter Twenty-One

"I heard that Orson Feeney is back in town."

Judy glanced at Eric, who looked back at her with the same wrinkled-brow expression. It was the first time Patrick had spoken at the dinner table since Sunday. With a shrug, Judy decided to take the bait. "Who?"

"Your old beau," Patrick said, pushing his chair back a few inches from the table. "He's a lawyer now, and he's divorced."

"I have no idea who you're talking about," Judy said with a slight shake of her head.

"Typical woman," Patrick said, balling up his napkin and tossing it on the table. "Breaks a guy's heart and doesn't even remember him."

"What are you—" Judy stopped as images of a certain Halloween came back to her. She had trekked through town as a scarecrow, and the hay stuffed into her pockets and jacket had made her itch all night. Orson's obsession with comic books was well known around town, so it wasn't a surprise he had worn the same costume he had the year before. Unfortunately, a year's worth of overeating had caused the bat on his chest to stretch, and before the night was over, the seams of his grey tights had given way. Entertained by the memory, Judy's eyes twinkled. "Oh my God, this is a stretch even for you, Pat," she said, placing her napkin neatly next to her plate. "I was seven years old, and it *wasn't* a date. We went trick-or-treating together because Mom didn't want me to go by myself, and you and Doug were at a Halloween party."

"Whatever," Patrick said, grabbing his cider. "The point is, he's back in town, and he has his own practice. You could do worse."

Judy's mouth went slack. She shot a look in Eric's direction, hoping he'd come to her rescue, but when she saw his amused expression, Judy knew she was on her own. She turned her attention back to Patrick, but before she could say a word, the blast of a ferry horn caused everyone at the table to jump.

"Jesus, could you turn that damn thing off," Patrick shouted. "We're trying to have a conversation here!"

"No, *we* aren't," Judy said, and getting to her feet, she pulled her phone from her back pocket and accepted the call. "Could you give me a sec?"

"Sure."

Just like before, Robin listened to muted voices and a bit of rustling before Judy spoke again.

"Sorry about that."

"No problem," Robin said as she sat down on the couch.

"And again, your timing was perfect."

"Well, I'd like to say it was just dumb luck, but I hedged a bet," Robin said, shifting slightly when Fred and Ginger decided to join her. "My mom and I always had dinner at the same time, and I figured your family might do the same, so I checked my phone records to see when I called the last time."

"Remind me never to play poker with you," Judy said with a laugh.

"If you do, I should warn you. I only play strip, and I *always* win."

It was lighthearted. It was meant as a joke, and then the line went silent. Unable to even hear the sound of Judy's breathing, Robin stiffened, and her mouth went dry. "So...uh...did you remember your gloves?"

"Sorry," Judy said. "I set my phone down for a second. I wanted to put on my gloves."

"Oh, okay," Robin said, sagging into the cushions. "No worries."

"So, what were you saying?"

"I was asking how it was going. Since you said my timing was perfect, I'm guessing not too well?"

"It's been hellfire and damnation around here since Sunday."

"What happened Sunday?"

"Five of my nieces and nephews called to bow out of this year's gathering."

"Oh, shit," Robin said, sitting straight. "I thought you said everyone shows up. Isn't it a tradition?"

"It's Pat's and Doug's tradition, and I guess it's starting to wear on their kids. I don't blame them. They all have their own lives, and their own interests, and it's not like they don't all come home for either Thanksgiving or Christmas. Asking them to spend what little hard-earned vacation time they do get working at the orchard isn't fair, which is something Eric and I have been trying to tell Doug and Pat for years. Not like they've ever listened."

"It sounds like they're going to have to listen now," Robin said, smiling as Fred and Ginger made themselves at home in her lap.

"Doubt it," Judy said, leaning back in the chair. "They'll just do the whole guilt trip thing when the missing ones show up at the holidays."

"Sorry."

"About what?"

"You told me you enjoyed going home because you could catch up with everyone, but it sounds like everyone's abandoned you."

"Not everyone. Trey, Pat's oldest, along with Doug's youngest two, Phil and Luke, all work here full-time, so I've been catching up with them and their families during the day. And Eric's here, too, which helps since Pat's been so moody. He hasn't said a word to anyone until tonight."

"Oh yeah?" Robin said, momentarily stopping Fred's back massage. "Should I ask?"

"Pat decided to play matchmaker. He got it in his head that some guy I used to know was an old boyfriend of mine, and he's apparently moved back to town. He's a lawyer now, and in Pat's words, 'I could do worse.'"

After waiting for a bit, Judy checked her phone to make sure the connection hadn't been dropped. "You still there?"

"Uh...yeah. I'm here," Robin said softly. "So...um...are you planning to rekindle the romance?"

"No, because I told you I'm not looking for a husband, and it was *not* a romance."

"It wasn't?"

"Robin, Orson and I went trick-or-treating together when I was seven. We never dated, and we were *never* an item," Judy said, relaxing back in the rocker. "But enough about me. What's going on with you? How's the painting going?"

"It's done," Robin said, grinning as she glanced around the room. "Everything is painted. The tile guy said I'll have a working shower by

Friday, and the countertop is being installed next Tuesday. Oh, and the best part is that the stuff I had in storage was delivered this morning, so tonight I get to sleep in a *real* bed with flannel sheets softer than you can possibly imagine, and enough space that I can actually roll over and not squish a cat."

"Sounds like *someone* is going to be a happy camper tonight."

"Tell me about it!" Although Robin's tone had hardly risen at all, it was just enough to send Fred and Ginger darting from her lap. As always, the tiny tips of their talons poked into her thighs, and as always, Robin took it in stride, her wince fleeting as she brushed a few strands of cat hair from her jeans. "I don't think my back could have handled much more of that sofa. Plus, with the run on Saturday, I need to make sure I'm ready for it."

"The run? Wait, let me guess. You're doing the Turtle Run."

"You've heard of it?"

"Of course. It happens every year. I've always wanted to try it, but I've never had the chance."

"Why not?"

"Because I'm always here, and it happens at the same time every year."

"That sucks," Robin said. "But wait. Why didn't you ever tell me that you ran?"

"You never asked."

"You could have volunteered the information."

"Yeah, but where's the fun in that? Besides, I haven't done it in a few years, so I'm not even sure these old bones still have it in them."

Robin frowned. "Why do you always do that?"

"Do what?"

"Talk like you've got one foot in the grave."

"Maybe not a foot, but definitely a toe."

"Bullshit."

"Robin—"

"Don't 'Robin' me. I'm serious, Judy. You aren't old. You're not even close, and when you get back, you and I are going for a run."

"I don't know. I could crap out on you, and you'd end up having to give me mouth-to-mouth."

Robin could do nothing to stop her mind from going into overdrive and images of soft lips locked in ecstasy swirled in her head. Long, lingering kisses that would leave them breathless, and tongues, warm and probing, tasting all they could. Robin shifted on the sofa, crossing her legs in an attempt to squelch her need as she became lost in her fantasy. "I'll look forward to it," she purred.

"What?"

Robin jolted upright. "Oh...I-I mean the run. I'll look forward to going on a *run* with you."

A few seconds passed before Judy said, "Are you doing the half-marathon or the short course?"

With her body still refusing to behave itself, Robin changed positions again and crossed her legs the other way. "The short course. I'm nowhere near ready to attempt a half-marathon."

"I don't know. You look in pretty good shape to me."

Judy's innocent compliment caused Robin's libido to surge like a tsunami. Dropping her chin to her chest, Robin held back a moan as she squeezed her legs together.

"You still there?"

"Yeah...um...I'm here," Robin said, pushing herself off the sofa. "But you know what? I've still got a...a mountain of totes to empty, so I think I'm going to try to get that done before I call it a night. Okay?"

"Oh...uh...sure."

"Thanks, Judy. I'll catch you later. Good night."

"Good night, Robin, and good luck with those totes."

Robin ended the call, and tossing her phone on the sofa, she stomped from the room. Glaring at the stack of empty totes in the foyer, Robin mentally admonished herself for what she was about to do.

She had looked forward to calling Judy all day. She wanted to tell her about all the discoveries she made, but one response, one *innocent* response from Judy had undone all Robin had tried to do. Since the day she had *almost* taken the matter of her need into her own hands, Robin had denied her imagination free rein. Over the years, her memories of Judy had been the driving force behind numerous self-pleasuring episodes, but now it seemed wrong. Now it seemed crude and exploitive, so she had turned to cold baths and binging on Netflix at night until it bored her to sleep, but abstinence was now impossible. Robin's body was on fire, and this time, there was no putting out the blaze.

As Robin went into the kitchen, wanton images, salacious and steamy swirled in her head, creating a savory cocktail too tempting to deny. Snagging a bottle of wine from the counter, she yanked out the cork and filled a tumbler to the brim. Taking a healthy swallow of the earthy

LYN GARDNER / 209

Cabernet, Robin topped off the glass before going to her bedroom, and pausing just long enough to set her drink on the nightstand, she stripped out of her clothes. Goosebumps sprang to life on her skin, the chill of room finding its way to her nakedness, and after one quick shiver, Robin climbed under the flannel sheets. She reached for her wine, taking a few more sips before she turned off the light. As Robin's hands began to wander, and her breathing began to quicken, she no longer cared if Isobel was watching or not.

***

Judy jumped up from the table as soon as the ferry horn blew, and without giving anyone so much as a half-hearted glance, she trotted from the dining room, grabbed her jacket and headed outside.

"Hi there," she said, cradling the phone between her ear and shoulder as she zipped up her jacket. "Long time, no talk."

Robin nodded. It had been nine days, and it had been the longest nine days of Robin's life. It had taken every ounce of energy she had not to pick up the phone. She had longed to talk to Judy again, to hear the lilt of her voice, imagine her smile, and fill Judy in on all the goings-on at the Inn, but every time Robin went to call, a memory stopped her. A memory of a night she spent giving herself orgasm after orgasm while fantasizing about the woman on the other end of the phone. She had awoken the next morning sated, but embarrassed, and it was that embarrassment that had driven Robin to almost near exhaustion every day since.

"Yeah, sorry about that," Robin said quietly. "I decided to knuckle down and get some stuff done. Hopefully, my timing is still impeccable though."

"It is," Judy said, getting comfortable in the rocker. "Thank God."

"Uh oh, that doesn't sound good. What's going on?"

"Oh, Pat and Doug have been flapping their feathers nonstop since the last time you and I talked, squawking about this and that, and doing everything in their power to convince me to move home. *And* the funniest thing of all is that they're basing everything on my age! Well, I have news for them. I may not be a spring chicken, but I'm sure as hell not an old cackling hen!"

"Wow. Th—"

"I swear to God, Robin. All they've done for the past week and a half is bitch and moan about their own children and how ungrateful they are for not coming home. Well, who the hell wants to come home to listen to all of their crap? What the fuck! When are they going to get it through their heads that some of us just *don't want to work in an orchard*?"

The louder Judy's voice became, the further Robin had moved her phone away from her ear, and it wasn't until a few seconds after the line went quiet when Robin decided to test the waters. "You done yelling?"

"Oh, shit," Judy said, her shoulders sagging. "I'm sorry. Was I yelling?"

"Let's put it this way. If you had cows, they'd surely be home by now."

Judy smiled into the phone. "I really like you."

It had been said in a breathy whisper, but with the phone pressed against her ear, Robin had heard every syllable, and her heart did a triple-twisting somersault. "Yeah?"

"I've been feeling shitty, and now I don't."

"You sick?"

"No, just tired. I haven't been sleeping well."

"Why not?"

"Just a lot of things on my mind and my brothers don't help. I've actually been thinking about cutting my vacation short and coming home early."

"Really?" Robin said, sitting up on her new, faux suede sofa. "That works for me."

"You sure? Sounds like you're getting a lot accomplished without me."

"Just little things."

"Like what?"

"Well, all the empty totes are now in the basement, and my apartment is completely finished *and* furnished. I raked up all the leaves and then weeded the raised beds around the house, so whenever we're ready to plant flowers, we can actually find the dirt. I also emptied the pantries in the big kitchen, washed everything inside, and then tried to put it back in some sort of order, but Jesus, I've never seen so many serving dishes, and there's an assortment of coffee urns that go from small to outrageous. Why in the hell would you need so many?"

"If I had to guess, it probably depends on the number of guests you have at any given time."

"Oh, you see, now that makes sense," Robin said, resting back on a stack of throw pillows.

"Glad you think so."

"I also asked the guy who tiled my shower to check out the bathrooms upstairs. He found three that needed to be re-grouted, so I hired him to do that, and I had a company come over and clean all the carpets on the first floor. I figure we'll wait to do the second and third until we get those rooms spruced up, but since I've got White Birch all cleaned and polished, the main floor now looks spiffy, just in case we get any guests."

"Robin, we're heading into winter."

"I know, and I was thinking about that. Since I live here, is there any reason why we can't say we're open?"

"Other than the fact the town is basically empty until spring?"

"I get that, but I was doing some reading, and it sounds like a lot of people come over for snowmobiling or cross-country skiing in the winter."

"That's right, but you forget that we still need to get the licenses—"

"Already done."

"What?"

"I told you I was busy," Robin said, grinning. "I went over and talked to Howard, and—"

"Who's Howard?"

"Adele's lawyer. He was the one handling all the estate stuff."

"Oh, okay."

"Anyway, I went over and talked to him, and even though Adele had closed this place, she kept up with the license, and because of the living trust, my name was already on everything. So, other than a couple of inspections—*which* I've already scheduled—we're golden."

"Are you serious?"

"Yes, indeedy," Robin said. "And I also bought a brand spanking new laptop, a couple of tablets, and that software you and I both liked, and it's all waiting for you in the office when you get here. Plus, while I was on the mainland, I hit the bank, got the accounts straightened out, so once you get back, you'll just need to stop in, fill out a signature card and choose a pin for your debit card. Oh, and before I forget, since I've been to Petoskey like a zillion times since you left, I already picked up the wallpaper, so there's no need for you to make a side trip."

"Good Lord, Robin. How much coffee have you consumed in the past week?"

"Why?"

"Because there's no way I'm going to be able to keep up with you if this is your normal energy level."

"Don't worry, it's not. I just had a little extra I needed to burn it off."

"Well, when I have extra energy, it usually means I'm anxious about something."

"Is that so?"

"Yes, and I have a feeling the same goes for you." When Robin didn't reply, Judy glanced at her phone. "What's wrong, Robin? Are you having second thoughts about all of this?"

Robin was racking her brain, trying to come up with a plausible reason to explain her behavior, so when Judy's words finally sunk in, Robin jerked to attention on the sofa. "What? No. No. *No*! I'm not having second thoughts. Not at all."

"Are you sure?"

"Yes. Yes, I'm positive. I'm looking forward to us getting this place in order."

"Then what's the problem?"

Robin let out a sigh, and as she did, she saw the magazine she'd put on the coffee table earlier that day. "It's my writing."

"What?"

"You're right about me being anxious, but it's got nothing to do with us. I mean, it's got nothing to do with Safe Harbor. I'm just a little antsy because I haven't found the courage to open my manuscripts yet, so I busied myself with lots of little things to keep my mind off of it."

"I'm confused. Why do you need courage to open your manuscripts?"

"Do you mind if we save that for another time? It's a long story, and there's more I need to tell you about the Inn."

Judy paused. It wasn't the first time Robin had hedged about her past, and Judy had a sneaking suspicion it wouldn't be the last. "All right. That's fine, I guess," she said softly. "So, what else is going on?"

"You know what? Never mind. You're just going to have to wait until you get here."

"That's not fair. You can't dangle 'there's more I need to tell you' and then drop it."

"I just did."

"Robin!"

"What? Don't you like surprises?"

Surprises can be pleasant like those found under Christmas trees wrapped in foil. They can be positive, grades reported at the end of semesters, or negative, grades reported at the end of semesters. They can create smiles or frowns, tears of joy or those of sadness, and responses can run the gamut as well. Startled, the unexpected can cause hearts to race, astounded can cause eyebrows to raise, and disillusionment can cause marriages to fail.

Judy tipped her face to the blue-black heavens freckled with silver sequins of radiance, the glint forming in her eyes putting them all to shame. Her mother once told her life was full of surprises, and Judy suddenly found herself eager for the next.

"Robin?"

"Yeah?"

"I'll be home Saturday night."

Chapter Twenty-Two

Robin turned this way and that as she stood in front of the full-length mirror on the back of her bedroom door. Her goal was to appear trendy, yet casual as if her choice of clothing had been spontaneous, even though it had taken her over an hour to pick everything out. The skinny jeans were perfect, hugging her like a second skin and the loose-fitting ribbed V-neck sweater, draped perfectly, ending mid-hip. She knew she couldn't go wrong with the suede slouch boots and her make-up, while minimal, added just the right amount of definition. The only remaining touch was to fix her hair, which had been giving her fits for the past twenty minutes.

Robin had worn her hair long for almost her entire life, except for one six-year-old moment when she found a pair of scissors and thought she could cut it herself. That resulted in a year of waiting until the mistake grew out, and Constance hiding every pair of scissors in the house.

In her teens, bowing to the pressure from her peers, Robin got a perm, hoping like her friends, to walk out of the salon with a mass of curls, puffed up as far as they would go. Instead, she left with a chemical burn across her forehead and a few lackluster waves in her hair, swearing she'd never make that mistake again, and she never did, much to her mother's delight. Other than having the length shortened to something a bit more manageable, Robin had always stuck with the tried and true, but right now, the tried and true was trying every bit of her patience.

One-by-one, Robin had worked her way through the hair accessories in the top drawer of her dresser. She had tried butterfly clips, bendy clips, claw clips, and jaw clips, and each had been flung back into the drawer when they disappointed her. Now, she stood staring at what remained.

The French combs seemed too upscale for the occasion, and the rhinestone tiara she had been forced to wear at a friend's wedding, she vowed would never see the light of day again, so that left her with Scrunchies or headbands. She drummed her fingers on her chin. The Scrunchies were undeniably laid-back, but with a sigh, Robin deemed them a little too laid-back, and pushing them aside, she grabbed her assortment of headbands. Fanning them out across the top of the cherry dresser, Robin was about to try the first when she noticed a chill in the air.

"Hi, Isobel," she said, looking around the room. "You're just in time to help me. Which one of these do you like?"

Amused she was again talking to a ghost, Robin waited for a moment before deciding Isobel had no intention of voicing her opinion. Glancing at the headbands, Robin reached for one, and a second later she was snatching her hand away as the entire collection was swept into the dresser, the ghostly demonstration ending with the drawer slamming closed so forcefully, the piece of furniture rocked.

"Whoa," Robin whispered as she took a step backward. "Well, headbands aren't for everyone, I suppose."

Robin stared at the dresser for another minute before she finally got the nerve to raise her eyes. She scanned the room, and while she saw no ghostly aura, the air was still cold.

"You know what?" she said, reaching for her hairbrush. "That's a good idea. I think I'm just going to leave it loose tonight. Why bother with all that other stuff—right?"

Robin turned back to the mirror to brush her hair one more time, but before she could, she felt the gentlest of breezes wash over her. She watched through widened eyes as a few strands of her hair lifted in the wind and then settled back into place perfectly. A few seconds later, as the temperature in her bedroom returned to normal, Robin gaped at her reflection in the mirror. "Freaky, but way cool."

***

A short time later, Robin was standing in her kitchen, admiring the table in the dining room. It was perfect. There was the right amount of glasses, plates, and cutlery, and the linen tablecloth and napkins also added to the mood.

"Shit!" Robin said, and hurrying over, she plucked the two candlesticks from the center of the table and rushed into the living room to place them on the mantle. "This isn't supposed to be romantic, you idiot. It's just a friend coming over for dinner. Geez."

Giving the candlesticks one last dirty look before she returned to the kitchen, Robin continued to snicker at her own stupidity as she looked in the oven. She breathed in the aroma of pot roast and potatoes, and glancing at the timer, she was about to turn it off when she heard the melodic chime of the new doorbell. "Crap," Robin said, hanging her head. "You really *are* an idiot. You forgot to unlock the flipping door."

It was basically a straight shot to the foyer, but as Robin tried to rush out of her apartment, the straight shot became anything but. Ginger met her in the hallway and when Robin veered to the right, so did Ginger forcing Robin to take a huge leap for womankind in order not to step on her cat. Careening off the wall, Robin continued on her way, only to meet her next obstacle as soon as she stepped into the big kitchen. Fred looked up at her, his eyes holding in their blackness defiance only found in a feline. Not to be thwarted, Robin glared back at him, daring him to move, and Fred didn't...until Robin did.

She went left. Fred followed her lead, and Robin ended up stumbling, scrambling, and swearing her way into the dining room, all the while sniggering at the impressionistic dance she just performed. She glanced at the table as she rushed by, and reaching the front door, she pulled it open.

For a split-second, Robin couldn't find her voice as she gazed at the woman standing on her porch. "Hi there."

"Hi yourself," Judy said, flashing a dazzling grin. "I'm sorry. I forgot to grab my keys."

"No, it's me who's sorry. I should have left it unlocked," Robin said, stepping back so Judy could come inside. "I guess I need to get used to doing that before we have guests—huh?"

"It's either that or you'll be forever running up here to open the door."

Robin's eyes creased at the corners. "Trust me. *That's* not as easy as it sounds."

Judy snapped back her head. "It's not?"

Before Robin could explain, the buzz of the oven timer reached her ears. "Oh crap, that's dinner," she said, turning toward the dining room. "I need to get it out of the oven, or we'll be eating leather."

"Take your time," Judy said, unbuttoning her coat. "I'll catch up."

"Cool."

Judy unzipped her parka, and hanging it on the coat tree, she draped her scarf over it and topped everything off with her knit cap. After adjusting her sweater and running her fingers through her hair, she headed toward the back of the house but came up short when she entered the dining room. Coming to a full stop, Judy tilted her head as she stared at something on the table. It was nearly three feet tall, but the blue plastic bag draped over it concealed its identity.

Intrigued, Judy moved a little closer, and noticing something red sticking out at the bottom of the bag, she lifted the plastic a few inches. Her smile began forming as soon as a pair of cherry-red oversized shoes came into view, and as she continued to raise the bag, Judy's smile grew even larger.

The doll was dressed in the costume of a circus jester, its onesie tied at the feet and hands, with ruffles surrounding its wrists, ankles, and neck. Half of the garment was striped in blue while the other half was striped in green, and where the two colors met down the middle was three jumbo buttons made from red puffs of cotton. Like his abnormally large feet, the clown's hands were also exaggerated in size, and raised in the air as if in exclamation, they were covered in four-finger canary yellow gloves.

Judy knew some people had a fear of clowns, but her attitude toward them had always been one of indifference. She had encountered some at fairs and carnivals, and over the years, they'd made appearances at a few toddlers' birthday parties she had attended, but Judy wasn't a fan of slapstick comedy. She found their buffoonery predictable and their antics rarely funny, so she had never paid them any attention, but she was paying attention to one of them now, and the longer she did, the more Judy's smile faded.

The clown's face was chalk white and above its two glassy, bugged out eyes were painted-on high arched eyebrows reaching toward his receding hairline. Sprouting from his scalp, through dozens of holes drilled into the plastic skull, were neon orange braided cords of yarn, and jutting out from underneath the thatch were two enormous ears. His lips were thickset and painted blood red, and with the corners of his mouth raised to the extreme, his grotesque grin was filled with Chiclet-sized teeth.

"Dinner just has to set for a minute and—" Robin came to an abrupt stop one step into the dining room, and spinning on her heel, she turned her back to Judy. "Could you please cover that back up?"

Judy glanced from the doll to Robin and back again. "Why?"

"Because it's a clown."

"I can see that."

"I don't like clowns."

"Then why is it here?"

"I found it in the basement. It was in the darkroom."

"There's a darkroom in the basement?"

Robin glanced over her shoulder and quickly looked away. "Yes, apparently Adele dabbled in photography. Now, could you please cover that back up?"

"Okay, so I'm still confused," Judy said, grabbing the blue bag from the table. "If you don't like clowns, why didn't you just throw it out or leave it in the basement?"

"Because it's the only freaking personal thing I found so far that belonged to my aunt, and I couldn't leave it down there because I wanted to keep an eye on it."

Robin heard the rustling of the plastic bag and believing it was safe to turn around, she did just that. Seeing the clown in all its macabre glory still standing uncovered on the table, she whirled back around. "Why didn't you cover it?"

"You *just* said you wanted to see it," Judy said, slapping her hands against her hips. "Make up your mind."

"I said I wanted to keep an *eye* on it. I didn't say I wanted to see it."

Judy pursed her lips as she looked back and forth between the doll and Robin again. "Okay, you're going to *have* to explain that."

Robin hung her head and let out a sigh. "You're going to think I'm stupid."

"I doubt it, but give it the old college try," Judy said with a laugh.

"This is *not* funny," Robin groaned.

"I'm sorry. I'll be serious," Judy said, fighting the urge to laugh again. "But you're going to have to explain what you mean by seeing it and not seeing it at the same time. That doesn't make any sense."

"I don't like clowns."

"You already said that."

"I'm not finished."

Judy snorted. "Sorry. Go ahead."

"I...um...I don't want to see it, but I need to know where it is."

"Because?"

"Because...um...I need to make sure it doesn't move."

"You need to make sure it...it doesn't *move*?" Judy said, the tone of her voice sliding up the scale.

"I told you, you'd think I was stupid."

"Stupid, no. Silly, yes," Judy said as she reached up and tugged the bag over the doll. "You can look now. The big, bad clown is hidden."

Before Robin even glanced in Judy's direction, she knew the woman was mocking her distress, but when she turned around and saw Judy's pouted lower lip, Robin's heart melted. It was the most adorable pout she had ever seen. "It's not funny," Robin said, trying to contain her smile. "Clowns are creepy!"

"I agree. They can be," Judy said, pointing toward the clown. "But this particular one is an inanimate object. It's a doll."

"Yeah, but it's a clown doll."

The dimples in Judy's cheeks appeared everlasting as she looked at Robin. "So, what are you planning to do with it?"

"I have no idea, but there was no way I could leave it in the basement. When I opened the curtains of the dark room and saw it staring back at me, I almost peed my pants."

"Did you?"

"No!" Robin said, before looking down at the floor. "But I screamed like a little girl."

"Oh, I would have given *anything* to see that."

"Can you please stop?" Robin said, looking up. "I seriously feel like a fool right now, and you're not helping."

"Okay, I'm done," Judy said, raising her hands in the air. "And dinner smells delicious, by the way."

Robin's face lit up as she turned toward the kitchen. "I hope you like pot roast," she said over her shoulder.

"I do," Judy said as she followed Robin through the house. "Oh. What's this about a darkroom?"

Robin suddenly came to a dead stop and turned around. "Wait!"

"What?" Judy said, taking a step backward to get out of Robin's personal space.

"We can't have dinner yet. You need to go up and take a look at Firefly."

"Why?"

"Just go up and take a look. It'll only take a minute. Please?"

The night before, when Judy broke the news about ending her vacation early, as expected, Patrick was livid. He blustered and bickered until his pockmarked face turned into a Better Boy tomato, but surprising even herself, Judy stood her ground. She didn't want to be there. She was tired of all the pestering, tired of all the same old, same old, tired of the silent dinners, the apples, and the market. Judy just wanted to go home. Back to familiar faces, back to the sounds of the water, and back to a job she had yet to even start, so when she pulled away from her childhood home early that morning, Judy was focused on her goal. Stopping at a local gas station, she topped off her tank, bought enough coffee to fill her thermos and grabbed something to eat. It was the first and last thing she would eat all day.

On the shelf, the prepackaged breakfast sandwich looked appetizing, but Judy quickly found out that looks can be deceiving. The perfectly round egg was rubbery. The flawlessly-browned biscuit was dry, and the bacon hidden inside tasted as if it had been boiled instead of fried. It sat in her stomach all day like a bowling ball, the weight squashing any thought about food for the rest of the trip, but the aroma of dinner had finally awakened Judy's appetite.

Her stomach was beginning to gurgle at the prospect of sustenance, but one look at Robin and Judy knew dinner was going to have to wait for a few more minutes. The woman's eyes were sparkling, and her smile was cheerful and impish, and Judy had a feeling if she didn't answer soon, Robin was going to explode from whatever surprise she was hiding.

"Okay, let's go," Judy said, doing an about-face.

"Oh...uh...I'll catch up," Robin said, gesturing toward her apartment when Judy looked back at her. "I need to go and make sure I've turned off the oven. I'll be right behind you. Promise."

"All righty, then," Judy said as she made her way to the stairs. "I'll meet you up there."

Firefly was the smallest guest room in Safe Harbor. Tucked into the far back corner of the third floor, it contained only a twin bed, a pair of minuscule nightstands, a small armoire, and two chairs nestled into an alcove. When they toured the house taking down measurements, Robin quickly deemed it her favorite room, and at first, Judy was surprised. The room was tiny. The bathroom was even tinier, and the walls were the color of an overripe peach, but when Judy went over and stood in the alcove, she understood the room's appeal. The niche jutted out over the side of the Inn, and with the neighboring homes being only two stories in height, the view of the Straits of Mackinac was uninterrupted and breathtaking.

Judy flicked on the hallway switch when she reached the third floor. Behind her, toward the front of the house, was Sterlingsworth. Deemed the honeymoon suite, it contained a bedroom, sitting room, and a gargantuan made-for-two bathroom. Their other high-priced suite, Georgian Bay, was directly ahead of her on the left. Large enough to hold two queen beds, it also included a sitting area and a comfortably-sized bathroom, but with a bit of rearranging, cots could be added so families of four, five, or six could easily be accommodated.

The room Judy came upstairs to see was opposite Georgian Bay, and she marched toward it with a smile on her face. With the knowledge their tastes in decorating were similar, Judy already knew that whatever Robin had done she would love, and when she noticed the small armoire pushed up against the wall in the hallway, Judy's suspicions were confirmed. Robin had started painting without her.

Judy waited for a second, glancing over at the stairs to see if Robin had yet to appear, and when she saw she hadn't, Judy decided there was no reason to wait and opened the door to Firefly.

"Boo!"

Judy leapt into the air and flailing backward, she placed her hand over her heart. "Geez-o-Pete!" she shouted from the hallway. "You scared the shit out of me!"

"I was going for a girly scream," Robin said, giggling.

"Well, you almost had one," Judy said as she looked back and forth between Robin and the stairs. "And how in the hell did you get by me?"

"I didn't," Robin said, motioning with her head to her right. "I took those."

Solely focused on a door she'd never seen before, Judy stepped into the room. "Where'd that come from?"

"It was behind the armoire."

"But how did you—" Judy stopped and looked around. The walls were the same yellowish-pink and as far as Judy could tell nothing else had been changed. "How did you find them?"

"They were hidden behind a bookcase in my spare bedroom downstairs, and wait until you see this," Robin said, motioning for Judy to follow her. "Come on."

Judy hesitated before following Robin through the newly discovered doorway, and a second after she did, Judy sucked in all the air existing in the stairwell. "Oh, my God!"

Robin smiled. "Yeah, I think I've figured out what Isobel was doing with all those pens and pencils."

When she was alive, it had kept Isobel sane in a world where she had felt threatened, and late in the night with only the glow from the hearth to brighten the paper, she would sketch until weary. Her father hadn't known about this secret either, for she drew what she thought and those thoughts could never be known.

Under her bed, in an old cigar box, were the scraps of paper she had squirreled away, a trove of treasures blank and printed on, she would remove one or two every night and allowing herself the freedom she craved, she would sketch. Many a pencil had been worn down to the nub and bits of charcoal, snatched before it found its way to the stove heating their home, had also been used until all that remained of it was the soot left on her skin. And when her eyes began to blur, and her limbs grew heavy, she'd place her sketches in the fire and watch as her truths turned into ash, but the correctness required of the breathing was no longer necessary to the dead.

Decades before, in the cramped confines of a stairway hidden from view, Isobel had found what would become her sketchpad, and she had put it to good use. Drawings in pencil and pen covered almost every square inch of the curved ivory colored plaster, and while most believed sketches to be born from speed and loosely drawn, Isobel's contained details Robin and Judy had yet to discover.

"This is amazing," Judy said quietly, fascinated by the drawings surrounding her. "I wonder how long it took her to do this."

"I have no idea," Robin said in a breath.

Both had felt the need to whisper for much like a cavern, the winding passageway amplified their voices, so when Judy's stomach growled, a lion's roar echoed off the walls.

Robin's face turned rosy, the reverberation of Judy's hunger almost as funny as the woman's wide-eyed expression at the rumble. "What the hell was that?" Robin said, laughing out every word.

"I'm sorry," Judy said, placing her hand on her belly. "I haven't had much to eat today."

"I have the *perfect* cure for that." Robin motioned for Judy to follow her as she headed down the stairs. "Besides," Robin said, looking over her shoulder. "There's a lot more I have to tell you."

"Yeah?"

"Oh yeah," Robin said with a snort. "*Lots* more."

Chapter Twenty-Three

"I can't thank you enough for doing this. It's delicious."

Robin looked up from her plate and grinned. "You're welcome. I just thought if you're anything like me, the last thing you want to do after a day of traveling is to come home and cook."

"Especially when you forget to stop at the market before getting on the ferry."

"Oh, no worries there," Robin said, reaching for her wine. "There's plenty of stuff in the freezers now. Feel free to grab anything you'd like."

"What freezers?"

"The ones downstairs."

"The chest freezers?"

"Yep," Robin said as she loaded her fork with some carrots. "The store was having a sale on...um...on some meat thingies, so I bought a few."

"Are you talking about meat bundles?"

"*That's* what they called them. Yes."

"How many is a few?"

"Oh, I don't know. Three I think."

"Three?" Judy said, her voice rising just a bit. "Robin, those things have like twenty pounds of meat each."

"I know, but winter is coming, and I heard once that happens, the ferries stop running."

"The ferries don't stop running unless the Straits freeze, and that's usually not until at least January, if not later. And even then, a plane ride is cheap enough, and there's always the ice bridge."

"Okay, you got me there," Robin said. "The ice bridge?"

"It's what they call it when the Straits freeze. Once the ice gets thick enough, we can just take a snowmobile over to St. Ignace."

Robin stared open-mouthed at Judy for a second. "Okay, first, unless Adele has a snowmobile hidden around here someplace, I don't own one of those, and second, are you *insane*? Who's to say the ice is thick enough, and you're not going to fall through and plummet to an icy, dark, and watery death?"

Judy was tickled by the author's embellishment, and it showed on her face. "Volunteers from both Mackinac and St. Ignace check it daily, and people on the island and the mainland hold onto their old Christmas trees, so once they find a route safe enough to travel, they drill holes in the ice, put in the trees, and away we go. It's only about three miles, which means it's a quick trip, and it also proves my point."

"What point?"

"There was no need for you to stockpile a ton of meat. There *are* ways off this island in the winter."

"I didn't stockpile a *ton* of meat. I just saved us some money by buying in bulk."

Judy's entire face crinkled into a smile. Stabbing her fork into a piece of meat on her plate, she popped it into her mouth and chewed merrily away without saying a word.

There was no way Robin could miss the twinkle in Judy's eyes. "What? I like meat. Not all lesbians are vegetarians, just to let you know."

"I wouldn't know if they were, or they weren't, but you bought enough meat to feed an army—*lezzzbian* or otherwise."

It was all Robin could do not to profess her undying love for the woman sitting opposite her right then and there. There wasn't a millimeter of Judy that Robin didn't adore, and the way she had just emphasized *lesbian* was as comical as it was captivating. She knew she was staring, and Robin knew it was rude, but for the life of her, there wasn't anything else in the world worth looking at.

"Oh, I think I'm done," Judy said, pushing away her plate. "If I eat anymore, I'm going to explode."

Robin slowly came out of her trance and drew a long, easy breath. "Sounds messy."

"I guarantee it would be," Judy said, placing her napkin on the table before relaxing back in her chair. "Hey, I forgot to ask you. How'd you make out on the Turtle Run?"

"I didn't do too badly. I finished twenty-second in my age group and managed not to kill myself in the process," Robin said, smiling. "Always a plus."

"I'd have to agree."

They gazed at each other for a long moment until the silence was broken by Judy. "Congratulations," she said, holding up her glass for a second before taking a sip. "Well done."

"Thanks."

"Now, let me help you clean this all up," Judy said, pushing out her chair.

"Don't be ridiculous," Robin said, getting to her feet. "Take your wine and go relax."

"I can help."

"I know you can help, but I don't want you to," Robin said, taking the plate Judy was holding. "You're my guest, and this isn't going to take any time at all. Now, go chill. I'll join you in a minute."

"Has anyone ever told you that you're pushy?" Judy said, looking up at Robin.

"Yes, but it didn't make a difference," Robin said with a grin. "And it's not going to now."

***

It was rare Judy would walk into anyone's home and not find something she'd have done differently. It wasn't that she was critiquing the homeowner's decorating abilities, but if conversations slowed or held no interest for her, her mind would drift to her surroundings. Sometimes it was just a crooked picture, and Judy would wonder why they hadn't noticed it, while in other houses, it would be a shade of paint she found less than appealing or a room crammed with furniture with no space left to breathe. Yet, since descending the stairs from Firefly, Judy had been hard-pressed to find anything she didn't like in Robin's newly redecorated apartment...and Judy was *really* looking.

For the spare bedroom, Robin had chosen earth tones, and using a shade similar to that of sand for the walls and repeating the color in the area rug, she had turned the once dreary room into something warm and welcoming. Given the space, or rather the lack thereof, the full-size platform bed had a bookcase as a headboard, and with drawers accessible from all sides underneath, there was no need for a bureau or a dresser. Two modest nightstands flanked the bed, and while all the wood was dark in tone, Robin had used brass accents in the lamps and hardware, giving the room an Old World charm even though everything was new.

When it came to the kitchen, Judy had almost let out a gasp when she saw what Robin had done. All the cabinets were now painted a dark colonial blue, but Robin hadn't stopped with just that color. Using a black glaze over top, the inky finish accentuated all the nooks and crannies of the old oak, and with the addition of a black quartz countertop, pewter hardware, and new stainless steel appliances, the kitchen was as modern as it was country.

Judy couldn't help but chuckle under her breath as she strolled into the living room. Once again, at first glance, there was nothing she didn't adore.

The orange walls were gone, replaced with a color halfway between gray and blue, and the once dismal bay window was now anything but. Robin had removed the shutters and in their place were white Roman shades, and steel-blue grommet-top drapes hung at the corners, framing the bay perfectly. Across the seat was an assortment of cushions, their upholstery holding abstract designs in blue, burgundy, and black, and centered in the bay was a small chandelier, perfect for casting just enough light to read a book after the sun had gone down.

The faux suede sofa was gray as well, albeit a few shades darker than the walls, and in front of the fireplace, Robin had placed a circular love seat complete with ottoman, perfect for lounging or falling asleep in front of a roaring fire. The tired and tattered metal screen in front of the hearth had been replaced by a new surround, its mesh fine and tight, and hugging the brick to ensure not a spark could reach the carpet or the cats. And the area rug now warming the floor was plush, the blend of thick piles a mixture of charcoal, black, and ivory.

Judy moved toward the fireplace, and scanning the items displayed on the mantle, she frowned. The candlesticks flanking the silver cremation urn centered above the hearth seemed out of place, but once she noticed a familiar face framed in pewter, her smile reappeared.

"I brought the wine in case you'd like some more."

Judy turned around, glancing at the empty glass in her hand before holding it out to Robin. "Actually, that sounds good, and I've gotta tell you, I love what you've done to this place."

Robin beamed. "Yeah?" she said, pouring some of the Cabernet into Judy's glass.

"Yes, it's amazing."

"Thanks. I guess it'll do."

Judy grinned as she faced the mantle again. "I was just looking at your pictures. Where was that one taken?"

Robin's expression grew even brighter when she saw the one Judy was pointing to. Handing Judy the bottle, Robin picked up the photo and motioned toward the sofa. "How about we sit?"

"Works for me."

A minute later, comfortable on the sofa, Robin looked at the picture in her hand. "This was taken twelve years ago during Pride in St. Pete. Mom surprised me with a visit, and when she found out I already had plans to go to Pride with some friends that weekend, she tried to bow out, but we wouldn't hear of it. We persuaded her to go with us, and I'd have to say it's probably one of my fondest memories of her."

"Why's that?"

Entertained by the memory, Robin shook her head. "I don't know if you've ever been to a Pride event, but they can be...well, they can be quite colorful and at times, over the top. It's a day we celebrate who we are and how far we've come, so almost anything goes. You've got gays prancing around, bare-chested and or wearing tutus, and drag queens on floats, belting out show tunes blasting from the speakers..." Robin's voice trailed off as she stared at the photograph.

"Something wrong?"

Robin shook her head and raised her eyes. "There are so many against us. So many who believe we're sick or evil or deserve to die because of our lifestyles, but I have to tell, the LGBTQ community is the friendliest, most loving group of people I've ever known, and it only took maybe an hour or two before my mom realized that."

"She wasn't comfortable with you...um...I mean—"

"No, she was fine with it, but she'd never been to Pride. She was suddenly surrounded by thousands of the gay community, and she was totally out of her element at first. She didn't know what to do or where to look, and I wish you could have seen her face when the women started hitting on her."

"Oh, my God. Are you serious?"

"Yes, I am," Robin said with a laugh. "And Mom had no clue as to what to say. She'd babble and stammer and then yank me over, quickly explaining to all who would listen that *I* was the lesbian in the family, not her, but that didn't stop some of them from continuing to flirt. It was all in good fun, and eventually, she got that." Robin paused to place the picture on the coffee table. "And as you can see, by the end of the day, she was wearing rainbow beads and had our flag painted on her cheek...just like me."

"Sounds like a wonderful day."

"It was," Robin said in a breath, looking at the photo.

Judy took a sip of her drink, watching as Robin continued to stare at the picture until Judy heard her sniffle. "Are you all right?"

"Yeah, I'm okay," Robin whispered. "I just miss her sometimes. Hell, who am I kidding? I miss her all the time." Feeling her emotions starting to get the better of her, Robin turned to face Judy. "We need a subject change."

Once Judy saw the tears in Robin's eyes, she understood the urgency, and scanning the room, she pointed to the left of the fireplace. "So, I already know you write, you run, and by the looks of it, you're a fantastic interior decorator, but when do you find the time to draw?"

Robin looked over at the sketch pad sitting on the rickety plastic easel. "That's not mine. I think Adele got it for Isobel, so she'd stop drawing on the walls."

"It could have belonged to Adele."

A knowing smile softened Robin's lips. "I don't think so, and I'll show you why." Robin got to her feet, and going over to the bay window, she lifted the lid of the seat. "The keys to the window seats were on one of the steps leading up to Firefly," she said over her shoulder. "The one in my bedroom had Stanley's shrine in it and—"

"Who? Oh, wait." Judy glanced at the fireplace for a second. "When I stayed here, there was a whole bunch of things on the mantle. It all revolved around Adele's husband. Is that what you mean by the shrine?"

"Actually, that's what Rita called it, and once I saw all the stuff, I have to agree. It really was a shrine of sorts," Robin said as she traveled back and forth from the window seat. "And I wasn't sure what to do with it. I mean, I didn't know the guy. Then again, I really didn't know Adele either, but getting rid of it didn't seem right. He was my uncle, after all, so, for now, it's packed up in one of the totes in the basement."

"Oh. Okay," Judy said, watching as Robin piled papers, notebooks, and a stack of sketch pads on the coffee table.

"Anyway, the reason I think the easel was for Isobel is because I found it in the window seat along with these," Robin said, handing Judy one of the sketch pads as she sat back down. "I didn't look through all of them yet, but the sketches in there look just like the ones on the walls in the servants' stairway."

Judy opened the drawing tablet and flipped through a few pages. "I see what you mean. They do look the same. Wait," Judy said, turning to Robin. "The servants' stairway? How in the world did you come up with that?"

"Because of this," Robin said as she pulled out a folded piece of paper from the stack. Opening it up, she spread it out so Judy could see. "This is a copy of the original blueprints for the house. I have no idea how Adele got it, but on here the third floor is labeled the playroom, and this apartment was called the servants' quarters, which would explain the need for the second kitchen. See?"

Judy read the notations. "Okay, but not the hidden stairs," she said, looking back at Robin.

"I don't think they were hidden originally. My guess is that the servants used them to get upstairs," Robin grabbed a packet of papers, and removing the clip holding them together, she said, "This is a photocopy of the 1894 census. It shows that Lyman and Flora Majors lived here with their children, Helen, Lyman Jr., Alice, Sarah, Emma, and Oliver."

"That's a lot of kids."

"It is," Robin said, resting back on the couch. "And I have a friend who's also a writer. One of his books was set in the late eighteen hundreds. Back then, especially in affluent families, children were supposed to be seen and not heard. It was all about appearances and because of that, you wouldn't have your servants carrying trays of snacks through the house, possibly disturbing guests or a meeting or whatever. You'd have them go up the back way so they wouldn't be seen."

Judy smiled. "I can see why you're a writer."

"Oh yeah? Why's that?"

"Because you have one hell of an imagination."

Robin reached for her glass. Downing what little remained in one swallow, she took the time to split the last splash of wine in the bottle between their glasses all the while hoping the blush forming on her cheeks would go the hell away.

Robin was well aware of her own imagination, and she had been having a hard time keeping it in check since Judy had walked into the house. Unlike any pair of jeans she had seen the woman wear before, the pair tonight was tight, hugging every curve Judy owned from her waist down. And from her waist up, the emerald green sweater, designed for an off-the-shoulder look, was being worn as intended, and the nakedness of Judy's right shoulder had been wreaking havoc with Robin's lower self all night.

"You have no idea," Robin said into her glass as she took another sip.

Judy pointed to the paper Robin was holding. "Can I see that?"

"Sure, here."

Judy squinted at the cursive penmanship on the page. "This is neat," she said, studying the document. "But it leads me to the next question."

"Which is?"

"The people called out as servants were Olga Hendrickson, Julia Cooper, Henrietta Zellen, and Thomas Skog."

"Okay?"

"There's no Isobel."

"She never lived here. I mean, not until she died."

"Then how did Adele know her name?"

"That's a whole other story," Robin said, and standing, she picked up the empty bottle. "Did you want me to open another or would you prefer something else? Green tea? Coffee?"

Judy placed her hand on her belly. "You know, tea sounds great. The last thing I think I need is caffeine."

"Cool. Give me a few minutes."

"You want some help?"

"No, I got this," Robin called from the kitchen. "Relax."

When Robin returned to the living room, she saw Judy standing in front of the barrister bookcase to the left of the bay window. "Oh, I see you found one of my other discoveries."

"Where did you find them?"

"They were also on the stairs leading to Firefly. That's another reason why I think the easel was for Isobel. Between the cameras and the darkroom in the basement, it looks like Adele's hobby was photography."

"May I?" Judy said, motioning toward the door on the bookcase.

"Of course."

Judy lifted the oak-framed glass to more closely view the collection of cameras filling the shelves. "Geez, these look old."

"That's because they are," Robin said, setting the two mugs on the coffee table before making her way to the bookcase. "I spent two nights researching them on the Internet. The boxy one is a Kodak Brownie, circa 1946."

Judy picked up the camera and gingerly examined the black steel box in her hand. "It's so...so..."

"Weird looking?"

"Yeah, a little," Judy said, placing it back on the shelf. "It doesn't even look like a camera."

"I know," Robin said, and picking up the next in line, she handed it to Judy. "But twenty years makes all the difference."

"Now, this looks more like it," Judy said, holding the Canon FT in her hand. "But it's a lot heavier than I expected."

"I thought so, too, but from what I read this one was made before they started replacing metal parts with plastic ones."

"Interesting," Judy said, returning the camera to the shelf to pick up the next. "This one looks newer."

"That's depending on what you mean by new. The Canon T90s came out in 1986, and by the amount of lenses Adele had for it, I think that was her go-to camera."

"Lenses?"

Robin took the camera from Judy and motioned to another shelf. "Check it out."

Judy bent down, and her eyes widened at the row of lenses in varying lengths. "She was serious about this, wasn't she?"

"Yes, it looks like she was," Robin said, putting the camera back on the shelf. "And there are two tripods in the basement, too. That's where I put the cases for these, but eventually, I'm going to have to pack everything up and take them somewhere."

"You're planning to sell them?"

"No, but I'm not sure if there's still film in them. I seriously doubt it would be any good, but I don't want to risk opening them either."

"Good idea," Judy said, and waiting until Robin closed the glass door of the barrister case, she led the way back to the sofa and sat down. "So...about Isobel?"

***

"Wow. I have to say, I'm with you," Judy said, a notebook on the coffee table. "Between Adele's research and all this documentation, Isobel Vallencourt has to be your ghost. It's kind of sad, though."

"Yeah, I know." Robin paused to take a sip of tea and then she found herself rushing to swallow it. "Oh my God, I forgot to tell you. I saw her!"

"Who?"

"Isobel."

"You *saw* her?"

Robin bobbed her head like a plastic statuette on a dashboard. "Yep. It was a few days after you left. I wanted to get some sleep, but she was upstairs stomping around. I stormed up there to give her a piece of my mind, and a few minutes later, I was running for my life. And just a heads-up, when she gets mad, it gets really, *really* cold and windy."

"Good to know," Judy said, eyeing Robin. "But I try not to get ghosts mad. Seems a bit like pushing my luck."

"Yeah, well I definitely pushed mine that night," Robin said with a laugh. "I got it into my head she was going to hurt Fred and Ginger, so I told her to fuck off, and then I promptly went in search of wine. I was in the kitchen, getting myself a drink, and when I turned around, she was standing there, or actually, I guess she was floating there. It was kind of hard to tell."

"And?"

"And I told her she was just going to have to get used to me. I was Adele's niece, and the house was now mine, and I didn't mean her any harm."

"What did she do?"

"She disappeared into thin air, which is totally freaky, by the way, but since then she's been okay," Robin said as she set her tea on the table. "And when I sense she's around, I talk to her, but if the temperature drops below freezing, I shut the hell up." Robin glanced in Judy's direction when she heard the woman giggling. "What's so funny?"

"You are," Judy said, doing her best to contain her mirth. "A few weeks ago, you were panic-stricken because of Isobel, and now you want to invite her to dinner."

"I do not," Robin said, trying to hide her smile. "I just came to the conclusion, since I have no plans of moving, I need to get along with her."

"I bet you wouldn't say that if she was dressed like a clown."

A second later, Judy burst out laughing at the sight of Robin's open-mouthed gawk. Throwing her head back, several guffaws echoed off the walls before Judy regained control of herself.

Robin peered at Judy. "You *had* to go there. Didn't you?"

"Are you kidding me? I've been trying to figure out a way to go up front all night, so I could move the damn thing just to see your reaction."

"Don't you dare!"

"But it's *soooo* tempting," Judy said, wiping the tears from her eyes. She glanced at her watch and got to her feet. "I should really be going. I still have things to unpack and laundry to do, but I can't thank you enough for dinner. It was great."

A tinge of disappointment washed over Robin, but she pushed it away. Judy had had a long day, and with two chest freezers now filled with food, Robin had more than enough reasons to invite Judy to dinner again. "My pleasure," she said, standing up. "I'll walk you out."

Robin followed Judy through the house, and as she watched the woman put on her coat, Robin said, "So...um...have you thought of when you might want to start working on the rooms upstairs? There's no rush. I was just wondering."

"Well, if I take tomorrow to catch up on things, I'm all yours come Monday morning."

Chapter Twenty-Four

"Patrick must have had a shit fit."

"To tell you the truth, there were a few seconds there when I thought his head was going to pop off."

"I bet," Rita said, snickering as she took a sip of her coffee. "And what about you?"

"What about me?"

"Any regrets? Guilt?"

Judy paused, running her finger around the edge of her coffee mug as she thought about the question. "Actually, no. I'm good."

"Hallelujah!" Rita said, waving her hands in the air.

"Did you think I wouldn't be?"

"I was just checking."

"Well, I'm fine," Judy said, relaxing back in her chair. "I'm where I want to be and doing what I want to do, but you know what's strange?"

"What?"

"Doug didn't say a word. He just sat there while Patrick went off on his tangent, and when it was all over, it was all over. Doug never chimed in once."

"Maybe he's finally given up," Rita said with a shrug. "You said some of his kids didn't show."

"Yeah, and I think that has something to do with it."

"Writing on the wall?"

"Exactly."

"What about Eric?"

Judy's face creased into a sudden smile. "He came up to my room later and gave me a high five."

"Typical Eric," Rita said before drinking what was left of her coffee.

"Yep."

Rita got up and walked across her kitchen to the coffee maker. Pouring a splash into her cup, she carried the pot toward Judy. "Would you like a refill?"

"Oh, no," Judy said, covering her mug with her hand. "I've reached my limit."

"Wimp."

Judy watched Rita begin prepping the coffee maker for another round. "I honestly have no idea how you can sleep at night after drinking as much coffee as you do."

"That's where Hank comes in handy. That son-of-a-bitch can really wear me out," Rita said, giving Judy a wink. "If you catch my drift."

"If I didn't, you'd probably draw me a picture."

"Would you like me to? It would give a whole new meaning to stick figures."

"Stop!" Judy said, sniggering as she pushed herself out of her chair. "I swear to God you have sex on the brain."

"Among other places," Rita said, waggling her eyebrows.

"I gotta go," Judy said, snagging her parka from the back of the chair.

"What's the rush?"

"I figured I'd head into town in a bit and see what all the Halloween hubbub was about?"

Rita's eyebrows drew together for a moment. "My God, that's right. You've never been here during Halloween."

"Nope, but since I am, I thought I'd give it a look. Maybe grab some dinner. You and Hank want to join me?"

"Oh, sweetie, I wish we could, but Trudy and Glen invited us over for dinner and cards."

"Let me guess. Honing your Euchre skills before the tournament at the church?"

"You know it," Rita said, holding her chin high. "Rose and Tommy are going down. There's no way those two can win every year without cheating. Nobody that's lucky."

"I can't believe you're honestly accusing them of cheating. What would they have to gain?"

Rita placed her hands on her hips. "Do I really need to answer that?"

Judy stood on her tiptoes and gave Rita a kiss on her cheek. "No, you don't. Have fun tonight. I'll see you later."

By the time Judy reached her bike, she had pulled on her gloves and knit cap. The sun was starting to go down, and it was taking the warmth with it, but the air was as fresh as ever, and for a moment, Judy stopped and took in the panoramic view before her.

Rita's family was one of the first on Mackinac to obtain permission to build their home on the East Bluffs. In the early nineteen hundreds, with their candy business thriving, they contracted to have a house built, and it became one of the most prestigious on the island. Three stories in height, the gorgeous Victorian cottage exemplified the elegance of the era. From its clapboard siding to its turret, and from its wrap-around porch to its terraced gardens, Rita's home was a stopping point for every carriage tour on the island. Tourists would gape open-mouthed at the magnificent house, but it wasn't until the coachmen informed them of one little detail, when their jaws would hit the ground. While the magnificent homes belonged to the owners, the land on which they were constructed...did not.

In 1875, believing the newly deemed Mackinac Island State Park would put a burden on the federal budget, the U.S. Congress determined that discretionary leases of land would be made available for those who wanted to build homes in the areas known as the East and West Bluffs. By doing so, the families could construct their homes, and the monies paid for leasing the land would assist in maintaining the park. However, politics being politics, it wasn't until 1884 when the Secretary of War, Robert T. Lincoln, son of the President, ordered the land surveys to be completed, and soon afterward Victorian cottages began to be built.

There was only one stipulation given to those who wanted to build on the bluffs, and it could be seen in every single dwelling. The Victorian heritage that encompassed much of Mackinac Island was to be maintained in perpetuity. Therefore, like Rita and her ancestors had done, the homes atop the East and West Bluffs stayed true to their original design down to the hand-blown glass in their windows, the incredible detail of their façades, and the grandeur of their landscaping.

Judy took a deep breath of the cool air before climbing onto her bike, and flipping up the kickstand she headed down Huron Road. In no rush to get back to an empty apartment, she meandered her way down the street, but as she approached a fork in the road, she slowed almost to a stop. Judy's expression grew pensive as she looked back and forth between the two streets, and with a shrug, she made a hard left and coasted down Truscott Street toward Main.

***

It's said that it takes more muscles to smile than to frown, and sitting on the floor in Firefly, Robin believed it. Her cheeks ached from the smile she had worn since waking up that morning, and it was all because of a few innocent words spoken the night before. *'I'm all yours come Monday morning.'*

The words danced their way into Robin's head again, and with a laugh, she reached over and cranked up the volume on the dock holding her phone. The upbeat mix was just what she needed to get the job done, and with the music now just below ear-splitting, she loaded her brush and went back to cutting in underneath the window.

Robin had spent the better part of the day painting the room, but her energy was now diminishing quicker than the level of paint in the can. Even after turning on all the lights, she was fighting the setting sun and the shadows it created, but she was determined to finish what she had started. Intent on creating a flawless division between the pale Air Force blue walls and the crisp white of the wooden moldings, concentration lines were etched into her forehead as Robin inched her way along. With the music blaring and hell-bent on finishing, she had no idea someone else had entered the room until she felt a hand on her shoulder.

Robin shrieked, and recoiling from the touch, she spun around and pushed herself up against the wall. She held up the loaded paintbrush, prepared to fight off the intruder with the only weapon she had, and just as quickly, she lowered her hand. "Holy Mother of God, Judy! You almost gave me a freaking heart attack!"

Judy pointed to her ears and then to Robin's phone, and a few seconds later, Robin was yanking her phone from the dock.

"I called your name a dozen times," Judy said, wearing a smile that added a thousand watts to the room. "But apparently you didn't hear me."

"Ya think?" Robin said, placing her brush on the rim of the can.

"And what's with the painting? I thought we were going to start this Monday."

"I was going to talk to you about this last night, but I forgot. Would it be awful if we didn't rent this room?"

"No," Judy said, looking around. "But why wouldn't we?"

"Well, if you don't mind, I'd like to use it as my office. Between the private stairs and the view, it would be perfect, and if we ever did need to rent it out, all I'd have to do is gather up my laptop and a couple of books."

Judy gestured toward the pile of furniture Robin had pushed into the center of the room. "What about all this?"

"Everything except for the chairs that were by the window can stay. It wouldn't be in my way, so we could easily flip the room into rentable space whenever we needed. What do you think?"

Judy looked around again. "That's fine with me."

"Are you sure?"

"Yeah. Like you said, it wouldn't take much to get it ready for guests. As long as you're open to that, I don't see why we can't try it. We can just keep the armoire off to the side, and block the stairs when we need to."

"Cool," Robin said and draping her hands over her raised knees. "So, are you here to raid the freezers?"

"Oh, um...no. Actually, I was...I was wondering how you felt about Halloween?"

"Halloween?"

"Yeah, you know. Ghosts, goblins...skeletons hanging from trees. Stuff like that."

Robin shrugged. "I've never been a fan, but I did get some candy to hand out just in case any kids show up on Tuesday night. Why?"

"I'm not into it either, but Halloween is huge on Mackinac and this weekend is when the locals get all dressed up and go into town to party. Since I've never been able to see it for myself, I thought I'd go over, grab some dinner, and check it out. I was wondering if you'd like to join me."

Robin's smile couldn't get any wider. "I'd love to," she said, but as she tried to push herself off the floor, she felt something tug at her hair, forcing her to sit back down. "Crap."

"What's wrong?"

"Um...I'm sitting up against the wall."

"I can see that."

"I just painted this wall."

Judy immediately pressed her lips together, taking the time she needed to still her laughter. "Are you stuck?"

"No, but I may lose some hair in the battle."

***

An hour later, Robin emerged from her bedroom, and as she reached the kitchen, she stopped to admire the woman in the distance. Judy was standing near the easel in the living room, casually sipping her tea as she regarded the sketch, completely unaware she was being watched.

Overtop a jersey turtleneck of burgundy, Judy was wearing an open knit dark gray sweater that reached her hips, and her jeans were again tight, fitting her petite form flawlessly, but Robin's perusal wasn't voyeuristic. It was fanciful. The unreal had become real. The unimagined was now before her, and the normalcy of Robin's life had become anything but.

Robin's skin had been warmed by the shower, the steam of the spray making its way to her bones and removing the chill that had settled throughout the day. Yet, as Robin made her way into the living room, she pushed up the sleeves of her own sweater and turtleneck in hopes her heated skin would cool.

"Sorry, it took so long," Robin said, reaching Judy's side. "I was hoping to get all the paint out."

"Turn around," Judy said, setting down her mug. "Let me check."

It was a simple request, and Robin did as asked, but even the simplest of things can cause unexpected results. With her back to Judy, Robin suddenly felt exposed, the visual examination more intimate than any doctor had ever performed, and when she felt Judy's fingers in her hair, Robin closed her eyes and tried to breathe.

"I don't see any blue. I think you're good."

Robin inhaled an uneven breath, and clearing her throat, she briefly glanced back at Judy. "So...you ready to go?"

"Sure," Judy said, walking by. "Let's head out."

***

They walked in silence, their hands stuffed in their pockets and their breath steaming in the air. The soft light from the lampposts dotting the street illuminated their way, and other than the sound of their footsteps echoing in the night, the only interruption to the silence was the water lapping against the rock-covered beach off in the distance.

They rounded the turn, ambling past the library, closed for the day, and the Iroquois Hotel, closed for the season. They passed homes darkened with vacancy and the ferry dock, now barren of workers and carts, and Robin suddenly felt on edge. It was as if they were the only souls on the island, left to fend for themselves and to survive however they could until eventually they, too, would become ghosts.

Robin had been in town several times over the past two weeks, and each time she had, another store had closed for the winter. It seemed to her like an odd, creeping disease of abandonment as one by one, shop windows were covered with plywood and decorations adorning doors and awnings were removed, leaving nothing behind but boarded-up shells holding treasures that would remain unseen until spring.

"This is weird," Robin whispered.

"What is?"

"It's so quiet and...and so empty."

Judy tugged Robin's sleeve to get her attention. "Are you okay? You seem scared."

"It's just...um...it's just that I haven't gone out at night up here, and this is straight out of a horror movie. All we're missing is the fog and the...and the—"

"Clowns?" Judy chirped.

Robin hung her head, and lifting her eyes to meet Judy's, she said, "This is going to be a constant with you, isn't it?"

"Maybe," Judy said, tittering. "But I haven't moved the doll yet, so that's a plus." Judy hooked her arm through Robin's long enough to get the woman moving again. "Come on. I'll protect you."

Robin could have easily marched right into a clown convention at that moment, but as quickly as Judy had slipped her arm through Robin's, she removed it. Disconnected from the warmth and touch that had made her heart sing, the corners of Robin's mouth drooped, but a few seconds later Robin found herself grinning. It's hard not to when you see a bunch of bananas walking across the street.

Mackinac's history, like that of Salem, Massachusetts, lends itself to the celebration of Halloween, for where better to observe All Hallows' Eve than on an island rich with the spirits of the dead. It is one of the few holidays enjoyed by the residents without the intrusions of thousands of tourists, and it only took an instant for Robin to realize that the Mackinac locals did indeed like to dress up...and they also liked to party.

The bananas, hooked peel-in-peel, sauntered down the street, singing the Banana Boat song at the top of their lungs while in front of them, with plastic parrots perched upon their shoulders, a group of pirates raised their mugs in acknowledgment as Judy and Robin walked by.

The further into town they moved, the more people filled the streets, forcing Robin and Judy to zig and zag through throngs of ghosts, skeletons, and the entire cast of characters from the Wizard of Oz. Music streamed out from the restaurants and bars, and white-faced corpses of Indians, soldiers, and ladies and gentlemen of yesteryear draped in historical finery entered and exited, and Robin couldn't contain her smile. She wasn't a fan of Halloween, but the more she saw, the more she started to think about joining in on the festivities next year.

Without warning, Robin felt someone grab her arm and force her toward a dark alley between two stores. For a second, she fought against the direction, only to quickly give up the fight when she realized it was Judy doing the pulling. Robin had been led into darkened pathways before by women wanting to steal a kiss just because they could, but Robin was fairly certain that wasn't Judy's intent. Damn it.

"So...," Robin whispered, surveying her surroundings before looking at back at Judy. "Any reason why we're standing in an alley?"

Judy looked past Robin to the crowd on the street and then lifted her eyes to meet Robin's. "Someone's dressed up as a clown, and he appears to be trying to make his way over here."

Robin's shoulders fell. "Seriously?"

"Yeah, but the Pony is just past that cycle shop," Judy said, pointing up the street. "Care to make a run for it?"

"You read my mind."

***

For anyone visiting Mackinac, it's rare that The Pink Pony isn't on their list of things to see. Situated inside the Chippewa Hotel, the bar and grill is known for its laidback atmosphere, imaginative cocktails, and its location. Built on the water, its massive patio juts out over the Straits, giving those dining under the umbrellas of pink a photo opportunity that all took advantage of.

When Robin reached the front door of the Pony, she only had to wait a few seconds until Judy caught up to her, and with the safety of the bar and grill at hand, they walked inside without a care in the world. Judy made her way to the host's podium, confirming the reservation she had made hours before, and within minutes, the two women were being led through the restaurant to a booth in the back.

Robin wasn't surprised to see the restaurant stayed true to its name. A pale shade of pink appeared in the upholstery of the bar stools, while the ceiling tiles were almost fuchsia in tone, and ponies could be seen on the glassware as well as on the T-shirts of the wait staff. But as she looked around, Robin realized the primary theme was boating. On every wall were posters of yacht races held over the years, and oars and lifejackets hung near tables, their surfaces worn and tattered, proving their authenticity.

As they walked by the singer on the stage, Robin grinned as she noticed the mural of high-stepping pink ponies on the wall behind him. With the noise level rising and falling as conversations in the restaurant grew loud and then quiet, for a moment, she could clearly hear the lyrics of the Monster Mash and then just as quickly, it was swallowed up by the boisterousness of the party atmosphere.

When they reached the table, they slipped into the booth and shrugged out of their coats, and before too long they had ordered their drinks and then their dinner.

"This is quite a place," Robin said, looking around. "You come here often?"

Judy giggled. "That sounds like a pick up line."

"Oh, sorry," Robin said, her cheeks instantly darkening one shade. "That's not what I meant."

"I know, and to answer your question, occasionally."

"And they close, too? I mean, for the season."

"Yes," Judy said, nodding. "There're only three that stay open all year round."

"I'm glad I filled the freezers then."

"You *over*filled the freezers."

"Say that when you run out of food and have to come begging to me for a handout."

Judy smiled as she reached for her wine. "And speaking of hungry, Adele bookmarked a few breakfast casseroles in one of the cookbooks. I was thinking about trying a few of them out so we could get an idea of what works and what doesn't before we're open for business."

"Technically, we could open for business tomorrow. White Birch is ready to go."

"You really want to open, don't you?"

Robin shrugged. "I just figured what's the harm if we do? I know we probably won't have anyone, but just in case..."

"All right, I'll see about putting a sign up at the Tourism Bureau before they close for the year. Just don't be disappointed when we don't get anyone, and you're left sampling all the recipes I'm going to try."

"I doubt you could ever disappoint me," Robin said quietly, and as she sipped her wine, she became lost in the gray-blue of the eyes gazing back at her.

"*Happy Halloween!*"

Robin and Judy both jumped at the clamorous greeting, and their heads turned in unison. Standing near their table were two people appearing as if they had just stepped out of *Lewis Carroll's Through the Looking-Glass, and What Alice Found There.*

Staying true to the mirrored characters, the Tweedledee and Tweedledum grinning back at Judy and Robin were dressed identically. Their dark mustard stretch trousers were pulled up well past their waists, disappearing under short jackets the color of sangria, and on their heads, both wore striped caps, topped with propellers.

"Happy Halloween to you, too," Judy said, gesturing toward Robin. "I'm not sure if you've met Robin yet. She's Adele's niece."

"Haven't had the pleasure," Tweedledum said, sticking out his hand. "Name's Tommy Conroy, and this is my lovely bride, Rose. It's very nice to meet you."

Robin's eyes widened just a tad. With their height, weight, and shape almost as identical as their costumes, Robin had thought both the people were men. She did a quick double-take, and that's when she noticed the subtle difference between the drape of Tommy's jacket and that of his wife. "Nice to meet you, too," Robin said, shaking Tommy's hand. "Great costumes."

"They're not only great. They're authentic," Tweedledum stated as he inched closer. "When *we* design *our* costumes, they're perfect down to the last detail."

Robin found the man's tone imperious, and with his rotund belly now resting on the edge of their table, she set her jaw. She quickly glanced at

Judy, and when she saw the woman roll her eyes in response, Robin turned back to Tweedledum. "Is that so?"

"Yes, indeed it is," Tweedledee said, and sashaying forward, the woman crossed her pudgy arms across her equally pudgy stomach. "We have a reputation to uphold. While some think store-bought costumes are good enough, Tommy and I know better. You can't win these contests with masks and painted faces. You need to put your heart and soul into it if you want to call yourself a winner."

Robin was at a loss as she looked back and forth between the two people, but thankfully, Judy came to her rescue.

"So, guys...are you hitting all the places tonight?" Judy asked.

"*Of course!*" Tweedledum bellowed. "We're planning to make a clean sweep." He turned to his wife and pointed toward the front of the restaurant. "Which reminds me, sugarplum, we really should be going. We still have a few more contests to enter before the night is over."

"You're absolutely right, dear," Rose Conway said, hooking her arm through her husband's. "We do hope you two enjoy your evening, and don't forget to vote for us!"

"We'll do that," Judy said, forcing a smile. "Good luck."

Robin looked over her shoulder, watching as the tubby twins waddled to the front door. "They're quite a pair," she said, turning back to Judy.

"That's putting it nicely," Judy said with a laugh.

"So, they *were* haughty then? It wasn't just me."

"Oh no. It wasn't you," Judy said, taking a sip of her wine. "Rose and Tommy are nice enough, but they're also a little over-the-top."

"Let me guess. They can trace their lineage back to the founding fathers of Mackinac, and they're very proud of the fact?"

"No, actually they're transplants."

"You're kidding."

"Nope," Judy said, placing her glass back on the table. "They used to just come to Mackinac for vacation, but about fifteen years ago they decided to move here. They opened up a place called Beads and Bangles, and they've lived here ever since."

"So why so...um...so snobby?"

"That's just who they are, and as you could see, they're also very competitive. Other than anything requiring one ounce of athleticism, if there's a contest on the island, Tommy and Rose will always be among the competitors."

"And I'm assuming they win a lot."

"Not as much as they'd like," Judy said with a chuckle.

Again, Robin found herself held spellbound by Judy's eyes. She had no idea how long she was staring, but when Robin went to take another taste of her wine, she found her glass empty. Feeling her cheeks begin to heat, Robin pushed herself out of the booth. "I think I'm going to visit the ladies' room. Be right back."

"Okay. It's up there on the right."

"Thanks."

Judy watched as Robin made her way through the crowd, and after finishing what was left of her own Cabernet in one swallow, she placed both glasses at the edge of the table and rested back in the booth. Most of the bars were holding costume contests, so Judy wasn't surprised that the liveliness of the restaurant had calmed a little. Like Tommy and Rose, many dressed for the holiday had made their way to the next stop leaving behind patrons more interested in food and drink, but a few costumed characters were still in view. Sitting at a nearby table was a trio of penguins enthusiastically rating the flights of beer in front of them, and at the bar stood a coven of witches holding brooms in one hand and drinks in the other. A lumberjack with a painted-on beard was standing near the restrooms, his arms draped over his colleagues' shoulders as they posed for a selfie, but the last in costume was alone...and heading straight for Judy in all his jokester glory.

"I've been trying to catch up with you since I saw you walking down the street, Jude," the carrot-topped clown said as he staggered up to the booth. "How 'bout I buy you a drink?"

Judy's shoulders sagged as she recognized the voice of the jester and one quick glance down at his greasy fingernails, confirmed Judy's worst fears. Behind the white makeup and the smeared black grin was Bubba Burdett.

A former employee of The Wheelhouse, Bubba had been a constant in Judy's life almost as long as Scott. Hired on part-time during his sophomore year in high school, Bubba had spent every free minute working at Scott's father's side, learning everything there was to know about bicycles. By the time Scott returned from college, Bubba was the best bike mechanic on the island, and he quickly became one of the reasons why The Wheelhouse was so successful. From antique Schwinns to streamlined racing bikes, there wasn't one Bubba couldn't fix or tweak...and the word spread.

From open to close, Bubba could be found at his bench in the shop. Located right outside the tiny office where Judy spent most of her time, she'd listen to him whistle and belch his way through the day, hardly giving him a moment's notice while she placed orders for stock. There were times when she'd look up to find him staring at her, his penetrating gaze causing goosebumps to appear on her skin, but offering her a yellow-toothed smile, he'd get back to work without so much as another glance in Judy's direction for the rest of the day.

On an island the size of Mackinac, it was inevitable that Bubba's path would cross with Judy's and Scott's after The Wheelhouse had closed for the day. A bachelor who liked sports bars and beer, in the evening when many of the tourists had returned to the mainland, Bubba could be found at the Pony or the Mustang, sampling the finest Michigan had to offer, and if Scott and Judy walked in for dinner, they'd always invite him to join them. It was what friends did, and Judy always considered Bubba a friend, or at least she did until she discovered Bubba wanted more than friendship.

Before the ink was dry on her divorce decree, Bubba asked Judy out on a date, and as politely as she could, Judy turned him down. Her excuse was that it was too early, too soon after her marriage had ended to think of anyone else, but it wasn't long before Judy was forced to tell Bubba the truth. She wasn't interested in going out with him. She was polite and apologetic, hoping not to hurt the man's feelings, but Bubba didn't seem to grasp the concept. No matter where Judy worked, at some point during the day, she'd look up to see him watching her. No matter what restaurant she'd visit, he'd appear and then invite himself to join her, and no matter how many times Judy would say no, he'd ask again...just like he was doing right now.

"Thanks, Bubba, but I'm here with a friend," Judy said, motioning toward the two wine glasses on the table.

"Well, then I'll buy you both a drink," he said, lurching into Judy's personal space. "How 'bout that?"

Judy recoiled as Bubba's beer breath washed over her. "I don't think so," she said, moving farther into the booth. "She'll be back in a minute, and we've already ordered dinner."

"Come on, Jude," Bubba said, and placing his plump, hairy hand on Judy's shoulder, he gave it a squeeze. "Jus' one little drink. What's wrong with that?"

"Other than the fact she said no, you mean?"

Bubba stood straight, wobbling for a second before turning around. "And whaz it to you if she did?"

If Robin hadn't just returned from the restroom, the need for one would have been forefront in her mind. Not only was she face-to-face with a ghoulish clown, this one smelled of stale beer and several apparently sloppy bathroom visits. Grimacing at the stench, Robin took a half-step backward before she managed to find her voice again.

"In case you haven't heard, no means no," Robin said, glaring into the clown's bloodshot eyes. "And she just told you no. So, either you walk away, or I'm going to call the manager over."

"I live on this goddamned rock," Bubba said, puffing out his chest. "They know me here. They won't kick me out."

"Maybe not," Robin said, and looking around, she motioned for a waiter. "But there's no harm in trying. Now, is there?"

Bubba rubbed his hand over his stubbly chin, smearing more of the black face paint into the white as he glared back at Robin. "Oh, fuck it," he grumbled, before gulping down what remained in his mug. "I'm out of suds anyway."

Robin took a step back so Bubba could pass, and as he wobbled to the bar, she slipped into the booth and immediately reached for her glass, slurping down the few drops that remained.

"Are you okay?" Judy said, leaning forward. "You look a little pale."

"Of all the guys in this bar, you *had* to attract a *clown*?"

"I'm sorry, but thanks for coming to my rescue."

"I would have been here sooner, except the lumberjack at the restrooms stopped me."

"Let me guess. He wanted to buy you a drink, too?"

Robin smiled. "Close. *She* wanted to buy me a drink."

Before Judy could respond, the waiter returned with their food.

"Here you go, ladies. Hot off the grill." Placing the steaming plates in front of them, he tucked the tray under his arm and picked up the two empty glasses. "Can I interest you two in a refill?"

Judy looked over at Robin. The color had yet to return to her cheeks, and by the size of the two slabs of prime rib in front of them, they weren't going anywhere for a while. "Make it a bottle, Ed," Judy said, picking up her silverware. "It'll save you some trips."

Chapter Twenty-Five

Robin had barely stepped out of her bedroom before she paused to breathe in the view. Judy was sitting at the dining room table with her head bowed as sunlight streamed in from the patio doors. It blazed its way into the kitchen, lighting up the entire room, yet as far as Robin was concerned, its warmth was no match for what Judy added to the space, merely by existing. "I could get used to this."

Judy looked up from the list she was making and smiled. "Good morning. Coffee's done."

"I smell that," Robin said, shuffling over to pour a cup. "How long have you been here?"

"About an hour, I guess. I was trying to be quiet. I hope I didn't wake you."

"You didn't," Robin said before taking a sip of her coffee. "What are you working on?"

"I figured since we have almost six months to get all the rooms ready, we could split our time between that and everything else."

"What's everything else?"

"Well, I need to learn the accounting software, so I can start entering all the information from Adele's old receipts and records. There's a lot of good stuff in there, and I don't think we want to lose it."

"I agree."

"We also need to look into getting a website, so I thought I'd do some research and see who's got the best plans. Once I figure that out and you and I agree on a template, I can start working on designing one. With your input, of course."

Robin flinched back her head. "You know how to build a website?"

"I did the one for The Wheelhouse. It's not that hard, and the sooner we get it done, the sooner our name's out there." Judy stopped long enough to take a drink of her coffee. "And I need to get a copy of that spreadsheet you made with all the room rates. That way, once the accounting software is up and running, I can start working on the booking and management program you bought so we have the right rates tied to the right dates."

"And you talk about *my* energy level," Robin said with a laugh. "Just how much coffee have *you* had this morning."

"This is only my second cup," Judy said, lifting her mug. "Thank you very much."

Robin grinned. "And while you're doing all of that, what exactly am I supposed to be doing?"

"Writing."

"Really?" Robin squeaked.

"Sure, why not?"

"But aren't you going to need my help?"

"Not at first, and besides, what are you planning to do? Hover over me at the computer?"

"No, but you forget. I still need a desk."

"We can move the one out of Georgian Bay," Judy said as she got up to get more coffee. "We both agreed it was out of place in there, and it would fit perfectly in Firefly. Let's just swap the chairs for the desk, and that way, you can write, and I can work."

"It's not fair for you to do all the—"

"What's the best time for you to write?" Judy said as she topped off her mug.

"Huh?"

"What's the best time for you to write? Morning? Afternoon? Night?"

"Oh...um...usually mornings," Robin said, scratching her head. "Why?"

"Then this will work," Judy said, slipping the carafe back into the coffee maker. "While I'm doing stuff down here, you go upstairs and write, and then we take a break, have some lunch, and spend the rest of the day doing whatever needs to be done."

"And you figured all of this out this morning?"

"Yes," Judy said, flashing a toothy smile. "It's amazing what you can accomplish when you don't sleep in."

Robin glanced at the clock above the sink. "It's not even seven o'clock yet."

"What's your point?" Judy said, folding her arms across her chest.

It was a good question, but as Robin looked at Judy, between the dimples in the woman's cheeks and her stance, whatever point Robin was trying to make was quickly forgotten. After taking a sip of her coffee, Robin placed the cup on the counter. "Let me go put on some shoes."

"Why?"

It was Robin's turn to flash a smile. "Because we have a desk to move."

***

Judy stood in the doorway of the office, sipping coffee while she looked back and forth from the small stack of records still needing to be entered into the computer and those she'd finished, now packed away in totes near the desk. It had been so easy on Monday to agree to change their plans for the day, but now it was Thursday, and Judy's eyes were beginning to cross. She dared not tell Robin, for fear she'd pull her away from her writing, so for the past day and a half, Judy had hidden her weariness behind false effervescence.

Tapping her fingers against the door frame, Judy considered her options. She still needed to find a website host, but that required sitting in front of the computer for yet another day. With a sigh, Judy returned to the kitchen long enough to refill her coffee, but as she made her way back to the office, something on the island caught her eye. Judy paused. She pondered. She shrugged...and then she smiled.

***

To be a successful writer, one of the first lessons learned is commitment. The unspoken promise an author makes to their story that it won't be forgotten or neglected. It *will* be written, and out of that dedication, a routine is born.

Like the masses, authors' work schedules normally include set times when they rise or slumber, but untethered by an employer's expectations, writers must create their own. For some, it's based solely on the amount of · time spent. They allot two, four, or more hours per day to their craft and no matter what is produced during that time, they are satisfied for they've reached their goal. Others use word or page counts as their targets and focused on them, whether it takes an hour or an entire day, it will be attained before they walk away from their desk.

Monday morning, Robin climbed the stairs leading to Firefly, and armed with the confidence she had once lost, when she opened her manuscript, she viewed it with an eye critical, but not condemning. Yes, her voice and style had been ensnared in a muck of adjectives, adverbs, and hastily written words, and no consideration had been given to telling versus showing, but amongst those words was a story...and it was a good one.

By the time she and Judy met for lunch in the kitchen Monday afternoon, both were bubbling over with excitement. Robin's novel wasn't nearly as crappy as she first thought and Judy was quickly getting the hang of the new accounting software, and before the last potato chip had been munched, they agreed to change their plans. Instead of working on any of the suites, Judy eagerly returned to what she had started, and Robin bounded back up the stairs to Firefly, a decision Robin hadn't regretted until now.

Robin's goal had always been four pages a day. To some, the number seemed trivial, but it gave Robin an attainable target while keeping her on a schedule that had proven itself time and time again. She knew if she could write at least four pages a day, in no time at all, a novel could be produced, but writing a book versus repairing a poorly written manuscript wasn't the same thing. Her mind no longer fogged with doubt and her abilities to weave words clearer than they'd ever been, Robin had already rewritten the first four chapters of the once gruesome manuscript. The fifth, however, had remained untouched on her computer screen all morning.

She sat at her desk, staring out the window as the rain pattered against the panes. The sky was thick with ashen clouds choking out all but the most dismal of light. The skeletons of oaks and birch, naked of leaves, swayed to and fro in the wind while tiny whitecaps broke the surface of the Straits. It was indeed a dreary setting, and it fit Robin's mood at the moment.

Instead of sticking to her timetable, for three straight days, from sun up to sun down, Robin sequestered herself in Firefly. She had taken breaks for lunch, joining Judy in the kitchen for sandwiches or leftovers, but fueled by her passion to write, Robin had willingly returned to it, and that was her mistake. She hadn't given herself time to reflect on what she was creating.

Unlike many, authors never leave their work at the office. Their stories, characters, and dialogue churn in their minds whether they're sitting at their computers, washing dishes, or eating dinner. They can picture their protagonists, and hear their voices thickened with accents, slurred by alcohol, or deepened by lust. They can feel the cold of winter chilling their skin or the summer sun beating down on their face, and as the crescendo of their scenes build, shivers run down their spines as well. And as writers mull over their creations, loopholes are found, better ideas come to mind, and dialogue once flat becomes crisp. Sadly, at the moment, Robin's brain was about as crisp as a head of wilted lettuce.

There were no words. There were no sentences or paragraphs or chapters inside Robin's head. There was only an empty space, a black hole where thoughts were lost before they could be formed because Robin was tired. Not in the physical sense as if she'd run the circumference of the island every morning for her jogs in the foggy hours of dawn had been short, but mentally Robin was spent.

Robin needed a break, and she knew the house was filled with distractions, but she didn't want to interrupt Judy. All week, the woman had practically skipped into the house every morning, anxious to get back to the office and her data entry, and Robin was afraid if she decided to start a project, Judy would put her own work aside to help.

Robin rubbed the back of her neck. She glared at her laptop, and with a sigh, she placed her elbows on the desk and prepared herself to read the words she knew she'd forget almost instantly. She took a deep breath, hoping as she exhaled her mind would clear, but instead, Robin found the distraction she'd been looking for.

***

"Looks like someone is being productive. What smells so good?"

"It's one of your aunt's recipes," Judy said, turning around from the sink. "Hey, I didn't know you wore glasses."

Robin snatched the black-framed spectacles from her face. "And you weren't supposed to."

"Why not? If you need them, you should wear them."

"I never *needed* them until a couple of years ago, and it kind of makes me feel old when I wear them, so I usually only put them on when I'm working," Robin said with a shrug. "Call it pride."

"You know, that's one of the deadly sins."

"And so is gluttony," Robin said, breathing deeply the aroma filling the kitchen. "What in the world is in the oven?"

"It's an egg, cheese, and bacon casserole. We had all the ingredients, so I thought I'd give it a try."

Robin glanced toward the office. "You finished with all the old paperwork? That's great!"

Judy's shoulders sagged. "No, I didn't, and I'm sorry, but I needed a break. My eyes were starting to cross."

"You mean it's not just me then?"

"What?"

"I've been upstairs all morning staring at my computer without typing a word."

"But I thought you wanted to write?"

"I did, and I do, but I need to get away from it every now and then to clear my head."

"Why didn't you tell me? We could have started working on the rooms."

"Because I thought *you* wanted to get the bookkeeping done."

Judy pressed her lips together to suppress her grin. "I'm thinking you and I need to work on our communication skills."

"Well, how's this for communication?" Robin said and going over to the island, she looked Judy in the eye. "I don't want to write today."

Judy's grin escaped, and she allowed it to fill her face. "I don't either. I don't care if we clean, paint, wallpaper, or rearrange furniture. As long as it doesn't have anything thing to do with paperwork, numbers, or computers—I'm in."

***

"How you doing in there?"

"Loving every minute of it," Robin called out as she dipped her brush in the paint again. "I'm finishing up cutting in again. Then I just have to roll the walls one more time, and we can cross this bathroom off our list. How about you?"

"I'm just starting the second coat," Judy said, slowly drawing her brush across the baseboard.

"Slacker!"

"Slacker my ass."

Robin smiled, and setting her brush aside, she grabbed the roller and began giving the walls their last coat.

By the time they had finished their casserole brunch, Robin and Judy had planned the rest of their day. Even though Judy doubted they'd have any guests before the season started in May, since paint had an odor and wallpaper didn't, it made sense to get all the painting out of the way just in case. They merrily ascended the stairs carrying two gallons of bright white paint and heading into Sunset Shores, while Robin attacked the bathroom, Judy carefully freshened up all the trim in the bedroom with a new coat of white.

"So, how did that woman know you were gay?" Judy called out as she dipped her brush into the paint can again.

Robin stopped mid-roll, her forehead furrowing as she glanced over at the doorway. "What woman?"

"The one at the Pony."

"Oh. I don't know," Robin said, shrugging. "Gaydar probably."

Judy tilted her head. "Gaydar?"

"Yeah, it means...um...crap." Robin set down the roller and went back into the bedroom, looking over the furniture blocking her view of Judy. "It's hard to explain. It's like an intuition that some of us have. We can figure out who's gay and who's not simply with a look or maybe a few words."

"And you can do this?"

Robin snickered. "Not usually. I mean, if the woman's butch or wearing a rainbow across her chest, it's pretty easy, but I've struck out more times than I've hit a home run, that's for sure."

"Oh," Judy said as she went back to painting the baseboard.

"Any reason you asked?"

"No. I was just wondering how she knew. I thought maybe you approached her."

"Not a chance."

"Why not?" Judy said, looking over her shoulder.

"Well, first off, I was with you."

"It's not like we were on a date, Robin, and I don't want to get in the way of you...um—"

"Trying to get some?"

Judy's eyes widened. "That's a little blunt, but yes, I guess."

Robin shook her head. "Why is it that heterosexuals think that all lesbians are attracted to every woman on the planet? Are you attracted to every man?"

"No, of course not."

"Then why would you think I was trying to pick that woman up?"

"I don't know. She didn't look bad from where I was sitting."

"*You* thought she was a *man*," Robin said with a laugh.

"Yeah, but I don't know your type."

"Wow," Robin said, placing her hand over her heart. "Not only are you going to be my business partner, but you're also planning to be my matchmaker, too. How cool is that?"

Judy narrowed her eyes. "I have no intention of playing matchmaker. I was just saying that if you found that woman attractive, being out with me shouldn't have stopped you from...from asking her out."

"Good to know, but you needn't worry about the lumberjack. She wasn't my type," Robin said before disappearing back into the bathroom. She loaded the roller with paint and managed a few strokes before her progress was halted again.

"What is your type?"

Judy's question brought a smile to Robin's face, and returning the roller to the tray, she stepped into the doorway. "I thought you weren't going to be my matchmaker."

"I'm not. I was just curious. That's all."

As Judy returned to painting the baseboard, Robin pondered how to respond. She had dated tall women, short women, slender ones, and those not-so-slender. Blondes, brunettes, and even a few redheads had been in her bed, and sports dykes and baby dykes had been seen on her arm more than once. Bois and butch had come and gone, and she had had her fair share of lipstick lesbians as well, but if Robin had to choose a type, it would be the one fitting the woman sitting on the floor across the room. "Chapsticks."

Judy froze for a second before turning around. "Huh?"

"Chapsticks."

"I don't know what that means."

"You know, if you're going to be my matchmaker, you really need to get up to speed with the nomenclature."

"Well, until I can find a book on the subject, how about you just enlighten me."

Robin paused for only a second before answering. "A chapstick is a lesbian who's halfway between butch and femme. I'm assuming you're familiar with those terms."

"I am."

"Okay, so a chapstick is comfortable in both of those worlds. She can be a girly-girl and wear makeup and dress to the nines, or she can just as easily go the other way and wear jeans and flannel shirts."

"So you're a chapstick then?"

"Very good," Robin said with a slight bow of her head.

"And that woman in the bar was too...um...too butch for you?"

"It wasn't really her style as much as it was her hardware."

"Her hardware?"

"I'm not into piercings," Robin said with a shrug, and returning to the bathroom, she picked up her roller one last time before continuing the conversation. "She had two in her eyebrow, one in her nose, and three hoops through her lip," Robin said, covering the last bit of plaster with its final coat. "And any butch having that many on her face normally doesn't stop there, if you know what I mean." Robin stepped back and inspected the wall, swaying to and fro to see if she had missed any spots.

"I have no clue."

"What?" Robin called out.

Judy huffed as she loaded her brush again. "I said *I have no clue what you're talking about.*"

Robin was sure Judy's interest was just the run-of-the-mill curiosity that most straight people had when it came to gays, but that didn't mean she wasn't enjoying the conversation. When they were student and teacher, their talks had been safe, centering on current events while leaving personal tidbits out of the discussions, but that was no longer the case. Judy wasn't the teacher. Robin wasn't the student. They were both adults. They were friends, and with friendships, walls come down, subject matters change, and each comes into their own.

Smiling, Robin didn't hold back her answer. "Let's just say, I don't like metal in my mouth and leave it at that."

At the very least, Robin thought Judy would have responded with her another 'huh,' but instead, all she heard was a long line of expletives being shouted from the bedroom. Robin rushed back to the doorway and then burst out laughing. Across the wallpaper, they *weren't* planning to change, was a wide brushstroke of white paint.

"Giving Isobel a run for her money?" Robin said while doing her best to swallow what was left of her mirth.

Judy hung her head, sniggering under her breath at her predicament. "No, but remind me never to be alone in the same room with you and Rita."

Robin's teeth gleamed in her grin. "Really?"

"Yes, *really*," Judy said as she grabbed some nearby rags and threw them in Robin's direction. "Now, if you're done embarrassing me, could you run those under some water, so I can clean up this mess?"

"As you wish," Robin said, snagging the old kitchen towels from the floor. "As you wish."

***

Other than when Robin was writing, and Judy was working in the office, they spent nearly every waking minute together for the next eight days, and their strategy was paying off. Robin was making progress with her manuscript. Judy was doing the same with all the management software, and Whitefish Falls, Forest View, and Sunset Shores were almost ready for guests. Ceilings, bathrooms, and trim had all been restored to a brilliant white. The rooms were cleaned, and the only thing left to do was to pick up the drapes at the dry cleaners in St. Ignace, contact a linen service, wash the quilts, and make the beds.

Shortly after five on Friday night, they made their way down the stairs, and as they reached the landing, Judy looked over at Robin and tutted. "How come you always manage to get paint in your hair?"

"I have no idea," Robin said, fingering the mass of blonde strands coated in paint. "I guess I just really get into my work."

"Maybe you should think of getting into a shower before that stuff dries," Judy said, continuing down the stairs. "Dinner won't be ready for at least another forty-five minutes. You have time."

"Are you sure?"

"Of course, I'm sure. All *I* need to do is wash my hands."

"'*All I need to do is wash my hands*,'" Robin whispered in a whiney voice as they reached the foyer. "Show off."

"It's not my fault you're sloppy."

"I'm not sloppy. I just need to get my hair cut short."

"Really? Are you planning to get it cut?" Judy said as they rounded the corner and headed toward Robin's suite.

"I've been thinking about it. There are a couple of styles I like, but my mother always loved it long, so that's the way I kept it that way. Why? Don't you think I should?"

"No, it's...it's up to you. Totally your choice."

"Well, I think the only choice I need to make right now is how many times I'm going to have to wash it to get the paint out," Robin said, reaching her bedroom door. "Are you sure you're okay with dinner?"

"Go!" Judy said, motioning toward the kitchen. "I can handle setting the table."

"All right. I'm going," Robin said, disappearing into her bedroom. "Oh, and that bottle of wine we opened last night is on the counter if you're interested."

***

Judy placed the lid back on the crockpot and opening a cabinet, she returned the chili powder to its place on the shelf. She reached for her wine, and taking a sip of the velvety Merlot, she turned around, leaned against the counter and let out an easy breath. It was another good day in a growing line of good days. It was nice to be active again, to be a part of something new and exciting, but it was more than that.

She no longer felt like a visitor possibly trampling on the privacy of another when she walked into Safe Harbor early in the morning, for Robin's smile always convinced her otherwise. Having helped make dinner more times than not, Judy now knew Robin's kitchen as if it were her own, and staying true to her promise, while decisions had been few over the past two weeks, Robin had included her on all of them. Judy wasn't sure when it happened, but Safe Harbor now felt like it was as much hers as it was Robin's...and it was also starting to feel like home.

Broken from her thoughts by the soft chime of the doorbell, Judy put down her wine and made her way to the foyer. Opening the door, she grinned at the stranger standing on the porch. "Hi. Welcome to Safe Harbor. Are you looking for a room?"

"Um...actually, I was looking for Robin Novak."

"Oh, she's—"

"*Eeeeeeeeeeeeeee!*"

Judy hunched her shoulders at the shrill squeal, and spinning around, she gaped as Robin ran toward the foyer, her arms high in the air as her joyous screech continued. Rushing past Judy, Robin jumped into the man's outstretched arms, and wrapping her legs around his waist, Robin planted kiss after kiss on his face. "Oh my God, I can't believe you're here!"

Declan held onto Robin as if a tornado was about to rip her from his arms, and breathing in the scent of her familiar cologne, he smiled into her wet hair. "If I didn't know better, I'd say you missed me."

Chapter Twenty-Six

"Damn, Judy, that was good," Declan said as he reached over and ripped off another hunk of sourdough bread. Sliding it around his bowl, he swept away any remnants of the remaining chili.

"Thanks, but how did you know I was the one who made it? Robin could have—"

"The hell she could have."

Judy looked back and forth between the people sitting to her right and left. Both were smiling, but while Declan's face showed off his dimples, Robin's showed off her blush. "Am I missing something?" Judy said to Declan.

"The last time Robbie made chili, I made her promise on her life that she'd never make it again. And before you ask, I'm not just being nice here," Declan said, ladling another scoop of chili into his bowl. "I love chili."

Judy's eyebrows grew together. "Then why—"

"Because it tasted like lumpy ketchup."

It wasn't intentional, but when Judy heard Declan's analogy, she scrunched up her face.

"It wasn't that bad," Robin said, rocking back in her chair.

"Robbie, it was crap and you and I both know it."

Robin hid her amusement as she tossed her napkin on the table. "Well, I never."

"Yeah, well according to the girls at our old haunts, never wasn't a word you used very often."

"Declan!"

"What?" he said as he filled his spoon with chili. "Truth hurt?"

"No, but you're going to hurt when I get done with you."

"Promises. Promises."

Over the past couple of hours, Judy's heart had swelled. Like her relationship with Rita, the friendship between Declan and Robin was loving and witty. They had played off of each other since Declan walked into the inn, tossing remarks and barbs between them like a ball in a tennis match. Yet through it all, neither had spoken a word without twinkling eyes or their faces glowing with love...just like they were now.

Noticing Declan had finished his third bowl and didn't appear to be going for another, Judy stood up. "If you two are done, why don't you go relax, and I'll clean this stuff up."

"Don't be ridiculous," Robin said, pushing out her chair. "I'll help."

"So will I," Declan announced as he straightened to six-feet-five.

"No, you won't," Judy said, pointing toward the living room. "Go relax and catch up, and I'll put on a pot of coffee." When Robin and Declan refused to budge, Judy placed her hands on her hips. "I said go. Now!"

Robin and Declan exchanged looks, and sighing in unison, they walked into the living room.

"Christ, she's as pushy as you are," Declan said, and sinking into the sofa, he glanced around the room. "*This* has got you written all over it."

"You like it?"

"Yeah, I like everything. Even the rooms upstairs with the shitty wallpaper have potential."

"We think so, too. Once we get everything done, I'll send you pictures."

"How about if I just see it in person?"

"Really?" Robin said, sitting forward on the couch. "You hate the cold."

"I wasn't talking about coming back in the winter. I was thinking maybe June or July."

"But that's eight months away!"

"I guess it could be sooner, but knowing Natalia, it'll probably be June."

Before Robin could speak, Fred appeared out of nowhere and jumped into Declan's lap.

"There's my boy," Declan said, running his hand down the cat's back. "You look none the worse for wear. Glad to see that your momma's feeding you."

"Like I wouldn't," Robin said, giving Declan the evil eye.

"And where's your sweet little sister?" Declan said, glancing around. "She's such a pretty girl."

No sooner had Declan spoke when Ginger jumped onto the couch and prancing across Robin's lap, she made a beeline for Declan.

"How you doing, baby," Declan said through puckered lips as he gave Ginger some attention. "Miss me?"

It came as no surprise to Robin when Ginger passed over her to greet Declan. Since the day her mother had given her the kittens, there had only ever been two constants in Fred's and Ginger's lives, and they were both sitting on the sofa. One they saw every day, and one they hadn't seen in weeks.

As the two felines slinked and slid all over Declan, welcoming their old friend back, Robin's grin continued to grow. She could easily hear their purrs, and flip-flopping in his lap, Fred and Ginger seemed eager for Declan's affection...almost too eager.

Robin lowered her chin as her eyes turned to slits. "Okay, what did you do?"

"You talking to me?" Declan said, momentarily glancing up before returning his attention to the cats now undulating against his corduroy sports coat.

"Yes, I'm talking to you. I'm not going to argue the fact that Fred and Ginger adore you, but what I'm witnessing right now is way beyond adoration. Hell, if it continues, I'm going to have to run out and buy them a pack of smokes."

"You really need to just accept that they like me more than they like you and move on. Not everyone is a cat person."

Robin snatched Fred off Declan's lap, and turning him around, she held the dangling kitty in front of her. It only took a moment for her to spot the bubble of spittle at the corner of his mouth, and with a laugh, Robin placed Fred on the floor and then turned to Declan. "You are such a bastard. Where is it?"

"Where's what?"

"The catnip."

"I have no idea what you're talking about?"

"Yes, you do. Fred's drooling, and the *only* time he drools is when he gets catnip."

"Maybe he's just excited to see me."

"Or maybe he's stoned out of his mind because my goofy friend coated his jacket with catnip," Robin said, and reaching over, she lifted Ginger from Declan's lap and placed her on the floor. "Go sleep it off, baby."

"That wasn't nice," Declan said, frowning as he watched Ginger saunter out of the room.

Without saying a word, Robin held out her hand, palm up.

A growl rose in Declan's throat as he reached into his inside jacket pocket. "Spoilsport," he said, tossing two fuzzy stuffed mice on the coffee table.

Robin regarded the catnip-stuffed toys for only a moment before shooting Declan a look. "Is that all of them?"

"What do you think I did? Buy out the store?"

"I wouldn't put it past you," Robin said, holding out her hand again. "Now, give me the rest."

"You really are a pain in the ass," Declan said, and standing up, he stuffed his hands into the pockets of his trousers and a moment later, two feathery stuffed canaries joined the mice on the table.

"I knew it!" Robin said, clapping her hands. "But I think you dropped something on the floor."

"I only bought four," Declan said, collapsing onto the sofa. "Now give it a rest."

"No, it was something else. It went flying. It looked like loose change."

"I didn't have—" Declan's eyes widened, and jumping off the sofa, he fell to his knees and began running his hands over the carpet.

"What the hell are you doing? Looking for a quarter to call someone who cares?"

"I can't fucking believe this," Declan mumbled, jamming his hand under the sofa. "Me and my brilliant ideas."

"Decl—"

"Found it!" Declan announced, and sitting back on his haunches at Robin's feet, he gazed up at his best friend.

"What was so important that—" Robin's words caught in her throat when she saw the diamond ring Declan was holding between his fingers.

"So...what do you think?"

"Oh my, God," Robin said in a voice barely audible. "It's gorgeous."

"I really wish you had been in the store with me. I don't know shit about—"

"Declan, it's beautiful. Natalia is going to be on cloud nine."

"She has to say yes first."

"Like there's a doubt," Robin said quietly, sniffling back a tear as Declan handed her the ring. Slipping it onto her finger, she smiled as her eyes met his. "She's one very lucky lady."

"Sorry it took so long," Judy said as she came into the room. "I wasn't sure what you took in your coffee."

Robin sprang to her feet. "Look!" she said, holding out her hand.

Judy glanced at the ring for a second before placing the tray filled with coffee and cups on the table. "I thought you were gay," she said, standing straight.

Robin's smile vanished for an instant before it reappeared. "I am. This isn't for me. Declan's going to propose to his girlfriend."

"Oh," Judy said, turning her attention to Declan. "It's beautiful."

"Thanks," Declan said, straightening his backbone just a smidge. "I hope she thinks so."

"I'm sure she will," Judy said before looking back at Robin. "And now I think I'm going to head home."

"What? Why?" Robin blurted. "I thought you'd stay and have some coffee."

"No, that's okay."

"Are you sure?"

"Yes, it's been a long day, and I'm a little tired," Judy said, and turning to Declan, she held out her hand. "It was very nice to meet you."

"The feeling is mutual," Declan said, getting to his feet.

"I'll walk you out," Robin said as Judy turned to leave.

"Don't be silly. You have a guest."

"Then how about if the *guest* walks you out?" Declan said, slipping the ring from Robin's finger. "My room is on the way, and I need to put this thing back in the box before I lose it."

Judy's left eyebrow raised just a tad. "Is there any reason why you two believe I need help finding the door?"

"This has got nothing to do with you finding the door," Declan said as he hooked his arm in Judy's. "This is about something covered in a blue plastic bag on the dining room table that Robin refuses to tell me about."

***

A short time later, Declan came back into the living room. "That is one fucking *ugly* clown."

"If you promise not to mention the clown again, I'll give you one of these," Robin said, holding up a snifter.

Declan's smile lit up the room, and going over, he sat down and took the glass from Robin. "What clown?"

"I'd thought you'd say that."

"Yeah, well you know me a little too well." Declan cupped the bowl of the snifter in his hand, allowing his body heat to warm the cognac for a moment. Breathing in the fragrances of honeysuckle and vanilla, Declan took a sip. "Oh, very smooth. Excellent choice"

"Glad you like it."

"Speaking of like, I like Judy. She seems really nice."

"She is."

Declan settled into the corner of the sofa and crossed one long leg over the other. "Can I be honest?"

"Always."

"I had my doubts about you moving up here."

"But you said you thought it was a good idea."

"What the hell did you expect me to say, Robbie? You were always so happy-go-lucky, and then Pam came along and managed to suck every ounce of happiness *and* confidence out of you like a fucking vampire. And even after you broke it off, and even *after* she was arrested, you were still so mired down in her muck, I just knew if you didn't get away, you'd always be looking over your shoulder, waiting for her to show her ugly head again...and I'd never get my Robbie back."

"And you think she's back now?"

"Are you kidding me?" Declan said as his mouth curled into a smile that reached his ears. "Abso-fucking-lutely! The minute I saw you running up that hallway, screaming like a banshee, I knew you were back. Hell, you're not just back, you're better than ever."

"How do you figure that?"

"Well, let's just put it this way. If I didn't know better, I'd swear you were pregnant."

Robin's eyes bulged. "What!"

"Kiddo, you're positively glowing, and you've been doing it all night."

"Did you ever think it's just because I'm happy to see you."

"Nice try," Declan said, eyeballing the woman. "And I would buy that if we hadn't seen each other in years, but it's only been six weeks, Robin, so stop trying to stroke my ego and tell me the truth."

"There's no other truth to tell, Declan. I'm writing again. I'm running again, and I'm just...I'm just happy."

Declan lifted his chin and looked down his nose at Robin. "I know you way better than that."

Robin silently damned the friendship she held dear as she took a long, slow breath. Unable to look Declan in the eye, she whispered, "She's the teacher."

Declan shook his head. "Who's the teacher?"

"Judy."

"How can she be a teacher and still manage to help you run this place?"

"No, I didn't say she's *a* teacher," Robin said quietly as she raised her eyes. "I said she's *the* teacher."

Declan's eyebrows drew together, Robin's words replaying in his mind while he reached for his drink, but just before he was about to pick up the snifter, he whipped around to face Robin. "Holy fucking Mother of God!" he shouted, bringing his hands together in a clap that echoed off the walls. "Are you shitting me? *Judy* is the one you've been crushing on for all these years?"

Robin sighed. "The one and only."

"Well, I'll be a son-of-a-bitch. Talk about a small world."

"Tell me about it."

"And does she know?"

"What? That I had a crush on her? No, and don't you *dare* tell her."

"You know me better than that, and you're using the wrong tense."

"What are you talking about?"

"You said you *had* a crush on her. You and I both know you still have it."

"Oh," Robin said, lowering her eyes.

"And that leads me to the next question." Declan stopped to pick up his cognac and take a sip, and when he turned around, Robin was looking back at him.

"Which is?"

"How in the hell are you going to work with her every day? I mean, Jesus, Robin, you've been infatuated with that woman since high school."

"It's been working so far."

"Yeah?"

"All right, so the first few weeks were a little awkward, but I got over it."

"And did she?"

"What do you mean?"

"Well, she was your teacher, and I think that could be a little weird for her, too."

"I guess it could have been if she had remembered me."

"*Ouuuuch.*"

Robin snorted. "Yeah, that kind of stung, but she was only my homeroom teacher. There's no reason why she'd remember a girl she spent just a few minutes with every morning."

"You remembered her."

"How could I not?"

Declan couldn't argue the point. Judy was an attractive woman, and knowing that twenty-five years had passed since Robin had last set eyes on her high school crush, he could only imagine what Judy had looked like a quarter century before. Yet, it wasn't just her appearance that made her pleasing to his eye. It was her persona.

For some, when skin begins to sag and wrinkles start to form, the weight of those changes affects not only appearances but attitudes as well. Shoulders slump, their droop caused by reflections no longer showing youth. Humor fades as aches and pains take precedence, and the new music of the day is merely noise, for the old holds in their melodies fond memories of a time long since gone. Others, however, embrace their age. Grateful for the experience gathered over the years, they stride through their lives with their heads held high and their shoulders square. Wrinkles define rather than disturb, and the twinges and pangs that come with age, like retirement, are simply rites of passage.

Declan was well aware of this type of person because he was raised by two of them. Even though his parents were on the cusp of turning seventy, they still went on a four-mile walk down the beaches of St. Pete every morning before spending their afternoons volunteering at their church. They had yet to slow down, and Declan doubted they ever would, and he also had a sneaking suspicion, Judy wouldn't either.

"Declan!"

The volume of Robin's voice caused Declan to jump, and he jerked back his head. "Why in the hell are you screaming?"

"I was trying to get your attention. Where were you just now?"

"What?"

"You looked a million miles away."

"Oh, sorry. I was just thinking about my folks."

"Are they okay?" Robin said quickly. "Is everything all right?"

"Yeah, they're fine. Judy just reminds me of them. That's all."

Robin narrowed her eyes. "She is *not* that old."

"I wasn't talking about her damn age."

"No?"

"No," Declan growled. "And if you stop acting all huffy, I'll explain."

"Fine," Robin said, crossing her arms. "I'm waiting."

"Jesus Christ," Declan mumbled under his breath as he scrubbed his hand over his face. "Kiddo, before I walked into this house tonight, the only thing I knew about Judy was that she lived on Mackinac, and she was older than you. Can we agree on that?"

"Yes."

"Hallelujah!" Declan said, waving his hands above his head. "So, I didn't know what to expect. Okay? But before dinner, when you guys gave me a tour of the place, the woman bounded up the steps like a kid, and I'm not talking one flight. I'm talking two! Then, she prattled on about all the stuff you two are going to be doing to this place, and all I kept thinking was where in the hell does she get all her energy, and *that's* why she reminds me of my parents."

"Are you saying I'm lazy?"

Declan sighed. "If I dig this hole any deeper, I'm going to hit China."

"Then bring me back some Peking Duck," Robin said, and jumping up, she stormed out of the room.

"Christ, I love women," Declan said, chuckling to himself as he got to his feet. Heading into the kitchen, he found Robin standing near the sink.

"What the hell is wrong with you," he said, taking Robin by the arm. "I like the woman, Robbie. She's nice. She's smart. She's funny, and she's not bad on the eyes. Not that that matters, of course, because she's only your business partner. Right? I mean, you're not expecting anything else. Are you?"

"Of course not."

"Are you sure?" Declan said, placing his hands on Robin's shoulders. "Because if you're doing all of this in hopes that...that something else is going to happen—"

"I'm not."

"Really?"

"Yes, really," Robin said, looking Declan in the eye. "I'm not saying it doesn't help that Judy's here, but I made the decision to stay *before* I knew that. And I'm not stupid, Declan. She thinks of me as a friend and only a friend, and that's okay."

"Is it?"

"It's better than nothing," Robin said, shrugging. "And honestly, it's enough. I didn't come up here looking for love. I came up here to regroup and to write and to just be happy again, and I am." Robin was surprised when Declan didn't respond. She knew he always enjoyed their little debates, and she couldn't remember the last time he'd given up so easily. Noticing the puzzled look on his face, Robin cocked her head to the side. "What's wrong? Can't accept defeat?"

"No, that's not it," Declan said as he glanced around the room. "Did you leave a window open because I swear to God, it just got cold in here?"

Robin moved out of Declan's hold and wrapped her arms around her middle to preserve what body heat she had against the chill in the air. "She's here."

"What? Judy came back?" Declan said, looking toward the hall leading to the front of the house.

"No. Isobel."

"Who the hell is Isobel?"

"Oops."

***

Robin tossed her cell phone on the sofa, and marching into the kitchen, she went to pour herself a cup of coffee. Seeing the pot she had just brewed nearly empty, she set her jaw. "Great. Just *fucking* great!"

For the next few minutes, Robin made enough noise to wake the neighbors. Opening and slamming cabinets to get coffee beans, a filter, and the electric grinder, once she was done, she put everything back and slammed the doors shut again.

"What the hell is all that noise?"

Robin's eyebrows drew together. She had yet to see Declan that morning, but he had somehow managed to drink all her coffee, and now he was shouting from somewhere else in the house. "Where the hell are you?"

"I'm in here."

After topping off her mug with some freshly-brewed coffee, Robin went into the spare bedroom and found Declan sitting on the spiral stairs halfway up, holding her biggest travel mug in his hand. "You could have left some for me."

"Sorry," he said while he continued to stare at the walls. "It was the first cup I found."

"No, it was the largest cup you found."

Declan's pearly whites were almost blinding. "Some things never change."

"I know," Robin said before taking a sip of her coffee. "What are you doing in here?"

"I'm spellbound by all of this. It's amazing."

Robin glanced at the sketches surrounding her. "Yeah, I know."

"There have to be over a thousand drawings in here."

"Probably."

"You know," Declan said, focusing on Robin. "This would make a great book."

"Don't get any ideas."

Declan's guffaw echoed off the walls. "I guess you already thought of that."

"It's crossed my mind, but I have a couple of others I need to finish first."

"Yes, you do."

For a few minutes, they remained silent, both entranced by the drawings on the plaster until Declan said, "Have you noticed that most of the women drawn here look the same?"

"Yeah. I think they're self-portraits."

"And she's really into eyes, isn't she?"

Robin gazed at the dozens of pairs of eyes drawn all over the walls. "Well, they say they're the windows to the soul, and if you look at them, you can see it in how she drew them." Robin began to point as she spoke.

"Like this pair looks happy. See the lines at the corners as if the person is smiling, but the shading on this set makes them look sad, almost teary-eyed. And I don't know who this pair belonged to, but look at the darkness, the intensity...pure anger. Don't you think?"

"Yeah," Declan said as he moved to within a few inches of the wall to study the sketch. "But what gets me are all the details. You can practically see every strand of hair on the mane of the horses pulling this wagon, every leaf on the tree in that forest scene over there, the clapboards on the buildings...every flipping detail. If it wasn't for the fact that most of these were drawn in pencil, they almost look like photographs."

"I know. I come in here sometimes at night to wind down before I go to bed, and I always walk away finding something else I didn't notice before."

Declan paused long enough to gulp down more coffee before he tapped on the wall. "So, who you do think this portly fellow with the clerical noose and the muttonchops is? I can see six or seven sketches of him without even getting up. Maybe her husband?"

Robin shook her head. "I'm thinking her father."

"Why?"

"Isobel died the day *before* her wedding."

"Wow, that sucks."

"Yep."

"And you got that little tidbit from the records you found?"

Robin nodded. "From what I can tell, Adele reached out to the Church of Latter-day Saints, the local churches, and newspaper archives, trying to find everything she could about the house and about Isobel. There were copies of microfilm records, census data, death and burial indexes, and even a copy of Isobel's death certificate."

"You're kidding."

"No. Her name was Isobel Vallencourt. She was twenty-six when she died. They labeled it an accidental drowning, but it wasn't."

Declan's eyebrows drew together. "What makes you say that?"

"Who goes swimming in the middle of the night wearing their wedding dress, the second week of December in Michigan?"

"No one, unless you have a death wish."

"Which is why Adele thought it was suicide, and honestly, so do I. It's the only thing that makes sense."

"I'd have to agree with you." Taking a deep breath, Declan drained what was left in his cup in one swallow and stood up. "Well, I think it's time for me to go grab a shower before Judy gets here."

"Take your time. She's not coming over."

"What?"

"She called a couple of minutes ago and said she was going to take the weekend to catch up on her own stuff."

"But I thought you two were going to give me a quick tour of the island before I have to catch the ferry."

"So did I," Robin said, flicking an invisible piece of lint off her pajama bottoms.

"What's with the attitude?"

"I don't have an attitude."

"The hell you don't. You're sitting there like a child who's just been told they can't play with their favorite toy."

"Judy's not a toy."

"That's right. She's not," Declan said, scowling at the woman sitting two steps below him. "And I hate to break it to you, but she's not your indentured servant either."

"I never said she was."

"Then wipe that pout off your face, Robbie. I get that you really like this woman, but don't like her so much that you forget she has the right to have her own life, too. This isn't all about you. You know?"

Robin's shoulders sagged and letting out a sigh, she shook her head. "God, I hate when you're right."

"When am I not?" he said, and as Robin stood up to let him pass, he hooked his arm through hers. "Now, get your ass in gear and show me around this rock you're living on."

Chapter Twenty-Seven

Robin smiled when Judy came into the kitchen. "You're late."

"I didn't know I had a schedule," Judy said, schlepping over to snag a coffee cup off the counter. "Sorry. It won't happen again."

"Whoa," Robin said, flinching back her head. "Is it me, or did someone wake up on the wrong side of the bed this morning."

"At least I woke up," Judy said pouring herself some coffee. "That's always a plus at my age."

Other than the phone call on Saturday morning, Robin hadn't seen or heard from Judy all weekend. It was odd not to have Judy around, but after taking Declan's reprimand to heart, Robin refused to allow her childish behavior to rise again. Instead, she enjoyed what little time she had with Declan before he climbed aboard the last ferry leaving the island that day.

Robin walked back to her house, her eyes misty with tears after seeing Declan off, but the memories Declan had given her were priceless. Having not ridden a bike since he was in his teens, she tittered as he wobbled and weaved up the road on a neon pink bike with plastic carnations woven into the baskets. She cringed when he came close to running into an unsuspecting bystander. She laughed so hard she almost fell off her bike when he rode directly through a pile of horse manure, and when they finally made it back to the house, Robin spent the rest of the afternoon hanging on every word he said. They spoke about writing, and they talked about ghosts, but there was one subject Robin knew Declan was avoiding, and she had avoided it, too. Unfortunately, Robin couldn't avoid the topic when the topic was currently standing in Robin's kitchen looking pissed off at the world. Robin frowned. "Okay. What's wrong?"

"Nothing's wrong. Where's Declan?" Judy said, putting down the coffee pot. "Sleeping in?"

"No, he left Saturday. Remember, he had to catch that flight to L.A."

"Oh, that's right," Judy said, and turning around, she leaned against the counter and stared at the floor. "I forgot."

"You also forgot we were supposed to give him a tour of the island together."

"Well, I'm sure you managed just *fine* without me," Judy mumbled as she brought the cup to her lips.

Robin eyed the woman who had yet to look in her direction. "What the hell is going on with you?"

"Nothing is going on with me, Robin. Nothing at all."

"Yeah, well I don't believe that," Robin said, placing her mug on the counter. "But it's time for me to go upstairs and get to work. See you later."

Judy lifted her eyes just in time to see Robin disappear into the spare bedroom, and hanging her head, Judy pinched the bridge of her nose. "Shit."

***

An hour later, Judy climbed the spiral stairs with a coffee mug in one hand and regrets in the other. She tapped on the doorframe, and it wasn't until Robin looked over her shoulder, that Judy walked into the room. Going over, she put the coffee on Robin's desk.

"What's this?" Robin said, motioning toward the mug.

"A peace offering," Judy said, quietly. "Hopefully, you'll take it."

"Thanks," Robin said as she picked up the cup. "I left mine downstairs."

"I know. I saw it."

When Judy didn't appear to want to leave, Robin said, "Is there something else?"

"Yeah, it's called an apology. I'm sorry I snapped at you earlier. I didn't have the greatest of weekends."

"Why? What happened?"

"Louise is planning a surprise birthday party for Patrick, and I'm invited."

"Who's Louise?" Robin said before taking a sip of coffee.

"Oh, I'm sorry. She's Patrick's wife."

"And let me guess, after the last visit, you don't want to go back anytime soon."

"Something like that," Judy said, plopping down on the edge of the bed. "I told her I didn't think I could make it, and I *thought* that was the end of it, but then Doug called."

"Laying on the guilt?"

"You know it," Judy said, running her hand over the quilt on the bed. "And unlike Louise, he wouldn't take no for an answer. He must have called a dozen times."

"Crap."

"Which is why I was less than happy when I walked in this morning, and I want to apologize. I took my aggravations out on you, and that wasn't fair."

"You already apologized," Robin said, placing the cup on her desk.

"I didn't hear you accept it."

"What makes you think I wouldn't?" Robin said, looking over at Judy. "I've had my fair share of bad days, so I know where you're coming from. You just want to reach out and piss someone off so they can be as miserable as you."

"That sounds really childish, doesn't it?"

"Yeah, but we all do it."

"It doesn't make it right."

"No, but at least you know you're not alone, and that I understand. So, if you're having a bad day, just tell me, and I'll give you some space."

"I had a whole weekend of space. It didn't help," Judy said, looking around the room.

Robin glanced at her laptop, the page on the screen being the same page she had stared at for the last hour. "Maybe it was because it was the wrong type of space," she said, closing her laptop.

"What?"

"Let's go for a run...or a ride. Your choice."

"No," Judy said as she stood up. "You're supposed to be working. I just came up—"

"To apologize, which you did, but you had a shit weekend and what better way to work out some aggravation than exercise? Besides, it's not like we're punching a clock. I wrote yesterday, and I normally take Sundays off, which means I'm a day ahead of schedule. So, if you want to do something that doesn't involve paint or wallpaper or...or paperwork, count me in."

"Are you sure?"

"The sun is shining, Judy," Robin said, pointing out the window. "Let's not waste it."

Judy paused and looked down at what she was wearing. "Well, if we're going to attempt to run, I'll need to go home and change."

"I'll go with you," Robin said and jumping out of her chair, she dashed past Judy and bounded down the stairs. "Just give me a few minutes to do the same, and I'll meet you up front."

***

Of all the things Robin had adapted to since moving to Mackinac, the weather had been by far the largest learning curve. In Florida, in the dead of what most believed was winter, days requiring layers of clothing were few and far between, but that wasn't the case in Michigan. It was only autumn, but layers were already necessary as were parkas, scarfs, and hats, most of which Robin hadn't owned in years. It took several excursions to the mainland to expand her wardrobe with the Michigan necessities, but when Robin stepped onto the porch of Safe Harbor, she breathed in the chilly air with a smile on her face. It was just ten degrees above freezing, but wearing compression tights, a zip-collar turtleneck, a down vest, gloves, and a headband, Robin mentally scoffed at the temperature as she made her way to her bike.

Self-confidence is a belief in one's own abilities. Achieved through repetitiveness and success, it boosts a person's opinion of themselves to a new height every time a feat is accomplished. Just as her return to her manuscripts had shored up any doubts about her talent as a writer, the many bike trips around Mackinac had boosted Robin's confidence as well. After all, she had leisurely pedaled her way around the island on the eight-mile stretch of M-185 more than once in the past several weeks, and towing an overloaded Burley behind her, she had made numerous trips to and from the ferry. Robin was in the best shape she'd been in for over a year, and it showed on her face.

"How far do we have to go?" Robin said as they walked their bikes to the street.

"Less than two miles," Judy said, pointing up the road. "That way."

"Piece of cake," Robin said, motioning toward the street. "I'll follow you."

Judy paused, her eyes holding a glint of mischief as she looked at Robin. "Oh, um...did you bring any water?"

"Yeah, a couple of bottles. They're in the basket along with some belt bags. Why?"

"Because you're going to need it," Judy said, and sniggering under her breath, she sped away.

"I'll show you who's going to need them," Robin said under her breath, and a moment later, she was racing after Judy down Lakeshore Drive.

***

Robin lay on the frozen ground outside Judy's apartment, staring up at the baby blue sky. Although she had believed her days of making a fool out of herself in front of Judy were over, Robin now knew differently.

Once they turned off Lakeshore onto Market, whatever lead Judy had given herself, Robin had taken back and then some. Smiling as she stood on the pedals, Robin had slipped her bike into a lower gear to make it up the short incline, and when they turned onto Cadotte Avenue, she did the same thing again. Robin managed the gradual rise with ease, but Judy had left out one detail, and it was that detail which soon caused the distance between them to lessen. While Judy's apartment was only two miles from Safe Harbor, she forgot to mention to Robin the ride was not only all uphill, there was also a two hundred foot change in elevation.

A few days earlier, Robin had jumped to the wrong conclusion with Declan, thinking he was somehow basing his opinion of Judy on her age, yet Robin realized she had done the same thing by the time they passed the Grand Hotel. Unknowingly, she allowed their age difference to play a part in their impromptu race, giving her the advantage, while totally forgetting that with age, comes experience.

Accustomed to the climb, and riding a streamlined bike with sixteen more gears than Robin's old Raleigh, Judy effortlessly made her way up the road while Robin struggled every inch of the way. With nary an ounce of strain on her face, Judy grinned at Robin as she passed her by the stables, and with every downward thrust of her pedals, Judy increased the distance between them. By the time they reached Judy's place, Robin was drawing in one hissing breath after another. The muscles in her legs were screaming, and as she pedaled onto the lawn, she caught sight of Judy's expression. The agony Robin was feeling was impossible to hide, and Judy had seen it.

Robin wanted to speak, say something flippant and witty to shrug off her near-death experience, but she had no more strength to speak and no more strength to stand. She climbed off her bike and fell to the ground as if shot by a sniper.

***

With the remnants of a less-than-pleasant weekend still on her mind, while Judy hadn't intended to leave Robin in the dust, her 'piece of cake' comment had rubbed Judy the wrong way. She had spent two days being badgered by her family and two days struggling with feelings she couldn't shake, and Robin's assumption, albeit innocent, had pushed Judy's button. Her life wasn't a piece of cake, and neither was the ride to Harrisonville. Setting her jaw, while Judy couldn't prove one to Robin, she sure as hell could prove the other, a decision she regretted when she came back outside and saw Robin still laying where Judy had left her ten minutes earlier.

"I am so sorry," she said, sitting down on the ground next to Robin. "I should have told you about the hill."

"That's not a hill. It's a mountain," Robin said, rolling her head to the side to look at Judy. "And I can't believe you bike that every day."

"You get used to it."

"Yeah, you made that fairly obvious," Robin said, pushing herself into a sitting position. "I must have looked like such a fool trying to keep up with you."

"The only foolish thing you've done is to stay out here while I got changed," Judy said, rubbing her hands over her arms as she stood up. "You should have come inside. These clothes are meant for running, not for sitting out in the cold."

"I needed to cool down," Robin said as she stood up. "And speaking of running, shall we?"

Judy gave Robin the once-over. "Are you sure? I mean, if you're too sore or—"

"The only thing bruised is my ego," Robin said, and resting her hands on her hips, she began to bend from side to side. "Just give me a minute to stretch out the kinks, and we can go."

"You read my mind," Judy said, and moving a few steps away to give Robin some room to flex, she began her own stretching routine.

Absorbed in recovering from her failure as a speed cyclist, Robin had yet to pay any attention to what Judy was wearing, so when the woman stepped in front of her to limber up for their run, Robin had to choke back a gasp.

Compression leggings encased Judy's lower half, the black shimmering sheath of fabric moving perfectly with every flex and stretch Judy made. Although opaque, through the skin-tight material Robin could see the clearly defined muscles in Judy's calves and as her eyes lifted, so did Robin's temperature. Eternally grateful for the moisture-wicking ability of her own compression tights, Robin shifted her stance and attempted to resume her half-hearted warm-up.

Robin knew right from wrong and what she was doing was wrong, but sometimes wrong was oh so right. Unable to stop herself, she continued her lecherous perusal.

The crisscross of the straps of Judy's sports bra was the only thing interrupting an otherwise unblemished view of Judy's back. The candy apple red turtleneck was as painted-on as her leggings, and Robin could see the outline of Judy's backbone through the fabric. It was straight as an arrow, and that arrow led to a waist, deliciously feminine.

Robin's eyes slowly slid south again, drawn to the gentle curve of Judy's bottom, and it was at that moment when she noticed something she hadn't noticed before. It shouldn't have been a big deal because Robin did the same thing, but going commando and knowing Judy was commando were two entirely different things, at least it was to Robin's body. A surge of awareness pulsed between her legs and unable to stop herself, Robin let out a lusty groan.

Judy stepped out of her lunges and turned around. "Is there something wrong?"

"What? Oh...um...no, nothing's wrong," Robin said, thankful the cold weather could easily explain her reddened cheeks. "I just finished, so I'm ready when you are."

"Okay, let's head out," Judy said, and jogging to the road, she waited for Robin to catch up. "Hey, I meant to ask you. Since this is my first time out in forever, do you mind if we do a walk-run combination? Walk a mile and then run a mile?"

"No, that's a great idea," Robin said, coming to a stop next to Judy. She looked to the right and left, and then pointed at the hill they had just climbed. "As long as we don't end up having to come back up that, I don't care if we run, walk, hop, skip, or jump."

***

Under a canopy of red, orange, and tan leaves, Judy introduced Robin to a part of Mackinac she had never seen, and it was a part as breathtakingly beautiful as it was profoundly peaceful.

Robin had always stuck to the road surrounding the island when she had gone on her runs, so as Judy led her down winding paths running through the forest, Robin was in awe. There wasn't a soul on the trail except them, and each tiny sound emanating from the woods got Robin's attention. A rustle of leaves and then a red squirrel would appear, darting here and there in search of winter's food. A branch would suddenly move, and her eyes would be drawn to a blue jay taking flight, and then just as quickly the staccato rhythm of a woodpecker would find its way to her ears, the ticking tap never-ending as he bored his way into a tree.

A mosaic of leaves covered the forest floor, its palette holding every shade of red and brown imaginable, and poking through the jumble were shrubs of emerald and spindly saplings bowing under the weight of their own existence. The air smelled of earth and decomposing foliage and the slightest of breezes brought with it the scent of pine and musty moss.

For two hours, they jogged, walked, jogged, and walked again, yet they hardly uttered a word. Captivated by their surroundings, they traveled in near silence, breathing in the serenity Mother Nature had provided until Robin saw what they were approaching. Arching an eyebrow, she turned to Judy. "Did you plan this?"

Engrossed in observing a squirrel munching on a pinecone, it took Judy a few seconds before she could tear her eyes away and when she did, she giggled. "Believe it or not, I didn't," she said, stopping to tie her shoe while Robin continued across the road.

"Sure, sure, sure," Robin mumbled as she sat down on the concrete and stone wall bordering the cemetery. "And I'll have you know, I'm no longer afraid of ghosts." With that, Robin yanked the bottle of water from her belt and took a sip.

As if on cue, a broken branch balanced precariously on another, lost its battle with gravity. It slipped from its perch and plummeted to the ground, taking with it loose leaves, small twigs...and Robin's poise.

Upon hearing the commotion behind her, as if shot from an invisible cannon, Robin flew off the wall, the water bottle in her hand going airborne as she sprinted toward the road like a deer jumping over high grass. It wasn't until Robin heard the sound of cackling that she skidded to a stop. She turned around and saw Judy standing in the middle of the road, laughing like there was no tomorrow.

Judy was doing her best to get herself under control, but the more she tried, the worse it got. Kneeling, she covered her mouth and swayed back and forth as she struggled to breathe.

Robin went over to Judy, her presence casting a shadow over the woman who appeared to be praying to Allah. "Are you done?" Robin said, crossing her arms.

Judy held up one finger in response, her heaving shoulders a testament to her current situation.

"It was *not* that funny," Robin said, failing to hide her amusement. Watching as Judy bobbed her head in reply, Robin stood over her for almost a minute before she finally held out her hand. "Come on, woman. Get up."

"I'm not sure I can," Judy squeaked, sniffling back some tears. "Oh, my God, I think I'm going to die."

"Well, then we're in the right place." Robin took Judy's hand and pulled her to her feet. "Let's go find you a nice shady spot. Shall we?"

Robin led Judy to the short border wall surrounding the cemetery, and while the woman composed herself, Robin went in search of her water bottle. Returning a minute later, Robin gestured down the road. "You want to keep walking?"

"Yes, please."

As they strolled past the cemetery, Robin took in the view. Sunlight streamed down through the branches of stately oaks, maples, and birch, illuminating headstones and monuments of every shape and size. "That's beautiful," she said quietly, pointing toward the graveyard.

"Yeah, they all are."

"All?"

Judy nodded. "There are three on the island. Two civilian and one military."

"Really?"

"Yep," Judy said as they passed the two small iron gates at the entrance. "This one is officially called The Mackinac Island Cemetery, but most of the locals refer to it as the Protestant cemetery."

"Some of the headstones look new, but others look really old."

"You're right, and if I remember correctly, the oldest one in there is from 1831."

"Wow."

"Oh, you haven't seen anything yet," Judy said, pointing up ahead. "That's the Post. It's the only military one on the island, and it always gives me chills."

"Why?"

"Come on," Judy said, motioning for Robin to follow. "I'll show you."

A minute later, they stood on a rise overlooking a small plot of land. Eight rows of headstones stood at attention within the boundaries of a white picket fence and toward the front was an old cannon standing on wheels with blue-gray rims.

In silence, Robin followed Judy down the path until they stopped in front of a sturdy wood turnstile situated under a simple timber archway announcing U. S. Post Cemetery Fort Mackinac.

"It's a lot smaller than I thought it would be," Robin whispered.

"That's probably because they closed it in 1895 after the Army abandoned Fort Mackinac." Judy turned to look up at Robin. "Legend has it that British and American soldiers who died in the War of 1812 are buried here, but others believe it holds only the remains of the soldiers who had been stationed at Fort Mackinac."

"Can't they tell that by the headstones?"

"Unfortunately, a lot of the graves were originally only marked by wooden crosses, and they disintegrated over time. From what I've read, they know there's just over a hundred graves here, but the identities of over half of them are still unknown."

"And that's what gives you chills?"

"No," Judy said, pointing over Robin's shoulder. "That does."

Robin turned around, immediately shading her eyes from the sun coming through the trees. She expected something out of the ordinary, but instead, she found herself looking at a flagpole holding the American flag at half-staff. "Don't get me wrong. I can be as patriotic as the next person, but I feel like I'm missing something here."

"Didn't you notice how it was hanging?"

"Yeah, at half-staff. Who died?"

"They did," Judy whispered, pointing at the graves. "And this cemetery, on this tiny little island I call home, is one of only four National Cemeteries having the honor to fly their flag at half-staff...*every* day of the year."

Robin instantly rubbed her arms, trying to calm the goosebumps that had sprung to life.

"Glad to see it affects you the same way," Judy said, smiling. "Or are you cold?"

"No, I'm not cold," Robin said as she gestured toward the road. "But I will be if we don't keep moving."

"Well, St. Anne's is right down the road. I'll race you."

Judy was already running down the path by the time Robin had processed what she had said, and with a laugh, Robin took off after her. She caught up just as Judy dashed past the stone entrance leading to St. Anne's and Robin jogged in silence until they turned down a side road and Judy slowed to a walk. "And this is the largest cemetery on the island."

Robin looked out over the sprawling graveyard, the numerous headstones and monuments nestled amongst the towering oaks and sugar maples dotting the landscape. "It's gorgeous. I can see why people would want to be buried here."

"Well, if you have any plans to join them, you better hang around for about fifteen years."

"I'm hoping to hang around for a lot longer than that. Thank you very much."

Judy grinned and bumped her shoulder into Robin's bicep. "That's not what I mean."

"Okay?"

"In order to be buried on Mackinac, you either have to be born here, or you've had to live here for at least fifteen years."

"Seriously?"

"Oh, you'd be amazed at how many tourists contact the cemeteries every year, trying to buy plots."

"Then I guess that means none of your family is here?"

"Nope," Judy said, shaking her head. "Scott's parents are buried here along with a few of his uncles and aunts, and I guess when he kicks the bucket, he will be, too, but as far as my real family, no, they'll never be here. And that's yet another bone of contention between Patrick and me.

He wants me buried in the family plot in Indiana, and I want my ashes interred here."

Robin frowned. "Is it me or has this conversation turned maudlin?"

"Yeah, it's definitely taken a turn for the worse," Judy said, chuckling. "But since we're talking about families, how do you feel about Thanksgiving?"

"Crap. That's coming up. Isn't it?"

"In two weeks, and I wasn't sure if you were thinking about visiting Declan or...or someone else, or just hanging out here."

"There's no one else to visit other than Gabby, and her folks retired to Arizona a few years back, so she usually goes down there for the holidays now."

"Who's Gabby?"

"Oh, she's my agent. Actually, she's Declan's, too. We all went to college together. Remind me, and I'll show you a picture of her. There's one on the mantle."

"Okay," Judy said. "So, does that mean you don't have any plans?"

"Not a one. Why?"

"Well, Rita and Hank usually invite me over on Thanksgiving, but I know they'll be in Cheboygan this year, so since I'll be alone, and you'll be alone, I was wondering if...if you'd like to spend it together? It doesn't have to be any big deal. I could run over to St. Ignace next weekend and pick up a small turkey. What do you think?"

Robin paused and looked at the road in front of them. "How far are we from your place?"

"Um," Judy said, glancing around. "Probably about a half-mile. Maybe a little less if we cut through the park."

"What park?"

Judy slowed her stride as she looked at Robin. "Great Turtle Park. At the end of this road, we just have to make a right and then a left into the park. My place is directly on the other side of it. Why?"

"Because the loser washes all the dishes on Thanksgiving," Robin said, and suddenly her brisk walk turned into an all-out sprint.

Chapter Twenty-Eight

After their run on Monday, Robin and Judy got back to their routine. On Tuesday, they continued painting upstairs in the afternoon until they ran out of rooms needing only that. On Wednesday, they began moving furniture out of their way and on Thursday, they started attacking what they agreed was their least favorite room.

Robin bounded up the steps, and as soon as she entered Central Lake, she grinned. "You're making quick work of this."

"We have Adele to thank for that," Judy said, stepping back to look at what remained of the fuchsia and pink wallpaper on two of the walls. "If she hadn't used sizing on this plaster, we'd be using a hell of a lot more elbow grease to scrape this stuff off."

"Which brings me to the bad news."

"The bad news?"

"This is the last one we have," Robin said, holding up a blue plastic bag. "And since we plan to go to the mainland tomorrow to get a turkey for next week, we either have to run over to Public Works today or wait until Monday. We have plenty of clear though, but you said you didn't want to use those."

"I'd be afraid to put this stuff in a compost bag with all the ink in it," Judy said, gathering a few scraps of paper off the floor. "And I've already sprayed down the next wall. Why don't you go get some more, and I'll keep going?"

"Are you sure?"

"Yeah, unless you can't handle the hill on Market Street," Judy said, her eyes creasing at the corners. "I know how much you *love* hills."

"Very funny," Robin said, tossing the bag to Judy. "I'll be back in a few."

"Hey, since you'll be out that way, do you mind going to the post office? I haven't checked my box in a few days, and it would save me the trip."

"No, I don't mind at all, especially since I keep forgetting to check mine. Where are your keys?"

"In my coat pocket."

"All right. See you in a bit."

"Be careful."

"What am I going to do? Get hit by a walker?"

"You're about to get hit by a wet piece of wallpaper if you're not careful," Judy said, wadding up a nearby strip. "Now get out of here and let me get back to my work."

"Yes, dear."

***

Pam stepped off the ferry and immediately wrinkled her nose. "Jesus, it smells like shit here," she mumbled under her breath. Yanking up the collar on her time-worn leather jacket, she strutted down the nearly deserted dock until she saw a man, bundled up in a puffy blue parka, standing near the locker area.

"Hey you," Pam yelled as she approached. "How about giving me a hand?"

Glen looked up from his clipboard. "Sure thing, miss. What do you need?"

"I need to know where this place is, and it's *mizz* not miss," Pam said, and bringing up the notes on her phone, she shoved the screen into Glen's face.

Glen cleared his throat, and rocking back in his stance, he glanced at the phone. "That's the Safe Harbor."

"What the hell does that mean?"

"It's a B&B."

"A bed-and-breakfast?"

"That's right," Glen said, tucking his clipboard under his arm. "But I'm not sure they're open."

"Well, don't you worry about that, old man. They'll be open for me. I guarantee it," Pam said, slipping her phone into the back pocket of her jeans. "Now tell me how I get there."

The tendons in Glen's neck tightened. He had been brought up to be courteous and respectful toward others, and on the rare occasion when someone stepped off the ferries wearing a frown, he did his best to turn it upside down. He loved his island, and he wanted everyone to enjoy it, but Glen doubted this woman enjoyed anything. Like a statue, she remained in his personal space, glowering back at him through eyes dark and hostile. The pungent cologne she had bathed in was making his eyes sting, and even though Glen knew he was older than the woman, someone displaying a road map of sun damage on their face shouldn't be throwing stones.

Glen took a step back, thankful for the breeze clearing away the essence of fermenting petunias. "You can take a taxi, or you can walk. Totally up to you."

"And just where in the hell do I get a taxi?"

Glen's lips thinned. Taking a slow, even breath, he motioned toward the carriage parked at the end of the dock. "Right over there."

"What in the world are you smoking? I'm not getting on a fucking wagon."

"Actually, it's a carriage," Glen said, lifting his chin. "I guess you're not up on your Mackinac history. We don't have cars on the island, and since all the bike shops are closed, it's either the carriage, or you walk. Like I said, it's *totally* up to you."

Pam huffed. "And I suppose that thing's going to cost an arm and a leg. Isn't it?"

"It's five bucks for the ride, and if you want them to wait, it's a dollar a minute."

"That's fucking robbery."

"It is what it is," Glen said, shrugging. "Now, I have some things I need to do so if we're done here—"

"How do I get there if I walk?"

Glen pointed toward the road. "Make a left on Main and a right at the end of the street. It's up on the right. You can't miss it."

"And how far, *exactly*, is that?"

"Oh, I'd say about four minutes, maybe five in those boots."

"Five?" Pam shouted, intruding on Glen's personal space again. "Are you fucking serious? You actually tried to talk me into paying for a taxi when it's that close?"

"I didn't try—"

"Don't bother!" Pam said, holding up her hands. "You tourist trap people are all the same. All you ever see are dollar signs. Well, I got news for you, pal. It'll be a cold day in hell before you get any of my money."

Glen watched as the woman lumbered toward the street, the clicking of her three-inch heels against the concrete echoing in the confines of the overhang. Scratching his head, he laughed as he pulled the clipboard out from under his arm. "Sure as shit takes all kinds."

***

It wasn't long after Robin left when Judy rocked back on her heels and set aside her scraper. She had already managed to fill the remaining bag with paper, and without another, she was left with either littering the floor with damp remnants of wallpaper or waiting until Robin returned. With a sigh, Judy got to her feet, grabbed a bag in each hand, and made her way downstairs. Placing them next to another, she was about to head back to Central Lake when the doorbell rang. After wiping her hands on her glue-speckled jeans, Judy went over and opened the front door.

"Hi!" Judy chirped. "Welcome to Safe Harbor. How may I help you?"

Pam gave the woman the once over. She had always imagined people who owned bed-and-breakfasts to be the retired type. Round at the waist, ruddy in the face, and with hair the color of salt, they'd spend their days pontificating to their captive listeners, who'd be forced to listen to all the tales about the good old days while they gobbled down their eggs, bacon, and biscuits.

The woman grinning back at Pam did not fit that bill. She wasn't fat. Her skin was clear and glowing, and while there was some gray in her hair, she felt no need to conceal it behind dye like Pam did. But even the sum of all those details didn't irk Pam as much as the vitality in the woman's Nordic blue eyes. Someone her age had no right to feel so good...or look so good.

"I'm here to see Robin Novak," Pam said with a syrupy smile. "Is she around?"

The hairs on the back of Judy's neck stood on end. The woman was smiling, but the emotion didn't reach her eyes. They were hard and piercing and held in their muddy brown nothing but arrogance. "Um...no. Actually, she...she just went to run some errands."

"Then I guess I'll just have to wait, now won't I?"

It was a standoff Judy wished they hadn't just reached. She either had to let the woman inside or make her wait on the porch. Inwardly, Judy sighed. "Of course," she said, opening the door wider. "Please come in. You can wait in the parlor."

Pam arched an eyebrow, giving Judy a half-glance before marching into the house. There was a lot to take in, but Pam was an expert in scrutinizing her surroundings. By the time she heard the door close behind her, she had sucked in every detail before she turned around and eyed the innkeeper again.

"My name's Judy Dunnigan," Judy said, and holding out her hand, she forced herself to continue smiling. "Now it's your turn."

Judy had expected the handshake to be quick and uneventful, but once she felt the strength in the woman's grip, she returned in kind. There was no need to show force, to squeeze until the other participant grimaced, but that's precisely what the woman seemed to be doing. It was rude, and it was uncalled for, so without one flicker of discomfort showing on her face, Judy continued to shake Pam's hand, all the while staring her directly in the eye.

Judy wasn't one who judged rapidly, and she never judged by the cover, but after the childish show of strength, Judy made an exception. At first glance, she found the woman unattractive. Her eyes, framed by a swath of eyeliner, were deep-set and shadowed in their sockets, and her lips were thin, barely hiding a slight overbite. Her hand was rough and calloused, and she was gaunt, the flare of her hips scarcely noticeable under the faded denim painting her legs. Separately, the elements that made up this stranger were hardly appealing, but like a recipe, when the ingredients were combined the result wasn't unpleasant, except for one thing. The woman's face was etched with defiance, and her beady eyes were currently trying to bore their way through Judy. She had yet to discover the stranger's name, but that no longer mattered. Judy already disliked her...no matter who she was.

Pam had begged, borrowed, and forced money out of everyone she knew in order to drive to Michigan, and she was too close to her end game to leave anything to chance. Without missing a beat, as their hands parted,

Pam honked out a laugh. "I'm sorry. My name's Gabby. Gabby Passarelli. I'm Robin's agent."

"Oh...um...it's very nice to meet you," Judy said, and taking a step toward the parlor, she motioned inside. "You can make yourself comfortable in here. Robin should be back soon."

"If it's all the same to you," Pam said, looking up the stairs. "I'd rather wait in her room."

"Her room?"

"Yeah. She does have one—right?"

Judy tilted her head. "Well, since she owns this place, she uses the innkeeper's suite. I would have thought you'd know that."

It was a misstep, the tiniest of stumbles, but Pam was a master of fabrication. Without so much as a hint of hesitation, she barked out another laugh. "Of course, I know that. *Duh!*" she said with an exaggerated eye roll. "But the last time we talked, she said she had a lot of cleaning to do. I just figured with all this trash piled up, she was still working on her place."

"Oh, I see," Judy said, glancing at the stack of blue bags.

"So, like I said, I'd rather wait there if it's all the same to you," Pam said, leaning in toward Judy. "Or is that a problem?"

"No," Judy said, locking eyes with Pam. "As a matter of fact, I was just heading back there to grab some water. Would you like some?"

"You got any beer?"

***

Judy rushed back down the stairs with her hoodie in hand, and when the front door opened and Robin walked in, Judy let out the breath she'd been holding for the past twenty minutes. "Where have you been?"

"Well, hello to you, too," Robin said, shrugging out of her coat. "And you know exactly where I was," she said, placing the stack of bags on the receptionist podium. "I went to Public Works and then to the Post Office. I ran into Maxine while I was there, so I stopped to chat. Why? And what's up with the sweatshirt? It's not cold in here."

"It's freezing in your apartment."

"That makes no—" Robin cut herself off as she glanced toward the back of the house. "Crap. Isobel must be visiting."

"She's not the only one."

"Huh?"

"You have a guest," Judy said as she put on her hoodie.

"Who?"

"She says she's your agent, Gabby."

"Gabby's here! Oh my, God, that's—"

"I don't think it's Gabby," Judy said, placing her hand on Robin's arm.

"What are you talking about?"

Judy looked over her shoulder and then began to whisper. "Remember how you said there was a picture of her on your mantle?"

"Yeah, it's the one on the far left. Why?"

"Because the woman sitting in your apartment isn't in any of those pictures. Not unless she's lost a shit load of weight."

A sucker punch couldn't have emptied Robin's lungs any faster. Frozen in place, it took almost a minute before she could find her voice. "Let me guess? Short? Thin? Wearing boots and...um...and lots of jewelry?"

"Yes," Judy said in a breath. "Who is she?"

"Someone you don't want to know," Robin said as she took off her jacket and handed it to Judy. "Stay here. I'll handle it."

"Robin—"

"Judy, please. This isn't your problem. It's mine."

Chapter Twenty-Nine

Robin now understood what it felt like to be on death row on that final day. To take that long, silent walk to a room where within its walls is the inescapable. Hearts race, the hammering in chests so rapid it drowns out even the loudest of sounds and ears become useless for the resonance of the world no longer exists. Breathing turns ragged, stuttered inhalations that grow even shorter as the distance is closed between life and fate, and palms sweat as strides shorten, finally ending in a shuffle for the end of the journey had been reached.

She stood at the doorway leading to her apartment, wondering what words of peace or harmony could bring this nightmare to an end once and for all, but as quickly as that thought entered her mind, Robin pushed it away. A year ago, that would have been her, trying to sooth through whispers of empathy and touches, soft and tender, the eruptions of anger and condemnation brought on by a Machiavellian skilled in the ways of duplicity, but that was then, and this was now. Pam had played Robin like a Stradivarius, but the horsehair of her bow was no longer intact. The strands had been shredded by truth, by a mind and a will that had returned in force, and it was that force which straightened Robin's shoulders, lengthened her backbone, and lifted her chin. She took the final steps, and filling her lungs with air, Robin rounded the corner leading to the kitchen of her apartment.

As she knew it would, Robin's stomach flipped when she saw Pam standing in the living room, but then she noticed the chill in the air, and it was exactly what she needed. It was a reminder of where she was. A reminder of how far she had come in healing herself from the wounds the woman in front of her had so expertly inflicted, and a reminder Robin had nothing to fear from Pam, at least not right now. Right now, Pam was sober.

Robin knew all the warning signs. The weaving stance, the droopy eyelids, and the crooked sneer, they were like lighthouse beacons signaling danger because drugs and alcohol were the fuel for Pam's temper. Like gasoline on a fire, they would ignite Pam's mood until it became an inferno of insanity. Without blinking an eye, everyone and everything would be dragged into the bonfire of her delusions, but *without* the propellant, Pam could be charming, conversational, and compelling. Of course, she was still a sociopath, and she still had her own agenda, but Robin wasn't concerned about that. She had seen through Pam's smokescreen months before.

Pam's face melted into a buttery smile as she ambled from the living room into the kitchen. "Hey there, baby. What's shaking?"

"You need to leave."

Hearing not one ounce of emotion in Robin's tone, Pam arched an eyebrow. She had expected, at the very least, a slight wavering in Robin's timbre, her response perhaps whispered, her body language, shielded and nervous. The groundwork Pam had laid out for so many months had always had that effect. It worked every time, and Pam set her jaw. It worked *every* time.

"Why would I do that, baby?" Pam said, placing the empty beer bottle on the counter. "I just got here."

"Leave, or I'm going to call the police. Your choice."

"What are they going to do? Show up on horseback?"

"I don't care if they show up on tricycles. The point is they *will* show up, and you'll be led away in handcuffs—again."

"Don't threaten me."

"It's a not a threat, Pam," Robin said, holding her head high. "It's called a restraining order."

"I just want to talk."

"You and I have nothing to talk about."

Pam cocked her head to the side. Robin's voice had remained calm and detached, nullifying Pam's belief this would be easy. She had always looked forward to challenges, and Robin *had* been a challenge, but once Pam had reached the apex of *that* mountain, returning to the summit was not in her plan. Running her fingers down the corners of her mouth, Pam sauntered over, opened the refrigerator, and pulled out another beer. "I'm going to get me a drink. You want one?" she said as she twisted off the cap and tossed it on the counter.

"No."

Pam shrugged, taking a long swig of her brew while she sashayed over and opened the door to the spare bedroom. She wasn't concerned with what the room held, but intrusion was always good for an emotional response, so Pam's annoyance grew when Robin uttered not one word. Pam brought the bottle to her lips again as she turned and propped herself against the wall. Crossing her legs at the ankles, she smirked. "Aren't you the least bit curious as to how I found you?"

"I wasn't hiding."

"No?" Pam said, pausing long enough for another gulp of her drink. "Then why wouldn't any of your friends tell me where you were?"

"I don't know. Maybe they were trying to protect me. If you had any friends of your own, you'd know what I mean."

"I have more friends than you can count."

"No, Pam, all you have is a bunch of unsuspecting, innocent women you've ensnared in your web of grandiose fabrications, bullshit threats, and half-assed attempts at blackmail. If you actually *had* any real friends, you'd know that friends don't have to tell their friends what to say and what not to say. It's one of the most fundamental things about friendships...thus the name."

Pam's eyes became slits. "Don't talk down to me. I'm not stupid."

Guns have triggers, and so do people, and Robin wanted to kick herself because she had just pulled Pam's. Robin knew the woman was intelligent. She had to be to manipulate and lie so effortlessly, but questioning her brilliance had always made matters worse. Then again, at the moment, it wasn't Pam's intelligence Robin was questioning. It was her own.

One word is all it takes to change the tide, the flow of convictions dissipating with the ebb of regret, and Robin's mettle washed out to sea in an instant. She was the one who was stupid. She was the idiot who had fallen for all of Pam's tales of gloom and fables of grandeur. She was the fool who had believed the endless promises of change, and she was the imbecile who had taken Pam back time and time again, freely giving up all Robin had held important until there was almost nothing left...except Pam.

Deep inside of Robin, a storm began to form as recollections of all that came before swirled together in a sickening stew of bitterness and loathing, yet in an instant, the tide changed again. Her regrets crashed against the shore, bringing with them all the words of hurt and anger she could muster, but Robin knew she had to fight against the strength of *that* current. The power of words unleashed and uncensored would only prolong this insanity, and it had to stop. It had to stop now. Pam wouldn't listen. Pam wouldn't hear. Pam would merely twist whatever Robin said into something bizarre and crazed. Truth would become fiction. Right would become wrong. Up would become down, and Robin no longer wanted to ride on the lunatic fringe of *that* roller coaster. No, she had to try to curb the velocity of what she wanted to proclaim, temper the sting just enough to get her point across because there *were* things Robin wanted to say. There were things she *needed* to say, and brainwashing herself into believing she could hide her contempt with carefully chosen words, Robin decided to say what was on her mind. As far as she was concerned, this was the only chance she'd ever get, and it was much too tempting to pass up.

"And neither am I, or at least I'm not stupid anymore," Robin stated, and going to the fridge, she opened it long enough to grab a bottle of water. She spun around as she loosened the cap, and lowering her chin, she looked Pam dead in the eye. "I've broken free of you, Pam. I'm free from your Svengali routine. Free from your lies. Free from your intimidations and your screams and your anger because I finally realized you're nothing special. You're not the be-all and end-all to every lesbian on the planet. You don't speak for every woman alive, and you sure as hell aren't the smartest person on the face of this earth. All you are is a liar and a thief, and..." Robin hesitated. The words were coming far too easily, and like a metaphorical snowball, they were rolling down a hill, gathering more pain, more shame, and more hatred with every syllable. She told herself to stop. She told herself there was no point in the path she was taking, and setting aside the bottle, Robin fisted her hands and dug her nails into her palms. She hoped the ache could somehow extinguish another and smother the need to give as good as she had gotten, but the snowball had become an avalanche.

Robin glared at Pam and finished her sentence. "And for shits and giggles, how about I throw in racist, too?"

"That's a lie!"

"Which part? It can't possibly be the lying part because I have a list a mile long of all the ones you told, and there's no doubt in my mind you broke into Declan's—"

"I am *not* a racist."

"Really?" Robin said, folding her arms. "Really, Pam? Do all those bosom buddies of yours know how you talk about black athletes, calling them boys and believing they're superior at sports *simply* because of their skin color? Or better yet, how about this? Have you ever dropped the N-word in front of them like you did in front of me?"

"It's just the way I was raised, and after you told me how you felt about it, I stopped using it."

Robin dropped her hands to her side and fisted them again. "Jesus Christ, do you *hear* yourself? Are you that stupid that I actually had to bring it to your *attention?*"

"Do not call me stupid!" Pam growled as the tendons in her neck grew taut.

Robin flinched. She had just stooped to Pam's level, and that wasn't who she was. Drawing in a slow breath, as she exhaled, Robin regained a modicum of control. "You're right. I apologize," she said, holding up your hands. "Name calling is your M. O., not mine. Mine's always been the truth, so how about I just stick to that, not that you'd know anything about truth."

"I told you the truth about *everything*," Pam said through clenched teeth.

"You wouldn't know the truth if it came up and slapped you in the face, Pam," Robin said, her tone rising slightly. "You lied about jobs you never had. You lied about an education you never received. You lied about never taking drugs. You lied about rarely drinking. Christ, you even lied about how you chipped your fucking tooth."

Pam ran her tongue over the tiny notch in her front tooth. "What the hell are you talking about?"

"The first night we met you pointed it out. Do you remember? You said you'd been mugged a few days before, and I fell for it hook, line, and sinker. I piled on the sympathy to this stranger with her woeful story, but it was all make-believe, and since in your eyes, sympathy is a weakness, I became your prey."

"It wasn't a—"

"Yes, it was!" Robin shouted. "Pam, think back to the night when we were talking about family. You went on and on about your sisters and how they had never amounted to anything. You even handed me your phone, and as I was looking at their photos, you kept rambling on, picking apart their looks, their clothes, their everything. Do me a favor, Pam? Open your phone. Scroll to the one taken with your family a few years ago. Zoom in on it. Look at your face. Look at your smile. Look at the *fucking* chip in your tooth and tell me again how you were mugged."

Pam's nostrils flared, her cheeks turning crimson as she glared back at Robin.

"What? Did you really think I didn't notice?" Robin said, rocking back in her stance. "I did, and for the life of me, I don't know why I didn't call you on it that night. Then again, I was fighting my own demons back then, but I'm not fighting them anymore, Pamela." Robin paused long enough to pick up her water and take a drink. "Now get out. I've said my piece."

"What about my piece?" Pam said, pushing herself off the wall and standing straight. "What about all the bullshit you put *me* through?"

"What, in God's name, did I put you through?"

"Everywhere I looked in your house was Declan!" Pam said, slamming her hand against the wall. "His books were all over the place and don't even get me started on all the fucking photographs! School pictures on one wall, party pictures on another, pictures of you and Declan, pictures of Gabby and Declan, pictures of your mother and Declan. Jesus Christ, it went on and on."

"He's my *best* friend, Pam."

"He's also the man you *fucked*!"

Robin shook her head. "You just *can't* let that go, can you?"

"It's true."

"Yes, it is, and I'm not ashamed of it. I never was ashamed of it. It happened. Not all of us are gold stars, Pam, but that doesn't make me any less of a lesbian than you are, and it sure as hell had nothing to do with what happened between you and me."

Pam lowered her chin as she considered her next move. "I'm not so sure about that."

Robin grinned. "Nice try, but that shit doesn't work on me anymore."

"I have absolutely *no* idea what you're talking about."

"Of course you do, Pamela," Robin said with a sigh. "Just like always, you're laying on the guilt, trying to make everything my fault so you can convince me that somehow it was the things I did or *didn't* do that were the problem."

"They were!"

"No, they *weren't*," Robin shouted. "You have lived your *entire* life piling one excuse on top of another. You always blame everything on everyone else. It's never your fault, Pam, because if it were, if one flipping thing *were* your fault, you'd have to admit you weren't perfect...and that would eat you alive."

"If you had been through what I've been through to get where I am—"

"Oh, here we go," Robin said, looking up at the ceiling. "This is the part where you moan about your life. Right? How you've always been misunderstood. How you were never treated the same as your sisters. How you were never given the breaks you deserved."

"I wasn't. I had to fight and claw my way—"

"Don't you mean lie and bully?" Robin said, placing her hands on her hips. "Because that's what you are, just a schoolyard bully who's gotten away with this kind of crap for way too long. Well, not anymore, Pam. Not with me. Now, for the last *flipping* time, get out of my house!"

Pam glared at Robin as she brought the bottle to her lips again, and she drained the rest of the beer in an instant. It felt good going down, cold and hoppy and her system welcomed its arrival. The drive to Michigan had been long and for the most part dry, and as Pam thought about that, the muscles in her neck began to strain against her skin.

Because of Robin, for the past four days, Pam had been forced to drive sober, and because of Robin, for the past four days, Pam had been forced to watch how much blow she snorted. And now, after four *fucking* days and traveling over a thousand *fucking* miles, Robin had the audacity to believe she could just dismiss her? Send her on the way with a wave her hand? Pam clenched her teeth as she prepared to launch a torrent of insults and threats, but suddenly her posture relaxed. Her eyes darted around the room, and a knowing smile slithered its way across her face. Bingo.

"That's right," Pam said, placing the empty bottle on the island as she scanned the kitchen. "The bitch who answered the door said this was *your* place. What did you do? Finally figure out you write like shit and decided to become a landlord instead?"

"She is *not* a bitch!"

Pam sniggered. "Well, now. It looks like I just hit a sore spot. I didn't know you were into antiques? Does she creak when you fuck her?"

Robin's entire body went rigid. She wanted to rant. She wanted to scream. She wanted to cram every word of what she wanted to say down Pam's throat because there was *so* much more to say, but Robin couldn't. She knew it was pointless. She knew this would never end unless she regained control of her emotions. Robin took a deep breath and let it out slowly. "I'm not doing this, Pam. Not anymore. Now, just get out and leave me alone."

Pam hid her glee. Alcohol and drugs weren't her only addictions, and Robin had been feeding the last for several minutes. Attention, whether it is good or bad, is what egomaniacs crave the most. As long as they're receiving it, the world is still revolving around them, as it should, and Pam wasn't done gorging. Robin's face was becoming mottled, stained by the simmering blood flowing through her veins, and she had clenched and unclenched her fists a half-dozen times in the past few seconds. Robin was now perched on the crumbling edge of a precipice, and Pam sucked in her cheeks. This was the most fun she'd had in weeks. God, how she had missed being the center of someone's universe.

"What's a place like this worth, anyway?" Pam said as she swaggered over and scoped out the living room. "I could use some money, and by the looks of it, you still have plenty."

Robin's shoulders slumped under the weight of Pam's tenaciousness. "It'll be a cold day in hell before I give you another dime."

"Speaking of cold, did you bite off more than you can chew, baby?" Pam said, and widening her stance, she looked down her nose at Robin. "Feels like you can't afford to pay the heating bill."

Robin unconsciously glanced around the room. Focused on having to deal with Pam, she had forgotten all about Isobel. She filled her lungs with the frigid air, and even though breath could not yet be seen, Robin knew if Isobel got any angrier, frost would begin to form. Robin looked back at Pam. It was impossible to miss the superiority oozing from every pore the woman owned, and Robin's blood pressure began to rise. Her only thought? Let it snow.

"Do *not* call me baby," Robin said through clenched teeth. "And what I can and can't afford is none of your business, and it hasn't been since the day you hit me."

"I never laid a hand on you!"

"Oh, and I suppose you didn't kick me or try to shove me over the sofa either?"

"That's a goddamned lie!" Pam yelled, taking a step closer to Robin. "I've never hit a woman, and I never will."

"Now who's lying?

"I never *fucking* hit you!"

"And how, exactly, would you know that, Pam? You were blitzed out of your mind on drugs and whiskey. The only reason you know *anything* about that night is because you called Gabby, wailing and pleading to find out what you'd done because you didn't remember one fucking thing when you woke up in jail the next morning. But I'll have to hand it to you, Pam, because even in that state, even when you didn't know shit, you continued to play your game. You called the one person you knew you could still manipulate, and you did, and Gabby told you what she knew, but she didn't know everything, Pamela. Gabby didn't know about you threatening to knock my teeth through the back of my head. She didn't know about you promising to take a baseball bat to Declan's skull, and speaking of Declan, Gabby sure as *hell* didn't know that you, the out and proud gold star lesbian, tried to *kiss* him!"

"That's a goddamned lie!"

Robin had finally gained the upper hand, and it was all she could do to keep her expression stoic. "No, it's not, Pam. You did it, and you did it three times, and each and every time, Declan backed away. He kept you at arm's length for I don't know how long as we tried to calm you down, but you were completely out of your mind."

"You fucking cunt! If you ever tell anyone, I'll—"

"What? You think it would taint your reputation? Tarnish the gold on your star? Well, let me enlighten you, Pamela. Do you want to hear the *best* part of the worst *fucking* day of my life because there's one little tidbit that no one knows about except for Declan and me? And honestly, every time I think about it, it *actually* makes me laugh."

"Let me guess. When you and your fucking bastard boyfriend watched the pigs take me away in handcuffs?"

"No, Pam. Believe it or not, I never found that funny, but if I did, it pales in comparison to this," Robin said as she walked out from behind the protection of the small island. "After Declan and I listened to your hysterics for over an hour, and after we watched you stumble and stagger your way from room to room gathering your shit while destroying everything of mine in your path, you came out of the bedroom wearing only a tank top and panties. And in the midst of your next tirade, in the midst of all the obscenities, threats and *spit* flying out of your disgusting mouth, you dropped your drawers...right...in front...of *Declan*."

Pam's jaw fell open, and she took a step backward as she glared at Robin. "That's bullshit! I didn't do that."

"Oh yes, you did," Robin said, slowly bobbing her head. "Do you honestly think I'd make something like that up? I write mysteries, Pam, not comedies."

"You're fucking lying."

"No, Pam," Robin said, eyeing the woman up and down. "I'm not."

Pam was an expert on distortion, molding her history and her life to her advantage, and while her education had not been as represented, she did own a PhD in Robin Novak. It had taken months, carefully jotting down observations in a mental notebook to discern her body language, her expressions, and even the slightest inflection in Robin's tone. Nothing had gone unnoticed, and Pam's heart began pounding in her ears. Robin was telling the truth.

Supreme beings do not make mistakes, but Pam had. A shameful, humiliating blunder that had been lost in the muck of a drug and alcohol-induced blackout, but now...now it would *never* be forgotten.

She could dilute its strength with alcohol and alter its memory with cocaine, but in the light of day, in the sobriety before drunkenness happened again, *this* would return. This misstep made Pam look like a fool, and she'd now forever be the brunt of someone else's joke. This *gaffe* would be the reason cackling, mocking and raucous, would fill living rooms and neighborhood bars, echoing off walls as tears of laughter rolled down cheeks.

Bile rose in Pam's throat, her gaunt face becoming almost skeletal as it twisted with malignant hatred, and as she was consumed by the indignity of it all, her lips curled into a venomous sneer. "You fucking *bitch*!" she bellowed. "This is all your fault! If your life wasn't so fucked up—"

"*My* life?" Robin screamed. "The only thing wrong with *my* life is that you were jealous it wasn't *yours*! It wasn't Declan's photos that pissed you off; it was the fact I *owned* the walls they hung on. It wasn't his novels on the shelves that lit your fuse; it was because *my* furniture wasn't hand-me-downs, left behind by the previous tenant. *My* friends, *my* way of living, *my* success...you wanted it all. Don't tell me you didn't."

"Because I deserve it all!" Pam howled. "And I'd have gotten it, too, if it wasn't for you. You drove me to drink. You drove me to—"

"Wait. *I* drove you to drink? And I suppose I shoved the cocaine up your nose, too? Or how about all the jobs you couldn't hold down? Was that because of me, too? Did I somehow warp your work ethic *years* before we even met?"

"Shut up!"

"What about the lack of friends, Pam. How exactly did I make them disappear?"

"I said *shut up!*"

"Why?" Robin said, waving her arms about. "If all the things wrong in your life are because of me, tell me how *I* did all these things! Tell me, Pam. *Tell me!*"

"Is everything okay back here ladies? It's getting kind of loud."

Pam whipped around and glowered at Judy. "*Get the fuck out of here!*" she screeched, and as her hands turned into fists, she took a step in Judy's direction.

"Don't you dare—" The rest of Robin's words were swallowed up in a gust of wind that ripped through the kitchen, its power funneled toward only one thing. The force knocked Pam back a couple of steps, and if it weren't for the wall stopping her momentum, she would have fallen on her ass.

It took a second for Pam to steady herself, and her eyes shifted between the two other people in the room, sizing them up with deadly glares of hatred and contempt. Judy was too far away to have shoved her, so that left only one other person. The woman she had momentarily turned her back on.

"You dare to lay a hand on me?" Pam shouted at Robin, and snatching up her empty beer bottle, she cracked it against the edge of the island. The glass shattered, sending shards all over the room. Judy and Robin both turned, trying to avoid the flying glass, but those bits and pieces were the least of their worries for Pam held in her hand the broken neck of the bottle, its edges jagged and razor sharp.

Spittle gathered at the corners of Pam's mouth as she fixed her eyes on Robin. "When I'm done with you," she growled, holding up what was left of the bottle. "Declan is going to puke every fucking time he has to look at you."

As soon as Pam took a step toward Robin, Judy launched herself at the woman, but the velocity of her intervention was no match for the momentum of Isobel's.

Again, a burst of wind appeared out of nowhere, its strength ten times stronger than it had been before. It knocked Pam backward into the wall like a feather in front of a fan, and as she slid to the floor, unable to move in the cyclone caused by a spirit named Isobel, the temperature in the room dropped below freezing.

This time, Isobel's onslaught didn't evaporate so quickly. The blast of gale-force winds kept Pam pressed hard up against the wall, and as her lips began to turn blue, the broken bottle fell from her hand, shattering into pieces when it hit the floor. In the blink of an eye, the air was still again.

Judy's jaw went slack, her eyes darting back and forth between Robin and the disheveled woman slumped on the floor. Her mind raced, random thoughts entering and exiting seemingly at the speed of sound, but none contained the answer she was looking for. What had just happened? *What had just happened?*

Like snakes pulsing under her skin, the veins in Robin's neck and temples throbbed. The beat of her heart hammered in her ears, the percussion growing louder as memory after memory engulfed her mind. Flashbacks to browbeatings that had left her cowering and condemnations that had left her contrite. The endless deceptions so cunningly orchestrated that Robin had questioned her own sanity, and then there was the humiliation and the feeling of being utterly helpless *and* utterly worthless. Robin had once been crippled by the woman on the floor. Turned into a human punching bag with each word a blow, each accusation a punch, each strike further disconnecting Robin from her own wants, her own needs, and her own life.

Robin's expression grew thunderous, her face contorting as she was consumed by bitterness. Her eyes blazed with fury as all restraint was lost, and taking two steps, she dropped to her knees in front of Pam. Grabbing the woman by the chin, Robin forced Pam to look at her.

"You are a pathetic excuse for a human being!" Robin shouted. "How long did it take, Pam? How long did it take for you to figure out how to get to me? A day? A week? *A fucking month*! How long before you had everything you needed to turn me into your puppet?"

Pam tried to twist out of Robin's reach, but Robin gripped Pam's chin even harder. "I'm not through!" she yelled, looking Pam in the eye. "You are the personification of evil. You're sadistic, and you're cruel. You take joy in hurting others, in tearing us apart, piece by fucking piece. You're nothing but a parasite, a blood-sucking insect that burrows her way into peoples' lives and leaves nothing behind except pain, but I'm still standing you *fucking* bitch!"

Robin let go of Pam's chin and took hold of her jacket, yanking the woman off the wall until their faces were only a few inches apart. "You spent months ripping me to shreds like a buzzard over road kill. You picked apart every detail of my life, pointing out everything you despised over and over again until I was like a top spinning out of control. I was running around like an idiot, trying to fix things that didn't *need* to be fixed because the only thing that *needed* to be fixed was *you*!" Robin released her hold on Pam's jacket, and the woman fell back against the wall. "You need help, Pam. You need doctors and padded cells and...and jackets that tie around the back because you're a fucking psychopath!"

Robin sprang to her feet and glared down at Pam. "Now, for the last *fucking* time, get out of my fucking house! What happened a minute ago, that wind, well that was a ghost named Isobel—"

"I don't believe in fucking ghosts, you stupid bitch," Pam snarled, clambering to stand. "I believe in teaching you—"

"Be careful," Robin said, glaring down at the woman. "Be *very* careful, Pam, because whether you believe in ghosts or not, I'm telling you right now if you lay one finger on me or lay one finger on Judy, Isobel *will* come back, and when she does, I won't stop her until you don't have any *skin* left!"

Pam took a step back, Robin's screech so loud it caused ringing in her ears. Her eyes darted back and forth between Judy and Robin as she thought about her options. Was there really a ghost? Would the wind start again? Pam straightened her spine as the slightest of tightlipped grins smudged its way across her face. Robin was no match for her, no match for the deviousness Pam could muster, the threats she could hurl, or the torment she could cause. Fueled by that grandiose perception, Pam took a step in Robin's direction, but before her foot found the floor again, strands of Robin's hair began to flutter...in a breeze.

Pam blanched, her palms dampening as she watched more of Robin's hair lifting in what was slowly becoming wind. Pam narrowed her eyes. She didn't like the feeling of fright, the feeling of weakness and uncertainty, but her heart had begun to race, and it wasn't because of the thrill of the hunt. Swallowing hard, Pam shook her head. "Fuck this shit," she growled as she glared at Robin. "This isn't over, baby. Trust me. You haven't seen the last of me!" Pushing past Judy, Pam stomped out of the apartment in her high-heeled boots.

Judy rushed over and touched Robin on the arm. "I'll be right back. I just want to make sure she leaves."

Judy didn't wait for an answer, and trotting after Pam, she held her tongue and her breath as she watched the woman's infantile display. In the big kitchen, Pam cleared the island of the pans Judy had set out to dry that morning with one sweep of her arm, sending them banging to the floor in every direction. In the dining room, the blue-bagged clown was sent flying with a shove, and the serving pieces nestled behind the plate rails of one hutch were snatched up and thrown to the floor, the old pottery shattering on impact. The reception podium was next, Pam hip-checking it into the stairs as she strode by, and as she yanked open the front door, she turned around long enough to give Judy a dirty look before kicking the coat tree to the ground.

***

Robin stood alone in the kitchen, loathing her own existence. This was the thing she had sworn she'd never do again, the thing she had berated herself for, condemned herself for, ridiculed herself for, and hated herself for, yet she *had* let it happen again. By allowing Pam to push her buttons, by allowing Pam to get her angry, Robin had once again become a puppet on Pam's strings. However, even with that awareness, Robin couldn't stop herself. Nothing she had learned over the past several months could prevent her rage from building. No knowledge gained could halt the fury that had invaded her mind like a cancer. No insight stopped the words she used because the only thing Robin wanted to do was hurt Pam as much as the woman had hurt her. She knew it was wrong. She knew it wasn't who she was and her stomach flipped.

She dashed to her bathroom, heaving up what little she had eaten that day, but her retching couldn't rid her of the shame. Robin pushed herself to her feet and seeing blood on the rim of her toilet, she looked down at her hands. When had she clenched her fists so tightly that her nails had broken through the skin on her palms?

Robin wiped her mouth with the back of her hand, and pulling her sweater and turtleneck over her head, she dropped them to the floor and rushed into her bedroom. The closet doors were no match for her mood, the bi-folds slamming open and then almost closed again before she stilled them long enough to grab a compression shirt. She tugged it on, but as she looked down at her jeans and the old sneakers speckled with paint, she shook her head. Why did it matter?

***

Judy closed and locked the front door, and turning around, she leaned against its surface. "Jesus," she said under her breath. A moment later, she saw Robin sprinting toward her.

"Christ, Robin, are you okay?"

"Get out of my way," Robin said as she tried to open the door.

"What? Why? Where are you going?"

"I'm going for a run!" Robin yelled, fumbling with the latch for the deadbolt.

"Robin, you're not dressed for a run," Judy said, grabbing Robin by the arm. "You need to just calm down and—"

"Don't tell me what to do!" Robin said as she yanked the door open, sending Judy stumbling backward. "You're not my fucking mother! You don't know what I've been through! You don't know *shit*!"

"Robin, listen to me," Judy said as she put herself between Robin and the open door. "It's cold, and it's supposed to rain."

Robin shoved her way past Judy. "Ask me if I care," she said, glaring at Judy through tear-filled eyes for a second before dashing down the stairs. "Ask me if I *fucking* care!"

***

The forecast hadn't been wrong, and a few minutes after Robin ran from the house, the rain began. It started as a mist, fine and barely noticeable, it drifted to the earth in silence, but it wasn't long before the drops of water could be heard hitting the road and the roof of the porch. With her breath steaming in the air, Judy stood just outside the front door, watching the water splash off every surface it touched. She flipped up the hood on her jacket more than once, going to the end of the walk to look up the road, but with shoulders slumped, she'd return to the protection of the overhang and sigh. Darkness soon fell over Mackinac, and as the sun traded places with the moon, and the day became night, Judy went back inside and began to remove every trace of Pam's visit.

The broken dishes and beer bottle were swept up and tossed in the trash, and the clown was returned to his place on the dining room table. Judy tucked his blue shroud firmly under his feet so even the red tips of his floppy shoes couldn't be seen, and returning to the foyer, she picked up the plastic bags Robin had brought home, now scattered all over the floor. The podium was beyond repair, the thin plywood sides no match for the oak of the staircase, and after stacking the wood off to the side, Judy righted the coat rack which had survived intact. She picked up all the pots and pans in the kitchen and gathered the papers that had been blown off the counter, and after it was all done, Judy poured herself a glass of wine and waited. It was excruciating.

She paced the rooms for the remainder of the first hour, traveling from the parlor to the kitchen and back again, and whenever she heard a sound outside, Judy would dart to the windows. She prayed to see Robin coming up the walk, but it wasn't to be, and eventually, she settled in the parlor, staring off into space as she sipped her wine.

She had so many questions, so many concerns about what had happened earlier, and so deep in her thoughts, Judy didn't hear the front door open. She did, however, hear it close.

Judy leapt from the sofa, dashing into the foyer to find Robin still facing the closed door. "Robin? Are you okay?" Judy waited, afraid to move for fear Robin would bolt again. "Robin, talk to me. Are you all right?" Again, Judy paused, and as she did, she noticed Robin's clothes. "Jesus, Robin, you're soaking wet. You've got to be freezing. You need to get out of those clothes." When Robin didn't move, Judy raised her voice. "Robin! God*damn* it, talk to me!"

Robin knew she should speak, but everything was out of focus. Blurred by exhaustion, fogged by the cold, and distorted by pain, Judy's words were muffled and distant as if she was at the other end of a long, dark tunnel. Robin could smell the polish on the door and the faint hint of the vanilla potpourri in the parlor. She took a slow, uneven breath. Thank God she made it.

Her nose was cold, yet the rest escaped her. She had no idea her clothes were soaked through. She had no idea her sneakers were filled with water. She had no idea how much damage she had done to herself, but when she turned around and heard Judy's gasp, Robin knew it was bad...and then her world went black.

Chapter Thirty

Judy sat with her elbows resting on her knees, staring at the floor. It wasn't the typical color found in a hospital. Instead of a muted pattern of varying shades of white, below her feet was a checkerboard of bright blue and yellow squares, but the vibrant backdrop did nothing to hide the flecks of color that did not belong. It was those flaws that held Judy's attention. Although some were smudged by feet and others, smeared by wheels, from the emergency entrance to the exam room was a trail of dark red.

She glanced at the clock on the wall. It had been fifty-two minutes since she first sat down in the chair opposite the exam room. Fifty-two minutes of listening to the click of the second hand as it made its way from one hash mark to the next. Fifty-two minutes of worrying. Fifty-two minutes of envisioning the worst. Fifty-two minutes sitting in a medical center with Robin's blood on her hands, on her jeans, and on her shoes.

"I brought you some coffee."

Judy jumped in her seat and then slowly looked up at Officer Kyle Ramon. The son of the dockmaster, she first met him when he was ten years old. He was spindly then and with a headful of unruly curls, and braces covering his teeth, he'd stand by his father's side on the dock in the summer, learning a trade he'd eventually leave behind when law enforcement began to interest him more. She had acted as his tutor for a few summers, using her education to broaden his, and over the years as his shoulders grew broader and inches were added to his height, their friendship continued, slipping effortlessly into one between two adults.

As Judy gazed into Kyle's familiar green eyes, she could still see the little boy she once raced on bikes around the island, and that memory brought the thinnest of grins to her face. "Thanks," she whispered as she took the cup, and welcoming the heat seeping through the paper, Judy took a sip of the steaming coffee.

Kyle had been at the station when her call came in, and hearing the frantic tone in Judy's voice, he jumped into the black-and-white SUV and made his way to the medical center. No crime had been committed, and no law had been broken, but Mackinac was a close-knit community, and friends need friends at times like these.

Open only during regular business hours, when Kyle arrived at the clinic, the doors were still locked. He paced in the darkness and drizzle until two people pedaled up on bikes, and while he recognized both, no pleasantries were exchanged as they rushed to prepare for an incoming patient. A couple of minutes later, the ambulance arrived. What transpired after that was a well-orchestrated scramble, as the doctor, nurse, and two EMTs did what they were trained to do, and rushing Robin into an exam room, they closed the door and got to work.

Kyle had been stunned to see the amount of blood on Robin's face, but he didn't allow his shock to show. Instead, he did what friends do. He assured Judy that all would be okay. He tried his best to downplay what appeared to be a serious injury, but the anguish of the unknown was etched into Judy's face, and as Kyle returned to his seat next to her, he couldn't help but notice that those lines were getting deeper by the minute.

"She's going to be all right, Judy," he said softly. "She was starting to wake up when they wheeled her in there. That's a good sign."

"I hope so," Judy whispered. "There was just so much—"

Judy's train of thought changed in an instant when the door to the exam room opened. Leaping to her feet, she rushed over to the doctor. "Liv, how's Robin? Is she going to be all right?"

Dr. Olivia Ingram smiled. "She's going to be just fine, Judy. Typical head wound. Lots of blood, but thankfully not a lot of injury. It looked a hell of a lot worse than it actually was."

"Really?"

"Really," Dr. Ingram said with a nod. "She's going to have one hell of a headache for a few days, and with all the scrapes and bruises, plus a sprained wrist, she's going to be sore for a little while, but Robin knows who she is, where she is, and she explained what happened. All signs lead me to believe that while she has a mild concussion, there's no permanent damage."

"Oh, thank God," Judy said, slumping against Kyle. "I was so scared. I thought any minute you were going to have to airlift her out of here."

"When I first saw her, that thought did cross my mind, but she's going to be fine," Dr. Ingram said, placing her hand on the doorknob. "Oh, you didn't by chance bring her a change of clothes, did you? We had to cut off what she was wearing."

"Clothes? Um...no. I...I didn't think about clothes."

"Well, we still have a few things to finish up. Why don't you go and grab her some, and by the time you get back, we should be almost done."

"Wait. Are you saying Robin can come home tonight?"

"Yes, Judy. She can go home tonight."

***

It was a night of firsts for Judy. It was the first time she had ever called 911. It was the first time she had ever ridden in the back of an ambulance, and it was the first, second, and *third* time she had ever been in a police car.

"I can't thank you enough for being my taxi tonight," Judy said, glancing at Kyle in the front seat.

Kyle Ramon looked in the rearview mirror. "Don't worry about it, Judy. I'm just glad I could help, and besides, she doesn't look in any shape to ride in the back of a carriage tonight."

"True," Judy said quietly and looking over at Robin, Judy placed her hand on her knee. "You feeling okay?"

"Yeah," Robin said in a whisper. "I'm just...I'm just tired. My head hurts."

"We're almost there."

"Okay."

"Is she doing all right?" Kyle asked, looking in the mirror again.

"Yeah. Just worn out."

It wasn't long before the police-issue SUV came to a stop in front of Safe Harbor. Judy glanced over at Robin, and thankful she wasn't attempting to exit on her own, Judy unbuckled her seatbelt and went to open the door, only to end up chuckling under her breath when the handle didn't move.

Kyle smiled, hearing Judy's failed attempt to escape. "They only open from the outside, Jude. Hold on." A few seconds later, Kyle opened the door and held out his hand. "Watch your head."

"Thanks," Judy said, and stepping out of the heated car, the cold air took Judy's breath away. "Wow, I can't believe how fast the temperature is dropping."

"And it's starting to get slippery, too, so be careful," Kyle said, closing the door. "You okay if I get the other door?"

"Yeah, go ahead," Judy said, looking down at the glistening pavement. "I'm fine."

The rain had stopped an hour before, but the frigid night air had turned what was left behind into an ultra-thin coating of black ice. Twice, Judy slipped as she made her way around the SUV, and by the time she reached the sidewalk, Kyle already had Robin standing safely on the frozen lawn.

"I figured the grass was safer than the sidewalk," he said as Judy approached. "And if you don't mind, I'll help you get to the porch before I go."

"We don't mind," Robin said quietly, looking up at the man standing next to her. "I think I've fallen enough for one day."

"I couldn't agree more," Judy said, grinning as she hooked her arm through Robin's. "Now, let's get you inside."

***

Judy guided Robin into the bedroom and flicked on the light. "Where do you keep your pajamas?"

"What?"

"Your pajamas. Where do you keep them?"

"Oh...um...hanging...hanging on the back of the door." Robin swiveled to point, but the simple movement seemed to spin the entire room. She reached out for the chest of drawers to steady herself at the same time she felt Judy wrap her arm around her waist.

"Okay, no more sudden movements for you," Judy said, motioning to the bed. "You need to sit down."

"I'm fine. It's just...it's just my head," Robin said, wincing as another invisible hammer crashed against her skull.

At a turtle's pace, Judy got Robin to the bed, and once she was sitting down, Judy rearranged the pillows until they were piled against the headboard. "Here, lie back."

"But I need to change."

"And you will, just not right now," Judy said, patting the pillows. "Right now, you're going to relax while I go get you something for that headache. Okay?"

"Yeah," Robin whispered, and pivoting enough to rest against the mass of down and foam, as soon as the softness swallowed her, she closed her eyes.

Convinced Robin didn't have the strength to do anything falling under the heading of stupid, Judy left the room, and when she returned Robin hadn't moved an inch. Sitting on the bed, Judy opened the bottle of ibuprofen and tapped out two tablets. "Here you go."

Robin opened her eyes long enough to pop the pills in her mouth, and after washing them down with the water Judy had handed her, Robin gave back the glass and then closed her eyes again. "Thanks."

"No problem. This should help, too."

Robin jumped when she felt something wet and cold against her forehead. "What—"

"Relax. It's just a washcloth. It'll help. Trust me," Judy said, keeping her hand lightly pressed against the cloth. "Just give it a few minutes."

One minute turned into two and then into three until Robin finally opened her eyes again. "You're right. It does help."

"Imagine that," Judy said softly, taking the washcloth away. "I'm going to go run this under some cold water again. Be right back."

While Judy was in the bathroom, Robin pushed herself into a sitting position. She dangled her feet over the side of the bed and waited for the crescendo in her brain to announce itself again. A few seconds passed before Robin let out a long, slow breath, the distant throb in her temples nowhere near as blinding as it had been.

"What are you doing?"

Robin looked in Judy's direction. "I need to get changed."

"You feel up to it?"

"Yeah."

"All right," Judy said, and draping the cloth over the water bottle, she knelt at Robin's feet and began untying the laces of her sneakers.

"You don't have to do that."

"Yes, I do," Judy said, looking up. "Because if you bend over, all the blood is going to rush to your head, and you're going to be right back where you were a few minutes ago."

"Oh, that would be bad."

"That's exactly what I was thinking," Judy said, tugging off Robin's shoes. Tossing them near the closet, Judy retrieved the pajamas from the hook on the back of the bedroom door. "Do you need my help with these?" she said, holding up the gray and blue flannel.

"No," Robin said, and inching toward the edge of the bed, she placed her feet on the floor and stood up. "I think I should be okay."

"Are you sure?"

"Yeah. I'll take my time."

"All right," Judy said, placing the pajamas on the bed. "I put some water on for tea, so I'll go check on that and give you some privacy. Call me if you need me."

"I will."

Robin appreciated Judy's choice in clothing as soon as she undid the tie to her sweatpants. She wasn't sure if Judy knew they were her baggiest pair, but as soon as the drawstring was loosened, the gray pants puddled around her feet. With one hand on the bed and the other on the nightstand, Robin stepped out of the fabric, and sitting down, she ever so slowly drew the flannel pajamas bottoms up her legs. Robin frowned at the patchwork of bandages covering her shins and knees, concealing the scrapes she had received earlier that night, but there was no hiding the splotches of purple appearing here and there, and everywhere.

Taking a deep breath, Robin got to her feet again, and unzipping the hoodie, she slowly shrugged out of it. With her right hand wrapped in an elastic bandage, Robin had no choice but to use her left, and as she repeatedly tried and failed to unclasp her bra, the temperature in the room seemed to increase.

"Shit," Robin said under her breath. There was no way in hell she wanted Judy to assist her with this task, so picking up the pajama top, she was about to put it on when she heard a gasp. Robin glanced over her shoulder and saw Judy standing near the door holding a cup of tea.

"My God, Robin, how many times did you fall?" Judy said, gawking at the bandage covering Robin's left shoulder blade and the impressionistic painting of red, blue, and purple bruises covering the other.

"Honestly? I don't know. Four, five...it could have been more. It all kind of ran together after a while."

"Jesus."

"But I'm okay, Judy. Just some bruises and a few cuts," Robin said, easing her arm into the pajama top.

Judy tipped her head to the side. "It's none of my business, but do you always wear your bra to bed?"

"No, I don't, but I'm right-handed, and I'm not ambidextrous."

Judy knew the feeling. Playing a game of tag football during college, a bad stumble ended with Judy's wrist in a cast for two months. It was a lesson Judy hadn't expected to receive while in school, but at the end of those eight weeks, although her right hand was still her dominant one, the left had stepped up and made her proud.

"I see," Judy said, and going over, as she placed the tea on the nightstand, she reached out and deftly undid the clasp on Robin's bra with her left hand. "Luckily, I am."

As soon as the fastener was free, Judy quickly moved away to give Robin privacy.

Robin was sore. She was tired. She was embarrassed, and her head hurt like a mother, but Robin wasn't dead, and neither was her sex drive. The feel of Judy's fingers on her skin sent a pulse of awareness through her body stronger than any ache or pain Robin owned, and her face reddened instantly. As fast as she could, she donned the pajama top, and climbed under the sheets on her bed, pulling up the covers until they were under her chin. "All done."

Judy returned to the bed and looked down at the woman snuggled under the blanket. "How's the headache?"

"Dull, but bearable."

"Well, just in case you need it, the bottle of ibuprofen is right next to your tea."

"Okay. Thanks."

"Is there anything else I can get you? An extra blanket? More pillows?"

"No. I think I'm set for now."

Judy stared wordlessly at Robin for a moment before patting her leg. "All right then. You get some sleep, and I'll see you a little later."

Judy was almost to the door when Robin called out, "Judy."

"Yeah?"

"Do you have any regrets?"

Judy paused and then slowly walked over to stand near the bed. "I suppose I have a couple. Why?"

"Most of mine revolve around Pam. I was so stupid, so—"

"Robin, stop," Judy said, again placing her hand on Robin's leg. "Now's not the time for that. You've beaten yourself up enough today without adding to it. You need rest, and you need to heal."

"I thought I was healed," Robin said under her breath.

"Healing takes time, and I don't know what went on between you and that woman, but there's no point in rehashing it right now. Now, all you need to do is get some sleep. Okay?"

"Okay," Robin said, closing her eyes.

"Sleep well, Robin," Judy said, and reaching over she turned off the bedside lamp before heading to the door.

"Judy."

"Yeah?" Judy said, glancing over her shoulder.

"Be careful going home."

A sliver of a grin appeared on Judy's face. "I will," she said, and leaving the door opened a crack for the cats to come and go, Judy went to the kitchen to make herself a cup of tea.

***

Judy's eyes fluttered open, and pushing aside the blanket, she sat up and rubbed the back of her neck. She moved her head back and forth, working out the stiffness that sleeping on a sofa can bring, and clearing her throat, she got to her feet and softly padded to Robin's bedroom.

She had checked on Robin practically every hour since they'd come home. Twice, the only occupants of the bed were Fred and Ginger, but a closed bathroom door provided Judy with the answer she was seeking. Other than that, under the blankets pulled to her chin, Robin had slept. And even though the level of the tea in the cup hadn't changed, Judy had refilled the glass of water more than once.

Judy crept into the bedroom, and after glancing at the closed bathroom door, she gathered the cup of cold tea and backtracked to the kitchen where she set up the coffee maker and put on some water to boil before making use of the powder room in the office.

When she returned, Judy opened the fridge for some juice, but before she could grab it from the shelf, she felt Fred and Ginger rubbing against her legs. "You hungry, guys?" she said, looking down at the cats at her feet. Her answer came in a chorus of meows. "I'll take that as a yes."

A few minutes later, Judy was doing her best imitation of the Pied Piper as she walked into the dining room carrying two bowls of wet food and one of dry. "There you go, guys."

Before Judy could fully straighten, Fred and Ginger began lapping up their helpings of today's selection which, according to the can, was salmon pâté. Hearing the squeak of hinges, Judy peeked around the corner of the dining room and for a split-second, she smiled. Robin was standing in the doorway looking far better than she had the night before. Most of the color had returned to her face, and the dark circles under her eyes had faded, but then Judy noticed something else and whatever color Robin lacked in her face found its way to Judy's. "I cannot *believe* you!"

"What?" Robin said, looking around. "What did I do?"

"Your hair's wet."

"Yeah, that usually happens when I take a shower."

"Robin, the doctor specifically said you had to wait forty-eight hours, and it hasn't even been twelve."

"Yeah, well the doctor didn't have dried blood in her hair," Robin said, shrugging. "And besides, I was careful. No harm done."

"Really? We'll see about that," Judy said, pointing to the dining room chair. "Sit."

"Judy—"

"Sit."

"Judy—"

"*Sit!*"

While the shower had felt good, the energy it took to take it had zapped most of what Robin had woken up with, so the eight steps it took to reach the dining room felt like eight hundred. When she finally got to the table, Robin gingerly lowered herself onto a chair, hoping she had hidden the discomfort caused by sore muscles, bruises, and cuts. She glanced over at Judy, prepared to assure her all was well through a counterfeit grin, except one look told Robin that was pointless. Judy's expression was pinched, and Robin sighed. Epic fail.

Judy's annoyance evaporated almost as quickly as the rosiness of Robin's cheeks. "Are you okay?" she said, lightly placing her hand on Robin's shoulder. "You look a little pale."

"I'm just sore," Robin said in a whisper.

Judy furrowed her brow, eyeing the woman before she wadded up the paper towel and dabbed it against the row of stitches and staples. "That's not all you are," she said with a sigh as she showed Robin the specks of red on the towel. "You're also bleeding."

"Crap."

"Do you have any antibiotic cream?"

"Yeah, in my medicine cabinet."

"Be right back."

A minute later, Judy returned. "This isn't going to sting, but I can't guarantee it's not going to hurt a little." Judy unscrewed the cap of the almost flattened tube of ointment and squeezed some onto the end of a Q-tip. "You ready?"

"Yeah, go ahead," Robin said, and closing her eyes, she bowed her head.

Judy winced as she applied the ointment. She heard Robin hiss a couple of times, but being a dutiful patient, she didn't say a word, and before too long, the sutures were coated with ointment.

"That should do it," Judy said, capping the tube. "I'm sorry if it hurt."

"And I'm sorry. I really thought I was careful."

"It's all right. It looks like you just loosened a few, but nothing broke open."

"That's good."

"You know what would be better?"

Robin opened one eye and looked up. "What?"

"If you promise me you won't wash your hair again for a couple of days."

Both of Robin's eyes popped open. "A couple of days? But—"

"Robin, please," Judy said, kneeling in front of her. "No more soaking that hard head of yours until it gets a little harder. Okay?"

"You sure you want my head to get any harder?"

"No, but I also don't want you bleeding all over the place," Judy said as she put her hand on Robin's knee.

For a long moment, Robin became lost in the eyes staring back at her. They gleamed with sympathy, the whirls of sapphire and sky holding in their hue compassion and kindness, but a flicker of challenge could also be seen. Amidst the amalgam of blue was a strength formidable and Robin was in no shape to take that on. And, if the truth was known, Judy had won the argument as soon as she placed her hand on Robin's knee. "All right, it's a deal."

"Good," Judy said, and standing up, she went back into the kitchen to wash her hands. "Now what do you want for breakfast? You've got to be starving."

When Robin didn't answer, Judy looked over her shoulder. "You doing okay over there?"

Robin took a long, slow breath and slowly shook her head. "I don't understand. I felt great when I woke up, but now...now I feel like I've just run a marathon. Hell, I've run marathons. I was never this tired when I finished them."

"Would you mind if I share a bit of something I've learned over the years?" Judy said as she dried her hands.

"No. Share away."

"The older you get, the longer it takes for you to bounce back."

"Ouch."

Judy laughed. "I'm not saying you're old," she said, returning to Robin's side. "I'm just saying—"

"I'm not as young as I used to be?"

"Something like that," Judy said, motioning toward Robin's room. "Now, go lie down, and when breakfast is ready, I'll come get you."

"Are you sure?"

"Yes," Judy said, watching as Robin stood up in slow motion. "Do you need my help?"

"No, I'll make it," Robin said as she finally stood straight. Pausing to gather her strength, Robin glanced over at Judy. "Wait. Aren't those the clothes you were wearing yesterday?"

"As a matter of fact, they are," Judy said, looking down at her wrinkled sweatshirt. "I didn't want to leave you alone, so I crashed on your sofa."

"Judy!"

"Don't 'Judy' me. You were hurt, and I'm not sure if you remember, but it was a little icy last night. The last thing I wanted to do was wipe out on the way home and end up needing a walker, too."

"I do *not* need a walker."

"Oh yeah," Judy said, dimples appearing in her cheeks as she pointed to the bedroom. "Then prove it."

***

"I've got to tell you," Robin said before gobbling down the last piece of bacon. "You're the first woman who's ever brought me breakfast in bed."

"Well, I figured if I waited until you reached the dining room, it would be cold by the time you got there," Judy said, grinning as she gathered the tray straddling Robin's lap. "I'm going to put this in the kitchen. Would you like another cup of tea?"

"That would be great. Thanks."

"Be right back."

Robin relaxed against the pillows propped behind her back and stared at the ceiling until Judy returned.

"Here you go," Judy said, and placing a mug on the nightstand, she sat on the edge of the bed. "So, if you think you'll be okay, the medical center called just after you fell asleep last night. The doctor wanted to start you on a round of antibiotics, but somehow they missed it on your chart when we left. I'm going to run up there to pick it up and then head home, grab a shower, and change my clothes. Is there anything else you need before I go?"

"Yeah, actually there is," Robin said quietly, placing her hand on top of Judy's. "I need to apologize."

"For what?"

"For everything. For running off in the rain. For worrying you, but mostly for yelling at you. You didn't deserve that."

"Well, from what little I saw and heard, I can understand how that woman got you so angry."

"I wasn't angry at her," Robin said, shaking her head. "I was angry at me."

"What do you mean?"

"I was angry at me...for getting angry."

"You were angry with yourself?" Judy said. "That doesn't make any sense."

"A year ago, I would have said the same thing, but not anymore." Robin took a deep breath, and as she slowly exhaled, she put her thoughts in order. "While I was still involved with Pam, I got an email from a woman who had read one of my books. She wanted to let me know how much she enjoyed it. She went on to say she was a psychologist, and she was impressed that my idiosyncrasies of the two characters were so accurate. One was flawed, and the other was a maniac, and according to her, I nailed their reactions, their behavior...their everything."

"Okay?"

"She asked if she could write to me again. She wanted to talk about a few things in depth, and so we began emailing back and forth. She was awesome to talk with. Smart, but not so smart that condescension dripped off the page, and she was truly interested in the whole writing process. Eventually, we stopped talking about my books and started talking about life in general. She told me about hers, and I told her about mine and somehow Ruth, that was her name, sensed I wasn't happy, so she asked me why, and I told her. I was dating a woman who continually made me angry, and she responded with only one line. 'She's not getting you angry. You're getting you angry.'" Robin grinned as soon as she saw Judy arch an eyebrow. "Yeah. Talk about cryptic—right?"

"Exactly."

"Of course, I asked her what she meant, and she told me that no one can make us *feel* anything. We own our emotions and how we react is on us."

"How so?"

"Well, have you ever been to a movie and not laughed at something everyone else found funny?"

"Sure."

"That's because your definition of amusement is intrinsic to you. No one can convince you something's funny if you don't see it that way. No one can *make* you laugh. You determine that, and on the opposite side of the spectrum, think about road rage. Some people become unglued when another driver does something they believe is stupid or reckless and others, like me, can't fathom reacting like that. I'll get there when I get there."

"Yes, but doesn't that have more to do with patience than an actual emotion."

"It does, but patience is tied to emotions. If you're tolerant, you don't explode, you don't react out of anger...which *is* an emotion."

Judy hesitated as she thought about what Robin had said. "Interesting."

"And it opened my eyes to a lot of things. It used to bother the crap of me when I'd go out to dinner with someone, and they'd sit there with their elbows on the table. I was brought up differently, but my reaction, my *annoyance* toward them wasn't based on anything they were doing. It was based on my own expectations. They weren't living up to them, so, therefore, *they* were getting me angry when, in fact, it was all on *me*. I'm the only one responsible for what I feel, or better said, on how I react. So, I could control my emotions and have a pleasant dinner, or I could fume the rest of the night and give up all control over *my* emotions to them."

There was no need to expound any further, but Robin needed to say what was on her mind. The most powerful emotion of them all had taken up space in her heart and in her head for a quarter of a century, and she needed to let it out just once. "And the same thing goes for love," Robin said softly. "No one can make you fall in love with them. No one can make you smile simply because they exist or somehow cause every love song you hear to remind you of them. They can't force your pulse to quicken when they're near or compel you to breathe deeply, craving the scent of their cologne. It's not in their power. It's only in yours. You're either head over heels...or you're not."

Seconds of silence passed between them until a yawn overtook Robin. It was only then when she realized her hand was still resting on top of Judy's. Removing it, she covered her mouth long enough to hide her fatigue.

"You're tired. You need to get some sleep," Judy said, and standing up, she ran her hands over her arms. "I'll be back in a little while. All right?"

"Okay," Robin whispered, and closing her eyes, she was asleep before Judy made it out the front door.

Chapter Thirty-One

Three hours later, Judy tiptoed into Robin's room to check on her for the second time since coming back to Safe Harbor. "Hey there," she said, finding Robin sitting up in bed. "I see you managed to get a nap."

"Yeah, I did," Robin said, putting her phone on the nightstand. "I woke up a few minutes ago."

"Are you hungry?"

"I'm going to get really fat if all you keep doing is feeding me."

"I doubt it," Judy said as she went over and picked up the empty mug on the nightstand. "More?"

"Maybe some water," Robin said, tossing back the bedcovers. "But I can get it."

"Robin, please...stay in bed. I'll get it."

Robin pursed her lips as she playfully glared at Judy. "Can I go pee or would you like to do that for me, too?"

"I already did *that* before I left my place, so you're on your own," Judy said, sashaying her way to the door. "Go pee to your heart's content. I'll be back in a few."

Judy stopped by the door, watching as Robin slowly extracted herself from the bed. "Are you going to make it?"

"Yeah, I'll make it," Robin said, shuffling toward the bathroom. "It may be tomorrow before I get there, but I'll make it."

"If you want," Judy said as whimsy flickered in her eyes. "I can always run back to the medical center. I'm sure they probably have some of those adult dia—"

"Don't you dare go there," Robin said with a laugh.

"Too late," Judy said, giving Robin a wink as she left the room.

Robin's smile remained for as long as she was in the bathroom and when she came out, it grew even bigger. There was a bottle of water sitting on her nightstand and the most beautiful woman in the world, sitting on her bed. "Hi there."

"Why did you unwrap your wrist?" Judy said, standing up. "If I'm not mistaken, the doctor specifically said to keep it wrapped for a few days."

Robin glanced down at her naked right hand. "I know, but I told you I wasn't ambidextrous, and it actually feels pretty good," she said, flexing her wrist this way and that.

"All right."

"What? You're not going to give me any grief?"

"Time will tell," Judy said, placing a pill in Robin's hand. "First things, first. Antibiotic, one every twelve hours until they're gone."

Robin paled at the sight of the pill meant for a horse. "It's huge!"

"Do you like when I give you grief?"

"Not particularly."

"Then take the pill."

With a huff, Robin put the tablet into her mouth and washed it down with half the glass of water Judy had handed her. "Satisfied?"

"Yes," Judy said, and taking the bottle back, she put it on the nightstand. "Now, sit down, turn around, and take off your top."

Robin froze, replaying in her mind what Judy had just said several times before she found her voice. "Um...excuse me?"

Judy held up a roll of gauze. "I need to change that bandage on your shoulder."

"Oh, don't worry about it. It washed off in the shower."

"Doctors bandage things for a reason, Robin," Judy said, motioning toward the bed. "Now sit."

"It really is—"

"Robin."

Robin's posture sagged, and sitting down, she turned her back to Judy. Noticing a basket overflowing with packages of gauze and tape sitting on the floor, she pointed at it. "Where'd that come from?"

"My place."

"Are you accident prone?"

Judy snorted. "No. Scott was, and I never saw a need to throw it out. It's not like they expire, but the ointment is new. I picked it up while I was out since your tube was almost empty."

"Lucky me."

"Top please."

Robin inwardly sighed and unbuttoning her top, she let it fall halfway down her back. A second later, she heard Judy hiss.

"Is it that bad?" Robin said, looking over her shoulder.

"Sorry. It just took me by surprise," Judy said, grimacing at the array of red, jagged gashes covering Robin's shoulder blade.

"The doctor said it was just a nasty brush burn."

"Nasty is right." Judy grabbed the tube of ointment from the nightstand. "Okay, so I know you said you fell, but do you remember how you did this?"

Robin had nothing to be ashamed of when it came to her body, but she still couldn't stop herself from clutching her loosened pajama top to her bosom when Judy reached around to grab the rest of the first-aid supplies. "Yeah. When I reached British Landing, there was a bunch of branches in the road. Instead of going around them, I decided in all my brainlessness to jump over them. I cleared them fine, but when my feet hit the ground, they slipped out from under me. I fell backward and landed right on top of a bunch of broken limbs."

"You're lucky you didn't break yours."

"Actually, I think I'm lucky they were there."

"Why?"

"Because it knocked some sense into me. Up until it happened, I had no idea it was raining, or it was getting so late, but lying on the ground, staring up at a rapidly-darkening sky with my shoulder feeling like it was on fire woke me up," Robin said, giving Judy another half-glance over her shoulder. "That's what made me turn around."

"Is that when you cut your head?"

"No, that happened on the way back. I was trying to outrace the setting sun, and I kept telling myself I could see, telling myself to just run a few more steps before I was going to be forced to walk and those few more steps kept turning into a few more until it was pitch black. It wasn't until I felt shrubs against my jeans when I realized I had veered off the road, and I tried to pull up, but it was too late. My momentum carried me into the brush, and then I tripped over something. The next thing I knew, I was flying, and a few seconds later, it felt like someone had hit me in the head with a hammer. I can't tell you how big the tree was, but it sure as hell took the wind out of my sails."

"And put stitches in your head."

"Yeah, that, too," Robin said, snickering. "Anyway, once I managed to get to my feet, I was clearheaded enough to know I had to keep the lights from St. Ignace to my right, so I got myself back to the road and kept going. I still managed to drift off the path a few more times, but since I was walking instead of running, the damage was minor."

"Define minor?"

"Relax," Robin said, glancing over her shoulder. "I'm not hiding some fatal, oozing wound. I just have a lot of bruises and a few scrapes on my legs."

"Do they need bandages, too?" Judy said as she picked up a strip of gauze now slathered with antibiotic cream.

"No, Band-Aids, which I put on after my shower. So there."

Judy smiled. "All right. Get ready. This is going to be cold."

As Judy expected, Robin flinched when she placed the bandage over the cuts, but she had no idea Robin's reaction wasn't based solely on the temperature of the cream.

Robin held her breath. Judy was lightly running her fingers over the gauze, ensuring it was in place before she taped down the edges, but while one finger remained on the bandage, another brushed against Robin's naked skin. Swallowing hard, Robin looked down and exhaled. The thickness of the flannel was hiding her body's reaction. Thank *God*.

"All done," Judy said as she began gathering up the supplies. After placing the first-aid basket near the door, she held up the packages of gauze and tape she had opened. "Do you mind if I put these in your bathroom? We'll need to change that bandage again."

"No, go ahead. There's plenty of room in the medicine cabinet," Robin said, and pulling on her pajama top, she fastened the buttons and then climbed under the covers.

A couple of minutes later, Judy returned to the bed and sat on its edge. "You feel up to talking?"

"Sure. About what?"

"I've been thinking about what you said, about owning your own emotions, and I have a couple of questions."

"Oh, okay. Shoot."

"If I understood you correctly, the reason you tore out of here yesterday was because you couldn't control your anger, but none of us are perfect, Robin. We all lose our temper every now and then. It's human nature."

"I agree, but not when it concerns me dealing with Pam."

"Why? What makes that so different?"

"Because I *know* better than to argue with her, but I still did it. I let her push my buttons, and I pushed back, knowing full well it was pointless. I fell into the same freaking trap she's set for me a hundred times, and it's something I swore I'd never do again. I know she feeds off reactions, so getting angry was the last thing I should have done. I *know* that, yet instead of starving her, instead of just allowing her to spout her bullshit and then leave, I gave her serving after serving of attention. I gave her back *all* the control. I fed her ego. I fed her anger...and you saw what my stupidity caused."

"But it wasn't your fault."

"Yes, it was."

"No, it *wasn't*. Stop blaming yourself," Judy said, raising her voice just a little. "There's only so much anyone can take, Robin, and I don't know what happened between you two, but you're condemning yourself for *her* reactions. How can you do that when they belong to *her*?"

"What?"

"*She's* the one who got angry. *She's* the one who went off the deep end, and *she's* the one who owns those things. Right? Isn't that what you said?"

"Yeah, but it's different—"

"The only difference is that you're of sound mind, and she's apparently not. She broke that bottle. You didn't force her to do it. She made those threats. You didn't put words in her mouth. She did those things all by herself, so blaming yourself for what happened directly opposes owning your own emotions. Could you have chosen not to speak your mind? Sure, but I'm sorry, from what little I saw, there's no way in hell I would have held back. No freaking way. Yeah, momentarily she was pulling the strings, but look around, Robin. She's not here, and if I get my way...if I get my way, she won't be coming back."

"What's that supposed to mean?"

"I'd like you to talk to the police."

"Why? I already have a restraining order against her. You saw how well that works."

"Wait," Judy said, jerking back her head. "What do you mean you have a restraining order? Robin, what the hell did she do to you?" When Judy saw Robin's eyebrows knit, she reached out and touched her on the arm. "Forget I said that. It's none of my business."

When trust is lost, to return to it is much like walking across a wooden bridge. Planks removed by others leave gaping holes, and through their apertures, pain exists. If weaknesses are spoken, would they be used against you in the future? If insecurities surfaced, would scoffs be heard, and would secrets be no longer secret if they were too juicy not to share with friends over drinks?

Robin took a deep breath and looked into Judy's eyes. Judy was *not* Pam, and it was time to step out onto that bridge again. "Maybe not," Robin said in a whisper. "But do you want to know anyway?"

***

"Gaslighting?"

"That's what they call it," Robin said. "And it's funny because I knew the term, but it wasn't until after the smoke cleared with Pam when I realized just how textbook she is. From the lies to the manipulation, trust me, if you Google it and read down the list of signs, it's scary just how accurate they are when it comes to describing Pam."

"Well, I have a few words that could be used to describe her," Judy said, patting Robin on the leg. "But I have a feeling, you've already used them."

"Probably…and then some."

Judy shook her head, her mind reeling with all Robin had told her, and then she snickered. Closing one eye, she tilted her head as she looked at Robin. "And she *actually* took off her underwear?"

"I swear to God," Robin said, holding up her right hand. "She was *totally* half Monty and *totally* oblivious to it."

"Geez, she must have been wasted."

"She was, and I can still hear Declan screaming 'no, no, no' as he ran into the kitchen. He was *so* funny."

"Why did he run?"

"I guess he wasn't interested in seeing her landing strip," Robin said with a laugh. "But he's also a gentleman. He's not perfect, mind you, but I couldn't ask for a better friend, and Pam couldn't handle that."

"And that's why she hated him so much?"

"Yes, that and the fact I slept with him."

Judy's expression went slack. "What? But I thought...well, I mean..." Judy's shoulders fell. "I don't know what I mean."

"Sure you do, and to answer your question, I *am* a lesbian, but not all of us shoot out of our mother's vagina knowing we're gay or actually *accepting* the fact we're gay," Robin said, grinning as she leaned into the pile of pillows behind her back. "It happened when we were in college. One of my short stories was accepted by a magazine. I was over the moon about it, and Declan took me out to celebrate. He's probably had a five o'clock shadow since he was four, so getting served was easy and getting drunk was even easier. Around midnight, we headed back to our dorms, and since my roommate had just flunked out and my room was closer, we ended up there. I was twenty, still a virgin, and totally confused about my own sexuality, and looking back I think I was just tired of wondering and worrying and having this virgin guillotine dangling over my head. So, I kissed him...and one thing led to another."

Robin stopped long enough to reach for her water, and after taking a swig, she looked Judy in the eye. "And in case you're wondering, I'm not ashamed of it, and I don't regret it happened, although, at the time, I did."

"Why?"

"Because when we woke up the next morning, things got really, *really* awkward. I couldn't look at him. He couldn't look at me, and for the rest of that semester, we were like strangers. God, it was awful."

"How did you get past it?"

"I kissed a girl."

"What?" Judy blurted.

"I kissed a girl," Robin said with a dazzling smile. "The details aren't all that important, but the bottom line was after I did it, the fog lifted. There was no longer any doubt in my mind as to what I was...what I *am*, and I told Declan the very next day."

"You told him you kissed a girl?"

"No, I told him I was a lesbian. He was *so* relieved," Robin said. "I think it was the longest exhale in history."

"Why was he relieved?"

"He thought he had destroyed our friendship."

"But *you* kissed him."

"I did, but the way he saw it, Declan was the one buying the drinks. Declan was the one who came into my room, and Declan didn't say no."

"I can see why Pam hated him," Judy said with a laugh. "He's a real loser."

"Yeah, he is," Robin said, chuckling. "I'm not saying he's a saint. Lord *knows* he's not a saint. He can be a royal pain in the ass at times, and we've had our fair share of arguments, but when push comes to shove, Declan's always been there for me, and I've always been there for him."

"Well, I'm glad he was there the night of the fight. Actually, in a way, I wish he was here right now."

Robin tilted her head to the side. "Why?"

"It doesn't matter," Judy said, and getting to her feet, she moved toward the door. "I'm going to make some tea. You interested?"

"I'm more interested in finding out why you want Declan here."

"It's nothing, Robin. Don't worry about it."

"Please, Judy, tell me what you meant."

Like a balloon with a slow leak, Judy's posture deflated. "Fine," she said, letting out a long breath. "I realized this morning when I was riding around that for the first time since moving to Mackinac, I didn't feel safe here."

"What?"

"She knows where you live now, Robin. She knows who I am. What's to prevent her from coming back and...and doing something else?"

Robin sat straight up in bed, and her jaw became as rigid as her backbone. Reaching for her phone, she said, "What was that cop's name?"

"What cop?"

"The one from last night. What was his name?" Robin said as she tapped away at the screen on her phone.

"Kyle. Kyle Ramon. Why?"

Holding up one finger, Robin waited for the call to go through. "Yes, hi. My name's Robin Novak. Can I speak to Officer Kyle Ramon, please? Yes, I'll hold."

"What are you doing?" Judy said, taking a step closer to the bed.

"Something I should have done a long time ago."

***

Robin spun around in the chair and held out the flash drive. "This contains copies of all the emails she sent me and screenshots of all the texts."

"Thanks," Kyle said, pocketing the USB drive.

"So what now?" Robin said, looking up at the man.

"Now, I'm going to head back to the station and call the probation department in Tampa to give them a heads-up, but they probably won't act on anything until you give them an affidavit," Kyle said, looking down at Robin. "Do you have a lawyer?"

"Yes. In St. Ignace. He handled my aunt's estate."

"Good," Kyle said while he ran a Google search on his phone. "You'll need to give him copies of the emails and texts, too, and he's going to also want a statement for the affidavit, so you'll need to write everything down just like you told me. After that, he'll handle the paperwork and then once you sign it, it goes to her probation officer, and they'll take it from there."

"Okay."

"Is this her?" Kyle said, holding out his phone for Robin to see it.

Robin blanched at the mug shot. "Yeah, that's her."

"Good. I just wanted to make sure."

"Why?" Judy said, taking a step closer to Robin's desk.

Kyle smiled as he looked back and forth between the two women. "Because we live on an island, Judy," he said, pocketing his phone. "And it's an island not only filled with your friends, but it's also one that doesn't have a bridge attached to it."

Judy paused for a moment. "Sorry, Kyle, but I'm not following you."

"I'm going to print out the photo and give it to the dockmasters and the people over at the airport. That way, if this Burton woman tries to return before the Tampa police pick her up, we'll give them a hand doing just that."

"Oh," Judy said, lightly touching Kyle on his sleeve. "That's a *great* idea."

"Thanks," he said, and picking up his clipboard, Kyle tucked it under his arm. "Now, I know we've already talked about this, but if you two want to press charges for what she did yesterday—"

"No," Robin said, looking over at the officer. "You don't know her like I do. She will twist and turn the facts until I become the attacker, and she becomes the victim. Seriously, what judge is going to believe that a ghost pushed her against the wall? She's going to swear I did it and then she's going to say she was defending herself, and she *will* make them believe her."

"Yeah, you're probably right," Kyle said, scrubbing his hand over the stubble on his cheeks.

Kyle Ramon was an easygoing man. He chose police work, not for the gun strapped on his belt or the authority given to him by the state. His calling had always been to help people. Whether it was carrying their luggage to a taxi, assisting in repairing a flat tire, or breaking up a barroom brawl, all he ever wanted to do was help. But even with that gentle side, the side that saved cats from trees, guided drunks back to their hotels, and chauffeured the elderly to church in the winter in his squad car, that didn't mean Kyle couldn't be stern. It took some rehearsal, some afternoons spent staring into a mirror while he practiced steely, staunch, and supreme, but all that practice was about to pay off...again.

Wearing the most menacing of scowls, Kyle took a step and focused solely on Robin. "One more thing before I leave," he said, crossing his arms as he widened his stance. "Part of taking out a restraining order is to follow through on it, which you didn't do and by doing nothing, you put someone *else* in danger."

"I know," Robin whispered, hanging her head. "It was stupid."

"Yes, it was, but you need to remember something." Kyle knelt down, and it wasn't until Robin looked him in the eye when he spoke again. "You're the victim here, and you have rights. You have the right to feel safe, to feel secure, and protected, but if you keep turning a blind eye, believing things will just go away if you don't do anything, you aren't doing *anyone* any favors. If that woman texts you again, if she tries to make *any* contact whatsoever, you are to *call* me immediately. Do you *understand?*"

No longer able to look the man in the eye, Robin kept her head bowed. "Yes, sir."

"Good." Kyle stood up and turned to Judy, and when he saw the stunned look on her face, his pearly teeth showed through his smile. Invading Judy's personal space, he lowered his voice to a whisper. "Sorry, if you thought that was too much. I was just trying to make sure she'll do the right thing the next time."

"Do you think there'll be a next time?"

"Not if I have anything to say about it," Kyle said, and bowing down, he placed a soft kiss on Judy's cheek. "See you around, Judy. I'll show myself out."

Judy waited until Kyle had left the room before going over and squatting next to Robin. "How you doing?"

"Other than the fact I was just admonished by a police officer, I guess I'm doing okay."

"Sorry, he was—"

"Don't. Don't apologize for him. What he said I needed to hear, and he's right," Robin said as she looked into Judy's eyes. "And next week, I'm going to make sure Pam never bothers us again."

Chapter Thirty-Two

Judy closed the booklet when she heard the passenger door open. "How did it go with the lawyer?"

"Good," Robin said, climbing inside. "You could have come in, you know?"

"I know, but then I wouldn't have had a chance to read up on your car," Judy said, and reaching over, she opened the glove box long enough to toss in the owner's manual. "Talk about state-of-the-art."

"Yeah, well when it comes to cars, I lean toward luxury."

"I can tell," Judy said, running her hand over the leather console between them.

"And I also can drive, by the way. I'm fine. I haven't had a headache for two days."

Judy slipped the SUV into gear and headed toward the parking lot exit. "Oh yeah? Then why were you taking Advil this morning?"

"That wasn't for headaches," Robin said, shifting in her seat.

It only took a second for Judy to understand. "Oh, *those* were the days," she said, grinning. "Not!"

"I seriously think there should be a way to just turn it off. Don't need it, flip a switch and shut her down."

"I would have signed up for that in a heartbeat," Judy said as she pulled out in traffic.

For a few minutes, Robin was entranced with the landscape whooshing by until she noticed how quiet it was inside the car. She glanced at Judy and saw lines creasing the woman's forehead. "You're awfully quiet. Something wrong?"

"No," Judy said, giving Robin a half-glance. "I was just thinking about Pam."

For a moment, Robin stared blankly back at Judy. "Can I ask why?"

"I was just...I was just trying to figure out what you saw in her. She didn't seem very chappy to me."

Robin's eyebrows squished together, and a second later, she smiled. "The term's chap*stick*, and you're right. She's not."

"Then why go out with her?"

"Just because I have a type doesn't mean I only date that type."

"Oh."

Robin picked at a loose thread on her jeans. "And I was in a bad place back then. My mom died. I was alone. All my friends had partners or wives or...or husbands, and there I was with no prospects. It sounds stupid now, but like I said, I wasn't in a good place. So, when I met Pam, I told myself to stop looking at all the little things that bothered me and start looking at the bigger picture. I know it's hard to imagine, but Pam's a chameleon. She can turn herself into anything or anyone, so with me, at least at first, she was exactly what I was looking for. She was smart, conversational, and had a lot of stories about her life that seemed to coincide with mine in one way or another. Of course, now I know they were all bullshit, but at the time she gave me exactly what I was looking for."

"Which was?"

"The makings of a perfect partner."

A few seconds passed before Judy spoke again. "So...you were in love with her?"

"At first I thought I was, or at least falling in love with her, but looking back, I wasn't even close."

"Are you sure? It sounds like you were together for a while."

"It was a little over a year, but yeah, I'm sure," Robin said, nodding. "And I know it sounds like a cop-out, like I'm trying to rationalize the biggest mistake I've ever made in my entire freaking life, but I'm not. I can't tell you how many nights I laid awake after I finally ended it, thinking about everything. I dissected our relationship like it was a frog in biology, and that's when I realized I was never in love with Pam. I was in love with the idea of *being* in love, which in its own way helps to explain why I overlooked so many things for so long. I kept trying to hold on to the dream."

"What dream?"

"The dream of a perfect life, a perfect mate, a perfect everything." Robin sighed and shook her head. "And even when her façade began to crack, and the true Pam started oozing out, I still refused to let go of the dream, but day by day, that dream turned into a nightmare...and I finally woke up from it."

"I'm glad you did."

"Me, too," Robin said, looking over at Judy. "But that doesn't mean I still don't kick myself almost every flipping day for letting it happen. I mean, Jesus, I'm a mystery writer. I've spent hundreds of hours reading about sociopaths, trying to get in the right mindset to write my villains, but reading about them and experiencing one firsthand...let me tell you, it's night and day."

"It sounds like it."

"You have no idea," Robin said, pivoting to look out the windshield. "Up until Pam, I can honestly say I was *fucking* clueless as to just how twisted they can be, and even now, even after everything I went through, I still can't fathom how someone can feel no remorse or guilt about *anything*. The sky's the limit with them, and whatever it takes, they fucking do. They don't look back. They don't regret. They don't *own* a goddamn conscience. They just plow through life, shoving the people they've *shattered* to the curb while they look for their next fucking victim!" Robin shouted as she slammed her fist against her thigh.

The longer Robin spoke, the louder her voice had become, and Judy was now hunching her shoulders against the volume. "Hey. I'm sorry," she said, placing her hand on Robin's leg. "I shouldn't have brought it up."

"It's okay," Robin whispered as she blinked away her tears. "Shit happens."

The corners of Judy's mouth drooped. "I wish there was something I could say or do."

Robin gazed out the window at the hotels and bars whizzing by, and as they approached a row of conifers lining the road, Robin looked toward the heavens. The sky was the bluest she'd ever seen and with nary a cloud to block its view, the sun was free to flood the earth with all its brilliance.

LYN GARDNER / 337

"You know what?" Robin said, turning toward Judy. "It's too pretty of a day to cloud it up with all my crap. How about we stop traveling down this memory lane?"

"Sounds good to me," Judy said, flipping on the left turn signal. "What would you think about making a right?"

"Um...I hate to break it to you," Robin said, quickly looking out the window. "But you're making a left."

"I know I am. I was talking about memory lane," Judy said as she made the turn.

"Oh," Robin said with a laugh. "What did you have in mind?"

"Let's talk about Thanksgiving. What's your favorite part?"

"The food. *Duh.*"

"Can you be more specific?"

"In what way?"

"Do you have a family favorite?" Judy said, shrugging. "Like with mine, my mom used to make homemade cranberry relish instead of getting the kind in a can, and we *always* had to have green bean casserole."

"Is that the stuff with those onion things on top?"

"Yep."

Robin tried to keep her lip from curling. "And you like that?"

"Hate it."

"Thank God."

Judy glanced at Robin. "You, too?"

"I tried it once. Declan's family always makes it, but smothering fresh green beans in mushroom soup and sprinkling sodium enriched fried onions on top just doesn't do it for me."

"I couldn't agree more."

"Well then, we can cross that off our shopping list."

"So, *was* there anything special you and your mom always had to have?"

Robin's smile reached her ears. "Celery stuffed with cheese and pimento spread, and sweet potato casserole with marshmallows on top. It just wasn't Thanksgiving without it."

"Okay. I've heard of the spread, but not the casserole."

"Seriously?"

"I mean I've had sweet potatoes before, but never with marshmallows. It sounds kind of weird."

"Oh, it's *so* good. Declan couldn't get enough of it. Although..." Robin stopped and tapped her finger on her chin. "Come to think of it, Gabby hated the stuff, which means it's not for everyone. I don't have to make it."

"No, I think you should. I'm up for trying new things."

Robin smirked as she glanced at Judy. "Are you now?"

Judy's cheeks turned rosy, and she shot Robin a quick look before turning her attention back to the road. "As long as you don't say you like oyster stuffing, I think we'll both be putting ourselves into a food coma in a couple of days."

***

Three days later, Judy came into the house and immediately knew Robin had started without her. Breathing in the aroma of freshly baked cornbread, Judy hung up her coat, gathered up the packages she had put on the floor, and made her way to the big kitchen. "Happy Thanksgiving," she chirped, entering the room.

Robin looked up from the cookbook she was reading, and her smile brightened the room instantly. "Happy Thanksgiving to you."

"I thought we were going to do this together," Judy said, placing the shopping bags on the counter on the island.

"We are, but the cornbread has to cool down before we crumble it up for the stuffing, so I thought I'd get it out of the way," Robin said before glimpsing at the assortment of cloth sacks in front of her. "What's all this?"

"While you took yesterday to write, I took it to shop," Judy said, fumbling in the bags for only a moment before pulling out a bouquet of red, yellow, and white mums. "And I bought these."

Robin did a double-take. "You bought me flowers?"

"Well, technically, I bought them for us. Thought it would add to the holiday," Judy said, glancing around the room. "Do we have a vase?"

"Yeah...um...pantry on the right. Bottom shelf."

"Thanks."

"So...what else did you get?" Robin said, peering into the bags.

"I bought a few bottles of wine since I'm always drinking yours."

"You didn't have to do that."

"I know. I wanted to," Judy said, shooing Robin away from the sink, so she could put some water into the vase.

The concept of reincarnation, like the existence of ethereal beings, weren't topics Robin had ever given much thought to until moving to Mackinac. But now, she was a firm believer in ghosts, and she was also convinced that in a previous life, she must have been a voyeur.

In place of blue jeans, Judy had on a pair of straight-leg corduroys, the charcoal shade a hair darker than the gray lace-up open knit sweater she was wearing, and Robin drank in the view as if she had spent a week in the desert. With Judy busy trimming the stems of the flowers, Robin took her time, her eyes raking over the woman standing at the sink, and it wasn't until Judy turned around when Robin awakened from her not-so-PG rated daydream.

"Something wrong?" Judy said, placing the vase on the island.

"What? No," Robin said, spinning toward the stove. "But I better break up this cornbread, so we can start on the stuffing."

***

When it came to dancing, Robin always preferred slow over fast. She adored holding her partner close, and in tandem, they'd glide across the parquet floor in breathless abandon. Breasts would lightly brush up against breasts and hands would rest on hips, curvaceous and soft, and although seldom labeled as a public display of affection, Robin found that dancing, with the right partner, very well could be.

The music playing on the radio was top forty, hardly what most would choose for a dreamy, sensual rumba, but throughout the morning, unintentionally, one was performed. Side-by-side they chopped and minced, stirred and seasoned, sampled and smiled, their arms or hips occasionally touching as one reached, one moved, one tasted. The kitchen was large, but more than once a hand found its way to the small of a back, a light, silent signal that the other was passing by.

Robin relished every touch. They had worked together renovating rooms, and each had easily guessed the other's move so they wouldn't get in the way, but this was different. This was personal. This was comfortable. This was...intimate.

Amidst the smell of onions and celery sautéing, Robin fell more in love with Judy as each minute passed. She tried to stop herself, tried to stop gazing, wondering, and wanting, but it would have been easier to stop a train without brakes from coming down a hill. Robin knew it was Thanksgiving, but it felt more like Christmas as one gift and then another was revealed, every detail about Judy growing crisper in the warm confines of the kitchen. The way the woman's eyes would light up a millisecond before a grin would appear. The way she'd poke her tongue between her lips as she chopped the last little piece of celery, and the way she'd squint, studying her mother's recipe for the cranberry relish were presents all the money in the world couldn't buy.

The deafening whir of the food processor jolted Robin from her thoughts, and her reaction was not lost on Judy.

"Well, now that I have your attention," Judy said with a laugh. "Could you hand me that bowl?"

"Oh, yeah, sure," Robin said as she reached for the Pyrex. "So what else needs to be done?"

"This is it," Judy said, scraping the cranberry mixture into the bowl.

Robin looked around at counters empty of pots, pans, and food. "Seriously?"

"Yeah, we put the turkey in the oven two hours ago, and the casseroles are in the fridge. So, once I finish this, we can relax for a few hours. Where have *you* been?"

"I guess I was just...I was just enjoying the morning."

An easy smile played at the corners of Judy's mouth. "I know what you mean."

***

"Too soon?" Robin said, holding up a bottle of wine as she walked into the living room.

Judy glanced at her watch. "It's almost one, so I'd have to say no," she said, reaching up to take a glass from Robin. "And thanks for finishing up in the kitchen. I could have helped."

"I know you could have," Robin said as she filled the two glasses. "But since you're cleaning up after dinner, I figured it was the least I could do."

"You cheated on that race."

"I did not. It's not my fault you dawdled," Robin said, and relaxing on the sofa, she took a sip of her Cabernet. "Very tasty," she said, looking at the dark ruby liquid in her glass. "Good choice."

"Thanks," Judy said, resting her head on the back of the sofa.

As the distant sounds of music from the radio in the kitchen made its way to their ears, almost in unison, both women sighed.

"This is nice," Robin said softly.

"I couldn't agree more."

"Yeah?"

Judy rolled her head to the side to look at Robin. "Holidays were never like this with Scott, or with my family for that matter."

"How so?"

"Well, with my family it's always hectic and loud, and with Scott, it was just another day."

"What do you mean?"

"He wasn't that much into holidays. He'd always get me something for Christmas, but the rest was just like any other day except for the food I made for us." Judy snickered when Robin raised an eyebrow. "I know that goes against the grain of all liberated women on the face of this planet, but sometimes it was just easier to do it myself than to have him underfoot."

"Gotcha." Robin paused long enough to take a sip of wine. "And speaking of that, what are your thoughts on Christmas?"

"Don't you think it's a little early to plan Christmas dinner when the Thanksgiving turkey is still in the oven?" Judy said, sitting up so she could take a drink.

Robin's heart didn't do a flip. It did a double axel with a twist at the mere hint of spending Christmas together. Robin knew she needed to get her grin under control before it jumped off her face and splattered all over the room in the shape of yellow smiley faces, so hiding behind her wine glass, she took a leisurely taste of the Cabernet. Several seconds passed before she reined in her excitement enough to speak. "No, silly," Robin said, putting the glass aside. "I wasn't talking about food. I was talking about decorating, because from what I saw in the basement, Adele loved it as much as my mom did."

A low chuckle rose in Judy's throat. "Let's just put it this way. I've been playing Christmas music since the beginning of November."

"Me, too!" Robin said, perking up in her seat.

"You didn't today."

"I wasn't sure if you liked it or not."

"Robin?"

"Yeah?"

"Go change the station."

Robin beamed, and she went from sitting to standing in record time. "Yes, dear."

Judy leaned back again, and stretching out her legs, her features softened. If she became any more relaxed, she was going to fall asleep, except a second later, Judy was scrambling not to drop her wine as an ear-splitting scream echoed through the house. Managing to set her glass on the table before she leapt to her feet, Judy rushed to the big kitchen and found Robin standing by the sink. "What's wrong? Did you cut yourself? Burn yourself? What's going—"

"It's snowing!" Robin screamed, spinning around.

"It's *snowing*?" Judy marched over and slapped Robin on the arm. "You scared the crap out of me."

"I'm sorry, but I haven't seen snow in forever."

Judy placed her hand over the heart pounding in her chest. "Your mom lived in Indiana, Robin. I'm almost positive they have snow there."

"I know, but once I moved to Florida, she always came down there to escape the snow, so I haven't seen it since I was a kid."

"Which explains why you just screeched like one, I'm guessing."

"Yep," Robin said, looking back and forth between the window and Judy. "So, do you wanna go out and play? Do you? Do you? Huh? Huh? Huh?"

Judy snorted as she looked at the large flakes drifting by the bank of windows. "I think I'm a little too old—"

"Oh, come on. Please? We can just go for a walk. What do you say?"

Judy glanced down at the suede ankle-high boots on her feet. "I don't have on the right shoes."

"What size do you wear?"

"Seven. Why?"

"I wear an eight and I have plenty of boots. With a couple pair of socks, they should fit you," Robin said, her words coming faster than the snow as she clasped her hands together. "*Pleeeease*? Pretty, pretty please?"

Feeling as if she would be stealing candy from a child unless the right word came out of her mouth, Judy caved. "Okay, but—"

"Yes!" Robin said with a fist pump.

"On one condition."

"Okay, anything."

"No snowballs."

Robin lowered her chin just a smidge and then raised her eyes. "Would I do that?"

A disco ball didn't hold a candle to the sparkle now appearing in Robin's eyes, and Judy tried her best not to keep her mirth in check. "I'm serious, Robin. *No* snowballs."

"Okay. No snowballs," Robin said with a pout.

"Promise me."

"I just said—"

"Promise me, or you're going alone."

Robin puffed out her cheeks. "Fine, I promise. I won't throw a snowball," she said as she made her way past Judy to fetch some boots. "Party pooper."

***

As they made their way up Market Street, Judy looked down at her feet. "How come you have so many boots? It's not like you needed them in Florida."

"Because I like boots, and there were always a few weeks every year I could get away with wearing them without sweating my toes off."

"But these look new," Judy said, glancing again at the insulated duck boots she was wearing.

"Okay, so I bought a few more pairs once I got here."

Judy's laugh steamed in the air. "You and your shopping. I'm definitely going to have to keep an eye on you."

Robin smiled as she shoved her hands deeper into the pockets of her coat. "Then you should know I'll probably go shopping next week. I keep forgetting to buy warmer gloves."

"Are you all right? Do you want to turn around?"

"Not a chance," Robin said, gazing at Judy. "I just want to take a walk in the snow. Okay?"

"Absolutely," Judy said, gesturing with her head. "Lead the way."

They continued up Market in silence, occasionally blinking away the lacy flakes attempting to settle on their eyelashes. Near Cadotte Avenue, the sound of children's laughter reached their ears and the giddiness of toddlers playing in the first snow of the season brought smiles to their faces.

Judy had glanced over at Robin a few times, but it wasn't until they reached the intersection of Hoban and Main to make their way home when Robin's expression seemed to darken. "What's wrong? Why so sad?"

Robin took a deep breath and shook her head. "I was just thinking about my mom, wondering if she ever walked down this street in the snow. She always loved this island, but I never gave it a chance...until now. Four years too late."

"You can't think like that."

"Also, too late."

Judy turned in front of Robin, blocking her path. "Stop."

"Yeah, well I kind of have to since you're in my way."

"No, I mean about regretting things."

"It's not that easy."

"Trust me, I know," Judy said, locking eyes with Robin. "But first it was Pam, and now it's your mom, and you need to stop it. It's not healthy, and there's nothing you can do to change things, so instead of constantly kicking yourself about all the mistakes you *think* you've made, concentrate on where those *supposed* mistakes have brought you."

"What?"

"Robin, if it hadn't been for what happened with Pam, if your life in Florida had been perfect, would you have ever really entertained the idea of moving here?"

"Probably not."

"And if your mother hadn't loved this place so much, would you see her in everything around here?"

"Of course not."

"You told me once that you believe in God, so I'm assuming you believe in heaven, too, and right now your mom isn't up there, pissed off because you missed a few vacations, she's smiling because you're living on Mackinac. You're walking down the streets she walked down, grinning at probably the same things that made her grin. You're biking the trails she biked and living at Safe Harbor, the place she stayed every time she was here, and to top it all off, today is Thanksgiving. It's a day to be thankful for what you *have*, so how about you think about *that* instead of whining about all your goddamned regrets!" Judy turned on her heel and strode down the street.

Robin spent more than a few seconds staring as Judy marched down the sidewalk before she jogged to catch up to her. "Um...I'm sorry. I didn't realize I was whining."

Judy hung her head and then glanced at Robin. "I'm sorry, too. I don't even know where that came from."

"Probably from my whining," Robin said with a laugh. "Which, by the way, I'm done doing."

"Good to hear."

As they approached the end of Main Street, Robin looked over her shoulder and her breath caught in her throat. There wasn't a carriage or bicycle in sight, and with a thin blanket of snow covering everything in sight, it was picture postcard perfect. "God, that's beautiful."

Judy stopped, delighting in the Thomas Kincaid painting brought to life. "Yes, it is. It can be batshit crazy in the summer, but this is what makes it special for me, especially once we get a real snow." Judy looked at her watch and then pointed down the road. "We'd better get back. We need to get the casseroles in the oven."

"What did you mean about a real snow?" Robin said, taking two quick steps to catch up.

"This is just a dusting," Judy said, running her hand over the top rail of the neighbor's iron fence, the delicate whiteness gathering like moss in her hand. "Wait until it really falls."

"Oh yeah?" Robin said as she looked out across the water. "What's the difference?"

"This will be a lot bigger," Judy said. Running past Robin, she turned around long enough to fire a small snowball directly at Robin's chest before she sprinted to the house, giggling like a little girl every step of the way.

Chapter Thirty-Three

A few hours later, two women in varying stages of food-induced catatonia were reclining on opposite ends of the sofa in Robin's living room. Their feet were propped up on the coffee table, and their eyes were closed, and the only sound to be heard was the Christmas music playing on the radio.

"Are you still awake?" Robin whispered.

"Barely."

Robin smiled without opening her eyes. "You know, I used to buy into all that stuff about something in turkey making you sleepy, but I researched it one day, and it's a myth."

"Is it?"

"Yep. It's got nothing to do with any amino acid. It's just the fact people usually overeat on Thanksgiving and on Christmas, and maybe even Easter. I don't know."

"So you're saying we've become a statistic?"

"Basically."

Judy took a deep breath and opened her eyes. "Speaking of Christmas, what were you going to ask me earlier today?"

"When?"

"You said something about Christmas, and then you saw it was snowing, and then all hell broke loose."

Robin forced her eyes to open, and flopping her head to the side, she looked at Judy. "Hell did not break loose."

"You screamed like a little girl."

"You should hear me when I see a clown."

Judy sprang to a sitting position. "Want me to go get him?"

"Don't you dare!"

"Now who's the party pooper?"

"It's not enough you slammed me with a snowball. Now you're threatening me with a clown?" Robin said, failing miserably at hiding her amusement at Judy's impish expression.

"Oh, my God, are you still pouting over that?"

"I'm not pouting. You promised—"

"No, no, no," Judy said, waggling her finger. "*You* promised not to throw one. I didn't."

"You do realize you could have hit me in the head. Undo everything that's healed."

"Oh, please," Judy said, rolling her eyes. "It was the size of a kumquat. My aim was perfect, and you got your stitches out on Tuesday, so stop trying for the sympathy vote, because it's not going to work."

"I liked you better when you were my dutiful nursemaid."

"Is that so?"

"No," Robin said softly. "Actually, it's not."

For a moment, they held one another's gaze until Robin reached for her wine glass. "So...about Christmas. Do you have any plans for the next few days?"

"Christmas is over a month away."

"I know, but usually, people get four-day weekends with Thanksgiving, and I wasn't sure if you had anything planned. Shopping or—"

"Oh, hell no," Judy said, waving off the idea with a flick of her wrist. "I made the mistake of going shopping on Black Friday once, and I swore I'd never do it again. As far as I'm concerned, I'd rather face a zombie apocalypse."

"Then you don't have any plans?"

"No, I just thought we'd be working on the house. Why?"

"Because Adele has a shitload of totes in the basement all marked for Christmas, and I thought instead of working on the rooms, we could spend the weekend decorating. That is if you want to?"

"I couldn't think of a better way to spend a long weekend," Judy said, getting to her feet. "And now, I think I'm going to call it a night and head home."

"Really?" Robin said, jumping off the sofa. "What about dessert?"

"That's going to have to wait until tomorrow. If I eat anything else tonight, the tires on my bike are going to flatten," Judy said, heading out of the room.

"Yeah, I guess you're right."

Judy turned, cocking her head to the side. "Excuse me?"

It took Robin a moment to replay the conversation in her head, and when she reached the end, her eyes flew open wide. "Oh crap, that's not what I meant."

"Of course, it wasn't."

Robin watched in horror as Judy set her wine glass on the counter and made her way toward the front of the house without so much as giving Robin a second glance.

"Judy, seriously, that's not what I meant. You're not in the least bit heavy," Robin said, rushing to catch up. Unable to stop herself, she eyeballed the sway of Judy's hips, the brief glimpse confirming what Robin already knew. "You're perfect. I mean...I mean you're totally proportionate to your height." Robin hung her head. It wasn't the stupidest thing she'd ever said, but it was close.

"Good to know," Judy said, turning as she grabbed her parka from the coat tree.

"That's not what I meant either."

"You know what, Robin?" Judy said, zipping up her jacket. "I sure hope you write better than you speak because I have to tell you, right now I'm not all that impressed with your way with words."

Judy held her breath, trying to contain what was building inside of her for a little while longer, but the sight of Robin's deer-in-the-headlights expression was too comical to ignore. Erupting in laughter, Judy barely got out the words. "Oh, my God. You should see your face."

Robin's mouth dropped open. "Are you serious?" she shouted, pointing toward her apartment. "I just did a walk of shame through this entire *flipping* house, and you were joking?"

"Yep," Judy said, bobbing her head. "And I'm sorry, but I couldn't resist."

Faced with Judy's devastating smile, Robin knew the feeling. All she wanted to do was pull Judy into her arms, hold her close and kiss her like there was no tomorrow, but she had to resist. Resist the urge. Resist the need. Resist the hunger, the passion, and the want. Robin swallowed hard as her body pulsed. Yes, to act on her feelings was impossible, but to resist them...was futile.

"You okay?" Judy said, tugging on her knit cap. "You look a thousand miles away."

"What? No, I'm fine. I was just...um...thinking about you going out in this weather."

"I'm used to it."

"Maybe so, but now you have to pedal up Everest on a full stomach."

"Well, it's not like I have another choice," Judy said, after pulling on her gloves and wrapping a scarf around her neck, she opened the front door.

Robin instantly hunched her shoulders at the burst of cold air, and snatching her jacket from the coat tree, she pulled it on and followed Judy outside. "Maybe you do."

"Oh yeah? What's that?"

"I have plenty of pajamas, and I'm sure I can dig up an extra toothbrush. Why don't you just stay the night? It's not like we don't have plenty of bedrooms."

Judy hesitated for a moment. "No, that's all right. It's tempting, but I'd have to go back in the morning to get changed anyway, and I'm already ready to go." Judy walked her bike down the porch steps, turning to face Robin once she reached the bottom. "I'll see you tomorrow, Robin. Good night."

"All right. Good night," Robin said, stuffing her hands into her jacket pockets. "But text me when you get home, so I know you're safe."

Judy flinched back her head. "Wait a minute. I thought you said you didn't text."

"I don't, but that doesn't mean I won't read them."

"I'll have to remember that."

***

"You did what!"

"Calm down."

"Don't tell me to calm down," Declan said, waving his hand in the air. "Six fucking days after the fact you're telling me you almost killed yourself."

"I didn't *almost* kill myself. I just...I just fell down."

"And busted open your head!"

"Well, nothing important leaked out, so that's a plus," Robin said, grinning.

"This is not funny, Robbie. Why the hell didn't you call me when it happened?"

"When it happened, I wasn't in any shape to call, and after that, I was afraid you'd try to come to my rescue, and I knew I wouldn't have been able to stop you."

"You're right. You wouldn't have."

A few moments of silence passed between them until Robin heard her best friend sigh. "Declan, I'm fine. The stitches are out. The bruises are all but gone, and I had a fantastic Thanksgiving. Okay?"

Declan huffed into the phone. "I suppose," he said, stroking his chin. "So...what did the lawyer say?"

"He said that with the holiday, he wasn't expecting her probation officer to do anything until at least next week. It sounds like they have to review everything and make their own determination, but Howard assured me this is cut and dry. They have my affidavit, the copies of all the texts and emails she sent after the restraining order was in place, and the copies of my phone records to prove the dates and times, so he said they'll have no choice but to put out a warrant for her arrest."

"Good!" Declan barked. "That bitch belongs behind bars, and I'm not talking about the ones that serve booze."

"But you need to do me a favor."

"What's that?"

"Watch out for yourself."

"Oh, Robbie, I—"

"I'm not kidding, Declan. Pam was practically frothing at the mouth when she was up here, and she wasn't even shit-faced while she was doing it."

"She wasn't high?"

"Yeah, maybe a little, but she wasn't circling the earth. And I don't trust her, Declan. Not after seeing her last week. She was a complete nut case."

"And that has changed how?"

"I'm serious!" Robin said, jumping off her bed. "You have to promise me to keep your eyes open, and if she shows up, sober or drunk, you need to call the police. Don't instigate. Don't even open the fucking door. Just call the cops. Okay?"

Declan didn't think he could hate Pamela Burton any more than he already did, but hearing Robin's voice tremble, he set his jaw. She was scared. "All right, Robbie," he said softly. "If I so much as get a whiff of her hairspray, I'll call the cops. I promise."

Robin sank onto the edge of her bed. "Thank you."

"Any time," Declan said, leaning back on his sofa. "So how did you explain—"

"Oh," Robin said, hearing a click on the phone. "Hold on for just a second."

Having no other choice than to do just that, Declan picked up his scotch and took a sip.

"Sorry about that."

Declan set his drink aside. "Problem?"

"No, Judy just texted to say she made it home okay."

Declan bolted upright. "Wait one goddamned minute! What do you mean she texted? If I can't text, she can't text!"

"You sound like a spoiled child," Robin said with a laugh.

"No, I'm a spoiled adult who you told months ago to stop texting, and now I hear you're texting with Judy? Oh...wait a minute," Declan said, stroking a non-existent beard. "Are you texting or *sex*ting? And if it's the latter, please send me examples to prove it."

"You're such a weirdo. I'm not texting *or* sexting. I just asked her to let me know she made it home okay."

"So I guess that means no examples—huh?'

"Get your mind out of the gutter."

"Like that's ever going to happen."

"Tell me about it."

Declan grinned for a moment, and then it faded away. "You know, when you told me about what you did after Pam left I thought...I thought you had fallen down the rabbit hole again."

"I did for a little while that night, but it's dark and dismal there, Declan, and I don't want dark and dismal anymore. Life's too short to brood over things you can't change."

"I'll drink to that," Declan said, reaching for his glass. "So you never said how you explained Pam to Judy."

"What do you mean?"

"A crazy woman comes into your house and threatens you with a broken bottle. That usually requires some sort of explanation."

"I told her everything."

Declan was in the midst of taking a sip of scotch when Robin's words reached his ears. With his lips on the glass, he paused and eased into a smile. "What did you just say?"

"I said, I told her everything. From how I met Pam to...to what she did to me. All the threats, the fights, the arrest, my depression...everything."

"Kiddo, trust hasn't been your strong suit ever since Pam came into your life. That's a big step."

"I know it was, but it felt good, and once I started telling Judy about Pam, I couldn't stop. I needed to let it all out. I needed to let her see inside of me. To see the hurt and the shame, the anger...the ugliness."

"You don't own an ounce of ugly."

"Thanks, but you know what I mean."

"I'm not sure I do."

"It's about secrets, Declan. It's about things you think you need to hide because you're afraid others aren't going to understand, or they're going to judge you, but when there are people in your life that you care about, you need to take that risk. You need to let your secrets out, because when you do you realize they aren't as big and bad as they think they are and life becomes so much better...so, so much better. My mom always told me to tell the truth, and she was right. The truth really does set you free. I haven't felt this good in a long time."

"I always said your mom was a smart woman," Declan said as he sat up. "So, how'd Judy take it?"

"She was a little shocked at some things, but all in all, she understood that—"

"I'm not talking about what went on with Pam. I'm talking about your crush. How'd Judy react?"

"Oh...yeah, well, I didn't tell her about that."

"But you just said—"

"Declan, there's a big difference between admitting to someone you're an idiot and confessing to them that you're in love—" Robin snapped her mouth shut like a mouse trap, but the bait had already been snatched.

"What was that?"

"Nothing."

Declan let out a hearty guffaw. "Oh, Robbie, it's not nothing. I've been waiting for over twenty fucking years for you to finally admit that."

"What are you talking about?"

"You have avoided that word since the day you first told me about Judy way back in college. You said you really liked her. Then, you said you were crushing on her, and somewhere along the line, I think you even added you had the hots for her, but you have dodged, evaded, and sidestepped the truth for years, which leads me back to a conversation we had when I was on Mackinac. How the hell are you going to keep doing this?"

"I just am," Robin whispered. "I won't risk losing her over this."

"*This* isn't exactly a small detail, Robbie. *This* is love, which in case you don't know, is the most powerful emotion we have. Are you seriously telling me that you can accept her never knowing how you really feel or having the chance to...to act on what you feel?"

"Not everything is about sex, Declan."

"I'm not talking about sex, Robbie. I'm talking about you being happy."

"I *am* happy. Why can't you see that?"

"I just don't want you to get hurt."

"I won't. I can't," Robin said, jumping to her feet again. "Declan, Mackinac has been like a good luck charm for me and—"

"Oh, so you think with a little luck you'll get her between the sheets?"

"Jesus! Get your mind out of the girl-on-girl porn movie!" Robin shouted. "Can you just let me finish instead of jumping to horizontal conclusions?"

"Sorry. Sure. Go ahead."

"Declan, think about it. Ever since I got here, my life has turned around. I'm writing again and running again. The nightmares have all but stopped, and I wake up looking forward to every flipping day. Yeah, I screwed up a little when Pam showed up, but I bounced back. And yeah, I've fallen in love with Judy, but so what? So what? She's already told me she has no plans to ever move off the island, and since neither do I, I can look forward to a life with her in it. I love it here, Declan, and all I see in my future is lots of time to be with her, so what's the harm in keeping my feelings to myself and preserving a friendship that means as much to me as the one I have with you?"

"I can't tell you if there's harm or not, Robbie, but a few minutes ago you said how great you felt after unloading all the bullshit about Pam. *And* you also said how your mother always told you to tell the truth, but now you're doing just the opposite."

"Then call me a hypocrite," Robin said, sinking down on the edge of the bed.

"Okay. You're a hypocrite."

"Fine, I'm a hypocrite, but I'm a happy one. I get to see her every day, Declan. I get to work alongside her, to joke with her, to laugh with her, to cook meals with her, and today we even went for a walk in the snow together."

"The snow?" Declan said, glancing down at his bare feet and shorts.

"Yeah, it snowed today."

"You've got to be shitting me. It's like ninety degrees down here."

"Well, not here, and tomorrow we're going to start decorating for Christmas."

Declan dropped his chin to his chest. "Oh, Christ."

"Stop."

"I totally forgot about you and Christmas. Suddenly, I'm *elated* you moved away."

"That's not nice."

"It may not be nice, but knowing I'm not going to spend endless hours turning your home into Rockefeller Center sure as hell puts a smile on my face."

"I'll have you know, Judy says she loves to decorate for Christmas as much as I do."

Declan snickered before taking a sip of his drink. "No one loves to decorate as much as you do, Robin. No one."

Chapter Thirty-Four

Robin stood in the front yard looking back at the house. "So, where do you want to start?"

"Probably the roof," Judy said, shading her eyes from the sun. "Start there and work our way down."

"Oh."

"Problem?"

"Um...two, actually. First, we don't have a ladder in the basement tall enough to reach even the porch roof, and second, I'm not a big fan of heights."

"How much not a fan?"

Robin sighed. "Right up there with clowns."

"Then I guess I'll be doing it."

"No, you won't. I'm not going to have you climbing all over the roof."

"Why not?"

"Because...because it's dangerous."

"Only if I fall," Judy said with a laugh.

"And that's *exactly* why we won't be decorating the roof."

"Robin, I'm not afraid of heights. I can do this. Trust me."

"Well, since we don't have a ladder long enough, it doesn't matter if I trust you or not," Robin said, folding her arms. "It's not going to happen."

Judy placed her hands on her hips. "So, you're saying you *don't* trust me?"

"No, I'm not saying that at all."

"Good!" Judy said, and giving Robin a wink, she headed to the side yard. "That's what I wanted to hear."

Robin caught up with Judy just as she was opening the doors leading to the underside of the screened-in porch, an area Robin had yet to investigate. "What are you doing?" she said, stepping back as the plywood panels swung wide.

"Getting something I'm going to need," Judy said, and reaching into the storage area, she began pulling out an extension ladder. "See."

"Shit," Robin said, squatting down to peer into the dark, earthy grotto. "I didn't know that was in there."

"I know," Judy said, smiling over at Robin. "But I did."

***

By Saturday afternoon, the outside of Safe Harbor was decorated, and Robin's delight showed on her face. Not only was Declan wrong, but Robin had met her match in Judy.

After admitting her fear of heights was stronger than her fear of clowns, while Robin looked through windows or stared up from the ground, Judy pranced around the roof with the confidence of a tight-rope walker. Wearing an irrepressible grin, courtesy of Robin's continual pleas to be careful, without slipping an inch, Judy clipped lights along the edge of every roofline she could reach without causing Robin to have a cardiac episode.

Lights intertwined with green garland were draped on the fence, and the railings and columns on the porch soon followed suit. Small plastic wreaths were hung on the windows, and a doormat proclaiming Merry Christmas was placed outside the door, and when they finally headed inside, both Robin and Judy were anxious for the day to become night.

More totes were brought up from the basement along with two long boxes containing artificial Christmas trees. It had taken all the strength the two women had to get the trees up the steps, and judging by the size of the boxes, they carried the largest to the parlor while the smallest was placed in Robin's living room.

The rest of their decorating efforts were put on hold for the remainder of the afternoon to turn what was left of their Thanksgiving turkey into soup. Robin stripped the carcass while Judy chopped up carrots and celery, and after the addition of a sachet of garlic, sage, thyme, and rosemary was added, they cleaned up what remained of the casseroles until all that was left of their holiday meal simmered on the stove.

After placing the last Pyrex dish into a cabinet, Robin turned to see Judy smiling back at her. "What?"

"You sure do get into your work. I'll give you that," Judy said, gesturing with her head at the splotches of water, suds, and probably even a few bits of errant turkey covering Robin's sweatshirt.

Robin looked down and frowned. "Crap."

"I told you to wear an apron," Judy said as she removed the one she'd put on.

"Yeah, well, you should have insisted," Robin said, holding her sweatshirt a little away from her body. "I'm a mess."

"Then go get cleaned up, and I'll find something to get into."

"You're not planning to start decorating again, are you?"

"No, I thought maybe I'd just go relax. Take a load off? Chill...or whatever they say nowadays."

"All right. Be back in a few."

"Take your time. Oh, hey, do you mind if I check out some of Adele's research on this place? I really like that kind of stuff."

"Of course not. Mi casa es su casa. You know that."

"Wait. You speak Spanish?"

"Just enough to order a beer and tell someone my house is their house." Robin reached her bedroom door and turned back around. "And speaking of drinks, I put a bottle of Gewurztraminer in the fridge if you're thirsty."

"Okay," Judy said with a laugh. "That's *definitely* not Spanish."

Robin grinned. "Nope, it's German, and before you ask, I don't speak German either. I do, however, know a good white wine when I taste one. I thought it would go better with the soup. Feel free to give it a try."

"I just may do that."

***

When Robin emerged from her bedroom twenty minutes later, she was wearing a pair of gray, relaxed-fit drawstring pants and a bow-neck sweatshirt to match. On her feet was her favorite pair of fleece-lined moccasins, and instead of any clip or band, her hair, damp and smelling of coconut shampoo, hung straight down her back.

Pleased to see the open bottle of wine on the counter, Robin filled the goblet standing next to it, put the bottle back in the fridge, and then headed into the living room.

"You look comfortable," Judy said as Robin walked into the room.

"So do you," Robin said, pointing at Judy's socked feet propped up on the coffee table. "Tired?"

"A little."

"You decorated out?"

"That'll be the day," Judy said before holding up her glass of wine. "And this is delicious."

"I'm glad you like it," Robin said, and slumping on the sofa, she pointed to a few of Adele's notebooks now sitting on the coffee table. "Did you find anything interesting?"

"Maybe," Judy said, looking back and forth between two papers in front of her. "These are copies of the newspaper articles about Isobel's death."

"Okay?"

"The one from the St. Ignace News is pretty basic, but the other one from the St. Ignace Democrat makes mention of another drowning the year before."

"Another one?"

"Yes." Judy put down her wine, and as she handed Robin the photocopy, she pointed to a paragraph. "It doesn't say who, but even Adele thought it odd. See her question mark in red?"

Robin looked at the photo and then pointed to the notebooks on the table. "Is there anything in those about it?"

"I don't know, but I think that'll have to wait for another day," Judy said, and placing the papers aside, she picked up her glass just as Robin began to rest her feet on the coffee table. "I wouldn't get too comfortable if I were you."

"Why not?"

"The sun's gone down."

A second later, Robin popped off the couch like a piece of bread from a toaster. Running to the bay window, she raised one of the Roman shades. "It's *dark*!"

The wine in Judy's glass splashed against the sides of the crystal as she burst out laughing. "You are so funny."

"I have to go get some shoes. Meet you up front."

Judy didn't have time to put her wine on the table before Robin was darting out of the room, and tittering to herself, Judy pulled on her sneakers and headed to the front of the house. Less than a minute had passed before she saw Robin racing toward her. "You're nothing but a big kid."

"Aren't you excited about seeing the lights?" Robin said, tugging on her coat, hat, and gloves seemingly all at once.

Time stopped. Blue eyes blended with blue eyes, each holding joy, excitement, and humor. Standing within inches of one another, their colognes blended as well, and then time started again. Without saying a word, they went outside.

At the end of the walk, they turned in unison and looked up at the house, its shape lost against the backdrop of the blue-black sky. The steam of their breath swirled in the air, the breeze bringing with it the faintest scent of logs burning in a distant hearth.

Robin held out the remote controlling the power block on the front porch. "You ready?"

"Do it."

They each held their breath as Robin pushed the button, and a second later, thousands of tiny bright lights reflected in their eyes...and in their smiles.

***

"I have a strange sense of déjà vu washing over me."

Judy waited for Robin to respond, but when she didn't, Judy opened her eyes and sat up from her comfortable corner of the sofa. She glanced over at Robin, instantly grinning when she realized the woman had fallen asleep, and as Judy listened, her eyes began to twinkle. It wasn't uproarious, and no wood was being sawn, but Robin was snoring ever so slightly.

Their dinner had been simple, but delicious, and while Judy couldn't disagree with Robin's findings about turkey and its inability to make one sleepy, after the table was cleared and the dishes were done, it was all they could do to drag themselves to the sofa. They sipped their wine in relative silence, their enjoyment showing on their faces for all that had been accomplished over the past two days and somewhere along the line, they closed their eyes.

As quietly as she could, Judy picked up her glass, and after draining it in half a swallow, she left to empty her bladder. Five minutes later, she was standing over Robin, debating on whether to wake her or not. Judy glanced at her watch, and letting out a sigh, she leaned down and placed her hand on Robin's shoulder. "Hey, I'm going to be heading home. It's getting late."

Robin softly sighed, pleased that her dreams had finally caught up with time. Judy appeared as she did now. There were streaks of gray in her hair, and tiny lines etched at the corners of her eyes, but of all the dreams, this was by far the most realistic. Robin could feel Judy's breath on her face and smell the hint of bergamot in her cologne. Robin forced her eyes to open just a little and seeing Judy bending over her, Robin's body pulsed. The rush of awareness caused her skin to tingle, and as she always did in dreams, Robin moved in close for a kiss that would be probing and wet, until she heard Judy's gasp. Robin's eyes flew open just in time to see Judy draw back. *Oh. Shit.*

A few awkward seconds of silence passed between them before Judy said, "Um...I...uh...I just wanted to let you know I was heading out. I'll...uh...I'll see you tomorrow."

"Okay. Sorry, I fell asleep on you."

"Don't worry about it. At least you got a good dream out of it."

Robin could feel her cheeks begin to heat. "Did I? I-I don't...I don't remember any dream."

Judy shrugged. "Well, it was just a guess." Judy held up her hand when Robin began to stand. "No, don't worry about it. I know my way out. I'll see you tomorrow, Robin. Good night."

Robin watched as Judy turned around and left the apartment. "Fuck!" Robin groaned, and throwing herself against the back of the sofa, she covered her face with her hands. "Fuck. Fuck. Fuck. Fuck. *Fuck*!"

***

"Good morning."

Robin jumped as she came out of the living room. The moment she'd been dreading since the night before was finally upon her, and it took all the strength she had to look in Judy's direction. Careful to avoid eye contact, Robin continued toward the dining room. "Oh. Hey. Um…good morning. I got your text. You know, you could have taken the day off if you needed one."

"No, like I said, I had some things to catch up on, but I wanted to give you a heads-up, so you weren't wondering where I was."

"Oh. Right," Robin said quietly, her eyes darting back and forth between Judy and the patio doors. "Um...well...uh...coffee's on."

"Thanks," Judy said, making a beeline for the coffee pot. "So what are you doing?" Hearing the patio door in the dining room open and then close, Judy turned around and found she was talking to herself. "Okay?" Judy mumbled under her breath, and leaning against the counter, she sipped her coffee and waited for Robin to return.

A few minutes passed before Judy heard the slider open again and taking a step closer to the dining room, she saw Robin coming back inside carrying an armful of logs. "What's all that?"

"Firewood," Robin muttered as she headed into the living room.

"Yeah, I got that part, silly," Judy called out. "But where'd it come from?"

For the first time in hours, Robin dared to smile. There wasn't a hint of anything other than friendship in Judy's tone. There was no anger. There was no animosity. There was only Judy being Judy. Letting out a long breath, Robin moved her anxiety to the back burner, deciding to let the day play out. If apologies were needed, they would be made, but for right now, life was good.

"I saw an ad in the paper a few weeks back," Robin shouted as she stuffed more logs in the two copper buckets near the hearth. "Mr. Booth up on Pine Avenue had firewood for sale, so I bought some. He called just after you left last night. His sons came into town for the holiday, but they're leaving today, so he asked if they could bring it down this morning since he had help."

"How much did you get?"

Robin jumped to her feet and returned to the dining room. "A couple of cords. Why?"

"Oh, I don't know," Judy said, shrugging. "For whatever reason, a vision of overfilled freezers came into my head."

Judy's eyes glittered with gaiety, and Robin inwardly sighed. Now more than ever before, Robin was convinced her heart was merely a puddle of goo in her chest, melted time and time again by the woman standing in front of her.

"The freezers aren't overfilled, or they wouldn't close. So there," Robin said, sticking out her tongue.

Judy laughed. "You are *such* a child."

Robin grinned as she headed for the patio door. "Well, this child has more logs to bring in and a few to rearrange."

"You want some help?"

Robin looked down at her damp, dirt and sap-stained jeans. "Did you bring a change of clothes?"

Judy's shoulders sagged. "No, I keep forgetting to do that."

"Then I think you should leave the dirty work to me."

"Okay." Judy glanced around the apartment. "Then how about I start assembling the trees? It'll give me something to do."

"Cool. That works for me," Robin said, stepping outside. "I'll see you in a little while."

***

"I think you're addicted to this."

"Oh yeah?" Judy said, putting aside the instructions. "Why's that?"

Robin went over to the tree and started fanning out some branches. "Because in the time it took me to finish with the firewood and change my clothes, a ten-foot Fraser Fir has sprouted in our parlor, and now you're back here, working on this one."

"Well, just to let you know. If it were an addiction, I'd be doing it every day," Judy said, poking another branch into a hole.

"Then how about compulsion?"

"Look who's talking."

"What do you mean?" Robin said, adjusting yet another sprig of plastic evergreen.

"You're re-spreading the tips of branches I've already done."

"There were some holes. You couldn't see them from where you're standing."

Judy narrowed her eyes. "Is that a short joke?"

"No, it wasn't," Robin said, doing absolutely nothing to hide her amusement. "But it could have been."

After giving Robin the evil eye, Judy got back to inserting branches into the faux tree trunk until a few more rows were filled. "I'm sorry I was late this morning, by the way."

"You had things to do. It wasn't a problem," Robin said as she moved around the tree.

"I was also trying to catch up on some sleep. For the life of me, I couldn't seem to get any last night."

Robin knew the feeling. She had spent until the wee hours of the morning staring at the ceiling in her bedroom, berating herself for almost destroying their friendship by acting on a dream that *wasn't* a dream. Robin took a deep breath. A few hours earlier, she had told herself if an apology were needed, she would make it, and it appeared that time had come. "Look, if it was because of...um...because of something I did—"

"What are you talking about? You didn't do anything wrong."

Robin's forehead creased. Was it a dream or wasn't it a dream? Nibbling on her lower lip for a moment, Robin decided to find out. "Well, I did fall asleep on you and when I woke—"

"Robin, by the sound of your snoring, you were exhausted. Don't worry about it," Judy said, plucking and fluffing the top section of the tree.

"I was snoring? Really?"

Judy smiled. "It wasn't like a three-hundred-pound linebacker. It was more just heavy breathing, sort of like an obscene phone caller."

"Oh, I feel *so* much better now," Robin said, and it wasn't a lie. She did feel better. Judy wasn't blind, and she wasn't stupid. There was no way in hell Judy wouldn't have realized what Robin had been about to do *unless* it had been a dream. In an instant, whatever weight remaining from what Robin believed to be a friendship-ending incident evaporated. It was *only* a dream.

Grabbing the nearby two-foot stepladder, Robin placed it near the base of the tree and held out her hand. "Here. I'll do it."

"Thought you didn't like heights?" Judy said, giving Robin the top section of the tree.

"I'm fine with this."

Judy watched as Robin took the two steps needed to reach the top of the ladder, but when Robin reached out to insert the last piece and wavered just a bit, Judy gasped. Quickly placing her hands on Robin's hips to steady her, Judy said, "Be careful please."

Robin stopped mid-reach, trying to figure out what was worse. Was it the fact that Judy's hands were on her hips or the fact her backside was in Judy's face? Deciding it was a tie, with her cheeks flaming, Robin jammed the pointed evergreen mini-tree into the hole drilled in the top of the seven-foot green dowel.

Escaping Judy's grasp, Robin took the two steps needed to reach the floor before sneering up at the tree. "It looks like a green stalagmite."

"It'll be better once we add some lights."

"Shit. That's right," Robin said, eyeing the spire. "It's not pre-lit, is it?"

"The one in the parlor is, but these instructions look like they were printed on parchment, so I have a feeling this tree is as old as I am." Seeing a glint in Robin's eyes, Judy's shoulders sagged. "Did you just add something else to your shopping list?"

Robin bowed her head. "Maybe."

"We just assembled it!"

"I don't mean for this year, but they always run sales after Christmas, and you have to admit it is kind of spindly."

Judy looked at the stick figure tree and then at Robin, and then resigned herself to yet another shopping trip. "Let me find some lights," she said, and moving past Robin, Judy lifted the lid of a tote. "Well, shit."

"What's wrong?"

"Look."

***

Sitting on the floor of Robin's living room, Judy looked up from the cobweb of Christmas lights draped over her lap when she heard Robin laugh. "What's so funny?"

"Oh, nothing. I was just thinking about my mom," Robin said, raising her eyes as she set aside another unsnarled set. "She would have hated this."

"I thought you said she liked Christmas."

"She did, but tangled lights gave her the fits," Robin said, and breaking into giggles, she paused until they subsided. "I can remember one year when she marched off to the store to buy all brand-new stuff because a few of our sets were knotted, and a couple of the others only lit halfway. Then, when Christmas was over, she got it in her head she was going to meticulously rewind the lights back into those plastic trays they come in so they wouldn't get tangled again."

"Oh, tell me you're kidding."

Robin held up her hand. "Swear to God, but after about an hour of trying to weave the wires into the notches, she finally gave up, but not before she colorfully discussed the lineage of those who invented Christmas lights."

"Well, it seems Adele wasn't as particular as your mom," Judy said, tugging another jumble of lights from a nearby tote. "Because this is a mess."

"I don't mind doing it if it's getting on your nerves."

"What?" Judy said, looking up. "No, I'm actually enjoying myself. I'm just wondering why the outside lights were so neat and orderly, and this is a rat's nest."

"I have no idea. Maybe she was in a rush."

"Speaking of rushes, since the Black Friday one should be over by Monday, I was planning to take the day to get my Christmas shopping done."

"You can do it in just one day?"

"Usually," Judy said as she worked on unraveling the strand of lights in her lap. "I started making a list while I was on vacation, so I basically know what everybody wants or needs."

"You still buy for your brothers? Not just their kids?" Robin said, getting to her feet with a handful of untangled lights.

"Unfortunately, yes," Judy said, raising her eyes. "I can't tell you how many times I've tried to persuade everyone to only get gifts for the kids, but unless you can't see the tree for the presents surrounding it, according to Pat and Doug, it's just not Christmas."

"Geez. That can end up being a little bit pricey."

"Yeah, but it's once a year, and it shuts them up for at least the holiday."

As Robin began threading the strands through the branches, Judy counted the piles of lights they had untangled. Figuring eight sets was enough to cover the lanky tree, Judy stood up and began opening the few remaining totes in the room. "If you're all right with the lights, I'm going to go downstairs and see if I can find some ornaments. This is all garland and stuff."

"Okay, but if you don't mind, can you start with the clear totes that have blue lids? Those are the ones I brought with me."

"I can do that. Be back in a few."

On Robin's fourth revolution of the tree, Judy came back into the room. "Do you have a flashlight?"

"Yeah, on the floor of the closet just outside my bedroom. Why? Did a bulb blow?"

"No. I was trying to get one of your totes out of the work area, and I backed into a stack of Adele's. They fell over, and ornaments rolled everywhere."

"They didn't break?"

"No," Judy called out as she made her way to the closet. "They're those Styrofoam things covered in sequins."

Robin curled her lip at the thought of decorating with bedazzled ornaments, and draping the strand of lights she was holding onto a branch, she headed for the basement. When she reached the bottom of the stairs, Robin began to make her way through the maze of totes, only to come to an abrupt stop when she saw Judy's feet sticking out from under the shelving along the wall. "What in the world are you doing?"

"I told you, they went everywhere." Judy backed out and held out a handful of the bedazzled balls. "Put these with the others, will you? There are only a few more under here."

"You're going to get filthy. Why don't we just pull out the other totes further down the row?"

"I was going to, but the first one I grabbed weighed a ton, so I figured this would be faster." Judy ducked down again and army-crawled under the wooden planks. She wouldn't call it a phobia, but Judy had no desire to have a tiny eight-legged creature crawling all over her in such tight quarters, so when she reached the next cobweb, she paused. As she had done for the first several feet of her travels, Judy examined it carefully before clearing it away with the flashlight, but when she reached the next, she didn't pause. Judy stopped and swallowed hard. The last two ornaments were nestled against a wall of ominous arachnoid filaments. "Crap."

"Problem?" Robin said, kneeling by the shelves.

"Um...no. Just need a minute."

Judy turned her attention to the web, and starting at the top corner, she shined the flashlight back and forth to make sure nothing small, hairy, and eight-legged was home. She wasn't expecting to see a spider because she hadn't seen any so far, and she also wasn't expecting what happened next. The beam of the Maglite suddenly flashed back at her, causing Judy to jump. "Shit!"

"What's wrong!" Robin reached under the shelves, trying to find Judy's legs. "Where are you?"

Holding her hand on top of her head, Judy waited for the stars to clear. "Give me a second," she called back. "I hit my head."

"Are you okay?"

Judy shone the light on her hand and seeing not a speck of blood, she chuckled. "Yes, I'm fine. No blood. No foul."

"You need to get out of there. If there's any more left, they can stay there. I'm not going to use them anyway."

"Now she tells me," Judy said, mumbling under her breath. Using the flashlight, she pushed away the cobweb to find what had acted like a mirror and a second later, her eyes opened wide. "Robin?"

"Yeah?"

"There's something else under here."

"If you yank out another clown, I swear to God, I'm going to—"

"Relax. It's not a clown," Judy said, struggling to crawl backward without dropping the Maglite, hitting her head, or losing hold of her find. "Here, take the flashlight."

Robin grabbed it and put it aside, her eyebrows knitting at the sound of scraping along the concrete floor. "What in the hell did you find?"

Judy backed her way out from under the shelves, and resting on her haunches, she looked up at Robin. "This," she said, and with one last tug, Judy pulled out what she had found.

Robin's eyes bulged. "Oh my, God," she said, pushing a tower of Adele's totes out of the way to make room for the trunk. "I can't believe you found that."

Judy grinned as she glanced at the chest. Its surface was army green and covered in dust, but the riveted metal edges were still shiny enough to give away its location. "That makes two of us," she said, dusting off her hands. "Do you want to open it now?"

Robin couldn't tear her eyes away from the footlocker. "Do you mind?"

"Of course, I don't mind," Judy said, waving her hand for Robin to sit. "I was hoping you were going to say that."

Robin dropped to the floor and shoved the footlocker just enough so it sat between them. She hesitated for a moment before wiping her hand across the lid, and as the dust cleared, Robin frowned. "Who's G. Anderson?" she said, looking at Judy.

Judy glanced at the G. ANDERSON stenciled in paint on the chest. "Good question. Maybe Stanley went by his middle name, and maybe, just maybe, if you *open* it, we'll find the answer *inside*."

"All right. All right," Robin said, holding up her hands. "Here we go. You take one side, and I'll take the other."

Both held their breath as they flipped down the latches, and pushing up the lid, they moved a little closer to view the contents of the divided tray at the top of the trunk. A few seconds later, their noses wrinkled in unison as the mustiness caused by confinement blossomed out.

"Phew," Robin said, waving her hand. "It smells like an antique shop."

"Yeah, it does," Judy said as she pulled out a crumpled paper bag and looked inside.

"What's in it?"

"Bottle openers."

"Seriously?"

Judy dumped the assortment into her hand and squinting, she tried to read the imprints. Suddenly, she smiled. "I'll be damned."

"What? Did you find something?"

"I'm not sure about the rest, but it looks like Adele named some of the rooms after places she'd visited." Holding up two of the church keys, Judy said, "Sunset Shores and Whitefish Falls. Both in Ontario."

"You're kidding."

"No, and the rest are from all over. Michigan, Wisconsin, Pennsylvania, and New York."

"That's still kind of a weird keepsake, don't you think?"

"I don't know. Maybe Adele just liked the places." Judy returned them to the paper bag and put it aside. "What do you have?"

Robin opened a bag and shook her head. "Coin pouches."

"What?"

Robin pulled out one of the oval squeeze coin purses and dangled it from its beady chain. "See."

"Okay, that's weird, too."

It was Judy's turn, and when she looked into the next bag, she laughed. "Key chains."

"You're kidding!"

Judy shook her head. "Nope, and by the looks of them..." Judy said, rummaging in the bag. "They're all from the same states. Pennsylvania, New York...and the rest."

"Wait." Robin fumbled through the coin purses. "Same here. Same states."

"I think we have a pattern."

Robin dove into the next bag. "Matchbooks. Same places."

"Refrigerator magnets. Same places."

"Postcards."

"Oh, what do they say?" Judy said, leaning toward Robin. "Is there anything written on them?"

Robin flipped each over and then sighed. "Nope. They're blank, but they're all from the same places, and add Central Lake, Michigan to our list," she said, holding up a postcard from that city.

"There's clearly a pattern to all of this, except for these." Judy reached into the next bag and then held her hand out for Robin to see.

"Pebbles?"

Judy shrugged and returned them to the bag. "She must have gotten this stuff on vacation or something."

"Well, this may give us a clue."

"What's that?"

"The eighties version of GPS," Robin said, holding up a wad of neatly folded road maps.

"Let me guess. Same states?"

Robin shuffled through maps emblazoned with logos belonging to Esso, Sinclair, 76, and Gulf. "Yep."

"Is there anything marked on them, like a route or...or a destination?"

A few minutes later, Robin was refolding the maps and sliding them back into the tray. "Nope. Nothing."

Judy scratched her head. "I don't know about you, but if I had a chest of keepsakes, it wouldn't contain stuff like this. I'd have pictures; maybe some books, a bible...even old school papers, but not coin purses, bottle openers, and key chains."

"Well, they must have meant something to her," Robin said, gesturing for Judy to lift her side of the tray. "Lift that, will you?"

"Sure."

The first thing they saw caused both women to grin, and reaching in, Robin pulled out two teddy bears. One had vibrant pink fur and the other, tangerine, but it was the hearts on their chests that gave them away. "Oh, crap. These were all the rage for a while. What the hell were they called?"

Judy pondered the question for a moment. "Care Bears," she said. "Big in the eighties."

"That's it," Robin said, glancing back and forth between the two before she placed them on the floor. "At least they're cute."

"Don't you mean at least they're not clowns?"

Robin was about to respond when she noticed what was under the bears. "Now we're talking," she said, pointing to the jumble of photographs. "Jackpot!"

Judy grabbed a stack, as did Robin, each flipping over the photos to see if inscriptions were written on the back.

"This is a nice one of your mom," Judy said, holding up a photo.

"And this is a good one of Adele," Robin said, doing the same.

"Here they are together." Judy handed Robin the photo. "Looks like it was taken at a school. See the building in the background. Maybe college?"

"I don't know. Mom never mentioned them going to school together, but they were only a few years apart, so it makes sense."

"Who's Virgil Jankowski?"

"Who?" Robin said, looking up.

"Virgil Jankowski." Judy turned the photo so Robin could see it.

"I don't know who Virgil Jankowski is, but that's Stanley."

"Not according to what's written on the back. It says Virgil Jankowski, 1973."

"No, that has to be wrong," Robin said, getting to her feet. "I'll show you. Be right back."

Robin went to the opposite side of the basement and returned with a couple of framed photographs. "These are the ones I found in the window seat with all of Stanley's other stuff," she said, handing them off to Judy before returning to her place at the other end of the trunk. "It's the same guy. See?"

Judy looked back and forth between the pictures for almost a minute. "This doesn't make any sense. Why would Adele lie about her husband's name?" Expecting a response, Judy lifted her eyes, her forehead furrowing when she saw Robin's stony expression. "What's wrong?"

"That's not the only thing Adele lied about," Robin said, looking up from the paper in her hand.

"What do you mean?"

"She wasn't my aunt."

Chapter Thirty-Five

Neither said a word as they were led through a house smelling of Ivory soap and pastel mints. The surroundings were to be expected, walls covered in photographs spanning generations, crystal bowls on end tables holding gumdrops and hard candy, and a crocheted blanket draped over the back of the sofa. Nestled between a recliner and a table was a wicker basket stuffed with skeins of yarn, and knitting needles stood at the ready, sprouting from the threads like off-shoots of a plant.

The essence changed once they reached the kitchen, the fragrance of cherry pie filling the room, and as seats were offered and taken, they waited in silence. One wanted to speak, to demand answers to questions ravaging her mind, and the other hoped the answers wouldn't hurt as much as she already knew they would. There was no other explanation.

The coffee maker hissed its final hiss, and coffee, steaming and dark was placed in front of them, and as soon as the last took her seat, Robin reached down and opened her backpack. Pulling out two pieces of paper, she slid one in front of Maxine. "You once told me that you and Adele had no secrets, so I need you to explain why this birth certificate lists George and Maureen Anderson as Adele's parents when those people aren't *my* grandparents. At first, I thought maybe she was adopted, maybe at such a young age that my mother never thought to mention it, but according to her high school diploma..." Robin pushed the other paper in front of Maxine. "According to *this*, Adele attended school in Grandville, Michigan while my mother, her supposed *sister*, went to one just outside of Fort Wayne, Indiana, two hundred flipping miles *away*!"

"Robin," Judy said, her volume only slightly lower than Robin's. "You're shouting."

"What?"

"You're *shouting*."

Maxine patted Judy's hand. "That's all right, dear. She has a right to shout." Maxine looked at the untouched mugs on the table and shook her head. "I think this is going to call for something a little bit stronger than my coffee."

Getting up from the table, Maxine returned a minute later with three glasses and a bottle of eighteen-year-old Chivas Regal. After pouring a splash into each squatty tumbler, she slipped back into her chair.

Robin paid no attention to the buttery toffee aroma, nor would she appreciate the mellow smokiness of the liquor. All she wanted to do was dull her senses, and picking up her glass, she drained it in one swallow and then slammed it down on the table.

Without saying a word, Maxine refilled it, before taking a sip of her own. She knew the truth, but there was no way to dull the edge of its blade. It was going to cut and cut deeply. Secrets do that.

Fact is based on logic. Deductive reasoning applied in science, medicine, or mystery games, it's used to solve the questions asked, to cure a disease, or to appease curiosity piqued. The world was flat until proven otherwise. Tens of thousands died until one man broke through the barrier of polio, and countless have announced it was Colonel Mustard in the library with the candlestick. For many, the words fact and truth are interchangeable, one swapped for the other at any given time, but there is a subtle difference between the two, and Robin knew it. Facts are more permanent and rarely do they change, but truth...the truth can change in an instant.

Robin exhaled ever so slowly. She knew she needed to say the words, to put them out into the universe and make them tangible, but once she did, there was no going back. She knew the truth, too. She could feel it inside of her, and like a flame to a photo, in Robin's mind, the edges of her life were curling up and turning to ash. Lies can do that.

Robin's eyes were glassy as she raised them to look at Maxine and when she forced the words from her throat, they came out in a ragged whisper. "They were lovers, weren't they?"

Judy winced. Two hours earlier, she had sat cross-legged on the basement floor feeling more helpless than she had ever felt before as Robin tore through the contents of the footlocker. The first nail of reality's coffin was a photograph of a husband who wasn't. The second, a birth certificate of a woman whose DNA would contain no markers matching Robin's, and the rest were the random photos of two women whose smiles were far too radiant, far too intimate. While Judy hadn't dared to pose the possibility, as preposterous as it seemed to be, it had existed in her mind nevertheless.

"Yes," Maxine said, bowing her head. "Yes, they were."

Robin's eyes overflowed with tears. Brushing them off her cheeks, she reached for her glass and emptied it again. "I can't believe this," she said, shaking her head.

Maxine covered Robin's hand with her own. "I'm sorry—"

"How long?" Robin said, snatching her hand away. "How long was this going on?"

Maxine sighed. "They met in college. Adele was in her third year. Your mother had just started."

Robin rocked back in her chair, and running her fingers through her hair, she glared at Maxine. "Keep going. I want to know it all."

"Robin, please understand—"

"Just tell me, Maxine. Just tell me."

Maxine took a deep breath and let it out slowly. "Like I said, they met in college. The way Adele described it to me, it was instant, like a...a flash of a match when it's struck. She saw your mother in a hallway. Your mother saw her, and that was it. At first, they were just friends, but during spring break of that year, they went on vacation together and...and things changed."

"I can only guess how," Robin mumbled.

Maxine nodded. "And they continued their...um...their affair until just before your mother graduated. That's when she broke it off."

"Why?"

"Because they had different dreams." Maxine paused to take a sip of her drink. "Since Adele was a child, her dream had always been to move to Mackinac. She used to visit her grandparents in Cheboygan during the summer, and they'd bring her here for fudge and carriage rides. She fell in love with the island, and that love never wavered."

"But my mother's did?"

"No, her love for Adele never wavered, but your mother wanted something Adele couldn't give her."

"What?"

"You."

Robin grunted. "Yeah, well, she had a funny way of showing it. You don't have a child and tell them that you love them, and then lie to them their entire life."

"Don't you ever—*ever*—doubt your mother's love for you, young lady!" Maxine said, raising her voice. "Constance walked away from the love of her life to marry your father because she wanted a child more than anything else in this world. So, put your petty hurt feelings where the sun doesn't shine because you have no right to judge your mother."

"I most certainly—"

"*No*, you don't," Maxine said, pointing her arthritic finger at Robin. "You need to remember that your mother knew what she was, and she *still* married a man...for *you*. If that's not love, if that's not sacrifice, if that's not what makes a parent a *parent*, then may God strike me dead right now!"

The only thing daring to make a sound in the kitchen was the cuckoo clock on the wall as it ticked off the seconds. Although no handprint was left behind, Maxine had just slapped Robin in the face with her words, and the sting momentarily put a damper on Robin's ever-increasing anger.

"I'm sorry," Robin whispered. "I know my mother loved me, but it's clear she...she never broke it off, at least not for long." Robin raised her eyes. "Were you a part of the charade? Part of this farce to make everyone believe they were sisters?"

"No, and it didn't start out being a charade. It was just a way to shut people up. Adele had no idea at the time she laid the groundwork for what was to come."

Robin narrowed her eyes. "What are you talking about?"

"I wasn't lying when I said your mother broke it off. She did, and Adele was devastated. I have never seen anyone so...so ravaged by loss. By then, she'd been living on the island for over a year, and everyone here is like family, so we all noticed it. She was losing weight she couldn't afford to lose. She was pale, withdrawn, and crying. God, she cried every day, and everyone kept asking her why. We weren't trying to pry. We were trying to help, but our questions were just making it worse, so one day when someone asked, Adele told them that her husband had been killed in Vietnam. Thousands of boys were killed over there, and anyone with one speck of decency knows you don't bring up pain like that if you know a person is mourning."

"So everyone stopped asking."

LYN GARDNER / 375

Maxine nodded again. "And, of course, when she began becoming herself again, we all thought it was because of the space we gave her, but years later I found out, it had nothing to do with us and everything to do with the letters she got from Virgil."

"Virgil?" Judy said, looking back and forth between Robin and Maxine. "As in Virgil Jankowski?"

"That's the one," Maxine said.

"Who was he?" Robin asked.

"Adele's best friend. They grew up together and went to the same schools all the way through college, which is how he met your mother. Adele told me that because of some sort of farming accident when he was a kid, Virgil wasn't eligible for the draft, so after they graduated, he took a job in California, but he never lost touch with either of them. When he found out your mother had broken off—"

"Wait. He knew about them?"

"Yes. Like I said, Virgil and Adele had known each other for years. He already knew she was gay, but since your mother was so guarded about her relationship with Adele, Virgil never let on to Constance he knew. When your mother broke it off, Virgil could tell by Adele's letters, she was circling the drain. I mean, imagine loving someone so much and then suddenly having no idea whether they were dead or alive or...or struggling. He knew he had to try to ease her pain somehow, so he began sharing what Constance told him in her letters. If I remember correctly, Adele said that went on for over four years."

Robin did the math and folded her arms. "So right after my father died, they got back together. That's just wonderful."

"No, they didn't. All Adele did was send a sympathy card. She didn't expect any response. She just did what people who care do. She sent her condolences with no strings attached, but a few weeks later, your mother wrote back."

"And that's when they came up with this scheme? This sister thing?"

"Adele said that once they started writing back and forth, it was obvious to both that their feelings hadn't changed. It was only going to be a matter of time before they could see each other again, and they knew they'd have to explain their relationship."

"Why not just be best friends?"

"That was your mother's idea except Adele knew that wouldn't work as long as Portia Kalos lived on the island."

Robin glanced at Judy and seeing her shrug, she looked back at Maxine. "Who was she?"

"An old, bitter woman who had more hate in her veins than blood. She moved to the island after splitting up with her husband. Since Portia lived off the proceeds of the divorce, she had lots of time on her hands which she used to turn everyone else's lives into pure hell if she could. She used to spread unfounded rumors, peppering people with assumptions and making up gossip just to see them squirm, and one of those was a young man Portia found...um...a little too feminine for her liking."

"In other words, she was homophobic," Robin said matter-of-factly.

"Yes, and Adele was smart enough to know that an explanation as simple as best friends would be like chum in the water for Portia."

"So they became sisters instead," Robin muttered. "Right?"

Maxine tipped her head. "By that time, your grandparents and Adele's parents were already gone, and since neither Constance nor Adele had any siblings, there was no one to disprove their relationship. So, Adele began slowly mentioning her sister around the island. Nothing too over-the-top, but just enough that people knew she had a sister, and when asked why she hadn't mentioned Constance before, she simply said they'd had a falling out, but they finally mended the fence."

Robin let out a long, audible breath and then ran her fingers through her hair. "They had an *argument*."

"What?"

"That's what my mother told me," Robin said softly as she closed her eyes. "She was sitting at the dining room table one night, writing a letter. It was after my father had died because I remember there were toys everywhere, and he didn't like that." Robin opened her eyes and looked at Maxine. "I kept...I kept asking her what she was doing, tugging on her skirt until she finally answered. She said she was writing to her sister. They'd had a bad argument a long time ago, but they made up and said they were sorry...and that was it. The seed was planted."

"Yes, but it still took a few more years before your mother dared to visit."

"Why?"

Maxine leaned back in her chair, and taking a moment, she thought about how to answer. "Robin, Adele didn't give a damn about what people thought. She would have walked down Main Street wrapped in a rainbow flag without blinking an eye, but your mother...your mother, was just the opposite. She was terrified of anyone finding out, so until she was sure Adele had covered all the bases, she wouldn't come here."

"So they just wrote back and forth for what...four, five years?"

"That's about right."

"Wow. My mom really knew how to string someone along, didn't she?"

Maxine pursed her lips as she glared across the table. "It's called patience, Robin. It's called knowing who you want and knowing what you'll do in order to have them."

"If you say so," Robin said, flicking a non-existent speck off the tablecloth. "And their affair? I'm assuming it started right back up once we came up here for vacation."

"Yes, and no," Maxine said softly. "Adele told me it was instant, just like when they first met. There was no denying their feelings for each other, but if you remember, her house back then was small. There wasn't a lot of privacy, so it wasn't until you stopped coming here with your mother when they...um...when they reconnected."

Robin huffed. "No wonder she put me in summer camp."

"If memory serves, Adele told me your mother did that because you never came out of your room when you were up here. Something about only wanting to read books, I think?"

"But it still gave them the opportunity to...to do what they wanted."

"Yes, it did."

"My mom must have been jumping for joy when I actually *liked* camp."

"She just wanted you to be happy and get out of yourself. It seems to have worked."

Robin set her jaw, glaring at Maxine for a second before picking up her drink and finishing it off in one swallow. "Wait," she said, placing the glass back on the table. "What about the men my mother dated? Rita said something about her seeing...damn, I can't remember his name."

"Ted Owens?"

"Yes, that's the one."

"He was the young fellow on the receiving end of Portia Kalos' rumors. I'm not sure how Adele knew the rumors were true, but she did. Without telling your mother, she approached him with an idea after you and Constance visited for the second time. To quiet Portia once and for all, and to cement their own secret, Adele asked him to pretend to date your mother whenever she visited. Ted was as fearful about being found out as your mother was, so he readily agreed, and the next time your mother was here, they went out to dinner together, and that was that."

"And the other men?"

"Seasonal workers," Maxine said with a wave of her hand. "Your mother was an attractive woman, so after Ted moved away, if someone asked, she'd say yes to a dinner or a lunch."

"And then she'd go back home to Adele."

"That's right," Maxine said before pushing herself out of her chair. "And now, I have something to give you."

Watching as Maxine left the room, Judy turned to Robin. "Are you okay?"

Clenching her jaw, Robin shook her head as she glared at Judy. "What do you think? I just found out my mother was gay, and she was...she was *screwing* Adele every chance she got."

"Robin, I don't think—"

"These are for you," Maxine said, placing a stack of white over-sized envelopes on the table. "Adele asked me to hold on to them for safekeeping. There's more I need to give you, but I think you should see these first."

Robin glared at the envelopes and shook her head. "I have a question for you."

"Okay," Maxine said as she slipped into her chair.

"A few days after my mom died, Adele called and told me she wasn't feeling well, and she wasn't going to make it to my mother's memorial service. If they were so much in love, how could a cold have stopped her from making that trip?"

Judy sat straighter in her chair. "Wait. She didn't have a cold," she said, glancing at Maxine. "It was because of that fall she took. I remember you telling me she was going to miss her sister's service because of it, and that's why I ended up working at Safe Harbor that year, isn't it?"

"Yes," Maxine said as she turned her attention to Robin. "After you called to tell Adele your mother had died, she collapsed and fell down the basement steps, but it wasn't those injuries that prevented her from making the trip."

"Then why didn't she go?"

"Robin, it's one thing when someone loses a brother or a sister, but when you lose the love of your life, mourning takes on a whole new meaning, and Adele knew she'd never be able to hold it together in front of you. She cried for weeks. I honestly can't remember Adele ever smiling again, ever...ever really talking other than a few words here and there. She walked around in a daze, staring out windows for hours, just...just an empty shell of who she once was. She lost all interest in everything, and when that season ended, and Judy checked out the last guest, Adele never reopened the Inn because it no longer held the promise it once did."

"What do you mean, promise?" Robin asked.

"I'm not sure if you're aware of this or not, but your mother was going to move up here after she retired."

"Yeah, I know that. She talked about it for years."

"What you didn't know is that Adele asked your mother to make that promise when they first got back together. Robin, I can't say it enough. Your mother was terrified of having anyone ever find out about their relationship, and she knew what she was asking wasn't fair, basically forcing Adele to take what she could get, but Adele worshiped your mother. Even if she'd had only one day a year to spend with Constance, she would have gladly taken it, but by asking your mother to promise to move here after she retired, Adele knew that one day they *would* be together. When your mother died, Adele's hope died with her. It's one of the reasons why I ended up closing up so much of Safe Harbor. Adele couldn't walk into any of the bedrooms anymore."

"Why?" Judy said.

"Judy, don't ask," Robin growled. "There are *some* things I don't *need* to know."

Maxine scrunched up her face. "Robin, it's not what you're thinking," she said, and rummaging through the long, slender envelopes, she grabbed one and opened it. "Does this look familiar?"

Robin found herself staring at a photo of Adele and her mother gazing at each other while they stood on a tree-lined beach. "No," she said, pushing it away.

"Look again," Maxine said, sliding it back toward Robin.

Robin cleared her throat and picked up the photo again. "Fine, well, let's see. We have my mother and Adele smiling at each other. No surprise there. After all, they were able to pull the wool over my eyes for over thirty flipping years. An empty beach. That's exciting, except there are nicer ones in Florida. A stand of trees. Now, there's a...a clue." Robin sat up in her chair, her mouth falling open as she studied the photo. "I've seen this before," she said, glancing over at Maxine. "But my mother and Adele weren't in it."

The slightest of grins appeared on Maxine's face. "Didn't you ever wonder how Adele came up with the names for the rooms?"

Robin shook her head. "We already figured that out by the mementos in the trunk. They were named after places she visited."

"Can I see that?" Judy said, holding out her hand. Taking the picture, Judy's eyes widened. "This is hanging in White Birch, but Robin's right. The photo in that room is a landscape. Adele and Constance aren't in it."

"That's right," Maxine said before pointing to the envelopes on the table. "All of these contain pictures matching the ones in the rooms, but unlike those, these will have your mother and Adele in them."

"But why?" Robin asked.

"Because they were in love and could only spend a few weeks together every year. This was a way for Adele to keep Constance close to her, and since Adele's hobby was photography, she didn't have to take them anywhere to be developed which, by the way, was something Constance wouldn't have allowed anyway. Whenever your mother visited, especially in the winter, they'd take a long weekend, and Adele would bring along her camera. She'd set up her tripod and take two pictures, one with just the scenery and one with them. That way, whenever Adele went into any of the rooms, she'd always be reminded of your mother and their vacations. She chose the names for the same reason. They were either resorts or towns they visited, and Firefly was named after the cabin they stayed in during their first...uh...their first vacation together. It's also the room your mother used whenever she was here."

Robin jerked her head back. "Why would she stay up there?"

"I told you, she was afraid of anyone ever suspecting their relationship was anything different than what they pretended it to be," Maxine said. "The hidden staircase gave her the opportunity to go upstairs like the rest of the guests and then—"

"Creep back down when the coast was clear," Robin said, shoving the envelopes away.

Maxine glowered at Robin. "Please stop making this sound dirty, because it wasn't. They were madly in love, Robin, and because of your mother's fear of being found out, Adele did everything in her power to make Constance feel safe. It's why she named the Inn, Safe Harbor. It was her promise to Constance that she would never have to be afraid there."

Robin flicked her gaze to the ceiling and counted to ten. "So, Maxine," she said, lowering her eyes. "What was your role in all of this subterfuge?

Did you run interference or just hover in the shadows, waiting until they needed to come up with another lie?"

"Believe it or not, young lady, I make a point of telling the truth, except when it comes to protecting those I love. And the only outright lie I've told you was the one about how Adele got enough money to buy the Inn."

Robin looked Maxine square in the eye. "That's right. You said she got it from Stanley's estate, but Stanley didn't exist."

"No, he didn't. Your mother is the one who helped Adele buy the Inn."

"What!"

"Between what she received after her parents died and your father's life insurance, she had more than enough to live on *and* to put you through school, so she gave Adele part of the money your father had set aside for his retirement. She knew this was Adele's dream. It was the least she could do knowing what she was asking of Adele."

"Meaning, to wait for her."

"Exactly, which is the reason Adele set up the trust. In her mind, the money Constance had given her should have been willed to you, but since it wasn't, Adele thought leaving you Safe Harbor would make up for that...and then some."

"I don't give a shit about the money."

"This isn't about you, Robin. It's about what *they* wanted."

"You sure as hell sound like you know a lot about them. You three must have grown as thick as thieves over the years."

"Robin, up until the early nineties, I had no idea that Constance and Adele *weren't* sisters. I found out by accident."

"How? No," Robin said, holding up her hands. "Let me guess. You walked in on them?"

"Yes. It was just after Christmas, your mother's usual visit, and since I knew she loved my cherry nut pound cake, I made her one and took it over early on a Saturday. I let myself into the house like I always did, and I found them in the kitchen...kissing."

"Jesus Christ," Robin said under her breath.

"Your mother became hysterical, and ran back to the apartment, crying like...like someone had just told her you died. Adele, on the other hand, just stood there, staring at me, a little defiant, a little hurt...and more than a little scared." Maxine paused to take a sip of her much-needed drink. "I knew it wasn't the right time to ask questions, not that I even had the right to ask them, so I went over and gave Adele a kiss on her cheek, told her that her secret was safe with me, and I left. A couple of weeks later, she invited me over for dinner and told me the whole story."

Tears welled in Robin's eyes as she shook her head. "Unbelievable."

"Robin, I know for a fact that if it had been up to Adele, she would have told you. She loved your mother so much, she wanted the world to know, but Constance was so, so terrified of being found out—"

"That she took it to the grave with her," Robin said, sniffling back her emotion. "That's just fucking great."

"But Adele didn't."

"Why?" Robin said, leaning forward in her chair. "Because we found the footlocker?"

"No, because Adele's the one who hid it, along with the keys and the cameras on the staircase."

"You knew they were there?"

"I told you Adele wanted the world to know how much she loved your mother, but Constance never found the courage. In life, Adele would never go against what your mother wanted, but in death, she decided to leave it up to fate. Adele was a huge believer in karma and how if things were meant to be, they'd be. So, before she put herself into that home, she packed up the footlocker and left behind a few other things, knowing if you found them, you'd either figure it out for yourself or if I were still around, you'd come talk to me."

"Then why weren't these pictures in the trunk? Why do you have them?"

"Because she didn't care if strangers found a trunk full of mementos, but these were too precious to her to have them fall into a stranger's hand. She actually told me to destroy them if...if you had no interest in the Inn."

"Why didn't you tell me this from the beginning? Why wait until we found the trunk?"

"Because that's not what Adele wanted. Like I said, she believed in fate."

Robin rested back in her chair, stretching her arms out before running her fingers through her hair. "You know what, Maxine?" she said as she pushed her chair away from the table and stood up. "Screw fate. Screw the secrets and the lies and all the head games that went with it. As far as I'm concerned, you can burn everything."

Chapter Thirty-Six

Judy flipped down the kickstand on her bike. Unzipping her jacket, she looked up at the house. "Fourth day's the charm?"

When they left Maxine's on Sunday, Robin hadn't said a word. Jumping onto her bike, she was down the street before Judy had time to pull on her gloves. After what Maxine had told them, Judy understood Robin needed some time to make sense out of everything, so she didn't return to Safe Harbor until the following day.

They had planned to go Christmas shopping, but on Monday morning, Judy knew in an instant, she'd be going by herself. She found Robin in the parlor, dressed in the same clothes she had worn the day before. Her hair hadn't been brushed and by the circles under her eyes, Judy knew Robin hadn't got much sleep, although she wondered why since there were two empty bottles of wine on the coffee table. The exchange of words was almost non-existent, Judy barely getting out the question before Robin growled back the answer, and Judy left only minutes after she had arrived...alone.

Tuesday was almost a reincarnation of Monday except Robin had changed into a baggy sweat suit and was camping out in her own living room when Judy came into the house. The kitchen was littered with crumpled chip bags, opened packages of cookies, and another empty wine bottle, and sitting on the island was a tub of ice cream, the melted mint chocolate chip contents leaking across the countertop. Judy tried again to get Robin out of the house, hoping a change of scenery would alter her frame of mind, but Robin was as unyielding as steel. Sitting cross-legged on the sofa, with her arms folded and her jaw set, the dozen words she muttered were dripping with disdain. She didn't want to talk. She didn't want to shop, and when Judy persisted, Robin jumped off the sofa, stomped to her bedroom, and slammed the door. Moments later, Judy left the house with an attitude that matched Robin's. She could understand Robin's anger, and Judy accepted it would take time to get past the hurt, but slamming a door in a friend's face wasn't the way to go about it.

The following morning, Judy phoned Robin to let her know she wouldn't be over. If Robin wanted space, Judy would give her exactly what she was asking for, but Judy's call went directly to voicemail. She tried again an hour later and again, an hour after that, but the results were the same. Robin had turned off her phone, slamming yet another door in Judy's face.

Judy didn't like being rebuffed. She was trying to be a friend, trying to lend an ear if that's what Robin needed, but in return, Robin was giving her the ultimate cold shoulder. Judy's calls had gone unanswered, and the few texts she knew wouldn't have been answered, had gone unread, so standing on the walk outside Safe Harbor on Thursday morning, while the air was frigid, Judy's annoyance was keeping her warm. Enough was enough. Stuffing her gloves into her pockets, she trudged up the steps and let herself into the house.

She wasn't sure what to expect when she came inside, but as soon as the aroma of coffee found its way to Judy, a small grin appeared. Coffee was a good sign. After all, it wasn't wine.

After draping her rain gear on the coat tree, Judy zigzagged through the totes still cluttering the foyer, pausing near the parlor to look inside. The tree in front of the windows had yet to be decorated, but the room was neat and tidy again, and Judy's grin grew a wee bit bigger.

Fred peeked out from under the table as Judy walked through the dining room, and pausing long enough for him to amble by, she followed the black-and-white cat to Robin's apartment. She couldn't help but hold her breath as she rounded the corner leading to the kitchen, but seeing not a crumb in sight on countertops spotless and shining, Judy exhaled, and her grin dared to become something more.

With a little more pep in her step, Judy strolled to the living room. Finding it empty, she turned around, and as she passed the spare bedroom, she saw that the door leading to the stairs to Firefly was open. As quietly as she could, Judy went over and listened, and when she heard a distant tapping, she beamed. Robin was writing.

Judy returned to the kitchen, and as she debated on whether to leave or work in the office, the fruit basket on the counter gave her the answer she was looking for. If there was ice left to be broken, *this* would do the trick.

***

"What are you doing?"

Judy smiled, and turning around she was about to answer, but instead, she scrambled not to drop the measuring cup she'd been washing. Given the number of days she had existed on only junk food and wine, Robin's pale complexion was understandable, and the black-rimmed glasses perched on her nose had become a familiar sight so Judy wasn't surprised by what she *could* see. She was shocked and somewhat saddened by what she couldn't. "You...you cut your hair."

Robin crossed her arms. "Yeah, I decided I needed a change."

Judy took a moment to adjust to Robin's new look. Longer in the front and shorter in the back, and parted far to the left, the asymmetrical pixie cut ended inches away from her shoulders. It was sleek and edgy, hiding in its chic style a few years of Robin's age while exposing her long neck and accentuating her strong jaw. It was perfect. "I like it."

"I didn't do it for you," Robin said, rubbing the peach fuzz on the back of her neck. "And you didn't answer my question. What are you doing?"

"I...um...I saw some overly ripe bananas in the fruit bowl. I thought you might enjoy some freshly-baked banana bread."

For two days, Robin had stewed in juices thickened by heartache and anger. Smothered by her rage, compassion had escaped her, the empathy needed to understand what her mother had done nullified by emotions she owned, but could not control. However, on the third day, Robin awoke with a different mindset. Fuck it. Fuck the years of deceit. Fuck her mother and her lies, and fuck the world.

More of a mantra than a mindset, it was nonetheless the fuel Robin needed to propel her through that day and into Thursday morning. She cleaned. She bathed. She ate. She escaped long enough to find a salon to rid herself of something she knew her mother adored, and she tried to write, but Robin's mantra hadn't erased the hurt. It only confined it, caging it like an animal, untamed and rabid. It had spent twenty-four hours pacing in its jail, patiently waiting for release and Judy's gesture, as heartfelt as it may have been, just opened the cage.

Robin didn't want comfort. She didn't want a friend or a confidante, and she didn't want an ally or a shoulder to cry on. All she wanted was to get Judy out of the house before Robin said something she'd regret. Unfortunately, Robin's agitation was about to leak out in her tone.

"Well, you thought wrong. I'm not hungry, and I don't want any banana bread," Robin said, turning to leave. "Just take it with you when you leave."

Judy's backbone stiffened. "Stop it."

"What?" Robin said, looking over her shoulder.

Judy set down the cup and picked up a towel to dry her hands. "I said stop it. Stop treating me like the enemy. Stop being rude. Stop wallowing in whatever you're wallowing in because it's not healthy, and it's not going to change anything. Your mother was gay. She didn't tell you. Get over it."

"Get over it?" Robin said, taking a step toward Judy. "That's your advice? Just...get over it?"

"Look, I know it's not that simple—"

"You know nothing!" Robin shouted. "Your mother didn't deceive you her entire life. Your mother didn't lie to your face year after year after year. Your mother wasn't *ashamed* of you!"

"What the hell are you talking about? She wasn't ashamed of you."

"Judy, she hid in the shadows, afraid of what people would think. You don't do that unless you're ashamed, and if she was ashamed of being a lesbian, then she was ashamed of me."

"She was scared, Robin. Times were different back—"

"I was her daughter!" Robin screamed. "And I *know* things were a lot harder way back when, but trust me, things haven't changed *that* much. Sure, we can get married now, and we can even adopt kids, but don't you think for one goddamned minute that makes everything else go away."

"I wasn't saying—"

LYN GARDNER / 387

"Do you think I haven't been discriminated against? Try going into a diner for months, thinking that all the people who work there are your friends, and then one day you show up for breakfast with a woman, and suddenly you can't get a table, suddenly you're not wanted because she's a little too butch for their tastes. Do you think I haven't been threatened? What exactly do you think skinheads promise when they shout at you while you walk in a parade or attend a march for gay rights? Do you think I haven't had guys tell me all I need is a good *man* when they see me out on a date with a woman? Do you think I haven't had Bible thumpers screech at me that I was going to hell? Do you think I haven't heard the sick jokes, seen the signs, or I haven't been called every disgusting name in the book? Do you? *Do you!*"

"Did you ever, for one minute, think your mother didn't have your courage?"

"This *isn't* about courage."

"It sure the hell is!" Judy shouted. "Tell me you didn't come out knowing you'd face some of what you just described. That it wasn't a surprise, sprung on you after the fact."

"Of course, it wasn't."

"And telling your mother? Didn't that take courage?"

"No, it didn't, or at least not as much as you think," Robin said, placing her hands on her hips. "I knew she loved me. Yeah, I was a little worried that I was somehow going to disappoint her, but I was never scared of telling her. She raised me to be honest and never to be afraid of who I was. I never saw her once judge anyone, so I knew she wasn't going to judge me."

"But you're judging her."

"That's different."

"No, it's not. It's the same thing, except your mother accepted your sexuality, and you can't accept hers."

"That's because I didn't *lie* about it!"

Judy's lungs emptied. "Robin, people lie. They lie for all kinds of reasons. Can you honestly stand there and say you've never lied?"

As Robin's cheeks reddened, she lowered her chin to her chest. "Of course not."

"And why did you do it?"

"What?"

"Why did you lie? Why didn't you just tell the truth?" Judy waited for Robin to answer, but when she didn't, Judy did. "I'll tell you why. It's because you didn't want to face the consequences if you spoke it, and that's exactly what your mother did for probably the same reason. It's called fear. Maybe, growing up, she had to listen to her friends bash gays, and she didn't want to be on the receiving end of their ignorance. Did you ever think of that? Maybe she went to church every Sunday and was forced to listen as the pastor spewed hatred supposedly based on passages of the Bible, except they had been edited by his own warped perspective. Did you ever think of that? And maybe your mom grew up in a home filled with homophobes, and if she ever *had* spoken the truth, if she ever *had* found the courage, she would have been ostracized, losing everything she held dear. Did you *ever* think of *that*?"

"My grandparents weren't like that."

"How do you know? You were a child when they died. You have no idea how your mother was brought up. You have no idea what she went through."

"You're right. I don't," Robin said, folding her arms. "But let me tell you what I do know. I am sick and tired of being lied to. Pam almost destroyed me with hers, and now my mother is doing the same from the grave, and I'm done being gutted by people I thought I could trust. It fucking *hurts* too much." Robin brushed away the tears rolling down her cheeks. "I'm done believing anyone, Judy. I'm done trusting anyone. I'm done assuming there's good in people when all I keep seeing is bad. You stand there, and you try to defend her. You say it was the way she was raised. I call that an excuse, not a reason. You say she was scared. I say *fuck* being scared. I was her daughter. If she loved me, she should have trusted me because if you love someone, you don't *lie* to them. You don't concoct stories, pretending you're something that you're *not* because it's convenient, because it's *easier*. Life is *not* easy."

"I doubt your mother would say her life was easy, but it *was* her life, Robin. Not yours."

"And from where I'm standing, she wasted it, and for what? For *what*? For a few weeks every year where, behind closed doors and shuttered windows, she could be herself? Sneaking down back stairs, dating men, and lying to her daughter. What kind of fucking life is that? Who the fuck would want to live like that?"

"Stop *judging* her! What gives you the right to say how people should live their lives?"

"She was my *mother*!"

"And it was *her* life. Why can't you see that? Why does this have to be all about you? Sure, you're hurt. Sure, you're confused, but goddamn it, Robin, your mother made a choice, and right or wrong, good or bad, it was her choice to make. You need to respect that, and you also need to start practicing what you preach."

"What's that supposed to mean?"

"Whatever happened to you owning your emotions, Robin, because from where I'm standing, they've been owning *you* for days. You've been acting like a spoiled child—"

"You need to leave," Robin said, fisting her hands.

"Robin—"

"You *seriously* need to *leave* right now!" Robin said, brushing away more tears. "You don't understand, Judy. You are so clueless. This goes against *everything* I thought she was, *everything* I thought she stood for...and it *hurts*."

"Robin, I know it does."

"You—know—*nothing*!" Robin screamed, waving her arms about.

Judy's heart was hammering in her chest as she reached around to untie the string of her apron. A cyclone filled with Robin's words, Robin's pain, and Robin's points spun in Judy's mind while she fumbled with the knot until it came free.

She was equally as culpable as Pam and Constance. Time had been wasted, and untruths had been told, and excuses were not reasons. They were merely lies Judy had told herself to get through the days, the weeks, and the years. Fabrications to blend and belong, she believed they'd give her peace, but instead, they became her prison. Walls thick with echoing voices, mortar made of false scripture, and barred windows draped with viewpoints unfounded, uneducated, and unfair had kept her captive and apathetic for far too long. Judy knew the consequences in facing her demons. It would destroy their friendship, and prove to Robin that still another had deceived her, but Robin was right. In friendship and in love...there was no place for lies.

"I know more than you think," Judy said, and neatly folding her apron, she placed it on the counter. "I know you were wearing a short, dark blue skirt with a jacket to match. They both had wide silver zippers running down the fronts, and I know your boots were suede and lined with fleece. It showed through at the stitching, and I know...and I know the turtleneck you had on was the same color as that fleece."

Robin's mouth went slack. "What in the *hell* are you talking about?" she said, flinching back her head. "You're not making any sense."

"You don't get it?" Judy said, her voice quivering with emotion. "It's what you were wearing on the last day of school before winter break. The last day we saw each other, the last day we spoke. You stand there in all your righteousness shouting your mother should have told you the truth, shouting that all you want is the truth, well, how's this for truth, Robin? *You* were the reason I left Heritage. *You* were the reason I married *Scott*."

Chapter Thirty-Seven

Rita looked up from the book in her lap when she heard the doorbell ring. She glanced at her watch before setting aside the novel and making her way to the front door.

As soon as Rita opened the door, her eyes began to sparkle. "This is a surprise," she said, seeing Judy standing on the porch. "What are you doing out and about on this chilly autumn night?"

"Sorry, I would have called, but I left my phone at Robin's," Judy whispered. "Can I come in?"

"Since when do you need to ask?" Rita stepped away from the door, her smile slowly vanishing as she watched Judy shuffle into the house with her head bowed. Rita eyed her friend up and down, and then she noticed what Judy was carrying. "And I see you come bearing gifts. What's the occasion?"

"Is Hank home?"

"Yeah, he's in the den watching TV. Why? Do you need him?"

"No," Judy said, staring at the floor. "I just...I just need to...to talk to you."

"All right. Let's go into the living—"

"No. Can we...uh...can we go somewhere else? Somewhere private. The Man Cave?"

Rita angled back in her stance as even the most delicate lines in her face deepened. "Yeah, sure. Just let me go grab my coat."

"Okay."

***

It wasn't a cave, and it wasn't only for men, but the Man Cave was what Rita affectionately called Hank's workshop. Located at the far end of their backyard, it was filled with gardening and woodworking tools, and it was where Hank liked to spend his days in the winter.

The walk through the house and yard happened in silence, and along the way, Rita gave Judy a dozen side-eyed glances. Like most, Judy had her moods and Rita thought she'd seen them all, but this one was new. This one was different.

This wasn't frustration, for Rita had seen that when Judy had dealt with customers returning bikes abused by carelessness. This wasn't annoyance. Rita had witnessed that numerous times over the years as Judy tried to put up with a husband who had never grown up. Cranky didn't fit either. Her friend was past the age where cramps came to call, and although Rita had only seen it once, she knew this wasn't anger. Anger was a wife erupting when she found out about her husband's affairs, and Judy wasn't erupting. Her expression was blank, closed, and passive. It held no clues, yet the vacancy of emotion was a clue in and of itself. What could have drained Judy to this point?

When they reached the shed, Rita turned on the light, and as Judy followed her inside, Rita reached up and turned on the forced-air electric heater mounted to the ceiling joists. "It shouldn't take long to warm up in here."

Rita pulled out two stools, wiping the sawdust from the top of both before offering one to Judy, but instead, Judy went over and hopped up on a workbench, setting the six-pack of hard cider down next to her.

For a minute, the only sound to be heard was the air blowing from the heater. One woman was eyeing the other, waiting for her to speak, while the other seemed a million miles away.

"Are you okay, Judy?" Rita said softly.

"No," Judy said, shaking her head. "Not really."

"Do you want to talk about it?"

Judy sniffled and shook her head again. "I do...and I don't." Pulling two bottles from the six-pack, she offered one to Rita.

"Thanks," Rita said, unscrewing the cap.

"You're welcome."

Rita took a sip of her drink and then noticed the label. "I didn't know Doud's sold this."

"They don't. I bought a couple of packs today in Lansing."

"Lansing? What the hell were you doing all the way down there?"

"I was on my way home until I realized showing up without any luggage would lead to lots of questions. Coming back here was the lesser of two evils."

"The lesser of two evils? Judy, what in the world is going on? You love this island."

Judy lowered her chin to her chest. "Yeah, but I ruined it. I ruined everything."

"How?"

"I did something...something really stupid. Something I can't take back. Something she'll never be able to forgive me for."

Rita's eyes narrowed as she looked at Judy. "By she, should I assume you mean Robin?"

"Yeah."

Judy's voice was barely audible over the stillness of the shed, and Rita's eyebrows became one for a long moment until relaxing easily back into place. "I have to say, this is a really interesting choice," Rita said, looking at the bottle again. "I think the last time I saw you drink this stuff was the night of the party. You know, the one Hank and I threw for you and Scott after you got married?"

"Is it? I don't remember."

A ghost of a grin appeared on Rita's face. "I'm not surprised. It was the first and last time I ever saw you get drunk. I mean, I've been around you when you've been buzzed, but that night...that night you were downright shit-faced."

"So what? It was a long time ago, and it was a party. I wanted to unwind."

"Well, you sure as hell did that," Rita said with a laugh. "And I have to tell you, up until then, I would have never labeled you as a magpie, but you were that night. Lord, have mercy. Going on and on about how stern and strict your father was and how overbearing your brothers were."

"Well, other than Dad being dead, the rest hasn't changed," Judy said, and bringing the bottle to her lips, she chugged down a few gulps.

"Yep, you were quite the Chatty Cathy," Rita said, before taking another sip of her drink. "And we even ended up out here, just like we are tonight, except back then you were the one doing all the talking, and I was the one doing all the listening."

"Times change."

Rita fixed her eyes solely on Judy. "Yes, they do," she said quietly. "Because back then I thought the student you had fallen in love with was a boy...not a girl."

Judy was about to have more of her drink, but the bottle never reached her lips. For a few seconds, she remained motionless and then her hand began to tremble. Barely managing to set the bottle down before she burst into tears, Judy covered her mouth as she tried to stifle her sobs. "No. No. No. No. *No!*"

Rita jumped to her feet and rushing over, she wrapped her arms around her wailing friend. "Judy, it's all right. Please don't cry. It's all right."

"No, it's not," Judy said through a strangled sob. "You must think I'm some sort of...some sort of pervert, some fucking pedophile."

"I don't think that," she said, holding Judy tightly. "I don't think that at all, Judy. Please, please believe me. I never once thought that."

"How could you not?" Judy said, pushing Rita away. "How could you fucking not?"

"Because I know you too well," Rita said with a snicker. "And that night...that night you kept saying over and over again that this Robin was eighteen, and eighteen doesn't make you a pedophile."

"But she was my *student.*"

"Did something happen?"

"No. I swear to God nothing happened, Rita. *Nothing* happened."

"And that's exactly what you told me that night. Actually, you said it about a million times if I'm not mistaken."

"I was telling you the truth."

Rita placed her hands on Judy's shoulders. "I never doubted you were telling the truth, but Judy something had to happen for you to...for you to quit your job and marry Scott."

Judy took a deep breath, her lungs emptying in a whoosh a moment later. "I don't even know how to explain it. I just know that from the moment I saw her on that first day of school, I couldn't get her out of my head." Judy paused and then looked at Rita. "Have you ever seen one of those photos they take nowadays where everything is black-and-white except for one thing? It could be a person or a flower."

"Sure."

"That's what it was like. I walked into that classroom, and everything went gray, except for Robin. She was sitting in the front row with perfect posture and the most amazing smile I'd ever seen, and all the hair on the back of my neck stood on end. It was the weirdest feeling."

"And then what happened?"

"Nothing," Judy said with a shrug. "School started. The kids went to their classes. I went to mine, and I didn't see her until the next morning. I showed up early to get some paperwork filled out, and when I walked into my room, she was already there, sitting at her desk bent over a book. We got to talking. Nothing serious, just mindless chit-chat, but I enjoyed every second of it, and it wasn't long before I was getting to work early every day, just in case she'd be there. And then one day I woke up and the first thing I thought of was her...and that's the way it's stayed."

"And that's what convinced you to change your entire life?"

Judy bowed her head. "No," she whispered. "As the weeks went on, I found myself thinking about her all the time. I'd be reading a book and wonder if she'd like it. I'd be watching a movie and wonder if she would laugh at the same places I laughed, and when I went shopping, I'd see something in a store window, and I'd picture Robin wearing it." Judy looked Rita in the eye. "I want you to know that my...that my thoughts weren't dirty or...or anything like that. They were just...thoughts."

"But?"

"But on the last day of school before Christmas break, she came into homeroom wearing an outfit I had never seen before. She looked really nice, and I told her that. She turned and smiled that...that damn, wonderful smile of hers, and she said 'Thanks. It's my birthday suit,' and in that instant, everything changed. She meant it as a joke, and she explained it was a birthday present, but my thoughts, my mind, my *feelings* were no longer platonic. And at that moment, I knew I had to get away from her. She was a student. I was a teacher. It wasn't right, and I wasn't going to allow something I had buried to rise again."

Rita's eyebrows became one again. "What the hell does that mean?"

"What do you think it means?" Judy said, locking eyes with Rita. "You know about my father. You know about my brothers."

"Oh, Jesus Christ," Rita said, rocking back on her heels. "How long have you—"

"Early teens," Judy said, shrugging.

"So, you've lived a lie practically your entire life?"

Judy flinched. They were the same words Robin had shouted over and over that morning. "I didn't have a choice."

"Of course you had a choice!"

Judy's head snapped back. "Really? What kind of choice did I have? Every time there was a news story about gays being killed or beaten, my father would bellow 'good riddance!' When Harvey Milk was assassinated, he threw a goddamned party because there was one less faggot on the planet. His words, not mine. People were getting beaten, brutalized or killed, all because they were gay, and you have the gall to stand there and say I had a choice?"

"Judy, I'm—"

"*You* grew up in a world that didn't give you a second glance walking down the street with Hank. *You* grew up in a world that applauded your wedding, your children...your life. *You* grew up in a world protected simply because *you* fit the norm, but yeah, I had a choice. I could either fit in or risk being beaten by my father or disowned by my family. Tell me, Rita, just how easy of a *choice* do *you* think that is?"

Tears trailed down Rita's cheeks as she wrapped her arms around Judy again. "I'm so sorry, Judy. I didn't mean it. I put my fucking mouth in motion before my brain was in gear. I can't...I can't possibly know what it was like for you, and it was stupid of me to say you had a choice."

"But you're, right, Rita. I did," Judy said, freeing herself from the hug. "I did have a choice. I just didn't have the courage. I didn't have the strength. I was fourteen and terrified that somehow my father would find out, so I buried all my feelings so far inside of me, they didn't come to the surface again until I met Robin. I know that sounds weird, unbelievable, ridiculous, but it's the truth. I never looked at another woman like I looked at Robin that day. I never had those types of thoughts, but all of a sudden my mind was flooded with them, and I knew I had to get the hell out. I was scared. I was in denial. I just wanted my life back, my humdrum, boring, *fucking* fake straight life back."

"Jesus."

The shed went quiet. Rita returned to her stool, and in unison, both women reached for their drinks. One swallow turned into two and then into three, and when their throats were finally cooled, and their nerves

LYN GARDNER / 397

settled, Judy looked over at Rita. "Why didn't you ever say something? Why didn't you ask—"

"Because it wasn't my place to ask, Judy. I figured if you wanted to talk about it, you would, but you never brought it up again. I can tell you that I *was* a little pissed off for a while, knowing you married Scott when you were in love in someone else, but then I realized in your own way you did love him, just not as much as you loved...her."

"He made me feel safe," Judy whispered. "Secure."

"And hidden?"

Tears filled Judy's eyes again. "Yeah, and hidden."

"I just don't know how you kept it together for all these years."

"It's called keeping busy, doing everything and anything I could do, just so I wouldn't think about her. I wouldn't have *time* to think about her."

"No, Judy. I was talking about her aunt living here and her mother—"

"I didn't know!" Judy blurted.

"What?"

"Rita, I didn't *know* Adele was Robin's aunt. She was your friend, not mine, and sure, I knew who Constance was, but only because people said she was Adele's sister. I was never actually introduced to her. I was always busy in the bike shop. I didn't have time to socialize."

"Then when in the hell did you find out?"

"The night I went over to talk to Robin about the job."

Rita's mouth fell open. "Holy shit. You've got to be kidding."

"Oh, trust me. I'm not," Judy said through a half-hearted grin. "And I'm telling you, Rita, when she opened that door, I swear to God, I almost took off running, but I figured if I did that, she'd realize I remembered her. I noticed she was working on the house, and that gave me the excuse I was looking for to leave, but she wouldn't hear of it. So, I ended up going inside, thinking we'd just chat for a little while before I turned down the job, but once we started talking, everything changed."

"What do you mean?"

"Like I told you, we used to talk before classes started. It was always so easy, so effortless, and it was the same way that night. She was bumbling around a little bit, so I guess she was nervous about talking to an old teacher, but I didn't feel like her teacher anymore. I didn't feel like...like it was wrong anymore."

"So, when we met for lunch on my birthday, that whole age thing was bullshit?"

"Yes."

"I knew it!" Rita said, slapping her hands on her thighs. "Thank God I'm a pushy old broad."

"What are you talking about?"

"When we were sitting in that booth, and you told me she was an old student of yours, your eyes lit up. Judy, I knew right then and there she was the same Robin you told me about the night of the party. I was a *little* surprised that she was a she instead of a he, but that type of thing has never been an issue for me, which I hope you know."

"I do."

"And since you've been honest with me, I'll be honest with you."

"Okay?"

"When I took all that food over to her, I kind of pulled that out of my ass. The ladies at church had every intention of delivering the stuff themselves, but once I realized who Robin was, I coerced them into letting me do it. I had to check her out."

"Why?"

"Jesus, Judy. My best friend in the whole wide world has been in love with this woman for a quarter of a century? How in the hell could I not check her out?"

"And?"

"And I already told you, I like her. What I didn't tell you, for risk of...um...showing my hand, is that she's as beautiful and charming as her mother. You have good taste in women."

Judy smiled. "I think I have good taste in friends, too."

"I'll drink to that."

Rita pulled two more bottles from the six-pack, and as she handed one to Judy, she noticed dark carmine blotches on Judy left sneaker. "Is that blood?"

"What?" Judy followed Rita's line of sight and sighed. Believing her day was only going to involve painting or decorating, Judy had pulled on clothes and shoes meant for the tasks, her sneakers being the same she had worn one night a few weeks before. "Oh, yeah. Robin got hurt—"

"I heard about it. She fell on the trail. Jesus, you must have been out of your mind."

Tears welled in Judy's eyes again. "That's putting it mildly. She came into the house with her face covered in blood, and the next thing I knew her eyes rolled back into her head, and she hit the floor. All I kept thinking was...was I was going to lose her, and I didn't even *have* her." Judy paused and looked at Rita. "And you know what the funny thing is?"

"What?"

"I held it together that night. There was so much blood, and I was scared like I've never been scared before, but I kept it together. And then this morning, this morning I fucked everything up."

"How?"

"We were having a...a fight. I guess that's what you'd call it. She's having a really tough time with this whole Constance and Adele thing."

"What Constance and Adele thing?" Rita said, setting her drink aside.

"Shit." Judy took a deep breath and looked Rita square in the eye. "What I'm about to tell you doesn't leave this shed. Okay? I need you to promise me it *never* leaves this shed."

"Judy, I've kept your secret for over twenty-five years. I never even told Hank, so as far as I'm concerned, this shed is Vegas and what happens in Vegas, stays in Vegas." When Judy continued to stare back at her, Rita held up her hand as if taking an oath. "I promise, Judy. Whatever it is, it stays here."

"Thanks," Judy said, before taking another gulp of her cider. "It seems that...uh...that Constance and Adele weren't sisters."

"They weren't sisters?"

"No, they were lovers."

Rita leaned far enough back on her stool that two of the legs came off the ground. "Holy crap-a-moly!" she said, clapping her hands to her head. "How in the hell did they ever hide *that* on this nutty gossip rock?"

"I have no idea, but they did, and Robin's not dealing with it very well. Long story, short, that's what we were arguing about this morning. She's pissed off because her mother never told her, and to make matters worse, again this stays in Vegas, the last woman Robin dated was a pathological liar. She really did a number on Robin, and now, the way Robin sees it, her mother did the same thing."

"Geez. I can see why she's upset."

Judy nodded. "Yeah, so can I, but as she stood there shouting her opinions, whatever empathy I thought I had went right out the window, and we started to argue. I told myself I was just trying to make her see that she was judging her mother based on her own life rather than on what Constance may have grown up with, and then I realized I wasn't defending Constance. I was defending me." Judy glanced at Rita. "And things went downhill from there."

"How so?"

"Robin began attacking her mother's choices, saying she wasted her life and that stung. I mean, looking back on mine, it's hard to argue the point. I spent years in a marriage that shouldn't have been, years running from something I couldn't outrun, and standing there, listening to her berate her mother for the lies she told, I realized Robin was right about one thing. When you love someone, you shouldn't be afraid to tell them the truth, so that's what I did. I told her the truth and destroyed our friendship in the process."

"What are you talking about?"

"I told her she was the reason I left Heritage and married Scott."

"Whoa," Rita said, her eyebrows raising a fraction. "And what did she say?"

"I ran out of the house before she could say anything."

"Why?"

"Because I knew I had just ruined our friendship. I didn't need to...I didn't need to hear anything else."

Rita crossed her arms, and cupping her chin in her hand, she tapped her finger against her lips. "Okay, we both know I'm a hopeless romantic, so I'm going to say this knowing you're going to laugh it off, but what if...what if she feels the same way?"

"What?"

"What if Robin feels the same thing for you as you feel for her?"

If Judy had had the strength to laugh, she would have, but instead, all she could muster was a blank stare. "She doesn't."

"Are you sure? She did remember you."

"That's only because some weird ass teacher talked her ear off every morning. That's probably hard to forget."

"But she is single, and she *is* gay."

"That doesn't matter."

"It doesn't?" Rita said, her face splitting into a grin.

Judy's blush was instant. "Well, yeah, of course, *that* matters, but Rita I'm fifty-five. I have more gray in my hair than brown, more wrinkles every day, more aches, more pains. What in the hell would a forty-something woman like Robin want in someone like me?"

"Christ, you're selling yourself so short."

"I prefer petite if it's all the same to you."

"Cracking jokes isn't going to make this go away."

"It's better than crying."

"Or running away, which is what you almost did today," Rita said, and getting up, she went over and stood in front of Judy. "Judy, running away is not the answer. You've *got* to know that."

Judy jumped off the workbench and snagged the almost empty six-pack. "I've been doing it my entire life, Rita. Why stop now?"

Chapter Thirty-Eight

"I don't blame her for storming out of the house."

"Yeah, but Declan, there's more—"

"Robin, talk about having your head up your ass!"

"If you'd just let me—"

"You have *no* right to judge your mother. No right to condemn her choices just because they didn't match yours. You're smarter than that, and I don't know why you couldn't see past your own goddamned feelings for one goddamned second to consider your mother's. And before you bring up that skank-of-the-year, yes, I know Pam did a fucking number on you, and yes, I know you carry the scars, but damn it all to hell, Robin, right now I'm ashamed to call you my friend."

"You won't be if you'd—"

"What the fuck were you thinking going off like that? Flaunting your supposedly superior choices and throwing stones when, all the while, you live in a fucking glass house! Because you *do* live in a glass house, Robin, or have you forgotten?" With the only sound on the line being that of Robin's breathing, Declan scowled. "Well, aren't you going to say anything?"

"Are you going to interrupt me if I try?"

"That depends on what you say."

"Well, how about I say that you're right. I was being a total ass and a total hypocrite, and you can even throw in idiot, fool, and a world-class moron, too. Will that work for you?"

"It's definitely a start."

"Declan, I was angry, and I was hurt, and I did every goddamn thing wrong. I didn't try to process. I didn't try to understand, and I sure as hell didn't try to put myself in my mother's shoes. From the moment I found out, all I could see was red. All I ever wanted was the best for her and—"

"What makes you think she didn't have the best? You're basing this on *you* again, Robin, instead of looking at the bigger picture. How much does someone have to love another person to...to do what your mother and Adele did? Jesus, they were willing to wait for decades, willing to steal time, willing to forego all those things couples in love do every flipping day. Hold hands, hug, the occasional PDA, not to mention living together or getting married."

"Declan, I know—"

"I don't think you do. Did you consider even for a *moment* what kind of strength it took to do what they did? What kind of commitment? How utterly amazing their love must have been, because I gotta tell you, kiddo, it sounds to me like they found what all of us want. Something so powerful, so all-consuming that you'd do anything to have it, and if you had to wait a lifetime for it, you would do it without question."

Declan's intensity brought a smile to Robin's face. "You know, I normally love your passion, Declan, but you're seriously beginning to try my patience. If you can give me more than just a few breaths to get out what I want to say, I think you'll see you and I are on the same page. Please?"

Declan rubbed the stubble on his face. "All right. Ball's in your court."

"Thanks," Robin said, and resting back on her sofa, she took a deep breath. "Like I was saying, at first, all I saw was red. I took a few days, trying to wrap my head around everything, and I thought I had it under control, but I was lying to myself. And when Judy showed up and basically told me to grow up, I erupted."

"And you two argued. I know that."

"Yes, but what you don't know is that Judy inadvertently put the shoe on the other foot, and by doing so, she gave me the swift, hard kick in the ass I needed. She made me see I was being a complete idiot, *and* I was being selfish, because once the roles were reversed, all of a sudden, nothing seemed catastrophic and nothing seemed insurmountable. Quite the contrary, actually."

"I'm not sure I'm following you."

"Declan, Judy told me she remembered me."

"What?"

"From school. She told me I was the reason she left."

Declan sat up straight on his sofa. "Are you saying what I think you're saying?"

"Honestly, I've been trying really hard today *not* to read more into it than what's there, but...but how can I not. Right?" Robin waited for a moment before glancing at her phone. "Are you still there?"

"Yeah. I'm just wondering why in the hell you're talking to me right now. I mean, this is your dream come true, Robbie, so why aren't you with Judy?"

"Trust me. That was my first thought, and a few minutes after Judy left, I tore off after her, but halfway up a hill the size of Kilimanjaro, I stopped and turned back around."

"Why?"

"Because my mother's secret sent me off the deep end, but Judy's made me euphoric, and I realized I can't have it both ways. Like you said, I live in a glass house. I can't condemn anyone for secrets when I have my own, and I sure as hell can't be biased, basing my reaction on whether it's to my advantage or not. It doesn't work that way."

"No, it doesn't."

"So, I came home, took my mom's cremation urn off the mantle, and she and I had a long talk. And before you think I'm off my nut, I talked. She listened."

Dimples appeared in Declan's cheeks. "How did it go?"

"A lot of tears, but they were good tears. I told her I'm still working on trying to understand, but I know I'll get there, and that no matter what, I will always love her. I'll always be proud to say I'm her daughter, and that she was the most amazing woman I've ever known." A hint of a grin appeared when Robin heard Declan sniffling. "Are you okay?"

"Yeah, kiddo. I'm good," Declan said, wiping the tears from his face with the back of his hand.

"After that, I went to Judy's, but by the time I got there, she was gone. I gave her a call and left her a message, then rode around the island for a while, hoping I'd find her. When I didn't, I called and left another message and then came home. That's when I saw her phone on the kitchen counter. She must have left it here this morning."

"So, you're planning to just wait there until she shows up?"

"It's either that or run around the island like a crazed stalker, and I've been on the receiving end of that, so waiting is my only option. Besides, I already told you, I'm trying not to jump to conclusions."

"Sounds like you really don't have to jump, Robbie." Declan waited for a few seconds and then frowned. "Okay, what's going on, and don't say 'nothing' because that's not going to fly? I understand the whole stalker scenario, but I know something else is going on in that beautiful head of yours, so spill it."

Robin sighed. "I'm a little scared."

Declan rocked back against the sofa and shouted to the ceiling. "Sweet Jesus, I will *never* in my *life* understand *women*. You have been in *love* with Judy since the dawn of freaking time, and now that it sounds like she feels the same way, you're scared? Of what? It's not like you don't have experience."

"There you go again—"

"All right. All right. My bad," Declan said, holding up his hand. "Everything's not about sex, but why on God's green earth would you feel scared?"

"Maybe apprehensive is a better word."

"Okay. Keep going."

"Declan, things too good to be true rarely come to fruition and that's where I am right now. I've been racking my brain all day, and I can't remember one time when Judy gave me even a sliver of an inkling as to how she may truly feel about me."

"That doesn't mean shit. You did it. Your mom did it. Adele did it. Why should Judy buck the..." Declan's voice trailed off as his mind took him down a different path. "Robin?"

"Yeah?"

"Judy doesn't know."

"What?"

"She doesn't know how you feel. You never told her, Robbie, and you sure as hell never showed her."

"What's that got to do with anything?"

Declan rolled his eyes. "Robin, your blonde is showing. Put the shoe on the other foot again."

"What?"

"It's one thing to have a crush on a teacher. It happens all the time, but when a teacher has a crush on a *student*, that's a whole different ball game. There are laws against that."

"But nothing happened, and I'm not her student anymore."

"I know that, but since Judy has no idea how *you* feel, right now all she knows is she's confessed to a former *student* that she's been crushing on you since *high* school."

***

When Judy attended Sunday School as a child, she was taught that confession was good for the soul. She was told it would help set free the stress. She was told it would help set free the guilt, but someone forgot to mention it did nothing for the pain. Stepping into her apartment, Judy flipped on the light, shut the door, and after placing the last two bottles of hard cider in the fridge, she went into her bedroom. She thought the tears had ended, but as she slumped to the floor, her eyes filled again. Judy had come full circle.

Much like the power in a battery, fading as the years had passed, before Robin had become a part of her life again, Judy's feelings for the woman had dulled. They always existed in the dark crevices of her mind, a place she rarely traveled unless urges too strong prevented her sleep, but in an immeasurable moment of time, they had returned. For years, she had avoided thinking about the past, but as Judy sat on the floor, crumpled and sad, reflections flooded her mind.

As she sat drinking wine and talking about a position she had no intention of taking, with a girl who was no longer a girl, a flutter deep within awoke. It was that flicker of awareness that convinced Judy *not* to take the job. She couldn't. She wouldn't...and then it rained.

A downpour from the heavens soaked the street and the sidewalk. A rider towing a Burley through the storm. A screech of fright. A muddy puddle, and the most adorable drenched woman she had ever seen, yet Judy's mind said no. It screamed it. It implored it. It *demanded* it, but in a whisper...her heart said yes.

Over wine, bar charts, and filing cabinets, Judy had stolen glances, and bit by bit the teenager she remembered morphed into a woman. Age is rarely subtle, but in Robin's case, it had made an exception. Her girlish prettiness had been replaced by a beauty only maturity can bring. The fine lines caused by laughter and happiness had yet to forever etch themselves in her face, but when amusement struck, they appeared, adding depth and charisma that took Judy's breath away.

The body language of youth, introverted and hesitant, had given way to an undaunted stride born from one who had walked enough miles to know the way, and the once angular teenager had gained just enough weight that her contours could very well have been sculpted by the masters. Judy left that night, never more aware of the heart beating in her chest, and when her head found the pillow, her mind raced. She wanted slumber to come for it would bring with it the dawn, but it would also bring a planned vacation one day closer. A vacation Judy no longer wanted...but duty was duty.

She awoke the next morning with the exuberance of a child at a birthday party with tons of sugar surrounding them. Judy had no idea what to expect that day, but any expectations she may have had, paled in comparison to what she received. The sight of a woman, sleepy-eyed and rumpled, and a glimpse of a stomach toned and flat had created a smile wider than any Judy believed she owned. Later, an accidental chest bump ended with her hands on hips, shapely and soft, and she managed only a few words before her mind emptied. Captured in the spell of winter-blue eyes variated with gossamer ribbons of silver, Judy took an indiscernible breath, inhaling the scent of a fragrance rich in amber and patchouli. It was to die for.

Throughout the day, her grins went unchecked. She watched as color drained at the mention of a ghost only for the lack to morph into scarlet from a playfulness unbridled by proximity. However, there *was* one moment of pause, a flicker of conflict when Judy heard the words 'I always have.' A quick escape was all that was needed to shake off the discomfort brought by bewilderment, but it reappeared again in another form.

Sexuality was known, splattered all over the Internet in biographies authorized, yet when Robin confessed the secret that wasn't a secret, its effect slithered through Judy's body and landed at her core. Had Robin noticed the slight shift, easing the pang brought on by the affirmation?

A spontaneous dinner invitation led to another spur-of-the-moment suggestion, a desire to show Robin the island Judy loved so much. Yet, beyond the history Judy could speak, beyond the trails and roads she knew would lead them to cemeteries and forts and homes lining the bluffs, and beyond all the ghost stories she knew by heart, there was something else driving Judy. A need she could not control, it was as old as it was new because attraction is formidable. Just ask a magnet when it comes upon a piece of steel.

That night, consumed by the nervous energy spawned from anticipation, Judy cleaned every crevice of her apartment. Her hope had been to quiet her mind, to still its travels down paths forbidden, but she had opened Pandora's Box when she accepted the job, and no matter how hard Judy tried, closing the lid was proving difficult. It had taken nearly three hours to dust, scrub, and polish, and three hours of mumbled scolding, growling condemnations, and shouted rebukes in her empty apartment before, showered and spent, Judy climbed into bed. Her thoughts were stilled. Her body was tired, and sleep came easily, and when she awoke the next day, Judy did it with a smile. How could she not?

But Mother Nature threw a wrench into Judy's plans. Winds too strong sent her mind into overdrive as she fought against gusts nearly knocking her over, but by the time she reached Safe Harbor, Judy had found her answer. It was easy, and the result would be the same. A day spent with Robin alone.

They easily conversed as they drove to Petoskey, but a shift in direction took Judy down a retrospective path. Blindsided, her world became tinted in green as she listened to talk about sports cars and women. Obscured by the emerald, Judy spoke the truth as she saw it and her extemporaneous compliment caused goosebumps to sprout. She rubbed them away and pushed aside her jealousy, only for it to return at lunch at the mention of numerous drawers being dropped numerous times. Unaccustomed to the green-eyed monster, Judy's reaction arrived without thought. Driven by envy, her tone became sharp and her attitude, curt, but seconds later, they were diluted by Robin's penitence. Judy knew Robin owed her no act of contrition, no bowed head or apology offered for it was Robin's right to have a life, to have a history that didn't include Judy…no matter how unsettling it was.

Her candor in the car hadn't been the only truthful blunder, the only divulgence spoken when Judy's guard was weakened. It *was* nice to hear Robin's voice that night in Indiana. Even a busy day hadn't lessened Judy's desire to be somewhere else, and 'funner' had plastered a grin across Judy's face so large, it took a moment before she could force a word through it. A clumsy question followed, and Judy's cheeks flamed, but continuing the conversation was worth every millimeter of the scarlet she wore.

A few days later, another phone call, and another night of awareness and honesty, and with the phone cradled, the card game preferred had been heard, and it had taken Judy's breath away. Her mind opened, and her mouth closed, and seconds ticked by before Robin's assumption gave Judy the answer she sought. A comment about resuscitation, while innocent, had brought an answer unexpected, and weakened by the possibility, Judy spoke the truth again. After all, she had covertly checked out Robin's form enough to know *exactly* what kind of shape it was in.

Eight days of dinners without the interruption of a ferry horn followed. Eight days of pacing the porch, debating whether she should call, but each time Judy went to do just that, she pocketed her phone instead. She walked the orchards at night, replaying their previous conversations in her head over and over again. Had her guard slipped so much that Robin had picked up on the truth, a truth that repulsed her, and a truth she would have preferred not to know? Is that why Robin no longer called? Was she sending a message with her silence?

Judy's answer came on the ninth day when the simplest of explanations erased over a week of worry in an instant. Robin hadn't read between the lines, and Judy's secret was safe, and when 'I really like you' slipped from Judy's lips, it carried with it a truth spoken from her heart...even though *like* was putting it mildly.

The decision to cut short her vacation was an easy one, and while no stop was needed for wallpaper, one was made for something else. Running with another would be in Judy's future, and she needed better than what she owned. Outdated and faded sweats were replaced by the latest in fashion, and color coordination became important for mismatched would no longer work, thus the need for a few new pairs of running shoes as well. Sports bras were also pulled from the racks as were sweaters, corduroys, and jeans, and even though Judy refused to acknowledge she was buying with only one person in mind...Judy was buying with only one person in mind.

Over the next few weeks, Judy's emotions continued to teeter-totter. They rose toward the heavens when she returned to Mackinac and exited the atmosphere when she was able to touch Robin's hair, the strands silky and lustrous between her fingers. But what goes up must come down, and a lumberjack upended Judy's euphoria, and a best friend's visit almost destroyed it.

It was a moment unforgettable. Awareness reminded Judy of the truth, and she regrouped almost instantly, but the wound of the original impression was gaping. Declan on one knee. Robin gazing at the ring. The inability to breathe followed by the excruciating pain of impending loss. The jealousy, the hatred, the embarrassment, the disgust, the anger, and the need to escape. As if looking through a child's kaleidoscopic toy, the images and feelings changed with every twist of the cylinder until Judy's stomach was in knots.

Repulsed by her own stupidity, Judy's need to leave was swift, and with the realization she *had* no entitlement, no right to feel the things she was feeling, she made it home in record time. It was a weekend filled with self-deprecating remarks mumbled out loud in an empty apartment and dealing with dogged brothers who wouldn't take no for an answer. At the time, Judy had no idea that those same brothers would give her the excuse she needed come Monday when her disparaging mood followed her into Safe Harbor.

Apologies and a childish race beat the last ounce of Judy's foul attitude into submission, and with the win came a day of running and whimsy spent in the sunshine, but on Friday, the abrupt arrival of a past lover turned Judy's world upside down.

Hatred was screeched, and vileness oozed, but the aftermath of the tempest is what left Judy reeling. Too much blood and a woman, unconscious in her arms. Tears that wouldn't stop until the sirens were heard. The agony of hiding emotions while others were near, and pretending she just entered the bedroom...when she hadn't.

Judy had stood there, blinking away the tears and gathering her wits. She told herself they were *friends*. She told herself she had to *be* a friend. She had to care and to tend without doing either too much, and she did until an unreachable clasp, and the feel of skin, warm and smooth sent Judy running toward the door. Privacy was important, but the effect had heated her face far beyond embarrassment.

The arrival of a new day brought with it walls that came down. Commentary followed and answers long sought were finally found, although one explanation hadn't been needed. Judy knew all too well what it felt like to be in love.

Wounds healed and the holiday arrived and with it came flowers, their purchase neither an afterthought nor haphazard. Each bloom Judy had handpicked from the florist's selection of autumn colors to guarantee one popular seasonal hue would *not* be included.

The perfect morning blended into an almost perfect afternoon, the only faux pas coming when Judy recognized a debt of gratitude was owed to a maniac. Robin's change of address coinciding with Pam's existence didn't sit well, but after an apology and a snowball, the day returned to being perfect.

Later that night, with bellies filled and wine bottles emptied, Judy was safe and content in Robin's world. Untroubled and relaxed in her surroundings her defenses weakened, and Judy became lost in the dream of another. Her purpose was to say good night, to bid farewell until tomorrow, but parted lips and shallow breathing beckoned Judy. An urge undeniable, she became the steel to Robin's magnet, but as she felt the warm caress of Robin's breath on her face, sensibilities returned and with them...they brought a gasp.

Judy's return to Safe Harbor the next day was slow, its pace set by a sleepless night replaying the memory of the near kiss she almost bestowed on Robin. It would have forever destroyed their friendship, and wary, Judy came into Safe Harbor not knowing what she would face, but firewood and decorating erased her worries.

Easy banter followed, and the day played out. Wood was stacked, and trees were erected, and then Judy found her hands on Robin's hips...again. God, how her body rushed at the touch, igniting her soul and her heart in a flash fire like no other, its embers refusing to die until she escaped to a basement, cool and quiet. And it was in that basement when secrets of another would eventually force Judy to reveal her own.

Judy wiped her nose with the back of her hand. She had been so successful at burying feelings that once stirred, evading at all cost the remembrances of the past that she had forgotten the strength of joy's embrace. Happiness was tenacious. Lust was potent, and love held in its grip the brute force of the undeniable and Judy shook her head. Disavowing was no longer possible. She had dug her own grave.

She glanced at the piles of gifts scattered around her apartment. All were wrapped in paper and ribbon and topped with bows shiny and new, but none had Robin's name attached to them. Judy had browsed in bookstores smelling of paper and coffee. She had contemplated in boutiques featuring the latest in fashion. She had pondered in shops featuring lotions, fragrant and soothing, and squaring her shoulders, Judy had even entered a store glittering with gold and diamonds.

That one had been her downfall for it held within its cases of glass so much she wanted to give. Judy knew love wasn't contained in necklaces or rings. It wasn't held in the amalgam that created platinum or silver. It was extravagant. It was corny. It was sentimental, and it was her...or rather it was who Judy had always wanted to be for Robin.

Judy sniffled again, and as she let out a long breath, she began pulling every suitcase she owned out from under the bed.

Chapter Thirty-Nine

Robin pedaled up to the little house, and gliding to a stop by a tree, she propped her bike against it. Taking a deep breath, she yanked off her cap, ran her fingers through her now shortened hair, and walked to the front door. Filling her lungs again, she pressed the doorbell, and as soon as the door opened, she quickly said, "I wouldn't blame you if you slammed the door in my face."

The two spots of rouge on Maxine's cheeks rose an inch. "Are you a Jehovah's Witness?"

"No," Robin said, unable to stop a grin from forming.

"Then you're safe," Maxine said, waving Robin inside. "And I love what you've done to your hair. Very stylish."

Robin rubbed the back of her neck. "Thanks," she said, and reaching into her jacket pocket, she pulled out a bag and handed it to Maxine.

"What's this?" Maxine said, taking the package.

"I seem to remember you enjoying the coffee we shared at my house. I blend my own beans, and...um...and I thought you might like some."

"Oh, you are a woman after my own heart," Maxine said, gesturing toward the kitchen. "But don't take that the wrong way."

Robin chuckled. "I wouldn't think of it."

A few minutes later, Maxine placed two empty mugs on the kitchen table and then slipped into the chair next to Robin's. "Coffee should be ready in about eight minutes."

"You've got it down to the minute?"

"When you're my age, every minute counts," Maxine said with a twinkle in her eye. "But I doubt you're here to talk about my age."

"I came here because I want to apologize for the other day. I was acting like an ass, and you didn't deserve that. It was inappropriate, and I'm sorry."

"Apology accepted," Maxine said, patting Robin on the hand. "But I think it was more than called for, Robin. Your mother should have told you."

Robin shrugged. "She had her reasons. It's not for me to understand them. I just have to accept them."

"My third husband used to say it was water under the bridge, and you either allow it to sweep you out to sea, or you swim to the shore. Your choice."

"Well, it sure as hell dashed me against the rocks."

"But it seems you survived intact."

"Not without a few aches and pains."

"Oh?"

"I had one hell of a hangover the next morning," Robin said, and then she jerked back her head. "Wait. You were married three times?"

"I was married four times," Maxine said with a laugh. "I divorced two of them and outlived the other ones."

"Wow."

"I wasn't always this old and wrinkled, Robin. I was quite the cat's meow back in the day."

"I'm sure you were," Robin said, and hearing the coffee maker beep, she pushed herself out of the chair. "I'll get that."

After filling their mugs, Robin sat down, taking a tentative sip of her coffee before raising her eyes to meet Maxine's. "I walked through the house this morning, looking at all the photos Adele had taken, and I couldn't help but feel a little sad."

"Why?"

"Because here Adele had all these memories hanging up all over the place, and my mother…my mother never did anything like that. It was as if Adele didn't exist in her life unless she was here."

"Robin, that couldn't be further from the truth. You just never realized it."

"Maxine, I'm telling you, my mom didn't have any photos like those. I packed up her house. I would have seen them."

"You're right. She didn't," Maxine said, warming her hands against her coffee mug. "Her fear of being outed was way too strong for her ever to do anything so blatant, and since you never knew about all those little vacations they took together, she wouldn't even hang up the ones without them in it."

"See, that's what I mean. There was nothing—"

"What did you do with your mother's paint-by-number?"

"Oh, it's in a box in the base—" Robin snapped back her head. "Wait. How did you know about that?"

"Because it was Adele's answer to your mother's dilemma."

"I don't understand."

"Adele knew all too well your mother would never hang up any of her photos or even take copies with her to stash away, so one year, Adele went out and bought two identical paint-by-numbers. The next time Constance visited, they sat down and painted them. The one your mother did, hangs in Adele's office and the one Adele painted—"

"Hung in my mother's bedroom."

"Exactly," Maxine said, smiling. "That way, your mother could always have something of Adele's around, and no one would ever be the wiser."

Robin grew quiet, drinking her coffee and staring off into space as she sorted her thoughts and her feelings. Placing her cup on the table, she looked at Maxine. "Tell me about them."

"What would you like to know?"

Robin paused for a second. "Did you ever see them together when they weren't pretending to be sisters? I mean, other than when you walked in on them kissing."

"Yes, I did," Maxine said as her mouth curved with tenderness. "It took some time before Adele could convince your mother I'd never share their secret, but once she did, they began inviting me over for dinner or cards, and sometimes shopping trips to the mainland. When we were out and about, they were obviously cautious, but in the house, behind closed doors, gosh, they'd dote on each other. I swear their grins were permanent. Sometimes they'd twitter like little girls when something struck them funny, and at others, they'd each get this look, and I'd know it was time for me to leave." Maxine smiled when Robin's eyebrows rose. "It's okay. They were in love. I didn't mind."

Maxine took a sip of her coffee and then relaxed back in her chair. "It always amazed me how they could hide their true feelings when they were out of the house because when they were inside, it was almost as if they were waltzing to a tune only they could hear. I felt very privileged to be a part of their world, Robin. Very privileged."

Robin sighed. "I know it was my mother's choice, but I still can't help thinking about all the time they lost being together because of it."

"Dear, when you get to be as old as I am, you're going to realize it's not about the quantity of time you spend with someone. It's about the quality. Sure, they didn't have a lot of days together, but the ones they had were priceless. They didn't have a lot of hours, but they made the most out of every one of them, and yes, they missed a lot of minutes, too, but I think they more than made up for them with *moments* they cherished. Far from prying eyes, those two women positively glowed when they were around each other, and you should have seen Adele as soon as Safe Harbor closed for the season. She'd be like a lighthouse."

"A lighthouse?"

"Positively beaming. As I'm sure you know, your mother visited at other times during the year, but that was always the longest vacation she took so it was extra special. Adele would tidy up the Inn and the yard and then tidy them again. She'd spruce and polish and fuss over every little speck until everything was perfect. And since, obviously, she knew how much your mother loved Christmas, she always went all out. She'd spend days working on the inside and then coerce some of her friends to come over and put up the lights outside since she didn't like heights."

"Now I know where..." Robin stopped, and hanging her head, she snickered. "I was about to say now I know where I get my fear of heights from, but I guess not—huh?"

Humor danced in Maxine's eyes. "No, I'm afraid not, but your mother was just the opposite."

"How did you know that?"

"She's the one who took them down."

Robin leaned back in her chair. "*Now* it makes sense."

"What does?"

"When Judy and I were decorating, all the lights for outside were wrapped perfectly, not one strand knotted with another, and that's got my mother written *all* over it." Robin paused and cocked her head to the side. "But the ones for the inside were a mess."

"That's because everything inside didn't come down until after your mother went home."

"Why?"

Maxine's pencil thin eyebrows drew together. "You haven't decorated the trees yet, have you?"

"Um...no. Once we found the trunk, everything kind of went south. Why?"

"I don't know when it started or who started it, but your mother and Adele always got each other ornaments for Christmas, but Adele saw no point in unwrapping them and putting them on the tree, only to take them right back down. So, the inside of the house was left decorated until after your mother left. Adele would eventually pack everything away, but I can remember a few years when that didn't happen until February."

"Geez."

"It made sense though. Every ornament held a memory, and I'm sure it was hard to pack them away. That's another reason why the photographs in the rooms were so important to Adele. She didn't *have* to pack them away."

"Oh, God," Robin blurted. "Please tell me you didn't do what I asked."

"What do you mean?"

"You didn't burn them, did you?"

"Robin, please. I may be old, but I'm not senile. Of course, I didn't burn them. They're in the other room with the rest of the stuff."

"What stuff?"

Maxine's mouth dropped open. "Oh, that's right. We never got that far, did we?"

"No, I huffed, and I puffed, and then I left."

"Come on," Maxine said as she stood up. "I'll show you. That is if you have time."

With Judy's phone held hostage in her back pocket, Robin grinned to herself as she got to her feet. "Yeah, I have time."

Robin soon found herself standing in one of Maxine's spare bedrooms. Minimally decorated with sensible contemporary furniture, tatted doilies covered the tops of the butternut bureau and nightstands, while the bed was protected by a mint green chenille bedspread. A crystal bowl filled with potpourri explained the scent of roses in the air, but the rest would have to be left up to Maxine.

"Is that the stuff you were talking about?" Robin said as she pointed to the boxes on the bed.

"Yes. It all belongs to you now."

Robin stared at the stack, but she didn't move an inch. "I'm afraid to ask what's in them."

"Don't worry, dear," Maxine said, patting Robin on the arm. "They didn't have a love child."

Whatever anxiety Robin was feeling disappeared in an instant and featherlike laugh lines appeared on her face. "That's good to know, although I always wanted a sister."

"Well, you won't find any in there," Maxine said, gesturing toward the pile. "The largest is filled with some books Adele preferred not to give away, including copies of all the ones you wrote."

"Really?"

"Oh, yes. Adele loved them," Maxine said, as she pointed to the next. "That one over there has a bunch of photos like the ones I showed you the other night, plus a ton of others Adele took over the years. And the last three contain mementos and gifts your mother gave Adele, except for that stupid clown, of course."

"Wait. What?"

"You did find the clown, didn't you?"

"Yes. It scared the crap out of me, but why in the world would my mother buy that for Adele? I know her tastes, and that clown doesn't even come close."

"She didn't *exactly* buy it," Maxine said with a laugh. "Adele told me that when they took their first...um...their first trip together, they were both a little nervous. They were driving into Canada, and when they came upon a town having a carnival, they stopped to grab some food and look around. Your mother ended up winning that hideous thing at one of those booths." Maxine shook her head as she began to titter. "God, Adele hated it, but she couldn't get rid of it to save her life."

"Why not?"

"It was the first thing your mother ever gave her, and before you ask, Constance thought it was ugly, too. She told Adele to toss it out dozens of times, but Adele wouldn't do it. She'd keep it stored in the basement until your mother visited, and then she'd bring it upstairs."

"Did my mother know—"

"Oh, yes. She knew. It ended up being a running joke."

Robin smiled for a moment and then slapped her hands against her hips. "Crap!"

"What's wrong?"

"That means I can't throw it out either."

"Oh, I'm sure Adele would understand—"

"No. Ugly or not, it meant something to both of them. I just don't know what I'm going to do with it."

"You'll figure it out," Maxine said with a wave of her hand. "It's a big house. You'll find a place for it."

"Here's hoping," Robin said as she glanced at the bed. "What's in the other boxes?"

"The shoe boxes have cards and letters they sent to each other."

"Love letters?" Robin squeaked.

"I don't know. I didn't read them, sweetie."

Robin sighed. "I'm not sure I can."

"You have all the time in the world to decide that. If and when you're ready, you'll have them."

"Wait," Robin said, looking back and forth between the boxes and Maxine. "You said letters and cards they sent each *other*. If Adele sent my mother letters, how could they be here?"

"Esther sent them to Adele after your mother died, and in turn, Adele gave them to me to protect when she went into the rest home."

"Esther? As in my mother's neighbor in Monroeville? How in the hell did she get them? I'm confused."

"So was I at first, but apparently your mother and Adele had one thing in common, which was thinking ahead. Constance never wanted you to find any of her keepsakes, but she couldn't bring herself to destroy them either, so she asked this Esther woman to keep them safe, and if anything ever were to happen to your mother, Esther was to send everything to Adele."

Robin shook her head. "My mother missed her calling. With foresight like that, *she* should have been the mystery writer."

"And speaking of mysteries, the last box contains all the research Adele did on Isobel that she didn't want to fall into the wrong hands. The poor thing was tormented enough in life without having to be tormented in death, too."

"What in the world are you talking about?"

Maxine jammed her hands on her hips. "You know, for such a prolific mystery writer, you sure do suck at solving them. You found the staircase and opened the window seat in the living room, didn't you?"

"Yeah. So?"

"So, didn't you *look* at anything?"

"Of course, I did," Robin said, the tone of her voice sliding up the scale. "There was a bunch of sketches which I assumed Isobel had done, a laundry list of people who had owned the house before Adele, census data, a copy of the original blueprint for the Inn, lots of notebooks and photocopies of newspaper clippings and stuff, pencils, pens...and...and an easel. What did I miss?"

"Did you *read* anything?"

"Yes, but no offense, I didn't *know* I was supposed to be trying to solve a mystery, now did I?" The dots of rouge on Maxine's cheeks darkened a few shades, and Robin grinned. "So, what exactly did I miss that I wasn't looking for in the first place?"

"Well, for starters, if you had looked at the laundry list as you called it, you would have seen that no one ever lived in that house for very long before Adele bought it."

"Okay?"

"Doesn't it strike you odd that a house as beautiful as Safe Harbor would change hands so often?"

"I guess. I didn't really think about it."

Maxine pursed her lips. "Obviously," she said, and opening one of the boxes, she pulled out a wad of manila folders. Thumbing through them, she finally fanned one open and turned it so Robin could see. "Now, I know for a fact Adele left a few photos in the window seat, and this woman was in one of them. She would have been standing with a lot of children. Do you recognize her?"

The photo in the newspaper clipping was grainy, and Robin wished she had her glasses. Taking a long moment to peer at the woman in the picture, Robin shook her head. "I'm not sure. The quality's not very good."

"Most tintypes weren't, but do me a favor and look again."

Robin did as Maxine asked and then sighed. "Honestly, Maxine, I just glanced at the photos. They were really old and in with the census data. I just figured they were some of the people who once lived in the house."

"True, they were, but if you found the stairway, it doesn't really matter if you paid attention to those old pictures or not. You should *still* know who this person is."

Robin took her time and looked at the photo again. "Oh, shit. This is Isobel."

"No, it's not."

"Of course, it is. This is the same woman whose face is sketched all over my walls. Trust me. I've sat on those stairs for hours, studying those drawings."

Maxine removed the newspaper clipping and unfolded the paper. Handing it to Robin, she said, "Take a minute to read this article and then tell me again, who this woman is. I have a feeling you're going to come to the same conclusion your aunt...um...I mean, Adele did."

Robin sat on the edge of the bed, reading the newspaper clipping dated over a hundred years before. As each word was absorbed, her brow began to furrow. "I know this name," she said, looking up at Maxine. "Julia Cooper was a servant for the guy who built the house. Her name was...her name was on the census Judy read to me."

"That's right," Maxine said. "And Adele believed—"

"I know what she believed," Robin whispered as tears began to cloud her vision. "That Julia didn't drown. That she killed herself just like Isobel. The same way. The same place." Robin raised her eyes. "And for the same reason."

***

"This is the last of it."

Sheldon Graham glanced at the suitcase in Judy's hand and then at the pile of luggage already stacked in the back of the carriage. Shoving a duffle bag to the side, he placed the last case next to it and began strapping everything in. "It seems what they say about women is right."

"Oh yeah? What's that?"

"If they can't decide what to wear, they bring everything they own."

Judy forced a weak smile. "Yeah, well, it is what it is."

"Okay," Sheldon said, yanking on the last tie-down to make sure it was secure. "We're ready to go."

They both climbed into the carriage, and as they started down the street, Judy said, "Shelly, can you do me a favor?"

"Sure, Jude. What's that?"

"I'm cutting things a little close to make the last ferry, so could you drop me off at Safe Harbor and then take my stuff to the dock? That way, we won't piss off Glen if we show up just when the boat's ready to leave."

Sheldon nodded as he guided the horses around the corner. "That's not a problem. You want me to come back and pick you up?"

"No, it's a short walk. I can make it on time. Thanks."

Chapter Forty

Robin sat on the step sipping her wine and looking back and forth between the old newspaper article and the sketches on the wall. The upturned nose, the compelling eyes, the genial mouth, and the full lips appearing in most matched the grainy photo, but moving to within a few inches of the plaster, Robin focused on a sketch that did not. The woman's eyes were sad, and in their melancholy, despair lurked, the weight of a world not ready for her ilk pressing down on her. There were others, camouflaged amongst the hundreds of Julia that showed a different Isobel. An Isobel who yearned. An Isobel who loved. An Isobel who laughed and who was joyous for a millisecond of her life, but Robin kept returning to this one. Unvarnished, the illusion of hope eradicated by truth was as potent as any she'd ever seen, and Robin's heart broke.

Robin knew the statistics of now, the amount of her community who took their lives because the stigma attached was cumbersome, yet she had never considered those who had come centuries before. Trapped in a world far too narrow to ever dare broach the truth of their own persuasion, they had no helplines to call. They had no shelters to seek, no outlets offering guidance or organizations crowded with the like-minded where they'd feel welcomed and normal. All they had were the shadows in which they hid, the lies in which they lived, and an abrupt end to their own existence…when denial was impossible.

"I'm sorry," Robin whispered, blinking away her tears as she looked up at the curved plaster covered in sketches. "I'm sorry you didn't have the chance to be who you were."

Robin had been sitting in the stairwell for over an hour. Her glass was empty, and her bottom was sore, so giving the wall one last glance, she got to her feet. "And she's beautiful, by the way. Not that I need to tell you that," Robin said over her shoulder as she started down the stairs. Out of nowhere, the slightest of breezes swept through the stairwell, and Robin smiled. "You're welcome."

She intended to refill her glass and then relax in the living room, but when Robin walked out of the spare bedroom, she noticed a light coming down the hallway. Changing direction, she headed for the big kitchen.

Judy moved like a thief in the night, carefully sliding the cookbooks on the counter out of her way before opening and closing every cabinet and drawer. "Where the hell is it?" she muttered under her breath.

As soon as Judy came into view, Robin's face lit up, but storm clouds rolled in seconds later when she noticed the backpack Judy hadn't bothered to remove. Thinking for a moment, Robin took a deep breath and summoned a grin. "Hi there."

Judy froze in place, bowing her head as the mere sound of Robin's voice did to her body what it had been doing for weeks. She squeezed her eyes closed, waiting for the last tingle to pass before she took a slow, even breath and turned around. "Hi," Judy said, her eyes finding the floor a split-second later.

"I didn't know you were here."

"Sorry. I...um...I didn't want to bother you, and I don't have a lot of time anyway."

Robin glanced at her watch. She knew the ferry schedule, and the last one for the day was leaving in twenty minutes. "You catching the ferry?"

"Yeah. Um...Pat's birthday."

"So you decided to go then?"

"Sixty. It's a milestone. I need to be there."

"Gotcha," Robin said, her eyes fixed on the woman who was intent on staring at the floor.

The hum of the refrigerator's compressor was the only sound to be heard as one gazed and the other avoided eye contact at all cost.

Seconds that felt like hours ticked by until Judy took a deep breath and turned toward the counter again. "I...um...I just stopped by to get my phone. I swear I left it here. Have you seen it?" she said, opening and closing drawers and cabinets she had already checked. "I really don't want to leave without it."

Robin took her time in answering. She didn't want to lie, but if she left the room would Judy be there when she got back? Robin sighed. "Yeah, I found it," she said quietly. "Give me a minute. I'll go get it."

When Robin returned, she placed Judy's phone on the island. "It started beeping last night. I was going to charge it for you, but we don't have the same phones, so I shut it off. Sorry."

"Not a problem. It's old, and the battery's been draining really fast," Judy said, and grabbing her phone, she slipped it into her back pocket. "And I have a charger in the car."

"That's good," Robin said, trying her best to mentally force Judy to look up. "So, when will you be back?"

Judy shook her head and moved to leave. "I don't know."

"Wait," Robin said, and taking two quick steps, she blocked Judy's path. "You *are* coming back, aren't you?"

"Robin, I can't...I can't do this right now. I'm going to miss the ferry."

"So miss it. There's another tomorrow and more after that, but don't...don't run away. We need to talk."

"No, we don't," Judy said, taking a step backward. "I should never...I should never have said what I said. Just forget it. Just forget everything."

"I can't do that."

"You have to," Judy said, looking up at the clock. "And I have to go."

As soon as Judy took a step, Robin touched her on the arm, and when Judy pulled away as if she'd been burned, Robin's face fell. "I'm sorry. I just want to talk."

"There's nothing to talk about, Robin. I made a mistake. Just leave it at that."

"No, I won't leave it at that, Judy."

"Robin, please—"

"Would you like me to describe everything *you* had on that last day at Heritage? Because I can, right down to the signet ring you used to wear."

Judy couldn't help but look down at her hands. It had been a present from her mother, but the band had thinned over time, and Judy had put it away. She hadn't thought about it in years, and she tilted her head. How odd Robin would have remembered something so small and insignificant. It *should* have gone unnoticed. It should have been forgotten with time. Judy flinched and taking a step backward, she bumped into the counter. The night before Judy had made up her mind, and she knew what she needed to do. She knew what she *had* to do, and she *was* prepared to do it, but absolutes can change in an instant. Up is up and down is down...until it isn't.

Judy's lungs emptied, and with it, she said the first word that came into her head. "Shit."

Robin's grin was automatic. "Not exactly the reaction I was going for."

Even though Judy had heard what Robin had said, she didn't say a word...because she was now under assault.

Conflict is derived from opposition. Battles are fought for land, for rights, and for freedom, and clashes turn into combat and morph into wars, but the discord between a heart and a mind can be the fiercest. Both work in harmony to breathe, to walk, and to talk, but when it comes to love, when it comes to yearning and passion, they can disconnect...and Judy's had done just that.

Her mind raced, and her thoughts swarmed like bees in her head, the buzz in her ears getting louder and louder until all went suddenly quiet. The truth hadn't changed. Robin's confession had only added to Judy's heartache, and for the first time, Judy looked Robin square in the eye. "It doesn't matter what you were going for, it's not going to happen."

Robin froze as Judy moved past her, allowing Judy enough time to reach the dining room before Robin caught up and stopped her again. "Judy, what's going on? It's obvious we feel the same way about each other. You admitted it. I just admitted it. What's the problem?"

Judy's jaw tensed, her hands fisting as she forced out the words. "I'm sorry, Robin," she said in a whisper. "I can't do this."

Robin's eyes turned glassy as she watched Judy walk across the foyer. "No!" she shouted, and in three long strides, she caught up with Judy inches before she reached the door. "You need to explain. You need to tell me what this is all about. Damn it, Judy. I'm in love with you, and I think...no, I *know* you're in love with me. I can see it. I can feel it, and I'm not going to let you walk out this freaking door until you tell me the truth."

"Robin, I'm too old—"

"Don't give me that crap. Age is just a number, and it's got *nothing* to do with this. You're just using it as an excuse, but I don't want excuses, Judy. I want the truth. I'm begging you. Please don't walk out that door like you walked out of that classroom. Please...*please* just tell me the truth."

As her eyes misted over with tears, Judy took a stuttered breath, and then she took another. "The truth is...the truth is the price is too high."

"What price? What price is too high? I don't understand."

"It's about choices, Robin," Judy whispered. "Just like back in school, I had to make a choice. You were eighteen. You were off limits. You were...*are* something I can't have, because if I do, if I choose you, if I choose *this* life, I lose my family."

All the air was knocked from Robin's body, and as she struggled to replace it, the fog lifted. "This is about what you said when we argued, isn't it? That family you were describing...that family was yours. Wasn't it?"

Judy brushed away the tears staining her cheeks. "Yes."

"And you agree with them?"

"Of course not," Judy said with a sigh. "But this isn't about agreeing with anyone. It's about things that are familiar. It's about family. It's about—"

"Duty?"

"No. It's not about duty. It's about deceit because whether you want to accept it or not, age *does* have something to do with this, Robin. I'm not saying it would have been easier if I had found the courage when I was eighteen or twenty or even twenty-eight, but I'm fifty-five now, and I've had fifty-five years of having a family. I've had fifty-five years of belonging. I've had fifty-five years of someplace I could always call home. And even if my brothers have softened over the years, even if they aren't as homophobic as they used to be, which I *seriously* doubt, once they find out that I've been lying to them for over *forty* years, they're going to tell me to get the hell out and never come back."

"But what about being happy, Judy? What about being loved and wanted, and living the truth instead of the lie? Doesn't any of that matter?"

"At this stage in my life, what's the point?" Judy said as she turned to leave.

Robin took another step closer. "Please don't walk out that door. Please don't walk out on us."

Judy bowed her head. Her heart was breaking and in the fissure was a love so strong her legs had grown weak. She knew she couldn't turn around. She couldn't look at Robin for the last time in her life and see nothing but pain. She wanted to remember her smiling, the blue of her eyes sparkling like pale sapphires refracting every ray of sunshine pouring from the heavens. She wanted to remember her mouth, tempting and sensuous, its arch conveying joy that took Judy's breath away, and she wanted to remember Robin's laughter, gleeful and sometimes childlike, holding in its melody something Judy could live off for days.

Judy put her hand on the doorknob. "There is no us, Robin. I'm sorry, but I have to—" Judy's shoulders sagged, and closing her eyes, she bowed her head until her forehead was touching the door.

Robin allowed herself a quick grin when the distant sound of a ferryboat horn found its way to her ears. "Sounds like you missed the ferry. Guess that means we have more time to talk."

"I don't want to talk anymore."

"Then stay the night," Robin said, her voice soft and breathy. "Give me the night, Judy. Give *us* the night. There's no tomorrow, no family, no prejudice or judgments. There's just tonight. Just you. Just me. Just *us*."

Judy shook her head. "Sex isn't going to change anything, Robin."

"I'm not talking about having sex, Judy. I'm talking about making love. I'm talking about giving in to what we both feel, what we both want, what we've both dreamed about for so very long. I'm not stupid. I know your mind is made up, and I know tomorrow you're going to break my heart. I know I can't live in closets, and I know you'd never ask me to, so this is it." Robin paused, wiping the tears from her face. "Tonight is all we have, Judy, so let's stop the world from turning for just one night. No apologies. No regrets. No tomorrow. Just tonight."

The ice had grown thin, and Judy knew if she fell through she'd be swept away in an instant. A glorious instant that would bring pleasure for a night, but when the sun appeared over the horizon, the memory would bring a lifetime of pain, and Judy was tired of hurting. She was tired of thinking, tired of being pummeled by emotions and responsibilities. Judy had made her choice, but as she placed her hand on the doorknob again, a chill ran down her spine. She hesitated, her eyes widening as she watched the latch for the deadbolt turn on its own, sliding into the keeper on the jamb with an audible click.

Judy froze, trying to wrap her head around Isobel's intrusion, and as she did, a current of cold air washed over her. A moment later, she felt the warmth of Robin's breath...on the back of her neck.

Chapter Forty-One

Attraction. Although not a branch of physics, the rules of attraction are much like those of electromagnetism. A physical interaction that happens between particles that are electrically charged, some objects are drawn toward one another, their need undeniable, their attraction...molecular.

The world stopped turning, and a mind fraught with thoughts emptied as a heart only ever belonging to one began to pound. The scent of Robin's cologne and the heat of nearness had broken the ice, and as Robin's breath washed over her neck, the surge of awareness rushing through Judy's body took her breath away.

In the throw of a latch, Robin's expectations were altered, and she moved to within inches of Judy in an instant. Her heart began to race, but with anticipation came apprehension. If she moved too fast, would Judy run? Robin pushed away her fear. She had no intention of moving too fast.

Robin slipped her hand under Judy's chin, her body pulsing at the mere connection of skin against skin. No effort was needed to turn Judy toward her, and Robin looked into her eyes. There was no longer a need to be covert, a need to hide the hunger, the ardor, or the desire, and when Robin saw the same gazing back at her, the air rushed from her lungs. She slowly lowered her mouth to meet Judy's, and as Robin's eyes fluttered closed, her dream became her truth.

By definition, dreams rarely contain certainty. A state of mind whereby the holder is released from reality, the situations conjured are often abstract and skewed based on the emotion. Hate generates an early demise. Revenge creates ingenious plots, and lust fabricates eroticism normally paling to the truth, but as far as Judy was concerned, there was nothing pale about their first kiss.

The brush of Robin's lips against hers sent a shock wave through Judy's body. Although the kiss was tentative and light, the feathery hint held in its brevity sensations unmatched in Judy's life. Every nerve awoke, every sense heightened, and instincts forever denied...could no longer be.

The kiss ended, and Judy opened her eyes, lifting her chin ever so slightly. It was a silent invitation for more, and Robin did not disappoint. Lips, supple and warm, found their way back to Judy, and while the kisses that followed were still brief, lasting only seconds, Judy cherished every one of them.

There are no guarantees in life, but when Robin kissed Judy for the first time, she knew it was the last *first* kiss she would ever have. There could never be another, and in that instant, she finally understood the love Adele had for her mother, and Isobel had for Julia. All-consuming and unwavering, Robin's love for Judy was unconditional, and as she turned her head this way and that, returning Judy's kisses with those of her own, Robin cherished her last second kiss, her last third, and her last fourth.

Passion brings with it many things. Hearts begin to race. Pulses start to quicken. Breathing becomes labored, and temperatures rise. Gasping for air, Judy pulled out of Robin's arms.

"What?" Robin said in a breath, her eyes widening as she glanced at the latch on the door.

"Hot," Judy said, her mouth falling open as she pulled in more air. "I'm hot."

Robin smiled. Judy had to be wearing at least three layers of clothing to protect her from the chilly autumn on Mackinac, so while the woman shrugged out of her backpack, Robin scrambled for the tab of the zipper on Judy's parka. A second later, Robin blurted, "It's stuck."

Judy burst out in giggles, her sex drive momentarily taking a back seat while Robin pulled, tugged, and cursed at the fastener. "Here, let me do it," Judy said, reaching for the zipper. "Unless you want to spend the entire night in the foyer?"

Robin popped up like a jack-in-the-box. Taking a step back, she held up her hands. "Not on your life."

"Yeah, I thought not," Judy said, and continuing to chuckle, she yanked the zipper up and then down. A moment later, Judy's jacket fell to the floor. The comical intermission could have easily broken the mood, but the woman Judy wanted to remember was now standing in front of her. *There* was the smile she never wanted to forget. *There* were the eyes, vivid and lustrous, and *there* was the beauty that would forever take her breath away. "Now," Judy whispered. "Where were we?"

Robin groaned. Other than placing her fingers on Judy's face when they kissed, Robin hadn't dared to allow her hands to stray. There had been a modicum of fear restraining her, concern about a lock that could easily be unlocked, yet it only took three little words to set Robin free. In one quick step, she pulled Judy into her arms. Again, the kiss was gentle, and again, the kiss was slow for when there's no tomorrow, memories have to be savored, and when Robin felt Judy's hands on her hips, pulling her even closer, Robin's body pulsed.

Judy moved her mouth over Robin's, answering in kind with whisper-light kisses until the urge for something else became too intense. Judy wanted more than whispers, more than gentle, and more than chaste, and when Robin lowered her mouth again, Judy ran the tip of her tongue across Robin's lips. The result took Judy's breath away. The ache of her arousal was like nothing she had ever experienced, and desire oozed from her core, soaking through her underwear and darkening the denim of her jeans.

Robin fisted the fabric of Judy's sweater. A hint of a tongue warm and wet had set her body on fire, and there was no putting out the blaze. She covered Judy's mouth in a kiss, hungry and deep, exploring every recess of Judy's mouth with her tongue. Her flavor was a blend of coffee, mint, and something entirely Judy's and Robin drank in the cocktail. Thirsty for the sweetness, Robin reclaimed Judy's mouth again and again, and when Judy's tongue began to dance with hers, Robin's knees almost buckled.

Judy was lost in a whirlpool of carnal need. She couldn't help but taste Robin as she, herself, was being tasted. She couldn't help but plunge her tongue into a mouth welcoming every stroke, losing herself to an essence intrinsic to Robin.

Invitation after voracious invitation was given and accepted, until fighting for oxygen, they both came up for air. Robin rested her forehead against Judy's, and both fought to regain control of their breathing as a few minutes went by unnoticed.

Robin lifted her head, licking her lips to replace moisture drained by an appetite shared. "Can we...can we take this somewhere else?"

"Yes," Judy said in a breath before sucking in another. "Yes, please. Yes."

Robin intertwined her fingers through Judy's. Slowly and silently she guided her through the house to her bedroom, and it wasn't until they stepped inside when Judy's grip tightened.

"What?" Robin whispered.

Judy motioned toward the many candles flickering atop the bureau, dresser, and nightstands. "Hedging a bet?"

Robin's eyes creased at the corner as she reached down for the hem of Judy's sweater. "No," she said, pausing as if waiting for permission. "Saying lots of prayers."

Judy's gaze met Robin's, and with an infinitesimal nod, she lifted her arms and a moment later, her burgundy V-neck was tossed aside. Still wearing a flannel shirt and long-sleeved tee, the coolness of the room hadn't yet found its way to Judy, but by the look in Robin's eyes, Judy knew it wouldn't be long.

A few hours earlier, Robin had changed into her lounge-around-the-house clothes. The drawstring sweatpants and long-sleeved thermal top hidden under a gray hoodie made sense at the time. The old house was sometimes drafty and cold, but Robin was anything but cold. She reached for the zipper on her sweatshirt, but before she could find the tab, Judy pushed her hand away and then ever so casually drew the zip downward. The fleece found the floor a second later, and a second after that, Robin began unbuttoning Judy's flannel.

Riveted by the need she saw on Robin's face, Judy stood motionless as yet another layer of her clothing was removed. Robin knelt at her feet for as long it took to untie her hiking boots, and after Judy kicked them off, while her height shrunk by an inch, her boldness grew by a mile. No longer wanting anything between them, Judy stripped off her long-sleeved T and threw it aside.

With the only light in the room coming from the candles, Robin couldn't tell if Judy's bra was pale blue or pale green, but edged in lace and thin in material, nipples pebbled and hard could be seen through the fabric. Robin's body tingled with awareness, and wasting no time, she rid herself of her own thermal. She pulled Judy back into her arms, and swooping down, Robin captured Judy's lips in a kiss, ravenous and wet, laying claim to what was hers...if only for one night.

Judy relinquished all control of her body to Robin, melting against her and relishing the feel of her fingers as they danced over her skin. Goosebumps would appear and then fade in an instant as Robin's hands roamed over her arms, her back, and her shoulders, and when they returned to a clasp, Judy craved for its release. Their lips parted, and through heavy-lidded eyes, she looked up at Robin. Her bra loosened, and Judy unconsciously held her breath as Robin drew the straps down her arms.

She expected to feel exposed, to feel somewhat bashful, somewhat disconcerted standing half naked in front of Robin, but instead, Judy felt emancipated. Freed from the burden of obligations and secrets, autonomy had finally found her, and it felt wonderful. For *this* moment in time, she could be who she was. For *this* moment in time, she could love who she wanted, and for *this* moment in time...she would.

Age *is* just a number for in the throes of passion, ageless minds and timeless instincts take over. Hands lightly speckled with spots are forgotten, wrinkles everlasting go unseen, and breasts no longer as perky as they once were remain breathtaking in the eye of the beholder.

Robin lowered her eyes and swallowed the moisture building in her mouth. Creamy and round, with peaks aroused and dark, Judy's breasts were faultless. They rose and fell with her breathing, Judy's gasps as shallow as Robin's were becoming, and as Robin locked eyes with Judy, she reached out and cupped a breast in each hand. In unison, they sighed, Judy's eyes closing and Robin's opening wider as she became entranced by the orbs in her hands. Velvety and warm, they fit perfectly against her palms, and she held them for a moment before running her thumbs over the tips. In an instant, the centers grew rigid, and Robin licked her lips. Sliding her hands to Judy's waist, Robin spun them around so she could sit on the edge of the bed, and pulling Judy close, Robin tasted the fruit no longer forbidden.

"Oh, God," Judy said in a breath, her head falling back as she buried her hands in Robin's hair.

Robin captured a nipple between her lips, gently tugging on the tip before sweeping her tongue around it, teasing it, tempting it, and making it grow even harder in her mouth while she tended to Judy's other breast with her fingers. Massaging and then tweaking the tip of one while she suckled hard against the other, Robin kept one hand firmly on Judy's back, holding her close while the woman arched and squirmed...but Judy wasn't the only one squirming.

With Judy standing between her knees, Robin couldn't close her legs to temporarily squelch her libido. Her inner walls were pulsing almost in time with the beat of her heart and with each throb, her titillation flowed. Glistening and thick, it had already soaked through her panties, and she knew without looking the light-gray material of her sweatpants had darkened to the color of charcoal. While the position afforded her a banquet of decadent delights, the raw ache in her core, although pleasurable, was rapidly becoming punishing.

Robin lifted her eyes and waited until Judy's fluttered open. The coolness of the room no match for the fever building between them, Judy's face was flushed, and her brow gleamed with perspiration, and Robin licked her lips again. One beat of her heart later, her fingers found the fasteners on Judy's jeans.

As Robin drew the denim down over her hips, Judy stepped away long enough to rid herself of something no longer wanted, but her eyes remained on Robin. Her bra was black, underwired and sculpted to present, and the fullness of hidden treasure rose above the spandex. Entranced, Judy watched as Robin stood up for a moment, and as she stepped out of her sweatpants, a wealth of the woman's cleavage came into view. When Robin straightened a second later, Judy swallowed hard at the magnificence before her.

Robin's skin appeared like that of a porcelain doll, flawless and ivory, and although the contrast was stark against the ebony of her underwear, it was nonetheless, stunning. Judy had seen Robin wear skinny jeans enough to know she was slender, but without clothes, new dimensions were now added.

Years of long-distance running could be seen in thighs defined by muscles, and a stomach thought toned became far more than that. Robin's waist was indeed narrow, and her hips, curvaceous and deliciously feminine, and Judy drew in a deep breath. She wanted to see more...and she wanted to touch.

Judy took a step, raising her mouth at the same time Robin's descended toward her and when their lips met, Judy found the clasp of Robin's bra and freed it. The sound of Robin's moan was all it took for Judy to deepen the kiss, and their bodies separated only long enough to allow the bra to slip away. They came back together, bare breasts pressing against bare breasts and feeding on the sweetness of Robin's mouth, Judy's urges grew wanton.

Robin succumbed to Judy's tongue, to her taste, and to her hunger until the aroma of their arousal was thick in the air. It rose from between them, a musky fragrance born from lustful fervor, and when she felt Judy's hands on her breasts, a lazy stream of sensual wetness began making its way down Robin's thigh.

Breaking out of the kiss, Robin's mouth dropped open as she sucked in air. "Oh, Jesus," she murmured, and grabbing the quilt covering her bed, she yanked it down. Lowering Judy to the sheets, Robin moved on top of her, and slipping her leg between Judy's, Robin slowly began to rock.

Judy arched instantly, reveling in the pressure of Robin's knee against the junction of her thighs, and a thin layer of cotton did nothing to dampen the sensation. She opened her eyes for a moment as Robin hovered over her. Her eyes had turned dark, and in the inkiness was lust and possession. At that moment, Judy knew she had become clay, and as she closed her eyes, Robin became her sculptor.

Robin blazed her way across Judy's neck and shoulder with a trail of kisses while never losing the rhythm she had set. Over the years, when Robin's fantasies had brought her to this point, her imagination had conjured up a utopian intimacy beyond compare. A world of make-believe where feelings and fluids were copious. A world where erotic wants were answered in kind, and a world where animal impulses went untamed. At the time, Robin had no idea the world her mind had created could possibly exist, but she did now.

With each slide of her body, Judy was moving against her knee, and with each kiss bestowed on skin dampened by sweat, Judy would writhe under her, rubbing her breasts against Robin's in a bawdy show of need. Gulping for air, Robin rolled to her side long enough to strip off her panties, and getting to her knees, she looked down at Judy, swallowing hard when Judy raised her hips.

Cotton now darker in areas than the blue purchased was drawn down Judy's legs, and Robin breathed in a scent that made her mouth water. The triangle of tight curls shimmered in the candlelight, Judy's ambrosia coating all that was near, and when Robin's knee found its home again, there was no fabric in the way.

Adrift in a sea of shameless and unbridled impulses, Judy wrapped one leg over Robin's bottom, meeting each of Robin's thrusts with one of her own. Never before had she been possessed by another, not like this. *Not* like this. Nights shared with Scott had been more giving than ever receiving, and the only possession was based on a license and matching bands. As hard as she tried to be what she wasn't, in bed, she could not deny the truth, and ecstasy had never been hers. He never knew. Just another lie to cover up another lie, her moans and movements had been false, but not any longer. *Not* any longer.

One devouring kiss was followed by another until Robin shifted and knelt between Judy's legs. Their eyes met, their needs matched, and opening her legs, Judy watched as Robin slithered up her body. On arms now locked at the elbows, Robin floated over Judy, and arching her back, she rubbed her sex against Judy's.

The feeling was overwhelming. Potent in power, like a surge of electricity it rushed from Judy's center like lightning. Her scalp tingled. Her fingers prickled. Her legs began to shake, and raking her nails down Robin's back, she grabbed Robin's bottom, silently begging her for more.

Robin was losing a battle, and she was losing it quickly. Her core was pulsating. Her juices were flowing freely, and a need, molten and animal was demanding release. Her arms began to tremble, and as she stiffened, knowing she was powerless to prevent the crescendo, she heard Judy cry out, the moans guttural and the meaning...crystal clear.

"Yes," Robin said in a breath, her pleasure erupting and sending shudders through her body. Her groans matched Judy's, and husky and unchecked, they rose in her throat again and again as she rode wave after glorious wave of release.

Chapter Forty-Two

It had been a night of love and lust, and a night of moans and uneven breaths, where skin gleamed with sweat and the words spoken were involuntary. Spontaneous utterances had slipped from their lips as the fury of their passion took them to heights unimaginable, but other dialogue wasn't allowed.

More than once, Robin tried to speak, tried to whisper what she longed to say, but each time Judy placed her finger on Robin's lips, quieting her with the slightest shake of her head. There was no tomorrow, and there was nothing to say.

Consumed by a dream that was no longer a dream, Robin would forget what the morning would bring until she'd look into Judy's eyes. At times, they held only rapture. Brimming with yearning or arousal, her pupils were dilated to the extreme, but at others, the pale blue had turned dull, subdued by a cloud, looming and steadfast.

Sleep had escaped them for hours, their needs taking precedence over all else, but just before the gray dawn streaked the sky, Robin closed her eyes. She told herself it was only for a minute, and she kept her fingers intertwined with Judy's ensuring any movement would wake her, but in sleep, bodies relax, and Robin's did. In a tangle of sheets and blankets, and in a room thick with the scent of sex, slumber took hold and pulled Robin into its darkness.

Exhausted from a night like no other, dreams played no part. Her mind was quiet and blank. There was nothing to rouse, nothing to startle, nothing to alert her to awaken, so for almost two hours Robin didn't move an inch, but bodies have clocks. Internal or warning they can bring consciousness in an instant. A distant sound unusual and sudden, a forgotten task remembered, or a decision dreaded, and the densest fog can dissipate in a fraction of a second...and it did.

Robin hid behind hooded eyes, not daring to view the morning. She listened to the room. The purrs of a cat no doubt snuggled at the foot of the bed. The occasional ting of the baseboard heating. The sound of her own breathing, and outside the windows she could hear the wind. The aroma in the air held in its bouquet the remainder of a scent, and Robin swallowed.

An anvil sat on her chest, pressing down with the weight of the inescapable, each inhalation was fought for, and each exhalation solidified in her throat before finally escaping. Robin swallowed again...and opened her eyes.

The sun had found its way through the gaps in the shutters, and the slashes of light streaking across the ceiling brought with it all the visibility Robin needed. She took a shuddering breath and rolled her head to the side. It was the side Judy had claimed, the side where she should have been sleeping with her hair ruffled and her face possibly puffy from slumber, and anguish rose in Robin's throat. Tomorrow had arrived.

Robin squinted, the rays of sunlight like lasers in her eyes, and blinking away the spots, she ran her hand over the void in the bed. The hint of the indentation no longer held any warmth, and Robin's chin began to quiver. Glaring at the emptiness, she willed it to be replaced by life again, demanding that time reverse itself and bring back the woman she forever wanted to hold in her arms, but it wasn't to be. That side of the bed was now barren and cold...and it would be for the rest of Robin's life.

Robin's chest grew tight, and as she choked back a sob, she saw something on the nightstand. She forced herself to draw in a breath as she picked it up, and tears began to stream down her face when she read the label on the key fob. Spare Front.

As if she wanted to annihilate the meaning of its existence, Robin clutched it in her hand as she pulled herself into a ball. Unchecked, sobs erupted from her lips, her strangled wails masking all other sounds in the house.

***

Like acts in a play, Pam had an order to her disorder, a finite set of steps she followed to win the game of domination. First was to assault character, to smear by words or photos the virtues of another, and as friends began to drift, she'd use her victim's weakness to her advantage, devaluing their existence and tainting their self-worth. If they wavered, if they stood stronger against the tide Pam was creating, she'd attack their lifestyle, her devaluation of their work and their personal life yet another scene in her theatrical production. Her pièce de résistance was the closing act, an act she had planned several times over her life, but there had never been a need for it to come to fruition. Up until now, no one had ever dared push Pam to that point. Up until now, no one had ever had the audacity to withstand her onslaught and dare shove her over the line. Up until now, Pam had never needed to unveil her final act for behind the drapes was only one thing. Revenge.

Pam was not a stranger to the feeling. Behind everything she did, reprisal played a part. Those rich were made poorer. Those successful were set up to fail, and those intelligent would eventually doubt their own abilities, but recovery was possible. More money could be earned. Successes could again be attained, and uncertainties could be eased over time, but there was one thing that once taken could *never* be replaced...and that one thing was life.

In movies and in books, when revenge is planned, often it is done in the gloom and shadows of night, yet Pam always thought that was odd. Actually, she thought it was stupid. One misstep and a motion light could illuminate even the darkest of yards, and a lone stranger ambling down a road lit by streetlamps is noticed by neighbors peeking through blinds or a pet owner, giving their dog one last sniff at a bush. But in the morning, awake and ready for their day, people exit their homes and those not toddling off to work can be found jogging, walking, or bicycling. So, if invisibility is of the utmost importance, how better to arrive at it than to blend in with your surroundings...and Pam had blended *perfectly*.

She stood on the porch with her head bowed, the hood of her jacket concealing her face as it had all morning, and reaching into her back pocket, Pam pulled out her wallet. The edges of the leather were worn, and the once slim billfold bulged to over an inch in thickness. Its contents were a mishmash of old pawn tickets for items she had never owned, vouchers and coupons for discounts at local stores and restaurants, and a healthy wad of credit cards. All but her lowly debit card had been canceled, their limits reached and never repaid, but Pam was not a fool. She knew looks can be deceiving and how easily it was to deceive when she could prove her wealth by flashing a stack of shiny, plastic rectangles…before deciding to pay in cash.

But Pam had long ago found another use for credit cards, and freeing one from her wallet, she slipped it between the door and the jamb, scoffing under her breath when the old latch released almost immediately. Entering, she closed the door behind her and paused. A smirk pulled at her lips. There was no smell of coffee or aroma of bacon, eggs, or pancakes with syrup hanging in the air, but nevertheless, Pam didn't move. She cocked her head to the side, concentrating on hearing even the slightest clink of silverware against breakfast dishes, and when none were returned to her, Pam's smirk grew wider.

She pushed the hood from her head and began to creep through the house, cautious of even the noise of her jacket rustling as she moved. As she approached the bedroom door, she reached into her pocket and pulled out her weapon of choice. Pam never cared for guns. She found them too bulky and noisy to bother with, but knives were different. Knives were like snakes…silent and just as deadly.

Pam pressed the button on the side of the knife, and like a viper thrusting to attack, the bayonet blade sprang to life. The sheen of the steel of the double-sided shank sparkled back at her, its surface unblemished and its edges honed to match that of a scalpel.

She moved closer to the bedroom, her knuckles whitening as she gripped the knife, and when Pam noticed the door wasn't closed all the way, she smirked again. This was going to be easy. Standing inches away from the opening, she listened for a moment. There was no sound. There was no movement, and placing the tip of her finger on the door, she pushed it open ever so slowly.

Pam curled her lip at the scent of sex, but that didn't slow her progress. She neared the bed, took a breath, and then raised the knife above her head.

***

When Judy reached the dock, she walked across the street and sat on the steps of a hotel, its rooms empty and its windows dark. The asphalt on the road slowly changed from black to gray as the glimmers of dawn breached the horizon, and in the distance, she could hear the faint hum of the ferry's engine.

Two hours earlier, in a room lit by candles, she had gathered her things, and refusing to look in Robin's direction, Judy crept into the big kitchen, naked and numb. Detached from the night and from the morning, she dressed slowly, cautious not to make a sound, cautious not to remember, cautious not to feel. Judy left the house with her head bowed and her mind blank, and as she walked to the ferry, she didn't lift her eyes. She knew the way, and if she had cared to look, she would have seen stores and restaurants covered in boards, but Judy didn't want to remember them that way, closed and vacant...just like her.

There was still no need to raise her eyes as Judy sat on the steps, the sounds of the ferry docking and people disembarking so familiar, although today it was crisper. The season was over, so there weren't many coming off the boat, and she could hear the faint chatter of friends planning their day and the steady rhythm of the tires on their bikes rolling over the boards of the pier.

Taking a deep breath, Judy pushed herself off the step and headed for the ferry. A few strangers ambled by without bicycles, but she didn't question their visit. Relatives of the locals always came to the island after the crowds had gone. She brushed shoulders with one and mumbled an apology, but the hooded visitor paid her no attention. Judy was glad.

As she walked past Glen, she paused long enough to listen as he explained her luggage was on the mainland having made the trip without her the night before. She nodded her acknowledgment. Glen said he'd see her later. Judy said goodbye.

Soon she was sitting on the ferry, one of only a few early-morning travelers, and distancing herself from them, Judy stared at the floor. The horn sounded. The boat glided away from the dock, and her eyes remained focused on her feet. She longed to look at the water one last time, the sunlight dancing on the surface, the waves rippling, and the gulls swooping, but if she did the feelings building inside of her would let loose. Judy kept her head down and prayed she'd make it to her car.

When she reached the mainland, luggage was gathered and packed into the trunk and back seat, and sliding behind the wheel, Judy barely had time to close the door before her eyes overflowed. Burying her head in her hands, she sobbed. Tears coursed down her cheeks in a never-ending stream as the violence of her wails wracked her body. She tried to smother off her cries, suffocate them with a clenched jaw and clamped lips, but her pain was too great. Overwhelmed, it was all she could do to breathe.

Throughout the night, Judy had tried to keep the ache in her heart at bay. When movements stilled, when hearts needed to slow, or lungs needed to calm, the truth would return, and her heart would break again. How many times had she choked back the words she longed to say? How many times had she stopped Robin with a quieting finger, hushing her before whispers of love could be heard? But it was in those moments of longing and of love unspoken when clarity came to Judy. Tomorrow she knew she was going to walk away, but tomorrow had yet to arrive, so she cherished the night. She let herself free. She let herself feel. She let herself love and give into all the yearning coursing through her veins, and Judy loved, as Robin had asked...like there was no tomorrow.

When the temptation of sleep was too great, and Robin's breathing slowed, Judy had stared at the ceiling and allowed time to slip by. Her body clock was as accurate as ever, and she wasn't going to miss another ferry, so she took what time was left and branded her mind with the memories of the night.

Memories of scents, new and evocative, and of skin milky soft and oh so warm. Memories of bodies meshed and limbs intertwined, and the glow of Robin's nectar shiny on her skin. Memories of kisses, addictive and intoxicating that had enslaved Judy throughout the night, and memories of the taste of a tongue, salty and wet, ravishing her mouth in abandon.

No boundaries had existed between them, and any hesitation was just that, a second of pause before letting their love guide them toward new discoveries, new textures, and new tastes.

Once surrendering to Robin's first kiss, Judy found it nearly impossible to break away from the power of Robin's ardor. She pillaged Judy's body, again and again taking with her lips, her fingers, and her tongue everything in her path, and while Judy was the most willing of victims, there were times when she became the victor.

Fraught with desire, Robin's eyes would plead for release, and it was then when Judy could capture a nipple in her mouth, suckling against it until it was stiff and swollen while Robin writhed under her. It was then when her hands could roam free, Robin so lost in a vortex, erogenous and unabated, she was helpless to thwart Judy's advances, and it was then when Judy could grind herself against Robin's most tender place, taking her to nirvana while Judy watched in awe.

Judy jumped in her seat, the blast of the departing ferry's horn interrupting her thoughts and bringing her back to now. She fumbled for her stash of fast food napkins in the glove box, and after drying her eyes, she tossed the crumpled napkin aside. She glanced at her watch. It was almost eleven. Where had the time gone? Six hours later, she would wonder that again.

***

At a rest stop just north of Marshall, Michigan, Judy sat at the furthest picnic bench she could find. At the very end of the property, it was away from prying eyes, dog walkers, and the ruckus of people streaming in and out of the restrooms as they chattered about their plans or yelled for their children to catch up.

Judy had made this trip countless times, and never in a rush to get to Pat's, she'd meander down the highway, stopping for food, fuel, or sometimes just to stretch her legs, but today she *should* have been in a rush. Today was Pat's birthday, and his party started promptly at five-thirty, but six hours into the trip, Judy had yet to make it halfway.

Time was spent in the ladies' room of a fast food restaurant in St. Ignace where, stripping out of clothes smelling of passion, Judy had scrubbed with paper towels and foaming restroom soap, trying to remove every trace of Robin's scent. Time was lost in gas station bathrooms, staring into cracked mirrors above sinks spotted with rust, demanding her reflection to grow up, to accept reality, and to stop acting like a fool. Time was wasted in convenience stores, walking up and down every aisle, mindlessly looking at food that didn't appeal before settling on yet another cup of what tasted like yesterday's coffee, and blinded by tears, time disappeared as Judy had sat in her car on the side of the road waiting for her vision to clear.

Judy closed her eyes and rubbed the back of her neck. Her head had been pounding for most of the trip, the pain dull at times and at others, piercing her skull like a railroad spike. She wanted to blame it on caffeine. She had had more than her fair share, but there are only so many thoughts a brain can handle, and Judy's had reached its limit. Much the same as protons in a particle accelerator, her thoughts kept colliding, bombarding off one another at a staggering rate. No sooner had one started when another would appear, countering her original conviction with arguments equally as voracious, and in a never-ending loop, they repeated and repeated and repeated. At times, the ache was so dizzying she wanted to vomit and at others, so grinding all she could do was pull off the road, pop a few more painkillers, and massage her temples until the vise loosened.

Judy pulled the crisp fall air into her lungs as she opened her eyes. She held her breath, waiting for the next shockwave to hit her skull, but instead, all she felt was a subdued throb. Exhaling, Judy picked up the vending machine cup and brought it to her lips again. She took a mindless sip, no longer able to discern strong from weak or good from bad. It was hot. It was wet. It kept her awake.

A gust of wind came out of nowhere, sending a chill down Judy's spine, and hunching her shoulders, she got to her feet. She told herself she didn't want to be late, but halfway to her car, she stopped and shook her head. She *really* needed to stop lying to herself. She *did* want to be late. She wanted to be late enough to miss the party. She wanted to be late enough to miss the people. She wanted to be late enough to miss whatever other lies she would have to tell, but with *that* truth, Judy unwittingly had started a trend. Although it wasn't a movement with placards or parades, it was a direction nonetheless. Judy just didn't know it yet.

Chapter Forty-Three

Judy sat near the door on a folding chair her family had borrowed from the church. Its sepia paint was nicked, and its seat, hard and unyielding, but comfort hadn't been its appeal. If a quick escape was needed to hide tears that had a mind of their own, in two quick steps, Judy could be out of view, allowed to mourn a loss she caused...again.

She raised her eyes for a moment and then averted them. She had no interest in the guests who remained, their belt buckles, bellies, and beer cans directly in her line of sight. Most were people she'd grown up with, gone to church with, attended weddings and funerals with, but they seemed like strangers now. They had smiled at her arrival, shaking her hand or giving her a hug that suggested she was contaminated, but their eyes stopped at her surface. Just a quick glance to check out how she had aged, a less-than-covert eyeballing of someone they once knew, and then they wandered away and got lost in the crowd, no doubt looking for someone more familiar.

Judy took a sip of her beer as she quickly scanned the room. With the guests invited numbering ridiculous, and seeing no need to spend money renting out a banquet hall, Louise had converted the orchard's market into the party venue. The pallets and tables usually scattered throughout had been moved to the storeroom, but the essence of the market still remained. The smell of beer and fried chicken couldn't hide the scent of produce and apples that hung in the air, and while banners announcing Happy

Birthday were draped everywhere, the blackboards revealing today's prices remained hanging all around. The blades of the ceiling fans were covered in a thick coating of dust and the concrete floor, although swept for the party, held the indelible stains of cherries, blackberries, and blueberries crushed under the footwear of oblivious shoppers.

Although Judy's headache still existed, its presence had almost gone unnoticed, but sitting where she didn't want to be, doing what she didn't want to do, with people she didn't want to see was having its effect. On any given day, the market could easily hold over a hundred people, yet Judy felt as if the walls were slowly closing in on her, and with every inch they stole, there was less air to breathe. Having arrived late enough to miss the throng, those remaining numbered less than thirty, but Judy felt stifled and compressed by all around her, and her headache kicked up a notch.

"You haven't missed much if that helps."

Judy glanced at Eric as he sat down next to her, trying her best to ignore the ice picks now poking at her temples. "What?"

"You look sad, and I was just saying you didn't miss much. This party's been kind of a bust."

It was well past nine by the time Judy had arrived at the party, and doing what was expected, she had sought out Pat and extended her birthday greetings. After kissing him on the cheek, she grabbed a drink she didn't really want, sat down, and for the most part, stared at the floor. It was a pose that was quickly becoming a habit.

Judy couldn't help but look around the room again. Along one wall was a row of tables, atop which were chafing dishes holding what remained of fried chicken, baked ziti, and pulled pork, and in between were large foil bowls of salad, rolls, and fruit, their contents now well below the rims. Coolers with beer, water, and soda were situated close by, and bottles of liquor and wine, along with stacks of plastic cups were strewn across the counters of the market's cash registers.

Judy turned back to her brother. "Why was it a bust? It looks like there was a party here to me."

"Oh, there was a party, just not the one Louise had planned," Eric said with a laugh. "Doug fucked up a couple of weeks ago and let it slip to Pat about the party. Once he found out, Pat invited all his buddies from the club, and when they showed up, everything went south. The more they drank, the louder they got until everyone was shouting over each other just to be heard. Someone broke one of Louise's favorite platters, and Doug ended up throwing up outside."

"Geez."

"Yeah," Eric said, frowning. "Bev managed to pour him into the car and get him home, and by eight o'clock all the grandchildren were gone since every other word was becoming the F-bomb. By nine, Louise had had enough, so all of Pat's cronies were shown the door, and after that, this place became a morgue. I think the kids are just waiting to help Louise clean up once the rest of these people get the hint the party's over."

Judy searched the room and finally noticed two of Pat's children sitting off to one side, both of whom were nursing their beers. Their expressions sagged with the weight of responsibility, but they dutifully waited as was expected. Judy sighed. She knew that feeling all too well, but as she was about to lower her eyes again, she noticed someone else in the room. Balancing a plate of birthday cake on his overextended belly, he shoveled forkful after forkful into his mouth while a piece of icing remained housed at the corner of his lips. Judy smiled to herself. He looked like a Buddha sitting atop a pin. "What's Orson doing here?"

"What do you think he's doing here?" Eric said, sniggering under his breath. "Ever since you mentioned to Pat on the phone you may be staying, he's been like an old Jewish grandmother."

"Huh?

Eric beamed, rocking back and forth as he broke into a whispered song. "Matchmaker, matchmaker—"

"Enough," Judy said, holding up her hand. "That's not going to happen."

Amused by his sister's predicament, Eric looked over at Orson for a second. "Oh, I don't know. What did Pat say? You could do worse?"

"Seriously?" Judy snapped. "You think that little of me to believe I'd be interested in him. That he's the *only* person I could ever attract?"

"Jude," Eric said, placing his hand on Judy's shoulder. "I was kidding. Relax. It was just a joke."

"Well, I'm not laughing," Judy said, and white-knuckling the bottle in her hand she stared off into space.

"Yeah, I can see that," Eric said, staring at his sister. "And by the way, what's this bullshit about you moving home? You aren't really considering it, are you?"

"I don't want to talk about it, Eric."

"Judy, come on. This is me you're talking to. There's no way in hell you'd ever want to move back here, so just tell me—"

"I said I don't want to talk about it," Judy said, glaring at her brother. "Now, drop it, Eric. Please, I'm begging you. Just drop it."

Eric's expression turned pained. He couldn't remember the last time he'd seen his sister cry, but in an instant, her eyes had misted over. He bowed his head, racking his brain to find a subject change. A minute passed and then another until the sound of Pat's gravelly voice carried across the room, jogging Eric's memory. "By the way," he said, inching closer to Judy. "Before you hear it from someone else, there *was* something that happened earlier today with Brett you should probably know about."

The mention of Pat's youngest made Judy look across the room again. Trey was still staring aimlessly into space, and his sister was now entranced by whatever was on her iPad, but their younger sibling was nowhere to be seen.

"What went on with Brett? Something at school? Is he okay?" she said, keeping her voice low.

"He's fine, but when he showed up with his girlfriend, his very *black* girlfriend, Pat went ballistic."

Judy winced as her headache, like an ice pick, pierced her skull. "What?"

Eric shrugged. "You know Pat. He went off like a crazy man. I think the only thing he *didn't* shout was the N-word before Brett managed to get the poor girl back into the car and drive away."

"And what did you do?"

"What?"

"What did you *do* about it?"

"Judy, I didn't *do* anything about it. I mean, I tried to calm Pat down, but it was like spitting into the wind. You know that."

"So you just let him do that to our nephew? You just turned the other cheek and looked away?"

Eric gawked at his sister. "Judy, have you forgotten how many times over the years we've argued with him, only to walk away with nothing to show for it except for sore throats and high blood pressure? And I'm not saying I agree with him. Lord knows I don't agree with him, but I'm tired of fighting the same old battle. What did Mom always say about that?"

"About what?"

"It was something about doing the same thing over and over again and expecting a different result."

Judy couldn't help but grin, remembering one of her mother's favorite analogies. "It's the definition of insanity."

"That's it," Eric said, slapping his knee. "But the point I'm trying to make is that Pat is never going to change, Judy. Okay? Just surrender and move on. You'll be a lot happier."

Judy knew all about surrender, and her stomach began to churn as she counted up the times. At fourteen, she yielded to pressures and fears and lost herself in the process. In her late twenties, her true self returned only to be abandoned when she gave into society's norms. In her thirties and forties, Judy had handed her life over to another, her desire for children and a house squelched with not so much as an argument, and now, in her fifties, she had once again raised the white flag, surrendering whatever years she had left...for what?

Absorbed in her thoughts, it wasn't until she felt Eric's hand on her knee when Judy realized he'd been talking to her. "I'm sorry," she said, shaking her head. "I was off in my own little world. What did you say?"

"I was saying that you shouldn't be worrying about Brett either because the girl couldn't have been all that special if he came back without her."

"What?" Judy said, sitting straight in her chair. "He's here?"

"Like a pariah in the corner," Eric said, pointing over his shoulder. "I went over earlier and did the uncle thing."

"The uncle thing?"

"Yeah, I made sure he knew I didn't agree with his father, and I assured him there were plenty more fish in the sea."

Judy whipped her head around. "But what if there isn't?"

"What do you mean?"

"What if, for Brett, that girl was the one?"

"Judy, he's twenty-two. He's got his whole life ahead of him to find the right girl."

"Don't you mean the right *color* girl?"

"Whoa," Eric said, holding up his hands. "You of all people know I am *not* a racist, but knowing how his father feels—"

"Who cares how his father feels?" Judy said through her teeth. "This is Brett's life we're talking about, and he should be able to..."

Judy stopped and stared wordlessly at her brother for a moment. Her lungs emptied and resting back in her chair, she took a swig of her beer.

She hoped the malty flavor would wash away the fetid aftertaste of hypocrisy, but its foulness lingered. Who was she to fight this fight? Who was she to claim unfair or speak words that weren't worth the air they were spoken on? They were true…but they were also weightless.

"Excuse me," Judy whispered and standing up, she snagged two beers from a nearby cooler before continuing across the room toward her nephew.

"Thought you might want a refill," she said, handing one of the bottles to Brett.

Brett turned from the window, weakly smiling at his aunt as he took the drink. "Thanks, but you may not want to get too close. It could send the wrong message."

Judy's mood came out in her tone. "I couldn't give a fuck about messages," she said, and unscrewing the cap on her beer, Judy brought the bottle to her lips, only to stop and grin when she noticed Brett's bug-eyed expression. "You're not twelve anymore, Brett. I think you've heard the word before."

"Yeah, but never from you," he said, and raising his bottle, he clinked it against Judy's. "And thanks, I needed that."

"The beer or my F-bomb?"

"Both."

A few minutes went by before Judy looked up at her towering nephew. "Eric told me what happened."

"And I suppose you think I'm an idiot."

"No, I don't. I think you're trying to live your life. I'm not quite sure why you chose today to do what you did, but then again, you shouldn't have to worry about bringing any of your friends here."

"She's more than a friend," Brett said softly. "And I brought her here today because I was stupid enough to think Dad wouldn't go off if people were around. Boy, talk about a swing and a miss."

"Yeah, I heard."

"Luckily, there weren't too many here yet, but he sure as hell made his feelings crystal clear to those who were. If it hadn't been for Uncle Eric and Tara, I honestly think I would have hauled off and hit him."

Judy widened her eyes. For those who didn't know her nephew, his appearance painted the picture of someone imposing. Tall, broad-shouldered, and with a perpetual five o'clock shadow, the only thing that softened his image was a mop of unruly sandy-brown hair and the dimples in his cheeks. But Judy knew better. She knew the boy who cried when he found a dead butterfly in the garden. She knew the teenager who saved cats from trees and ushered spiders out of the house instead of stomping on them. And she knew the man whose DNA was similar to his siblings, yet thankfully he didn't inherit all the same markers. Trey and Gayle were go-getters and mulish like their father while Brett was as laid-back as the day was long. Keeping his drive to succeed quietly in the background, he had aced every class he had ever attended, and while his siblings struggled to find colleges that would accept them, by the time it was Brett's turn, he accepted one and turned down a dozen more.

"That's not like you, Brett," Judy said, eyeing the man. "And I'm glad you didn't."

"Are you?"

"Why would you say that?"

"Because I've seen the way Dad and Uncle Doug treat you. I would think you'd like to see at least one of them get put into their place."

"No, not my style," Judy said with a snicker.

Brett snorted. "Yeah, not mine either. Thank God Tara and Uncle Eric stopped me."

"I hope you don't mind me saying this, but I'm a little surprised she'd do that. I mean, I don't know the girl, but...but geez, facing that kind of hatred. How could she *not* want you to defend her?"

"Because she's marvelous," Brett said, his chiseled features instantly softened by a glow only love can bring. "And if you ever get to meet her, you'll see she doesn't need defending. Tara could have easily called Dad out on his bullshit, but that wasn't why we were here. We weren't here to start any fight, and even though I didn't think Dad would do what he did, Tara and I both knew we could be walking into a hornet's nest, but that didn't matter to her. She just wanted to see where I grew up and have at least one shot at meeting my family."

"What do you mean one shot?"

"When I leave tonight, I won't be coming back," Brett said, following it with a swig of his beer.

"That's a big step, Brett. This is your home."

"No, this is where I grew up, but my home is where I choose to make it. I'm not saying I don't love my family, and I'm not saying this place doesn't hold a bunch of good memories, but memories aren't static. They don't only exist when I'm here. They go wherever I go. Whether I'm a part of the family, or I'm disowned, I'm always going to have them."

Judy ran her hands over her arms to calm the goosebumps that had just sprouted. "When did you get so smart," she whispered.

"Knowing what we both know, it sure as hell wasn't from Dad."

Judy raised her beer bottle to tap it against Brett's. "I'll drink to that."

"Me, too."

For a minute, both sipped their beers in silence until Judy turned to Brett. "So this girl must be pretty special for you to...well, for you to walk away like this."

Brett studied his aunt for a moment. She was a foot shorter than him, but in his mind, she had always seemed so much taller. "Do you believe in love at first sight?" When Judy's eyebrows rose, Brett said, "Stupid question coming from a guy—right?"

"No, not really. It just surprised me."

"Well, do you?"

Judy rubbed the back of her neck, calming the hairs now standing on end. "Yes, I do," she said softly. "Why?"

"Because that's what happened. I walked into the library at school one afternoon, and there she was at one of the tables. She saw me. I saw her, and *bam*, that was it. It was like...like someone flipped a switch. And I know I probably sound like a complete idiot right now, but in that instant, I just knew Tara was the one for me. I just knew it. No getting around it. No changing it. No fighting it. No nothing. It just...it just was." Brett looked at Judy and leaned in a little closer. "And I'm not a sappy romantic, Aunt Judy. I never believed in love at first sight or...or—"

"Soulmates?"

"Yes, soulmates, and Jesus Christ, in the blink of an eye, my whole world changed. I knew in a *split*-second she was my one and only." Brett paused and shrugged. "When you know, you know. You know?"

Judy smiled at the redundancy, but she understood all too well what Brett had just described. Whether it's a gut feeling or one that can be put into words, when you know...you *do* know.

Corners are turned, and choices are made, but throughout Judy's life, roadblocks had swayed her direction, taking with them her hours, days, and years. She could never get them back, never rewind the clock to choose more wisely, but Judy was done wasting time. A few silly words had just changed her outlook for good because in their meaning was a powerful truth. Judy *did* know what she was. Judy *did* know who she loved, and Judy knew that *both* would never, *ever* change...and why the hell should they?

"And if Dad would just stop playing his stupid games, I could say my goodbyes and get back to the woman I love."

Judy jerked out of her thoughts. "What? What do you mean? What games?"

"Oh, he's been running interference all night. Mom has tried a couple of times to come over here, and he's pulled her back, and if anyone else tries, he gives them that famous snarl of his, and they tuck their tail between their legs and scurry away. I've become a leper apparently, which is why you shouldn't be talking to me. He's just going to give you a lot of shit when he gets you alone."

Judy set her jaw. She was well aware of the shit Patrick could shovel. He had entombed her in it for years, tossing shovelful after shovelful on top of her as if he was trying to bury her in a grave, but graves are for dead people, and Judy had never felt more alive.

"How about I turn the tables before he gets the chance?" Judy said, handing Brett her beer. "And I'd hold onto your hat if I were you because I'm about to bring this party to a close in a big way. Hope there's room for me in Leperville."

"What in the world are you going to do?"

Judy's face split into a grin and standing on her tiptoes, she kissed her nephew on the cheek. "I'm going to live my life, Brett. I'm going to *finally* live my life!"

Once Judy turned to face the room, it took only a moment to spot Patrick standing next to Louise near the buffet. Making her way across the room, Judy had every intention of starting the conversation, but Patrick beat her to it.

"What were you doing talking to him?" Pat growled, gesturing with his head toward the corner where his son was still standing.

"He's my nephew. Why wouldn't I talk to him?"

"Because he's no longer your nephew."

"Is that so?"

"Yes, that's so," Patrick said, perching his folded arms across his potbelly. "And after Monday, he's going to have to figure out how to pay for his precious master's degree because I've written the last check out to Princeton."

For a moment, Judy was dumbstruck, and she caught herself looking at Louise, trying to see if her sister-in-law felt the same way. The tears Judy saw welling in Louise's eyes told her that she didn't. They also told Judy she was on her own.

Louise was once statuesque. Her chin always held high, her eyes bright, and her voice lyrical, but somewhere along the way she had changed. Louise now had the demeanor of someone beaten down over the years, forever slouching, forever talking in whispers or not talking at all just like she was doing now, except Judy didn't need to hear her voice. She heard all she needed to hear from the anguish she saw in Louise's eyes.

Judy glared at her brother, striking the same pose, although she had no potbelly on which to rest her arms. "Well, then you're a *fucking* fool."

Housed in a metal building, there were no panels in the market to absorb noise and prevent it from carrying, so Judy's words were heard by all. Behind her, in unison, Pat saw every head turn his way, and his cheeks flamed crimson. "*You* need to watch your language, Judy," he growled, glaring down at her.

Judy looked over her shoulder at all the people gaping back at her. Their eyes were wide, and their mouths were open, but amongst them, she saw no children. "Why?" she said, returning her focus to Patrick. "We're all adults here. If I want to say fuck, I'll say fuck. What are you going to do, Patrick? Fucking disown me?"

"Are you drunk?"

"No, Pat, I'm stone cold sober. As a matter of fact, I don't think I have *ever* been more clear-headed in my life."

"Well, I don't know what the hell's gotten into you, but this is no way to talk to your brother."

"Really? Because I think this is *way* overdue," Judy yelled, taking a step closer to Pat. "That man over there is your son. You and Louise created him, and when you did, you took on the responsibility of a parent, *not* a tyrant. You're supposed to love him and cherish him, not banish him like an infidel just because *he* decided to live his own *life*."

"I'm not stopping him from living his own life, little sister. I'm just choosing *who* I want in *mine*," Patrick said, leaning in toward Judy. "And if that little prick can't stick to his own kind, he is no son of mine. Period!"

"Oh thank *God*!" Judy shouted, waving her arms in the air. "That means I'm safe."

"What the hell are you talking about?"

Judy froze for one beat of her heart. She had just shot from the hip, saying the first thing that popped into her head, but instead of scrambling to create a lie to cover her tracks, Judy realized she didn't need to scramble anymore, and suddenly she felt free. Her headache was gone. Her energy had returned, and she felt lighter than air.

Taking a deep breath, Judy smiled her best smile at Patrick and gave him a wink. "Hold that question, bro," she said. "I'll be right back."

Judy made a beeline for her social media junkie niece, and she was tickled when she saw the twenty-four-year-old's eyes grow wider and wider the closer Judy got. "Can I borrow that, Gayle? Promise, I'll bring it right back."

Gayle's gulp was audible. She quickly glanced at her brother for guidance, and after Trey gave her a half-hearted shrug, Gayle mimicked his gesture as she tapped on the screen to exit her Twitter app. Handing the tablet to Judy, she said, "Here you go."

"Thanks."

Judy opened the Google app, and typing into the search bar, she viewed the results. Clicking on the one she knew all too well, she tapped on the Gallery tab, brought up a picture and then marched over to Patrick. Flipping the tablet around, she said, "What was that you were saying about sticking to your own kind?"

Patrick pinched his lips together. He didn't know what kind of game Judy was playing and his annoyance was rapidly darkening his cheeks. After giving the attractive blonde on the screen a cursory glance, he shoved the tablet back at Judy. "And who in the hell is that supposed to be?"

"My own kind, of course. Isn't that what you said? We needed to stick to our own kind?"

"You're talking in circles, Judy."

"Well, then let me straighten the line, no pun intended," Judy said, pointing to the picture. "Her name's Robin Novak. She's my lover, Patrick, and God willing, one of these days...she's going to be my wife."

Judy took a moment to watch as Patrick's face morphed into what appeared to be a giant pimple waiting to burst before she flashed him a toothy smile and walked away. She was well aware all eyes in the room were on her, but ignoring the gawks and whispers, Judy strode back to her niece. "Here you go. Thanks."

"Um...yeah," Gayle said, taking the tablet. "Uh...no problem."

Judy went to leave, but before she could take a step, she turned back around and knelt in front of Trey and Gayle. "You two have a choice. If you want to disown Brett, if you want to disown *me*, that's on you, but *everyone* has the right to live their life without judgments. You do. I do. Brett does, and I hope you remember that."

Judy straightened and headed for the door, slowing down only to grab her jacket draped on the back of a chair. As she tugged it on, she looked over at her nephew, still standing in the corner. "By the way, Brett," Judy called out, giving Patrick a half-glance before focusing on Brett. "Give me a call. I'll see what I can do about helping you out with your tuition. Love you."

Brett's dimples cratered in his cheeks. "Love you, too. Aunt Judy."

Across the room, Gayle waited until she saw her aunt go outside before rushing to open her tablet. A moment later, her smile matched Brett's. "Wow."

Chapter Forty-Four

As she was heading out of town, Judy stopped at a gas station to top off her tank, buy some energy drinks, use the ladies' room, and call Robin. The last thing on her list had actually been her first. A few minutes after leaving the orchard, she had pulled off the road to call Robin on her mobile, only to find out that her rapidly draining battery had been a sign. Her ten-year-old phone had finally become a paperweight.

Judy pocketed her change, and snagging her coffee and her purchases, she smiled at the clerk. "Do you have a pay phone?" When the craggy-faced man raised a bushy eyebrow, Judy laughed. "My cell phone died."

"Out the door, make a right. It's around the side of the building."

"Thanks."

A minute later, Judy stood in front of the pay phone with the receiver in one hand and quarters in the other staring at the keypad. It was the standard configuration and had all the numbers and letters just like her phone, but unlike her phone, this one didn't have Robin's number programmed into it. Judy hadn't memorized a number in years, and the only time she'd seen Robin's was when she had added it to her contact list. Judy drummed her fingers on the shelf under the phone for several seconds before hanging her head. "Seriously?" she said under her breath. "Do you really want to tell her you love her for the first time on the phone? Idiot."

Judy gathered her things, dropped the quarters in her pocket, but as she rounded the corner to return to her car, she stutter-stepped to a stop. A pickup truck had pulled in behind her car at the pumps, and on the door of the old red Ford was a faded Lawton Orchards decal. Judy took a deep breath and headed to her car, slowing to a snail's pace as the door of the truck opened, and Eric stepped out.

"What?" he said, holding up his hands. "You're not going to say goodbye?"

"I thought it best I got out of there before Patrick imploded," Judy said, placing her coffee on the hood of her car.

"Well, he did down a couple of quick ciders as soon as you left."

"Did you?"

Eric shut the truck door and walked toward his sister. "No, because I don't suffer from the same rectal dysfunction like our brothers."

"What?"

"I don't walk around with my head shoved up my ass."

Judy couldn't help but laugh. "Oh."

"But I'm not going to lie," Eric said, stopping a few inches from Judy. "What you said back there, it really took me for a loop, but I'm not going to pepper you with questions. I just want to know you're happy, and this is what you want."

"I am, and it is. Even if I hadn't found Robin again—"

"Again?"

A faint smile graced Judy's face. "Long story."

Eric arched an eyebrow. He was curious, but whatever the story was, he somehow knew it would be worth waiting for. "Maybe when I visit in the spring then?"

"Still planning to?"

"Still want me to?"

Judy took a deep breath, her smile growing wider. "Yes, very much."

"Come here," Eric said, and pulling Judy into a bear hug, he kissed the top of her head. "I love you, Judy, and no matter what, you'll always be my sister. Okay?"

Forever the runt of the litter, Judy stood on her tiptoes and kissed Eric's cheek. "And I love you, too. A lot."

"Good to know," Eric said, holding Judy at arm's length. "So, you're heading out tonight?"

"Yeah. I got my coffee and a couple of energy drinks. I should be fine."

"You look a little wiped out."

"That's mostly from...from just a very long day," Judy said, opening the car door to toss in the grocery bag. "But I'll stop if I need to."

"All right. Well, I better get Pat's truck back before he realizes it's missing," Eric said, turning to leave. "Let me know when you get there. Okay?"

"Absolutely." Judy grabbed her coffee cup off the hood, but as she was about to climb into her car, something in the back seat caught her eye. "Shit!"

Eric spun around. "What? What's wrong?"

Judy glanced at her brother and then back at the car. "Hey, can you do me a favor?"

"Sure. Anything. What do you need?"

Judy opened the back door and rummaged through the luggage covering the seat. Yanking out the largest, she trotted around the car and opened the trunk, and in a minute, there were three suitcases on the ground.

"What's all this?"

"Christmas presents," Judy said, picking up the smaller case. "It was the easiest way to pack them. Can you take them back to Pat's with you?"

"Not a problem," Eric said, and grabbing the other two suitcases, he headed for the truck. Tossing them in the back, he did the same when Judy handed him the last. "Wait. What do I tell them? I mean, you didn't exactly leave on the best of terms."

"You don't have to tell them anything. They're still my nieces and nephews, and the little ones won't care. Just ask Louise to stash the stuff until Christmas."

"Do you think Louise is an ally?"

"I'm not a hundred percent sure, but Brett said she had tried to talk to him a couple of times, so I'm hoping that means she's a little more open-minded than Pat."

"Actually, she always struck me as pretty down-to-earth."

"Me, too. Oh, and just tell her to change the tags on the things I got for Doug and Pat. They won't figure it out."

"Are you sure?"

"Eric, even if they suffer from...what did you call it?"

"Rectal dysfunction?"

Judy chuckled. "Yeah, even if they suffer from that, they're still my brothers. They're still the ones that held my hand when I was a kid and I had to cross a street, and who taught me how to ride a bike when Dad could never find the time. I still love them, Eric. Like you said, that will never change."

"But they do try our patience, don't they?"

"That they do," Judy said, giving Eric another quick hug. "And now, I gotta go."

"You sure you're okay to drive?" Eric called out as Judy went to her car.

"I'm fine," Judy said, opening the car door. "And if I get tired, I'll stop. I promise."

Judy pulled the door closed, and after taking a few gulps of coffee, she headed out. Traffic was almost non-existent until she reached the interstate, and then it was sporadic with tractor trailers and RVs outnumbering the cars on the road, but two hours later, Judy had to keep her promise.

It only took one time drifting onto the shoulder of the highway for Judy to realize she wasn't as fine as she thought. Opening the windows to let the frigid air intrude, she turned up the radio and headed to the next rest stop.

Even with coffee and energy drinks in her system, Judy hadn't slept in over forty hours, and once she parked the car and reclined the seat, within minutes sleep took hold. Since her phone was dead, she left one window cracked open, believing the chill of the night wouldn't allow her to sleep too long, but three hours later, it was her reaching-maximum-capacity bladder that jolted her awake. A quick trip to the ladies' room averted the catastrophe, and after visiting the vending machine kiosk, Judy climbed back into her car with another cup of coffee and made her way north.

***

Judy took a deep breath and slowly stretched to work out the stiffness that had seemed to settle throughout her body.

By the time she had stepped foot in Safe Harbor the day before, every part of her plan had gone awry. She missed the first ferry and had almost missed the second due to an excruciatingly drawn-out visit at a phone store in St. Ignace. When she finally got to the house, Robin wasn't home, and no longer having a key to get inside, Judy had to test every door and window before eventually gaining access through the basement. Although she had wanted to shower away the two days of grime that had settled on her skin, Robin's bed was far too inviting to ignore, so kicking off her shoes, she stripped off her jeans, and the rest was a blur.

If Judy's mind hadn't been fogged by exhaustion, she would have questioned why the bed was so disheveled, and if her mind had been clear, she would have been concerned about why Robin wasn't home, but that clarity had only just arrived...after sixteen hours of sleep.

Judy's eyes flew open and sitting up, as soon as she saw the light from the kitchen streaming into the bedroom, she jumped out of bed and ran from the room. A second later, she slid to a stop. "Rita?"

"It's about time you woke up," Rita said, placing the cat bowls on the floor. "I was starting to worry."

"But...but how did you know I was here?"

"Because when I came by last night to feed the cats, I almost tripped over your backpack. It didn't take long to find you, and I saw no point in waking you up, so I fed Fred and Ginger, called Hank to let him know I'd be hanging here for the night, and then I crashed on the sofa."

Judy shook her head. "I...I don't understand. Why are you feeding the cats? Where's Robin?"

"Robin's in Florida."

"What!"

Rita held up her hands. "She called me on Saturday and asked if I could watch the cats. She said a friend of hers got hurt, and she needed to leave."

"Oh."

"And when I asked why she wasn't having you take care of them, she started to cry. She managed to say that you had left the island, and then she hung up." Rita crossed her arms and glowered at Judy. "So, that leaves me with three questions. Where in the world have you been? Why didn't you return any of my messages, and what the *hell* is going on?"

***

"What's all this?"

"This," Declan said, waving his arm over the counter. "This is our breakfast."

Robin gave Declan a dirty look as she made her way to the coffee pot. "It's beer and sandwiches."

"It is, and we're going to enjoy them on the beach."

"Declan, I'm not in the mood to—"

"I don't give a shit what kind of mood you're in. All I know is that you're not going to spend any more time hiding in the bedroom watching stupid TV. You and I are going to head down to the beach, put up an umbrella and enjoy our beer and sandwiches."

Robin snagged a mug from the counter and filled it to the top. Taking a hesitant sip, she shook her head. "But it's only ten."

"And by the time you get showered, it'll be eleven, which is close enough to make it brunch. So get your ass in gear, Robin, because I'm not taking no for an answer. I get that you're hurting. I get that she crushed you. I even get the appeal of watching endless hours of brain-numbing TV, but I stood by once and watched as another woman pulled you into that rabbit hole, and I'll be damned if I'm going to let that happen again."

"This isn't the same thing, and you know it."

Declan took a deep breath and going over, he took the mug from Robin's hand, placed it on the counter, and then pulled Robin into a hug. "I know it isn't, kiddo. Judy didn't fuck with your head. She broke your heart, and I'm sorry that happened, but hiding isn't helping so the sooner you get your scrawny ass into the shower, the sooner you and I can get wasted on the beach. Okay?"

Robin freed herself from Declan's hold and shot him a look. "My ass is *not* scrawny."

"I know," Declan said, chuckling. "I was just trying to get a rise out of you."

"All right," Robin said and reaching into the pocket of her PJ bottoms, she pulled out her phone. "Just let me have some coffee and call Rita to check on the cats and—"

"Nope," Declan said, snatching the phone away. "You're not going to stall until you can figure out a way to get out of it. Take your coffee with you, and I'll call this Rita person."

"Declan."

"Robin...*go!*"

***

"You know, if I didn't love you as much as I do, I'd tell you that you're a special kind of stupid," Rita said, reaching for her coffee cup. "Why in the world, after all these years of loving that woman, would you walk out on her?"

"I was scared," Judy said softly. "I thought I'd lose my family and—"

"Screw your family!"

"I kind of did. Don't you think?"

Rita shot Judy a knowing smile. "You sure as hell did, and that *almost* redeems you for leaving this island without even as much as a goodbye. I gotta tell you, that really hurt."

"I'm sorry. I wasn't thinking too clearly."

"Well, thankfully you are now," Rita said, and getting to her feet, she began gathering the breakfast dishes. "I still think you should call her, though. I mean, I understand why you don't want to because that's really a romantic gesture, but Robin's somewhere in Florida right now probably feeling like shit, and that's all because of you."

"But I thought you said she left because...wait. You said someone got hurt. Did she tell you who?"

"Yeah, a guy named Declan."

"Declan!" Judy shouted, jumping to her feet.

"Relax, he's fine," Rita said, motioning for Judy to sit back down.

"How do you know?"

Rita brought over the coffee pot and refilled the cups. "Because when Robin called yesterday to check on the cats, I asked if everything was okay and she yes, he was fine. Then she asked if I was going to be around for a while, so she didn't have to come back right away."

"What did you tell her?" Judy said as she picked up her coffee to take a sip.

"I told her to take her time, the cats were no problem, and as long as she got back before Hank and I left to spend the holidays with the kids, that would be fine."

"Oh, okay," Judy said, placing the cup back on the table. "So when's that?"

"The twentieth," Rita said, returning to her seat.

"The twentieth! But that's over two weeks away."

"Which is why you should call her," Rita said, and fishing into her back pocket, she put her phone on the table. "Her number's in my contact list."

Judy eyed the phone as she nibbled on her lip, but before she could make up her mind, the phone began to vibrate against the table.

Rita glanced down and tried to hide her smile when she saw the name on the screen. "Well, I think that's my cue to head into the living room and relax for a while," she said, standing up. "Don't think you need to answer that, by the way. I'm sure she'll leave a message. It doesn't matter if she has to wait for a few more weeks before you tell her that you love her. Nope, that doesn't matter at all."

"Shit," Judy said and jumping to her feet, she picked up the phone.

The drive back to Mackinac had provided Judy with more than enough time to get her thoughts in order. She knew she had made mistakes. She knew she had a lot to apologize for, and Judy knew she was prepared to spend the rest of her life making it up to Robin, but when Judy accepted the call, her mind became a blender and her thoughts, the fruit in a smoothie.

"Robin, it's me, Judy." Rolling her eyes, Judy started again. "I'm home. I mean I'm back on Mackinac, and I don't ever plan on leaving again. I fucked up, and I know it, but...well, listen. There's something I've never said to you, and I really didn't want to say it on the phone, but Rita told me you aren't planning to come back for a few weeks, and I'm done wasting time. I've wasted enough of it, so...I love you, Robin. I love you more than I can say, and I promise when you get back I'm going to show you just how much I love you by—"

"Keeping those *particular* details to yourself until you're actually talking to Robin," Declan said as he slid the door closed behind him.

"Declan?"

"The one and only," Declan said, his eyes narrowing to avoid the glare of the sun gleaming off the Gulf of Mexico. "I called to check on the cats, but so far this has been *way* more enlightening."

"Are you okay? Rita said you got hurt."

"I'm fine. It was just a scratch," Declan said, moving to the far end of the balcony. "But Robin's been a fucking mess since she got here, so I'm glad you've come to your senses. I was having a really hard time hating you, but that doesn't mean I couldn't have got there."

"I wouldn't have blamed you if you did."

"Well, thankfully it sounds like I don't need to practice my scowl, but it also sounds like you may be between a rock and a hard place."

"What do you mean?"

"Robin's not planning to come back for a few weeks, so all those sentiments you just rattled off are going to have to wait, because you're right. If you haven't told her you loved her yet, you sure as hell shouldn't do it over the phone. Not after all the years she's loved you, and especially not after running out on her the way you did."

"I know," Judy said, and plopping down on a chair, she sighed. "But sixteen days seems like a lifetime."

Declan unconsciously nodded as he looked down at the beach, dotted with vacationers and locals enjoying a day in the sun. Parasailers could be seen off in the distance, their multi-colored kites vibrant against the cerulean sky, as life-jacketed riders on jet skis skipped across the emerald green Gulf. Declan's face eased into a smile. "Of course, there is *another* option."

"Oh yeah? What's that?"

"Are you afraid to fly?"

Chapter Forty-Five

Declan made his way across the sand, the insulated beverage cooler in his hand swinging with the rhythm of his steps. Reaching the cherry red umbrella, he ducked under the fringe and slipped into his beach chair. "Sorry, that took so long. My phone kept ringing."

"Problems?" Robin said, looking over her shoulder.

"Not a one. Natalia called to check in and—"

"I cannot *believe* she went back to work."

"She went back to work because she knows I'm okay, and I don't need a babysitter, plus there's a big convention happening in Tampa this weekend. Her hotel is expecting a couple hundred VIPs, so she wanted to make sure her staff had everything handled."

"Yeah, but after what she's been through—"

"Robin, if there's one thing about Natalia you need to understand, it's that she's plucky as hell. Sure, it was frightening, but after everything was said and done, she was fine."

"I suppose so," Robin said quietly.

"And how are you doing?"

"I'd be better if you'd stop asking me that, and besides, I should be asking *you* that."

"Lord have mercy, woman. It's just a scratch," Declan said, glancing at the bandage wrapped around his forearm.

"A scratch doesn't take twenty-eight stitches to close."

"Robbie, we've been over this already. I'm fine. My arm's fine. Natalia's fine. No harm. No foul."

"But there was harm, Declan," Robin said, fighting to control her emotions. "If—"

"Kiddo, *if* I hadn't walked out of the bathroom when I did, you're right, there would have been harm, a shitload of harm, but the Gods were in our favor, so drop it. Stop blaming yourself for what happened. It wasn't your fault. Pam's a fucking nut case."

"I couldn't agree more, but why the hell go after Natalia instead of me?" Robin said. "That doesn't make any sense."

"Natalia wasn't her target. By the look on Pam's face when I came out of the bathroom, she didn't even know Nat was there. She was coming after me."

"But why?"

"You know, at first, I thought it was because of what you told me about Isobel knocking Pam down when she was in Mackinac. I figured Pam was afraid to go back, but when the cops were dragging her away, Pam had a complete meltdown. You know the one? Her usual bullshit hissy fit where she threatens anyone within shouting distance what she's going to do to them, and then makes it sound like she's the victim."

"Oh, I know all about those."

"Well, during her tantrum, she let it slip that she came after me because killing you wouldn't hurt you as much as if she killed me."

Robin scrunched up her face. "Say what?"

"It actually makes sense when you think about, Robbie. We both know Pam is all about paybacks. When you broke up with her, she tried to hurt you in every way possible. She lied to your friends about the type of person you were. She made up stories about you and me. She basically did everything in her power to destroy you, and what better payback is there, then to kill me and let you live with the guilt, because that's precisely what would have happened."

The color drained from Robin's face. "It would have destroyed me," she said in a whisper.

"Exactly, and if Pam had gotten away with it, like she obviously thought she was going to, she could have kicked back and wallowed in yet another victory. Luckily for us, the only thing she's going to be wallowing in is a prison cell, and by the sounds of it, it's going to be a *very* long wallow."

"What do you mean?"

"Oh, that's the other reason why it took me so long to come back with the margaritas," Declan said, grabbing the jug. "Detective Sanchez called, too. Pam was well enough to be arraigned, so they took her in front of a judge this morning."

"And?"

"As it stands right now, the charges are trespassing, breaking and entering, carrying a concealed weapon, two counts of aggravated assault, two counts of attempted murder, a shitload of parole violations, and drug trafficking."

"Wait. Drug trafficking?"

"She had a bag of oxy in her pocket along with one holding enough cocaine to charge her with trafficking both of them."

"Shit."

"Yeah, I know," Declan said, and filling a plastic cup, he handed it to Robin. "And what's really funny is I kind of feel bad for her."

Robin glanced at Declan. "Me too."

"Seriously?"

"Yeah," Robin said, swiveling back to stare at the Gulf. "We both know she's unstable, but I think a psychiatrist could have probably helped her more than prison ever will."

Robin and Declan sipped their drinks in silence until Robin glanced at Declan to see his expression had turned dark and hawkish. "What's wrong?"

Declan shook his head. "I was just sitting here thinking about that morning."

"What about it?"

"About how you think you know yourself until something pushes you over the edge. When I saw Pam holding that knife, I didn't think. I didn't consider. I didn't weigh options. All I knew is that I needed to stop her. No, that's not right," Declan said, shaking his head. "I didn't *need* to stop her. I was *going* to stop her...and I launched myself at her like some sort of fucking superhero. I didn't care about the knife or...or anything else. Hell, I didn't even know she cut me until after it was all over. All I knew was there was no way in hell she was going to hurt Natalia. And when Pam kept fighting, kept struggling to get back the knife, Robbie, I slammed her face into that lamp with all the strength I had." Declan hung his head. "So much for never hitting a girl."

"You were protecting Natalia, Declan. The cops said you had every right to do what you did to stop her."

"I know, and I'd do it again if I had to. I just wish I hadn't fucked up her face."

"How bad was it?"

Declan thought for a moment before letting out a long sigh. "Think Picasso."

Robin took a few gulps of her drink in hopes of diluting that image, and shifting in her chair, she looked out across the Gulf.

***

Judy made her way down the access ramp to the beach, across cracked planks partially covered by sand. She breathed in the briny air, and as she reached the end of the walkway, she kicked off her flip-flops, knocked off the sand, and dropped them into her netted beach bag. The carryall was one of many recent purchases. At first, she thought she could do without, but mentally tallying up only the most necessary of items, the lightweight sack was just large enough to carry the keys to her rental car, her phone, a towel from the hotel, a bottle of water, and now, her sandals. The rest of the things Judy needed at the beach she was wearing.

The kiss of the sun's warmth caressed her shoulders as Judy stepped onto the fine white sand and moved between the dunes. Iconic sea oats swayed in the breeze along with the cordgrass and beach-elder, and weaving its way through the brush was a vine dotted with lavender flowers, its color distinct against the surrounding green.

Emerging from the protection of the dunes, Judy pushed her mirrored aviators to the top of her head. For a moment, she squinted at the brilliance of the sun, its radiance streaming down from a cloud-free sky of blue, but without the darkly tinted lenses, the magnificent crystalline cyan of the Gulf came into view. "Wow," Judy said in a breath as she took it all in. A minute later, she filled her lungs again with the salty air and readjusting her sunglasses on her face, Judy set off down the sand.

Given the fact it was a weekday, the beach wasn't crowded, and she meandered past sun worshipers who, like squatters, had claimed their places in the sun with chairs, umbrellas, coolers, and boom boxes. Children wearing vividly-colored water wings ran to and fro carrying plastic pails and shovels in their hands and a few parents, with reddened faces, blew into inflatable toys and floats hoping to provide even more entertainment for the youngsters.

Judy veered toward the water, enjoying the balmy breeze off the Gulf as she watched plovers and terns scamper and dance near the waves while, in the distance, gulls swooped and cried as they dove for their food. She stepped around the occasional piles of beach wrack, the entangled seagrass, reeds, and algae common where water meets the shore, but when she came across a section covered in broken shells, Judy headed back to dry sand.

Although to onlookers, it would have appeared she was in no rush, her movement casual and her attention all-encompassing, Judy was merely focused on her goal. Somewhere down the beach was the woman she loved, and once she found her, Judy had no intention of ever letting go. She also had no intention of forgetting anything that had brought her to this point.

From the three flights and sixteen hours of delays and layovers to the time spent at the International Plaza shopping mall in Tampa buying what she didn't pack, Judy had committed everything to memory and today was no different. She never wanted to forget the smell of the salt air and the feel of the warm sand under her feet, or the intensity of the sun heating her skin and the sounds of the waves lapping against the shore. Judy burned every detail into her mind because she knew she'd never repeat this day…for it was the first day of the *only* life she had ever wanted.

The blast of a ferry horn broke Judy from her thoughts, and hunting through her bag, she pulled out her phone. Unable to see the screen because of the sun, Judy darted under a vacant umbrella and read the text.

"Where the hell are you!!!!"

Amused by Declan's overkill of punctuation, Judy replied, "No place to park at condo. Found a lot about a mile north. I'm on the beach, heading your way now. 10-15 minutes max."

**

Declan pocketed his phone and stretching out his legs, he crossed them at the ankles as he reached for the margarita jug. "So, have you given any thought as to what you're going to do?"

Robin gave Declan a side-eyed glance. "About what?"

Declan shrugged. "Are you planning to stay on Mackinac or…or sell it all and move somewhere else?"

"I'm not going to sell," Robin said, holding out her cup for Declan to refill. "It's hard to explain, especially now after...after what's happened, but it feels like home up there. I know it's not going to be easy, and it'll be a while before I can ever sleep in that bedroom again, but Mackinac holds a lot of good memories." Robin paused and took a deep breath. "And I finally understand something Maxine said to me once."

"Which was?"

"That Adele would have taken only one day a year if that's all my mother could have given her because I feel the same way. I only had a few months with Judy and...and only one night, and I'm not saying it was enough. God, it *so* wasn't enough, but everything we were together is a part of that house and that island, and I can't walk away from it. I just can't."

As Robin sniffled back her emotions, Declan quickly glanced down the beach before he topped off Robin's drink. "I get that. I really do, but aren't you a little young to live like a nun?"

"I don't care about that, Declan. I've had my one true love. I'm done."

"Okay, we need to do something to get you out of this funk," Declan said, scrubbing his fingers through his hair. "Hey, how about we play that game we used to play? We're not drunk yet, but we're close enough. What do you say?"

"What in the hell are you talking about?"

Declan was in his forties, but his grin belonged to an impish little boy. "Rate the Babes on the Beach."

Robin stared blankly back at Declan. "That wasn't my game. It was yours, and you're off the market."

"I'm not off the market until I propose to Natalia, and that won't be for another few weeks."

"*Excuse* me?"

"Okay, you're right," Declan said with a laugh. "I'm happily off the market, but that doesn't mean we can't find *you* someone. I mean, come on," he said, spreading his arms wide. "The Gulf coast is a mecca for lesbians."

"I'd hardly call it a mecca," Robin said, giving Declan the once-over. "And I am *not* interested."

"Then humor me. After all, you're not the only one who's had a hell of a week," Declan said, tenderly running his fingers across the bandages encasing his forearm.

Robin's mouth went slack, Declan's overt play on her sympathies as transparent as it was triumphant. "Okay," Robin said with a sigh. "Whatever. Go for it."

"Great!" Declan said, briskly rubbing his hands together. "Now...let's see."

Declan scanned the beach, shading his eyes as he searched for the least likely of candidates. "Got one," he said, leaning closer to Robin. "At your ten o'clock. Cargo shorts. Halter top. Undeniably gay."

Robin adjusted her sunglasses lower on her nose, and changing her focus, she saw the woman almost instantly. Cargo shorts well past her knees. A halter top straining to hold back 44DDs, and enough lambda and labrys tattoos covering her beefy arms to make her sexuality more than known. "Are you serious?"

"What? You've dated large women before."

"I have, but after Judy do you really think—"

"Yeah, I suppose you're right. Okay, cross her off the list," Declan said as he scoured the beach for his next nominee. "At your nine. Board shorts. Striking style choices."

Robin turned her head. Down the beach was a woman wearing a sleeveless T-shirt with Proud to be Gay painted in red across the black-and-white stripes, clashing effortlessly with her green and blue plaid board shorts. The combination should have been enough to grab anyone's attention, but her blue Mohican hairstyle guaranteed it. "That's strike two. One more and me humoring you is over."

Declan faked a frown. "All right. Guess that means I've gotta find a good one."

"Or we could just stop playing."

"Nope. The rules are I get three strikes." Declan looked to his right and surveyed the beach, and a second later, every laugh line he owned made an appearance. "Okay. I've got a winner. Your three o'clock. Aviators. Prismatic wrap."

Robin let out a long, exaggerated sigh and peering over the top of her sunglasses, she looked down the beach. Again, Declan's description was scant, but amidst the people dotting the sand, the woman's sarong in the colors of the rainbow flag stood out. The black one-piece she wore dipped provocatively in the front. With no embellishment Robin could see, it was chic and understated, yet the seductive flash of one thigh peeking through the wrap as she strolled down the sand amplified her gender nicely. And even though the colorful stripes announced her proclivity, they weren't accompanied by tattoos, spiked hair, or hoops of metal pierced through her skin.

Robin's cursory once-over lasted only a few seconds before she turned back to face the water. She calmed the hair on the back of her neck and just before she was about to take a drink, she said, "And that's strike..."

The diluted mixture of tequila, Cointreau, and lime juice in Robin's cup began to ripple. She told herself her mind was playing tricks on her. After all the hours Robin had spent over the past few days thinking about only one person, why wouldn't a woman with salt-and-pepper hair remind of her of Judy? It was just a coincidence the woman had the same hairstyle, the same petite frame, the same...walk?

Robin's breath caught in her throat. Whether encased in denim or in corduroy, Robin had ogled Judy's bottom enough to have memorized the swing of the woman's hips. A casual sway combining confidence and femininity, there had never been an ounce of flaunt in the movement, never an ounce of exaggeration to catch someone's eye, just like the woman walking toward her. *Exactly* like the woman walking toward her.

Declan moved closer until his chin was almost resting on Robin's shoulder. "If I were you, I'd give that last one another look," he said, taking the cup from Robin's trembling hand. "And I have a funny feeling I'm about to become the third wheel, so I'm going to head out." Kissing Robin on the cheek, he whispered, "I love you, kiddo. Be happy. You deserve it."

Choked by emotion, all Robin could do was bob her head in reply. For a few seconds, her shoulders continued to heave as she fought hard against her tears until taking a deep, ragged breath, Robin pushed herself to her feet. Tossing aside her sunglasses, she wiped the tears from her face with the back of her hand before ducking out from under the umbrella. For a second, she had to shield her eyes from the sun, but with Judy now only a few feet away, once Robin saw the face she thought she'd never see again, the dam let loose for the second time. Cupping her hands over her mouth, Robin tried to quiet her sobs as tears trickled down her cheeks.

Judy pushed her sunglasses up and smiled at the woman bawling in front of her. "Not really the reaction I was going for."

Robin huffed out a laugh between her sobs. "What...what are you doing here?"

"I'm here because I finally figured out that when you know who you want, when you know who you love, when you know who you need to feel complete, you find that person, and you tell them. You tell them you love them more than anything else in the world. You tell them you can't live without them, and you tell them if a choice has to be made, no matter what that choice is, you'll choose them and only them...and I have. I love you, Robin. I love you beyond any words, any sonnets, or any universe, and I have loved you since the first moment I saw you...and there was no way in hell I was going to say that over the—"

Chapter Forty-Six

Unlike the night they had spent in the shadows of a room lit only by candles, no shadows existed today. The blinds on the patio door were opened to the extreme and sunlight flooded the room. It was one of four bedrooms in the third-floor condo, and overlooking Longboat Key beach, there was no worry about prying eyes or nosy neighbors with binoculars...not that the two women cared.

Judy smiled into the kiss, just as she did when Robin had pulled her into her arms on the beach. Just like she had done in a shower lasting only long enough to wash away salt, sand, and SPF, and just like she had done when their towels dropped to the floor seconds before they fell onto sheets, crisp and white.

In photographs, the difference between black and white is called contrast. Without it, no image would exist because it would be lost in the gray of nothingness. In life, contrast brings with it a new definition. It can be the difference between tall and short, round and lanky, or reserved...and unrestrained.

In the dimness of Robin's bedroom on Mackinac, Robin had taken Judy to orgasm more times than she could remember, but through it all, Judy had barely said a word. A few had slipped out, unpreventable as passion soared, but hesitant to speak for fear words of love would emerge, Judy had bit her lip more than once. She had silenced her breathy encouragements and censured her throaty directives, and even though she had opened her eyes at times, she had closed them just as quickly. She had wanted to remember the touch of Robin's hands and the feel of her mouth and tongue on her body, but amidst the yearning on Robin's face, there had always been a modicum of sadness, a tinge of dread at what the morning would bring...but no more. No more.

Before Robin had a chance to cover Judy's body with her own, Judy took the upper hand, and straddling Robin's thighs, she gazed down at her victim. "I love you," she whispered seconds before she claimed Robin's mouth in a wet, probing kiss. She ravaged Robin's mouth with her tongue, sucking on Robin's when it was offered until they were both out of breath. Judy broke out of the kiss and sitting up, her eyes roamed over what was before her.

Robin's skin had been honeyed by the sun, her fairness now showing only in areas once protected by a periwinkle bikini, and it was those areas which held Judy's focus. Perfect breasts tipped with rose-hued nipples rose and fell in time with Robin's breathing, and as Judy's eyes locked with Robin's, she reached out and covered the mounds. Judy watched in awe as Robin's expression began to change as Judy fondled and squeezed the orbs, and when she scissored her fingers around the points, they grew even more rigid, much too stiff to go to waste.

Judy rocked forward, covering one delectable tip in her mouth and circling the beaded nipple with her tongue as she continued to knead Robin's other breast, she felt Robin's hands on her waist. For a moment, they were still, but as they started to travel, Judy stopped what she was doing long enough to capture Robin's hands and trap them under her own. "No," she said, smiling down at Robin. "Right now...right now, this is all about me loving you."

This was a Judy she had yet to meet, and Robin couldn't contain her grin. "Is that so?"

"Yes," Judy said, lowering her face to Robin's breast again. "That's so."

Judy teased and tasted her way across Robin's torso, leisurely taking her time as she ever so slowly made her way down her body. A kiss here, a kiss there, a kiss almost everywhere until Judy had to nudge Robin's knees apart to continue her journey, and when Robin's glistening womanly flesh came into view, Judy licked her lips.

Robin spread her arms wide, reaching out across the bed for something, *anything* to hold onto. She grabbed at the tightly fitted sheet, hoping she could release some of the fabric, and when it loosened, Robin held on for dear life. This was a surprise. This was going to be a first, and as Robin felt Judy's breath between her legs, Robin knew...*this* was going to kill her.

There were no curls to conceal the dark pink furrows and ridges, and no clothing to hinder the aroma of need, and as Judy breathed in the exquisite fragrance, she drew her tongue through one of the crevices.

"Oh, my God," Robin said, arching her hips. "Oh...God."

Robin's flavor was as ambrosial as it was intoxicating and Judy dined on the blend of salty and sweet, using her tongue to taste, to investigate, and to probe. She could hear Robin's breathing growing louder as each minute passed, but a gourmet meal such as this had to be savored, and Judy was doing just that. The satiny flesh against her tongue was delicate, warm, and slick, and each nook and cranny was enjoyed. Judy sucked on the tender lips and poked into secret spots, investigating every millimeter before her as Robin writhed and moaned until there was only one thing left to be tasted.

Judy paused just long enough to take a few quick breaths before zeroing in on something now only partially hidden for it was swollen with need. Judy tenderly pushed aside petals glazed with want and circled Robin's clit with her tongue.

Robin's gasp filled the room, and bending her knees, she opened herself up to Judy. "Please. Oh, God...you're killing me."

A brief smile crossed Judy's face before she returned to administering torturous pleasure on the woman she loved. Again and again, she traced Robin's clit with the tip of her tongue, occasionally suckling gently against the engorged organ while Robin writhed on the bed. It wasn't until Robin's words turned unintelligible, and her breathing became shallow and fast, when Judy fully uncovered the swollen nub and began flicking her tongue against Robin's clit. She gradually increased the pressure and the speed, and within seconds, Robin's guttural moans filled the room.

Overwhelmed by sensations deep within, Robin could do nothing but give herself to the climax Judy created. Her nectar oozed from her core as ripples of ecstasy morphed into shuddering explosions, and plunging over a crest, Robin's soul was shattered by an orgasm stronger than any she'd ever imagined.

Mesmerized, Judy listened to Robin's guttural moans, enthralled as much with the sound as with the woman herself. Perspiration had soaked the strands of Robin's hair, turning it dark, and her face glowed, heated by the flames of passion. Her torso shimmered with sweat, and her nipples had yet to calm, the erect tips rising and falling as Robin gasped for air. Love brings with it many privileges, and Judy swore at that moment, she would never, *ever* take any of them for granted. They were much too precious. Much, *much* too precious.

Judy had no idea how much time had passed, but when she heard Robin's breathing finally slow, Judy crawled up the bed and straddled Robin's waist again. "Are you okay?" Judy said with a laugh.

Robin opened her eyes. "You're pretty pleased with yourself. Aren't you?"

"I've been thinking about doing that for a few days now, so yeah. I'm good."

"Are you now?"

"More than I can put into words," Judy whispered.

For a long moment, they gazed into each other's eyes until Judy saw a devilish glint appear in Robin's. "Don't even think about it," Judy said, waggling her finger. "I have the upper hand here, and I plan to keep it."

It was true that Judy's position gave her somewhat the advantage. Robin was, after all, pinned under her, but it did provide Robin quite the view. In the brightness of the day, Judy was even more beautiful. Brazenly exposed, her pert breasts were tipped with nipples, distended and pink, and her hour-glass waist led to hips, curved and soft. "This is new," Robin said, raising her eyes as she ran her finger across a bit of satiny skin where once was curls.

Judy could feel her face begin to heat. "I could lie and say it was because of the French-cut bathing suit."

"You could."

"But I won't. I'm never going to lie to you again."

"So, this was for me," Robin said, again running her finger over the smoothness.

"Do you mind?"

"I'll tell you in a minute."

Judy knew chicanery when she saw it. Mischief danced in Robin's eyes, and if her grin became any more lopsided, it was going to slide off her face. So intent on trying to solve the puzzle, Judy paid no attention when Robin slipped her arms through the small gap between Judy's thighs and Robin's waist, but a second later, she wished she had.

Robin quickly pushed Judy upward, lifting her just enough so Robin could slide down the bed, right between Judy's legs.

Instantly recognizing Robin's intent, all the air rushed from Judy's lungs. "Oh, no."

A hum with diabolical intent slipped from Robin's lips. "Oh...yes," she whispered and breathing in Judy's carnal bouquet, Robin sampled the copious divine dew coating Judy's sex.

For a moment, Judy remained rigid, keeping herself far enough away that Robin had to reach for what she wanted. The position was raw and salacious, giving a new meaning to being exposed. Judy was hovering over Robin's face as if she was an offering, but when she felt Robin's tongue lapping against her folds, there was nothing Judy could do but sacrifice herself to it. As she relaxed her legs, lowering herself just enough so Robin could rest her head on the bed, Judy closed her eyes...and it began.

Judy was dripping with excitement, and Robin regaled in running her tongue through the wet folds, drinking in the heady delicacy that already was coating her cheeks. She sought out every valley, burrowing into the slippery softness to pillage its secrets and succulent flesh was tenderly nibbled along the way. At times, Robin would tease, pausing for a moment to build the anticipation before she'd start again, and then she'd plunder, drawing her tongue in long, drawn-out strokes over Judy's puckered fissures.

Robin's attention to detail was sending Judy spinning out of control. No longer concerned with the bawdy and unchaste arrangement, Judy leaned forward and placed her hands on the upholstered headboard. In an unbridled and erotic invitation, she lifted her hips and opened herself even more for Robin.

One marginal shift of position was all Robin needed to take full advantage of what Judy was offering. She nuzzled against Judy's opening, taking great pleasure in tasting the savory juices flowing freely from Judy's center before Robin finally probed the opening with her tongue. Judy instantly bucked against the intrusion, but with her hands on Judy's hips, Robin held her in place, ravishing yet another part of Judy's body in sensual abandon.

Instincts, primal and uninhibited took over as Judy began moving against Robin's tongue. At first, her undulations were subdued, slow slides matching the rhythm Robin had set, but before too long...slow was not enough.

Insatiable, Robin continued to lick, suckle, and taste until she felt Judy tap her on the hand. Robin stopped instantly. Fearing she'd done something wrong, as Judy moved above her, angling away from the headboard, Robin watched in silence and then her breath caught in her throat.

Judy's face was flushed, and her lips were parted as she gasped for air. A shimmering hint of sweat covered her brow and upper lip, but it was what lived in the blue of her eyes that held Robin's attention. The pale blue had darkened to that of the deepest sapphire, and in the facets of the gems was a wanton urgency. It wasn't an appeal, a wordless plea to end the exquisite distress Robin had produced. It was a demand, and when Judy threaded her fingers through Robin's hair, taking hold and pulling her face toward Judy's center, Robin didn't wince at the yank of her hair. She rejoiced in the privilege of loving Judy.

Burying her face in Judy's luscious folds, Robin was ravenous in her assault. Licking, suckling, and probing, she was unforgiving in her pursuit, and Judy soon began to grind herself against Robin's open mouth. With both of Judy's hands now in her hair, Robin was being guided to where Judy needed her most, and covering Judy's clit with her mouth, Robin swept her tongue over it again and again.

Unchecked and libertine, Judy gyrated above Robin until her shattering release was upon her. Dizzying bursts and spasms rushed through her, taking with them her breath and her sanity, and for a split-second, she stiffened against the onslaught. A moment later, Judy gave herself to the waves of splendor crashing her against the shore, riding each to the sweetest of deaths.

***

"I brought you some water. You look parched," Robin said, handing Judy a bottle.

"That's because you sucked me dry," Judy said and rearranging the pillows, she relaxed against the stack.

Robin's eyes creased at the corners, and sitting on the bed, she folded her legs under her. "Coming out becomes you. That is...if you did come out?"

Judy chuckled, downing half the bottle of water before she spoke. "Oh, trust me. I did."

"And?"

"I probably lost a few members of my family, but—"

"I'm sorry."

Judy shook her head. "Don't be. The way I see it is we all have choices. They're choosing to forget who I am. They're choosing to forget the person they grew up with. All they're seeing is this," Judy said, waving her arm over the bed. "And if their minds are that limited, that parochial, then they don't deserve me in their lives. They don't deserve *us* in their lives because I will always and *forever* choose you. End of subject."

Robin's smile lit up the room, and leaning over, she gave Judy a kiss. "I love you."

"I love you, too," Judy said before taking another sip of water. "By the way, where are we?"

"Huh?"

Judy twirled her finger in the air. "Whose place is this?"

"Oh, it belongs to Natalia's parents. It's their winter home."

"It's nice."

"Speaking of nice, how about I take you out for a nice dinner? I don't know about you, but I'm starving."

"Worked up an appetite, did you?"

"You should know," Robin said as she climbed off the bed. "So, you game?"

"Yes, but we have a problem."

"Which is?"

"All I have is the bathing suit. The rest of my stuff is in the rental car."

"Where is it?"

"Um...in a public parking lot about a mile from here."

"All right," Robin said, and gathering up their bathing suits, she handed Judy her one-piece. "What say we take a walk down the beach, grab your things, come back, shower, and get some dinner?"

Judy grinned as she stepped into her swimsuit. "Do you honestly think we'll make it past the shower?"

"No, but we can try."

Chapter Forty-Seven

A few weeks later...

"I think we're going to need a bigger closet."

"What?" Robin said, and watching as Judy pointed to the far corner of the room, Robin looked over her shoulder at the Christmas tree in the corner. Surrounding it were the numerous gifts they had unwrapped that morning, the lids on many now inverted to reveal new clothing still nestled in red, green, and white tissue paper. "I don't think we went crazy. Do you?"

"Not like my brother's house. That's for sure."

"And all the clothes from your apartment are already here, aren't they?"

"Yeah, there's nothing left up there except for the furniture. Why?"

Robin glanced over at tree again. "Then we should be fine," she said, turning back around. "We have the armoire in the guest room, and we have the storage under the window seat. Plus, I'm not opposed to buying another armoire and putting it in our room. There's plenty of space for one."

"There you go shopping again," Judy mumbled into her wine glass as she brought it to her lips.

Robin snorted. "And there's no twelve-step program for it so you may as well get used to it."

Judy gave Robin a quick peck on the cheek. "I already have."

"Good."

"Oh, I was thinking about asking Larry and Kay if they want me to leave the sofa and tables for whoever rents it next, and if it's okay with you, I thought maybe we could use my bedroom set in Willow Bay once we redecorate it."

"I forget," Robin said, narrowing her eyes. "Which one's Willow Bay?"

"End of the second-floor hall. Gray and purple wallpaper. Heavily painted black bed frame."

"Oh," Robin said, faking a shiver. "Done deal, but we may want to snag that bookcase from your apartment. Between what you brought over and what I already have, there's no way we have enough shelves to fit all the books."

"That works."

"And speaking of books, I'll try not to take it too personally that you don't have any of mine in your collection."

"That's where you're wrong," Judy said, putting her glass aside. "Once I found out your pen name, I bought all of them. They're on my Kindle."

"And?"

"Are you asking me if I liked them?"

"Yes, and you can tell the truth. Part of being a writer is having a thick skin."

"I will always tell you the truth, and the truth is I only got a few pages into The Butterfly's Sting before I had to put it down."

"Ouch."

Judy giggled. "So much for having a thick skin."

"Well, my style isn't for everyone."

"Robin, I didn't say I didn't like it."

"Then why put it down?"

"Because it was right after I took the job, and I was still fighting with myself over how I felt about you. I opened that book, and I found myself smiling like a fool only a couple of pages in."

Robin raised an eyebrow. "Um...that book starts out rather grimly."

"Oh, it does, and you do gruesome really well, let me tell you, but I wasn't smiling about the story. I was smiling because *you* wrote it, and I loved every word. The only problem was I didn't *want* to love every word because it was just going to make me love you more, which, at the time, I didn't want to do."

Robin sighed seconds before giving Judy a slow, feathery kiss. "I think that may possibly be the best review I've ever received."

"Cool," Judy said, snuggling against Robin.

"Speaking of cool, I could get used to this," Robin said, and draping her arm around Judy's shoulders, she pulled her closer and planted a kiss on her head. "I love you."

"I love you, too." Having had enough of the light whispery kisses, Judy tipped her face to Robin, but before she could accomplish her mission, a ferry horn stopped her mid-kiss. Pulling her phone from her pocket, Judy looked at the screen and got to her feet. "Um…I need to take this. Okay?"

"Sure. Everything okay?"

"I'll tell you in a minute," Judy said as she left the room.

***

Twenty minutes came and went before Judy came back into the living room, slipping her phone into her pocket as she did. "Sorry. I didn't think it would take that long."

"Don't worry about it. As soon as you left the room, Gabby called, and then Declan called," Robin said as Judy sat down next to her.

"Am I ever going to meet Gabby?"

"As a matter of fact, she asked that we hold a room for her in June. She's going to send me the dates in an email."

"Well, I look forward to meeting her," Judy said, and reaching for her wine, she took a sip. "And how's Declan doing?"

"He's fine. He and Natalia wish us both a very Merry Christmas."

"And?" Judy said, looking out of the corner of her eye as she put her glass down.

The glow of Robin's face warmed the room. "He's officially engaged."

"That's great," Judy said, her expression mirroring Robin's. "And he's not the only one."

"What do you mean?"

"That was Louise on the phone."

"Louise? As in Pat's wife?"

"That's the one. She wanted to thank me for the gifts I left with Eric and to let me know that Brett's engaged. He called her this morning."

"That's awesome, but I'm afraid to ask. How'd it go over?"

"Actually, she sounded really happy, but she didn't say a word about how Pat took it. I'm not even sure he knows, but..." Judy stopped and smiled. "She said they're planning to get married this spring, and *we* should keep an eye out for the invitation."

"We?"

"That's what she said, and I'm pretty sure Louise doesn't speak French."

"Well, how about that. You surprised?"

"Not as much as when she told me she moved out of the house."

"What?"

Judy nodded. "She said she was staying with Gayle, and she wasn't going to lose her child over this. I think her exact words were 'either he comes to his senses, or he's going to lose more than just his son.'"

"Holy crap. Good for her."

"Yeah, I was thinking the same thing, but talk about an interesting day—right? I mean lots of couples get engaged on Christmas, but this is the first I've ever heard of someone separating—"

"Shit," Robin said, bolting upright on the love seat.

"What's wrong?"

"Nothing," Robin said, standing up. "Be right back."

Judy relaxed into the cushions and looking at the flames dancing in the hearth, she drew a slow breath. Her life had changed dramatically in only a few short weeks, but there had never been a moment of hesitation or a flicker of awkwardness. It was as if they had lived a previous life together and now, reincarnated, they were together again. From walking hand-in-hand on a beach under a moonlit sky to moving in with Robin the day after they returned from Florida, no effort was needed to blend their lives. No effort at all. Smiling, Judy ran her hand down her thigh and a moment later, she winced.

"Did you just pinch yourself?" Robin said as she came into the room.

"Yes," Judy said with a laugh.

"I didn't know you were into self-harm."

"I'm not," Judy said as Robin sat down next to her. "But does it ever feel like a dream to you? Like you're going to wake up and all of this...all of this is just going to be in your head?"

"More than once," Robin said, folding her leg under her as she faced Judy. "And there have been a couple of times when I've woken up, and you're not near, and I'm afraid to open my eyes, afraid to find out you're gone again or...or like you said, you were never there. But then I hear you breathing, and I wrap myself around you, and all is right with the world again."

"I'll never leave you again, Robin," Judy whispered, sealing the deal with a velvety kiss. "You're stuck with me now."

A grin overtook Robin's features. "Good, then I guess I'll still give you this." Robin placed a black, velvet ring box in Judy's hands. "I hope you don't mind."

Robin watched as Judy's expression went from blank to bright, her eyes darting back and forth between the ring box in her hand and Robin. In an instant, Robin understood every blonde joke she had ever heard. "No!" she blurted, placing her hand over the box as more words poured from her mouth. "No, no, no, no, Judy. Oh, gosh...that is *so* not what you think."

Judy's face fell. "It isn't?"

"Yeah, no," Robin said, her cheeks now flaming. "And that would bring a whole new meaning to U-Haul jokes."

"It would, would it?"

Robin's shoulders sagged past her hips. "Great. You don't know lipstick or chapstick, but you understand U-Haul?"

"I've heard the joke before," Judy said, placing the box on the ottoman. "And you think we're moving too fast."

"No. I don't think we're moving too fast at all," Robin said, grabbing the ring box and returning it to Judy's hand. "But when I propose, and I *will* propose, it's not going to be on a holiday or...or a birthday. It's going to be on a day when there's nothing else to celebrate except for that day. Okay?"

"Are you sure?"

"That I'm going to propose?"

"No, that you don't think—"

"We are *not* moving too fast, Judy. We have loved each other for over twenty-five years, and I don't know about you, but I wouldn't exactly label that lickety-split."

"Yeah, I guess you're right," Judy said, her smile brighter than all the lights on the tree.

"You know I am. Now open the box. It wasn't supposed to be for today anyway, but between finishing the Christmas decorations and shopping, and well..."

"Sex?"

Robin beamed. "Yes, that *definitely* came into play, so I totally forgot about it until we were talking about the engagements."

Taking a quick breath, Judy opened the box and her eyes misted over with tears.

"I hope you don't mind," Robin said, moving a little closer. "When we were moving you in, I knocked over your jewelry box, and that fell out. I saw how thin the band was, so I had it repaired."

"My mother gave me this on my sixteenth birthday," Judy said, gently extracting her signet ring from the velvet. She slipped it onto her right ring finger and gazed at the gold, now polished to a high sheen. The faint scratches from years of wear had been removed and the calligraphic J once lost amidst them had returned to prominence.

"Thank you," Judy whispered, and sliding her hand behind Robin's neck, she pulled her into a kiss. It started out light and tender like a summer breeze, but it didn't take long before it became hungry and wet.

"We have sex on the brain," Judy said as their lips parted.

"Yes, we do," Robin said as she slipped her hands under Judy's sweater. "And we're about to have it on the love seat."

Judy was inclined to agree, but as she moved to kiss Robin again, she noticed something in the corner. "Crap. We forgot something."

"We don't need protection," Robin said as she began to kiss Judy's neck.

Judy couldn't prevent a gurgle of mirth from escaping as she stopped Robin's advances. Pointing over Robin's shoulder, Judy said, "We forgot about what we locked up in the window seat last week."

Robin didn't need to look behind her and resting her forehead on Judy's shoulder, she sighed. "Okay. Let me go get the key. You get the stuff out of the bedroom."

"All right."

A couple of minutes later, Robin returned to find Judy removing the pillows covering the seat of the bay window. "Do you think she knows?" Robin said, unlocking the latch.

"I don't how she could. We had it covered when we brought it into the house, and the table wouldn't give her any hints."

"What about the—"

"It was all the way in the back of the closet, and as much time as we've been spending in the bedroom, I can't remember once when I felt a chill."

"Kudos to me!"

"I'm talking about Isobel, silly," Judy said, moving toward the fireplace. "Can you handle that one while I move this one?"

"Yep. Almost done."

It didn't take long before the two women had rearranged the living room, removing the old easel and replacing it with another almost twice the size. Instead of plastic, the new one had mahogany framework and accents in brass, and with the addition of a tiny, long-legged accent table just large enough to hold a cup of charcoal pencils and one filled with colors, Isobel's studio was almost complete. Judy placed the drawing pad they had kept hidden in their closet onto the rail, and returning to the love seat, they plopped down on the cushions. In unison, they propped their feet on the ottoman before Robin picked up their wine glasses and handed one to Judy.

"This has been a good day," Judy said before taking a sip.

"Yes, it has," Robin said, draping her arm around Judy's shoulders. "So, I have a question, and I want your honest answer."

"That's all you're ever going to get from me, sweetheart," Judy said, giving Robin a peck on the cheek. "So ask."

"Are you worried at all about when everyone comes back to the island in the spring?"

"You mean about us?"

"Yeah."

"No. Not at all."

"Really?"

Judy turned slightly and looked Robin in the eye. "The people I call my friends wouldn't be my friends if they were like Pat. I'm sure they'll be a little surprised, but as for being worried about them being hateful, I can't see that happening."

"I hope not."

"Well, when Woody helped us bring all my stuff down here, he didn't seem to have a problem with it."

"That's true."

"And Glen didn't either."

"Glen? As in the dockmaster? How would he know about us?"

"You kissed me on the dock right in front of him when we got back from our last Christmas shopping excursion."

Robin flopped her head back and stared at the ceiling. "Crap, I didn't even think about it."

"I know, and I loved that you didn't," Judy said, grinning. "And since his reaction was to give me a wink when we walked by, I'm thinking he doesn't care."

"Why am I just hearing about this now?" Robin said, rolling her head to the side.

"I don't know. I guess, like I said, I just know my friends."

"Yes, it seems that you do."

"But Rose and Tommy will probably be all bent out of shape. I can almost guarantee it."

"Remind me again. Which ones are they?"

"Tweedledee and Tweedledum."

"Oh," Robin said, sitting up. "Well, by the looks of them, they can't bend very far."

Judy burst out laughing as she slapped Robin on the leg. "That's not very nice."

"Sorry."

"Don't be. It was funny," Judy said, picking up her empty glass. "I think I'm done with wine. You want some coffee?"

"Yeah, that works," Robin said as she handed Judy her glass. "And while you're doing that, I'll put another log on the fire."

"Okay. Be careful."

"Always."

Robin got up and opened the screen on the fireplace, taking a few minutes to rearrange what remained of the burning logs before placing another on the stack. Returning to the sofa, she propped her feet on the ottoman and watched as the fire slowly began to consume the fresh timber.

"Hey, speaking of my friends. I may have one who's going to need a job once the season starts," Judy called from the kitchen.

"Oh yeah?" Robin said, looking toward the kitchen. "Who?"

"Have you ever met Zayne Johnson? Young guy. Dock porter."

Robin paused and then smiled. "Yeah, he was the one who brought over my luggage when I first came to the island," she called back. "Why would he need a job? He looked pretty happy doing what he was doing."

"That was before his bungeecide a few weeks ago."

"His what?"

Judy walked in carrying two steaming mugs of coffee, and when she saw Robin's bewildered expression, she grinned. "Sorry. You probably don't know what that means."

"Haven't a clue," Robin said, taking the mug Judy was offering her.

"It's a funny term for a not-so-funny accident," Judy said as she sat down. "It's what the porters call it when one of the bungees break, and it gets caught in the spokes of the bike tire."

Robin's eyes flew open. "God, that sounds awful."

"It is, and Zayne went down hard. Broke his collarbone and snapped his arm in four places. His mom told me they put in a bunch of screws to get everything back together, and since this is the second time Zayne's broken that same arm, the doctor suggested he find a new job or risk permanent damage if he does it again."

"Shit. That sucks."

"Yes, it does, but it gives us an awesome opportunity to help out a great kid and ourselves in the process," Judy said, and after taking a hesitant sip of coffee, she put the mug aside. "Zayne's an islander, and since he knows the island like the back of his hand, if he came to work for us, we'd not only get someone to haul luggage or clean rooms or...or build a website, but we'd also get someone who could offer our guests insight on what to do or where to go."

"I thought you were doing the website."

"I am, or I can, but Zayne's always been a geek when it comes to computers, so I thought...um...well, I thought a younger mind, more up on today's technology, could build us a better one." When Judy saw Robin instantly scowl, she snickered. "Before you say it, I know I'm not old, but we have a lot of things to do around here before we are officially open, and I don't know about you," Judy said, placing her hand on Robin's thigh. "But I don't want to spend all my time all alone in the office learning new technology when I could be with you...doing other things."

A low chuckle rose in Robin's throat. Judy had purred the last few words, making her intention perfectly clear. "Sold," Robin said, placing her mug on the floor next to the loveseat.

"Yeah?"

"Did you honestly think I was going to say no?"

Judy gave Robin a quick kiss and then moved a little closer. "I love you."

"I love you, too," Robin said, once again draping her arm over Judy's shoulders.

The room smelled of pine candles and the fire in the hearth, and with Christmas music softly playing on their newly purchased sound system, and Judy nestled against her, Robin closed her eyes for a moment. She took a deep breath, letting it out slowly as she opened her eyes. Smiling to herself, she pinched her leg.

"I see I'm not the only one into self-harm."

Robin kissed Judy on the top of the head. "You weren't supposed to see that."

"Too late," Judy said, turning to rest her head on Robin's chest. "And if this is a dream, I don't ever want to wake up. I just want to sit here with you, in front of a roaring fire…forever."

The flames flickered in the hearth and minutes slipped by without notice as both women became lost in their thoughts until Judy finally broke the silence. "Do you ever wonder if Adele picked out hers before she died?"

With Judy's head on her breast and the woman mindlessly running her hand up and down Robin's thigh, it took a few seconds for Robin to answer. "Um…what?"

Judy pointed to the urns sitting on the mantle. "They're almost identical."

Robin glanced at the two brass urns holding the ashes of Adele and her mother. Other than one being a little more polished than the other, there was no difference. "I don't know, but there was no way Adele would have known what I had picked for Mom."

"Interesting."

"I've actually been thinking about what to do with them."

"Why? I like them there."

"No, not the urns. I'm talking about what's inside of them."

"Oh. Why?"

"After all the years they spent apart, I'm not sure I want them separated in death, too. I thought about scattering their ashes on the island, but…but I don't want people trampling on them."

"Good point. There aren't many places on Mackinac where people don't go. That's for sure."

"Do you think it would be crass to split the ashes? Leave some in the urns and then…I don't know…scatter the rest somewhere else?"

"That's a great idea," Judy said, a soft grin gracing her face. "I like the way you think."

"Yeah, well, keep that thought," Robin said, removing her arm from Judy's shoulders.

Judy missed Robin's touch instantly, and she tipped her head to Robin. Noticing the twinkle in her eyes, Judy said, "What?"

Without saying a word, Robin swung her leg across Judy and a second later she was straddling the woman's legs. "I don't want to talk about urns anymore if that's okay with you" she whispered as she began kissing Judy's neck. "It's Christmas. I love you, and I want you."

A lusty feeling of warmth spread throughout Judy's body, ending at her core with a pulse that took her breath away. Judy turned her head to the side, sighing as she felt Robin's lips softly follow the curve of her neck. "Has anyone ever told you, you have a one-track mind?" Judy murmured.

"You really want me to answer that?" Robin purred, continuing her sensual onslaught. "Or are you complaining?"

Judy groaned as Robin nibbled on her ear lobe. "Um...no...definitely not complaining."

"Good." Robin rested back long enough to take off Judy's sweater, and tossing it aside, Robin quickly rid herself of not only her sweater but her bra as well. "Now, where were we?" she whispered a few seconds before her lips found Judy's.

The kiss was wet and probing, and Judy relished every stroke of Robin's tongue as it danced with her own, but when she felt Robin unclasping her bra, Judy broke out of the kiss. "You're incorrigible," she said with a laugh. "And we have a perfectly good bedroom for this."

"I know, but it's so far away," Robin said, gazing into Judy's eyes as she drew the straps of the bra down Judy's arms. "And I think we can both agree...we've wasted enough time."

***

Later that night, when the house was quiet, Isobel Vallencourt stood in front of an easel larger than she'd ever been afforded and with charcoal, she sketched. Death brought with it no stains on her fingers, no smudges of soot as she drew, and the purity of her dress remained intact as it had for so many years.

She looked over occasionally and smiled at the cats who had become her friends. Why they didn't run, why they didn't scamper in fear from her existence or rather her non was an answer she'd never find, but their company, in purrs and piercing green stares gave her more substance in death than she'd had when she was alive.

It had taken her over a century to understand that death had not been her answer. Yes, it had given her freedom from duty, and yes, it had protected her from hands, rough and hard, but the peace she had sought hadn't been found in death. It had been found in life. It had been found in the strength of two women who, like her, chose to hide, but unlike her, they still had lived. They had loved and laughed. They had touched and kissed, and while time spent was short, every minute they shared was a lifetime.

She had seen it in their eyes and heard it in their whispers, and high in a stairwell, she had drawn them, keeping their secret safe yet rejoicing in something she had only had for one summer more than a hundred years before.

It was a summer when a family moved to the island, bringing with them servants and a caregiver for their children. Her hair was dark and flowing, and her eyes the shade of cinnamon, and in one glance, Isobel's heart no longer was her own. It was a summer of discovery, of ardor new and compelling, and in the shadows of a stairway leading to a playroom when their hands touched for the briefest of moments, denial was no more. And it was a summer when in the depths of the forest their lips first met, and afterward, in a house not yet inhabited by the owners, they made love, touching and tasting all that was forbidden.

There were countless moments of joy when they shared their rapture without abandon, yet as the months moved slowly by, their guilt and fear became oppressive. They were breaking the laws of their church, and exposure would bring shame upon not only themselves but their families as well. If discovered, they would be deemed filthy and unnatural, yet disavowing their love was impossible, so they carried the strain of their secret until winter was almost upon them.

On an afternoon with rain misting through the trees, they stood under a canopy of branches, and as their breath steamed in the air, they shared a kiss like they had done so many times. They hadn't noticed the man walking the path until he was almost upon them, and while they managed to separate in time, the terror Isobel saw in Julia's eyes said it all. Never again would they hold each other close. Never again would their lips meet. Never again would they love in earnest, and when the first snow of the season blanketed the island in white, Julia stepped into the water of the Straits to forever quiet her mind of feelings and thoughts unstoppable.

A year later, Isobel had made the same choice, but the tranquility she sought wasn't to be. A rift, unexplainable and random, had settled her soul into a house. She had wanted sleep, deep and endless sleep where dreams and memories wouldn't exist, but instead each day *they* haunted her. Her era was a time when women were quiet. Refrained and refined, they dared not speak their minds, but in death, Isobel quickly found her voice. Despising the families that came and went, their existence continually reminding her of all she could never have and of all who would have condemned her, she ensured their visits would be short. Slamming doors, dislodging ceramics from shelves, and creating wind when no window gaped, she forced them all to leave until one afternoon, a woman tall and pretty walked into the house. Her jaw was square, and her eyes dark and piercing, but there was something else. She held her shoulders high and walked and talked with confidence and determination, and unlike all the others, *this* woman didn't answer to a man.

It wasn't long before Isobel discovered why and that knowledge brought with it a modicum of tranquility, but it wasn't until a niece who wasn't a niece moved into the house when Isobel finally and forever found her peace.

This one had no shame, no guilt attached to her lot in life for she viewed it not as a burden. Isobel had listened while she had spoken freely about it, with no concern for condemnation or banishment in the timbre of her voice and in an instant, serenity was Isobel's. And that was the reason for this gift.

Their love would not be hidden high on a wall, lost amongst hundreds of sketches, old and new. Their love would not be viewed as unworthy or unwelcome by any who walked into this house for Isobel would protect them until the day they joined her beloved Julia.

Isobel ran her finger down a line slightly darker than she wanted, adding definition to the intertwined bodies on her paper as she went. She found their embrace while sleeping gloriously honest. Even in slumber, they melded unconsciously, craving the other's touch, the other's warmth, and the other's existence for without it, they were not whole.

Her cheeks heated when she realized she had left a hint of a bosom exposed, but adjusting the drape of the sheet with a smudge of her finger, its beauty was concealed. Taking a step backward, she viewed the drawing with a critical eye, tilting her head this way and that until she slipped the charcoal back into the cup. Their future would hold more sketches for her mind was no longer filled with what she had lost, but rather what she had gained.

Isobel silently glided through the room, and as she reached the doorway, she looked over her shoulder and tittered at the clown she had placed on the coffee table. She had forgotten how much she loved to laugh.

Epilogue

"Maybe it's time we start considering turning around."

"Why?" Robin said, looking over at Judy for a second before returning her eyes to the road.

"Because it's called a snowstorm."

"It's not too bad, and we've been planning this trip for weeks. Besides, we're over halfway there. It would be kind of silly to turn back now. Don't you think?"

"Yeah, I guess you're right. Just be careful."

"Yes, dear."

Judy grinned. "I love you."

"I love you, too," Robin said, glancing at Judy. "Where did that come from?"

"From nowhere in particular. I just do."

"Well, I do, too."

"Good to know."

A few moments of silence passed between them before Robin said, "By the way, I think I've figured out what we can do with Isobel's sketches."

"That's great," Judy said, turning slightly in her seat. "Because the one she left for us this morning is gorgeous."

"I agree, so I thought maybe we could get some of them framed and put them in the bedrooms."

"The guest rooms?" Judy said, her voice traveling up the scale. "Robin, I have no problem being out, but I think that's a little too *out* for me."

Robin's mouth dropped open as she shot Judy a look. "I'm not talking about the ones where we're sleeping in bed, you goof. I was thinking about the others, like the one this morning where we're just snuggling on the window seat."

"Oh. Whew."

"Did you honestly think I'd want drawings of you and I sleeping in bed displayed all over the house?"

"Well, since some of them are only *bordering* on sleep, I was praying you wouldn't."

"Give me some credit, darling."

"Sorry."

"Apology accepted."

"Thanks, and I like your idea, but I don't want to lose Adele's landscapes. They belong in those rooms."

"Actually, I was thinking about replacing them."

"What? Why?" Judy said, turning further in her seat. "Robin, those pictures are meant for those rooms. They're all named after the places Adele and your mother stayed, and they loved each other so much. It wouldn't be right to take them down. Please, please don't do that."

Robin smiled. "God, I love your passion."

"Does that mean we're not going to change them?"

"No, that means we are."

"But Robin—"

"To the ones that actually *have* Mom and Adele in them."

"Really?" Judy squeaked.

"Why not?" Robin said, shrugging. "Like you said, those pictures belong in those rooms, and so do the women in them."

"Gosh, I wish I could kiss you right now."

Robin was tempted to lean over and grant Judy's wish, but the wind had changed direction, and the snow was now flying straight at the windshield. "Sorry, sweetheart. That's going to have to wait for a couple more miles."

Judy looked between the swipes of the wiper at the swilling, near whiteout conditions. "How can you tell where we are?"

"Positive thinking."

A second later, Judy felt the rear end of the SUV swerve just a hair, and white-knuckling the grab handle above the dash, she glanced over at Robin. "Then how about letting me drive? I'm used to driving in the snow."

"Sweetheart, I grew up in Indiana and driving in the snow is like riding a bike. You never forget how."

No sooner did the words slip from her lips when the rear end of the SUV began to slide. Overcorrecting, Robin ended up driving on the wrong side of the road for almost a minute before she guided them back to safety. "Sorry about that."

"I cannot *tell* you how much confidence that little bit of stunt driving just instilled in me."

"All right," Robin said with a laugh. "Let me just find a place to pull over, and you can drive."

"No need," Judy said, pointing in front of them. "That's our turn up ahead."

"Are you sure?"

"About the turn or your snow skills?"

"Both."

Judy glanced at her phone. "According to the GPS, that should take us to the parking lot, and as for you driving in the snow, we'll switch on the way back. All right?"

"Okay."

Before too long, Robin was carefully driving down a dark, two-lane road lined with trees, the headlights of the SUV providing the only illumination along the way. "Now where?"

"Um...up ahead on the left. There," Judy said, pointing at a break in the trees.

Robin slowed the SUV to a crawl as she made the turn and a few seconds later, the darkness of night morphed into a sunlit day. In front of them, brightened by high-intensity lighting, was a substantial parking lot and the only spaces taken were those filled by four pickup trucks covered in snow.

"Crap. They're supposed to be closed this time of the year."

Judy peered through the window. "I think they're workers."

"What?"

"Like on Mackinac. The people who own this place probably do all the repairs or renovations on the cabins during the winter. That way, it doesn't get in the way of the guests."

"Well, shit."

"Maybe we need to rethink this?"

Robin sighed and looked around. "No," she said, pointing to the furthest corner of the lot. "I'll park over there. It's far enough from the lights, no one should see us."

"Robin, seriously, maybe we should go back to the hotel and call them in the morning. Just ask if they'd mind—"

"Hello?" Robin said, splaying her fingers into an invisible phone. "Yes, my name's Robin Novak. What? You've heard of me? Yeah, that's right, the mystery writer. You enjoy my books? That's great! So, the reason I'm calling is to ask if you'd mind if I spread the ashes of my mother and her lesbian lover around one of your cabins. You wouldn't? You think it's a great idea? That's awesome. See you in the morning."

Judy's face creased into a smile. "Nice try, but they wouldn't know you're R. C. Novak."

"They would if they were a big fan and had all my books. It's mentioned in a few of the earlier ones."

"Fine. Okay, I'll admit you have a point, but what if someone sees us and calls the cops? I don't know anything about the laws in Canada, and any way you cut it, we're at the very least trespassing. They could deport us."

Robin parked the SUV in the shadows and glancing at Judy, she grinned. "For trespassing? Really?"

"Yeah, it sounded pretty lame to me, too," Judy said with a snort.

"But if you're worried, stay in the car. It won't take me long."

Judy looked over her shoulder. With the lights reflecting off the snow, she had a clear line of sight to the trucks and to the snow plowed around the edge, but beyond that, there was a curtain of blackness. A second later, Judy's eyes began to sparkle. "I don't see any ominous sewers, but what if a scary clown is lurking in the bushes?"

Robin dropped her chin to her chest, and trying to ignore the sound of Judy's giggles, she shot Judy a look. "You just had to go there. Didn't you?"

"Sorry," Judy said as she tried to stifle her amusement. "I couldn't help myself."

"After what happened this morning, I wouldn't think you'd find my fear of clowns funny anymore. I dropped a whole bottle of orange juice because of Isobel's antics."

"I remember. I helped clean it up."

"And how in the hell did she get that stupid thing in the pantry?"

Judy snickered. "I think we'll need to chalk that up to ingenuity."

"Well, she needs to stop being so clever. I've lost count of how many times she's moved that flipping doll, and if she doesn't knock it off, I'm going to need a freaking pacemaker."

A fit of laughter overtook Judy, and several seconds passed before she could speak. "And when you started jumping around and screaming like a little girl with uncontrollable jazz hands, I swear, I almost peed myself."

"It really wasn't that funny."

"Trust me. It was," Judy said, sniffling back the rest of her amusement. "But I don't think she's trying to be mean. We've both heard her laughing, so I think she's just having some fun."

"Yeah, at my expense."

Judy placed her hand on Robin's leg. "Okay. When we get home, we'll ask her to stop. How's that?"

"See, that's the thing. I can't bring myself to ask her to stop. Like you said, I think she's just having fun, and her sketches are...well, they're wonderful. So much detail, so much...love. Maybe it's me, but I think Isobel's happy."

"Then I guess that makes three of us—huh?"

Robin leaned over and gave Judy a kiss. "Definitely, but keep your eyes open for a good deal on a defibrillator."

"I'll do that," Judy said, unbuckling her seat belt. "And now what say we go do what we're here to do?"

"You sure? After all, if we're caught, we could be deported. Who knows? They could just toss us in the slammer and throw away the key. Bread and water for the rest of our days. A metal cup to rattle against the bars when we want attention."

"Drama queen," Judy said with a laugh. "And I told you I would never leave you again, so I guess I'm just going to have to take my chances."

Whatever heat existed in the car was sucked out by the frigid wind as soon as they opened the doors, and hunching their shoulders against the chill, Robin and Judy quickly zipped up their jackets. Gloves and knit caps followed, and after grabbing the backpack and a couple of flashlights, they made their way across the lot through the newly fallen snow.

As soon as they scaled the snow piled along the perimeter, Judy and Robin froze in their tracks. Not too far in the distance were cabins, easily seen in the pitch of night because there were lights in the windows.

"Shit," Judy whispered. "That must be where the workers are staying."

"That's okay," Robin said, quickly scanning the area. "From the map on their website, it should be right around here. It was really close to the parking lot."

"All right," Judy said, and turning on her flashlight, she aimed it at the ground. "Should we split up?"

"No. We'll just walk along the edge and check the ones we find."

"Okay. Lead the way."

Fox Point Resort had been around for almost a hundred years and nestled in and around trees dotting the acreage were endless cabins and cottages. Some were tucked away, their secluded locations affording honeymooners privacy, while others stood in the open, their porches facing the nearby lake and their size accommodating even the largest of family gatherings.

Carefully making their way through the trees and snow-covered brush, Judy and Robin took turns climbing the stairs leading to the tiny homes, raising their flashlights only long enough to read the signs above the doors until they found Firefly.

"Are you still sure you want to do this?" Judy said as she came down the stairs.

Robin shined her flashlight on the cabin. It was smaller than she imagined, barely the size of her own bedroom, but then she remembered Adele and her mother had been in college at the time. Young, vital, and falling in love, the accommodations no doubt hadn't mattered to either.

"Yeah," Robin whispered. "This is where they first...where they first came together. This is where it all started, and they'll be safe here. The wind can carry them away if it likes, but they won't be trampled on." Using her foot, Robin cleared away some drifting snow before holding out her hand. "You did leave some in the urns—right?"

Judy couldn't help but smile. "Of course. I did exactly as you asked, sweetheart," she said, placing two plastic bags in Robin's hand.

"I can't thank you enough for doing that by the way. For the life of me, I just couldn't...I couldn't—"

"Robin, it's okay. You already thanked me, and I totally understood your reluctance. It's one thing to scatter ashes and allow the souls of your loved ones to go free, but...but dividing them up? I can see how that would bother you."

"I love you so much," Robin said, her breath steaming in the air. "I hope you know that."

"I do," Judy said, hunching her shoulders against a sudden breeze. "Do you want me to go with you?"

"No. I got this. Be back in a few."

A moment later, Judy watched as Robin crawled under a cabin built atop piers of masonry and concrete.

Dried leaves and twigs littered Robin's path, and brushing them away, she army-crawled under the tiny house. Laying her flashlight off to the side, Robin opened one bag and then the next, scattering the ashes together in a row far enough from the edges of the cabin, so they'd be safe until time and wind swept them away.

Tears stung at Robin's eyes. Silent and motionless, she was unaware of the minutes that came and went as she got her thoughts in order. "I love you, Mom," she whispered. "I always have and I always will. You were always my strength. You were always my hero...and you still are. You were fair when you had to be and strict when I was being a pain in your backside, and the woman I've become is all because of you. You taught me to stand tall, but not too tall as to ever look down on other people. You showed me that grace and kindness takes a person further than ugliness and hatred ever could, and it's okay to stand up for myself, as long as I don't trample others along the way."

Robin paused and cleared her throat. "You also taught me to admit when I was wrong, and I was wrong, Mom. I was wrong to get angry when I found out about you and Adele. I was wrong to feel slighted because you didn't share that part of your life with me, and I was wrong, so very wrong to ever judge you, to ever condemn you for the decisions you made, and I know that now because I...well, I started reading your letters."

Robin stopped to sniffle back her emotions. "Now, before you get all pissy, yes, I know I'm prying and yes, I know I'm intruding on your most private thoughts and feelings, but your letters to Adele made me realize that everything I always wanted for you, you had. I wanted you to be happy, and you were. I wanted you to find love, and there's no doubt in my mind, you did. I saw it in every stroke of your pen, Mom. In every syllable you wrote, your love for Adele lifted off the page...and so did you.

"While I was reading your words, it was like your arms were around me again. You had me wrapped up in one of those big, never-ending hugs you always used to give me. You know the ones? Where I'd tried to get away and you'd pull me closer and laugh? I could smell your perfume, Mom, and I could almost...I could almost feel your cheek pressed up against mine as you told me how much you loved me or...or how much you missed me. And I can't tell you how many times I smiled as I read what you wrote. Defiant and sometimes funny, sarcastic and sometimes...well, let's just say flirtatious and leave it at that, I saw the woman I knew, *and* I saw the woman you were with Adele, and that's a privilege I never thought I'd have."

Robin bowed her head, allowing her tears to fall freely for a few moments before raising her head again. "Okay, so I think I need to stop talking now. I hope you don't mind what I'm doing tonight. I wanted you and Adele to be together, but I couldn't fathom losing either of you totally. Yeah, I know I didn't know her that well, but from what I read in her letters, she loved you to the moon and back, and that's good enough for me. So...I love you, Mom. Be happy and take care of that woman of yours. By what you wrote, it sounds like she was really special...just like you."

Judy held out her hand as Robin crawled from under the shed, and helping to her feet, Judy saw the tears in Robin's eyes. "Are you all right?"

Robin wiped the tears from her cheeks and then gave Judy a kiss. "Yes, I'm fine," Robin whispered before filling her lungs with the frigid air. "Let's get back to the car before we freeze to death."

They walked across the parking lot in silence, and Judy grinned when she saw Robin heading for the passenger side. Climbing inside, Judy started the engine, and turning on the defroster and heater, she waited as the windshield cleared.

"Okay, I think we're ready," Judy said, placing her hand on the gearshift.

"Not yet," Robin said, covering Judy's hand with hers.

"Why? What's wrong?"

Robin looked at Judy and smiled softly. "I know I said I didn't want this connected to any other day, but in that cabin over there, my mother and Adele started a love affair that I'd like to think is still going on, and that's what I want. I want to be with you for this lifetime and the next and the next after that. I want us to be together until we're ghosts, until we're ashes floating in the wind, forever swirling and dancing in the currents." Robin paused and stretched, lifting her bottom off the car seat to get her hand deep into her jean's pocket. A moment later, she turned to face Judy, holding a radiant solitaire diamond ring between her fingers.

"Oh, Robin," Judy said in a breath.

"I'm an author," Robin whispered, gazing into Judy's eyes. "I'm supposed to be able to write words that make sense, but there are no words to describe how I feel about you that do it justice. You have redefined everything I thought I knew about beauty and grace, about the intensity in a look, about the power of a touch, and about the absoluteness of love because what I feel for you, Judy, *is* absolute. It's unconditional and infinite, expanding every minute of every day we have together, and the most amazing thing is, looking back, I was never given an option when it came to loving you. From the moment you walked into that classroom, my heart belonged to you and only you." Pausing long enough to hold up the ring, Robin said, "Judy, I love you. I always have. I always will, so...would you do me the honor of becoming my wife?"

Judy's chin began to tremble, and her eyes welled with tears as she held out her hand. Watching as Robin slipped the ring on her finger, Judy moved in for a kiss, and a hairsbreadth before her lips touched Robin's, she whispered, "Like I have a choice."

The End

Thank you for reading Choices. As an independent author, I have no publicity department or publishing company to depend on to spread the word about my books, so if you liked Choices, I hope you can find a few minutes to return to where you purchased it and leave a comment or a review.

It took me over a year to write this book, and as you know, it contains a few surprises. If you're kind enough to leave a review, please don't include spoilers. Don't ruin it for the next reader – or for the writer who spent countless hours trying to make this book worth the ride.

If you want to contact me personally, please drop me a line at Lyng227@gmail.com or catch me on Facebook https://www.facebook.com/lyn.gardner.587

Lyn

Acknowledgements

As always, I would like to say something to those who spent their days, nights, and weekend reading my words. They are my editors, they are my proofreaders, but more importantly –they are my friends.

To Susan, Marian, Mike, Marion, Ro, and Bron, thank you more than words can ever say. I couldn't do this without you. You speak your minds. You keep me in line (not an easy task), *and* you keep me sane. You are the best!

Other Titles by Lyn Gardner

Born Out of Wedlock

** WINNER – 2017 International Book Awards – LGBTQ Fiction
** SILVER MEDAL – 2017 Global Ebook Awards – Gay/Lesbian/LGBT Fiction
** SILVER MEDAL – 2017 eLit Book Awards – LGBTQ Fiction
** FINALIST – 2017 National Indie Excellence Award – LGBTQ Fiction
** DISTINGUISHED FAVORITE – 2017 Independent Press Award – LGBTQ Fiction
** FINALIST – 2017 International Author Network Book of the Year – Romance
** DISTINGUISHED FAVORITE – 2017 NYC Big Book Awards – LGBTQ Fiction
** RUNNER-UP – 2017 Rainbow Book Awards – Best Lesbian Contemporary Romance

Two women. Two worlds. Two problems...and two attitudes.

Addison Kane does not want for much. With a touch equaling that of Midas and a confidence overstepping the borders of arrogance, Addison's ability is vast, yet her focus is narrow. Her vision tunneled by haunting memories of her youth, she is blinded to the peripheral. She doesn't care that life is passing her by. She doesn't notice as friends fall to the wayside, and the finery that comes from wealth holds no importance for Addison is single-minded. Her goal is the ultimate of paybacks. She needs to succeed like no other before her and prove someone wrong.

Joanna Sheppard lives a simple life because she can afford no other. At the age of seventeen, her father falls ill, and for the next eleven years, Joanna's sole focus is providing for the only parent she has ever known. For the man she loves with all her heart, she gives up her dreams and doesn't look back. She goes about her days with no complaints, working three jobs so she can pay off her father's creditors, but there is no light at the end of Joanna's tunnel...or so she thinks.

When an edict from the grave threatens all Addison holds dear, two women from two different worlds are brought together, and a deal is struck. In exchange for uttering a few words, both get what they need...but not what they bargained for.

There is a thin line, as they say, but when it is crossed, can love survive when more family secrets are revealed?

***

Give Me A Reason

** WINNER – 2015 National Indie Excellence Awards – LGBT Fiction
** SILVER MEDAL – 2014 Global Ebook Awards – Gay/Lesbian/LGBT Fiction
** SILVER MEDAL – 2014 eLit Book Awards – Lesbian Fiction
** FINALIST – 2017 – International Network Book of the Year – Romance
** FINALIST – 2015 International Book Awards – Fiction: Gay & Lesbian
** FINALIST – 2014 GCLS Ann Bannon Popular Choice Awards
** FINALIST – 2014 GCLS Awards for Contemporary Lesbian Fiction

Intelligent, confident and beautiful, Antoinette Vaughn had it all until one night she went to help a friend and paid for it...with a life sentence in hell.

Four years later, Toni's judgment is overturned, but the damage is already done. She walks from the prison a free woman, but she's hardly free. Actually, she's hardly alive. A prison without rules can do that to a person.

She was raised amidst garden parties, stables and tennis courts, but now a dingy flat in a decrepit building is what Toni calls home. It's cold, dark and barren just like her heart, but it suits her. She doesn't want to leave much behind when she's gone, but the simplicity of her sheltered existence begins to unravel when a beautiful stranger comes into her life.

How does anyone survive in a world that terrifies them? How do you learn to trust again when everyone is your enemy? How do you take your next breath and not wish it were your last? And if your past returned...what would you do

***

Ice

** GOLD MEDAL – 2014 Global Ebook Awards – Gay/Lesbian/LGBT Fiction
** WINNER – Indie Book of the Day – April 19, 2013
** FINALIST – 2015 National Indie Excellence Book Awards – LGBT Fiction

Ice begins when a boy is kidnapped from a London park and Detective Inspectors Alex Blake and Maggie Campbell are brought together to work on the case. While their goal is the same, their work ethics are not. Intelligent, perceptive and at times disobedient, Alex Blake does what she believes it takes to do her job. Maggie Campbell has a slightly different approach. She believes that rule books were written for a reason.

Unexpectedly, their dynamics mesh, but when her feelings for Alex become stronger than she wants to admit, Maggie provokes the worst in Alex to ensure that they will never be partners again.

Three years later, fate brings them together again. Their assignment is simple, but a plane crash gets in their way. Now, in the middle of a blizzard, they have to try to survive...and fight the feelings that refuse to die.

***

Mistletoe

** WINNER – Indie Book of the Day – December 28, 2013

Four-year-old Diana Clarke sends her wish to Santa Claus, but lost in the lining of a sack, it isn't discovered for thirty years. Now, Santa has a problem. No child's wish has ever gone unanswered, but the child isn't a child anymore.

Believing there is nothing in Santa's Village to satisfy the little girl's wish now that she's an adult, he calls on a Higher Power and is given a suggestion. Although most of Santa's workshops contain only toys for boys and girls, there is one that holds a possible solution to his problem. Learning that Diana will be attending three upcoming Christmas parties, Santa calls on his lead elf to deliver three sprigs of mistletoe, hoping that under one, Diana Clarke will find what she asked for thirty years before.

Made in the USA
Columbia, SC
21 November 2020